The
Return
of the Elves
Collection

Books 5-7

Bethany Adams

The
Return of the Elves
Collection 2
Includes bonus short story The Sentinels
by Bethany Adams

Copyright © 2020 Bethany Adams
All rights reserved
ISBN: 978-1-953171-00-9

First Edition

Abyss first published 2018
Awakening first published 2019
Ascent first published 2020
The Sentinels first published 2020

Edited by Jody Wallace at www.jodywallace.com
Paperback design/illustration by The Illustrated Author Design Service at www.theillustratedauthor.net
Interior design by Gaynor Smith of Indie Books Gone Wild www.ibgw.net

Published in the United States of America

ISLE OF DRAGONS

UNCHARTERED LANDS

MORANAIA

THE NORTHERN MOUNTAINS

BRAELYN

SOUTHERN MOUNTAINS

ROYAL PALACE

THE PLAINS

THE CITADEL

FIORN

SOUTHERN DESERT

Table of Contents

Abyss

Character Pronunciation Guide

Abyss

Places:

Braelyn (BRAY-lynn)
Moranaia (MOR-uh-nai-uh)

Main Characters:

Aris (EHR-iss)
Kezari (ke-ZAHR-ee)
Selia (SEHL-ee-uh)

Secondary Characters:

Baza (bah-zah)
Caolte (KWIL-chuh)
Eri (EHR-ee)
Iren (EAR-ehn)
Lial (lee-ahl)
Kien (KEE-ehn)
Meren (MEHR-ehn)
Naomh (NAY-om)
Perim (PEHR-im)
Tynan (TIE-nehn)

Other:

Gwragedd Annwn (GRA-geth A-noon)
Gwraig Annwn (grag A-noon)

Prologue

Shudders wracked Aris's body as the blade sliced across his outer thigh. He hissed at the sting, but the pain numbed quickly in the frigid cave. The longer Aris dangled against the icy stone, his arms bound above his head, the more the burn of exposed skin faded. But the cold was not an oversight, nor was it mercy.

Frostbitten skin would be agony to regenerate.

"You have the power to end this."

He squeezed his eyes tight against the sweet, cajoling voice. "No," he managed to gasp through his raw throat.

"Just bond with me," she said, slashing her knife along his side. "That's all it would take. Our souls were made to be together, but your stubbornness keeps us apart."

He didn't bother to answer. If he didn't goad her, she might leave him alone for a while, possibly even lengthen his chains so he wasn't bound so closely to the wall. Sometimes weeks would pass between her torture sessions. She could give him a measure of freedom, even a few small kindnesses. Water to bathe. A walk to the mouth of the cave. If she interpreted his silence as weakening resolve, she would go easier on him.

Maybe.

She removed the blade from his flesh, but he didn't move. "You're no fun today, Aris," she said, a pout to her voice.

Finally, he opened his eyes and glanced at the beautiful woman. Lips pursed, his captor stared at the blood dripping down his body before her gaze captured his. A tremble shook him at the coldness of her eyes, the window to her wicked mind. Her expression never changed. Her soul might be a match to his, but she was twisted inside.

What did that say about him?

She tucked her hair behind her ear, leaving a smear of his blood on the pale strand. "Start the bond, and I will treat you as the king you should be."

Aris held back a snort. She led a small band of outcasts who'd made their home with the dragons, but she certainly wasn't a queen. "Not this day."

Her green eyes narrowed. "Then I'll leave you to the cold."

His captor spun away, and anger rang through her footsteps as she marched from the cave. He slumped against his bonds, a soft groan slipping free despite his resolve. Void take her, he shouldn't have spoken. There would be no small kindnesses now. She would leave him hanging for days, and that was the best-case scenario.

At least she hadn't lowered him into the crevice.

The light that streamed from a hole far above faded until the cave darkened into night. The unrelenting cold numbed the newest cuts but barely slowed the blood flowing from the wounds, and Aris could no longer contain the shivering of his body as he weakened. Maybe he would die this time.

Gods willing.

Then something shifted in the shadows. Had his captor returned? His heart leaped in alarm even as he peered into the darkness. An illusion meant to torture him further? She never arrived in the dark herself—the night was purely for the dragons, and any fae who wandered free risked death. That was their pact. Who would risk coming here?

A small flame sparked to life, and Aris cried out at the unexpected pain that speared his eyes. But he didn't dare to blink. Someone had come, and he wouldn't be caught unawares. As the light moved closer, his vision began to adjust.

He wasn't reassured.

The flame hovering above the woman's palm cast a soft glow across the sharp features of her face. Her golden eyes sparkled vividly as they stared into him, seeming to weigh his soul. Long brown-gold hair flowed around her otherwise naked body. His blood chilled at the blank, unnatural expression of her face. Then her head tilted in an almost birdlike gesture, and clarity hit.

A dragon in the guise of a woman.

"I refuse to wait any longer," she said, her voice resounding oddly through the cave.

His brows wrinkled together. "What?"

"Your mate has delayed me for years, but—"

"I have no mate," he snapped. He couldn't stand the thought of anyone associating him so intimately with his captor. "Certainly not the *drec* who has held me here."

The dragon's uncanny gaze lifted to his wrists, manacled to the stone by thick iron shackles. "Perim said you were training."

Rage heated his insides and caused his muscles to tense. "Is that her name? The blond woman who torments me?"

The dragon tilted her head again. "You've been with your mate for years, and you must ask me this?"

"She. Is. Not. My. Mate."

The flame hovering over the dragon's hand grew brighter. "I see. You are here unwillingly."

"Very," Aris answered, though her words hadn't sounded like a question.

"Then Perim must pay." Her other hand lifted toward his manacles. Power built in the air until every hair on his body stood on end. With a sharp crack, the metal split and fell away, freeing him. "You'll be coming with me."

Aris dropped hard to his knees as feeling roared back into his limbs. Heat washed through him, banishing the earlier cold, and he bit back a yell at the harsh pain. His muscles quaked, but he braced his hand against the floor and shoved himself to his feet. Though he had to lean against the cave wall, he faced the dragon standing.

"Who are you?" he demanded.

"I am Kezari," she answered. "Your dragon."

He shook his head, certain he hadn't heard correctly. "My what?"

"Have your kind forgotten the bond we once shared?"

His stomach lurched at the mention of a bond. "Like a soulbond?"

"Not typically," she answered in a flat tone. "But it has happened. No, I speak of a synthesis of elements. Magic most compatible. I am earth. You are earth."

Aris frowned as he tried to understand her words. He had the feeling that she hadn't been around many people—her grasp of the language was off. "You are here because our elements are compatible?"

"There are more links than soul to soul." Her head tilted again. "You understand this?"

Unbidden, Selia's laughing face flickered to life in his memory. Then an image of his son, Iren. His heart twisted at the memory of his family. Gods knew where they were now. "Yes."

"Let us go, then."

Before he had time to consider her words, Kezari stepped back, and the fire winked out. Fear sliced through him like his captor's blade. Had this been some strange trick? A new method to torment him? Power built in the air once more, stronger than before. Aris shrank back against the wall as his head throbbed with the force of the rising energy.

A rough slithering filled the cave. Then a gust of air rushed over him, tossing his sweat-slicked hair around his face. Another flame sprang to life, but it was too far away to hurt his eyes. It glimmered near the far ceiling of the cave—beside the massive golden head of a dragon.

Aris froze like prey at the sight of the huge talons only an arms-length away. As the dragon lifted her claw and rested the tip of a single talon against his chest, Aris forced himself to remain still. If this was how he died, he would greet the moment with courage.

Power roared through him without warning. Thank the gods he'd braced himself against the wall. A slight pain flared across his skin, but the sensation was swept away by the glorious energy filling his depleted body. His muscles strengthened and his mind cleared. For the first time in years, he could detect the life in the cave around him as clearly as his own breath.

Then it was done.

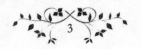

The flame above Kezari's head brightened, and he felt the surge of power in his own blood. She'd linked them. Bile rose up the back of his throat. Aris dug his fingers into his palms and breathed through his nose before he vomited. Linked against his will. The dragon was as bad as his captor.

"Leave me alone," he rasped.

Kezari's wedge-shaped head lowered until all he could see was her golden eyes. *"You are distressed,"* she said into his mind.

"You stole my choice."

"I offer freedom." Her heated breath warmed the rock behind him. *"You were too weak to choose. Once a cycle of the moons has passed, you may sever the link. If you wish."*

Aris studied the dragon's face, but he couldn't tell if she was lying. Her slit pupils focused, unwavering, on him. In fact, the only movement came from her nostrils as she breathed. Then she tilted her head, much as she had in her elven form, and he caught a hint of uncertainty.

"The war between our peoples was millennia ago. Do you still hold animosity?"

Aris frowned. *"Of course not."*

"Only elves who link with a dragon may ride one." Her long neck arched upward as she pulled her head back. *"Do you want to live? I can take you from this place."*

He swallowed at the thought. Freedom. He'd believed he would die here once his captor grew tired of trying to force their soulbond. How many years had passed? Four? Six? He'd tried to keep count of the days, but he'd lost more than a few to unconsciousness. His people probably thought he was dead. Selia would have moved on, and his own son would barely remember him.

Worse, he was damaged. Broken.

"Do not cast aside the millennia of life you could have because of your torment." Smoke puffed from between Kezari's lips. *"Perim is not worth it. And we can do great things, you and I."*

Aris held the dragon's steady gaze. He didn't trust her, but he no longer trusted anyone. What did he have to lose? Better if Kezari killed him than his wicked potential soulbonded. Dragons were typically straightforward creatures, so the former would be a quicker death than the latter. And if his soul was twisted like Perim's, Kezari would know. She could end him before he caused harm.

He took a deep breath and nodded. "Then let's go."

Kezari circled the village stretched out along the coast below, descending gently to avoid upsetting Aris as he clung to her back. Though it was night, she could identify each stone dwelling with ease. More buildings had fallen into disrepair since she'd last flown by, though it had only been a year. The once-proud population of fae, descendants of the dragons' riders during the war with the elves almost forty thousand years prior, continued to dwindle.

No wonder Perim wanted to gain her freedom from the island.

But the fae woman had gone too far. It was one thing to interrupt council meetings to demand redress from the queen—that had earned Perim a month's imprisonment a few decades ago—but something else entirely to torture a dragon's *skizik* under the guise of training. Of course, Kezari had allowed herself to be fooled. She swallowed down the acrid taste of flame rising up the back of her throat at that reminder.

Perim would pay.

Kezari glided lower, though she wanted to dive as though catching prey. Even at this slow pace, Aris's arms tightened around the base of her neck, and his legs dug his saddle into her shoulders. She couldn't risk tipping him into madness by hasty actions.

But finally, she hovered near the house she sought. Her wingbeats resounded around them, echoing off walls and rattling glass windowpanes. Kezari cried out, a shriek of challenge, and blasted a stream of flame just above the tile roof. It was a traditional summons, though one never given at night when the fae remained indoors.

"*I smell Perim,*" Kezari said into Aris's mind. "*Is it a remnant, or do you sense her presence?*"

Aris trembled against her, and his mental voice was a faint whisper. "*I feel her near.*"

She hadn't wanted to risk the reminder, but she had to be certain. She shrieked again, more loudly now that her target was certain. They ignored her at their peril.

One of the windows lifted, and a man gaped at her through the opening. "My lady?"

"*Send forth Perim,*" she sent into his mind.

His expression shuttered. "She is not here."

He dared to lie? Kezari shot a stream of flame high into the sky. "*Then she breaks the law by wandering in the night?*"

"No. I didn't mean…" the man stuttered.

"*I will have justice.*" Kezari lowered her head until the smoke from her nostrils curled through the open window. "*Send her out, or I will melt this rock into a puddle of lava.*"

A deep, harsh scream echoed from the other side of the village as another dragon plunged from the sky. Tebzn. What was she doing here? Kezari whipped her head around and hissed as her cousin hovered a neck's length away, her forearms lifted in challenge.

"This is beyond the bounds of law," Tebzn snarled in their tongue, too high-pitched for the fae to easily discern.

"Perim tortured my *skizik*." Kezari gnashed her teeth. "She will pay."

Her cousin's claws lowered. "If that is the case, then justice will be delivered. But not now. The fae are to remain undisturbed in their homes at night."

"Tebzn—"

A cry from the window interrupted her cousin's words. "What have you done to my bonded?"

Perim. Steam poured from Kezari's nostrils as she focused on the wretched woman. *"I have saved him from you. Come out and face me."*

Tears leaked from Perim's eyes as she peered out the window, the man no longer in sight. Her guileless expression might have fooled Kezari under different circumstances, but not after finding Aris chained and bleeding. Not after connecting to him and examining his memories.

"You must return my bonded to my care," Perim said, her voice shaky.

A clever ploy, but a wasted effort.

Unfortunately, Perim's demand proved too much for Aris. Though only a shadow in Aris's mind, Kezari felt the exact moment his hold on reality shattered. His unending mental scream filled her own head until she sent him hurtling into sleep with a quick spell. Another flex of power ensured he would not topple from the saddle, but she could only hold this spell for so long. She had to get him away from here.

Kezari pinned Tebzn with her gaze. "She lies."

"Regardless, we do have laws."

Without warning, Kezari sent a single memory of Aris's torture into her cousin's mind. Tebzn reared back, her wingbeats faltering before she recovered control. "As you can see, I speak the truth."

"In the morning, we can haul Perim before the queen," Tebzn answered.

"I must get my *skizik* out of here now." Kezari's nostrils flared. "Now. His mental health is fragile."

Below, Perim let out a sob. "You cannot take my soulbonded."

Neither dragon answered her.

"Go," Tebzn said to Kezari. "I will ensure that justice is served."

Through her connection to Aris, Kezari detected his thoughts beginning to stir. She had to get him somewhere alone. "See that you do," she conceded. "I will check with you soon."

Perim's shriek sounded below as Kezari propelled herself into the sky, faster than she would dare with Aris awake. There was a small, abandoned island a short flight away. She could take her *skizik* there. And she would do her best to help him heal.

1

Selia opened the door to her son's room and sighed to see him awake, still curled up in his favorite reading chair. Iren startled, slamming his book closed and jumping to his feet with a guilty expression pinching his face. But his contrition faded quickly. As he placed the book on a side table, he tried for an innocent grin.

"I just wanted to get to a stopping point."

"Bed," Selia said with an impatient gesture. "Now."

Huffing, he trudged across the floor. "*You* stay up late reading sometimes."

She couldn't help but smile at that truth. "And I usually pay for it. You're sharing a magic lesson with Arlyn tomorrow, and I want to be certain you are rested and focused."

Iren paused beside his bed. "I thought she was traveling with Kai."

"They leave again tomorrow evening."

Her son crawled beneath the covers, and Selia resisted the urge to tuck them up around his shoulders and smooth his hair. At eleven, he had become resistant to such shows of affection. All too soon, he would be a man grown, and even these moments would end. A point she reminded herself of when he was being particularly difficult.

"I guess you and my father weren't soulbonded like Kai and Arlyn," Iren said sleepily. "The bonded couples here seem to travel together all the time, but you and *Onaial* didn't."

Selia froze at the unexpected comment. Even after seven years, the loss of her beloved cut deeply. "Our lack of bond had nothing to do with that. Your father traveled to wild places, and I had students to train besides."

Iren twisted the blanket between his fingers. "Do you think you have a soulbonded out there somewhere? I hate to think you're lonely. I thought about asking Eri, but it didn't seem right."

"Do not bother your friend about such things," Selia said, a bit more sharply than she'd intended. She didn't like to think about her possible soulbonded. "She might be a seer, but she's still younger than you are. If you want to be her friend, you'll not ask about the future."

Iren nodded. "I kind of thought that, too."

"About the possibility of a soulbond…" Selia took a deep breath. "I don't think about it. I loved your father dearly, bond or no. I'm not certain when I'll be ready for another relationship."

"I understand," Iren said.

Unable to resist, she pushed a strand of his light brown hair out of his eyes. "What has you thinking about this, beloved?"

Iren nibbled at his lip. "I don't want you to be unhappy."

"I'm not," Selia said firmly, although she wasn't certain it was true. An uneasiness had been growing inside her, a feeling closer to glum loneliness than she wanted to admit. But overall, she was content. Wasn't she? "Moving to Braelyn was an adjustment, but I enjoy my work. Are you homesick?"

She and Iren had lived at her father's estate, Fiorn, until she had accepted the role of teacher for Lord Lyr's newfound adult daughter, Arlyn. Iren had struggled at first, but Selia had thought her son was happy here, especially once he'd befriended young Eri. Maybe she was mistaken? Worried, she studied her son's frowning face.

"Why would I be?" Iren asked. "I don't get lectured here."

Selia laughed at that. "I know your grandfather is gruff, but surely you miss your Aunt Niasen."

"Sure," he said. Then he shrugged. "But she's the heir. I could visit through the portal and see her just as often." Iren tugged the blanket close to his chin, his eyes growing heavy. "I like it here. I want you to like it, too. You find a soulbonded, maybe we can stay."

His words trailed off as his eyelids slid closed. Smiling softly, Selia waited until his breathing slowed and his body went lax before she dropped a kiss on his forehead. So he wanted to stay here at Braelyn, did he? As she slipped out of his room and down the stairs curling around a broad tree trunk, she could understand why. The plains of Fiorn were beautiful, but the forests and mountains of Braelyn held their own unique power.

At the bottom of the stairs, Selia glanced across the entryway at the massive side of Eradisel, one of the nine sacred trees. Perhaps it was the tree's influence. Fiorn did not house one of the nine, but Braelyn was built around the very trunk. Lord Lyr, Myern of the Callian branch, guarded the sacred tree and the priests who tended her. Her power permeated everything.

Selia found herself stepping closer to the tree as though she were being pulled. Did Eradisel wish to communicate? Only once, when she and Iren had first arrived, had the tree spoken to her. Well, sent feelings of joy and welcome more than words, but it was communication nonetheless.

When Selia was close enough, she extended her hand, palm outward, until she could almost touch the bark. Then she waited. A sense of peace filled her a moment before the tree's thoughts flowed in, more concept than true words. *Prepare yourself. They come.*

Selia jerked back, stumbling slightly with the motion. The image had been vague and blurred, but she'd discerned the form of a dragon and rider gliding across the mountains to the east. That couldn't be good. Dragons had originally shared territory with the elves after their migration from Earth to Moranaia, but after a long, brutal war, the dragons had retreated to an island on the other side of the world, too far away for the mostly land-locked elves to reach. They'd only taken a few of their fae allies with them.

Why would they return after millennia of peace? The elves hadn't had contact with the dragons for so long that few if any people had even seen one. She hoped war wasn't brewing, but Eradisel's warning to prepare didn't bode well. Still, it didn't make sense. Lyr was lord of this estate. If there was danger of war, wouldn't the tree have told him instead?

Selia spun away and strode across the entryway, sending her mind out in a sweep to try to locate Lyr. She found his energy in his study, as she'd expected, and headed that way even as she gave him a gentle mental nudge. Her steps rang out on the wooden floor as she waited for him to connect.

He completed the mental link almost immediately. *"Good day to you, Selia."*

"Good day. Please forgive me for interrupting your work," she sent back. *"I hope I have not caused undue disturbance."*

"Of course not," Lyr answered. Not that he would be so impolite as to say otherwise. *"Is all well?"*

"I believe so." She took a deep breath. *"Eradisel provided me a vision. I am near your study and would like to discuss it, but I thought it best to ensure you were available."*

"I am. Come straight in."

When Selia pushed through the door and stepped into the long oval room, Lyr already waited, leaning against the edge of his desk. She glanced around, but aside from a pair of people beyond the large windows, she saw no one else near. Not even his soulbonded, Meli, who often read in one of the chairs situated in the center of the room.

Good. She had a feeling her vision didn't need to be general knowledge.

"Thank you for seeing me so quickly," Selia said.

"It is truly no trouble." A slight smile crossed Lyr's face though he stood with crossed arms. "You needn't have been so formal, you know. I'm getting used to disruptions. *Clechtan*, but Ralan has practically made it a hobby."

Her cheeks warmed. "He's the prince. The king's own heir."

"He's something," Lyr muttered, though affection colored his tone. "Please, sit."

Selia hesitated only the briefest moment before settling into one of the center seats. Maybe someday she could be as casual as Lyr, but the informality here had been a difficult adjustment after Fiorn. She had never enjoyed her father's stern, cold household, but she still struggled to slip free from the hold of her early training.

Lyr sat across from her, brow furrowing as he focused on her face. "Am I to assume the vision was a bad one?"

"I'm not certain," Selia admitted. "Eradisel said only to prepare myself. They come. I caught a vague image of a dragon and rider flying over the mountains. I'd guess from the look of the area that it's the eastern side of this mountain range."

"A fair distance if we weren't talking about a dragon." Lyr's fingers whitened around the chair's armrests. "This doesn't bode well."

Selia shook her head. "No. But why did Eradisel warn me? She said 'Prepare yourself' not your*selves*. There must be something I'm supposed to do."

"Do you have spells for dragon containment?"

Selia considered her options. She knew a fair number of pre-set spells, enchantments prepared in advance for easy use, but none of those had been designed with dragons in mind. However, she was adept enough at magical containment. Given a bit of time, she should be able to devise something suitable.

"I can come up with something." She glanced at the water clock on the wall and sighed. "Even if I must sacrifice sleep. But do you think containment is wise? If the dragon comes in peace, using magic against them could cause more harm than good."

Lyr nodded. "I wouldn't do so unless necessary. But after all that has happened over the last few months, I automatically prepare for trouble."

Selia winced in commiseration. When she and Iren had first arrived, one of the lords under Lyr's command had been trying to kill him. No sooner had that threat been ended than exiled prince Kien had attempted to send more assassins through the portal between Moranaia and Earth. Prince Ralan had finally defeated his evil brother a couple of weeks ago, and none of them had settled into the apparent peace.

Perhaps that was a good thing.

"I understand," Selia said. "I hope we're concerned for nothing. Eradisel might have wanted to keep us from acting rashly when the dragon arrives. After all, neither Ralan nor Eri have warned us of danger. Surely one of them would've had a vision."

Lyr's gaze flicked to the door. "I suppose we'll know it's bad if Ralan bursts into my study without knocking."

Selia half-expected him to do so, but after a few moments of silence, she chuckled. "Guess we're on our own."

"It appears so," Lyr answered with a grin. "I'll have the *Taysonal* standing guard in the trees pay close attention to the skies, and I'll contact some of the estates to the east for news. My House was the diplomatic liaison with the queen during the dragons' time here. If they seek to contact the current monarch, it makes sense that they would come here first."

Selia stood, smoothing the fabric of her long gown. "I'll work on a containment spell just in case. Do you think we should be concerned about the harvest festival? I could contact my sister and see if she would send extra mages so that you don't have to ask my father. As his heir, she has the authority."

"That's a good possibility." Lyr pushed to his feet and started toward his desk. "We have four days until the festival. I'll see what Lady Imai to the east has to report.

As the duchess just above me, she has a good portion of the eastern coast under her command. If the dragon and rider have made it that far, she will know. It's possible your vision hasn't happened yet."

"That is true," Selia said, considering. "I didn't get a strong sense of time beyond *soon*. Perhaps you'll learn more details on this situation from Lady Imai. And I'll report back once I've completed my own work."

After a quick detour to her room to grab her cloak, Selia headed out the back door and into the chilly gardens. It was almost the end of the month of Eln, which marked the middle point of autumn, and the promise of winter blew in with the nighttime breeze. She tucked the warm cloak tightly around herself and marched along the path toward the magic workroom at the bottom of one of the outside towers. Fiorn rarely grew colder than this at any time of year, and she'd first arrived at Braelyn during the summer. None of her other teaching assignments had been in places with deep winters, either.

Walking to lessons would be much more unpleasant in the snow, but such was life.

As soon as she entered the workroom, she adjusted the cooling spell to warmth. Some days, like this one, were still hot when the sun was out, so the room needed cooling during the afternoon. Fortunately, it only took moments for the magic to work. By the time she hung up her cloak and seated herself on one of the cushions in the center of the room, the temperature had grown comfortable. Thank the gods for the long-dead elf who had first designed the enchantment.

Now it was time to design one of her own.

In the sky, Aris could almost forget the fractured mess of his life. The wind tugged at his hair, pulling strands across his eyes, but the power of it was more relief than annoyance after being confined for so long inside a cave. Far below, the mountains rolled by, the peaks growing gentler the farther west they traveled. His life was nothing compared to this ancient range. A single drop in the endless measure of time.

Thousands of heartbeats thrummed in his own blood as his magic connected with the creatures below. Stone held no interest for Aris, but animals and plants were altogether different. He could sense living things and even link with them to varying degrees. If he wanted to, he could manipulate and change them—or snuff out their spirit if they proved to be a threat. During his capture, the spells somehow worked into the iron shackles had cut him off from the life he'd always felt around him. Isolation of the worst sort.

"How much longer?" he sent to Kezari.

"We should arrive by the sun's zenith."

Aris studied the golden scales on her long neck. The light struck them, making them glow amber in the sun. With each wingbeat echoing through the air, her shoulder muscles shifted beneath him, but she peered ahead with no sign of effort or concern. As far as he could tell, in any case. Every once in a while, she turned her head enough to check on him, but he had no idea how to gauge a dragon's facial expressions.

Perhaps he would learn during the next month—if he made it that long. How simple would it be to shove himself free of the dragon's back? No healer would be able to save him from such a fall, and his torment would be over. They'd already lost a week to his madness. Kezari had taken him to a small isolated island, working with him until he'd returned to himself. Or as close to himself as he would ever be again.

Before they'd left the island, Kezari had told him that she had to travel to Braelyn to speak to the lord or lady currently in charge there. She claimed to need Aris's aid. Was she worried that the elves would hurt her? Although their peoples had remained separate for millennia, there was a peace treaty. She didn't need Aris to make it through. In his current state, he could only be a liability.

His gaze flicked to the ground so far below. A tempting release, but no. He was unlikely to hold onto his sanity for a month, but he could ensure that his rescuer reached her destination. She might not be harmed, but a guide would make the journey easier. He owed the dragon a few more days at the least.

Then he could end his torment for good.

He gave Kezari's neck a pat to catch her attention. *"What message is so urgent that you rush to Braelyn?"*

"Can you not feel it?"

"Feel what?" Aris asked with a frown.

"The Earth weeps. The energy seeps."

He glanced past the dragon's shoulder at the ground. All seemed well to both his eyes and his magic. *"I don't understand."*

"Not Moranaia," she said. *"You do not explore our link. Join with me and know the Earth as I know your animals and plants. This will tell you."*

His muscles seized at the suggestion, and he tightened his legs reflexively on the small saddle Kezari had conjured. Explore their link? This wasn't the first time she'd implored him to do so, but each time the thought of being bound to another made him want to vomit. He shoved the knowledge of their connection to the back of his mind as he had when she'd mentioned it before. No way he could access a link. No.

"It is not a soulbond. I am not Perim."

Bile scalded his throat at the name. *"It doesn't matter."*

"We will need to link," Kezari said, her tone implacable. *"But you have time yet."*

"You should have found someone else," he muttered aloud.

Although the wind whipped his words away, she still heard. *"That is not how this works, skizik. Your kind has forgotten the closeness we once shared."*

"I was taught that the dragons began the war when we would not yield the portal to their control. And they wanted too much land."

Kezari huffed, and smoke whirled from her mouth and nose. *"Convenient. There was wrong on both sides, I will allow. However, keeping the portal from our control was foolish. We are still bound to the Earth. The elves are not."*

Aris smiled at the indignation in her tone. *"The Veil leads to more places than Earth."*

"Irrelevant." Her wings beat harder. *"This is a useless discussion."*

"I don't think so, but if you want to drop it, I'll grant you the same grace you do me," Aris said. *"I take it your link with Earth has revealed something dire?"*

"Yes." A pause. *"We are essential. I can alter stone and mud. You can help the life of Earth. Together, we may fix. A mage would help, but Baza refused to leave the island. Useless reptile."*

Aris shook his head. Even in her dragon form, Kezari's body emitted warmth. He wouldn't classify dragons as mammals, but they were warm-blooded, more like birds that had scales instead of feathers. The best he could tell, dragons used the association with reptiles as an insult. The gleaming blue dragon he'd seen in her thoughts had earned Kezari's rancor. If they'd been friends, they weren't any longer.

"Perhaps an elven mage would help. My wife..." The mental image of Selia's face sent a wave of pain through him until he clenched his fingers around the saddle. His weak left arm protested the strength of his grip, but the ache was an effective distraction. *"You'll be able to find help, I'm certain."*

Kezari turned her head, her gaze fastening on his face for a moment before returning to the skies. *"I thought you were unmated."*

"I was married before my capture." Aris closed his eyes and let the wind wash around him. *"I have no doubt she has chosen another after so much time."*

"I am sorry, skizik," Kezari said. *"I will rend Perim myself. There are ways to prolong the pain so that—"*

"If you manage to find her, kill her quickly." Aris shuddered. *"I'll have no part in torture. Neither of us should be like her."*

"If you insist," Kezari answered placidly.

Aris wasn't certain he believed her easy acquiescence, but he didn't want to dwell on it. He didn't want to dwell on anything, really. As the mountains rolled by, he tried not to imagine what would happen when they reached Braelyn—and not because of the dragon. He'd learned from Kezari that seven years had passed since he'd left home. Seven years without seeing any of his own people. But he didn't want to be around any of them now.

He could only hope that no one would try to confine him. Losing control around Kezari was bad enough, but doing so in front of some of the most important people in Moranaia would certainly lead to disaster. Especially after arriving on a dragon. Then again, it might be a quick way to die. The *Taysonal* guarding Braelyn would be skilled and efficient archers. An arrow to the eye and—

Kezari's voice cut sharply across his mind. *"No. Die and I go with you. We are linked this cycle of the moons. Longer, if we should decide such."*

"A soulbonded often survives the death of his or her mate unless the bond is incomplete," Aris argued. *"Why couldn't you?*

"As I've said before, this is not a soulbond." The dragon's wings snapped sharply with each beat. *"Live out this cycle or kill us both."*

His body shook with the helpless anger her words brought. Days. He'd planned to give her a few days. *"Why not break the link now?"*

"I cannot," she said. *"Only the moons' full turning brings the time of choice."*

"Choice," he snarled aloud.

She'd taken away his final and best escape from this hell. Consigned him to suffer through this nightmare of a life for another twenty days when he hadn't been certain he could even make it to Braelyn. His fingers quivered around the edge of the saddle as darkness teased the edges of his vision. *Control yourself. Control this.* He'd survived years of torment. He could last a month to save Kezari.

"We'd better be camping in the woods," Aris sent. *"I am uncertain how much I can handle."*

Her lack of response was no reassurance.

2

Selia spun the glowing ball with a quick thought, examining each side of the enchantment. She'd started with a spell she'd learned for subduing the wild plains cats, but that was far from strong enough to contain a being as powerful as a dragon. She'd added enchantments designed to nullify magical talents and immobilize powerful prisoners. What else might the spell need?

After searching through her mental catalogue of prepared spells, Selia grasped a sleep spell and cobbled it carefully onto the ball. On a creature with the size and strength of a dragon, it was unlikely to work as intended, but it might provide drowsiness or dulled senses. If she had to use this spell, they'd need all the help they could get.

Another mark passed before she was satisfied with her work. Swiping away the sheen of sweat from her forehead, Selia settled the enchantment into a neat mental compartment. She would only need to trigger the symbols of power to release the spell when necessary. Whether it would work on a dragon was anyone's guess. She had been well-trained, but not even the most conscientious teacher had thought to prepare for something like this.

They'd been at peace with the dragons for almost forty thousand years, after all.

Selia slumped, glancing at the water clock with a frown. After all of her fussing at Iren, here she was, awake at the twenty-fifth mark. In five more marks, it would be dawn. Well, at least her lesson with Arlyn and Iren didn't begin right at dawn. If she went to bed immediately, she could get the rest needed to handle two inexperienced students.

She shoved to her feet and grabbed her cloak from its hook before heading back out into the gardens. The second moon was near to setting, so the forest had gone dark. Only a few dim mage lights illuminated the trails as she returned to the main part of the estate. Cold rushed around her, and she huddled more deeply into her cloak.

With the hour so late, a guard stood sentry at the back door. Ah, Febith. He smiled and nodded, a gleam of attraction in his eyes, but Selia only gave a polite smile and nod in return as she hurried inside. She didn't know him well, and she hadn't been able to summon any interest during their few exchanges. She might never be ready for a relationship, at least not for a few more decades, and she didn't want to give a false hope.

She wouldn't risk hurting someone the way she'd hurt Aris.

Selia tried to bury that thought the way she had for the last couple of years, but Iren's earlier words haunted her. Her son would never say so, but she could tell that he missed having a father. Some day he would want to know more about what had happened with Aris, and she would have to confess the truth.

Iren's father might still be alive if not for her.

Her beloved had had a wild, free spirit, perhaps because of his link with nature. He'd been an explorer before they'd met and remained an explorer after. Selia hadn't begrudged him his expeditions, even when they'd lasted months at a time. Those trips were essential for his soul, and she'd had her own work as a magic teacher. She'd missed him, of course, and she had worried, since there was a fair bit of danger in the unexplored parts of Moranaia, but few had the talent and desire to uncover the secrets of their world the way Aris had. Over the centuries, he'd discovered and catalogued several species of plants and animals. Some of the maps their people used bore his signature.

Then Iren had been born. Aris had been happy to stay close during the early years, but around their son's fourth birthday, the first of the great ocean ships had been completed. He'd been invited to go on the initial voyage, a month-long journey to test the ship, and for days, they'd debated what he should do. Her beloved had wanted to remain behind with his family, but Selia had seen the tension radiating through him, that drive to explore that often came upon him.

And she understood it. Despite tens of thousands of years on this planet, her people had still barely explored a quarter of the world. They reproduced so slowly that it had taken millennia before the Moranaians had settled throughout the more habitable regions of the continent where they'd emerged. Only then had they looked toward the oceans and given real effort toward crossing. But they were not natural sailors, and the sea was too rough for fishing boats. Their new ships were revolutionary. Of course Aris had wanted to go.

So she'd talked him into the journey he'd decided against.

When a storm blew up unexpectedly, the vessel had been dashed on one of the western islands, leaving only two survivors. Aris hadn't been one of them. How could she tell Iren that his father wouldn't have been on that voyage if not for her? The accident itself had been out of her control, it was true, but she couldn't help feeling responsible. Even after all this time.

Drooping with weariness, Selia pushed into her room and flung her cloak across a chair. She would pick it up in the morning—hopefully before Iren noticed her carelessness and used it as an excuse to clutter his own room. Right now, she needed rest. Maybe sleep would give her the strength to rebury the past.

There was nowhere to go but forward.

"If you insist on coming with me, then you'll have to wear clothes," Aris said.

Kezari's head tilted. "Elves are not ashamed of their bodies. Or they once were not."

"It isn't shame." Or for most, it wasn't. If he considered the question for himself, his mind might fracture. Again. "In this weather, a naked woman would cause as much comment as a dragon. And as much as I appreciate the care you have given me, I would like to eat something not roasted by your breath. I'll go alone if you don't create yourself some clothes."

Her hair rippled as she shifted her shoulders in a motion almost like a shrug. "Very well."

Aris glanced away as power glowed around her, then checked her appearance once the light settled. A thin sleeveless dress flowed around her, beautiful but insufficient for the weather. "Kezari…"

"I cannot bear much in the way of bindings," she said. "I produce too much heat."

He winced at her choice of words but forced his mind away from the images that *bindings* had evoked. Not now. *Not now.* "It'll do," he answered. Better to get on with their tasks than to think. "No stranger than I look, I imagine."

The long-sleeved tunic and cloak Kezari had made for him didn't match the pants he'd found in the cave, and they no doubt resembled nothing in current Moranaian fashion. His ancestors might have worn something in this cut and fabric—if a dragon had designed it. Severe, almost scale-like… Between his clothes and her dress, he and Kezari were certain to draw notice.

Well, nothing for it.

They'd landed a fair distance from the village huddled in a small valley, so it was a long, chilly walk to find the tavern likely to be in the center. Though the cold increased the ache in his already sore muscles, Aris didn't pull his cloak tight. Nothing tight. He'd experienced worse conditions over the years, before and after capture. Kezari appeared unbothered by the weather, but he'd come to realize that she didn't always show what she felt. She might be able to shapeshift, but she hadn't yet learned the non-verbal expressions that he took for granted.

The late time meant few people wandered the trails even in the center of town. Those who did invariably stopped to stare, but Aris ignored their rudeness. Their opinions meant nothing. So long as he and Kezari didn't draw enough attention to get the local lord or lady involved, he didn't care. The dragon had her own goals, but for himself? He wanted a solid meal and a set of clothes created by elven hands. It was the least he deserved for agreeing to this mad journey to Braelyn.

Only two of the ten tables were occupied in the tavern Aris found. Four pairs of eyes turned his way as the door swung shut behind him, and he scanned each face for signs of hostility or danger. He found only surprise and curiosity. After a

few heartbeats and a sound from the barkeeper at the back, the four returned their attention to their drinks.

Aris skirted around them, careful to remain out of reach, and settled at a table in the far corner. Though he was able to sit with his back to the wall with the door in sight, a sheen of sweat broke out on his forehead at being enclosed, even in a building. He'd hoped an elven-made structure would be different. But no. He swallowed down the rising bile and took steady breaths until the feeling passed.

Then the woman appeared.

He barely heard Kezari settle into the chair beside him. The scrape of wood against floor was drowned out by his heartbeat as the pale-haired female approached from an archway in the other corner. Nothing about her was threatening. Her face held a friendly smile, and she weaved her way jauntily through the tables. The energy flowing from her was open and kind. But that white-blond hair...

As his vision began to gray around the edges, Kezari's warm fingers wrapped around his wrist. "It is not Perim."

"I know," he whispered. "But she's still free. Maybe tracking me. What if—"

"I would detect her, *skizik*." Heat surged from Kezari's hand, shocking him abruptly from his panic. "My cousin hunts her while we seek the leader of Braelyn. Justice will be served by claw or tooth."

She'd said so before, but her assertion did nothing to ease his fear.

Shame flooded him until he averted his face from the dragon's astute regard. He would never be whole again. If he couldn't even go into a blasted tavern, how could he survive for another month? It was impossible.

What did any of it matter, anyway? It wasn't like he could return to his family if he did prevail over his inner turmoil. Selia had surely remarried. So many had died in the shipwreck that had sent him drifting on the sea that he would have been counted in their number, especially after his long absence. It was better not to bring chaos and conflict to her current life or that of his son.

Better for Aris to *be* dead than that.

"Good day to you," a cheerful female voice said, but Aris didn't glance up. He couldn't. "What may I get for you?"

"I will have only roasted meat," Kezari said. "He will have a variety of other elven foodstuffs."

Unexpectedly, Aris found himself stifling a laugh. A laugh, of all things. They'd better eat and go, for there was no way the local authorities wouldn't be contacted at this rate. When the silence began to stretch, he risked a look up at the woman. Her befuddled stare shifted between Kezari and him.

"Elven foodstuffs?" she asked slowly.

Aris focused on her eyes—brown, not green—and tried to ignore her pale hair. "Please forgive my friend. She is not from Moranaia. I'll take whatever warm meal you have available. She meant to say that I'm not picky."

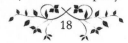

The woman relaxed, and her smile returned. "It's getting late, but there's still plenty of stew. I'll need to see about the roasted meat."

As the serving woman headed back toward the kitchen, Aris slumped in his seat. This had been a terrible idea. He'd considered camping in the forest beyond the village for the rest of the night, but after the disaster of this trip, it would be better if they moved on at once. In such a small village, their oddness would not go unremarked for long. And it was a small step from being noticed to being challenged by the guards.

Perhaps he and Kezari could camp on a distant mountain. A *very* distant mountain.

Thankfully, the tavern keeper had a portion of roasted *daeri* left over from the evening meal, so both Aris and Kezari were able to eat. Aris kept his head down, trying to savor the stew but ultimately shoveling it in as though he'd just returned from a long mission to the southern desert. A simple stew had never tasted so divine.

As they stood, Kezari dropped two valuable gems, sought after for their rainbow hues and durability, on the tabletop. He lifted a brow. "Food does not cost that much."

She frowned. "One should always pay well for excellent nourishment."

With a shake of his head, Aris pressed one of the gems back into her palm. Even one was excessive, but he had a feeling she wouldn't take both. "Fine. Let's go."

Because once the serving lady found the treasure, the rumors about him and Kezari would grow exponentially.

They reached the exit before the woman hailed them. "Milord. Milady. This is too—"

"Please keep it," Aris interrupted before she could mention the value of the jewel. Best if the other patrons didn't overhear the woman's good fortune. "Your kindness is well appreciated."

He urged Kezari out the door before he received an answer.

A few marks later, Kezari circled a remote portion of the mountains and then landed in a large clearing. Tiny flakes of snow drifted around them, tossed from the clouds by the cold air, but the ground wasn't yet cool enough even at this elevation for the flakes to stick. Miserable regardless, but he'd faced worse.

"I'll gather wood for a fire," he said.

"No need." Kezari nodded her wedge-shaped head toward the nearby line of trees. *"Let's settle by the forest. If you sleep against me, you'll be more than warm enough."*

The ground vibrated beneath his feet from the weight of her steps as Aris followed the dragon to the tree line. She curled up beneath a large tree, the branches still holding enough leaves to block some of the snow. After a brief hesitation, he settled in the space between her foreleg and chest, and sure enough, blessed warmth suffused him, easing the ever-present ache in his body. She curved her wing in front of him, enough to block the wind but not confine.

He couldn't quite relax, but he wasn't panicking, either.

Aris tipped his head back against her chest. There was much he didn't understand and even more he wasn't sure he wanted to know. But if he closed his eyes, he would be back in the cave, tormented once more. He gripped his knees until his hands stopped shaking. Asking Kezari questions could prove painful, but it was also a needed distraction.

"Tell me about the mark on my chest. About being a *skizik*. I'm not even sure what the word means."

"*Ah, yes.*" Kezari turned her face toward the forest, though her mental voice sounded thoughtful more than upset. "*Long ago, dragons recruited helpers. We are elemental, more so than your kind, but our elements are frequently…incomplete. A* skizik *is the other portion of the element, one you've joined magics with. It requires no mating or soulbond, but you do have to merge minds and powers.*"

He frowned at her explanation. "It makes no sense for your kind to be reliant on elves for complete powers."

Kezari's eye pinned him again. "*I did not say we were. A* skizik *can be another dragon. However, around the time of the war, no small number were elves or fae. We began to mark our non-dragon allies lest they be confused in battle. The tradition remains.*"

"This is madness, Kezari. You know that, right?" Aris heaved a sigh. "I almost lost control ordering food in a tavern, and you want to merge minds with me. There must be another who could become your *skizik*."

Her answer was a few moments in coming, and her voice was thoughtful when it did. "*Compatibility is not always so easy. But even if we didn't have to wait for the moons to be full to break the link, I would not. I like you.*"

He snorted. He wasn't particularly fond of himself right now, but a dragon had decided she liked him? Nonsensical. "Perhaps you are as crazy as I am."

"*You are not crazy.*" A puff of smoke escaped her nostrils. "*There is greatness in you, Aris, but you'll have to forgive yourself before you find it. Give yourself a chance to heal.*"

"Sure."

He fell silent, considering her words. She believed he'd recover, but she couldn't know the extent of his wounds. He could give her what she wanted and fully link— his memories would disillusion her quickly. But he refused to inflict that on Kezari, especially after all she'd done to help.

That kind of pain should die with him.

Aris closed his eyes and shifted against her smooth scales. "Help me sleep? I need rest if we're to reach Braelyn tomorrow, but the dreams…"

"*Of course, skizik,*" she answered, her voice echoing in his mind as he drifted toward oblivion.

3

Selia noticed the exact moment Arlyn faltered. Unfortunately, so did Iren. As Arlyn lost her grip on the group shield they'd all been holding, Iren sent his own energy forward to try to fill in the lack. But he overestimated, unbalancing the half-globe of power shimmering around them. Selia steadied the spell and then dispersed it safely. The hazy room beyond the shield came back into focus as the magic disappeared from around them.

"I was just trying to help," Iren said in a rush.

Selia nodded. "I know. It was a good instinct, but this type of work takes a light, steady touch. It was a shield of illusion only."

"I'm sorry," Arlyn said, her face almost as red as her hair. "I'm not feeling myself this morning."

Selia peered at her student. Before embarrassment had blushed her skin, Arlyn had looked a bit wan. Selia had assumed she was nervous about training with Iren. Although Arlyn was grown, she had lived most of her life on Earth and hadn't reached Moranaia until a few months ago. She'd barely started her magical training. Iren had a great deal more experience despite the gap in years. But she hadn't mentioned that. Perhaps she was ill.

"Do you need to go see the healer?"

One corner of Arlyn's mouth tipped up. "No. I've seen him about this. There's not much for him to do about my condition."

Arlyn's expression had Selia lifting her brows. Her condition, hmm? "You're pregnant!"

Iren's mouth fell open, but Arlyn chuckled as Selia lifted her hands to her own burning cheeks. "And now I am embarrassed," Selia said. "Please forgive my lack of courtesy. I should not have blurted such a supposition, especially since we are not alone."

Arlyn grinned. "You know I'm not formal, and I'd like to think we're friends."

"Of course," Selia answered. "Still…"

"Don't worry about it. Seriously." Arlyn glanced at Iren's stunned face. "I should have mentioned it outright, but I wasn't certain if I should with a child present."

Iren rolled his eyes at that. "I'm eleven years old. Why wouldn't I know all about babies?"

"Customs vary," Arlyn answered with a shrug. "Just please don't tell my father. I…maybe haven't mentioned it to him yet."

Oh, that couldn't be good. Were Arlyn and Lyr fighting? They hadn't seemed to be at odds, but one never knew. "Might I ask why not?" Selia ventured.

"I'm a chicken."

Selia blinked, not certain she'd heard correctly. "A…what?"

Arlyn laughed again. "Sorry. A chicken is a kind of bird."

"You're a bird?" Iren cried.

"No," Arlyn said, chuckling. "There's an Earth phrase. If someone is being chicken, it means they are acting cowardly."

Iren's expression grew thoughtful. "I'm a chicken," he whispered, probably putting the phrase back for future use.

Selia's lips twitched, but she stifled the laugh. "So why are you being a chicken about this?"

"He was upset that Kai and I bonded so quickly. I don't know how he'll react to this news," Arlyn said. "Besides, Kai is being annoying enough. I'd rather not have two people worrying about every little thing. Please tell me *you* won't do that."

Selia shook her head. "Of course not. I know well enough how frustrating that can be. We'll need to go back to meditating and connecting with your energy, though."

Arlyn groaned. "I thought I'd finally mastered that."

"Sure." Selia remembered her own struggles with magic when she'd been carrying Iren and winced in sympathy. "But as your baby grows, their magic will develop along with their physical body. It'll mess with your energy in the process. You'll need to re-center yourself periodically or your power might do strange things in the middle of a working. Like today."

Arlyn's shoulders drooped. "Figures."

"Before we try the shield again, we should—"

Selia's words cut off as the protections around Braelyn shrieked a warning into her mind. She wasn't fully linked to the estate's magic, but she'd helped reinforce the spells that detected intruders—such as the one sounding the alarm now. She sent her power into the spell and found what she'd already suspected. The threat came from the sky.

Arlyn shot to her feet, her brow creased in alarm. "That's not the portal."

"The dragon is here." Selia stood at the same time as Iren, though without the whoop of excitement her son released.

"A dragon?" Arlyn's eyes widened.

"Didn't your father mention it?"

"No, he absolutely didn't mention a dragon. You're kidding, right?"

Selia brushed at her pants in case she'd picked up any stray dust and then headed for her cloak. "Eradisel warned me last night. I assumed you would know."

"I haven't seen my father since yesterday afternoon. Guess that's what I get for avoiding him," Arlyn muttered as she retrieved her own cloak.

"Sounds like it." Selia gestured for Iren to hurry. "I want you to stay inside the main building, Iren. Watch from a window if you can't contain your curiosity, but don't come out. And don't dawdle. The only place clear enough for the dragon to land is the ridge above the valley, so we should be safe crossing the garden. But I'd rather get into the shelter of the main house even though we should be fine under the trees."

Her son nodded and rushed out the door behind her. She wasn't happy with the gleam of excitement in his eyes, but there wasn't much to be done for it. Iren had an adventurous spirit, much like his father, and little beyond tying him up would do much good if he was interested enough. But he was also smart, and he'd grown more cautious about danger after having to use his magic against an assassin to save Kai and Arlyn a few months prior. He would at least wait to analyze the danger.

She hoped.

By the time they arrived in the entryway, Lyr and Kai already waited. Iren rushed immediately to the window despite Selia's sharp warning, but she relaxed slightly at the calm expression on Lyr's face. Kai didn't appear nearly as collected. Frowning, he placed his hand on Arlyn's shoulder.

"You should stay in here with Iren."

Arlyn's mouth pinched. "You'd better rethink that."

"We don't know what the dragon wants. There's a chance—"

"How many *Taysonal* will have arrows trained on the dragon?" Arlyn demanded. "If you thought it was here to attack, none of you would be going out. I am my father's heir. Unless you have evidence of danger, I'm going, too."

Kai scowled. "I don't like this."

"She's right," Lyr said. "I've spent the night thinking about this. There's no way a single dragon would come here intending to attack. They are powerful, but they are neither invulnerable nor foolish. And in Selia's vision, the dragon had a rider. According to lore, only a dragon's linked *skizik* would be allowed astride except in an emergency."

"So?" Kai asked.

"If they were hostile to non-dragons, there would be no rider." Lyr spun toward the window beside the double doors as the throb of wingbeats began to drum against the walls. "This is almost certainly an act of diplomacy."

In the end, even Kai shifted close to the glass to watch the dragon land. Selia's breath caught at the gold shimmering from the massive body. Branches swayed in the tempest as the dragon alighted on the ridge outside the door. When it stilled, pulling its wings against its body and waiting with wedge-shaped head held high, its beautiful

scales gleamed like a thousand tiny flames. They were so blinding in the midday sun that she could barely make out the shadowed form of the rider.

"You have your spell prepared, Selia?" Lyr asked.

"Yes, but I cannot guarantee how well or how long it might hold." Selia tore her gaze away from the mesmerizing sight of the dragon and made sure the spell she'd created was ready. "I can also put up a fire-resisting shield. It seems like a reasonable action even during a diplomatic mission."

Lyr nodded. "Please do. Meli and my mother are in the library searching the archives for information about the initial peace treaty with the dragons and anything else pertinent. I've studied it, but my memory is hazy. Meli will relay word of anything they find."

"Arlyn should help them," Kai said.

Lyr shot his friend a quizzical look. "*Clechtan*, Kai, what is your problem? Do you not have faith in your bonded?"

"Of course I do, but—" Kai's words cut off when Arlyn grabbed his arm and glared at him. "Forget it. Let's just get this over with."

"If there wasn't a massive dragon outside that door, we'd be discussing this now," Lyr grumbled. Then he shook his head and started for the entrance. "Well, come on. Except for you, Iren. Do not put yourself into danger."

Selia pinned Iren with a glance as she followed the others. "If you don't listen to me, you'd better listen to the Myern."

"Okay," Iren said.

It wasn't precisely agreement, but it was the best Selia would get in such a short amount of time. *"Don't make me give you extra lessons. Or ban you from watching the warriors train,"* she sent to her son.

"I'm smart enough to understand real danger, Onaiala."

Selia snorted at the indignant frustration in his tone. *"I love you, Iren. Stay safe."*

"I love you, too," he answered.

As the group passed through the double doors and out into the clearing in front of the estate, Selia squinted against the flashes of light reflecting from countless scales. The autumn sun hung a bit lower, the perfect angle to strike against the dragon's body in a blinding display. She fought the urge to shield her face and stiffened her spine instead, not wanting to show weakness.

Thankfully, her eyes adjusted by the time Lyr halted, Arlyn and Kai to his left and Selia to his right. They stood just out of reach of the dragon's long neck and massive head. Selia hoped. Despite the nerves that danced in her stomach, she gathered energy and cast the flame-resisting spell in an arc in front of their group. The dragon's warm breath hissed over them, but it made no complaint about the use of magic.

"I bid you good day, honored visitors from the Isle," Lyr announced, no hint of worry in his tone or expression. "It has been millennia since one of the fabled dragons has graced us with their presence. I hope this is an occasion of peace and not of strife."

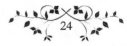

The dragon's voice—a female-sounding voice—poured into Selia's head despite not establishing a link. *"I have come to demand passage through the portal for myself and my skizik."*

Lyr didn't so much as blink. "Such passage was forbidden as part of the treaty."

"Forge a new treaty," the dragon sent. *"We must pass through."*

At the implacable tone and the puff of smoke from the dragon's mouth, Selia drew the containment spell into her mental hand. The dragon didn't appear ready to budge, but Lyr didn't, either. "Does your council know of your presence?" Lyr asked.

Selia barely managed to contain a shiver when the dragon snapped her mouth in annoyance. *"I will go through,"* she insisted.

"Calm down, Kezari," another voice said. A male voice, and one that sounded oddly familiar.

Selia narrowed her eyes against the sun and peered at the dragon's rider, but he bent down, obscuring his face. He threw his leg over and slid off. When his feet hit the ground awkwardly, he stumbled and leaned against the dragon's massive leg. A chill passed through Selia at the sight of his long braid. Light brown hair striped through with dark green. Just like...

He settled himself and spun to face them.

Aris. He looked like Aris. But that was impossible. Selia's head reeled and her knees grew weak. She darted out a hand, gripping Lyr's shoulder for balance. Seven years. Aris would not have stayed away from her if he was alive. He'd loved her and Iren. Perhaps this man was a relative.

Had to be.

Shock lined Lyr's face as he turned her to face him, taking her wrists and squeezing gently. "Selia?"

"It's impossible," she said aloud.

"Are you unwell?"

"That man looks like my husband," Selia whispered. "Iren's father. But he's dead. I..."

Lyr's expression softened. "You can go inside if you need to. We can manage."

For a moment, the temptation was almost too strong. But no. Selia had promised to use her magic to aid Lyr, so that was what she would do. She forced strength into her legs and shoved her shoulders back. "I can stay."

Lyr let her go, though he gave her a sidelong glance before returning his attention to the dragon's rider. "Please state your name and purpose here."

But if the man heard Lyr's words, he gave no indication. He stared at Selia, his eyes so shadowed with pain she could almost feel it across the distance between them. His mouth thinned into a line, and he turned his face away, resting his weight against the dragon's leg. In the shadow of the dragon, she could examine him more easily, but it didn't make her feel better.

Oh, Gods. It *was* Aris. With every breath, suspicion grew into certainty. She'd caressed those sharp cheekbones. Kissed that generous mouth. Tapped her finger

playfully against the small cleft in his chin. Her fingers had twisted in those long locks as she'd marveled at the green, a gift from his dryad grandmother.

She still dreamed about the shifting hazel of those eyes.

At the surge of hurt, Selia clenched her fists and locked her knees. She wanted to run into the house or crumple into a ball beneath the weight of her pain. But she would not do that. She had a duty to protect the rest of the group. Even as her heart shattered into dust.

For one long moment, Aris considered throwing himself over the edge of the ridge behind him. Only Kezari's warm bulk at his side grounded him. Supported him. Of all the things he'd expected to happen when they reached Braelyn, seeing Selia hadn't been one of them. His love. His light.

She had moved on.

"Your impoliteness does you no favors," their leader said, an edge of annoyance entering his voice. "What is your name, and why have you come here?"

It was gravely rude not to answer, but Aris couldn't force a single sound through his aching throat. Selia must have married or bonded to the lord here. As soon as she'd recognized Aris, she'd reached for the other man. Who had held her arms gently, whispering to her out of the range of hearing.

He hadn't been ready for this. Theory was one thing, but the reality… His stomach roiled as he struggled to think of what to do. Kezari wasn't going to give up on her mission. Maybe she would fly him to another location until she received approval to use the portal. She could return for him, and he'd help her solve her Earth problem.

Then he could be free.

He cleared his throat. "Forgive me, I…"

His throat seized, and his lungs burned with the shallow breaths he tried to force through. Each pair of eyes trained on him was a weight strangling away his very air. Wooziness blended with nausea until Aris had to settle his face against Kezari's leg to regain his equilibrium.

"I wish to shift, skizik.*"*

That shocked him out of his daze. *"What? Now?"*

"They cannot relate to me in my natural form. Perhaps an elven body would provide reassurance."

"Maybe," Aris answered. *"But by Arneen, wear some damn clothes."*

"Warn them. I do not wish to have an arrow to the wing."

Aris made himself look at the small group, but he couldn't meet anyone's eyes. "Kezari is about to shift into a smaller form. Please do not be alarmed by the surge in energy. I give my oath she intends no harm."

He could have sworn he heard a soft snort from Selia's direction, but her expression was blank when he ventured a glance. But then, she'd always been good at hiding her emotions. Her father had demanded his children master the art, and she'd

excelled at that task as expertly as every other. Of course, the more impassive she appeared, the more emotion she was typically containing. Unless she had changed. A lot could change in seven years—he shot a glance at her new lover—obviously.

Lyr nodded. "Very well."

Power expanded around them as Kezari's form began to blur and shrink. Aris shielded his eyes against the flash, but it only lasted a moment. Then she stood beside him in her elven form, her body barely covered by a thin, short dress. Without her larger body, the space between their two groups grew into a chasm. An abyss he wasn't certain he could cross.

Kezari said nothing, only wrapped her hot fingers around his wrist and tugged as she started forward. Instinctively, he balked, his feet digging in when she pulled. He couldn't do this. Even in the open sky, he couldn't. His chest tightened with each reluctant step, and his vision grew blurry at the edges. He needed to stop. He didn't want to break again, not here.

But Kezari's unrelenting grip dragged him forward.

"I am Kezari," the dragon said when they drew to a halt. "I wish to seek shelter for myself and my *skizik* while we resolve this matter. He needs a healer's aid."

Aris's muscles seized with the shock of her words. His throat closed around his denial.

"And I am Callian Myern i Lyrnis Dianore nai Braelyn," the lord answered. "I am willing to offer shelter so long as you vow to maintain peace and to not attempt to go through the portal without my permission."

"I vow such," Kezari answered.

Lord Lyrnis inclined his head. "Very well. In what way has your *skizik* been injured?"

Kezari peered at the trees ringing the clearing and then at the small group before them. "He would not wish to say at this moment. I would not. There are many ears."

"Perhaps we should continue this discussion in my study," the lord said. "Provided you are able to maintain your current form for that long."

Her nose wrinkled. "I can stay this strange shape for the needed time."

The door to the estate opened, and a woman with light blond hair exited. She held a book, not a knife, but her resemblance to Perim had Aris's chest constricting with the force of a great jungle snake. He gasped, a strangled sound of pain slipping free, and his vision wavered. With barely a glance his way, she rushed over to Lord Lyrnis, but her lack of attention wasn't comforting.

Kezari's fingers tightened on his wrist. *"It is not Perim."*

"I know." The woman stopped beside the Myern, the corners of her mouth curving as she leaned close to whisper. *"But they could be sisters. Even her energy is similar. What if she… A trap. This may be…"*

The clearing faded from his vision, replaced by memories of the cave. His captor's wicked smirk as her cajoling hands ran along his body. The sudden surge of pain as her knife sliced into his flesh. Aris attempted to dispel the images, but he couldn't

seem to find his grip on the present. She was here, and he would suffer for these weeks of freedom.

Something squeezed his wrist and shook, causing a twinge of pain, and he tried to tug his arm away. Too strong. The chains had always been too strong. Aris gasped for breath, but his chest hurt too much to take in air. Chills wracked his body as his mind splintered.

"Aris," a female voice snapped. "Stop, *skizik*."

"Told you…couldn't…"

Power flashed painlessly through his mind, and he fell into blessed dark.

4

Before Selia had quite processed what was happening, power surged and Aris crumpled. The dragon woman caught him in her arms and lowered his slack body to the ground. Beside Selia, Meli's words cut off, and Lyr hissed out a low curse. For a drip of time, they stood unmoving, the very air taut with tension.

That had been a spell of incapacitation—not something typically cast by a friend.

Selia rushed across the space between them. The dragon, Kezari, glanced up from where she crouched at his side, and power built around her. Selia readied her own magic, but she didn't stop. Not until she dropped down next to her husband and placed her hand on his cheek.

"What kind of dragon attacks her rider?" Selia demanded.

"Guard your words, elf." Kezari's head drew back as if she were about to breathe fire or consume prey, but on the shorter neck of this body, the motion threw her off balance and she had to catch herself on her hands. "Cursed useless form."

Aris let out a groan, and Selia studied his face. His eyes fluttered, but they didn't open. "What did you do to him?"

The dragon leaned closer, her voice dropping to a bare whisper. "The memories held him in their grip. I am uncertain how to heal him."

Memories? Selia recalled how the birds and other forest creatures had begun to make sounds of distress. Then the blind panic in Aris's eyes moments before the dragon had used her power. Selia's own heart had pounded with the frenzied rhythm of his, a sure sign that something was dreadfully wrong with her husband. He only lost control during times of extreme duress or pleasure, and his reaction hadn't been the latter.

Something terrible must have happened to him.

"You know the cause," Selia accused flatly.

Kezari gave a sharp nod. "But I do not know you."

Selia's hands shook as she brushed a strand of dark green hair from Aris's forehead. "I am his wife. Unless he rescinded his vow. I…I don't understand. He's dead. Was."

"He was on our isle for some years," the dragon said. "But not voluntarily, I discovered."

Aris had been held against his will? A frown creased Selia's brow as she stared down at her beloved's face. The survivors of the shipwreck had claimed to see Aris sink beneath the wreckage and never emerge. He must have been swept away by the currents and somehow ended up on the dragons' island. But who would have kept him captive for seven years—and why?

Why hadn't he run to her when he'd recognized her?

His eyelids flicked open, and his hazel eyes collided with hers. For a heartbeat, joy surged in his gaze, only to morph into pain. "Selia," he said, his voice rough.

"I can't believe it's you," she whispered. She wanted to throw herself across him and hold him close. She wanted to shake him and demand to know what had happened. Neither option seemed like the best plan considering his earlier breakdown. "I don't know what to ask first."

Aris winced. "Perhaps you should return to your husband."

"What are you talking about?" Selia blinked in confusion. Had he lost part of his memory? "You are my husband."

Aris shifted restlessly. "Lord Lyrnis."

That startled a short laugh out of her. "I am not married to Lyr. He's bonded to the blond lady who just joined us."

"Bonded to the…" Aris stiffened, his eyes going wide. "Who is she? What is her name?"

"Meli," Selia said quickly, hoping to stem the panic building on his face. How odd that Meli's presence caused him such distress. "She is one of the Ljósálfar, but I don't understand why that would upset you. I've never known her to be anything but kind."

Aris let out a breath. "She looks like—"

"Perim," Kezari hissed. "I will rend that reptile limb from limb. But I will not consume her. Oh, no. Her wicked body would give sickness, not nourishment."

Selia sat back on her heels. A reptile who looked like Meli? It made no sense. She started to ask for more information, but Aris distracted her by sitting upright. His cheeks reddened as he caught sight of the group watching them from a few paces away. Shame tinged his expression before all emotion left his face.

Aris had always loved people. To have reacted like this to such a small crowd… Whatever had happened to him must have been horrific.

Selia made quick contact with Lyr. *"Meli's appearance caused him distress. Literally."*

"Meli? You must be joking."

"I don't know the full story," Selia sent. *"But it seems he was captured at some point by someone who looks like her."*

Lyr gave a slight nod. *"I'll ask her to go back inside."*

After a moment, Meli's mouth fell open. Then she grimaced, and without a word, she spun and darted back inside. Once the door had closed behind her, Aris

relaxed slightly before shoving himself to his feet. But as Selia studied his harsh pro-
file, she had a feeling the man she'd known was gone.

Would she get the chance to learn who he'd become?

Aris forced his emotions to blank as he stared at the lord of Braelyn. Despite
the humiliation of falling prey to panic in front of the Myern, focusing on him was
a better alternative than Selia's stunned, hurt gaze. Once, he'd yearned with all of his
heart to be with her again, but that longing had been severed at Perim's hand. Selia
deserved far better than this broken shell.

"As Kezari stated earlier, I am…unwell," Aris said carefully. "Please forgive my
lapse."

Lord Lyrnis's expression remained placid. "It is of no consequence. However,
I must insist you accompany me to the healer's tower before negotiations continue.
Once you have properly introduced yourself, of course."

Aris hesitated. Who was he, really? He could no longer define his place, but
one's title described that very thing. Selia called him husband. Could he step back into
that role? He had no idea, but it was the closest thing he had to give. "Taian ia'Kelore
ai'Flerin ay'mornia Ayern Aris Baran ne Selia nai Fiorn."

Lyrnis inclined his head. From the Myern's lack of surprise, Aris assumed Selia
had somehow told him. "Follow me, Aris Baran. I have a feeling we need you well."

With that cryptic statement, the Myern strode back toward the building. The
other two who had been with him, a red-haired woman and a black-haired man,
stared after him for a moment before following. Then Lord Lyrnis cut left down a
side path and paused, glancing over his shoulder with a raised brow.

"Kezari?" Aris asked softly, knowing she would understand.

"You will see this healer." She reached for his wrist again, but he shook his head
in denial. He would move forward on his own this time. "I can shift into an elven
form, but I do not know how to fix one. Your body may be unwell. I cannot tell."

Avoiding Selia's gaze, Aris made himself take a step. Then another. Although his
heart pounded in his chest, he managed to shuffle toward the others without another
breakdown. Kezari and Selia kept pace with him, one on each side, but he couldn't
think about them. He had to concentrate on advancing.

How pathetic was this? He'd spent years traversing deserts and hacking through
jungles. He'd helped blaze trails and establish settlements in the remote areas of their
continent. Now, he could barely stand to cross a simple clearing in the heart of his
homeland. He had nothing to fear here—he'd never heard an ill word against Lord
Lyrnis or his father before him, and Aris sensed no hostility.

Too bad fear wasn't logical.

Or perhaps it *was* logical. The other half of his soul had been willing to torture
him for years. How could he trust strangers to treat him any better? His heart knew
Selia, at least, wouldn't hurt him, but he had no faith in anyone else. And being
around Selia brought its own agony.

Just as he reached the others, the estate door opened again, and another, smaller form slipped out. Aris halted, his muscles locking at the sight of the boy frozen in the doorway. Light brown hair flopped around his young face, a few strands shading his wide hazel eyes. Aris didn't need Selia's strangled groan to know who it was.

His son.

In a flurry of movement, Iren dashed across the distance between them and threw his arms around Aris. "*Onaial!*"

Aris's heart twisted and then pounded hard at the constraint. Even as joy surged through him, a thousand knives pricked at his nerves until his whole body thrummed with the need to push Iren away—but also to pull him close. Memories swelled of the last time he'd seen his son. Iren had curled his small body around Aris's leg and begged him not to go. Now his son's arms spanned his waist. *Miaran.* He would not let his sickness ruin this moment.

Even as Aris shuddered, he wrapped his arms around Iren and hugged him back.

Aris would never under any torture reveal the relief he felt when Iren finally pulled away. "You have grown too much," Aris whispered through a throat gone raw.

Iren swiped tears from his cheeks. "I thought you were dead."

"I did, too, but it seems I must live." Aris sighed at the frown the comment inspired. There was no way he could explain to his innocent son all of the horrors he'd been through or the times he'd longed for death. "I was a prisoner, Iren. I did not abandon you."

Trust gleamed in Iren's eyes as he smiled. "Now you're home."

What could he say to that? He hadn't thought to live beyond the next month. But seeing his family—perhaps he could find a way. Somehow. "I..."

"Your father was just rescued," Selia said softly. "He needs to see the healer."

Iren nodded. "Let's go."

Before Aris could think of a way to discourage him, Selia solved the problem. "You have studies to focus on, and I am certain your father would like privacy for his examination."

"But everyone else is going," Iren cried.

The red-haired woman stepped toward the estate, dragging the other male with her. "Kai and I will wait in the study. Come on, Iren. We can work on our history together."

Though he protested, his son was finally nudged back through the door by the unknown woman. Aris peered after her for a moment. She wore the medallion of the one named Kai, so she was clearly bonded. Why would she still be studying basic history at her age? With a shake of his head, he shoved the question aside. The mystery would have to wait.

"If you are ready?" Lord Lyrnis asked with a polite motion toward the trail.

Aris wanted to groan. They watched him like an invalid, and he couldn't even argue the point. Not when he could fall into madness at any moment. "Yes."

As he followed the Myern, Kezari gave him a pointed glance. "You did not mention that you have spawn."

Selia made a choked sound, and he winced. She had to think the worst of him despite his capture. If she even believed that part. "Speaking of my lost family brought me pain, and I did not want to spark another breakdown."

"I do not know what to do," Kezari said. "I would not put one with young into danger, but I must have your help. You are important."

His lips twisted. "I'm not an asset to anyone."

Kezari squeezed his shoulder. Though her fingers closed like talons, the gesture brought an odd sort of comfort. "Give yourself a chance, and you will be."

Once they reached the tower standing alone in the trees, the Myern stopped. The door was open, but Aris didn't see the healer. "I will stay outside," Lyrnis said.

Aris gave a small grateful smile. "Thank you, Lord Lyrnis."

"Please, call me Lyr." The impassivity faded from the Myern's face, replaced with lines of concern. "The sacred tree Eradisel Herself warned us that you would be arriving. Considering that and your connection to Selia, I suspect we'll attain more than a passing acquaintance."

The sacred tree? Aris blinked. He'd assumed the gods and their emissaries, the trees, had long forgotten him. "Very well."

"I will go into this place with you," Kezari said.

Aris stared at the gaping hole that was the door. It was too bright outside to see into the interior darkness of the tower. "I'm not sure I can go inside, regardless," he admitted.

"I could..." Selia began, but her words trailed off uncertainly when he met her eyes. Gods knew what she saw there. "Perhaps my presence would no longer bring comfort."

He lifted his hand to brush his fingers across her cheek, longing to smooth away her pained frown, but he let his arm drop. His fingers curled into his palm. Aris could never touch her again, not with hands as dirty as his. She wasn't some pure and perfect creature—no one was—but she deserved better than him. Once she learned the extent of his torture, she would surely agree.

"If I am to attempt to enter, it must be alone," Aris said. "Not even you can come, Kezari."

Her nostrils flared. "That is unwise."

His laugh held little humor. He had no idea if he could bring himself to go through the door, but if he couldn't perform that simple task under his own power, he had little hope of making it in this world. "Perhaps, but it is my choice."

Aris focused on his goal and took a resolute step forward. Then another. He had to do this. Now that he'd found Selia and Iren, Aris couldn't simply give up. It was one thing for his family to have never known he still lived. If Aris had killed himself, well...they'd already thought he was dead. But returning to his family only to leave them forever was a cruelty he couldn't inflict. The trust, joy, and love in Iren's eyes

haunted him, but they also propelled him. If nothing else, Aris had to discover if there was any hope of fixing his broken mind.

And maybe the healer would be able to tell if Aris's soul was as twisted as Perim's.

Selia stared after Aris and tried to shove down the pain that threatened to choke her. For the briefest moment, he'd almost touched her. Love and concern had flickered across his face, and he'd reached out to comfort her the way he'd always done. Then he'd shut down and pulled back.

Aris had told the dragon that thinking of his family caused pain. He hadn't mentioned Iren. Had he even intended to return to them? Perhaps he had decided to start a new life on Earth with the dragon. Selia eyed Kezari. She was certainly beautiful in her elven form. Selia would never have thought it of Aris, but anything was possible.

Kezari leaned close. "The female who tortured him claimed to be his mate."

Selia went cold as she processed the dragon's words. The implications of that whispered statement tore into her heart. "Tortured by his mate?"

"He rejected the claim," Kezari said. "I do not know more."

Selia had no idea how dragons used the word, but mate implied a soulbond. Gods, that couldn't be true. No one would do that to the other half of their soul. Bonding wasn't always as perfect as the idealized view so many held, but *torture?* It made no sense.

As Aris paused in the doorway of the tower, Selia had to hold herself back from running after him. If he believed she would reject him because of the torment he'd gone through, he was mistaken. And if he had bonded, she needed to know. Either way, one thing was perfectly clear—she would never stop loving him.

5

Aris reached the entrance before his resolve gave out. He dug his fingers into the wooden door frame and peered into the dim interior of the tower. But it wasn't dark now that he'd moved out of the sunlight. High windows allowed natural light to stream in, giving the room a soft glow. There was a long workbench along the left wall, a stone table at the back, and a bed near a staircase to the right. No healer, though.

As soon as he'd had the thought, someone started down the spiral stairs. Aris froze, hoping the healer wasn't another woman with Perim's coloring, but it soon became obvious that the healer was neither female nor blond. A stern-faced, auburn-haired male came to a halt a few paces from the door, his brow raised in question.

"Are you coming in?" the healer asked.

"I cannot tolerate being enclosed in the dark," Aris found himself admitting beneath the healer's steady regard. "I was kept in a cave for over six years."

"I am Lial," the other man said. At a quick gesture, the mage lights dangling from sconces brightened until the room was filled with light. "Lyr gave warning of your arrival, but he was unable to tell me much about your condition beyond what happened outside."

Aris snorted. "I think it was fairly obvious that I had a breakdown."

"Panic attack," Lial corrected softly. "I am not a mind-healer, but I have seen the results of trauma. How long has it been since your escape?"

Aris's grip loosened on the door frame. "One week."

"Five days of freedom would hardly be sufficient for your mind to recover." Lial took a cautious step closer. "Do you have physical injuries? Would you allow me to examine you?"

Suddenly, a helpless rage surged through Aris, stealing his breath. The healer, the others in the clearing—they looked at him like he was a wild animal, ready to snap at any moment. Next, the healer would hold out a treat and try to coax him. Was he really that messed up? Aris lifted his chin and shoved away from the door, striding toward a wooden stool beside the workbench. The bed was too far from the exit, but he would sit down and be examined, iron blast it.

"If this causes you discomfort—"

"Everything causes me discomfort," Aris snapped.

"Fair enough." The healer chuckled. "No need to be angry at me. At least not yet. I'll annoy you legitimately if you stay around long enough, or so I'm told."

"Healers often have that effect."

"Ah, but I have a talent for it." If the confession bothered Lial, his wry smile gave nothing away. Shrugging, he moved closer. "No more evading. May I scan you with my magic? I assure you that it causes no pain."

"I know that." Aris lifted a brow. "I have been healed before. I'm not a child."

"I've had patients from beyond Moranaia of late," Lial said. "I've learned not to assume."

Interesting but irrelevant. Aris braced himself, fighting the anxiety of being in contact with another person's energy. "Just get it over with."

Despite his initially tentative approach, Lial didn't hesitate. Aris squeezed his eyes closed against the blue glow and gripped the bottom of the stool as the light settled around his body. Peace rushed in with it, easing his clenched muscles. His mind floated, much as his body did when Kezari carried him across the sky. He let go and drifted.

Lial had grown adept at stifling anger while working, but for the first time in centuries, he struggled to maintain control. Aris's body was riddled with signs of abuse, from a just-healed gash across his thigh and side to bones that had been broken and improperly set. Typically, elven bodies healed from even serious injuries with a modicum of care. For Aris's bones to be misaligned, his tormentor would have had to warp his limbs out of alignment and leave them there while they healed. Probably stretched out while chained.

Stifling another surge of fury, Lial proceeded to Aris's mind. The maelstrom there would need a mind-healer to fix, preferably with a mage present to guard against Aris's power overflowing. Lial had a small amount of mind-healing talent, but not enough to touch this. So many pathways created by torment and fear. Aris must have a strong will to be so lucid. With a sigh, Lial did what little he could to ease the panic. If there hadn't been a dragon outside, waiting impatiently, he would have rendered his patient unconscious until a mind-healer arrived. It went against his every instinct to allow Aris to suffer more, but in this, he had no choice.

Lial gathered more energy and healed the cuts and strained muscles he'd found on his first pass. Then he did what he could for the misaligned bones. Most would cause no active trouble, only leave a weakness that would make future breaks easier, and a few others he was able to smooth out. But the large bone in the right thigh and one in the left forearm would need to be rebroken and set again.

Not today. With his patient's permission, Lial would undertake that after the mind-healer arrived—and while Aris was sedated. Lial had had plenty of recent practice restructuring bone after fixing Lynia's spine, so the task itself would be more draining than difficult. Hopefully, Aris would agree before the damaged bones caused him trouble.

After a quick pass to ensure that any injury to the organs had healed, Lial pulled his consciousness fully back to his own body. But he didn't remove his healing magic while he opened his eyes. How could he reawaken his patient to the torment of existing with such scars? The tension and stifled fear had smoothed from Aris's face, and his half-slitted gaze was clear of stress. It would be a difficult return to awareness, but neither of them had a choice.

Muttering a curse, Lial lowered his spell as slowly as he could. It was always his nature to heal, no matter his joking threats to the contrary, but for the first time in a long time, he wanted to hurt someone. As each line of anxiety returned to his patient's face, the urge to annihilate Aris's tormentor grew. Too bad Lial would never have the chance.

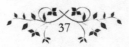

As the light faded, so did Aris's moment of peace. He tumbled back into his body in a slow fall, and though he could tell that the healer tried to give him time to adapt, there was no stopping reality. He felt…different, and his heart gave a hard leap until he realized that it was a good different. He'd grown accustomed to a constant ache, varying degrees of pain that shifted rather than disappeared. Almost all of that was gone. Even his emotions seemed a bit steadier.

Emphasis on *a bit*.

Aris focused on the healer's angry face. "That bad?"

"I was able to fix everything but two misaligned bones." Lial's lips thinned. "And the bulk of the damage to your mind. That will require a specialist."

Aris frowned. "Bones?"

"Do you not remember having them broken?"

"I do." Aris shuddered as he tried to concentrate on the knowledge of the events rather than the actual memories. "I thought such injuries heal quickly."

Lial gave a sharp nod. "They do, but it was not a boon in this case. You must have been held in a position where they couldn't realign correctly."

His very bones. Aris's shoulders slumped as despair rather than anger filled him. If the healer couldn't fix them, he would carry those remnants of her always. "Will it cause me future trouble?"

"Not if you let me correct the problem." Aris glanced up at those words. "Your mind is damaged enough that I must bring a mind-healer here. Once you've undergone that treatment, I'll render you unconscious, rebreak the bones, and heal them properly. I will not do that in your current state. Even unaware, it resembles torture too closely. It's bad enough that you must remain awake and aware until a mind-healer can be found."

Aris winced at the blunt truth, but it was preferable to the alternative. "I appreciate your candor. I did not expect it after your initial caution."

Lial's brows rose. "Did you expect me to be rough with a patient suffering such severe anxiety?"

"I did not give it much rational thought," Aris admitted.

"Do so in future." Despite the gruffness of his tone, Lial's eyes pinched with concern. "And do not give up. I sense the risk of that in you, and I will warn your dragon as such. Were she not insistent on your presence, you would be in a deep sleep instead of speaking with me. Do anything rash, and I will be dealing with a dragon's wrath over your unconscious body."

Kezari's voice popped into his mind as though summoned. *"The wrath will be at you, skizik, if you attempt to harm yourself."*

It seemed she hadn't quite left his mind after all.

Aris rubbed the back of his neck. "I will do my best. But I must know this. Was there…other damage? I worry that this darkness has spread to my soul."

Lial's eyes narrowed. "I am no priest, but I detected nothing like that in you. Being abused does not make you an abuser."

But having an evil soulbonded might. Aris opened his mouth to voice that concern, but his throat closed around the words. He couldn't confess that. Everyone already regarded him warily. If they knew the other half of his soul was a twisted, torturous woman, they would watch him with fear, too. He couldn't bear it.

"Thank you," Aris finally managed.

"Send for me at any hour." Lial gestured at the door. "Now, I suggest you rejoin your dragon before she storms my tower. I will search for a suitable mind-healer."

Aris shoved himself off the stool. "There are things… I would prefer another male."

With a grimace, Lial nodded. "I will see that it is so."

The benefit of the healing became obvious when Aris strode for the door. Now, only a slight ache in his right thigh remained, and his muscles flexed easily with each step. Some pain wasn't obvious until it was gone, he supposed. Although anxiety still threaded its claws into his heart, his physical body felt so much better that his mental burden grew lighter, too.

Perhaps he could make it. Perhaps there was hope.

Selia tapped her fingers along her crossed arm and watched the dragon pace. The longer she was in Kezari's presence, the more obvious the dragon's otherness became. She bore an elven form, but she lacked typical facial expressions and physical motions. Although pacing, it seemed, was universal. Kezari's feet slammed down with a force that would have razed buildings in her dragon form. Wordlessly, she'd circled the clearing in front of the healer's tower countless times in less than a mark's time.

"Did Meli find something useful?" Selia asked Lyr softly. "She was quite intent on bringing you that book."

Lyr nodded. "A record of the treaty, complete with commentary."

Well, that was curious. A forty-thousand-year-old record in their library? "I did not expect that to be housed here."

"It is not the original," Lyr said. "That is at the palace under preservation. But my ancestors deemed it prudent to keep a full copy close to the portal. My mother found the passage I thought I remembered from my studies, and Meli rushed it over. I suppose she could have taken her time."

"Poor Aris." A lump formed in her throat. "The way he reacted to Meli. To all of us, really. I don't know what's going to happen next."

Kezari drew to a halt, her head whipping around. "He's going to come with me through the portal."

Lyr frowned. "We will have this discussion later."

"You are a mage?" Kezari asked Selia, not acknowledging Lyr's words. "We will need you, too. This will be easier. Faster. You will come. But perhaps we must bring your young to guard."

Selia stared at the dragon's closed expression. "Do dragons jest?"

"Not in this manner." Kezari startled her with a toothy grin. "We need a mage, but young must be guarded."

"Enough, Kezari."

Aris strode from the doorway of the healer's tower with more confidence than he had entered, and although his face was still lined with tension, something about him was more…himself. She wanted to ask how much the healer had been able to help, but he avoided her gaze when he drew near.

Perhaps she no longer had the right.

"We need to explain the situation rationally to the Myern," Aris said. "And to Selia. She is a powerful mage."

Kezari stared at him. "I will go into the dwelling if it is required, but I do not like it. I do not feel safe under so many trees."

"I am not fond of the concept, myself," Aris said.

"It is the most private option," Lyr interjected smoothly. "Which I believe you both desire. This is a large estate with many guards, not to mention residents. My study is secure."

"Very well," Kezari said, and without another word, she started down the path toward the main estate.

Lyr turned to follow, and suddenly, Selia was alone with Aris. She flicked a look through lowered lashes, but he barely glanced her way as he started walking. She hurried to keep pace, her jaw clenching in annoyance. Was he going to pretend she didn't exist? If he'd bonded or otherwise decided to end their marriage, he could at least have the grace to tell her. There was no need to treat her like the ghost he'd been.

"You cannot avoid me forever," she murmured.

A hitch marred his stride. "I don't know what you mean."

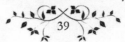

"By the Great God Meyanen—" Selia began, cutting off her words before she could threaten bodily harm. That would be the worst thing she could say. "I understand that you are not ready to speak of what happened, but after three centuries of being together, I would have expected the common courtesy of looking at me and acknowledging my presence."

Selia had his attention then, but the dark annoyance lining his face was far from what she'd wanted. "If you understood, you would not say such things," Aris said.

"Maybe." Selia drew her shoulders back, bracing herself. "But I want you to know that if you have decided to end our relationship, you may simply say so."

Mouth pinched tight, Aris ran his fingers through his hair. "I have not. When I am able to tell you what happened, however, you will cast me aside. I am not whole, Selia. I have no idea how effective mind-healers are, but I doubt they can fix this."

"Aris, you know I—"

"Would not hold my capture against me." His hand lifted as though he would touch her, but once again, he lowered it without making contact. "I want to be here for Iren until he reaches manhood, but I don't know if I can. Each moment is agony. The endless stretch of years before me breaks me inside. I refuse, *refuse,* to drag you into this madness."

Selia wanted to scream, but she had no idea at whom. Him, in part, but shame filled her at the impulse. It wasn't his fault he'd been traumatized, and it would be wrong of her to push him. If she ever encountered this Perim, Selia would blast the *drec* with a spell so violent that ballads would chronicle the event for millennia. Then the dragon could chew up the remains.

As the front doors came into view, Selia leaned close to Aris but was careful not to touch him. "Speak to me as a friend, if you must, and we will resolve the rest when you are able. You know you will always have my love and support. Just treat me as though I exist."

"I did not intend to upset you," Aris said. "But it hurts. It hurts to see you and to know all that was lost. If I seem to ignore you, it is only to avoid a breakdown."

Tears burned in her eyes, for him and for herself. She'd believed his disappearance and death had been the worst thing that could ever happen to her and Iren, but she'd been wrong. Oh, that had been horrible. But nothing compared to the joy of finding him alive intertwined so painfully with the knowledge of his broken state. He was as dead to her as he'd been that morning even though he walked beside her.

Far too close to be so out of reach.

6

Aris had expected to feel trapped by the estate, but entering the large double doors filled him with a curious sense of comfort. Perhaps it was the fact that the massive house had been constructed quite literally around the largest of the trees. Just ahead, a staircase spiraled up a broad tree trunk in the middle of the room. Then he glanced to the left, and his breath caught. On the far end of the entryway, the wall had been cut away to reveal the most massive trunk he had ever seen, its energy unmistakable.

Eradisel, one of the nine sacred trees.

The reason behind the steady flow of comfort solidified in his mind. Because of his gift, he'd always resonated with the Great Trees. In fact, he'd considered becoming one of the priests that tended the sacred nine, but he hadn't felt a true calling for that path. The gods were a distant concept, worthy of reverence but not as immediate as the life his magic detected. Why be bound to one place, meditating on divine favor, when he could be discovering the gods' creations? Or so he'd once thought. Roaming the world had lost its appeal after his latest adventure.

Aris sensed the soft brush of Eradisel's energy against his mind. Lyr had said that the sacred tree had warned them of Aris's arrival. But why? His feet wanted to carry him to Her to ask, but the task at hand kept him from following his desire. The Myern certainly would have allowed time, Aris knew, but Kezari was low on patience. If the sacred tree affected her, she didn't give any sign of it. She slunk after Lyr with hunched shoulders, her uneasy gaze darting everywhere.

Why was she so bothered by Braelyn? Kezari hadn't been this uneasy in the tavern or the clothing shop. Concerned, he connected to her mind. *"What is it? Do you sense danger?"*

"This place curves in little tunnels. You will see."

He found his brow lifting. Tunnels? Then Lyr pivoted down a corridor that did curve here and there to accommodate trees, though the hallway was hardly a tunnel. *"Don't dragons live in caves?"* he asked, trying to hide his amusement. *"With narrow passages, too, I'd wager."*

Kezari let out a small but pointed snort. *"Those are inside mountains. What if one of these trees crashes on this puny structure? There is no bulk. The other structures we entered might have been flimsy, but they weren't so ill-placed."*

Aris chuckled at that, earning a questioning glance from Selia. "How many spells would you say fortify this place?" he asked aloud.

Selia's brow furrowed for a moment before she answered. "There are seven types upholding the walls themselves, mostly preservation against natural degradation but some for fortification. A solid twenty-two maintain the roofs, and approximately fifty are layered carefully to prevent damage to and from the trees. Why do you ask?"

"Dragon taming," Aris answered as Kezari lifted her chin and pretended not to hear. "Kezari was concerned about the possibility of collapse with so many trees."

"Reasonably so," the dragon sent to him alone. *"This form squishes easily."*

As Aris choked back another laugh, Lyr peered at Kezari. "Braelyn has stood on this spot for thousands of years. In fact, the main entry and the rooms above were built just after the war with your kind."

"After we burned the original, I suppose," Kezari said stiffly.

"There was no ill-intent behind my comment." Lyr paused in front of a door and caught the dragon's eye. "We are not our ancestors. Even had our own parents warred, I would not hold you in poor regard because of it. I meant only to highlight the security of the building."

Kezari inclined her head. "I thank you, then."

Lyr opened the door and gestured for them to precede him. Aris followed Kezari through a short hallway that opened into a large oval room. Bookcases and tall windows lined the longer sides of the oval, with a short dais and large desk on the farthest end. The couple from earlier rose from two of the chairs in the center as the group entered. From their tense body language, he had a feeling the pair had been arguing, but he was hardly one to judge.

Quickly, Lyr made the introductions. Aris processed the formal titles with a smile, although the information prompted more questions he wouldn't ask out loud. The tall red-haired woman with green eyes was Lyr's daughter and was soulbonded to the frowning male with black hair. Arlyn and Kai. Seven years ago, before Aris had left on the expedition, the Myern hadn't had children. At least he didn't think so. Either Aris hadn't been paying attention, or something strange had happened in the last seven years.

"It is an honor to meet you," Aris said, keeping his curiosity to himself. "I appreciate your assistance with Iren. I hope he didn't give you too much trouble."

Arlyn grinned. "I had him go study with Lady Lynia. My grandmother will keep him in line."

He knew nothing about the lady in question, but from Selia's low laugh, he assumed it had been a good decision. "Thank you," he said.

Aris studied Lyr's tense posture as he strode across the room and opened a book on his desk, frowning down at the pages. Something was obviously bothering him.

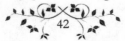

Were the terms of the Moranaian treaty with the dragons so dire? Kezari's request hadn't sounded like a problem to Aris, but his knowledge of the war didn't go beyond the basics every child learned. It seemed that hadn't been the case for Lyr, who flipped through the tome like he knew what he was looking for.

"It is as I thought," Lyr said. "No dragon can pass through the portal without the permission of both rulers. Even then, there are very specific conditions listed."

Aris took a step closer to Kezari, who had stopped her pacing to glare at Lyr. "Our queen could not feel the scope of this danger. She did not believe. You must be wiser."

Lyr placed his hands on his desk and leaned forward. "Perhaps you should explain what is going on."

"*Skizik?*" the dragon demanded.

"Oh no," Aris answered, shaking his head. "I barely understand this myself."

Kezari shifted on her feet. "I am of the Earth and the earth. I can work with the rocks and soil here, but my connection to our original world remains strong. Something is wrong there. It is terrible."

Lyr's lips turned down. "I have guides who travel there regularly. Although there was trouble with poisoned energy, that was resolved about a month ago. Is this feeling recent?"

"It is now," Kezari insisted. "It grows. It seeps into the ground. The plants and living creatures must be affected. Aris and I, we can heal it, especially with his mage."

Beside him, Selia let out a soft sound, a sure sign of her annoyance to any who knew her. "I have not agreed to such a thing."

Kezari turned her golden eyes their way. "You will. You must."

"This requires more investigation," Lyr said as he straightened. "I will not send any of you through with so little information. I do not mean offense, but it is difficult to believe that none of my guides would have noticed this kind of danger."

"It can't be too bad if Ralan isn't here giving orders," the one named Kai muttered.

"Prince Ralan?" Aris stared at the other man, uncertain he had heard correctly. The prince had left Moranaia centuries ago. "Why would he be?"

Lyr grimaced. "I'm sorry, Aris. You wouldn't have heard of his return during your…absence. The prince has been back for a couple of months now. Ralan, his daughter Eri, and his bonded Cora are currently staying in my home while a secondary palace is being built to the south of my lands. They are at the site consulting with the builders today."

"Eri isn't," Selia said, giving the door an uneasy glance as though someone would rush through at any moment. "She asked to stay and play with Iren after lessons."

"She was with my grandmother," Arlyn said.

Silence fell, and Aris pursed his lips at the oddness of it. He could deduce that Eri was a child, but why would that make a room full of adults nervous? Suddenly, he felt like an outsider in the land where he'd been born. Important events had ob-

viously occurred, things the others knew well. As an adventurer, he'd always tried to keep up with the news from the larger estates—it was how he'd found some of his best missions. Now he was a tree with no roots.

"I do not care who is here," Kezari said, her voice rising in annoyance. "Something must be done. Contact your ruler. Work out a new treaty."

Lyr's expression turned sympathetic. "I understand your concern. I do. There has been much to handle here, so I have grown accustomed to crisis. A rogue Moranaian caused the initial energy poisoning, and it affected quite a few fae realms as well as Earth. That foe has been defeated and a counter-spell activated. In truth, I have experienced enough chaos lately to know better than to dismiss your words."

"But?" Aris demanded.

"I must obey the law." Lyr gestured at the book still open on his desk. "This treaty is older than any of us, save perhaps Kezari. Ralan could negotiate on his father's behalf with the king's permission, but unless you are dragon royalty, Kezari, there is nothing to be done."

"I am not a princess." Kezari sniffed. "Nor am I so old. That happened in my grandparents' time, thank you."

Aris smiled slightly at the dragon's vanity, but he didn't want to hurt her feelings by calling her on it. "What would you suggest, Myern?"

"I'll send Kai and Arlyn through the portal to see if they can detect any hint of trouble. Arlyn destroyed the other spell, so she might be more sensitive to new problems."

"No," Kai said at once.

"If we weren't bonded, I'd shove you off the top of the brooding tower." Arlyn poked her finger against Kai's side. "Stop it."

Brooding tower? Bemused, Aris glanced between them. The group's arrival had definitely interrupted an argument, one that appeared ready to erupt again. Arlyn glared at her bonded, who stood with crossed arms and set jaw. If the Myern thought she was skilled enough to take on such a mission, why would her bonded protest? How unusual.

"This is not the time for such a disagreement," Lyr snapped. "We can discuss this in greater detail once I have found our guests shelter."

Kai clenched his jaw tighter, but Arlyn's face reddened. "Of course," she said.

Though Lyr's eyebrows were lowered in frustration, he strode easily around his desk, and the emotion had smoothed away by the time he stopped in front of Kezari. "I assume you will want a place where you can shift back to your natural form?"

"Oh, yes," Kezari said emphatically. "This skin itches after a time. Far too small."

Aris frowned. His mind had been too muddled to consider this problem. There'd been fewer trees on their other stops, but the area around Braelyn was largely ancient forest. They'd learned to build their houses in, around, or on those trees, but Kezari's dragon form wouldn't fit in any of those structures. The few clear places along the ridges weren't particularly secure.

"The stone beneath Braelyn is fairly solid, but there is a small cave system on the north end of the ridge," Lyr said. "If it does not cause offense to be so removed from the bulk of my home, I would suggest you stay there. You are more than welcome to make subtle changes to the caves if they are not large enough."

Kezari's head tilted back. "You would trust me to make modifications?"

"Dragons are renowned for such work," Lyr answered. "And it would not be in your best interests to destabilize the land above you."

Cave...land above... Aris's shoulders jerked in an involuntary shudder. At Selia's concerned glance, he shook his head. He did not want to reveal yet another weakness, but he had no choice. Kezari was certain to be upset by his refusal. Still, what else could he do? Not even under the prompting of the Nine Gods of Arneen would he go into a cave voluntarily. "I will have to beg a different kind of shelter."

Kezari spun, her nostrils flaring. "I will not leave you unguarded. We should be close."

"I cannot." Aris let out a shaky sigh. "A cave would be living torment. Perhaps I could camp on the ridge just above? Anything out in the open."

"You are not considering the season. The nights are turning chilly, and the cold rains are almost upon us. Late autumn is an unpleasant time to camp," Lyr said.

Fiorn, where Aris had lived most of his life, didn't suffer through autumn rains—at least not in the same way. The plains did flood off and on through autumn and winter, but it was warm throughout both seasons. However, he'd been on several expeditions to climes like Braelyn's, and those had been sheer misery. Too bad he wouldn't be able to abide a tent. Fabric close to his face, blocking any view... No.

Selia stepped forward, catching his attention. "What about the brooding—I mean, the observation tower?"

Shame and frustration curled through his insides and sharpened his tone. "What, you think I need space to mope?"

"No." Selia lifted a hand in conciliation. "It's a nickname that has nothing to do with you. I wasn't trying to insinuate anything."

Lyr chuckled even as his daughter winced. "Arlyn has caught both myself and Kai atop the tower in times of distress, so she dubbed it the brooding tower. The name stuck."

Aris rubbed the back of his neck. He'd grown too sensitive during his capture, and he had a feeling it would cause him more than a little embarrassment. Selia wouldn't have been so rude. She, unlike his so-called bonded, had never insulted him like that. Well, besides a few well-placed barbs during arguments, but he'd never held that against her. He'd said his own share of foolish things.

"Forgive me," he said.

"Of course," Selia answered softly, but the tense set of her shoulders told him she was still upset. Nothing to be done about it now. "I suggested the tower because the walls of the top floor are largely glass. You can see from any angle but still be

inside. And Kezari could perch on the top when she wished to be close to you. The roof is flat."

Lyr nodded. "Excellent suggestion. Would you mind showing Aris and Kezari the tower while I speak with Kai and Arlyn?"

"It would be my pleasure," Selia said.

Oh, he just bet it would. She was probably eager to reprimand him for thinking ill of her. "We would greatly appreciate it," Aris said.

Selia gestured toward the door. "Then let us go."

Hoping she wouldn't be too hard on him, Aris nodded and then followed.

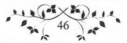

As soon as the door closed, Lyr rounded on Kai. "That's it. What is wrong with you? Don't try to tell me everything is normal, either. Clearly, it is not."

Kai's nostrils flared. "I don't want Arlyn put in danger again. Last time was bad enough."

"You're joking." Lyr stared at his friend, aghast. Kai had never reacted this way before. He was treating Arlyn the way he'd seen some human males act toward their women, possessive and overprotective. "Would you say the same for Kera or any of our other female warriors?"

Kai gaped at him for a moment before shaking his head. "You think it is because Arlyn is a female? That's not it at all. Well, I suppose it's related, but—"

"I'm pregnant," Arlyn blurted, her words ringing into a sudden silence.

It didn't hit Lyr immediately. Then the full import trickled through, along with a shock so profound it rattled him to the core. His daughter was expecting a child? But she'd only been here for three months, had only been bonded with Kai the same length of time. Few elves conceived so quickly.

Joy sparked inside him as the news settled in.

"I should have waited a few more weeks to tell you," Arlyn mumbled.

Lyr's gaze shot to his daughter, his rising happiness stifled a little by her statement. "How long have you known?"

She nibbled at her lower lip. "Since just before Ralan went to Earth to find Cora."

Hurt pinched Lyr's heart, warring with joy. She'd kept something this important from him? It explained Kai's growing protectiveness and reluctance to travel to the Sidhe realm of his own father. Had they told Naomh? Anyone else?

Such amazing news—and only Kai's snit had revealed it to him.

"Why didn't you say anything?" Lyr forced himself to ask.

"Because of this. Your reaction." Arlyn sighed. "I knew you wouldn't take it well."

Comprehension dawned as Lyr stared at her worried face. "You think I'm upset that you're pregnant? No. I'm thrilled beyond telling about my first grandchild. But I am hurt that you didn't trust me enough to tell me sooner."

Frowning, Kai crossed his arms. "You were furious when we bonded."

Lyr made a sharp, impatient gesture. "Not at the bond itself. Only your haste in starting the bond. I thought we resolved that two months ago."

"I'm sorry," Arlyn whispered.

At the sight of his daughter's upset face, Lyr's hurt, and his heart, melted. He wrapped his arms around her in a gentle hug. "Ah, *tieln*, I'm the one who is sorry. This shouldn't be about me. Let's not mar such wonderful news with worry."

"I should have told you," she said with a sniffle. "Only Lial knows. I had to see him to check, of course. Well, Selia guessed this morning when my energy went awry during a lesson. I don't know why I was so worried. Hormones, maybe."

Smiling, Lyr gave Arlyn's shoulders a reassuring squeeze. "Don't stress this. Are you well? Is Kai so protective because there's a problem?"

Arlyn took a step back and glared at Kai. "No. We're perfectly fine."

"If she and the child are healthy, why would she not continue her duties?" Lyr peered at his friend curiously. Color had leeched from his face along with any hint of anger. "What is this really about?"

For a moment, Kai didn't answer, his expression twisting with an odd sort of pain. "I didn't know my own mother beyond my first few days of life. I can't abide risk to either you or our child, Arlyn. My family is so fucked up, but this…I want better for us. The fear isn't rational, but I can't silence it."

"I never said I wanted to go on this mission," Arlyn said with a shrug. "Unless there is truly no one else, I'd rather not. I don't think it's a good idea to expose our child to poisoned energy."

Kai scowled. "Then why—"

"I didn't want you speaking for me, either," Arlyn interrupted, giving her bonded a pointed look.

Lyr couldn't help but laugh at Kai's chastised expression. "You deserved that, my friend. As to our current crisis, I'll see if Inona is ready to resume her duties. If so, she and Delbin can travel to Earth. Delbin can seek out Fen and see if he knows what is going on. Hopefully, he isn't involved."

"I don't think he is," Kai said. "But our acquaintance was admittedly short."

"I suppose we'll see. Now…I won't tell you to rest, Arlyn. I'm sure Kai does that countless times already." Lyr grinned at his friend's disgruntled frown. "I'm sure you'd rather take Kai to task a bit more in private. Or have my mother work with him on his manners."

Kai groaned. "Can I just grovel?"

Lyr made a shooing motion. "Not here. I have work to do."

As soon as Kai and Arlyn closed the door behind them, Lyr sank into his chair and rubbed his hand across his eyes. Dragons had been denied access to the portal for a reason. The few dragons who had opted to stay on Earth instead of migrating to Moranaia had lingered for millenia and had caused a great deal of trouble. And during the war, some of the Moranaian dragons had raided Earth with impunity to bolster their resources. The humans had their dragon

myths for a reason—dragons did not live well with other species.

But Lyr had a bad feeling that the dragon would have to go to Earth, and navigating the situation was a mess he'd rather not handle. Too bad it was his job. With a resigned sigh, he prepared to contact Inona.

7

By the time they neared the tower, Selia was ready to scream. Eradisel had told her to prepare herself, but there was no way to get ready for this. Her beloved husband walked beside her like a near-stranger, asking polite questions about the scenery. Who cared how many different kinds of blasted flowers were in the gardens or how long it had been since the last rain? No one in this situation.

"How long have you been here?" Aris asked.

"About three months." Gritting her teeth, she shoved the words she wanted to say to the back of her mind. "Lyr's daughter arrived unexpectedly from Earth. Her gift was strong but untrained, so he sought a teacher for her. Iren and I came to live here then."

Aris frowned. "How did Iren take the move?"

"He has loved being away from Fiorn," she answered. "We've had a few rough days, but he's thrived away from my father's strict rules."

"I imagine so." Aris grimaced. He'd never gotten along with her father, either. "There is so much I want to know about Iren. So many years… I'm not sure how I can ever make up for that."

Her heart pinched. She'd wanted him to talk about something more serious, but now that he'd broached the topic of his missing years, she wasn't sure how to continue. "It wasn't by your doing," she ventured.

Aris shook his head. "It doesn't matter. The result was the same."

She twisted her fingers together. "I don't know what to say."

"Selia," Aris said softly. "Don't get upset on my account."

She snorted at that. "Sure."

As they stopped at the door in the base of the tower, he surprised her by taking her hand. His hold was light, but it was there. Voluntarily. "I mean it. I don't know if the mind-healer can help. I don't know if anything can. But I will do my best to keep from hurting you more. That would never be my intention."

Her shoulders drooped. "I know."

"*Skizik*, this tower is broad," Kezari said from a few paces away, seemingly oblivious to their conversation. "I could maybe sleep on top."

The wide stone tower stretched up high in the middle of the clearing. But though the top was at the same height as the branches of the nearby trees, it didn't appear big enough for a dragon to sleep on. At least not to her eyes. "Let's go up. It's a bit of a climb, though, and the staircase is enclosed."

His hand jerked in hers before he abruptly let go. As he peered at the stone, Aris shivered. "With few windows."

"Were you…" How could she ask about his captivity without throwing his mind into chaos? She didn't want to, but it was difficult to suggest suitable shelter if she didn't know how he'd been held. "Do such structures bring back bad memories?"

His lips thinned. "Anything enclosed, which is nonsensical. The cave was large enough to hold Kezari in dragon form. But I was rarely free to explore it."

Although his words were even, Aris's pupils had begun to dilate, and his breathing was growing shallower. Her instinct was to reach out to him, but she held back. "Perhaps I can help," she offered softly.

"Selia—"

"Not with mind healing. I have an idea, if you'll indulge me."

His nod was sharp, but he gave it. Quickly, Selia sent a mental request to Lyr and stood with bated breath until he gave his assent. She hadn't been sure he would approve such a major modification, but he was eager to see Aris settled. All she needed now was energy. As she stepped through the doorway into the small landing at the bottom of the stairs, Selia reached out with her senses and connected to the power of the world around them.

Magic streamed through, burning in her blood like purest sunlight. Selia smiled with the joy of it, but she didn't take the time to bask. Instead, she funneled the power through the proper channel in her mind and stretched out her hand. She started up the steps, letting her hand rest on the wall, and forced the image in her mind outward.

Her body jolted as the magic poured free, bringing her inner vision to life. Beneath her fingers, the stone heated, and the slight resistance of rock gave way to the smooth glide of crystal. Although her body shook with the force of it, Selia took another step up. Then another. Trembling, she climbed and transmuted until her chest ached and her fingers stung from the constant heat.

Once she reached the upper landing, Selia slumped against the inside wall and stared at the shimmering crystal that now bordered the stairwell. It wasn't as clear as a window, but light poured through with hints of the outside world beyond. Would it be enough? Her transmutation abilities weren't strong enough to change rock to glass, only one kind of stone to another. She swiped the sweat from her forehead. It had been challenging enough to manage so much of that.

Selia drew in energy to replace some of what she'd used, but only sleep would fully rejuvenate her. It would be more than worthwhile if it gave Aris some relief. What else could she offer him? She wasn't a healer, and he didn't want her touch or even to talk. But this she could do.

Once her energy settled, Selia pushed away from the wall and started down the stairs. Only to halt halfway down at the sight of Aris climbing up, his hand—and gaze—on the hazy crystal. Surprised wonder filled his face instead of the fear he'd shown earlier. A few steps below, Kezari came into view, a toothy smile widening her mouth she stared at the crystal.

"Do you like it?" Selia asked softly.

Aris paused on the step beneath hers. "I am in awe of it. And you."

"No need of that," Selia said, smiling. "I hope it helps."

His hand rubbed absently at the crystal. "It does. I cannot tolerate the thought of being cut off from nature again. I was denied even the sight of it for so long."

Oh, how that must have hurt him! Selia's heart pinched, and she was glad to have eased that burden for him, if only a little. "Let's go see the top."

As Selia climbed again, she felt his presence behind her with each step. His energy was as familiar to her as her own, so she could sense his tumult without much effort. The alteration might have eased his panic, but his struggle was still evident. And why wouldn't it be? With Aris's connection to living things, it must have been pure agony to be cut off. Not just because of his magic, either. He might have scaled back his expeditions after Iren had been born, but he'd never wanted to stay indoors for long periods of time. He'd spent hours outside each day.

Selia paused when she reached the top landing again, an alcove that opened into the circular tower room. Sitting on one of the padded benches built into the base of the windows, Iren and Eri waited for Selia and the others. How in the world had they known…? She gave a soft snort at her own thoughts. Eri was there, so of course they'd known the right time to be in the tower.

She expected Iren to run up to Aris, who'd frozen at Selia's side, but their son stayed still. "Eri suggested we help set up the room," he said.

Selia huffed. "You were supposed to be studying with Lady Lynia."

"Our help eased things," Eri said, not a hint of chagrin in her tone.

After a glance around the bare room, Selia lifted a brow. "What did you do?"

Iren did jump up then. Excitement lit his face as he pointed at the ceiling. "We added a door."

"Irenel Baran," Selia breathed when she caught sight of the wooden rectangle angled awkwardly overhead. "Please tell me you did not modify Lord Lyr's property without express permission. I must be mistaken since you have very little of the artisan's gift and surely would not have tried such a thing."

Of course, Selia knew very well he would have done it, especially with Eri's encouragement. He might be the older by five years, but he wasn't a mature influence. Sure enough, a guilty flush stained his cheeks as he studied his feet. Selia took the opportunity to pull in a few deep breaths. He would admit it fairly quickly if she let him stew. He might be mischievous, but he was honest.

"Answer your mother, Iren," Aris said.

Although he didn't raise his voice, Selia and Iren both startled at the sound. Annoyance at his interference flashed through her, followed promptly by guilt. She might have grown accustomed to disciplining Iren herself, but Aris still had that right. It certainly motivated their son, who snapped to full attention.

"I did do it," Iren said, lifting his chin and squaring his shoulders. "I didn't think about asking, but I guess I should have. Eri said that if there wasn't a way for the dragon to get up there, they'd move to the cave area, and—"

"And they don't need to know that," Eri interrupted cheerfully. "Trust that it would be bad."

The brush of Aris's mind against hers was so light, Selia almost missed the request for communication. *"What's wrong?"* she asked.

"Is this the child everyone seemed worried about earlier?"

As the smooth timbre of his mental voice filled her mind for the first time in years, heat slammed into her, low and hard. Gods, she'd missed him. But she was careful to keep her reaction from crossing through their faint connection. *"Yes. Eri is Prince Ralan's daughter. She is a seer, same as he, but I wouldn't be surprised to find she's stronger."*

"Wonderful," Aris answered wryly before ending the link.

That loss hurt, but she didn't have time to dwell on it. "How in the world did you two manage this, Iren?"

"Well, Eri showed me an image of what we needed and where we could find it," Iren said. "I did a dual transport spell to switch the stone of the ceiling with a hatch from another tower. Eri said it wasn't being used."

"A hatch from…" Selia counted to ten. Then twenty. She choked down a bubble of laughter as she wondered what Lyr's reaction was going to be. "Did it not occur to you both that this might cause a problem?"

Eri shook her head. "I checked. No one is going to need that tower for three months and nineteen days, and that's not even the most likely strand."

"Perhaps Lord Lyr does not want a ladder to the roof in this location," Selia said, struggling to control her tone. Shouting would not solve the problem. "Did you consider that?"

"He only yells in one strand." Eri shrugged. "In three, he is frustrated, and in two, he's amused. In all of them, he'll assign artisans to fix both towers. No big deal."

"*Miaran,*" Aris muttered softly beside her.

Selia had to concur with the use of an expletive in this case. Eri was a force all her own. "I hope your assessment is correct. However, I fail to see why you couldn't wait if you knew the Myern could solve the dilemma himself."

"They are clever younglings," Kezari said before either child could answer. "There are too many trees nearby for me to land on the ground. I would not be able to check on Aris without this hole. How does it work?"

Iren pointed at an indention in the wood. "Direct a bit of magic there, and it'll slip down to release a ladder."

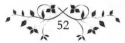

The dragon hurried forward, her curious gaze on the spot. Energy trembled through the room, raising little bumps across Selia's arms, a moment before a click sounded. As Iren had said, the wood angled down, and a ladder slid free. A breeze wafted through the hatch, bringing the sound of birdsong and the sharp scent of forest with it.

"Well," Selia said.

Part of her wanted to punish Iren for his actions, but an equal part was proud. He'd only been studying magic for a couple of years, yet he'd managed a complicated set of spells on his own. He was innovative and quick-thinking, traits that would serve him well in the centuries of training to come. But he also had to learn not to act rashly.

"I wanted *Onaial* to be close," Iren said.

Aris crossed the room to kneel in front of their son. "I appreciate your effort. I have missed you more than I can say, Iren, and it lightens my heart to know you want me near. But I must be honest and tell you that I am not well. Inside my mind, where you cannot see. If there are times when I am distant, know that it is not your fault."

"I'm eleven now." The solemn expression on Iren's face made Selia want to weep. "I've learned enough about war to guess the kinds of things that happen to prisoners."

"I may not always be able to fight back the darkness," Aris said. "I am not the father you deserve. Not anymore."

Iren averted his gaze. "I haven't exactly been great myself."

Selia shivered as a cool tendril streamed through the open hatch. What was he talking about? Iren might have a bit of a wild streak, but he was an excellent son.

"I can't imagine you've done anything too bad," Aris said.

Iren bit his lower lip. Then he met his father's gaze, and his next words came in a rush. "I think I killed someone a couple of months ago. He was shooting arrows at Arlyn and Kai, so I used fire magic to stop him. I'd never used that kind of fireball, though. It was only supposed to burn the bow, but I lost control. Sometimes I wake up hearing his scream."

Selia gaped at her son, disquiet sliding through her at his words. He'd saved Kai and Arlyn, it was true, and she'd known he struggled with it. But why hadn't he told her he was still having nightmares? Tears filled her eyes. She should have insisted on a mind-healer, at least for a quick check. Some mother she was.

"Did you eat him, too?" Kezari asked, missing the undertones of the conversation. "That is not always best. There are some beings it is better not to ingest."

Iren's eyes widened, and Aris gave the dragon an exasperated look. "Kezari."

If the dragon noticed the warning in his tone, she ignored it. "Fire is an excellent first attack. Your young one is strong, *skizik*."

Aris sighed. "Thank you, Kezari."

"I...I didn't eat him," Iren said.

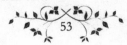

Smiling slightly, Aris laid a hand on his son's shoulder, and Selia's heart squeezed at the sight. "I am proud of you, Iren," he said. "You acted to save others. How could you think I would be upset at you for that?"

Iren's lips turned down. "Because *I* am, I guess."

"Understandable," Aris said. "Killing should never be easy, but sometimes it's necessary. I'm certain your mother would have told you that."

"Sure. But I worried… I thought your spirit was maybe watching. Disapproving," Iren blurted.

Selia crossed her arms over her stomach, an inadequate wall for the pain churning inside. "I didn't know that," she whispered.

Iren scuffed his foot against the floor. "I wasn't sure if I should say."

"Well, you should've said something to me," Eri said suddenly, giving Iren a quick nudge. "I could have told you that you didn't kill anyone."

Selia's brows lifted, and her son spun back to face his friend. "What do you mean?" Iren asked. "You weren't here."

"I Saw stuff about Moranaia before we came here from Earth." Eri shrugged. "In the vision, the man you attacked ended up at a bad guy's house. The bad guy killed him."

Aris's forehead furrowed. "I fear I have missed a great deal these seven years."

"Nah, it was pretty boring until the last three months," Eri said with a chuckle.

Relief etched Iren's expression as he threw his arms around his father, laughing, but he pulled away when Aris stiffened. "Sorry. I just can't believe it. It wasn't me."

A little pale, Aris stood. But he didn't run away. "I am glad to hear it for your sake. And please don't be afraid to show affection. Even if…even if it is a struggle for me. It is not your fault."

"I know. Eri told me—" Iren's words cut off at another shove from his friend. "Never mind. I understand."

Suddenly, Eri tugged at his hand. "Let's go play."

"But I want to see my father," Iren argued.

"You'll see him more later." Though half his size, she dragged him toward the stairs. Her voice echoed behind their retreating backs. "Lord Lyr will be here in a quarter mark, and now he's yelling in two strands instead of one. Those odds aren't good."

Selia couldn't help but laugh. She probably ought to make them face Lyr's disapproval, but Iren needed some relief after the burden he'd carried for so long. She could give him his punishment later. Besides, Lyr would no doubt lecture both children, as would Ralan and Cora upon their return. Selia's gaze landed on Aris. A hint of a smile curved his lips as he stared after Iren. She had a feeling they'd both go easy on their son.

Just this once.

8

After a solid mark spent staring out the window, Aris could understand why they'd named this place the brooding tower. He could watch the limbs of the surrounding trees as they swayed in a gentle breeze and let his mind roam where it would. Here, he was apart from the world. Even the occasional person walking through the garden below didn't mar the feeling, for no one even glanced at the windows at the top of the tall tower. He could have been invisible.

The room had grown chilled with the open hatch, but Aris welcomed the coolness. The breeze carried the scent of fallen leaves and damp moss, the essence of autumn. A reminder that he was alive and free—and for the moment, alone. Kezari had flown in search of a stray *daeri* for her dinner after an exasperated Lyr had left with Selia to discuss the estate shielding. Thank the gods the Myern was a steady soul. Instead of shouting, he'd peered at the ladder, shaken his head, and said he'd find a proper artisan to situate the hatch correctly and replace the one now missing from the other tower.

He smiled at the memory of his son's guilty but proud expression. When Aris had left for his last expedition, Iren had only begun to show the promise of future power. Now he was using complicated transportation and alteration spells with a skill beyond his years. Aris's smile dropped. Iren had also been forced by circumstance to seriously injure another.

Would it have happened if Aris had been here?

Foolish thought. If assassins had shot at the Myern's daughter in the heart of Braelyn, then the danger must have been extreme, not to mention unusual. But he couldn't dismiss the notion. Nor could he shake the sinking feeling that he'd failed his son in more ways than he could ever know.

Aris spun away from the window and frowned at the round, empty room. Could he tolerate sleeping here? With so much glass, he didn't feel trapped, and if he kept the ladder down, he could see the canopy of trees and the gleam of moonlight after dark. But would the place trigger nightmares once the sun set?

He would have to hope not. The girl had said something bad would happen if he camped near Kezari's cave, and atop the tower it was too cold. Though he wouldn't usually give credence to the words of a child he'd never met, there was something uncanny about her. He'd never met Prince Ralan, either, but Aris had heard enough tales about his skill as a seer. If Eri was more powerful than her father, as Selia seemed to believe, then Aris would do well to take her seriously.

Whether he wanted to or not.

Selia stared at her reflection in the softly glowing mirror with barely restrained impatience. Why wasn't her sister answering? Selia's time was limited. Lyr had asked her to add more nuanced dragon detection to the estate's existing shield and to expand its range in case any followed Kezari. That would take several marks and a lot of energy, something she was short on as it was. She also wanted to check on Aris, and she needed to have a long talk with Iren about today's actions.

All before bed.

Abruptly, the light from the mirror flared and then settled into her sister's image. They could have been twins, despite the couple of centuries separating them in age, except that Niasen's hair was closer to brown than gold. But their dispositions differed greatly. Her sister was more bold and assertive, but she lacked Selia's patience.

"Selia!" Niasen called. "I did not expect to hear from you today. I hope all is well."

Selia studied her sister's harried expression with a frown. "I could say the same for you. You look frustrated."

"Father chose a poor time to take one of his little trips." Niasen grimaced. "Erek and Temeth ran off together before Erek could formally dissolve his marriage bond to Bothen, and Bothen is understandably furious. And Erek and Temeth each had three students who have to be reassigned. Nothing that I can't handle, but the drama is monumental. Odes will be written about this mess, I've no doubt."

Selia barely heard most of what her sister said. She was stuck on the first part. "Father took another trip? Where?"

Niasen drew back in surprise. "Earth, of course. I thought you knew."

"No," Selia said through gritted teeth. More hurt to layer on the day's pain. "He must have decided not to visit me before he traveled through the portal."

Regret and sympathy crossed Niasen's face. Braelyn guarded Moranaia's only portal to Earth, so her father would have passed through here to take one of his jaunts. On one of his previous trips, he'd conceived and then abandoned a son with a human woman, but neither Niasen or Selia had known. They'd only discovered the truth after Selia had tested Lyr's newfound daughter, Arlyn. That abandoned child had been Arlyn's grandfather. No doubt her father had feared Selia's anger, which still hadn't cooled after his long deception.

Even knowing that, his lack of contact hurt.

"I hope he behaves himself this time," Selia simply said.

Niasen's lips thinned. "He swears he will take more care."

"We shall see."

"Is everything fine otherwise?" Niasen asked. "You do not tend to connect in the middle of the day."

"You aren't going to believe the news I have to share." Selia took a deep breath as her sister stared in confusion. "It's about Aris. He's…he's alive."

Niasen's mouth dropped open. "What?"

"Aris is alive," Selia repeated. "He just arrived."

"That *drec*," Niasen said with a snarl. "He abandoned you?"

Selia hurried to explain before her sister became truly angered. "No. He'd been captured and held against his will."

"Sure."

"He's with the dragon who saved him," Selia said. "She confirmed it."

Her sister's brows shot upward. "A dragon? If you are jesting with me—"

"No, I'm not," Selia interrupted. But she hesitated, uncertain of how much to say. "If you'd seen them, you would believe. Aris… He is severely traumatized. I don't know the entire story, but I'll tell you what I can when I do. Just…don't tell Father if he returns without stopping here. He never liked Aris, and I don't want to deal with him in the midst of everything else."

Niasen peered at her for a moment before finally nodding. "If you believe Aris, I'll take your word. The dragon, of course, would be tough to fabricate. And you may be assured that I will not tell Father when he contacts me tomorrow to check on estate business. I am still angry at him, myself."

"Thank you."

They chatted a little longer, Selia offering advice on finding teachers for Niasen's abandoned students, before her sister had to rush off to solve another problem. Once the connection ended, Selia leaned back against her seat and rubbed her eyes. The discussion could have gone worse. Niasen was fiercely loyal, and Selia had half-feared that she'd storm Braelyn to take Aris to task. One crisis averted, at least.

Blowing out a long breath, Selia pushed to her feet. Transmuting the stone tower had taken a good half of her reserves, but she had enough left to tackle the estate shielding. Barely. If Arlyn's magic wasn't going awry, Selia would have asked for her help, but her student would need to practice attuning her power while pregnant before taking on such delicate work. And Iren didn't have enough experience, tower adventures notwithstanding.

Of course, if Aris were well, he could have shared his life energy with her. His rare talent provided one of the few types of power that didn't require transmuting, and they'd once worked together often when she had need of more magic. Her heart squeezed at the memories. They might never be able to work together like that again.

After a moment's hesitation, Selia opened a small chest on her desk and grabbed an energy crystal. Pulling in natural energy and converting it to something she could use took a good bit of her inner reserves, but the crystal held her stored power. She hated to use one, but it seemed prudent. If more dragons arrived or Kezari wasn't

as friendly as she appeared, Selia might need her magic to stop them. She couldn't afford to drain herself completely.

Perhaps a thought she should have had before transmuting a tower, but Selia didn't regret it. She would never regret helping Aris.

She hurried from her room and down the staircase to the lower floor. She'd just turned the corner to the hall leading to the library when she spotted Ralan striding her way. He must have returned from the building site. Had he spoken to Eri yet? Judging by the crease between his eyebrows, Selia had a feeling he'd either heard or Seen something.

"Ah, Selia," he said, coming to a halt at the same time she did. "I am glad you took the most likely path. I wanted to offer my apologies for my daughter's behavior as well as my own absence this day."

Selia smiled. "Eri hardly acted alone. And you can't be everywhere."

"I had intended to be here for this had the strands not shifted," Ralan muttered. "I should have been paying more heed."

"Is the situation that serious?" she asked.

His lips twisted wryly. "Is it ever otherwise? I can't say much, but I suggest you speak with Arlyn about Earth. And have Inona find you suitable clothes. A future visit is a high probability."

Excitement and fear streamed through her in equal measure. "So the dragon is correct?"

"More correct than she knows." Ralan sighed. "You'll likely go, as will Aris when he is able. Possibly Iren. And *that* is all I will say."

Absently, Selia bid the prince good day as he departed. Her mind was on the news he had delivered. Her, go to Earth? Some of her kind, like her father, traveled there to explore the human world without the humans' knowledge, but she'd never really considered it. Still, Arlyn's descriptions of the Earth realm had piqued Selia's curiosity. The elves had magic, but they didn't have moving vehicles, computers, or space stations circling the planet.

Because of magic, her people had never needed to create the type of physical devices the humans had. Why burn natural resources fueling vehicles when one could step through a transportation portal? Moranaians rarely even rode horses for long distances, though they were more common outside the mountainous regions.

Lost in thought, Selia slipped out the back door and headed for the training room, the best place to perform detailed magic undisturbed. Was it any wonder they hadn't created ships capable of sailing the rough eastern ocean until the last decade? Travel had become easy once magical transportation was established, and the population grew too slowly to make expansion to new continents necessary.

From what she'd heard, Earth was teeming with people. Humans everywhere. Did she have it in her to take this journey? She'd moved around over the centuries to teach, but she'd never been particularly adventurous otherwise. Frowning, she

entered the training room and hung up her cloak. No, she hadn't been adventurous, but the idea held an odd appeal.

Selia settled on a cushion in the center of the room and placed the energy crystal in her lap. There was a lot to consider, but she would have to do it later. She wanted to complete the shielding quickly so she could check on Aris and get his thoughts on Ralan's words. They would have to think very carefully about what to do with Iren.

But first, work.

By dinner, Selia wanted nothing more than to curl up in bed and sleep, preferably wrapped around Aris, but she'd long ago learned that wants often went unrealized in reality's domain. Instead, she sat at the table with the others as they discussed the day's events over the evening meal. She'd come to enjoy spending time with her new friends each day, but today was different. Today, she felt alone.

Lyr sat at the head of the table, Meli at his right and Arlyn at his left with Kai next to her. Ralan and then Cora were beside Meli. That left Selia on her own at Kai's left. The only other person at the table without a mate was Lynia, who'd settled beside Selia instead of her usual place at the other end from Lyr.

Selia hadn't given much thought to all the couples until Aris had refused to attend the meal, too concerned about another breakdown. Now she felt the lack most acutely. What would it be like to share a secret glance with him over some point of discussion? To have his hand brush hers and linger? She could lean into him as she told an amusing tale or simply smile into his eyes, secure in the knowledge of his love.

If he hadn't gone on that expedition, everything would be different. Selia curled her hands in her lap and stared down at the food on her plate, her appetite stifled by the turn of her thoughts. Aris never would have been tortured if she hadn't insisted he go. He acted concerned that he would hurt her, but she'd caused the most harm of all. How could he not be angry at her for that?

"Are you unwell, Selia?" Lynia asked softly. "It has been a difficult day."

"I am not certain what to think of it all," Selia admitted.

Cora leaned forward, a sympathetic smile on her lips. "It wasn't helped by our children."

Selia chuckled at the reminder. She'd ended up making Iren eat dinner in his room and do two marks' extra studying, though she really wanted to let his actions pass. Judging by Eri's absence, she'd been given a similar punishment.

"Indeed not."

"I like the changes," Kai said, surprising her. "I didn't go up, but I've long thought it would be nice to have a ladder to the top. I did see the crystal walls, though. I hope you don't transmute them back."

Meli nodded. "Oh, yes. It reminds me of Alfheim."

Selia lifted a piece of bread and took a half-hearted bite. She was glad that Meli found comfort in the tower, but the knot in Selia's stomach hadn't disappeared. "I am happy to hear it."

"There are no interior rooms besides the one at the top, so the new walls won't interfere with anyone's privacy," Lyr said. "I imagine we will keep it."

An awkward silence descended as they all avoided broaching the most serious topic. Finally, Prince Ralan cast a serious look around the table. "I know you are all wondering, and the answer is no. I do not know all that is to come. At least not as well as I would like. There are quite a few future threads, all with different outcomes."

"At least your Sight has returned now that your brother is dead," Cora said.

Ralan shrugged. "Sometimes there are too many options for it to be useful. But you know I will help as I can."

"Delbin and Inona left two marks ago," Lyr said. "I'm not certain what, if anything, they'll be able to find. They are going to check with Cora's half-Sidhe friend, Maddy, and then see if they can track down Fen or Vek. With Fen's earth magic, he might have already detected the same thing Kezari has."

Selia shifted in her seat. "But what then? Finding a problem won't negate the law forbidding Kezari from going through."

"It is my hope that if we gather enough evidence, the dragons' queen will reconsider her refusal," Lyr answered. "Provided I can find a suitable way to communicate with her. It hasn't been attempted in some time."

Ralan leaned forward. "My father can. You may be the liaison between Moranaia, Earth, and those fae we speak with through the Veil, but our ruler is ultimately in charge of negotiations with the dragons. The king has the only communication mirror to them, so far as I am aware."

"I will contact him as soon as possible," Lyr said.

Selia took a long drink of her wine, a wasted effort since it wasn't the type to easily intoxicate. "I hope Lial will be able to find someone to help Aris. I don't think either of us should travel to Earth until then."

"Lial will succeed, likely by tomorrow." Ralan smiled. "But I would have guessed that without my Sight. Mind-healers are accustomed to traveling quickly."

The conversation drifted to other topics, as did Selia's thoughts. Would this day never end? She still needed to speak to Aris about their possible trip to Earth and what to do about Iren. Would it be better to try tonight or to wait until the healer arrived? Maybe there would never be a good time. There was a chasm between them that their love once filled.

Selia had no clue if that hole could ever be healed.

9

Delbin skidded to a stop at the door to The Magic Touch, Inona close behind. He sighed with relief at the sight of the Open sign hanging at a tilt against the glass. The Veil had been unexpectedly turbulent, or so Inona had said, and he believed it. He hadn't experienced the strain of trying to grasp the strands and pull them through, but the journey had taken longer than usual, and he'd been sick to his stomach by the end. Then he'd had to charge his phone with a bit of magic before they could call for a ride into town.

"Looks like we made it," Inona said.

His insides clenched at the strain in her voice. On their last trip to Earth, Inona's throat had been slit in a confrontation with Kien, and only Cora's quick healing had saved her. Inona was cleared by the healers to resume duty, but Delbin still worried. She'd been remote and contained since her near-death. Understandably, of course, but he couldn't help but fear that she blamed him in some way. Maybe this return trip reminded her of the trauma—and her anger at him.

"Well?" Inona's head cocked, a question in her eyes, before she shrugged and opened the door. "No need to stand here staring at the entrance."

Delbin shoved his concerns to the back of his mind and followed her inside. They passed several racks of clothes on their way to a long counter in the back, where the red-haired, half-Sidhe Maddy perched on a stool.

"Inona! Delbin!" With abroad smile, she jumped down and rushed around the counter. Delbin halted beside a display of shirts, just in time for Maddy to launch herself at him for a hug. Surprisingly, she did the same for Inona, although they hadn't had much time to get to know one another during the previous trip.

"What are you two doing here?" Maddy asked as she pulled away. "Please tell me this is a friendly visit and not some other disaster?"

Delbin grimaced. "I wouldn't call it a disaster, but I'm afraid we *are* here for more than just a visit. I don't suppose you know where Fen is?"

"His Uncle Vek's house, I think," Maddy said, her nose wrinkling. "He just bought it."

Delbin's brow quirked. Vek had a house? He'd only arrived a couple of weeks before, hadn't he? "He must've used magic to get a sale through that fast."

"Probably. An Unseelie like him wouldn't have any qualms."

He almost reminded her of how Fen had been willing to sacrifice himself to save her from Kien, but she'd scowled enough at his name that Delbin decided not to. Whatever was going on between them was none of his business. Unless, of course, either of the Unseelie males hurt Maddy or Jase, the other full-time employee here.

"They haven't caused you trouble, have they?" Delbin asked. "Or bothered Jase?"

Maddy waved her hand. "No, nothing like that. But I'm Seelie. I don't trust how nice they've been."

"They've given us plenty of cause to doubt their intentions," Inona interjected. "Especially Fen, since he worked with Kien for a time, but we may need their aid. Have you noticed anything odd in the last couple of weeks?"

"Odd how?"

"Wait," Delbin said as a hint of unfamiliar magic drifted across his senses. A chill went through him. He peered around the room and out the front windows, but he didn't see an obvious source. "How long until you close?"

Maddy tugged her phone out of her back pocket. "Fifteen minutes. Would you mind doing a quick check of the floor to make sure the displays look okay? Doesn't have to be perfect. I'll start closing out the register, at least as much as I can while we're still open."

Delbin almost laughed as a hint of panic pinched Inona's face. Maddy might as well have asked her to give a report on the current state of human fashion. "Why don't you scan for any threat, love?" he asked Inona. "I'll work on the shelves."

"Yes. Thank you," she said under her breath.

It wasn't a difficult task, not after all the jobs he'd done during his hundred-year exile on Earth. Really, straightening purses and shoes was more natural than practicing magic or learning Moranaian history. He was finished with the task before Maddy locked the door and headed back to the counter.

"Come on," Maddy said, grabbing the till from the cash register. "We can talk in the back."

Delbin and Inona followed her through the door behind the counter and into the small office beyond. Past the desk and the small safe, the space became a stock room, with tall shelves full of shoes and other merchandise. Maddy pulled a couple of extra chairs up to the desk and then sat at her own. As she sorted through the money, she flicked a glance at Delbin.

"Okay, why'd you tell us to wait?"

He lifted his brows. "You didn't sense that strange energy moving through the room?"

"I did, but I didn't give it much thought." Maddy shrugged as she copied numbers into a book and put some of the bills into a bank bag. "Those have been hap-

pening lately. The first time was maybe a few days after you left? Jase and I wondered if someone was spying, but then other fae mentioned the same thing. It's like a pulse. A wave that flows through and then is gone. No one knows what's up."

Inona straightened in her seat. "Has anything else unusual happened?"

"Well." Maddy's hands stilled. "Jase thinks it's my imagination, but I could swear there are more brownouts. Anna said the power went out at our house twice while I was working yesterday. I mean, it happens, but when I looked at the outage map online, the affected area seemed pretty large. The website said they are doing maintenance, but I still think something isn't right."

Random waves of magic and possible interference in the electrical grid? Delbin's lips pursed. It could indicate a problem, but neither sounded serious enough to have a dragon from Moranaia ready to storm the portal. They definitely needed to speak with Fen and Vek. Especially Fen, since he'd helped Kien poison the local energy fields not that long ago.

"What do you mean by outage map?" Inona asked, reminding Delbin that although she traveled to Earth as a guide, she wasn't familiar with human technology.

"Here, I'll show you." Maddy turned to the computer and wiggled the mouse, waking the monitor. After a bit of typing, a website popped up with a map of Chattanooga. "See all those reddish dots? That shows where the electricity is out."

Frowning, Inona leaned closer. "How does this map know?"

"I have no idea," Maddy said. "I guess the electric company has sensors. But look how many dots there are on the west side of town. The neighborhoods and businesses near Prentice Cooper State Forest keep losing power, especially near the mountain where Fen set up that spell for Kien."

Delbin studied the screen for a moment. "I don't suppose you'll show us where Fen and his uncle live? If you know the exact place."

Maddy's cheeks reddened. "I might have driven by after Vek mentioned it. Once. Or twice."

He let out a low chuckle. "I hope Anna's not too mad about that."

"I'm trying to build up the nerve to really thank Fen for saving me," Maddy muttered.

"Whatever you say," Delbin said, but as his friend squirmed uncomfortably in her seat, he dropped the teasing. "You can just give us the address. I'll blame Ralan, so Vek won't know who did it."

Inona shoved his arm. "You're going to cause a multi-dimensional incident if you make the princes annoyed at each other."

Delbin smirked. "Couldn't be too bad or Ralan would've told me not to do it."

"What if Prince Ralan wasn't checking for these future strands?"

"Then he'll have a fun surprise," Delbin quipped. Then he sobered. "Seriously, I'm not going to cause trouble. After all that has happened lately, I don't think Prince Vek will be upset at our arrival, especially not after we explain."

Maddy gestured at the desk. "Let me finish this, and I'll drive you there myself. I really do want to tell Fen thanks. Maybe having you two there will give me the courage."

"Sounds good," Delbin said. "Anything we can do to help?"

"Make sure the front door is warded with magic and turn off the lights." Maddy picked up another stack of money. "I'll add the final count to the books and prepare the deposit. Then we can go."

As Delbin returned to the front room to finish closing up, Maddy's words circled in his mind. *I still think something isn't right.* Maddy was a healer, although a barely trained one, so if her intuition hinted at a problem, it was worth investigating. Could the energy poisoning be seeping back in, too slowly for non-healers like him and Inona to notice? Did Maddy's power have some connection with Earth? The dragon might be mistaken—or lying.

But Delbin would trust Maddy with his life.

The wind bit into the skin of Aris's face, but it made a welcome contrast to the heat of Kezari at his back. The dragon had curled up on the top of the tower after her hunt, leaving just enough space for him to climb up through the hatch. She wasn't at her full size, but she didn't complain as much about this as she did her elven form.

Not that he could blame her.

Aris hugged his knees closer and snuggled deeper into the space between the dragon's front leg and her chest. What would it be like to completely change size and body structure? She must have practiced before their first meeting, for she hadn't struggled to walk. If he managed to turn into a dragon somehow, he'd probably fall flat on his snout in less than a moment.

"I have faith in you, skizik," Kezari sent.

His sigh puffed into a cloud of frost. *"Do you read my mind constantly?"*

"Almost." She tilted her head enough for one eye to focus on his face. *"I worry about what you might do."*

"You should have chosen someone less broken."

Kezari hesitated before answering. *"What makes you think I am so whole?"*

Aris stared at the side of her wedge-shaped head, but her unblinking eye gave no indication of her mood. Only the rustle of her wings betrayed any agitation. *"I'm admittedly no judge of dragon behavior, having met only you, but you seem well enough. You have the confidence to cross half the world, and I can barely go into a room without panicking."*

"There's more than one type of scar." Kezari lifted her head, breaking eye contact. *"I do not have the support of the dragon queen for a reason."*

His fingers dug into his legs at her words. *"You led the Myern to believe that it was the queen's error."*

"It is." A tiny flame slipped from Kezari's mouth before she continued. *"Most do not believe me, but what I sense is the truth. You see, we are born with the call of Earth in our veins. No one is certain why after all these years, but it is so. But as we grow, it fades. Most choose*

to have the connection severed or stifled since it no longer serves a purpose. I did neither, and instead of fading, my link grew stronger."

"*Ah.*" The tension eased from his shoulders. "*You believe you are broken because you are different.*"

Kezari's chest heaved beneath his back with her sigh. "*It is true.*"

"*It is not.*" Aris lowered his hand to her leg and gave a gentle squeeze. "*Sometimes the very thing that seems a hindrance is our salvation. I believe it will be so with you.*"

"*I hope you are correct. I am uncertain we can convince the queen, but I cannot deny the Earth's cry for help.*"

"*We'll figure something out,*" he reassured, though he had no clue how they would.

They both went silent as the frigid wind swirled around them, bringing the scent of rain. The cold approached from the north, and the yearly autumn battle between seasons would begin. Would he be here when the rain turned to ice and snow? At this rate, he wasn't certain he could make it to the equinox in a few days' time.

Before his thoughts could drift too far along that line, a shiver of awareness traced his skin as the protections he'd placed on the tower alerted him to another's presence. It was poor form to add his own shielding to the building, but he hadn't been able to stand the thought of anyone approaching him without his knowledge. He connected fully to the spell, seeking the information it held, and followed the warmth of Selia's energy as she ascended the steps. She'd taught him this spell and could have unraveled it easily, but instead, her presence halted at the top of the inner stairs.

Aris shoved to his feet but hesitated to move toward the hatch. That clawing fear that had been eased by the healer's magic itched at the back of his mind, waiting to engulf him. Anytime he entered an enclosed space, he risked releasing it. Love, guilt, regret—they converged on him each time he saw Selia. But she'd said before dinner that she would return to speak to him about Iren and their possible trip to Earth. He couldn't hide up here and avoid that discussion.

No matter how much he wanted to.

"*Should I transform?*" Kezari sent.

"*No,*" he answered. "*Some things I must do myself.*"

In truth, he wanted to be alone with Selia as much as he feared it. He'd been able to speak with her before dinner, even survived rejecting her invitation. He could do this. Resolved, he edged around the dragon's arm, lifted the hatch in the floor, and descended the ladder. Cold air followed him down, but he didn't close it. At least not until he peered through the dim light at Selia to see her shivering. He shoved aside the thought of being trapped and pulled the hatch closed. He could shatter a window or rush down the stairs. Kezari could break through the top with a single claw. It was fine. He would be fine.

"I can go back down and get my cloak," Selia said softly. "I left it on the hook without thinking. Or I could ask permission to alter the spell so you can leave the hatch open without freezing."

His heart warmed at her concern, but he pulled his shoulders back and shook his head. "I must learn to be inside. The windows help."

Selia shifted a step closer, into the glow of the single mage light he'd activated. "If you say so. But the offer stands."

He stared at her beloved face as uncertainty flooded him. What could he say to her? Seven terrible years filled the chasm between them. Did he deserve to have a say in Iren's life anymore? He hadn't been there for the two of them, and it didn't matter that his absence hadn't been by choice. He didn't know anything about his son's life in the interim. How could he say whether Iren was capable of traveling to Earth?

"If you are not ready, we can have this discussion tomorrow," she said.

"Why do you want my input?" he found himself asking. "Am I even really Iren's father?"

Oh, clechtan. He hadn't meant that the way it had sounded, but it was too late to recall the words now. Selia flicked her fingers, and the mage lights ringing the room leapt to life. Her tan skin had gone ashen, but her lips had thinned until they were white. Nostrils flaring, she stomped across the space between them.

As she came to a halt, the color rushed back into her cheeks. "I may not know what happened to you, but I can't believe you would—"

"I'm sorry," Aris said. "That came out wrong. Truly. I was wondering if I had the right to call myself his father, not questioning that he is mine. I would never do that."

Her eyes narrowed, and her chest heaved. "I don't know if I can believe you."

He couldn't stop staring at her flushed cheeks and parted lips, not even to defend himself. Except for the anger in her gaze, she had always looked much the same after he'd kissed her. Well, there had been a few arguments where he'd pulled her into his arms and… Groaning, Aris spun away and shoved his hands into his hair. Waves of memories both good and bad beat at his mind, but he built his mental wall ruthlessly higher. He *would* make it through a single discussion.

"Aris?"

"I give my word that I meant no offense," he answered, though he wasn't ready to look at her. Not yet. "But how can I call myself a father? I don't know what Iren is capable of. I haven't been here to see his character form. There is no way I could decide this."

Selia stepped close enough for her energy to brush his. "I wouldn't expect you to make the decision, but you deserve to give input. You will always be his father. It's up to you to earn the name *Onaial.*"

A smile ghosted across his lips at the word. *Onaial,* a blend of the words 'heart' and 'father.' Iren already called him that, but Selia was correct. There was much Aris could, and should, do to earn it. He'd missed too much time with Iren already. If there was any chance of healing, of moving forward, Aris had to take it.

He took a deep breath and turned around to face Selia once more. Their bodies nearly brushed, she was so close, but he forced himself to hold his ground. "If you want my opinion, well… I believe we should bring him with us."

Her brows rose. "You do? But with your dragon so upset, I can only imagine what we'll find. You want to bring him into danger?"

"I don't think we'll have a choice."

"He has barely started his training." Selia crossed her arms beneath her breasts, and he forced his gaze away. "Iren is very powerful, but he has no discipline. Just today, he modified the tower without a thought to the consequences."

Aris let out a soft laugh. "Didn't you, too?"

"I asked permission first," she said with a huff, but he could tell by the twitch of her lips that he'd made a point.

He gestured at the hatch. "What he did today? That's why we need to take him."

"I don't understand," Selia said, frowning.

"He has your confidence and strength, but he has my personality." Aris smiled. "If we tell him he has to remain behind, he'll find some way to follow. His best friend's a seer, so he might even succeed. I don't want to have to worry about that. Do you?"

"By Arneen," she muttered. "You might be right. But the danger… I'll have to think about this."

At the worry pinching her face, the urge to hold her rose like fire within him. Once, he wouldn't have hesitated to offer comfort. Now, his hand shook as he lifted it to cup her cheek. Her soft skin warmed his chilled fingers until her heat seeped into his blood. He'd never experienced this kind of connection to another, not even—

No. He wouldn't think about her.

"Ah, Selia," he whispered, "If only…"

Her breathing grew ragged, and her arms tightened around her ribcage, pushing her breasts higher. Gods. He needed to hold her. He had to. In this moment, the darkness was locked away. He could be normal, right? Her gaze, full of longing, met his, and he was lost.

His hand slid from her cheek into her hair, and his other hand dropped to her waist. Aris took a deep breath and pulled her against him. Her head settled in the hollow between his shoulder and neck, just as it always had, and she wrapped her own arms around him. Home. He'd finally made it home.

For a few heartbeats, he savored the feel of her body against his. Then her hold tightened. Softly, but as her breasts pressed into his chest, her hips came into alignment with his. He went hard, painfully so, and the wall he'd tried to build crumbled into dust. Memories rushed over him, but not of Selia. His vision went black.

Perim's hands squeezing. Caressing. Demanding. The rock beneath his back as he was shoved down to the cave floor. Chained.

Bile scalded his throat, and he jerked back from the female wrapped around him. A cry sounded, then a soft thud. Maybe he'd hurt her this time. She'd thought using his body for her pleasure would force the bond, but she'd been wrong. Maybe he'd hurt her too badly for her to try again. Please, gods.

Please.

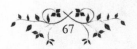

Rock bit into his knees as he dropped, shoving his hands against his eyes. Why couldn't he see? Had she hit him again? He hadn't refused her demands, had he? His body would cooperate even if his heart and mind screamed in denial. But she only hit him hard enough to blind him when he'd said no.

A thud resounded from overhead, and the female let out a sound of pain. Good. Then the world went dark.

10

As her spell hit Aris, Selia shoved herself to her knees from where she'd fallen and shuffled over to catch her husband as he toppled. She let out a soft *oomph* as his dead weight hit her, knocking her over. As her body crumpled backward, her lower legs became trapped beneath her, her heels digging painfully into her bottom. Her upper thighs stung from being stretched into an unnatural position, and her breathing shallowed beneath his weight.

What had just happened?

Aris had stunned her by drawing her close, after he'd avoided touching her as much as possible since his return. Then, just as abruptly, he'd tensed and shoved her away with enough force that she'd lost her balance. He'd gone insensible. As a thud resounded from the hatch above, Selia had acted on instinct and cast a spell of unconsciousness at him.

A sob slipped from her lips. Once he learned that she'd used her magic against him, he would never forgive her. Not after he'd suffered at the hands of that other woman. Why had she done such a thing? She should have tried to reason with him first. Maybe. She'd never seen such panic before. His eyes had lost focus, and he'd clawed his hands across his chest as though trying to scour his flesh.

But that was nothing to the low, tortured moan ringing in her memory.

Selia tried to wiggle out from underneath him, but he was too heavy. Drat. She needed to get out from under him before he came to and lost control again. She had to think of something… Her lips twisted as she pulled in energy for a levitation spell. Too bad she hadn't considered doing that instead of shoving her body beneath him like a blasted cushion. She sucked in a breath as his weight lifted off of her and then shifted him to the side while she still had the strength.

Before she could get up, the hatch crashed open, and the bottom of the ladder hit the stone floor with a crack. Kezari rushed down, completely naked in her elven form, and knelt beside Aris. "What did you do to him?" the dragon snarled.

"Me?" Selia blinked up at the dragon. "He went from pulling me close to shoving me away. With force. I didn't hurt him."

"Why is he not awake?" Kezari leaned over Aris to glare down at Selia. "I had to shift and learn the way of opening the hatch. Your magic hit him, and he fell."

Selia uncurled her legs and groaned as she straightened them along the cool floor. The dragon leaned back, and Selia sat up. Pain shot through her thighs and up her back from the awkward strain of her previous position. Wincing, she twisted in a slow, tentative stretch to ease the twinge in her back.

Kezari's brow furrowed. "You move like a decrepit *daeri*. Were you injured, too?"

"I caught him when he toppled over." Selia rubbed her hands across her thighs. "I'm not injured, just sore."

"I know your magic was to blame for Aris's current state."

Selia sighed, her shoulders slumping. "It was instinct. He was so lost, and I...I didn't know what else to do. You can see for yourself that he's only unconscious."

The dragon lowered her hand to Aris's forehead, and the solid, earthy thrum of her power vibrated against Selia's shields. But Selia detected no threat, no hint of attack magic. It was a probing spell, though not one that she had ever used. Like a tune a few notes off, the enchantment was just familiar enough to be disconcerting without causing true alarm.

Kezari drew back, her posture easing as her magic winked out. "A different version of my own spell. Forgive my assumption."

She couldn't blame the dragon. She would have been suspicious, too, under similar circumstances. "Of course. Were you connected when he lost control? What happened?"

Kezari's lips turned down as she glanced at Aris. "You should not have pulled yourself so close."

"*He* hugged *me*," Selia insisted.

"Lightly," the dragon said. "Then you curled together like lovers entwining necks."

Bemused, Selia stared at Kezari. "What?"

"Your bodies wrapped together."

Ah. Perhaps dragons hugged with their necks? Despite the situation, Selia smiled. "It was an innocent embrace, not uncommon among our kind."

"There is no innocent hold for Aris," Kezari said sadly. "I will not tell his tale, but consider everything the woman might have done to him as part of his capture."

Selia's stomach lurched as she studied Aris's sleeping face. She could think of one thing in particular that would have caused her touch to break him, and it wasn't pretty. Anathema. Punishments for rape varied, but they were always harsh. If she had Aris's tormentor in front of her now, Selia would cast a spell of pain so convoluted a healer would spend a solid week unraveling it.

Not that Lial would. In truth, he would probably help her devise the proper punishment.

"Aris must believe I'll blame him. Reject him," Selia whispered, caressing him with her gaze. The only touch she dared offer right now. "That's why he can barely look at me."

Kezari's expression gave nothing away. "I cannot say."

Selia peered at the dragon. The history books she'd read had contained very little about the bond between dragon and rider. Was the dragon usually so protective, or had Kezari and Aris formed a true friendship? "Thank you for guarding him so well. And for saving him. You couldn't have known you were returning him to me, but I appreciate it regardless."

Kezari gave a toothy smile. "I would have made sure he found you despite his fears."

A voice echoed up the stairwell, and Selia scanned with her magic to find Lial approaching, an unknown presence behind him. "It's the healer. I suspect he found another to help."

"I smelled him," Kezari said. "The tinge of herbs and frustration. The other carries the scent of flowers and smoke."

Selia raised a brow. "Your nose is so keen in this form?"

"Some benefits I will not relinquish. It would be a quick shift if the prey smelled tasty." The dragon's shoulders lifted. "And scent reveals much."

If the prey smelled tasty? Selia focused on the top of the stairs and tried not to wonder what qualified as prey. She'd read a few tales about the war. None of them mentioned the dragons eating Moranaians. Of course, she'd not paid a great deal of attention to the finer details, being more concerned with more modern events.

A scowl already marred Lial's face as he appeared at the top of the stairs. He barely glanced at Kezari, naked though she was, and his stride didn't break as he crossed the floor. Another man trailed behind, his short white hair bouncing with each step. The flower-embroidered robes of a priest of Bera, Goddess of Protection and Healing, flowed around his body like the peaceful energy that surrounded him.

"What happened?" Lial snapped.

Selia's cheeks heated as she described the events leading to Aris's current state. She should have known better—should have seen the signs. The way he'd drawn back from her. His shame and avoidance. If she'd considered the extent of his abuse, she might not have held him as tightly when he did reach out. Maybe she wouldn't have let him hug her at all.

"Do not follow that river," the stranger said softly. "You'll be swept into the rapids."

Her gaze jerked to his as Lial made an exasperated sound. "Dispensing wisdom before I've introduced you, Tynan?" he asked.

The priest smiled. "Please forgive my lapse in manners."

"So long as you don't have a method of reading minds without breaching shields," Selia answered.

"I needed no such skill to guess where your thoughts were headed." Selia scooted back as Tynan knelt beside Aris. "Only experience."

Lial dropped to his knees on Aris's other side. "I do not believe we should move him to my tower while he's unconscious."

"No. An abrupt change in environment—"

Aris groaned, and his head rocked gently against the floor. Too bad her spell hadn't lasted longer, but it was only designed to give the caster a chance to escape— or a head start on preparing an attack. Prolonging such a state was too dangerous for a non-healer. As Aris's motions became stronger, Selia stood and backed away until her calves brushed against one of the long benches circling the room.

He wouldn't want to see *her* when he woke.

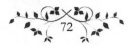

The deep murmur of voices—male voices—broke through the haze, one of them familiar. Aris struggled to catch hold of any words, some clue as to what had happened. Where was he? Smooth stone pressed against his back, but he was warm and dry. No…no chains. What had he been doing? He searched his memory, but his mind was slow to provide the answer.

He'd been talking to Selia. Hadn't he?

Aris pulled upon the magic welling fitfully in his chest, feeding him information about the life around him. The healer he'd seen this afternoon perched beside him, Kezari leaning over his shoulder. A stranger knelt at Aris's right, and the man's life-force pulsed with the comforting steadiness of a priest. And yes—Selia was present, but she was at the far end of the room.

Why had she moved away? They'd discussed Iren, and although he'd unintentionally offended her, she'd accepted his explanation and apology. Then…what? He had touched her cheek. Drawn her into a tentative embrace. She hadn't been upset by that. She'd curled close, and…

His eyes flew wide, and his breath hissed out as memory returned. He'd lost his senses entirely. A female had yelped in pain—twice. Gods, he must have hurt her in his madness. He cried out as grief and shame burned in his blood, and red tinged his vision once more.

No wonder she was on the other side of the tower room.

"Do not," the stranger said, pressing a finger to Aris's forehead. Power flowed into him until his vision began to clear and his heartbeat to steady.

"Selia," Aris forced out through parched lips.

The healer, Lial, stared down at him. "She's fine."

Lial might be correct that she was physically unharmed, but mentally? His mouth went even drier as a new thought hit. "Gods, I'm like Perim. I pushed Selia. I can't believe I—"

"No," the priest interrupted, the flow of his magic increasing.

"I can't believe she didn't flee entirely," Aris whispered. "I am tainted."

The scuff of her shoes sounded across the stone a moment before her face appeared alongside the others. "Is that what you think? I…didn't think you'd want to see me. After what I did."

He lifted his shaking hand to swipe a hair from his damp cheek, and the priest shifted back. "What *you* did?" Aris asked.

"You don't remember? I used my magic to put you under." She nibbled on her lower lip. "I'm sorry."

"I'm not." He shuddered. "I thought you were Perim in that moment, ready to…ready for more torment. I don't know what else I might have done."

"You didn't hurt me," she said.

His brow furrowed. "I heard you cry out."

"I stumbled and fell on my bottom when you pushed me away, but I was more surprised than injured." Selia glanced at Kezari. "And a bit frightened when a dragon started slamming on the hatch."

"You were in distress, *skizik*."

A choked laugh escaped Aris at her tone, a blend of contrite and chiding. "Sorry."

"You must stay at the top of the tower," the dragon said. "You will be warm on me."

The priest coughed into his hand. "That type of comfort is not wise right now."

"You think that…" Shaking his head, Aris pushed himself upright. "Kezari was not offering sex. Did you miss the part about her being a dragon?"

Tynan flushed. "Lial mentioned the dragon's presence, not a naked woman's."

Aris ran his hand through his tangled hair. "This is not her natural form."

"Forgive me for my earlier assumption," the priest said. "Perhaps you should formally introduce us so that I might begin to repair the others' impression of me."

Aris lowered his trembling arms to his knees. Though shaky from his attack, he had to agree with the newcomer. Once the introductions were complete, Aris could request treatment, as this evening's disaster proved how much he needed it. He would not risk harming Selia again. He might never be whole or healed, but the priest would know better than anyone if he could ever be trusted around others.

"The sooner the better," Aris said.

Fen paced in front of the bank of windows overlooking the city of Chattanooga, but he'd stopped being fascinated with the view days ago when the odd waves of energy had begun. How much longer was his uncle going to keep him here behind this blood-magic shield? Fucking ridiculous. So he'd helped that bastard Kien escape to Moranaia in order to save Maddy. The prince of Moranaia had ordered him to do it.

Sure, Fen had once been part of Kien's crew. Fen's Unseelie mother had abandoned him as a baby, leaving him to fend for himself with little guidance. Sticking it to the fae had sounded like a great idea at the time. How could he have known that Kien was a sick fuck? As they'd traveled the world setting up nodes for the energy poisoning web, the guy had been normal enough. At first.

Then Kien had started dismembering the people in the group who displeased him.

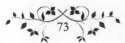

Fen had tried to ease himself from the gang then. But escaping a guy who decorated the camp with body parts was easier said than done. Safer, he'd thought, to pretend to go along with the poison web, send Kien back to Moranaia, and then dismantle the bastard's work. Too bad Fen sucked at planning.

"Don't you enjoy my new home?" Vek asked smoothly.

Fen swiveled to face his uncle where he leaned against the broad archway leading to the kitchen. "If you're going to kill me for my part in the energy poisoning, just do it."

Vek laughed. "You know very well that I'm not going to kill you. You would've been dead days ago if that were my intent. I don't play with my prey."

"That's all I am to you?" Fen couldn't stop himself from asking, the old hurt surging within him. "I should've expected no better treatment from my *family*, I suppose. You've never paid me any heed."

Eyes narrowing, Vek shoved himself to his full height and strode closer. "I admit I should have done more for you after my sister's coldness, but I dared not approach you too often lest my father notice. The king's attention would not have been the boon you believe."

Fen snorted. "Sure. Must be a hardship growing up in a palace. Hell, you bought this house from a fairy with a handful of diamonds. You probably have a chest full of the damned things."

"Material wealth is nothing." Vek waved his hand dismissively. "You're barely twenty. Were you not wasting your time on revenge, you could have acquired some of your own."

"Spoken like someone born with money."

"Enough, Fen," Vek said. "This argument wastes time."

Fen lifted a brow. "You started it."

"How did I—" Vek's eyes closed for a moment before he glared at Fen. "Never mind. I have my reasons for holding you here. Get used to it."

"You are such a bastard," Fen muttered.

"Technically," Vek countered, shrugging. "But it isn't a point of importance to our kind."

Vek was a child of one of the king's many affairs? Fascinating. Fen didn't know a great deal about the Unseelie Court, but by all accounts, it was a cutthroat place, full of people vying to be named heir. The queen's two children from her marriage to the king had little advantage in the contest, as strength and purity of magic counted more than being born from a wedding alliance.

"I don't suppose your reasons have something to do with gaining the crown?" Fen asked. "You were supposed to take me back to face the king's judgement. Or kill me yourself."

Vek's cheek muscles flexed. "I don't give a fuck about the crown, no matter what my father... No, it isn't that."

"You owe me an explanation." Fen speared his fingers into his hair. "None of this 'I have my reasons' bullshit. You may think of me as a child, but I'm an adult in this world."

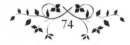

"Not a well-trained one," Vek said. "Or you could break free from your confinement."

That was *it*. Fen darted across the space between them and shoved his uncle's chest. He would probably die, but whatever. "Dammit, Vek. Don't you feel the storm building? The energy is warping, changing, and I'm stuck in here like a toddler in a playpen. The energy poisoning spell should have been destroyed, and Ralan sent word that Kien is dead. But I have to get back to the cave to make sure."

"Well, well," Vek drawled, a mocking smile crossing his face. "Maybe you'll figure it out after all."

What the hell was that supposed to mean? Fen took a step back, studying his uncle. Only one explanation made sense—Vek wanted to keep him from the cave. But why? If something was wrong with Earth's energy, Fen was well-suited to find and fix the problem. He'd worked with those energy fields extensively when he'd helped create the initial spell.

But perhaps his uncle didn't want the potential crisis solved.

"What game are you playing?" Fen demanded.

Vek's lips pinched. "Not the one you're thinking."

A series of chimes rang out, interrupting the question Fen was about to ask. Vek cursed, eyeing the front door with a scowl. "Visitors," he said. "That Seelie girl and her friends."

Fen's brows rose. "Maddy?"

"Yes." Grumbling beneath his breath, Vek headed for the door. "And from the feel of their energy, I have a feeling this visit isn't for pleasure."

Would it ever be? Maddy was taken, he reminded himself as he braced to see her once more. And she'd shown no interest in him even if she hadn't been. It didn't matter that he'd been drawn to her from the moment he'd seen her huddled in that cave, held captive by Kien. Fen had tried to help her as much as he could without blowing his cover, but so what? She would never see him as anything but the asshole who'd helped start this whole mess in the first place.

Seeking absolution would be an epic waste of time.

11

Maddy wiped her damp palms against her pants as she waited for the door to open. Night had fallen hours ago, and the porch light wasn't on. Only the bare glow of a single street light at the end of the driveway illuminated the area. The house's windows were mostly dark, a single a line of dim yellow gleaming between the nearest curtains. Figured that the Unseelie would prefer the shadows.

Delbin's sigh sounded from behind her left shoulder, and beside her, Anna shuffled her feet. Poor Anna. When Maddy had called to tell her where they were going, her love had insisted on joining them. She wanted to thank Fen, too, she'd said, but her eyes had been shaded with fear as they drove toward Vek's house. Thanks to Maddy and her friendship with Cora, Anna knew a few non-humans, but she'd never met any of the Unseelie before.

"Perhaps they are not home," Inona said from behind Maddy's other shoulder.

Wouldn't that just figure? But before she could worry too much about that, the door jerked open. The pale light from within barely illuminated the person blocking the opening, but the man's dark energy was unmistakable—Vek. Maddy squinted until she could make out the scowl on the prince's face.

"Well met, Maddy," Vek said, though his expression indicated otherwise. "I trust you are not abusing the knowledge I gave you of my home."

She hid a wince and pulled her shoulders back. "Not intentionally. We need to see Fen."

"I gave you his phone number," Vek said with a smirk.

Her cheeks heated, and anger surged as she felt Anna's questioning gaze. Now she would think Maddy had been hiding something. "Some thanks should be delivered in person. Anna wants to thank Fen, too."

"At..." Vek glanced down at an expensive gold watch. "Eleven o'clock at night?"

"Stop giving her trouble," Fen said as he nudged his uncle aside and took his place.

The shadow of an arm lifted beside the door before light flared from the porch light. Muttering a curse, Maddy covered her eyes until they adjusted and glared at a laughing Fen. "Warning would've been nice."

He grinned. "Probably."

"Blasted Unseelie," Inona muttered from behind her.

Fen's smile faded as he took in the others. "This really isn't a pleasure visit, is it?"

Delbin stepped up to Maddy's left side. "Nope."

"Come in, then," Fen said with a resigned sigh.

The line between Vek's brows deepened as he glared at them over his nephew's shoulder. "You cannot simply invite people into my home without permission."

"So you're going to lower the weird-ass blood shield you put up?" Fen demanded. "Because I have a feeling that this isn't business that should be discussed on the doorstep."

Wait, Vek was keeping Fen captive? The last time she'd seen Vek at the shop, he'd made it sound like his nephew was staying voluntarily. Something was definitely up. "Delbin told us about why he's here on the ride over," Maddy said. "You really don't want to talk about it out here."

"Fine," Vek said. "But do not attempt to leave the main room. I was not prepared for visitors, and I cannot be bothered to adjust the protective shielding on the more private areas. You will find unpleasant surprises if you venture far."

Well, that sounded charming.

"We'll stay in the living room," Maddy answered. "We're not here to cause trouble."

Fen's eyes crinkled with his smile. "Too bad."

He stepped back, gesturing for them to enter, and the light from inside caught against his fangs. She probably should've been afraid to enter a home with two Unseelie blood elves, but if either had wanted to hurt her, they'd had ample opportunity. So they required a sip of blood every so often to replenish their magic. They didn't have to hurt anyone in the process.

Of course, once they sampled your blood, it allowed them to drain your energy reserves using the connection, but she chose not to think about that.

Maddy entered the large main room. The right wall was almost entirely windows, and across from her, a blank flat screen television hung on the wall in front of a massive sectional couch. To the left, a broad arch led into a sleek modern kitchen. Only a few lamps brightened the space, giving it an almost empty feel.

Delbin whistled. "How did you score a place like this so fast?"

"Connections," Vek said smoothly.

Anna followed Maddy to the center of the room, sticking close. The amazing view beckoned, but Maddy refused to turn her back on Vek and Fen. Delbin stopped at Maddy's left and Inona at Anna's right as the Unseelie neared. Vek's scowl had faded, but his jaw was still clenched. Fen just looked bemused.

"Why did you bring Anna?" Vek's eyes narrowed. "Your mostly human girlfriend has no seeming place in this discussion."

"How do you know her name?" Maddy demanded as Anna squeaked out, "*Mostly* human?"

Vek's smile held little humor. "You didn't think I'd investigate you after your experience with my nephew? I assure you he has become my utmost concern. And yes, I said mostly. Something stirs in you, girl. Don't you feel it?"

Maddy glanced at Anna's pale, beautiful face. She'd expected instant denial, but there was a knowledge there that twisted Maddy's heart. "Anna?"

"I..." Anna shoved a strand of her blond hair behind her ear. "I didn't want to mention it. Then you'd have used your healing magic to check me, and I know you hate doing that. It's just a bit of odd tingling. It happens when I get near the river."

How could she have missed something so important about her love? Tears stung the corners of Maddy's eyes, but she blinked them back. "How long has this been going on?"

"Only a week or two." Anna grabbed her hand. "I didn't want to upset you after the kidnapping. I was going to tell you if it didn't go away soon."

"It's okay," Maddy said softly.

"Your non-human blood is stirring, what little there is." Vek crossed his arms. "But your Gwraig Annwn ancestor is a discussion for another day."

Her what? Maddy's forehead wrinkled as she tried to remember anything about the Gwraig Annwn. She'd heard of Gwragedd Annwn, Welsh fae. Maybe they were similar. Her father had mentioned the fae maidens who lived in the lakes and streams of Wales, sometimes emerging to marry human men. It made sense if Anna was being drawn to water.

"This is intriguing," Inona said, breaking the silence. "This tingling rises in her blood at the same time Earth is experiencing unusual energy surges and...what was it? Brownouts? We also have a dragon showing up at Braelyn claiming something is wrong on Earth."

"A dragon?" Vek's arms tightened across his chest. "Explain."

Maddy let Delbin and Inona handle that, since her knowledge was secondhand anyway. Instead, she closed her eyes and reached for her healing magic. It stuttered and shifted, as unpredictable as always, but she finally grasped it well enough to send her senses around Anna. Maddy couldn't heal anyone without risking harm, but if she strained, she could detect things about their health.

Sure enough, Anna's energy had shifted. A silver thread ran through her normally placid blue aura, and it throbbed periodically to Maddy's inner sight. What the hell? Magical blood didn't just...awaken, not without some major exposure to energy, which was rare and generally traumatic. But nothing had happened to Anna. Her beloved might not have wanted to bother her, but she would have mentioned something like that.

"Maddy?"

At the sound of Fen's voice, Maddy opened her eyes, and her magic flared. Color swirled around him. Not red, as one might expect from a blood elf, but the deepest greens and browns. Except...there. Right above his heart, a thorn of reddish-black speared, unmoving.

"You're sick," she said without thinking.

"Fuck," Vek muttered.

"Sick?" Fen asked, an eyebrow lifting in surprise. "I feel fine. Well, except for low energy since my uncle hasn't deigned to feed me."

"You'd better keep your energy low, or you will make yourself sicker." Maddy shivered as she examined the magical thorn. If she was a true healer, she might be able to help, but she had no idea where to begin. "Your low power must be why you don't sense the sickness in yourself. That poisoned energy in the outer world? There's…there's a bit of it in your heart."

Selia slumped in her seat, rubbing her hand across her eyes. She'd helped teleport a bed to Aris's tower room while he spoke with the healers, and then she'd stood by as Tynan had nudged her husband into a deep sleep so he could recover from his panic attack. After that, she'd had to force an excited Iren to go to bed. She hadn't been this drained in years.

She ought to go to bed, but her mind was too restless. So many worries swirled through her that she felt tossed by the rapids Tynan had warned her about. He was right, but that didn't exactly help. By Arneen, she needed to get herself under control if she hoped to help Aris. But could she ever help? Maybe he would never be able to bear another person's touch. And though she would still choose him regardless, he might feel resentment that she'd told him to go on the journey that had cost him so much. He might…

And around the rocks she spun.

Selia shoved her palms against her brows and groaned. So much for control.

When the mirror on her desk chimed, she lowered her arms with a frown. Who would be contacting her at this hour? Sighing, Selia reached out and activated the link with a tendril of power. Her sister's worried face swam into immediate view.

This couldn't be good.

"Good evening," Selia said. "Is everything well?"

"I don't know." Niasen winced. "I'm sorry for the late hour, but I wondered if… Has Father shown up there?"

Selia sat back in her seat. "Father? No. I thought you said he was on Earth."

"He's supposed to be. I am growing concerned, however. It is two marks past when he was planning to contact me to catch up on estate business."

"That doesn't seem very long," Selia said.

Niasen shook her head. "He's not usually more than a few moments off our usual time. He calculates the time differences very carefully to make our weekly meetings."

"As far as I know, he has not traveled through here." Selia glanced at the water clock. Several marks had passed since dinner, but it wasn't unusual for Lyr to be in his study at this hour. "I'll check with the Myern. If he is unavailable tonight, I will ask him in the morning. Unless you think there is an imminent threat?"

"I do not yet have reason to believe there is," her sister answered. "This did happen once before, a few centuries ago, when he decided to return to Moranaia ahead of schedule. But with you so near the portal…"

Selia shrugged. "We both know he's avoiding me. Still, I will check."

"Thank you." Some of the tension drained from Niasen's face. "Then I will bid you goodnight."

"Goodnight," Selia answered before the connection winked out.

She dropped her head against the back of the seat for a few precious breaths, but she couldn't afford to relax. Her father was very…exact. Proper. He would not abandon his meeting with Niasen without cause. It was possible that he'd miscalculated the time shift between the worlds, but it was worth checking with Lyr to see if he'd heard of any trouble. Just in case. With so many unusual events happening lately, anything outside the norm deserved attention.

Groaning, Selia scooted the chair back gently from the desk, not wanting to scrape the floor and wake Iren next door. A quick scan revealed that Lyr was in his study, as she'd hoped, so she started in that direction as rapidly as her tired feet would allow. For politeness's sake, she should send a mental request for a meeting, but she didn't want to waste more energy. Unlike her father, Lyr wouldn't hold such a lapse against her.

But to her surprise, she was halfway down the stairs when his energy brushed hers in a request for contact. *"Good evening, Lyr. Is everything well?"*

"Debatably," he answered. *"I need to speak to you if you are available."*

The coincidence wasn't promising. Had something bad happened to her father? Lyr certainly wouldn't deliver that kind of news across a telepathic connection. *"I'm already on my way to your study. I will be there in a moment."*

"Thank you," he said, cutting off the link.

Her heart pounded as she hurried, ignoring the ache in her feet and the leaden weight of her muscles. She might have a complicated relationship with her father, but she didn't want anything to happen to him. Far from it. With trembling hands, she pushed open the door to Lyr's study and strode into the large, oval room.

Lyr slumped against the back of his seat, his face lined with exhaustion. His eyes opened as she neared, and he straightened. "You look the way I feel," he grumbled.

Selia smiled, far from offended. If he spoke so plainly, he must truly consider her a friend. "Either you feel terrible, or I look better than I expect."

He shoved his braid of dark brown hair over his shoulder. "It has been a long day, and the night promises to be longer yet. Dare I ask why you were on the way here?"

"It's about my father," Selia said as she stopped in front of the small dais holding the desk. "He's on one of his trips to Earth, and he failed to check in with my sister at their arranged time. I told her I would ask you if he'd returned, since he is avoiding me."

Lyr frowned. "He passed through the area quietly, then, for I have heard nothing. I will check the scouts' records for the details of his travel."

The lump in her stomach uncurled. "Then you weren't contacting me about news of him?"

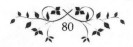

"No," Lyr said. "But I wouldn't recommend relaxing. I spoke to the king."

Her forehead wrinkled. Wouldn't he have summoned Ralan about that? "I'm afraid I don't understand what that has to do with me."

"Nothing and everything." He leaned forward. "The dragon queen contacted him, and the news is not good. Kezari is on her way, as is Ralan, but Lial forbid me to wake Aris under threat of pain most dire. You know Aris best, so I thought you might give input on his behalf."

Just like that, the knot in her stomach squeezed tight once more. "I am not certain that is a good idea. I don't feel comfortable speaking for him."

"I would not ask you to do that," Lyr said. "Only give your opinion."

The door opened, and Ralan strode in. "Stay, Selia," he said.

She held back a groan. From the sharp command in his tone, his words obviously hadn't been a request. "Of course."

Before Ralan was halfway across the room, Lyr's third in command, Kera, entered with Kezari. The dragon appeared paler than before, apparently no more eager to be indoors than she had been before. She gripped her hands into the thin dress she'd donned, and she scanned the walls like they were hiding enemies within. Was it Aris's absence that had the dragon nervous or something else?

"Thank you for joining me," Lyr said as Kera left. "Let us recline in the center chairs as we discuss the matter at hand."

Kezari's arms drew in close to her body before she darted to the nearest chair and perched on the edge. Selia took the seat to the dragon's right. Ralan sat across from the dragon with Lyr beside him. The steady drip of the water clock filled the silence as they stared at the agitated dragon.

"I cannot abide this enclosed space," she said. "Not without my *skizik*. Why have you called me here?"

"I am afraid we have a problem." Lyr sat up straighter. "Your queen contacted our king. She declared you a renegade and refused any possibility of negotiation on the matter of returning to Earth. Something the other dragons apparently do not want after so much time."

A wave of power thrummed through the room, shaking the chair and floor before cutting off abruptly. Selia's heartbeat pounded in her ears as she observed the raw fury on Kezari's face. "Our queen has grown too soft. She neglects the needs of the young ones, those not old enough to sever their connection to Earth. She blames their agitation on boredom, but I know the truth. This must be stopped for the dragons' sake."

"That may be," Lyr said in a quiet, even tone. "However, the result of breaking the treaty would be war. The queen has decreed it. At this point, the only option left is to send Aris and Selia through without you."

Kezari hissed. "No. I must not be left behind."

"I'm not sure Aris will agree to it, either," Selia said. "Have you heard from Inona and Delbin yet?"

Lyr shook his head. "I expect them to return soon. Perhaps we will understand more then."

Heat trembled on the air, fighting against the cooling spell imbued into the room. Kezari's fingers dug into her legs as her piercing gaze moved to Ralan. "Who is this one? You have brought a stranger here to witness my shame. I do not like it."

Selia stretched out her hand, but the dragon's angry look had pulling back. "Please be at ease, Kezari. This is Prince Ralan, heir to the throne. I am certain he will help if possible."

Despite the dragon's anger, Ralan's expression remained relaxed. "Forgive my intrusion. As a prince, I spent more time studying the treaty than the others. I believe we may have one other option, one neglected by our ancestors and current monarchs alike."

Kezari leaned so far forward that Selia feared the dragon would fall from her chair. "Yes?"

"In declaring you renegade, am I correct in assuming that the queen has cast you out?" Ralan asked.

Kezari nodded. "That is correct. If I return without causing harm, I could petition to be reinstated. My cousin Tebzn will care for my hoard until my banishment is certain. If I am not reinstated, all but a small percentage of my collection will be hers."

"Then you have a choice to make." A sly smile crossed Ralan's face. "The treaty gives no guidance on dragons who wish to join Moranaian society."

Lyr huffed out a breath. "You're certain? I do not recall the treaty sufficiently to say."

Frowning, Selia tried to remember her own school days, but she hadn't read the document since her early studies. "Nor do I."

"You believe I should become one of you?" Horror rang in the dragon's voice. "I cannot tolerate this form for so long. No, never."

"That would not be a requirement," Lyr said. "We have a variety of fae who have journeyed here over the centuries, like Kera, whose family is Dökkálfar. None have been required to change forms for any reason. One must only request entry into our society and swear allegiance to our king and laws. If your queen has disavowed you, there would be no reason not to accept."

Kezari sucked in a breath. "But my hoard…my cave…"

"Think on it tonight while we wait for my people to return," Lyr said.

Poor Kezari. The dragon gave a sharp nod and jerked to her feet, marching from the room without another word. Selia exchanged a tired glance with the other two before she, too, stood. "If you don't need anything else from me, I will rest. I have a feeling I'm going to require all of my energy."

"Of course," Lyr said. "Good eve, Selia."

With a parting smile, Selia hurried toward the door. If she was lucky, she could get a complete night's sleep before another disaster struck. She sent up a quick prayer and sped up her steps.

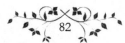

12

I can't be poisoned. No way.

Once again, Fen paced. Along the wall of windows and then around, circling the large sofa where the others sat. Even Vek was surprisingly quiet. But then, he'd been hiding a big fucking bombshell, hadn't he? It would explain why Fen's uncle hadn't wanted him to consume much blood or leave the house. If it was true, taking in more energy would increase the size of the sickness affecting him.

If.

"I feel fine," Fen said for probably the twentieth time. "Those waves of energy make me lightheaded sometimes, but that doesn't mean anything."

"Nephew…"

Fen rounded on Vek. "Oh, don't give me that regretful tone. If you thought I was ill, why wouldn't you want me to solve it? Maybe Kien left something in that cave. I can unravel it."

"There's nothing there to find. At least nothing you can fix." Vek drummed his fingers on his knee. "I went to the cave. It's…there's nothing poisoned there."

"I can tell the waves of magic originate in the cave where we fought Kien," Fen argued.

"They do." Vek's gaze encompassed everyone. "There's a crack there. Not one you can see, of course, but a crack in the wall restraining the bulk of Earth's magical energy."

Delbin, who'd been exiled to Earth for much of his life, shook his head. Like Fen, there was a lot of magical lore he didn't know. "What are you talking about?"

"I do not understand, either," Inona said, appearing just as confused.

Maddy and Anna exchanged equally blank looks.

Vek let out a low chuckle. "Ah, how the so-called greater races have fallen behind. You didn't know we saved you so many millennia ago, did you? According to legend, the fae races began to abandon Earth because the magic started to fade. They slipped into different dimensions or journeyed through the portal to new lands. Even humans talk about the magic disappearing, but they attribute it to belief. Or the lack thereof. We Unseelie have been happy to have the stories say so, but it's time for that misapprehension to change."

"You make no sense," Inona said, her brows drawing together. "Our historians would have recorded the cause of decreased energy."

One corner of Vek's mouth tipped up. "They didn't know. We Unseelie have always been masters of shadow, you see. We understand better than others what happens when power goes unrestrained. Earth's energy was growing, not leveling off, enough that humans learned to use it. With magic so easily accessible, small wars broke out constantly. The fighting never would have stopped. So we bound and sealed much of the magic in a parallel dimension without the other races' knowledge."

Fen dropped heavily onto one side of the sectional. Was Vek serious? "Why? Your kind crave conflict."

"*My* kind, hmm?" Vek asked with a smirk. "We don't shy from a fight, but a cataclysm makes even the shadows unpleasant. To lessen the chance of a catastrophic war, we bound the energy with blood. Now something has cracked it. You drew blood from Kien, did you not?"

Fen nodded.

Any hint of humor left Vek's face. "He must have done something to the barrier when he died. He was linked to Earth's energy...and to you. The power trapped behind that wall chips away at that crack with every moment, releasing magic with each fragment that shatters. Those with latent fae blood, like young Anna here, will awaken, and gods know what else will happen. Provided we aren't all killed by the force when the dam breaks. I'm no Earth mage, and you're weakened by the poison even if you were trained. In short, we're all fucked."

What in the hell were they going to do? The others' faces echoed the worry that slammed Fen's heart. Then Delbin cursed beneath his breath, and Inona pinned Vek with a glare. Anna gripped Maddy's hand, making Fen's insides twist in unexpected but acute longing. As the desire to wrap a comforting arm around both of them swamped him, Fen averted his gaze.

One hopeless situation at a time.

"I hope you have some evidence of this story," Inona said.

"I suppose you can create your own myth for it if you need to." Vek shrugged. "You are welcome to explore the cave yourselves to feel the crack, but good luck sealing it without a dragon."

Pain replaced the anger in her eyes. "I am uncertain I am prepared to return to the cave."

"That was not a taunt," Vek said evenly. "By my own blood, I swear that I have spoken only truth in this matter."

Fen's lips twitched. If the others didn't know how many shades of the truth there might be, he wasn't going to tell them. He had more important things to consider. Number one? Find a way to heal himself. Then he could see about averting

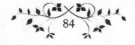

the coming disaster. Vek might think a dragon was required, but Fen had his doubts. He'd inserted poison into Earth's energy field, manipulating it in the process. How different could some magical barrier be?

Maybe stopping an apocalypse would impress Maddy and Anna, provided he didn't die. Ah, well. He could deal with either outcome.

Panic and fear clawed through the layers of quicksand clouding Aris's mind. Why? Through the morass he dug, seeking something to hold, until he gripped the fear itself to pull his way out. Why did he feel this terror? Why did he follow it? The sand gripped him, but he fought through each layer until finally he was free.

A frenzied tapping met his ears as he opened his eyes against the dim light. For a moment, Aris processed his surroundings. The bed beneath him. The glow from the globe near his headboard. His sleep-stiffened muscles. Footsteps—the source of the tapping. He stretched each leg and then his arms before carefully sitting up.

Across the room, Kezari paced. Her form appeared different somehow, and he squinted against the dim light to try to discern why. Was her body larger? Taller? Her fingers extended farther than an elf's should, her nails curved into dragonesque claws. Her skin gleamed with the dark golden hue of her natural form, and he thought he caught a hint of scales along one arm.

Did he want to know what had led to her current state?

Really, he didn't have a choice. Her panic curled through him, threatening to trigger his own. Gods help them all if they both lost it. "Kezari?"

She stopped, her chest heaving as she stared at him. "You are no longer at rest."

"How could I be when you are so upset?" Aris pushed his hair from his face and stifled a yawn. "What happened?"

"The queen banished me," Kezari answered, her voice emerging in a deep rumble. A puff of smoke curled from her nose. "I must abandon this quest and petition to return, or I will be cast from my home. Your leaders say I could live here. Here, with the elves? Our kind did not cohabit well before. I do not know what to do. The Earth screams. Violation. Explosion."

"Slow down," he said. "When did you hear from your queen?"

Kezari hissed. "She did not contact me. She gave her decree to your king. But I could become Moranaian. I do not know if I want this thing. Where would I live? I would lose most of my hoard. This is a possibility most distressing."

It took a moment for his groggy mind the comprehend the import of her words. "My leaders? Do you mean Lyr or Ralan?"

"Both," she answered.

"They offered you citizenship? A new home?"

"But I will have no home. No place. No cave. No hoard," Kezari moaned.

Aris grimaced in sympathy, but at least he could help in this regard. "All Moranaians are provided with the basics for survival so long as they contribute to our society. We can work together to rebuild your hoard. I've gained enough wealth exploring over the centuries to contribute. Besides, wouldn't being a Moranaian citizen free you to fly anywhere you want to seek treasure? You'd no longer be restricted to the dragons' isle."

Her head tilted in thought. "That is so."

"More importantly, it would allow you to go through the portal." He smiled. "Moranaians may do so, provided they follow the rules."

"It is much to consider," she said.

"Yes." Had the scales faded from her skin? Her coloring appeared a little less gold, he was fairly certain. "Is the threat you sense from Earth severe enough that you must give up everything?"

Kezari pressed her palms against her temples and let out a low groan. A wave of magic pulsed around her, rumbling through the floor and up the walls. Aris scrambled from the bed as her eyes went blank and her flesh changed color once more. Instinctively, he connected through their bond in an attempt to calm her as she had so often done for him.

Only to be swamped in sensation.

If he'd been in quicksand before, now it was a mudslide. A mountain's worth of screaming darkness tinged with the slow thrum of the Earth's heart. But something wasn't right. *Beat, beat, groan. Beat, beat, crack.* The burn of raw energy seeped into his core, shifting. Changing. Insects cried. Birds screeched a warning.

Something is coming.
Something is coming.
Something is coming.

Cold fingers brushed against his forehead, and the sensations cut off like a broken mage globe. He became aware of his frantic breathing and the heat of his own skin. As the haze left Aris's vision, Tynan's face solidified in his view. Aris blinked rapidly as the healer's magic flooded him with serenity. He stood in the same place, his legs shaky but holding his weight, yet his outlook had changed.

"Gods," Aris said under his breath.

But Kezari heard. "I am sorry, *skizik*. I did not know you would do that. But now you see?"

Aris nodded. The dragon still paced, but the healer's presence seemed to have given her some comfort since she'd returned fully to her elven form. After experiencing what she felt, he couldn't imagine how. And she'd been living with this for over a week? She was far stronger than he was.

"I'll help rebuild your hoard and find you a cave. Anything. We need to get to Earth before whatever that is erupts," Aris said.

"Yes," Kezari said sadly. "There is no choice. There never was."

Perim tugged herself through the narrow passage, ignoring the scrape of rough rock. She would heal quickly, as always, and the day's pain had been well worth the effort. The air vents hewn through the queen's own mountain were rarely considered by anyone, least of all the useless fae content to die off waiting for some dragon to claim them. Fools. The dragons rarely chose partners anymore, the bonds not happening as they once had.

Well, Perim wasn't waiting.

She'd almost had a way off the cursed island with Aris, but now that chance was gone. Why had the dragon claimed him now? Time passed so slowly for the dragons that Kezari hadn't even noticed how long Aris was "training." Hah. The wyrm knew so little about the fae that she hadn't questioned the little tradition Perim had made up. But as soon as she'd fished Aris from the sea and heard the dragon's roar at a *skizik*'s presence, she'd known what to do—hide him until she could use him.

If only he'd bonded with her. Why had he refused? Perim had tried pleasure and pain. Incentive and deprivation. Anything. Everything. She'd broken his bones, carved at his flesh, and claimed his body. Still, their souls remained separate. Curse him and his stubbornness. Why didn't he understand that she needed that bond? None of the dragons would link with her so she could escape this terrible place, but she could have used her soulbond with Aris to coerce Kezari.

She would've let him go after that. Probably.

Perim hissed as a protruding rock bit into her side, drawing blood, but she pulled herself forward without pausing. She had a solution now, and it was all thanks to Kezari. Based on the council meeting she'd overheard, the stupid dragon had enemies. What good fortune that Baza and Tebzn had paused near the air vent to discuss the...disposition of Kezari's hoard if she decided not to return.

Baza was a mage. If any dragon knew a way off this useless island, he would. And Perim could give him plenty of incentive. She could locate Aris, and thus Kezari, through their potential bond. They would never expect her to find a way off the island to track them down, so Baza's aid and a well-placed blade would solve everyone's problems. Maybe she would kill Aris, too.

No need to leave loose ends.

By the time Inona pulled Delbin through the portal onto Moranaian soil, she was ready to drop. She might not believe all that Prince Vek had claimed, but there was no doubt something important was happening. As with their previous journey, the strands in the Veil had twisted and turned, sometimes snapping back on themselves, until her head had ached with the strain. But finally they were through.

At least now she knew the cause of the Veil's increasing tumult.

She leaned against Delbin's steady form and ignored the stares of the portal guards as she regained her strength. A shiver went through her with each bit of energy she gathered. Nothing could compare to the power of their home world, especially not Earth. Although if Prince Vek could be believed, Earth had once been far richer. Could that magic truly be breaking free?

"Are you okay?" Delbin asked softly.

Inona straightened and then curled her fingers around his. "I'm only tired. Let's go report in."

He frowned. "It's the middle of the night."

"The Myern will want to know what we learned immediately, even if we must wake him." Inona gave a gentle tug as she started down the trail. "He urged me to do so before we left."

Delbin fell silent as they walked, and her heart twisted at the hesitant way he held her hand. He claimed that the scar seared into her throat didn't bother him, but he hadn't acted the same toward her since she'd awakened in the healer's tower three weeks ago. They needed to talk about it, of course. Once she gathered the courage to ask.

"Was it bad?" Delbin asked. "Being back on Earth?"

A cold gust of wind blew around them, and a frigid drop of rain plopped on Inona's arm. Shivering again, she huddled closer to Delbin as they walked. "Yes and no."

Delbin released her hand, only to curl his arm around her waist and tug her close. "I wish you'd talk to me."

She halted in the middle of the trail to peer up at his face, barely visible in the dim moonlight. "What?"

"I'm sorry that I failed you in the cave." His jaw clenched. "I tried to take control of Kien, but I wasn't strong enough."

A low laugh burst from her lips before she could contain it. "Surely you don't think I blame you. I am a warrior, Delbin. I should never have put myself into a position where Kien could grab me, and I paid for that lapse. It had nothing to do with you."

"You're so quiet and withdrawn," Delbin said. "I thought you were upset at me."

She brushed the backs of her fingers against his cheek. "No. You've been different, too, and I thought...my scar..."

With a chuckle, he lowered his forehead to hers. "We've been reacting to each other's reactions. I don't care about scars. I love you regardless of the appearance of your neck."

Her heart warmed even as relief made her shaky. "As I love you."

Delbin lowered his mouth for a quick kiss. When he pulled away, he was smiling. "Let's go give that report. I'd like to finish this discussion in our room."

Though more rain began to fall, the chill couldn't cool the heat pooling within her. She had a feeling she was about to give the fastest report of her life.

13

When the knock sounded on her door again, Selia considered burying her head beneath the pillow. The room was too dark to see the water clock, so the sun couldn't be up yet. Could she ignore the disturbance? Just as she began to give the matter serious debate, she detected Arlyn's energy brushing against her privacy shield. If her student was being this persistent, there must be something wrong.

"Fine," Selia grumbled, shoving the covers aside and lowering her legs over the side of the bed.

She rubbed her eyes and opened a mental connection with Arlyn. *"What time is it?"*

"Not long before dawn," Arlyn answered, her inner voice just as sluggish. *"Sorry to wake you. Onaial sent Kai to consult with his father less than a mark ago. Now he wants us to meet him downstairs."*

"Now?"

"Delbin and Inona returned from Earth not long ago," Arlyn sent. *"The dragon's suspicions were correct."*

Selia rubbed her fingers across her nose. *"I'll be down in a moment."*

As Arlyn's presence faded, Selia jerked to her feet and rushed into the dressing chamber. Thank goodness she'd decided to have a soak last night before sleeping, since she wouldn't have time for a bath this morning. Instead, she brushed her long hair and braided it. Then she shucked her nightdress and tugged on a thick pair of pants and a long-sleeved tunic with practical boots. She grabbed her cloak on the way out the door in case she had to go outside in search of Aris. From the sound of the rain plopping against the windows, the weather would be wet, cold, and generally unpleasant.

Fortunately, Aris and Kezari had already joined Arlyn and Lyr in the study by the time Selia hurried in and hung her cloak on a hook. Her steps hitched when she focused on her beloved's face. There was an intensity there that she hadn't seen since he'd left on his last fateful journey. That unusual blend of curiosity and adventurousness that had so often propelled him to places unseen, far different from the shattered pain of the night before.

Selia took the only free seat in the center of the room, Aris to her left and Arlyn across from her. Lyr leaned forward in his chair next to Arlyn as Kezari shifted restlessly by the window. "Thank you for joining us, Selia," Lyr said.

Wordlessly, Arlyn grabbed a mug of tea and handed it over. Selia took a tentative sniff and then smiled. An energetic blend, perfect for morning. "I surmise that the news is not good," she said after taking a quick sip.

"No," Lyr said. "According to Inona's report, Prince Vek of the Unseelie claims that a crack has formed in the wall blocking much of Earth's magical energy. He told them that his people set up the block millennia ago to stop the fighting between the fae and humans, but I've never heard of any such thing."

Kezari snorted. "Leave it to one of *them* to claim such."

Lyr glanced over his shoulder. "What do you mean?"

"It was a joint effort," the dragon replied. "The power grew unchecked. Many frail humans hurt themselves trying to learn to harness it. The human use of magic required action."

Selia stiffened. Surely, they hadn't meddled with an entire world's energy to prevent a single race from accessing it? Humans struggled to connect with natural magic and thus required a stronger flow. Walling off enough would leave them fairly powerless.

Arlyn's eyes narrowed as she seemed to come to the same conclusion. "So the Unseelie and the dragons decided that humans were unworthy?"

Kezari shook her head. "Oh, no. I do not believe so. Humans live such short lives, and their magical channels are terribly small. And they do not require magic to live, as we do. We did not want them to die out."

"I suppose it didn't occur to you," Arlyn ground out, "that the human race might have evolved, shaped by the magic?"

"Evolved?" Kezari asked.

"Been changed by their environment, as all living creatures are."

The dragon stared at Arlyn for a long moment. "I do not believe dragons do this thing."

Arlyn's lips pinched. "It takes generations. Perhaps you live too long to notice much of a difference."

Varying degrees of horror filled the others' expressions, and Selia imagined hers was no exception. The Unseelie and the dragons had cut the humans off from any chance of evolving to be more like the magical races. Would they have changed to survive partially off of energy, as did many fae, and begun to live longer lives? According to myth, their natural lifespan had once been greater.

Walling off the magic might have harmed the human race.

"We didn't mean…" Kezari whispered.

"Good intentions often go astray," Lyr said. "In any case, if Vek is to be be-

lieved, the human race may be getting another chance. Provided the release of that much magic at once doesn't flatten them all."

"We must go now," Aris said, his voice low and urgent.

Selia peered at her husband. "Why now? You were unsure before, but suddenly, you're ready to go?"

His hands clenched in his lap, but he nodded. "I connected to Earth through Kezari's link. Smaller lifeforms are already crying out for help, and I cannot neglect them. The Earth's heartbeat stutters."

Selia set her cup down on the side table with a decisive click. She had no idea what she was supposed to do—Repair the wall? Mitigate the damage?—but she was willing to try. "I'll help."

"Not so fast," Lyr said. "For one thing, there's still the matter of Kezari's citizenship. I'm afraid she can't go through without it."

The dragon marched over from the window and halted between Aris and Lyr. Lifting her chin, she stared down at the Myern. "I ask for a place among your kind. A home. I will make no war and will consume no sentient creatures. If there are areas where I may not hunt, I will abide by that law. All laws I will heed. I do not know if we can live in peace, unlike our ancestors, but I will put forth effort to do so."

Lyr smiled. "House Dianore welcomes you to Braelyn as one of us, although I recommend being confirmed by Ralan in this sensitive situation. He should—"

The door opened, and Selia almost snorted as the prince sauntered through. "Done," Ralan said. "I bid you welcome to Moranaia. Would you like to keep your clan's name, or do you wish a rebirth?"

Kezari's gaze flicked to Aris. "If I might be counted among my *skizik*'s people, I would be pleased. He is now my clan."

"Then you will be known to all as Callian iy'dianore tenah i Kezari Baran nai Braelyn." Ralan winked. "For now. If you return to Fiorn with Aris and Selia once Arlyn's training is complete, you'll have to petition Selia's father for entry to their branch, but your family name is the same. And you might yet earn a title besides *tenah*—dragon friend."

Kezari's body shuddered, though her expression was too closed for Selia to determine why. "I must fly," the dragon said. "My feelings ride close, and I must fly."

Aris frowned. "Should I—"

"Stay, *skizik*," Kezari interrupted. "I am not distressed like last night, but this form is difficult to maintain in my current state."

"So long as you remember your vow not to eat anyone, I see no issue," Lyr quipped.

Selia gaped at him and Arlyn's eyes went wide, but Kezari surprised them by laughing. "Not unless you have a citizen *daeri*."

The Myern chuckled. "No, we do not. And hunting is not restricted on my land if care is taken to avoid domesticated herds."

Kezari nodded once and spun away, rushing toward the outer door. Selia caught a hint of golden scale on the dragon's arm as she darted out the side entrance. A moment later, a sharp snap sounded, and the tree branches swayed with the dragon's wingbeats. Well, at least she hadn't changed forms in the middle of the study. That would have been unfortunate, indeed.

Before anyone spoke, Ralan plopped down on the floor where Kezari had stood and crossed his legs. Selia's brows lifted at the sight of the heir to the throne in such a humble position, but the prince appeared at ease. Would she ever be comfortable with his unusual blend of informality and authority?

"We do have more chairs," Lyr said wryly. "Kezari might have refused, but there's no reason for you to sit on the floor."

Ralan shrugged. "It is no hardship. Now, about this journey to Earth. You need to—"

"Don't start," Lyr said with a wave of his hand. "Unless you've Seen a highly probable future strand. You promised to stop interfering without being certain of the course. After last time…"

"Fine." Ralan's lips turned down. "I'll give you the chance to choose the least messed up option."

When Lyr made another gesture, this one much less polite, Selia had to cough to hide her surprised gasp. No, she might never get over the bizarre informality here. Her own father would have lost his mind at such a show of disrespect, but the prince only laughed and returned the gesture. Changes would almost certainly come to the kingdom when Ralan ascended the throne.

Lyr focused on Aris, ignoring the prince. "As I was about to say next, there is another matter of importance before you travel through the portal. Your health, Aris. Tynan reported that he had to interrupt another episode in the middle of the night."

A flush crept up her husband's neck. "Not the way you think. I connected to Kezari, and the combination of her distress and the Earth's pain almost pulled me under."

"You don't think that kind of vulnerability might be a problem during a crisis?" Lyr asked. "I mean no offense, nor do I minimize your trauma. I know a bit about such things myself. But you need a few sessions with the mind-healer before you leave for another world."

Aris's nostrils flared. "We do not have that kind of time."

"What do you think might happen if you have a breakdown while connected to the Earth?" Lyr asked softly, though his fingers tightened around the arms of his chair. "Consider that. Also, Lial has reported that your body still needs repair."

"A few poorly healed bones—"

"Aris." Selia dared to lower her hand to his arm, and despite a slight flinch, he didn't remove it as he glanced at her. "You have said many times that undertaking an expedition in a poor state of mind or body, and without proper preparation, is a certain path to disaster. I know it is difficult for you not to follow your magic's call, but it will not serve you well to make everything worse."

His jaw clenched, and for a moment, she thought he would argue. But then his shoulders slumped as he let out a breath. "Thank you, Selia. Hard to argue with you *and* myself."

"You'll work with Tynan and Lial for the couple of days until the autumn festival," Lyr said. "I've sent Kai to check with his father, Lord Naomh of the Sidhe, a powerful earth mage. Depending on his advice, I may send Selia, Kai, and possibly Arlyn through for an initial analysis while you heal."

"Me?" Arlyn asked.

Lyr gave a sharp nod. "Consult with Lial on the possible repercussions to the baby. If he believes this may cause harm, then no. But being part human, you might be able to detect something the others miss. We'll have to see."

"Oh. Okay." Arlyn stood and ran her hands nervously down her tunic. "I'll go find Lial now. The sooner we know, the better."

As Arlyn hurried from the room, another thought occurred to Selia. "What about Meli? She draws upon magic when she's divining, but she doesn't carry a large store of internal energy. That could be a boon if the energy fluctuates. Plus, she could use her runes to guide us to the best location."

Lyr's lips pinched until they whitened. Selia could sympathize with his plight. He'd lost his soulbonded, Arlyn's mother, before they'd been able to join many years before. He'd found her reincarnated in Meli less than two months ago, and his fear of losing her again had to be intense. Finding Aris after believing him dead sparked a similar reaction in Selia's heart.

"As much as I hate it, you are right," Lyr finally said. "I'll ask her what she wants to do. She has grown more confident with the runes as she has worked with my mother, so I imagine she will agree."

"Kezari will not be happy," Aris grumbled.

"Then pose to her the same question I did you," Lyr snapped. "About losing control while connected to the Earth. Cooperate with the healers, and it will all go faster. Trust me."

Ralan stood in a single fluid motion. "I didn't have to interfere. Good job. Now let's get to it."

Laughter edged with worry echoed through the room, but no one argued. Even Aris headed for the door without another word, although he'd tensed up again. Selia gripped her fingers in her tunic to keep from running her hand down his back in an attempt to soothe. He wouldn't welcome her touch, not now.

But maybe someday. Maybe.

"So," Naomh drawled. "You come to me for help now?"

Kai bit back the words he wanted to say and kept his gaze locked on his father's. "If you have sensed a problem with Earth's energy, just say so."

Naomh leaned back in his seat with a slow smile. "If only you'd been more eager to return for your studies, hmm?"

Fuck it all, he didn't have time for this. Lyr was waiting on him to make a final decision on the coming mission. There was too much at stake. "Arlyn's pregnant," Kai snapped without meaning to. *Miaran.* "It has hindered our travel."

His father's expression went blank, his sly humor gone. "Another of our blood already?"

"Yes," Kai said sharply. "And I'm afraid Lyr might be thinking about sending Arlyn on this mission. It's her choice, but we need to know more about what's going on with the energy. Right now, we have only a dragon's concern and an Unseelie prince's word on the problem."

Naomh merely stared. "You would trust me in this?"

"Stop stalling," Caolte, Kai's uncle, said as he strode into the massive dining room. "When *you* consider breaking the ancient covenant, it's time to drop pretense."

Kai's head reared back at that. Thousands of years before, the Sidhe had agreed to remain in the underhill dimensions and leave the surface to the humans. Naomh had been so adamant that the deal be honored that he'd worked briefly with Kien to try to keep his brethren underground. Only something major would make him consider breaking that law.

"Your dragon friend is right. There is a schism in the wall regulating Earth's energy. Though the Unseelie think we don't know, we are not fools," Naomh said softly. "We've let the barrier stand because it serves our purposes, too. But this fissure…it's tinged with poison, same as the kind Kien tried to use. This has his mark all over it."

Kai went cold at those words. "Kien? He's dead. Beheaded by the king himself."

"He must have found some way to inject his poison before he died," Naomh said, his gaze never wavering. "Others might not have detected it building, but I know this sickness all too well. More is released with each surge of Earth's heart. Do not send Arlyn there. In fact, I recommend evacuating any vulnerable fae—pregnant women, children, elderly."

"I thought the greatest risk was the wall breaking, releasing the energy," Kai said.

Caolte settled his fists on the table and leaned forward. "Oh, that'll definitely be bad."

"Now imagine the greater catastrophe of poisoned energy flooding Earth." Naomh sat up straight, and for once, true worry lined his face. "Forgive me for giving you grief. I've been considering what I could do for days now, but perhaps my thinking was incomplete. Maybe we need to work together."

For once, Kai fully agreed with his father.

Clechtan, he thought. *Didn't see that coming.*

14

Aris made no effort to block the rain that dripped onto the hood of his cloak, penetrating the fabric until a few chilly runnels made their way down his neck. The door to the training room beckoned, but it also repulsed. Aris had circled the tower twice as he searched for his courage, but no matter how many times he perused the walls, the current two windows were the only ones. Small windows, too, barely enough to let in light.

It might be the best shielded room on the estate, but it looked like a prison.

The mind-healer had insisted on meeting here in case Aris lost control of his magic during the session. Reasonable—if he could manage to go in. His fingernails dug into his palms, and he recoiled, the ill-timed pain tipping his mind toward darkness. Aris took a deep breath. It was a room, not a cave.

The door opened, and Tynan stepped beneath the doorframe. Beyond him, light from several mage globes filled the mostly empty stone room. The priest eased back and gestured silently toward a pair of cushions situated in the center of the floor. Though Aris's shoulders ached with tension, he forced his feet to carry him through the door and into the room. Creatures needed saving, and cowering outside wouldn't do it.

"Thank you," Aris said as he hung his sodden cloak on a hook and shook the rain from his hair. Then he shuffled toward the cushion and sat. "I appreciate your quick action on my behalf."

"Opening the door?" Tynan asked wryly before taking the other cushion.

If the question was designed to lighten the tense mood, Aris had to admit it worked. A little. "Your arrival. And helping last night. I don't know what would have happened if I'd broken while Kezari was so upset."

The priest smiled. "As a mind-healer, I am accustomed to quick action. Mental injuries can be dangerous for all involved."

"I never…" Heat crept into Aris's cheeks. "I never thought I might need this type of aid."

"Who does?" Tynan asked, his eyes crinkling with his grin. "Trust me, I am accustomed to such a reaction. Our thoughts form the base of our existence, and no one wants to contemplate a weak foundation. But it is the part of us most in need of care, lest everything else crumble."

"I would think the base would be the soul."

"No." The priest's smile faded. "The soul *is* existence. The structure and base change with each incarnation, but our spirits flow on, retaining only an echo of the shape before."

Aris averted his gaze. He must have done terrible things in his past lives to shape his soul into its current form. "I met my potential soulbonded," he whispered.

"Did you, now?"

At the calm curiosity in the priest's tone, Aris glanced at him. Tynan sat cross-legged, his palms upturned on his knees. For the first time, Aris detected the steady flow of cool, calming energy emanating from the other man. It didn't stop the nausea creeping up his throat or the tension in his muscles, but the admission wasn't threatening to suck him into madness.

"My captor," Aris said. "She tortured me." He gripped his hands together until his fingers stung. "And violated my body. All to try to force me to complete the potential bond. What does it say about me that my soul is a match for hers?"

Despite Aris's words, the priest's expression remained neutral. "Absolutely nothing. It isn't the shape of the soul that makes the bond, it is the flavor. Her actions must stem from a broken mind, for I can tell that your spirit is whole and untarnished by that kind of evil. If her soul was evil, it would not be a match for yours. The bond would not be possible."

Relief flooded Aris's body until his head spun with it. Only when he'd steadied did the full import of Tynan's words hit. "How could she torture me for almost seven years and not blacken her soul?"

The priest's brow lowered in thought. "It is difficult to say without examining her. However...we all have darkness within us. Echoes of poor choices in this life or the ones before. It doesn't prevent bonding. But a soul is not turned to evil easily. Perhaps it is her mind that is broken but not her very core. Insanity sometimes leaves its mark for the next life."

Aris shoved his fingers through his hair as he tried to process the priest's words. Could Perim be redeemed? His stomach lurched as the image of her cruel face flickered into his thoughts. If so, it would not be done by him. She'd forfeited any right to his aid. She could be responsible for her own poor choices.

And she never would have gained his love in any case.

"I don't understand soulbonds," Aris finally said. "I would swear Selia is the other half of me, but some cosmic force decreed otherwise. The gods? Fate? I don't know."

"It is true that some souls are able to join, but plenty of others are perfect complements." Tynan let out a long sigh. "I would be well pleased to find either."

Aris peered at the healer, and the reason for the longing he'd noticed on Tynan's

face when he'd been near Kezari came clear. He wanted a relationship, and for some reason, he was drawn to the dragon. If they were friends, Aris might have asked if that were true, but it was too intrusive of a question for a near stranger. Even one who would soon know his darkest secrets.

"So what do we have to do to heal the damage to my mind?"

Tynan grimaced. "The process is unpleasant, and I must warn you that the mind doesn't heal without scars. There is no cure for the type of trauma you've experienced. I can help you reroute the worst of the mental connections, but doing so will trigger terrible memories. It is more painful than physical healing."

"Will I be able to…" Aris swallowed against the lump in his throat. "I couldn't even hug Selia without losing myself. I worry that sexual intimacy will not be possible."

"I'll help as much as I can," the priest answered. "However, much of your ultimate recovery will rely on establishing positive patterns to replace the trauma, and that includes sexual experiences. Some mind-healers offer that kind of aid, but I'm afraid I can't help with that. I'm afraid I do not favor men. No offense intended."

Aris summoned a slight smile. "None taken."

"Good." Tynan gestured toward the floor. "I recommend you lie down during the healing. You might collapse from the intensity of the memories."

Lie prone on the stone floor, vulnerable to another? Fear erupted through his blood and reddened his vision. Was there another choice? Not the wall. He'd been chained there all too often. Leaning against it…no. A chair. Why were there no chairs? Perim had never granted him one.

A touch against Aris's forehead followed by the cool, soothing rush of magic sent the panic skittering away. He cursed as clarity returned, shifting quickly to lie on the smooth floor before the sense of peace disappeared. He rested his head on the cushion, a luxury he'd never enjoyed in the cave, and stared up at one of the mage globes overhead.

He hadn't been allowed much light in the cave, either. The small variations made such a big difference. He could remain here in this time and space instead of being sucked into madness—barely.

Just barely.

Tynan moved his own cushion so that he could sit at Aris's head. As the healer settled his hands on each side of his temple, Aris pressed his palms against the cool stone and fought the urge to run. But even if he flew away with Kezari, he couldn't escape his own mind. Instead, he panted against his fear and tried not to be sick.

At first, the healing magic soothed his dread. The tension in his muscles eased, and the nausea faded. His eyes drifted closed when he sensed the healer's presence at the edge of his consciousness. Aris's breath puffed out on a sigh as he established the connection. For endless time, Tynan examined the countless channels in his mind, an unusual ruffling sensation but hardly painful.

Then it hit.

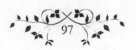

The sea roiled above the side of the ship in a solid wall. Unnatural. Deadly. How had they sailed so far from shore? Miaran, it shouldn't be like this. Tessen should've known better. But Tessen had been swept overboard with the last wave. Aris knotted the rope around his waist and leaned his weight against the wheel in a desperate attempt to turn the ship.

The wall of water crashed over them before he had a chance. Snapping. Screams. Aris gripped the wheel as the world turned to liquid, dark and cold. The rope bit into his waist, snapping him back when the sea tried to tug him away. His head cracked against something hard, and water rushed into his lungs as he cried out.

Darkness.

Aris thrashed, gasping for breath. The faces of the lost flashed through his mind, and he moaned. All dead. He should have monitored Tessen. What three-hundred-year-old was ready to captain a vessel? All Aris's fault, every death, but he'd survived. Ice seeped into his body until his teeth chattered with it.

"What have we here?"

The smooth female voice crawled inside him, waking him from his doze. Where was he? The board, his endless home, buoyed him. His arms dangled over the side, trailing in the water. He must have fallen asleep. His fingers brushed against something solid, and he cracked his gritty eyes open. His vision filled with the sight of the woman, pale hair falling across her beautiful face as she bent toward him.

His soulbonded?

Aris recoiled at the thought. He'd never wanted to bond. He had Selia and Iren. Perhaps the woman hadn't noticed the connection. Gods, he hoped not. As soon as he figured out where he'd landed, he'd be on his way back. Selia would be worried sick. Still, he didn't want to hurt the woman now gripping his arm to pull him onto land. Rejecting her would be poor thanks for the rescue. But there was nothing for it.

In the distance, a roar sounded, and the woman jerked. Her fingernails dug into his flesh, drawing blood.

Aris's arm twitched, and pain crept from the remembered spot along his skin, arrowing toward his heart. Power surged, and he cried out at the ache blooming in his head. What had he been dreaming? He reached for the memory, but another took its place.

His captor grabbed his left arm in both hands, lifting it high. Aris gurgled out a scream, his throat sore from begging, as his raw, bloody back slid along the rough floor. Red coated her naked body as she glared down at him. She hadn't been sated. She never was. No matter how often she forced him, the bond wouldn't form.

He wouldn't let it. Please, Gods, never let it.

"Say the bonding words, Aris," she demanded. "Say them now."

He turned his face away and thought of the cool stream outside the mouth of the cave. The ocean where he'd drifted. But a sea of water wouldn't wash him clean. His tormentor screamed, the shrill sound echoing through the cavern, and air rushed around his arm.

Crack.

The pain.

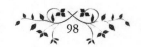

He bit his lip to hold back the cry, but a strangled moan slipped free. He barely felt the bite of the chain around his wrist. It was drowned by the agony crashing through him when she tugged, drawing his battered body along the stone until his arms were pulled wide.

"Bond with me, or I'll let it heal like this. It's a simple thing, really."

Every nerve in his body screamed at him to accept, but his spirit held firm. It was all he had left. "Eat iron."

She laughed. "Enjoy being misshapen."

He barely knew when she left. He screamed into the darkness then. Agony. Fury. Prayer.

Gods, let me go. If you are there, let me die.

Pain was his only answer.

Aris convulsed against the tower floor as the pain echoed through muscle and bone. And the shame. How could he have let her take his body, even knowing she would torture him afterward? She shouldn't have been able to arouse him, but he hadn't been able to stop it. Maybe some part of him had wanted her. Could he be that sick inside?

Sweat prickled his skin as he fought to keep hold on sanity. The foundations of his being shook until the wall holding in his power crumbled. His shout sounded through the room as raw life magic streamed from him in a flood, cracking against the shield and tormenting him anew.

It would never end.

Never.

"You should carry your walking stick," Lial said, knowing it would bring a delightful flush of anger to Lynia's cheeks.

The ploy didn't disappoint. "I've been walking in the garden without trouble for several weeks now. Although it might come in handy for whacking annoying healers."

He hid his humor in a wicked smirk. "Then—"

Pain crushed into Lial's skull, temporarily blinding him. He sucked in a breath, then expelled it on a yelp when his knees crashed into the stone. Aris. Ah, *miaran*, why hadn't Tynan warned him? Didn't he know that Lial kept a link with all of his patients? His head drooped, and his hands sank into the grass beside the path.

How could anyone bear this?

Fingers gripped his shoulders. Delicate. Tentative. "What happened?" she asked, panic edging her voice. "What do I do?"

"Rebound. Aris." He gasped against the pain and struggled to pull back from the link enough to form solid thoughts. "Workroom."

Lynia pressed against him, linking an arm around his waist as she tried to haul him to his feet. He jerked away, almost falling into the grass in the process. "No, Lynia. Your back. No."

"Can you stand? I'll brace you while you walk."

"A moment."

Lial let his mind sink into the cool earth beneath him, grounding himself as best

he could. Distancing himself from the link had done little. *Miaran*, but the images pouring through alone… His muscles spasmed in sympathy.

Nothing for it. For the first time in years, he severed a healing link completely. The crushing agony ceased, but the echo never would. Shaking, Lial pulled in lungful after lungful of fresh air. The chilly mist was a welcome relief on his skin.

Then he stumbled to his feet, wavering there while the world solidified around him. Lynia stared at him, her beautiful face almost as pale as her white-blond hair, and he reached out a trembling hand to brush his fingers against her cheek. A weakness for a weak moment.

"I need to lie down," he whispered through lips gone dry.

Her brows furrowed. "You mentioned Aris."

"Tynan is with him."

He should stumble to his tower as quickly as possible before he cracked beneath the weight of all he'd seen, scaring Lynia away for good. But when she kept pace beside his careful steps, he didn't have the heart to tell her to leave. Not even when a few rogue tears escaped from his eyes and crept down his cheeks.

Why did the world hold such pain? Why couldn't he bear it as he usually did?

Lynia followed him into his workroom, closing the door softly behind her. He studied her beloved face, now filled with sadness, and took a step back. This pain was a healer's burden, not hers, and one he usually guarded well. He should have known that Tynan would work quickly and stayed close to his workroom.

"Tell me," she whispered.

"Tynan is working with Aris." Lial swallowed. "You do not want to know, Lynia. Trust me on this."

She stepped closer. "I don't have to."

Then she held him in her arms as he wept.

"You dare a great deal to step foot in my cave," Baza announced before Perim had even cleared the entrance.

Perim froze at the harsh bite to the dragon's mental voice. His red-and-gold scales glinted in the light from countless globes suspended from the ceiling, highlighting Baza's hoard of crystals, more types than she could ever count. She shifted her gaze quickly away from the treasure, though, lest the dragon believe her intent was to steal.

Nothing so simple as that.

"Please forgive me," Perim said. "I have heard rumors that suggest we might have a mutual enemy."

They both knew that there weren't any rumors. Dragons guarded secrets as securely as any other hoard, but that very quality meant that Baza was unlikely to ask how Perim had gained her information. Not unless the source became relevant.

"Elaborate."

Perim braved another step forward. "Kezari. She stole my potential soulbonded."

Baza lowered his wedge-shaped head, the spines around his eyes tilting at an ominous angle. *"That is not what I have heard."*

"Her claims about me are lies." They weren't, of course, but she was counting on the dragon not to care. "But they hardly matter. Help me escape this island, and I will ensure Kezari's death."

Baza snorted. *"The barrier around our isle is mere formality to any decent fae mage. You should not need my aid."*

Impotent fury surged through her, but Perim shoved it down. "I don't know why my ancestors journeyed here with you when you care so little for us. Yes, we could get through the barrier. But none of us can construct boats. Even if we could, our population lessens every year. I want out before we are nothing but a memory, easily forgotten by dragonkind. I'll do anything."

"I suppose that includes torturing your own soulbonded," Baza answered, baring his teeth in a grin.

Perim snapped her mouth closed. She would admit nothing.

"Where will you go if you succeed?"

"Far from here." Her nostrils flared. "The other fae won't leave, but I hope to seek asylum with my distant ancestors, the Ljósálfar. My line traveled from Alfheim to Earth, departing for Moranaia with the dragons. Perhaps our family will be re-membered."

The slow hiss of Baza's breath filled the chamber as he seemed to consider her words. She fought the urge to fidget. He couldn't know how much this meant. This island was death, and she would not go down without a fight. She hadn't been lying about doing anything—torturing Aris was proof enough of that.

Her patience was rewarded by Baza's nod. *"Very well. But you will have to journey farther than you imagine. Are you willing?"*

Perim smiled. "More than willing."

15

Selia pinched the strange, thick fabric between her thumb and forefinger and gave a tentative tug. The stuff felt coarse and restrictive around her legs, and the metal closure sat uncomfortably against her waist, pinching oddly. Her nose wrinkled in distaste as her skin itched beneath the uncomfortable cloth.

A few paces away, Meli wore a similar expression. She'd braided her light hair back in a simple plait before she'd donned the dark blue pants and thin, stretchy tunic. Selia glanced down at her own similar top. What had Arlyn called it? A tee shirt? These had been made on Moranaia by an elven artisan based on samples the scouts had brought back from Earth, but the clothes still felt foreign.

At least the metal button was made with *peresten* instead of steel. It wouldn't interfere with magic or cause any allergic reactions. Selia could deal with a little iron, thankfully, but it could sometimes make things go awry.

Arlyn glanced between her and Meli and laughed. "Don't look so thrilled."

"Why do humans enjoy being uncomfortable?" Selia asked.

"You need Earth jeans," Arlyn said. "Modern styles are stretchier. If there wasn't the chance you'd be going into a cave, I'd say just wear a sundress."

Meli picked at the sleeve of her shirt. "We're going to be cold."

"I put a light sweater in your backpack." Arlyn gestured toward the bags on the bed. "Inona said it's still summer on Earth, so you'll just need cloaks to get to the portal. The sweater is for the cave."

"Are you upset that you're staying behind?" Selia asked.

Arlyn smiled. "Nope. Lial didn't think there would be any issues, but when Kai reported what Naomh had said, I decided on my own to stay. I'll help my father manage estate business and coordinate the efforts here. Such things are just as important."

Selia hadn't spoken to Lyr since earlier that morning, so perhaps Kai's news wasn't relevant to her part of the task. Still. "What Naomh said?"

"I believe *Onaial* was going to mention it at lunch," Arlyn explained. "According to Kai's father, there's poisoned energy in the fissure, and it's starting to seep out. I'm not exposing my unborn child to that."

Well, that was unfortunate news. "Blast it," Selia said. "Iren will have to stay here for both missions. Aris was worried that he would try to follow and get into trouble. We'll have to hope he's wrong."

"Maybe I'll make Iren help me sort through the latest reports on the final harvest." Arlyn grinned. "If you don't mind."

Meli let out a long groan. "Oh, that's cruel. I offered my aid last week and regretted it sorely."

"You'd better keep my father in good health," Arlyn joked. "Not gonna lie. I'm not looking forward to being charge of all this. I'd rather wait a few thousand years."

The sound of Meli's open laughter warmed Selia's heart. The young Ljósálfar woman had been too afraid of mages after her experiences in Alfheim to be comfortable around Selia at first, but that was slowly changing. In time, they might even become friends.

"I'll only gently scar him after our next argument," Meli said, still chuckling.

"Good enough for me." Arlyn's smile held a wicked glint. "Now. Do you want to wear these clothes until time to leave?"

Selia rubbed her hands along her pants, hoping to stop the tingling itch spreading up her torso. Even her scalp had started to prickle. She examined her forearm, but there was no physical rash. "I...I don't know. Something doesn't feel right."

Arlyn's eyes narrowed on her face. "What do you mean?"

Pulling the fabric away from her waist, Selia glanced at her stomach, but it was clear, too. A tremble built in her limbs, spreading until she sank down on the side of her bed. What in Arneen? She focused her attention inward. Her personal shields were undisturbed, but a faint reverberation echoed along the link to the training room. Iren was studying next door, and Arlyn was here with her. Who else could it be?

"Someone's in the training tower," Selia whispered.

She reached for the shield that kept rogue magic safely within the tower. The disturbance there shrieked along her senses until the itching threatened to drive her mad. But she shoved the physical sensations away and focused on merging her consciousness into the spell. If someone was causing trouble, she needed to know. Especially after all that had happened over the last few months.

Without warning, pain slammed into her mind, raw and elemental. A strangled sound choked in her throat as Aris's energy filled her with the speed and heat of a plains fire. Selia doubled over, trying to contain the surge within her own body before it seeped out to the others. The screech of birds, the drone of insects, the cry of animals—all filled her head under the grip of the powerful life energy.

But that was nothing compared to the memories.

Her stomach lurched, and Selia surged to her feet. She struggled to disconnect from the tower's shield as she stumbled toward the refreshing room, barely managing to reach the closest basin. Footsteps rushed behind her, and someone reached out to pull the plug and let water into the bowl to wash the vomit away.

As her insides settled, Selia lowered her hands into the cool stream and gathered a small pool into her palms. She took a drink to rinse out her mouth before splashing the rest across her face. Then she leaned against the basin as her legs shook beneath her. Gods above. Why hadn't anyone warned her that Tynan would be treating Aris in the training tower? She was responsible for upholding the shields there and could have reinforced them. The current protections would never hold against such an onslaught.

A hand settled between her shoulder blades. "Is there anything I can do to help?" Meli asked.

"No, thank you. That was…" Selia swallowed against another wave of bile. "I need to get to the training room."

Arlyn's voice came from somewhere behind her. "Please don't tell me there's another intruder."

"There isn't." Tucking a strand of hair behind her ear, Selia straightened. "Aris was being healed, and I inadvertently intruded. He probably won't want me there. But I have to help."

"Go on," Arlyn said. "I have a feeling you won't be in the mood for lunch, anyway. My father can share his plans later."

Selia gave a grateful nod and hurried to gather her cloak along with a pouch of empty energy crystals. The twisting hallways seemed eternal, but she finally burst out the back door and rushed down the garden path. Overhead, the snap of wings sounded, and Selia glanced through the few remaining leaves to see the dragon circling overhead. Did the workroom block Aris's distress from Kezari? Selia would have expected her to be with him.

Some of the birds began to shriek warning cries, and the branches swayed as others launched themselves into the sky. Aris's power hadn't technically escaped containment, but his connection with life was strong. Soon, the people preparing the gardens for the coming festival would be overcome with the same fear and pain swamping the birds.

"Is the dragon causing this tumult?" a male cried, dropping his side of the table he carried to stare up at the canopy. "The birds are not usually this restless."

His partner bit her lip. "Maybe we should go in. The table can wait."

Selia paused long enough to offer reassurance. Mass panic would help no one. "It isn't the dragon. Please, continue your tasks. I'll take care of the source of discord."

She didn't stay long enough to see if they believed her, but she did send a quick warning to Lyr about the current crisis.

When Selia reached the tower, she braced herself and sent her senses delicately toward the shields. Prepared this time, she let her magic settle in just enough to integrate without engaging Aris's power. Now she needed to bolster her own defenses. Layer by layer, she built the counter shield around herself until the bubble shimmered around her form.

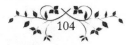

Only then did she dare open the door.

Tynan's gaze snapped to her, panic filling his expression as she closed the door behind her. She waved toward Aris where he lay convulsing on the ground. "Don't stop. I need to channel this power or the shields will shatter. I wish you'd warned me."

"This is not safe to be around," he said, his own shield glowing like water glinting in the sun.

Her trained eye caught a hint of weakness in his defenses. "You'll be the first to find that out if you don't hush and get to work. I am a mage and teacher. You do your job, and I'll do mine."

Without another word, Tynan nodded, his eyes closing as he returned to the maelstrom of Aris's mind. Selia tried not to look at her husband's thrashing form. When he screamed, his leg jerking violently, she averted her gaze and settled just out of reach. Then she grabbed her pouch of crystals and emptied them into her lap.

She gripped the first in her palm and opened herself slowly to his magic as it swirled through the room. She did her best to blunt the memories, but the occasional image slipped through as she channeled the raw life energy into herself. Only instinct born of training let her push those aside to be examined later. Converting another's power to one's own use generally took more effort than it was worth—unless the other person was like Aris. They'd done this very thing before when she had a lot of work to do, but he'd been in control then. This…this was like trying to pull a waterfall into a tea cup.

Well, she'd just have to go one scoop at a time. If she failed, his magic would escape containment and upset everything living within a half-day's radius of the tower.

Endless moments passed as Selia funneled the energy whirling around them, purified and converted it, and transferred it to a waiting crystal until it hummed with fullness. The warm stone nearly slid out of her sweaty palms before she set it aside and gathered another. Then another. Even as a headache built at the base of her skull, she continued.

Suddenly, it was over.

Aris's magic stuttered, then flickered out. She peered at him as she converted the remnants of power, and her heart twisted at the sight of him huddled on his side like a child. His shoulders heaved as he wept silently, his knees curled up close to his body. The mind-healer better have been successful after making Aris relive that nightmare. She lowered her forehead to her own knees as shadows of his memories paraded through her mind. How was her husband even close to sane?

"Thank you, Selia," Tynan said, his voice rough as though he'd been the one screaming.

She pinned him with her gaze as anger flooded her. "Did you have to do everything at once?"

The priest rubbed both hands across his face. "Not by preference. I was told the situation is urgent, and this particular method only works when all of the memories are confronted at the same time."

"You should have warned me." Selia scooted until she sat at Aris's back, but she didn't try to touch him. "Even if he told you not to. You should know better than to work on someone like him without a mage's aid."

Tynan's jaw firmed. "I was *also* told that this room was well-protected."

"For most things." She glared at him. "Are you a novice to act so rashly? I cannot believe Lial would request your presence. And speaking of Lial, I'm surprised he hasn't rushed in himself. He keeps a connection with those under his care, you know."

"Iron blast it," Tynan muttered. "I should have thought… It's that dragon. I wanted to complete the healing before she returned."

Selia lifted a brow. "You muddled this because of Kezari? Do dragons frighten you that much?"

The priest's cheeks reddened. "Fright has not been my experience with her. But she wouldn't…" He sighed and rubbed the back of his neck. "Forget it. I will endeavor to keep my thoughts in order in the future."

Before she formulated a reply, Aris groaned and rolled onto his back. His eyes crept open, and his empty gaze scanned the room. Then he blinked a few times before focusing on her. "Selia?"

"Forgive my intrusion," she whispered. "There was too much power for the shields to contain."

A slight smile crossed his lips. "You are never an intrusion."

"How do you feel?" she asked.

"Raw," he answered honestly. "But…different."

Tynan leaned forward to catch his attention. "I repaired what I could, but you'll have to build positive experiences on your own. The mind is complex and ever changing."

Aris nodded, though his attention seemed focused on her rather than the priest. "Selia, I want…" His voice trailed off, uncertainty entering his gaze. "I'd like to hold you. I can think of nothing more positive than that."

She sucked in a breath. "You're sure? Before…"

"I need to try," he said softly. "I need you."

Though she trembled, Selia stretched out beside him and let him gather her close. Shudders still rippled through his muscles as she rested her cheek against his chest, but he didn't go tense and his breathing remained even. Slowly, she wrapped her arm around his waist and tucked her body nearer. His heartbeat sped up beneath her ear, but it settled back to a steady pace after only a moment.

She barely noticed when the healer stood and let himself quietly out.

"You gave me more strength than you know," Aris whispered.

Selia stiffened. "Me?"

"You gave me a reason to keep going, even when I didn't realize it. It didn't matter that I wouldn't see you again. Knowing you existed in the world was enough." His lips brushed her hair. "You will always be my heart."

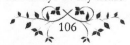

A lump formed in her throat. "You should've hated me."

"What?" he asked, his arm tightening around her back.

Now might not be the best time, but it felt right. Selia's hand gripped the fabric of his tunic as her greatest regret poured free. "If not for me, you wouldn't have been on that ship in the first place. It's all my fault."

Her whispered words dug into his heart, turning it over. Aris caressed her soft cheek with shaky fingers. "No, love. No."

"You were going to stay, but I convinced you it would be fine."

He cursed the weakness that kept him from sitting up and lifting her into his arms where he could look into her eyes. But his nerves groaned with the echoes of pain, and his muscles refused to do more than shift her a little closer. "You knew my heart's dream and encouraged me to seek it. I've always wanted to be among the first to successfully sail the seas. Do you know how much your support means to me?"

Her head moved against his chest. "You wouldn't have landed in such torment if—"

Aris placed his finger against her lips. "Stop. You aren't a seer. I hope you haven't carried this for seven years."

"Of course I have." Selia snorted softly. "How could I not?"

He smiled at that. Yes, she would have. Selia had always taken responsibility for more than she ought. "Well, drop that burden. It isn't yours."

She fell silent, but he didn't mistake that for agreement. He wouldn't argue the point, not now. Not when he could savor the feel of her against him for the first time in years. Although spasms still shot through his muscles and his body felt as heavy as a mountain, the priest's work held.

Mostly.

As Tynan had said, the healing wasn't perfect. A thread of unease wound through him as Selia shifted higher, closer to being on top of him than beside. He knew by the tension winding into his shoulders that he might never be able to bear her completely above him, but having her this close so soon after reliving his past was enough of a miracle.

If he'd learned anything, it was that miracles should be cherished.

"How did you end up in here?" he asked.

"I prepared the bulk of the shields on this room, and after I caught Iren experimenting with lightning one day, I set it to alert me to excessive power," Selia said, her tone dry. "The whole thing would've shattered if I hadn't brought crystals to fill."

Aris trailed his fingers through her hair and smiled again to remember the times they'd worked together in the past, loading energy crystals so she'd have extra power when she needed it. "At least my suffering will serve some good."

She gasped. "I wasn't thinking of it that way. You may have the crystals if you like."

"No," he said quickly. "No, they are yours. We would have had to fill them anyway in case we need them on Earth. I imagine this was faster."

"I would not have them in exchange for your pain," she whispered.

"My pain was inevitable." He kissed the top of her head even as he gave her hair a slight tug. "Anyway, I like the thought of creating something out of this. Stop overthinking it."

Her sigh caressed his neck. "Fine."

There was so much they needed to discuss, so much still between them, but for the moment, he didn't care. He wanted to ignore the last seven years and just be. Tomorrow, he could begin to tell her bits of his torment—and that Perim had been his soulbonded. But not now. One day's torture was enough.

16

Selia breathed in Aris's wild, woodsy scent as she twisted a lock of his brown-and-green hair around her finger. There was a tension to his muscles despite the peace of the moment that told her there were things unsaid—things beyond the terrible images she'd already seen. She wouldn't ask now, though. He'd gone through more than anyone should suffer in this day alone.

The door clicked open, and Lial's and Tynan's energies flowed in before their footsteps sounded on the stone. Selia nuzzled into Aris for another moment before she reluctantly pushed herself up with one arm. She glanced up, hiding her surprise at Lial's red-rimmed, solemn eyes. Oh, yes, he'd been linked. She'd never seen such a haunted look on the cranky but self-assured healer's face.

"How is he?" Lial asked.

"I'm alive," Aris murmured. Selia blinked at the hint of humor in her husband's voice. His lips curved up as he stared at her for a moment. Then he winked. "Can't complain about being able to hold my wife without going insane."

Lial's expression barely lightened as he crouched on Aris's other side. "For so much trauma, you deserved a complete healing. I am sorry you had to suffer."

Aris sighed. "You'd have to wipe my mind for a complete healing. I have a feeling you know that well enough now."

"Unfortunately," Lial said, flinching before he could smooth out the reaction. "Tynan's haste prevented me from severing our link as quickly as privacy would demand."

Tynan huffed. "I feared the dragon would try to—"

"So you said." Lial's voice could have frozen the sweltering plains in the height of summer. "I was assured of your skill despite your being out of your apprenticeship for such a short time. You may have treated many in those seven years, but you were obviously not ready for a task of this magnitude. Were any others available, I would call on them before attempting to fix Aris's poorly healed bones."

Selia lifted her brows at that. Training and apprenticeship for a healer lasted hundreds of years, but even after that, they often worked alongside someone with more experience for the first quarter century. She peered at Tynan's ashen face as he stood a few paces away, his eyes averted. He should have known better, but he was young. Despite his lapse, she found herself hoping Lial didn't go too hard on him.

"Torture isn't something our people often see," Aris said suddenly, his soft voice carrying across the silence. "Those inclined to that kind of cruelty are brought to justice before they reach that level of depravity. The shock of my trauma couldn't have helped."

His first assertion was certainly true—or at least she'd always believed so. But the whispers she'd heard of Kien's depravity trickled through her mind. He'd tortured Ralan's beloved for weeks before being discovered, and he had been a prince committing his foul acts near the palace at the very heart of their kingdom. Then there had been Allafon, a lord under Lyr's command. He'd hidden a great deal of damage before he'd been caught.

Perhaps there was more darkness in their society than any of them wanted to believe.

"One might think so," Tynan said softly, reinforcing Selia's own thoughts. "But I have seen my share of terrible things. Lial is correct to berate me."

"It remains to be seen if I will report this matter to your superior," Lial said. "I am strongly considering it."

The door opened again, and Kezari in her elven form slipped through. She glared at Lial as she strode toward Aris. "Do not threaten Tynan."

Selia's mouth dropped open at the dragon's angry demeanor. Kezari wasn't breathing fire, at least, but it might not be far off based on her expression. Aris groaned and shifted, and when Selia glanced at him, worry lined his forehead. He shoved his hand against the floor, trying to push himself up, but he dropped back down without making much progress.

Lial cursed. "Don't move. Your body is weak, and it would be best to let me heal the strain to your muscles before you hurt yourself worse."

"Kezari…" Aris began.

"Will certainly know what her *skizik* needs," Lial finished, his eyes narrowing as the dragon halted.

"Do not berate Tynan," Kezari said.

"I can't…" The priest shook his head. "I shouldn't have…"

Kezari thrust her shoulders back and glared at Tynan, too. "Your actions were necessary. Elves waste too much time, and a quick, hot flame cauterizes best. You were correct."

Lial's lips pinched. "There is more to consider than his methods."

Aris lifted a hand and then let it drop heavily on his chest. "I would appreciate it if you'd heal me enough so I can get up instead of arguing? Please?"

"Yes, heal him," Kezari said. As she sank to her knees behind Aris's head, her thin dress bunched around her legs, and she almost toppled before she caught herself. "His body must be in good health for our mission."

After a few muttered expletives, Lial got to work, and Selia glanced away from the bright blue light surrounding Aris. Her gaze landed on Tynan, who stared at Kezari's back with unmasked longing—until he noticed Selia's regard. Then he spun away to pace a circle around the room.

Was there something between the two? Selia tried to remember if dragons and elves could bond, but she didn't think any of the histories she'd read had mentioned it. She'd heard a ballad about such a pairing once, but then, she'd also listened to a song extolling the virtues of running naked outside in the season of ice. One never knew what the *omree* would put into verse.

As soon as the healer finished, Aris shoved himself up to a sitting position, drawing Selia's attention. His long hair shifted around him, more than a little tangled. He braided it as best he could in a few quick motions and let his hands drop into his lap as he studied her. His gaze trailed down her body before returning to her face.

"What...what are you wearing?"

Oh. Selia found herself chuckling despite the situation. "Earth clothes."

"They look good on you, of course." He flicked a glance at her breasts. "But definitely different."

Selia smiled. "You'll have to admire them later. I have a mission to do now that the crisis has passed."

"I should go with you," Kezari said. "I am Moranaian now. That solves the problem."

Aris frowned at the dragon. "Not without me. You said our magic would work best together. We're a team."

An unexpected sliver of pain sliced Selia's heart. He didn't protest her departure, but he didn't want Kezari to go without him. There were plenty of good reasons for that, of course. Selia knew that. Just preventing the dragon from behaving rashly was difficult enough in Morania where dragons were known to exist. But on Earth, without Aris there to guide Kezari? Visions of humans running in panic from a flame-breathing wyvern flickered through her mind.

But feelings weren't rational.

"I do not like this delay, *skizik*," Kezari muttered. "The crack widens with each day."

Aris rested his arms on his knees. "Lial. While Selia and the others are on this first mission, I would like for you to repair my bones."

"No," Selia said before the healer could respond. "What if that sets off bad memories and your magic leaks out again?"

Lial's nostrils flared. "That will not be a concern. Aris will be placed into a deep sleep, his nerves deadened during the procedure. Tynan will ensure that memories are not triggered while I work."

Selia frowned. "Why didn't Tynan block the pain today?"

The priest's pacing cut off abruptly as he spun to face her. "I could not. Mental pathways formed by pain cannot be rerouted while sensation is blocked. Please do not think I am cruel in addition to inept."

"I meant no offense," Selia said.

Tynan nodded, but doubt shadowed his expression. Unfortunately, she didn't have time to deal with his insecurities. Meli and the others would be waiting on her to journey to Earth. Selia glanced at one of the small windows and frowned at how dim the light appeared. It was well past the midday meal. Why hadn't anyone come looking for her?

Aris stood, still wavering on his feet despite his healing session. Kezari shifted beneath his shoulder to help support his weight. "We can discuss my bones later. I want rest," Aris said.

"I'll see you to your room," Lial said. "If necessary, I can put you into a light sleep."

Selia stared at her husband's back as he limped across the room with Kezari. He wouldn't leave without saying anything to her, would he? Surely not, especially with her impending mission. Her throat tightened. She wasn't jealous of the dragon, exactly—not in a romantic sense—but she did envy their closeness. He'd formed this connection alone, a symbol of the new life they didn't quite share.

Then Aris looked over his shoulder, his brows lowering. "Aren't you coming with us, Selia? I want to see your face as I fall asleep."

A bit of the heaviness left her chest at the pleading in his eyes. The mission would have to wait. Aris needed her.

Water sucked at Perim's body as the waves surged in frenzied eddies around her waist. Salt stung the healing cuts from her crawl through the tunnels, but it was a small discomfort. *Twenty. Twenty-one. Twenty-two.* She stopped at the proper number and studied the sea around her. Baza had claimed there was an outcropping twenty-two steps from the shore. A quick swim from there, and she was supposed to find a fissure of energy that connected to the Veil.

What a delicious secret that had been. All this time, Kezari had sought a way to convince the queen to petition the Moranaians for use of the portal while Baza had quietly been expanding a newly developing fissure. Like the other dragons, he had no desire to leave the island—or so he claimed—but gathering control of a valuable resource like a new portal would give him a great deal of power.

If he didn't want Kezari's hoard of earth-magic gems so badly, he never would have revealed the truth to Perim. He'd even shared that Kezari was likely to head to Earth with Aris to solve a problem with the energy there. Perim grinned. The dragon wasn't likely to get anything useful out of Aris after he'd been so thoroughly broken.

Perim shoved her hand over her eyes and squinted against the sunlight striking the sea. The only outcropping she could see was at least another thirty paces away, maybe more. Had Baza lied about the whole thing? This was far more than twenty-two. Although… She groaned. How did dragons count steps? Not the way elves did, it seemed.

She straightened her spine and started walking again, ignoring the pull of the water. She'd swim if she had to—anything to escape the living death of the island.

As she exited the brooding tower, Selia gathered the edges of her cloak in her hands, blocking the sight of the strange Earth clothes from others' view. With the dragon gone and the birds settled, the workers had resumed their preparations for the autumn festival. Only two days away now. Soon, crowds would gather to hear the *omree* practice their songs.

Warriors from surrounding areas would also arrive to compete in the tournaments the day after the main festival. There would be archery and swordplay for certain, but Selia wasn't sure what else they did here. At home, the mages held contests for the most innovative spells, but that probably wouldn't happen at Braelyn.

She'd been looking forward to experiencing the festival, and now she might not see it at all.

Selia ducked into the door near the library and hurried toward the study. Once she'd checked in with Lyr, she could talk with Iren. It would be just like him to try to follow the group to Earth, especially considering his fascination with Arlyn's stories. He'd already considered and discarded several ideas on how Moranaians could use magic to create a space station circling the planet like Earth had. She smiled. Elves in space—what a thought.

To her surprise, Iren was already in the study, bent over a stack of papers in the seat next to Arlyn. She'd certainly wasted no time in recruiting his aid with those reports. When Arlyn cast a sheepish look her way, Selia grinned and inclined her head. She had no problem with other adults giving him tasks, within reason. It was good for him.

Lyr stood with Meli beside his desk. His hand rested at her waist, and his face was pinched with worry. But as soon as he caught sight of Selia, resignation replaced it. His hand lingered for another moment before he sighed and straightened. Meli leaned up to give him a quick kiss on the lips before walking over to Selia.

"Ready for our grand adventure?" Meli asked.

"Now?" Selia's brows drew together. "I thought we'd need to do more preparation."

Meli shook her head. "We're only waiting on you. Kai, Inona, and Delbin are already at the portal with our packs."

Her cheeks heated. "Forgive me for holding everything up."

"It was necessary," Lyr said, striding over. "Lial reported to me already. But now that Aris is settled, it seems best to proceed quickly. I didn't want to say this in front of Kezari, but I would like to have a better idea of the situation before sending a dragon to Earth. Although I don't doubt her honesty…"

Arlyn glanced up from the report she held. "I wouldn't send her without good reason, that's for sure. There are lots of ways to explain pointy ears on Earth, but a dragon is sort of hard to pass off as something else."

"Just so," Lyr grumbled.

"Perhaps it will be unnecessary," Selia said. "If I am capable of correcting the problem, would you like me to do so, or should I stick with gathering information?"

Lyr's lips pursed. "If you are certain you can fix it, please do. I would be happy to avert another crisis."

"Me, too." Selia smiled at Meli. "Well, then. I'm ready when you are."

The younger woman nodded, turning to give her bonded another kiss. Selia walked over to Iren's chair and knelt to look into his eyes. He grinned at her, no hint of the nerves twisting her stomach in his eyes. "I'll be good, *Onaiala*. I want to go to Earth, but I don't want to be poisoned. Then I'd have to see the healer."

Selia chuckled at the dismay in his tone at the last word. In this case, it wasn't just because of Lial's grumpy nature. Iren balked at any healer. "Remember that, love. Perhaps you could check in on your father later?"

"I will," Iren said, his humor fading. "I promise."

"Good." Despite the others in the room, Selia leaned forward to kiss Iren on the cheek. He groaned at the display, but his arms wrapped around her neck for a hug. "I love you."

"I love you, too," he answered as she stood.

Then Selia joined Meli by the door. Selia gripped her cloak together with shaky hands, took a deep breath, and stepped out into the hall.

Toward her first real adventure.

17

They emerged into darkness.

Selia squinted against the sudden night, her eyes taking a moment to adjust after the dim glow of the Veil. After a few heartbeats, the thin trickle of moonlight resolved the world into shades of black and gray. She followed the others from the narrow passage in the wall of a ridge, and a bit more of the world came into focus.

The small ridge followed a hill that sloped upward to their left and downward to their right. Beyond the small clearing where they stood, sparse tree-shadows stood against the navy sky, but the branches looked far smaller than the trees at Braelyn. Still, this wasn't too different from the foothills on the edge of the plains. Hadn't Arlyn said there would be cities on this world? Difficult to believe in this location.

"It's late," Kai said, peering down the hill. "I doubt your friend would appreciate us calling her for a ride."

Delbin pulled a thin, rectangular device from his pocket. A phone, she thought it was called. He pressed on the side, and the glassy surface filled with light. The thin beam illuminated the frown creasing his brow. "Yeah, not at one in the morning."

"This does not look like morning," Meli said from beside Selia.

"Humans count the start of the day in the middle of the night." Delbin shrugged. "You get used to it. But hey, I have a ride-sharing app. Once we reach the end of the driveway on the other end of the ridge, I'll request pick-up."

"You don't think that'll look suspicious?" Kai asked.

Delbin smiled. "Eh, maybe. We could say the party up at the house got a little wild. It's too far away to see from the road."

Inona nudged Delbin's shoulder with her own. "You just want a chance to use Ralan's money."

"He's a rich bastard. And I'm not stealing," Delbin added when Kai frowned. "He gave me permission to hook his card to the app."

App? Card? Selia exchanged a confused grimace with Meli. "This sounds difficult."

Kai expelled a long breath. "And dangerous. We don't want to keep showing up out of nowhere with no obvious means of transportation. Even Maddy's periodic pick-ups may be causing notice."

"It's not too much of a jog to reach a few human businesses," Inona said. "I've found people willing to drive me places from there when needed."

Delbin spun to face Inona. "You hitchhiked? Ah, hell, that's not a safe way to—"

"I may not have your strength when it comes to telepathy, but I can tell when someone is dangerous. I can give them a bit of a nudge, too," Inona grumbled.

"Learn from your elders, man." Kai grinned. "You might have lived here the last hundred years, but we've been doing this type of thing for centuries. It's best in this case. We'll find some place public, and you can take control of someone with a large vehicle. From my understanding, the cave isn't near well-travelled areas. Your app would keep a record of our unusual destination."

Delbin shook his head. "There's an official trailhead and a small campsite near the cave."

"Do humans begin such activities in the middle of the night?" Inona asked sweetly.

"Not usually for legit reasons," Delbin muttered, rubbing his neck. "All right, fine. I'll let the elderly lead the way."

Selia studied their surroundings as much as the light permitted as she and Meli followed Inona and Kai. The insects' chirps sounded a different tune, and the air carried an unusual blend of nature and…something else. A hint of something acrid, but she had no name for it. Even the energy felt different.

What little she could pull in. It was like trying to grasp something on a tall shelf. She could brush it with her fingers, but she couldn't get the leverage to pull. When Selia did finally manage a link, the flow was but a trickle. Drips from a water clock compared to a steady stream. Her fingers wrapped around the pouch of energy crystals she'd shoved in her pocket. If she had to do magic, she was going to need them, though she hoped she didn't have to waste the one containing pure Moranaian energy. That one was a last resort.

By the time they reached a road, Selia was out of breath. They'd alternated between walking and jogging, and the scouts' paces were definitely faster than hers or Meli's. More than once, she'd exchanged exhausted but resolved glances with the other woman. They might not have trained for this, but they weren't going to hold the group back.

Still, she was more than grateful for a short break.

Selia bent over for several long moments, trying to steady her breathing. She stared at the odd, smooth material of the road as she gasped in more air. A harsh scent emanated from the…rock? Shaking her head, she straightened, and only then did she notice what was on the other side. Light poured from a squat metal-and-glass building situated in a sea of more smooth stone. A variety of conveyances sat between lines all around the place.

Cars. These must be what Arlyn had called cars.

"What is the ground here?" she asked softly.

"It's artificial," Delbin explained. "This stuff is asphalt. It's a mix of small stones and pitch. Humans spread it all over the place for cars to drive on. Sometimes, you'll see concrete, which is made in a similar way to the walls of some of our houses. I think."

All along the road to the right of the building, more structures sat, little grass to be seen amidst the asphalt. Tall metal poles stretched into the sky at regular intervals, connected by a series of thin ropes, and little arms stuck out from the top with lights attached. Selia sent out a tendril of power, curious to see how the lanterns differed from mage lamps. But she retreated quickly at the intense energy surging through them, like lightning contained.

Fascinating. She might be able to work with human electricity if it was similar to lightning, but it would take some research. "Remind me to speak to you later, Delbin, about how you use magic to charge your device. There may be more compatibility than I'd thought."

"Sure," he said.

"Come on." Kai gestured toward the brightly lit building. "Let's cross the street before someone drives by."

Selia and Meli followed Inona and Delbin, Kai falling behind to guard their backs. As they hurried across the road and onto the broad expanse of asphalt, an odd sound like a buzzing whoosh echoed off the trees. Frowning, Selia spun around, only to step back with a cry when a large conveyance—car—rushed past with such force that her hair was tossed about by the wind. Gods, those things went fast.

Without magic, too.

"We're supposed to ride in one of those?" Meli whispered.

Delbin chuckled. "You get used to it."

Selia stared at the retreating red lights, her heart pounding against her ribs. Get used to it? No. She'd ridden horses on the plains, but they couldn't approach that speed. It couldn't be safe. Were humans insane? Fear crawled up her throat and coated her mouth with bitterness. She shouldn't have come here. She wasn't an explorer like Aris.

"Selia," Inona began softly, settling her hand on Selia's shoulder. "It's a lot to get used to. Don't give yourself grief over it."

With a nod, Selia spun back toward the metal and glass building, though she wasn't so certain Inona was correct. They were all at risk if she couldn't handle this. Why shouldn't she be hard on herself? But she didn't give voice to her doubts, lest she affect their confidence, too.

"I'm ready," Selia said.

As they resumed walking, Meli gave Selia a quick smile. "She's right, you know. Shifting cultures is tough. In some ways, it was harder for me to go from Alfheim to Moranaia than it is to travel here. I get flickers of my past life sometimes, so I've seen some of these things in my head. You haven't."

Selia arched a brow. "You seemed just as worried about the car's speed as I was."

"The image in my mind wasn't moving," Meli said with a grimace. "Transportation portals are much safer and more efficient."

"You have the right of it." Selia lowered her voice. "If I can gather enough energy after we find the breech, I'll transport us back to the portal."

Kai spoke over Selia's shoulder. "It would be nice if you can manage it despite the energy limitations."

Selia shrugged. "We shall see."

She followed Delbin and Inona through a set of doors that slid open as they approached, but she was too busy blinking against the intense light of the interior to marvel over that. Once her eyes adjusted, she stumbled to a halt, stunned by the shelves full of brightly colored packages. A tall display stood directly in front of her, purple and orange bags lined up in little compartments. The bag had words, but she didn't recognize them.

Selia's brow furrowed. Lyr had used a spell to give her the English language, and he'd said the written form was included. Had there been a mistake? "What do they speak here?" she asked Kai.

"English."

She frowned. Languages did change all the time, so these words might simply be new. "I thought that was what I'd been given, but I don't understand the words on some of these items."

"Probably product names," Kai answered. "A special name intended to differentiate between similar items created by different people."

The knot in her stomach began to ease. She didn't want to consider not being able to read in a world she already didn't understand, not even for such a short mission. "Hopefully that is it. Thank you."

Selia headed over to the others where they stood beside a display filled with shelves of more colored packets. Some had pictures of oval or triangle-shaped food. Thin bread? She studied the packages more closely for some clue, and though relief coursed through her to recognize some words, they weren't exactly helpful. *Cheesy. Crunchy. Original.*

But cheesy, crunchy, original *what?*

Meli picked up a yellow bag. "This looks familiar, but I can't remember why."

"Try it," Delbin said. "We should buy something while we wait for our friend to pick us up."

Inona crossed her arms. "What are you talki—"

"They'll kick us out if we're just loitering." Delbin flicked a meaningful glance to the left, and Selia noticed the human woman scrutinizing them from the end of the aisle as she placed supplies on another shelf. He raised his voice slightly for her benefit. "It's bad enough that we had to walk all this way to avoid Kai's dad. It's just a party."

Kai's brows rose, but a small smile pulled at his lips. "Hey, my dad is a hard ass. Barely around except when he wants to tell me what to do."

"I just wish you weren't so cheap." Delbin's eyes shone with humor. "It would've only been another twenty or thirty dollars to get a big enough car to take us all from my house."

"Why pay when you can get a free ride? Just takes a little extra effort."

Selia, Meli, and Inona exchanged amused looks. As Inona's lips twitched, Meli grabbed Selia's wrist and tugged her down another aisle. "I wonder if they think that was convincing?" Meli whispered, chuckling under her breath.

"Probably." Selia grinned. "Where are we going?"

Meli paused beside a row of glass doors and pointed at the closest one. "These bottles look like they have water in them. I don't know about these other drinks, but it sounds like fun to try water from another world."

Selia frowned at the rows of bottles. "Will it make us sick?"

"I don't know." Meli jiggled the bag she still held. "But it can't be worse than this. Come on." She lowered her voice. "Who knows if we'll ever get another chance to try this kind of Earth stuff?"

Meli was right. If she did return with Aris and Kezari, Selia would be able to cast a transport spell back to the spot they needed—or at least, she hoped she could. Aris would be disappointed to miss the adventure, but it would be safer than trying to sneak a dragon past countless humans. Even in elven form, Kezari didn't exactly fit in, so it wouldn't be worth the risk. When would she get another opportunity like this?

Resolved, Selia yanked at the handle and ignored the blast of cold air within as she pulled a glass bottle from a shelf. But when it dented beneath her hand, she realized that it wasn't glass at all. Yet another unusual human contraption. She held the door open for Meli to grab one of her own before turning her attention to the other displays.

An unusual cabinet caught her eye. This one was glass, lit softly from within, and several shelves held rows of round, bread-like objects with various forms of frosting. She wandered closer. One of them was only lightly frosted, and except for a hole in the middle, it looked very much like the cakes her people ate during the summer solstice festival.

"I would like to try one of these," Selia said to Meli. "But I'm not sure if I can buy just one."

Delbin stepped up beside her. "You can. Here, I'll get it."

Selia watched as he picked up a thin, clear bag and a white piece of paper. After he opened the case, he grabbed a cake with the paper and slipped it into the sack. "It's called a doughnut," he said as he handed it over.

The small bag rustled as she wrapped her fingers around it. Selia lifted the bag and the bottle. "And what are these containers made of?" she whispered

"Plastic." Delbin's attention shifted to the window behind her. "I'll tell you about it in the car. Looks like our friend is here."

Selia glanced over her shoulder. On the other side of the window, a man stepped

out of a large, boxy vehicle. He appeared human, and a quick energy scan confirmed it. "You know him?" she asked Delbin.

Delbin winked at her. "I'd say we're about to become best friends."

"Are you sure about doing this?" Selia asked, keeping her voice low. "It doesn't seem quite…fair."

He sobered. "I don't like it, but there isn't a lot of choice. We have to get to that cave. But I'll make sure the human is fairly compensated."

He left her standing there as he approached the stranger entering the main doors. The human's steps hitched and his expression went a touch slack, but those were the only signs that Delbin had taken control. Their new friend walked right up to Kai and Delbin with a smile.

"Hey, guys. Ready to go?" the human asked.

"The ladies just need to buy their snacks," Delbin said. "Then we can get going." The man nodded. "Sure."

It only took a few moments and a swipe of Delbin's card before the group headed for the door. While the human purchased a drink, Delbin leaned in toward the group. "I've implanted memories as much as taken true control. I'll remove them once we get where we're going. Still, try not to say much. Less for me to deal with that way."

Inona eased closer to him, her own voice going low. "You've done a lot of work with Ralan in such a short time. It didn't seem this easy for you before."

Delbin slung his arm over Inona's shoulders. "Yep. Guess it was worth working with the arrogant ass after all."

Heat climbed into Selia's cheeks at his words, though he'd spoken them with true affection. Ralan and Delbin both needled each other like friendly competitors in a magic contest, but despite the lack of rancor, it made her uncomfortable. One didn't call the heir to the throne an arrogant ass—whether he was one or not.

The human joined the group outside the glass doors. "You guys are lucky I'm borrowing my dad's van. Climb on in, and we'll head out."

Kai hopped into one of the front seats as Delbin grabbed a handle on the side of the van and tugged. To her surprise, a portion of the vehicle slid back, leaving a large hole for them to enter. "Why don't you and Meli sit in the back? I'm probably the only one who knows how to close this door," Delbin said with a laugh.

Biting her lip, Selia hesitated for only a moment before ducking into the van. She crawled between the two inner seats and plopped down on one in the back. She gave a quick bounce as Meli settled beside her. The cushioning was adequate. Otherwise, there wasn't much to note about the unusual conveyance. Lights in the ceiling illuminated the seats and a few small panels with knobs and buttons, but the interior was overall bland. No carving or embroidery. Why not decorate something so important?

But as soon as the human placed a key into a slot and twisted, such thoughts were forgotten. Selia clutched the water bottle to her chest and leaned back against her seat for balance when the vehicle began to move backward at an angle. A quick pause, and then the human directed the van forward with a jolt. Her heartbeat pounded in her ears as they turned onto the street and accelerated.

Delbin pulled some kind of strap over his shoulder and glanced over the seat. "Grab one of the buckles on the wall and pull the seatbelt over you. There's a small place by your hip to secure it."

Selia shifted her possessions onto the seat between her and Meli and reached for the strap beside her that matched Delbin's. It took a bit of fumbling, but she finally got it latched with a small click. "What is this for?"

Delbin smiled. "It's a safety measure. These things do go pretty fast, after all."

She gave a jerky nod and peered out the window. Her stomach immediately lurched at the sight of the trees rushing by. No wonder she had to wear a belt for safety—if this thing crashed, anyone inside would be flung gods knew where otherwise. It was foolhardy, bold…and amazing. And very, very human.

"Let's try our food," Meli said, lifting her bag from between them.

"Now?" Selia grabbed the package holding her cake. "I'm don't know. My stomach is uneasy enough."

Meli frowned. "Are you sure you aren't hungry? When did you last eat?"

"This morning, I suppose." Selia had missed the midday meal helping Aris and had been too busy after to consider food. With so much magic to perform, that could be a problem. Proper nourishment was vital to energy production. "Let's do it."

Selia pulled the round cake from its bag and stared at it. Though flattened in places from being tossed around, the cake made her mouth water. She took a tentative sniff and was rewarded with a sweet yeasty scent that produced a yearning for home. Despite the slight sharp smell of something else, some component uniquely human, she pinched off a bite and popped it in her mouth.

It was… Selia wrinkled her nose as she tried to determine if the treat tasted pleasant. It was missing the fuller, more savory taste of the grains on Moranaia, and the sweet hit her tongue with greater intensity. As she chewed, she noticed an aftertaste, too. Brow furrowing, Selia tore off another bite. Then another. Unusual, but not unpleasant.

Meli tore her bag open, almost spilling the contents. She steadied it in her hands and lifted a piece from inside. A golden, curved oval caught the light from a passing streetlamp. Probably not bread, but what did they know? Meli studied the bit of food for a moment before taking a tentative bite.

Selia lowered her own treat at the unusual look on the other woman's face. Eyes wide, Meli worked her tongue against the roof of her mouth. Without a word, Delbin reached over the seat and grabbed the water container from between them. He did something to the top handed it over. Meli drank deep before lowering the bottle with a grimace.

"I don't know if I can eat the rest," she admitted.

Selia eyed the bag. "That bad?"

"Feel free to try one," Meli said.

Although the other woman's tone wasn't promising, Selia accepted a golden disk from the bag. Before she could second guess herself, she took a quick bite. The food crunched loudly, but that wasn't too bothersome. The intense, sharp taste that permeated her mouth? That was altogether different.

When Delbin handed her the other water bottle, Selia took a grateful sip, barely noticing the tinny flavor. "What was that?"

Delbin lifted the bag and then laughed. "Salt and vinegar potato chips. Plenty of humans aren't even fond of that combo, and they invented it. I wish I'd looked more closely. I would have warned you."

"Oh, certainly." With a small smile, Selia tore off a large piece of her cake and passed it to Meli. "Good thing I don't mind sharing."

The sweet dulled the remaining bitterness lingering on her tongue. But despite the unpleasantness of the snack, Selia didn't regret trying it. Eating Earth food was a small enough thing, but she couldn't help but feel brave. Exhilarated.

Perhaps she had adventure in her after all.

18

Aris stirred to awareness beneath the weighty feel of someone's regard. Although he tensed, he was able to scan with his senses before panic set in.

Iren.

Aris cracked his eyes open to see his son sitting in a chair beside the bed. Where in all the worlds had Iren found a chair? The bed had been the only furniture here when Aris had fallen asleep. He had a feeling he didn't want to know where the new addition had come from, but as a father, he also didn't have a choice.

"Did you teleport that from some hapless person's room?" he asked, then cleared his throat to try to ease some of the roughness. "I'd rather know before they come looking for it."

Far from worried, Iren grinned. "No. Well, I did teleport it, but I asked Lyr's permission first."

"You're too young to be using your power so casually."

"Yeah, probably." Iren shrugged. "But *Onaiala* makes me go too slow."

Aris sat up, shoving his hair out of his face as he studied his son. There wasn't anger in his expression, precisely, but he exuded a certain frustrated mulishness that Aris had seen in the mirror more than once. "Constraints are necessary in magic."

"Sure, but sometimes I just want to…" Iren's shoulders slumped. "I don't know how to describe it. *Onaiala* is a great teacher, but I still want to…"

"Do things your own way," Aris filled in for him. He'd felt the same often in his life. "You don't fit the steady, formal mold of your grandfather. Selia doesn't, either, but she's never had a good reason to realize it."

"Is that why you left?" Iren blurted.

"What?" Aris's head jerked back. "No. Not because of your grandfather. He never approved of me, but we reached an accord. And I didn't leave you. It was supposed to be a quick, low-risk expedition. I had no intention of being away from you for long."

Though Iren nodded, he nibbled on his lower lip for a moment before speaking again. "I thought maybe we weren't, you know, enough."

Aris's spine stiffened. "That is far from the truth. My last trip was also the first I'd taken since a couple of years before you were born, and it was only supposed to take a month, two at most. I would not have gone otherwise. Your mother knew I'd always dreamed of sailing the ocean and encouraged me."

"She wanted you to leave?" Iren said, anger lacing his voice.

"Do *not* take it that way." Aris captured his son's gaze. "I mean it. Your *onaiala* loved me for myself, not what she wanted me to be. She loved me enough to make sure I was able to fulfill a dream. I hope you find a partner like that someday, too."

After a few heartbeats, Iren nodded. "I wish we'd known Ralan and Eri then. They would have known you'd have trouble."

"Doesn't mean they would have stopped it." Aris sighed. "I'm glad I don't have to be the one to decide what information to withhold."

"Surely they would have prevented all the horrible things that woman did. You were tortured and…"

Aris froze as his son's mouth snapped closed. "You saw."

"It was an accident," Iren said in a rush. "There was so much energy coming from the training room, so I hooked in. But only for a few drips of time. I'm sorry."

His throat closed up. He might not have liked knowing that Selia and the healers had seen so much of what had happened, but his own son? Once again, Aris had failed his child. No eleven-year-old should know about torture. More than torture, if the flush on Iren's skin was any indication.

"Perhaps you should speak with Tynan," Aris whispered. "You should not have seen that."

Iren rolled his eyes. "You think I don't realize bad things happen? This kind of stuff is in my history books, you know. And I've heard some of the whispers about Kien and Allafon, whose servant I fought."

Aris's lips pinched. It was true, but… "It's altogether different when it's your father."

"I'm glad I know," Iren said. This time, the stubborn set of his son's shoulders reminded Aris of Selia. "You told me it was bad, but I didn't really get it. Now I do."

A rustling sounded from the top of the stairs, and Aris glanced up to see Tynan stride into the tower room. Perfect. The mind-healer could examine Iren for any sign of trauma. Gods, Selia would never forgive him if this mess had caused harm to their son.

Or maybe she would, but he wouldn't be able to forgive himself.

The healer smiled as he neared. "Good, you're awake."

"Where's Lial?" Aris asked.

"He will be here in a moment." Tynan paused at the foot of the bed. "I wanted to apologize for my lapse in judgement earlier."

Aris shrugged. "It worked out."

But those words didn't ease the frown on the healer's face. "Yes. However, the more I consider it, the more I am inclined to agree with Lady Selia. We should wait

for her return to proceed with the secondary healing. I do not want to risk more trouble."

Iren perked up. "Trouble?"

"Oh, I'd say you've had enough of that," Aris said. Then he took a deep breath and plunged ahead. "Tynan. My son connected to the training room's shields and caught a few of my memories. Could this have caused harm?"

"Let me see."

Tynan rounded the bed and stopped at Iren's side. As he reached out a hand, Iren glared. "Do not erase anything. I am old enough to deny you permission for that."

In that moment, Iren looked far older than eleven, the resolve hardening his face that of a man. Tynan obviously agreed, for he gave a sharp nod. "I will not. But no one of any age need suffer trauma when help is available."

Aris smiled as Iren grudgingly allowed the healer to use his power on him. He'd once felt the same about having someone meddle in his mind, but he'd learned the folly of that pride. Tynan was correct. There was no reason to leave the mind unhealed. Unhappiness, stress, sadness—these were necessary parts of life, if unpleasant. But there came a point when the damage was beyond normal, a muscle torn instead of strained. Then healing was required.

Tynan's hand lowered. "He is handling it well. I believe he disconnected quickly enough to avoid the worst of it."

"See?" Iren said, crossing his arms. "I'm fine."

Relief slackened the muscles in Aris's shoulders. "I had to know."

"So are you going to tell me about the extra healing thing?" Iren asked.

Aris sighed. Clearly, his son was not one to give up. "Lial intends to reset and properly heal a couple of my bones. I'll be unconscious with the pain blocked and Tynan monitoring my mind, but they are concerned my magic will react again. Your mother had to filter the last leakage into energy crystals. But I wasn't able to be unconscious then."

Tynan's jaw tightened. "I do not want to make another error."

"And I want to get it over with," Aris snapped. "We don't know what they will find on Earth. Kezari and I may be needed at any time."

"I'll help," Iren said.

"No," Aris and Tynan said simultaneously.

Iren's eyes narrowed, and he sat up straighter in his chair as his arms dropped to his sides. "I'm not four anymore, *Onaial*. I can do this."

Aris studied his son's face. Yes, he wasn't four, but eleven was far from manhood. That said, energy transference was one of the earliest skills taught since the ability to manipulate energy was vital to all other skills. But could Iren handle raw life magic? Selia could only transfer it, but his son might have inherited—

"I can feel it," Iren blurted. "I couldn't sense much when I was younger, but over the last couple of years, I've started connecting to living things. *Onaiala* is wor-

ried about finding someone to teach me about it, but it hasn't caused any problems yet."

Aris's heart thumped with alarm. "Please tell me you haven't tried to use that energy."

"No," Iren answered. But he ducked his head, avoiding Aris's gaze.

"What did you do, Iren?"

His son squirmed in his seat. "There was this flower. I...tried to make it grow faster."

Worry curled through Aris. He'd tried something similar as a child, hoping to encourage the growth of a tree his mother had planted. Within days, the poor sapling had been dead, and he'd felt the loss he'd caused so deeply that he hadn't touched life magic for a solid year. His mother had found a teacher for him after that.

"Creation and destruction stand a hairsbreadth apart," Aris said softly. "A flower may be just a beautiful plant to most, but it is different for us. And that's the risk of our talent. You can let yourself merge so deeply with the life around you that it's difficult to function. You can't even walk without feeling the pain of the grass crushed beneath your feet, and no death is easy at that level. I hope you learned that lesson well."

Iren nodded, sadness beyond his years filling his eyes. "I haven't touched it since."

"I will teach you," Aris said.

Hope lightened Iren's expression, twisting into Aris's gut. Suddenly, he couldn't sit still under his son's regard. He leaped to his feet and pushed past Tynan to stare out the window. Why had he promised such a thing without stopping to consider the ramifications? The healer's work on his mind had been impressive, but there was no guarantee it would be permanent. Aris had barely been awake for half a mark, and he was making promises to his son that would take centuries to fulfill.

But few were skilled in life magic, which went beyond earth-healing and into the heartbeat of nature itself. Aris could force plants to grow or die. He could find the unique energy signature of any living creature, and if he were so inclined, he could alter the physiology of smaller animals. But the hardest to deal with was the power to kill. With enough power, he could kill even one of his own kind.

He'd extinguished more than one spark of life, a weight he would forever carry.

"I do hope you won't choose to focus on it to the exlusion of your other talents," Aris said as he stared at a group of people setting up a small table in the garden below. "Life magic can be heady. All-consuming if you let it be. I spent centuries traveling the wild places to appease it. My path is not one you should take."

Iren's footsteps sounded against the stone. "Why not? I mean, except for the last few years."

"It is a difficult thing to handle, Iren."

Like the time he'd had to kill one of the few *merk* they'd managed to find during their research trip. The great beast had stood three times his height, and it had pinned

Ter against a tree with claws longer than his forearm. None of which had eased the pain of draining its life with his own mind.

"Maybe," Iren said. "But right now, I want to help you while you're being healed."

Aris turned to face his son. "No."

"This is important to me." Iren's hands curled into fists, but his downturned lips trembled as he glared. "You don't trust me."

Tynan stepped forward, one hand lifted. "Be calm, young Iren. Your father is correct."

Aris shot the healer an annoyed glance. "I am, but it has nothing to do with trust. If you have my abilities, then too much exposure to my power could trigger yours. Awaken them further before you are ready. It's too risky."

"I thought you said you wouldn't lose control while unconscious," Iren said, lifting a brow.

Aris smiled. "Then I won't need help."

Lial's voice echoed across the room. "No, he won't. I am more than capable of cutting off pain receptors, and if Tynan monitors his mental pathways, there will be no risk. I respect your desire to help, Iren, but your aid is unnecessary."

"Yeah, sure." If Iren had been a few years younger, he no doubt would have stomped his foot the way he had as a toddler. Instead, he crossed his arms and scowled. "I'll just get out of your way."

"Iren—"

"Forget it," his son said sharply before darting toward the stairs.

Aris moved to follow, but Lial halted him with a hand to his chest. "Let him go. He's a good lad, and he'll see the sense in our words once he calms down. He only needs a bit of time."

For once, the anxiety in Aris's stomach had nothing to do with his torture. Would alone time help Iren think through the problem, or would dwelling on it make his anger worse? Aris raked his fingers against his scalp. He would have to trust the healer's assessment, for Lial likely knew Iren better than he did. That a stranger might have more understanding of his son…well, it was galling.

"You have plenty of time to rebuild your relationship," Tynan said, perhaps guessing Aris's thoughts from his expression.

"A fine start I just made."

"Parents must deny as much as indulge, as well you know." Lial pointed toward the bed. "Now go lie down. As the senior healer, I've decided to go ahead with the procedure, and I would like to get it over with."

Aris choked back the arguments running through his mind. They could debate parenting styles for the rest of the afternoon, but it wouldn't fix his poorly healed bones. "Fine. Then once you're finished, I'm going to find Iren."

The healer was probably right—Iren needed space. He'd certainly required time away from his own parents at that age, especially after an argument. But as Aris stretched out on the bed, he couldn't shake the feeling that he'd made a terrible mistake.

The cave's entrance was smaller than Selia had expected. Her friends had confronted Kien here, of all places? From the moment their unwitting driver had deposited them at a small roadside area and driven away, she'd been struck by the absolute peace surrounding them. Through the darkness, they'd climbed the side of the small mountain to the sounds of droning insects and chattering wildlife. Selia had scanned for turbulent energy, but she'd sensed nothing but the occasional gentle ripple. In the light of the mage globe hovering overhead, the narrow cave opening appeared almost welcoming.

But beside Selia, Inona stood as still as a stalagmite, except for her hands rubbing anxiously across her upper arms. Meli eased closer and gave the scout's shoulder a squeeze. "Do you want to stay outside?"

Inona's fingers slid to her throat before her hand dropped to her side. "Of course I want to. But I won't."

Delbin nodded, a slight smile on his lips. "Good for you, love. If anyone can conquer this, it's you."

"Thank you," she whispered.

Inona lifted her head high and marched toward the opening. Although Kai outranked her, he shifted aside and let her take the lead. He fell to the back of their group as Delbin and then Meli followed Inona. Selia gathered as much energy as she could, sending the mage light ahead as she took her place behind Meli. Blast it all, but it was tough to pull in power here. Like running honey through a finely knit sieve, possible but slow.

They wound their way through a thin tunnel that opened abruptly on a broad cavern. Fragments of stalactites lay scattered across the uneven stone floor, and a few scorch marks and one dark stain shadowed the rock in the center. The hairs on Selia's arms lifted at the remnants of the malevolent energy lingering in the space. So much for peaceful.

Inona's steps hitched and then ground to a stop. Delbin lifted his arm slightly, gesturing for the rest of them to wait, as his love stared at the dark blotch on the floor. Though her chest heaved, Inona stumbled forward until she reached the spot. Then she knelt down and brushed her fingers against the stain. Power trembled on the air, and the mark disappeared.

The scout's blood would remain here no longer.

After a few moments, Inona stood and cast an inscrutable look over her shoulder. "I don't sense any sort of rift here."

"Nor do I," Selia said after a quick scan. "Your friends were certain it's the same cave?"

Delbin's shoulder lifted. "Seemed to be sure."

"It is here."

At the harsh sound of Kai's voice, Selia turned to stare. His expression had

gone slack, but his eyes burned with an emotion she couldn't quite name. Not anger, pain, or fear but some unpleasant mixture of all three. Then he shook his head and scrubbed his hands across his face. When he met her gaze, he looked like himself once more.

"Sorry." Kai's lips twisted wryly. "No matter how much Naomh tried to teach me, I never could connect to the Earth. I feel the trauma in this dimension's energy itself, but I can't get a hold on it. The schism is near. But I don't know where."

Meli lifted a small pouch from her pocket and gave it a slight shake. "That's what my runes and I are here for, remember?"

Selia glanced around the cavern. There were a few shadowed places against one wall, and the rows of stalagmites could conceal more passageways. Any number of chambers could branch off from this room. Without Meli's aid, it would take forever to find the way. Including her had been an excellent idea.

Smiling, Selia nodded at the younger woman. "We're ready when you are."

Something tickled Perim's nose as she forced her eyes open. Tall green stems fluttered in front of her face, one of them brushing her nostrils until she almost sneezed. She batted the grass away and pushed herself upright. Where was she? The last thing she clearly recalled was plunging from the water into a world of gray. She'd stumbled through endless mist, reaching for to the strands Baza had directed her to find.

How had she ended up here? She rested on an incline in the middle of a forest, but the trees were smaller than the ones she'd seen on the island. She pinched one of the blades of grass. It caught roughly against her fingers, so unlike the smooth glide of the grass at home. She'd explored most of the island, and this area was nothing like that horrible place.

Perim reached out a mental hand to replenish her energy, but instead of a deep pool of power, she found a nearly dry well. She pulled harder at the tiny trickle of energy and groaned in frustration at the lack of response. But as her mind cleared, realization set in. She might have reached Earth.

Well, she wouldn't find out if she was correct by sitting here. Perim stood and took a tentative step through the trees. If she'd reached her destination, then Aris had to be near—or would be soon. Baza had claimed that Kezari and thus Aris would be searching for a source of poisoned energy, so that was what she would look for.

She had a soulbonded to kill.

19

Selia studied Meli as she stood in the center of the cavern with her eyes closed, her cupped hands aglow with the light from her runes. When Selia looked with her other senses, she could see energy flowing up through Meli's feet and into the stones, using very little of her own magic.

Among the Ljósálfar in Alfheim, Meli had been an outcast because she had little natural capacity for energy and could not perform many spells. Foolish mages. Meli might not be able to hold a great deal of power, but she was a diviner, able to channel energy through objects like the runes. Not that the younger woman knew the extent of her ability. If Prince Corath constructed a sword with the proper enchantments, Meli could be deadly. Or with the right kind of staff… Selia had been doing a bit of research on the topic but hadn't had a chance to bring it up yet. Perhaps soon Meli would be comfortable enough around mages to consider becoming a student.

The light in Meli's hands faded to almost nothing, pulling Selia from her thoughts. Meli slipped the runes back into their pouch and tucked the pouch into her pocket. Her eyes opened, and although her gaze was distant, she was able to focus on the group waiting expectantly.

"We need to slip between a pair of stalagmites in the back left corner," Meli said softly. "But the way won't be easy. Some of the tunnels we must follow require climbing."

"You can still see the path?" Delbin asked.

Meli's lips curved upward as she nodded. "I've been practicing. Much better than wandering around like a sleep-walker, wouldn't you say?"

Behind Selia's shoulder, Kai chuckled. "Much better."

"Let's go," Meli said, waving toward the back of the cavern.

Selia hitched her bag more securely on her shoulder and followed Delbin, Inona, and Meli into a narrow passage tucked between two stalagmites, just as the other woman had seen. The path was clear for a time, but after they reached another, smaller cavern, they had to huddle close to avoid the cave formations. As far as Selia could tell, the trail ended here.

Meli pointed to a narrow shelf of rock barely visible behind a grouping of stalactites clustered on the ceiling. "We need to climb up the side of that lumpy column and behind the stalactites. A short distance along that shelf, we'll find another tunnel. We have to crawl through that before we get to another room."

Though Selia grimaced, she didn't complain. Not even when she scraped her forearm on a sharp stone as she wiggled along the narrow stone shelf. Instead, she used a precious tendril of energy to seal the wound and kept going. The sooner they reached the rift, the better.

Why did it have to be in a cave? Hopefully, they'd be able to take care of the problem today because this would be pure misery for Aris. Great gods, what if he had a meltdown in the middle of the return mission? Mind-healing was typically accompanied by weeks of therapeutic treatment, and even then, it wasn't perfect. Much could be done to return muscle and bone to their original state, but minds were too malleable.

The coming mission was at risk of failure from the beginning.

As they gathered in the next, even smaller, cavern, Meli pointed out a thin gap angled in the floor. Down. They had to slither down the passage one at a time. Selia muttered a curse as she watched Delbin try to fit into the gap, grumbling a few choice words of his own as he squeezed through. What were they going to do when it was Aris who had to try that?

Once it was her turn, Selia fought back a shiver and squared her shoulders before lowering herself in. As she eased down, balancing on one foot while searching for a hold with the other, the tunnel walls seemed to close around her. It was difficult to breathe, and she didn't even have trouble with enclosed spaces.

When she finally dropped onto the floor of the next chamber, she shifted out of the way for Kai and bent down to catch her breath. Then she straightened to study the area while they waited. The long, uneven tunnel curved like one of the corridors in Lyr's home, but the rock itself had a smoothness that suggested the cave had been formed by water, not trees. Their small mage light glinted against the tiny drips of moisture forming along one side of the ceiling in a thin line.

Kai landed beside Selia with a soft oomph. "We're close," he said. "Something is building. Both the energy and this sense of...wrongness. But I still can't pinpoint the exact location."

"It's just past the curve up ahead," Meli said absently.

Delbin tossed a glance over his shoulder. "You think Kien climbed all the way through these passages to set this up?"

"Maybe," Selia said, trying to examine the energy flowing around them. "I get a hint of the darkness I felt up above, but not enough to know for sure."

Inona and Meli rounded the corner first, and at a sharp exclamation from the latter, Delbin sped up, Selia and Kai quickly following. At first, Selia thought Meli had cried out because of the jagged line of energy suspended in the center of the large circular cavern like red lightning frozen mid-strike. But then the figure leaning against a column of rock straightened to his full height, the arrogant tilt of his head tumbling his flaming hair across his forehead.

Selia blinked, so taken aback she couldn't even summon alarm.

Pol?

He'd been one of the people who'd traveled with Meli from Alfheim, but he'd returned there weeks ago. What was he doing here, smiling for all the world like they'd met in the gardens for tea?

"And to think you almost rejected those runes," Pol drawled.

As Inona slipped a knife from…somewhere, Selia wrapped her hand around an energy crystal in her pocket. Pol grinned, his thumbs tucked casually into a couple of loops on his Earth-style pants. Despite the appearance of the knife, his casual demeanor hadn't changed.

"Lo…I mean…" Meli lifted both hands in the air and then let them drop. "What are you doing here?"

"You know him?" Inona demanded.

Kai stepped up beside Selia. "Wait, Inona. Pol is a friend to House Dianore, or so I was told."

Pol inclined his head. "As it pleases us."

Selia had a feeling that she didn't want to know who he included in the "us."

"You left so abruptly," Meli said, "and haven't spoken to me since. Are you here to cause trouble, or do I still have your support?"

"Don't hold my absence against me, little diviner." Pol smirked. "I had a bit of a dalliance. A brandy so fine should be savored, so forgive me for not rushing back."

Meli's forehead wrinkled. "That still doesn't explain why you're *here.*"

"True." Pol's face tipped up, and the crack of energy tinted his pale skin an eerie red. "You know, I'd hoped this would happen. But nothing is guaranteed."

Eyes narrowing, Meli took a step forward. "Did you make sure I reached Moranaia for this very purpose? I've spent a lot of time wondering why you helped someone so unimportant as me. At least, unimportant in the grand scheme of things."

Pol chuckled softly. "All of life is a grand scheme. However, I must remind you that I only help people I like. Voluntarily, at least."

Without warning, energy throbbed through the cavern, hitting Selia's shields so hard she stumbled. She grabbed for a stalagmite to steady herself as she reinforced her protections with help from the crystal in her hand. Meli wavered on her feet, only Pol's hand keeping her upright. Delbin tripped and fell against the side of the cave, and Kai dropped to his knees, his palms shoved against his temples. Only Inona kept her footing completely.

As quickly as it had hit, the wave of power was gone.

"Fuck," Kai muttered.

A few paces away, Inona glared at Pol. "What did you do?"

"Inona…" Meli began.

"That was no coincidence," Inona said as Delbin limped back to her side, rubbing his hip. "It was an attack."

Selia's brows rose at the hint of panic creeping into Meli's eyes. The younger woman tried to shake her head at Inona, but the scout ignored the signal. "Step away from Meli, stranger, or I will—"

Laughter rang out, and although Pol released Meli, it was only to brace his hands on his knees while he gave in to his mirth. Little sparks drifted from his hair as he chuckled, but he didn't seem to notice. And when he finally grew quiet and straightened, his lips still twitched with repressed humor.

Inona, on the other hand, tightened her grip on her knife until her knuckles whitened—the only part of her not flushed red with anger. "You should not mock me."

"Come now," Pol said. "I like you too much to exclude you."

The scout opened her mouth, but no sound emerged. Meli stepped between the two, offering Pol a smile. "She doesn't know you, of course."

"No one does." He waved his hand dismissively. "I'll spare your friend and get to the point. If you try to tap into this rift right now, you will die. All of you."

Fear slammed into Selia more effectively than the energy pulse. She'd considered doing that very thing when they'd discussed this mission, and even now, that jagged line of power beckoned. If he was telling the truth, she might have killed them all attempting to access it. But why? She hadn't intended to do anything that would widen the crack in the spell holding the rest of Earth's energy back. A probe should have been simple enough.

Kai stood, swaying slightly as he frowned at Pol. "My...father seemed certain he could connect to the fissure. I should be able to, as well."

Pol snorted. "You are not Naomh, and he's a fool if he treats you as though you are. But then, his father wasn't very bright, or he would have realized that Caolte's mother was...more than she seemed." He gestured at the walls around them. "Do you feel the energy of this place the way he believes you should? No."

Kai's eyes narrowed. "You know a great deal about my Sidhe father for one of the Ljósálfar."

"One of the Ljósálfar? Perhaps foolishness *does* run in your bloodline." Pol shook his head, a mocking tilt to his lips. "Listen, for I will say this only once. Kai will guard the strands binding Earth to the other planes, Aris and Kezari will heal the poison, and Selia will stand as guard."

Selia froze, her blood chilling at the man's words. If he was a man. For he had been long gone before Aris and Kezari had arrived, and as far as she knew, he had no reason to be aware of their names. Pol could be a seer, Selia supposed, but it didn't seem likely. The way Meli had reacted to him told a tale all its own.

"What do you mean by that?" Kai demanded.

"Just what I said." Pol glanced at each of them in turn, and when his eyes met hers, Selia froze like a *daeri* in Kezari's sight. "Bring him here tomorrow," he said, and there was no mistaking that he was talking to her.

Between one heartbeat and another, he was gone. No blur of movement or puff of smoke. If the others didn't appear as stunned as she felt, Selia would have believed his presence a dream. Whoever he was, Pol was no Ljósálfar. He was no elf at all as far as she could tell.

"Oh, this can't be good," Meli whispered. "Not if Loki is involved."

Selia's brow creased. That name sounded familiar, but she couldn't quite place it. Did anyone else besides Meli know him? Inona appeared as puzzled as Selia, Delbin's expression shifted between amused and concerned, but Kai... Kai's entire demeanor had turned stony. Was it because of the stranger's identity or the words he had said? She wasn't certain she knew him well enough to ask.

"Who is this Loki?" Inona said.

Delbin laughed, though a hint of worry lingered around his eyes. "He's the Norse trickster god."

"That's one way to put it." Meli's lips thinned, but Selia couldn't tell if it was with concern or annoyance. "In any case, where he goes, change happens. Whether it's good or bad is anyone's guess."

Wonderful. Selia stared at the rift in the center of the chamber and tried not to think too hard about what would have happened without Pol's—Loki's—warning of danger. Ignoring a random elf was one thing, but a god? No.

Now she just had to figure out how to get Aris down here without driving him insane.

Double wonderful.

Iren grabbed another pebble and ran his fingers along the smooth surface. He wanted to fling it at the nearest tree, but he couldn't bring himself to risk harming it. So instead, he skipped the stone along the stream as he had the others and watched as it sank after two hops. Not bad over moving water.

He'd wanted his father to come home for as long as he could remember, but now that he had him, nothing was going right. Iren didn't care about the torture. Well, fine, he cared, obviously. But it didn't change his opinion of his father. As much as Iren had suffered from the loss, now he knew it was nothing compared to what *Onaial* had gone through. That brought a terrible kind of comfort.

When Iren had first seen his father standing in front of the entrance to Braelyn, his heart and his hopes had soared. His mother loved him, as he did her, but she babied him. His father the adventurer wouldn't do that. *Onaial* would see how big he'd become and encourage him to push beyond the rules. Maybe he would even find Iren worthy of training.

Iren snorted. Apparently not.

"I thought your father would pick this future strand."

At the sound of his friend's voice, Iren spun. Eri smiled at him from the garden path, tendrils of her dark hair peeking from beneath her cloak. "That bad?" he asked.

"No." Her nose wrinkled. "Really, Iren, what were you thinking? If his life energy triggered yours, it could make you lose control of your other powers. Unlike you, he doesn't have the talents of the traditional mage, too. Did you want to blow up the estate?"

Heat climbed Iren's neck. "I...no."

Her smile turned impish. "Oh, don't get upset. There are other ways you can prove yourself."

His heart pounded harder at that. If Eri suggested an alternate method, she always had a good reason. Sometimes, it was great having a seer as a friend. Well, all the time, as far as he could tell. "Like what?"

"Come on." She darted forward and grabbed his wrist in her small hand. "My parents are at the construction site today, so we can talk in my room."

Curious, he let her pull him along. This was going to be good.

20

Aris was really, really tired of waking up dazed after some procedure—or after being rendered unconscious during a fit of madness. But this time, he felt… different. He extended one arm and then the other. No sign of strain. He flexed his legs and rolled his ankles before drawing his knees up.

His breath eased out, and his body sagged into the mattress. No pain. None.

"Feeling better?"

At the sound of Lial's voice, Aris opened his eyes. The healer leaned over him with a somber expression, but he sounded calm. "Much," Aris said. "All went well?"

"It took a fair bit of time to accelerate the healing, but your bones are knit properly and should stand up well to activity." Lial shoved a damp tendril of hair aside, and it was then that Aris noticed the sheen of sweat on his brow and the lines of exhaustion bracketing his eyes. "Though if I can avoid having to break someone's body on purpose for a few centuries, I'll be well pleased."

Aris winced. "Sorry."

Lips twisting wryly, Lial straightened. "Try not to get captured and tortured again and we'll call it even."

Aris surprised himself by chuckling. He pushed upright and stretched again as the healer stepped back. When had his muscles last felt so good? For a moment, he let himself savor the feeling of wholeness. If the Myern held a running competition during the coming autumn festival, Aris could likely win it.

Then his gaze landed on Tynan on the far side of the room, almost hidden in the shadows cast by the setting sun. His body was turned away from Kezari, who sat cross-legged on the floor a few arm-lengths away. *I hope they haven't been arguing.* Kezari stared at Aris, not seeming to notice the mind-healer, but her shoulders angled a bit toward Tynan.

Aris lifted his brows. "Did I lose control of my magic? You two look somber."

"We…almost had an incident," Lial said, his nostrils flaring at the words. "But Kezari and Tynan kept it under control. I still do not understand why that segment of your brain was activated with all sensation cut off, but I am glad I followed my instinct to have a mind-healer present for the procedure."

"It is good that your spawn was not present," Kezari said. She jerked her head toward Tynan. "This one was complication enough."

The mind-healer bristled. "I did not make an error this time."

"You are a distraction," she grumbled.

Aris smiled—until their words sank in. Iren. Would his son still be upset by their earlier disagreement? He tugged his hands through his tangled hair until it was something resembling smooth. Then he leaped from the bed. Lial's lips turned down, but Aris lifted a hand before he could say anything.

"I want to check on my son." Aris shifted on the balls of his feet and sighed in satisfaction when his muscles flexed smoothly. "I don't suppose you could give me directions through the twisted maze of this place?"

Lial's eyes narrowed in thought for a moment. Then he nodded. "I sense him with Eri in her family's rooms. I'll walk with you to the base of their tower if you like."

Aris nodded. "Please."

Although the healer wasn't unfriendly, he spoke little as they descended the stairs and traversed the winding garden paths. That was fine with Aris. It was awkward enough that a virtual stranger knew the worst details of his life—inane small talk would only make it worse. A cold, damp gust of wind flowed around them, and Aris shivered, suddenly regretting not grabbing his cloak. Luckily, Lial stopped at the base of a stone tower before he could grow too chilled.

"Ralan's rooms are at the top of the stairs," the healer said.

"Thank you," Aris said, holding Lial's gaze. "For everything, I mean. Not just the escort. If you ever have need of my aid, I offer it freely. I might not be able to heal, but life energy is a powerful force."

The healer's eyebrows rose, a sign that he hadn't expected such an offer. "Let us hope I never encounter anything that requires such strength."

"Indeed," Aris said with a smile.

Then Aris turned away and strode into the tower.

A scream ripped from Fen's throat as he jerked upright. He clawed at his heaving chest, but no physical wound marred his flesh. The pain was inside, splintering beneath his heart. Frantic, he dug his fingernails into his skin in a futile attempt at distraction.

But nothing eased the agony.

When the wave of pain finally passed, he came to slow awareness. His forehead was pressed to his upturned knees. When had he curled up? Something wet trickled down his leg and slid beneath his fingers. His face and chest felt damp, too, as though someone had dumped a bucket of water over him while he slept. The tinny but sweet smell of blood wafted around him.

What the hell?

Every muscle in his body protested when he unclenched his hands enough to straighten. He groaned as pain shot up his shoulders and down his legs, but it had to be done. The longer he stayed curled up, the stiffer he would become.

Fen rubbed at his eyes and then glanced down at his chest, only to freeze in horror. Partially dried blood coated his skin in rivulets from where his nails had dug in, the furrows barely closed. After a quick examination, he found similar marks on his legs.

The price he paid for ingesting Kien's blood, it seemed. The bastard must have sent the rending spell through his own blood link to Earth, and since Fen bore a bit of that blood within him, he'd been linked to the process. Nothing else made sense. But what had caused such unexpected pain? He'd borne the pulses of energy for over a week with only mild discomfort.

The door clicked open, and Vek strode in, only to halt as soon as he caught sight of Fen. "I hope you killed whoever did that to you."

"I'm not suicidal, so no." Fen gave a self-conscious shrug. "You took your sweet time coming in here. Pretty sure I made a lot of noise."

Vek's expression shuttered. "I was out."

Ugh. He could just imagine what his uncle had been doing—finding blood. Fen's stomach rumbled in envy, even though blood did nothing for his physical hunger. His energy was getting low enough that he was tempted to lick his own leg in search of sustenance. It wouldn't provide him any extra magic, but...

"Your fangs are out," Vek said.

"I'm fucking starving." Fen shoved himself to his feet, ignoring the agony movement brought, and rushed past his uncle into the hall. If he didn't shower soon, the smell would drive him crazy. "I've had enough. I'm going to go feed. Then I'm going to find Maddy and see if she can do something about this poison."

Vek grabbed Fen's upper arm, pulling him around. "Aren't you forgetting something? You're bound here, and feeding will only make the poison worse."

"Says who?" Fen jerked free of his uncle's grip. "I'm covered in my own god-damned blood from marks I made in mindless agony. Obviously, hunger didn't prevent that, did it? So fuck off with your patronizing shit. If it takes the last of my energy, I'm busting out of here. I'm not going to die screaming in bed."

Vek's lips pinched tight, and for a moment, Fen thought he would argue. But his uncle surprised him by nodding. "Fine. There was an energy pulse not long ago. If they're starting to hurt you, then...then I am not certain what we can do. My shield is apparently not enough. We need to go to the cave."

Fen stared at his uncle's pained expression. Vek actually appeared concerned, and that was almost worse to Fen than waking up in his own blood. His uncle typically alternated between cold arrogance, cool disdain, and exasperated annoyance. He must be consumed with worry for it to show.

"Let me shower," Fen said softly. "Then we'll head out."

138

Vek nodded and turned toward the living room without another word.

His uncle's easy capitulation drove Fen's fear deeper. He rubbed his hand across his aching chest and hurried into the bathroom. The answer had to be out there.

Somewhere.

The little girl opened the door before Aris reached it. Unlike the cheer she'd displayed on their last meeting, her lips curved down like a bow, and a thin line of annoyance hollowed between her eyebrows. What was her name again? Eri?

"Yes, I am Eri," she said, making a shiver trace through him. "And I am mad at you. There were eleven better strands you could have taken, you know. Now everything is going to be harder."

How...how old was she? Aris studied her young face, far too small to bear such words. She crossed her arms, staring back boldly, and even if Selia hadn't told him, he would have guessed she was a princess of Moranaia. It wasn't just her unusual golden eyes and dark black hair, traits shared by Prince Ralan and his siblings. It was the authority she carried at such a young age.

Gods help her parents.

"Perhaps I will do better next time," he said.

She grinned, a child once more. "There's a good chance of it. Come on. Iren is pouting in my room."

Aris followed her through a living area, tidy save a couple of abandoned dolls. He eyed those doubtfully. Did the prince have another child? Because Aris found it difficult to believe that a powerful seer like Eri played with something so mundane, even at her age. Though maybe she used them to practice delivering prophecies to hapless adults.

When she pushed open the door to her bedroom, Aris's gaze went immediately to Iren. His son glared out the window into the fading light. "Guess you didn't destroy anything without me there to help," Iren said.

Eri tugged at Aris's wrist to get his attention. "I'll wait in the front room."

"Thank you, Eri."

Aris waited until the door closed behind him to approach his son. Without a word, he lowered himself into the seat next to Iren. Then he waited. They sat that way for several drips of time, both of them staring into the dusk-coated branches beyond the window.

"I'm not a baby," Iren finally said.

"No, you aren't," Aris agreed. Gods, how he'd hated being this age himself. That feeling of growing confidence twined with a lack of control over one's environment. He wouldn't repeat those years even if he could. "But you aren't an adult, either."

"I know," his son mumbled.

Aris kept his gaze on the gnarled curves of the nearest branch, unwilling to break the moment. "Iren, I loved you at your birth, and I love you now. Even if centuries passed before our next meeting, that love would hold. I am aware that you may not believe me, but it is true. And I will not risk your life for mine. Not under any circumstances. My refusal of your aid was for your sake and nothing more."

Silence descended, drawing out until he worried that he'd said the wrong thing. At the scrape of chair on stone, Aris finally dared look at Iren, and his heart burned at the sight of the tears on his son's cheeks. He had said the wrong thing. *Miaran.* He opened his mouth to apologize, but an *oomph* slipped out instead as Iren threw his arms around his neck and squeezed.

Aris pulled his son as close as he could with the arm of the chair between them. Though tears dampened the top of his shoulder where Iren's head rested, Aris let out a small, relieved breath and hugged his son tight. And unlike before, only a hint of discomfort itched beneath his skin at the close contact. Far more than that was the joy.

"I only wanted to make you proud," Iren said.

When Iren pulled back, Aris rested his hands on his son's shoulders. "You need not do anything special for that."

Iren rolled his eyes—but some of the tension eased from his muscles. "Parents always say that kind of thing."

"They do not." Aris lifted an eyebrow. "Can you imagine your grandfather doing so?"

Iren's nose wrinkled. "Good point."

A knock sounded on the door, and after a brief pause, Eri ducked her head through the opening. A sunny smile lit her face. "You might want to get your dragon and head to Lyr's study, Lord Aris," she said. "Lady Selia will be back soon, and that's where you'll meet. I want to play tag with Iren."

"I'm too old for tag," his son grumbled.

Eri only laughed. "Not what you said yesterday."

Iren shrugged and cast his Aris an apologetic smile. "May I go play?"

"Sure."

Aris had barely given permission before the children darted out of the room, the earlier tension gone as though it had never been. For a moment, he almost wished he could join them, but he'd rather go find out what Selia had discovered. Despite having a strong feeling it wouldn't be good.

21

By the time their group stumbled through the portal, Selia was ready to curl up in bed for a solid week. But although five days of blissful rest might be enough to ease her aching muscles, it wouldn't touch the turmoil of her thoughts. Stand guard, the god named Loki had said. What did that mean? She knew little about the dangers of Earth, and he'd claimed that tapping into the rift would bring death.

This was a magical dilemma she might not be able to solve—and that galled.

Dawn had been breaking on Earth, but night had fallen again here. Traveling through the Veil helped the body shift between time streams somewhat. Still, they'd switched from light to dark so many times that her mind couldn't keep up. Sleepy, she trudged along with the others down the path to the estate. At least the guards had kept the cloaks dry by the portal, for it was cold here in comparison to Earth's late summer.

"I am more tired than I ought to be," Kai confessed as they rounded the front of the building. With so much festival preparation happening in the garden, the private entrance to Lyr's study had seemed more prudent. "Especially with Inona taking part of the burden of navigating the Veil."

The female scout stifled a yawn against her hand. "Both crossings were rough."

"Probably because of the rift," Selia said, covering her own yawn.

A snort from Delbin caught her attention, but he grinned at them despite the frustrated sound. "The long hike and the caving didn't help. Some of us aren't trained scouts accustomed to hours of physical exertion."

"Please," Inona said. "I saw the type of labor you did at that carnival."

"That doesn't mean—"

Kai lifted a hand to silence Delbin as they reached the outer door to the study. "We can determine who is more drained later. I'd like to give this report and go get some sleep."

"Agreed," Meli whispered from Selia's right side.

The younger woman had gone quiet after leading them back to the main entrance of the cave. But as they entered the study, her expression brightened. Lyr straightened from his perch on the edge of his desk and rushed across the room to meet her, wrapping Meli in his arms despite the audience. Selia averted her gaze, only to connect with Aris's eyes.

Concern shadowed his face, but there was also something closed about his expression. Some aloofness they might never bridge. Exhaustion swamped Selia, weighting her muscles, as everything seemed to crash in at once. From the strangeness of Earth and the effort of doing magic there to the distance between her and Aris…it was all too much.

An abyss she wasn't certain she had the strength to cross.

"Your mate appears tired," Kezari said from her place by the window.

Aris's brows drew down. "Did something happen?"

"We weren't attacked, if that's what you're asking," Selia hedged. How could she admit her uncertainty to him when he'd faced so much already? "I'm fine."

His frown deepening, he strode over, and the rest of the room faded from awareness. Then he brushed his thumb gently across the curve of her cheekbone. "You've never made it a habit to tell me an untruth."

Selia squirmed beneath his touch, and not just because of the heat that flowed through her from the contact. "I wasn't lying. I *am* fine, and we *weren't* attacked. I'm simply tired. I transported the group from the cave back to the portal on Earth, and even with the use of two energy crystals, I'm drained."

"I know you, Selia," Aris said, his eyes narrowing. But it was true—he did know her. Well enough not to press her for more in front of others. "Perhaps you will join me in the tower once this meeting is complete?"

She swallowed an instinctive denial. She'd been bare before him in more ways than one, and she wasn't going to start hiding from him now. No matter how much she wanted to. "Certainly."

Aris stepped back, and the rest of the room returned to focus. Thankfully, the others had made an effort to ignore the exchange. Lyr and Meli leaned against the edge of his desk as she spoke to him, her hands fluttering with her excitement as she recounted her part in the mission. Kai slumped in one of the center chairs, his head tipped back and eyes closed. And Delbin and Inona stood beside Kezari. Inona's voice was too low to hear their discussion, but the dragon listened attentively.

"This energy rift…" Selia began. "Perhaps I should warn you before the main discussion."

His frown returned. "Warn me about what?"

"It's deep in a cave," she blurted.

The color drained from his face, and his mouth pinched white. He gave a sharp nod, his throat bobbing as he swallowed. But although he didn't speak, panic didn't appear to consume him. He breathed in and out, the air hissing softly through his teeth, but he remained lucid. The mind-healer's work had kept him from a breakdown at least.

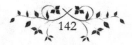

"Thanks," Aris whispered.

Lyr stood before she could answer, his discussion with Meli complete. "Well," he said. "I admit I didn't expect a god's involvement, but I suppose I should have. Why not at this point?"

Selia's lips twitched at that. With one crisis after another occurring lately, the Myern had clearly lost patience. "I wish he'd given more specific instructions." Selia grimaced. "What am I supposed to guard?"

"Makes as much sense as my advice," Kai muttered, not bothering to open his eyes. "He seemed to know more about my lineage than I do. Not that it helped. He implied that I can't touch earth energy the way my father can. But protecting the strands connecting dimensions? It didn't make sense."

Kezari took a few steps closer, her head tilted in curiosity. "Why would you try to touch the flow of earth? It is not your calling."

Kai jerked upright, peering at Kezari through narrowed eyes. "How would you know that?"

"My soul sings with soil and stone and my *skizik*'s with plant and animal." The dragon let out a soft huff. "I can identify one of my own kind. You do not share this link."

"Then what does my father sense in me?" Kai's fingers tightened on the arms of the chair. "He is a Sidhe lord and master of earth magic. He claims to detect the same talent in me, but..." His shoulders slumped. "What little training I've done with him has not gone well. If you have insight, I would love to hear it."

The dragon studied him, unblinking, for so long that even Selia wanted to shift restlessly. "It is believed that there are other worlds out there with their own linked dimensions," Kezari said slowly. "But for us, Earth is central. Those strands link through the heart of our home planet. The Veil."

Kai frowned. "The Veil can't be in the center of the world. That is the realm of heat and flame."

"Not the physical center." Kezari's toothy grin took on a sly cast. "You elves may use the Veil, but you do not understand it. It's the core of all linked worlds, Earth at its center. And you, Kai, guide others through the mists without understanding your potential to manipulate them. Perhaps even the Sidhe have forgotten how to identify that flavor of earth talent."

Mouth agape, Kai leaned forward. "You're saying I can alter the strands themselves?"

"The order mages made an art of it at one time."

Selia's brow wrinkled. "I know of no Moranaian mages who refer to themselves—"

"Neor," Kai said, an odd tone to his voice. "The People of Order. They were almost decimated by the poisoned energy that swept through a couple of months ago. Not to mention by the Seelie army unhappy with them for seeking our aid. But I have no connection to them. In fact, that place creeps me out."

"I cannot answer the questions you do not speak." Kezari lowered herself to a chair, and Selia hid a grin at the dragon's posture. She sat on the edge, her toes digging into the floor as though she was trying to gain purchase on a cliff. "Even if you spoke them."

Kai let out a strangled laugh. "Wonderful."

"Seems you need to consult with Lord Naomh," Lyr said. "Last I heard, the Neorans have not returned to their previous home."

"I wouldn't, either," Kai said.

He hadn't said much about the mission he'd completed a few weeks ago, but Arlyn had let slip a few details. When Kai had gone to rescue those suffering from the energy poisoning, he'd found a massacre. Neor was a colony of the Seelie Court, and someone there had decided to eliminate the ill instead of save them. It couldn't have been a pleasant discovery.

"There is no time for that." Kezari pinned Lyr with her gaze. "I am Moranaian now, and the rift on Earth has been checked. Aris is as healed as he will be without time. We must go."

Surprisingly, it was Meli who argued. "No. Pol...Loki...said to return tomorrow."

At her words, the dragon shot to her feet. "You said we could leave once they scouted the area."

A strangled noise from Aris caught Selia's attention. He stared at Meli, his breathing a little more shallow than it had been. He'd ignored her during the rest of their discussion, but he must have turned to her instinctively when she'd spoken. Oh, blast it all. Would his healing hold well enough at the sight of the Ljósálfar woman?

His fists clenched, and his pupils dilated.

Maybe not.

Aris could have looked away. Perhaps he should have. But thought made habit, and habit made thought. As Tynan had warned, he would need to create new pathways for his mind to follow. Healing hadn't erased the old ones, but they blocked them enough for him to bypass them. So although his mind almost verged down the trail of madness, he yanked himself back from the brink.

The woman might have pale hair and a similar build, but she was not Perim.

He forced himself to study her pale face, her expression frozen into lines of alarmed concern. His tormenter had never shown either of those emotions. And this woman's eyes were light blue, not green. Instead of an arrogant posture, the Myern's bonded stood with shoulders slightly hunched. Everything about her spoke of kindness and youthful vulnerability.

The woman leaned closer to Lyr. "Perhaps I should go," she whispered.

"Do not," Aris said, though it was rude in the extreme to interject. "Please forgive my impertinence in speaking so plainly when we have not been introduced, but I do not wish for you to go. I can do this."

A slight smile lightened her face. "No need to apologize to me. My people are not so formal about strangers. Well, my previous people."

"It is I who should beg forgiveness," Lyr said with a wince. "Good thing *Laiala* is not here to see my poor manners. I should have presented you to one another immediately, especially considering the importance of this meeting."

The Myern might joke about upsetting his mother, but they all knew the real reason he hadn't offered immediate introductions—Aris's sanity. He had a feeling that if she hadn't gone on this mission, the lady would have stayed away entirely. Considering how he'd broken down at his first sight of her, he wouldn't have blamed her.

"It is no matter," Aris said politely. "These are unusual circumstances."

Lyr inclined his head. "Even so, I will remedy the lapse now."

Aris kept his gaze on the woman, processing her full name out of habit. Once Lyr finished, Aris gave a slight bow. "It is a pleasure to meet you, Myerna Ameliar."

Color flooded her cheeks. "Ah. Just Meli, please. I still don't understand why my full given name must be included."

"A custom long ago formed, I'm afraid." Aris smiled. Yes, Meli was nothing like Perim. How could he have thought otherwise? "May blessings grace your House this day, Meli."

"Yours as well," she answered.

His muscles unclenched, his relief intense enough to make him dizzy. Not only had he looked at Meli, but he had interacted with her. Although his heartbeat still pounded a bit faster in his chest, he wasn't at risk of breaking down. A grin broke across his face, crinkling his eyes, and the woman in question frowned in confusion at his sudden humor.

Aris couldn't help it—he laughed. "Sorry, Lady Meli. I never thought I would be so happy to make it through a simple introduction."

She smiled. "I understand."

"Good. You know one another," Kezari snapped as she stepped to Aris's side. "Now we go."

Aris spun to face the anxious dragon. The skin of her right forearm was almost all scale, and a hint of steam escaped her nostrils. He settled his hand on her shoulder and squeezed, providing her the anchor she had so often given him. "Kai and Selia need rest if they are to return with us."

He swallowed as her golden gaze pinned him. "The Earth cries. Join magic fully and you will know."

"I don't have to, Kezari," Aris said. "I can see that it is urgent. But we cannot have half of our group too exhausted to complete their tasks."

Meli took a small step forward. "It was not yet dawn when we were advised to return tomorrow, and I don't think he meant Moranaian time. A little sleep but not a full night should satisfy that."

Kezari's growl rumbled through the room, but she nodded. "No more than six marks."

"Then it is settled," Lyr said. "Go get some sleep. Kezari, Aris, Selia, and Kai, all of you return in five marks to discuss your plan."

"Of course," Aris agreed before turning to leave.

He caught Selia's eye as he strode away from Lyr, forming a mental connection with her out of habit. *"You'll still meet me in the tower?"*

She twisted her fingers together. *"Briefly. After I make sure Iren goes to bed."*

Aris couldn't quite hide his smile. *"Perfect."*

22

Selia stood at the base of the tower stairs, her fingers clenching against the smooth crystal of the doorframe. Iren was settled, and she'd taken a moment to eat a bowl of stew before heading to Aris's tower. Fatigue enveloped her shoulders like her cloak, but that wasn't stopping her from the short climb up the stairs. There was only one thing it could be.

Cowardice.

Wincing at the thought, she forced her feet to move. It was time for her and Aris to settle the issues that remained between them. Now that he was more himself, perhaps he'd decided he no longer wanted to be with her. Maybe he worried that he'd changed too much or that she wouldn't be able to accept everything that had happened. Selia sniffed at that thought. He should know she wasn't as narrow-minded as that.

She spotted Aris as soon as she rounded the last curve of the stairs. Legs and arms crossed, he leaned one shoulder against the wall a few paces away, his gaze fixed on her as she advanced. She came to a halt just out of his reach. Her heart fluttered at his inscrutable expression, but she tried her best not to reveal her nerves.

"Why didn't you tell me what was wrong earlier?" he asked softly.

Selia let out a sigh. "It is foolishness."

One corner of his mouth tipped up. "You're not given to foolishness, Selia. I don't want you to stop confiding in me when you used to tell me everything."

If only he knew.

"You've suffered so much, but you are still so ready to proceed with what needs to be done no matter the cost," she blurted, crinkling the smooth fabric of her shirt between her fingers. "And there I stood, doubting I was equal to the task on Earth. I feel ridiculous admitting such a thing."

His head tilted. "Why? You have a right to your feelings."

How could he remain so impassive? Why couldn't he see? "You. Were. Tortured," Selia said. "I could have no challenge equal to that."

Aris smiled, and she suddenly wanted to hit him. A poor impulse, considering.

He unfolded his arms and pushed away from the wall, moving closer. "We can each only live our own lives in our own bodies, Selia. My past pain won't ease your current doubts."

"I don't understand how you can be so calm," she grumbled.

"You think I'm calm?" Aris grasped one of her hands in his. "I'm not. I've grown…adept at hiding my feelings."

Grief filled her at what those words implied. He had learned to do so for self-preservation. "What are you feeling, then?"

Aris lifted her palm to his chest, and the rapid thumping of his heart met the frantic pace of her own pulse. His head tipped down until their breaths mingled. "Many things. Desire. Pain. Fear. Love."

"An unusual mixture," Selia whispered. "And a sad one. Are you afraid of me now?"

His lips thinned. "Not exactly."

"What is that supposed to mean?" she asked, her fingers twitching beneath his.

"I want to be with you, but there is much…" His eyes squeezed closed. "There is a lot you don't know."

Her heart ached for him so sharply her breath caught. But perhaps she could spare him. "I saw what she did to you when I accidentally connected. If you think I would hold that against you, then you are the foolish one. You did not break our bonds of fidelity by being forced."

"Selia…"

She tugged her hand free, only to place both palms on his cheeks. Aris glanced down at her, then, and the fathomless pain held within his eyes pierced her deeply. "You *do* think I hold it against—"

"She is my soulbonded," he said, his voice stark with emotion. "My potential one, at least."

Selia's arms dropped to her sides, and she took a step back. "What?"

"I was lost at sea, barely alive when she found me." He shoved his hands through his hair, and the long strands snarled with the motion. "She took me to a cave and kept me there. When I refused to bond with her, she chained me. And…you've seen too much of the rest."

By all the gods. He'd been tortured by his soulbonded? She'd never considered that horror. "That's abhorrent."

Aris flinched and crossed his arms again. "Yes."

Oh, no. He thinks I meant—

"Not on your part," she hurried to assure him. "You can't think I would reject you because of her."

His expression hardened. Perhaps he could.

"Selia," he began, his fingers whitening where he gripped his arm. "So many believe a soubonded is the perfect mate, but the other half of my soul is evil and twisted. Tynan claims my own soul is unmarred by such darkness. It doesn't seem

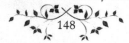

possible. I should believe him, I know, but I can't. I don't see how you could, either."

She closed the distance between them and barely resisted pulling him into her arms. "I don't need to hear anything from Tynan. We've been together for more than five hundred years, Aris. You are not evil. Soulbonds might link, but they don't define. They are not always the perfect love, and we are not more or less because of them. That's why our priests can and will sever those bonds."

His lips twisted. "When you haven't faced something like this, it's easy to say such things."

"Aris." She shouldn't tell him. She had to tell him. "I met my potential soulbonded a hundred years ago."

For a moment, he simply stood there, a confused frown creasing his brow. Then he moved, so quickly his hands were gripping her shoulders before she'd registered the motion. "You *what?*"

He wasn't hurting her, but the tension in his fingers twisted something in her heart. "I know I should have told you. I wasn't trying to lie, honestly. But I didn't want you to be noble and demand our marriage be severed."

"Why?" he demanded.

Selia didn't need to ask what he meant.

"I didn't like him." She grimaced at the memory of their first meeting. "Gods, that sounds so trivial. But he was arrogant, dismissive. Nothing like your potential bonded, obviously, but I had no desire to be linked to him. He even tried to ignore my denial of the bond, insisting I accept his necklace until I threatened to find a priest of Arneen. It was…not a pleasant encounter. I knew then that soulbonds weren't always ideal, and I spent a great deal of time attempting to figure out why my soul could join with his. It haunted me for years."

Aris released her arms and spun away. She watched him wordlessly as he paced the tower, knowing from experience that he would need a moment to work through his emotions. *Miaran*, she should have told him at the time. She'd never kept anything else from him in all their years together.

"You might not forgive me," she said as he drew to a halt an arm's length away. "But I am sorry. I…I loved you more than any soulbond. I still do. Even when I believed you dead, I had no desire for another. I don't care what the gods may have planned for my soul."

Aris scrubbed his hands across his face and then let them drop. "Aren't we a fine pair."

"I truly didn't know how to tell you." Selia's shoulders slumped. "Not without losing you."

He wrapped his fingers around her wrists and tugged. As she settled against him, he lowered his forehead to hers. "Perhaps there was a divine mistake. A confusion of souls. I wouldn't have bonded with Perim even if she'd been perfection itself. No type of link could compare with my love for you."

Selia swallowed. "I thought you'd be angrier."

"I'm upset that you didn't tell me." He brushed her lips with his, drawing out a gasp. "But I'm not in a position to judge. At least yours didn't keep you chained in a cave for almost seven years."

A choked laugh slipped free. "There is that."

"I love you, Selia," he whispered. "If you still…"

"Didn't I already say I love you? Because I do. Always." She wrapped her arms around his waist and let herself relax against him. "Kiss me."

His fingers speared through her hair as his lips descended on hers. No gentle brush this time. Selia whimpered, her hands sliding up his back to grip his shoulders as he consumed her. Their tongues tangled, dueled. Against her belly, he hardened, and a shudder rippled through his muscles. But he didn't stop.

She startled when his hands slid down her neck and headed toward her waist, his thumbs brushing the sides of her breasts along the way. Heat flared within her, an inferno she'd thought she would never feel again. A moan slipped free at the perfection of his mouth and hands. His body against hers. She wrapped one of her legs around his to bring herself closer.

He froze, panting as his lips jerked away.

"I'm sorry," she managed around her own frenzied breaths.

"I want you," Aris said, his voice rough and low. "But you'll have to let me lead. I can't…I can't bear weight on me. Or too much aggressiveness."

An image of his torture tried to flicker through, but she shoved it aside. They had a lifetime of memories to choose from—and she knew just the one. "Remember the morning we conceived Iren?"

His gaze grew heated, and his fingers gripped her bottom. "Very well. I was a bit rough, though. I don't want to hurt you. I know what that's like. I—"

Selia pressed her fingers to his lips. "Being abused doesn't make you an abuser. You didn't hurt me then, and you won't hurt me now. But this time, we'll leave off any bindings."

Aris lowered a kiss to the vee of her neck, and she felt his lips curve against her skin before he nodded. Then his tongue traced a line along her pulse as he boosted her against him, his hard length trapped between them, just where she wanted it. When he spun around and strode toward the bed, she cried out from the pleasure of the contact.

"Have any empty energy crystals?" he whispered against her flesh. "Gods, I hope you do. I'm not certain of my restraint."

She let out a breathy laugh. "Didn't think I'd be grateful for the low energy of Earth. I had to use a few crystals there, so yes. In my pocket."

His low groan was answer enough.

The sound sent a shudder down her spine, for when he truly let himself go, they created magic. Literally. Ah, how she loved making him lose control of his power! It was dangerous, especially if she had nothing to channel the overflow into, but so, so worth it.

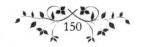

Aris lowered her to the bed. His arm muscles flexed as he held himself above her and stared into her eyes. "With this much life magic…"

"It's probably the wrong time in my cycle." Selia tugged at a strand of his hair, bringing his face closer to hers. "But I'd welcome another child with you. Provided you stop worrying and make love to me."

He kissed her softly. Once. Twice. Then he plundered, his mouth taking hers as his hand cupped her breast. He pinched at her nipple, arrowing heat straight into her core, and she couldn't stop herself from gripping both hands in his hair. When he trembled against her, she loosened her hold until he relaxed.

Aris broke their kiss long enough to tug her strange Earth shirt over her head and toss it away. Selia worked at the clasp of her pants, barely remembering to grab the energy crystals from her pocket before helping him remove the rough fabric from her legs. He lifted away again to free himself from his own clothes until nothing remained between them but air.

Her lungs seized at the sight of his chest, pale scars marring the skin in a few new places. No need to ask where those were from. But then her gaze landed on the image of a curled dragon painted across his left pectoral muscle. Frowning, she traced her finger along the curve of a wing. A tattoo, she realized. Not paint.

"What's this?" she whispered.

He flicked a glance down at his chest and then smiled. "You'd have to ask Kezari. It appeared when she rescued me."

"For which I'll be forever grateful." Selia slid her hand down his side, and a tendril of energy escaped his control, sending a zing through her blood. "Ready?"

"For you?" The green threading his hazel eyes brightened. "Always."

Without warning, Aris flipped her over, and that earlier zing turned to lightning. Selia lifted to her hands and knees, offering herself to him. Open and vulnerable. His hands traced the line of her back before slipping around to her breasts, and the feel of him almost made her cry out. It had been far, far too long.

He touched her entrance, then, and his groan echoed around them as his control snapped. Between one breath and the next, Aris entered her. Her breath left her in a rush, and her back arched. Not from pain, but he went motionless inside her.

"Selia," he whispered. "Did I hurt you?"

"Gods, no." She couldn't stop herself from shifting against him, and they both moaned. "If you need to stop… I hope you don't…"

"I need you," Aris said.

And then he took.

He rushed into her—his body, his magic, his mind. Her home. Her fingernails dug into the bedding as she moved with him, and her heart soared even as she shattered with pleasure that seemed to last forever. Behind her, he stiffened and cried out, and combined with the feel of his fingers caressing her skin, his release triggered another of her own.

The crystals heated between her hand and the mattress as she poured the excess through by instinct. She barely noticed. Aris leaned over her, kissing a line down her spine, and she shuddered. She could have stayed like that forever. But all too soon, he withdrew.

Was he okay? Worry awoke as the pleasure faded. Then he dropped onto the bed and pulled her against his chest, nestling her close. Selia glanced over her shoulder, and some of her tension eased at the relaxed expression on his face. Sensing her regard, he cracked one eye open.

"What's wrong?" he asked.

Should she ask him? She didn't want to ruin his mood, but… "I was worried about you."

His arms tightened around her waist. "Thank you. There were times…" A sigh ruffled her hair. "I had a few rough moments, but you seemed to know what to do to ease them."

"Good," she whispered. She let her head drop and settled against him. "I suppose we'd better rest. I have a feeling your dragon is counting every drip of the clock."

Aris's low laugh echoed around her, following her into sleep.

As Selia's breathing slowed, Aris tucked his face against her shoulder and let himself bask in her presence. Unlike his beloved, he was too energized to sleep; he'd had a fair amount of that already with all the healing sessions. Perhaps, in a way, this could be counted as one of them. There'd been a few times when he'd almost had to stop, but he'd managed to steer himself away from panic. A promising sign.

Still, how long would it be before she could ride him once more? Even as his body stirred at the thought, his stomach lurched. *Clechtan.* They'd always been adventurous and uninhibited with one another, but he couldn't offer her that freedom anymore. He might never be able to, but she appeared to love him anyway.

She'd chosen him over her soulbonded, by the gods.

His arms tightened, and he had to force himself to relax when she shifted restlessly. He'd been angry, and he still hated that she hadn't told him. But once his emotions had settled, the one that had filled him most clearly was awe. Smart, talented, beautiful Selia hadn't wanted to risk losing *him*, a reckless adventurer who hadn't had a home for centuries before her. His own parents hadn't contacted him in decades, but Selia loved him without condition.

For the first time in seven years, hope sparked and simmered. More delicate than new love, the feeling settled in his chest, warming him. It might take years, but he could heal. He would never be the same, and for once, he didn't want to be. His spirit felt more settled now. But then, being tortured on the other side of the world tended to kill a bit of that zest for adventure.

It was time he found something better to do with his talents.

Aris's hand shifted to Selia's stomach. He could sense without effort that she'd been correct—she wasn't at the right point of her cycle for them to have another child. Maybe sometime in the near future, when he was better healed, they could try. He'd felt the moment Iren's new life had begun, and he would love to experience that once more.

Family. He never wanted to lose them again.

23

The rock smoothed beneath Kezari's claw as she finished the last wall of the small hollow she'd created for herself within the cave system. She'd shifted to three different sizes to fit through the twisting tunnels, but she refused to make the entrance easy to find. Moranaian she might now be, but dragon she had always been. Some elves would not trust her as readily as the ones she'd met.

She settled on her haunches and let her claws dig in to the cool sand beneath her. She had some time, since the others required rest. Hah. A puff of smoke left her nostrils, but it was more amusement than anger. Some rested more than others, and her *skizik* was not one of those few. Not that she begrudged him his pleasure—he more than deserved it.

Kezari closed her eyes and gathered energy through her talons. The cool flow of the stone's power surged in, chilling the natural heat of her body until it neared the cave's steady temperature. Her heart slowed, and she let her senses drop away one by one. No more taste of minerals on her tongue or soft sand beneath her stomach. Only self and thought.

In that moment, she reached. Space ceased to exist. Distance was nothing. Through the thread of earth that bound them all, her consciousness flowed. Until she reached Tebzn and connected with a jolt. And in that moment before her cousin censored herself, Kezari tasted the betrayal. She might have hissed, but she paid no heed to her body. None at all.

"Why have I been named a renegade?" Kezari demanded, not bothering with a greeting.

A brief hesitation. *"You left with little warning. There is no proof of your claim that your skizik was held against his will or even that you have one. The fae had no clue who this Perim could be."*

"You were there. You saw my skizik. How can you deny knowledge of Perim when she spoke to you at our last meeting?" Kezari wanted to rend her cousin to pieces. If only she could. *"You gave your word that she would be hunted. Could you not find your own hoard? I did not believe you so inadequate that you would need to steal mine."*

"*Reptile,*" Tebzn muttered. "*Your blood is cold to say such a thing. I am glad that the queen declared you a renegade. All this talk of Earth. Why should we care about a planet long discarded?*"

There would be no reasoning with her cousin. That, she could tell. "*You will know soon enough. Guard the young. Shield them if the wall breaks.*"

"*Go away, Kezari.*" Tebzn's tone turned mocking. "*You'll not see Earth no matter how you try to scare us. And do not contact me again.*"

Her cousin severed the connection and slammed up a strong mental barrier. Kezari had no desire to try to break it, though she could. Tebzn had always been sloppy, more prepared to hunt *daeri* than practice her magic. All too many of the dragons followed the same pattern. Hunt. Bury oneself in a cave and hibernate. Mate. Hunt. Their once proud kind served little purpose now.

Kezari returned to her body with a jolt. The air steamed around her, flames licking from her mouth in time with her breath. She centered herself. Anger had no place now, and she had almost lost control more than once in front of the Moranaians already. Soon enough, she and her *skizik* would solve their problem.

Then it seemed she would have the pleasure of hunting Perim herself.

"You still look like hell."

Fen flicked a dirty look at his uncle but didn't bother to flip him off. The bastard probably wouldn't understand the gesture, and in any case, he was probably right. Fen felt like hell, so chances were good that he looked the same. He should never have taken Vek's blood. It had seemed reasonable to save time by doing so, but the rush of energy from a single sip had made Fen's chest burn as magic flooded the shard of poison near his heart. Even his breathing was shallow from the effort of hiking to the cave.

He rubbed a hand across the ache that remained. It had been pure agony to drive to the parking lot near the base of the mountain, but Vek had no clue how to operate a car. Or much of any technology designed by humans. Despite the splinter of pain digging into his chest with each step, Fen smiled. Showing his uncle how to use a television had been one of the few highlights of this mess, though they'd mock-argued the whole time. Maybe eventually, Fen could taunt him into trying video games.

Hope I'm alive to do it.

"We're almost there," Fen said, pulling a deep breath into his straining lungs.

Vek eyed him worriedly. "I can't believe you let that remark pass."

"Hard to argue with the truth." Fen paused to examine the small clearing in front of the cave entrance. Flowers waved in the wind as they soaked up the mid-morning sun, and birds chirped in the nearby trees, unconcerned with their presence. "We should have been here hours ago. I hate approaching this place in the sunlight where anyone can see."

"It took far too long for your scratches to heal," Vek said. "With my blood, they should have been gone in moments."

Another truth Fen couldn't dispute. He glanced at his uncle, who studied the clearing with his own frown of concern. Vek's face and neck had reddened with the climb despite being under the cover of trees. Hadn't anyone ever told him about sunblock? Damned Unseelie thought they knew everything, but they couldn't even keep themselves from getting a sunburn.

Vek caught him staring and scowled. "What?"

"Have you seriously not devised a spell to protect your skin from the sun?" Fen let a sneer wrinkle his nose, though he was more amused than anything. "The humans have a cream to help with that if you're not up to it."

His uncle made a dismissive gesture. "Why bother? We are never above ground."

"I hate to be the one to break it to you, but…" Fen waved his own hands at the clearing and leaned closer, lowering his voice. "We *are* above ground. There. I said it."

"Fuck off," Vek muttered before striding toward the cave's entrance.

But Fen caught a hint of affection in the insult.

He smiled again as he followed his uncle across the small meadow. He had to admit that Vek was growing on him, too. After Fen's mother had abandoned him, he'd assumed the rest of his family didn't care. Vek's sporadic visits had seemed to confirm that, but now he couldn't help but wonder if there'd been more to his uncle's lack of attention than Fen had understood as a child. Perhaps someday he would ask.

They made their way through the short tunnel easily enough, but Vek halted just inside the cavern opening, so abruptly that Fen almost crashed into him. It didn't take long to see why. In the center of the large expanse, two men stood.

Well, shit. Not them.

One had short red hair and a ready scowl, but despite his unfriendly expression, something about him had always triggered an affinity in Fen. Not so the other. He hovered just off the floor of the cave with his shoulders back and chin tipped up, his noble aloofness a fine complement to his long pale hair. Caolte and Naomh, the Seelie nobles who'd helped Kien enact his foul plan.

Fen shifted to his uncle's side, but Vek lifted a hand in warning. "If it isn't Lord Naomh and his little brother Caolte," his uncle drawled. No affection in his tone now. "I should have expected to find you here. You Seelie love to talk about how good and honorable you are, but I've sensed your energy in this mess more than once."

Caolte stepped in front of his brother. "You should not be here."

"I've as much right as you do," Vek retorted.

"Stand down, Caolte." Naomh waited for his brother to return to his side before speaking again. "One of Kien's toys is with the Unseelie. Here to finish what that fiend started, boy?"

Fen snorted. "You're one to talk. Didn't you help create that invisibility cloak that the others used to slip into Moranaia? One of those cloaks was used in the assassination attempt on your own son. Kai, right? He seems like a nice guy."

Naomh stiffened, his hands clenching at his sides. "What did you say?"

"Kai is a nice guy. He deserves a better—"

"Before that," Naomh snapped.

"One of the half-bloods Kien sent to Moranaia was ordered by Allafon to kill Kai." Fen thought back to those terrible days in Kien's camp. He'd been so ready to escape but so helpless to figure out how. "Kien was furious about it. Of course, if any of us had known that Kai was your son, I'm sure he would have been much more pleased about the attack."

Caolte let out a low growl. "How does someone like you know of our relation to Kai?"

"When you live with a maniac, you learn how to listen to the right people." Fen met Naomh's heated gaze. "Guess you weren't aware of what happened to your son. Not close, I take it?"

Naomh lifted a hand, and a stalagmite speared up from the ground a few inches from Fen's right side. Jeez. The Seelie Sidhe had such a poor sense of humor. But Fen refused to be intimidated, especially after an infusion of energy from his powerful uncle. He flicked his fingers, and the stalagmite crumbled into dust. Unfortunately, his heart ached as though it might shatter, too. Only his years with Kien kept the pain from his expression.

Far from upset, the Sidhe lord let his hand drop and granted a slight smile. "Well done, youngling. I can see why Kien recruited you."

"What are you doing here?" Vek demanded suddenly, and Fen got the distinct impression that Naomh's praise bothered him. Which made no sense. "By all accounts, you cut ties with Kien when you discovered the scope of his plan. Are you here to prove that rumor false?"

Naomh grabbed Caolte's shoulder, halting his brother when he attempted to rush forward. The Sidhe lord studied Vek and Fen with his cool gaze before he surprised Fen by letting some of his noble veneer drop. "You know why we're here. If that wall shatters, many will die. Our people. Humans. The wave of energy won't discriminate."

"I may be able to help," Fen said.

The Sidhe's eyes narrowed. "Not in your state."

Fen's skin heated in a flush, but he refused to cave. "I had to ingest some of Kien's blood, and I was the one who connected him to Earth's energy. Not that I wanted to," he hurried to explain at Naomh's scowl. "Prince Ralan ordered it to save Maddy. A young half-Sidhe, as a matter of fact."

"Surely not from the Seelie side," Caolte said with a sneer.

Vek's hands clenched. "You iron-blasted hypocrite. You're about as much Unseelie as Seelie. But I suppose you'd rather not claim your mother with her *tainted* blood."

Not even Naomh could hold him back then. Caolte shoved past his brother and launched himself across the cavern. Vek bared his fangs as Caolte flicked a ball of

flame into his palm, but Fen was too surprised to do more than stare. A Seelie lord's brother was part Unseelie? That sounded like a story he'd love to hear.

"Stop," Naomh called out.

For a moment, the other two ignored him. But there had been an unusual edge, an urgency, to his tone. Then Fen sensed it—another wave of energy coming from the rift.

"Vek," Fen warned as the dizziness hit. "We're too close. Shouldn't have…"

A surge of power. Pain.

All he could do was scream.

Aris woke with a start, Selia wrapped in his arms. *Clechtan.* He hadn't meant to fall asleep, but he'd been more exhausted than he'd thought. According to the small water clock on the wall, they still had a mark before they were supposed to meet in Lyr's study.

The hatch in the ceiling rattled and the windows shook as Kezari's wingbeats resounded above. Carefully, he disentangled himself from Selia and tucked the blanket around her as she burrowed into his pillow. It took him a moment to retrieve and don his clothes before he could head for the hatch. He cast a regretful glance at Selia, warm—and naked—in his bed and almost turned around. But he needed to talk to Kezari, and there wasn't much time before they had to go.

As he triggered the stairs to descend with his magic, Aris combed his fingers through his hair and tied it back with a strap from his pocket. Then he climbed up into the cold night. The wind whipped more snarls in his long hair almost instantly, and his clothes dampened with the thick mist. He dismissed both sensations as he edged around Kezari's large form to settle next to her foreleg.

Without comment, she lifted her wing and curled it in front of his body, blocking the worst of the weather. Her wedge-shaped head bobbed as she stared into the trees around them, and if not for the wing shielding him, he might have assumed she didn't know he was there. Something had to be bothering her.

"What is it?" he whispered as he braided his hair with a few deft motions.

One golden eye turned to face him. *"My cousin betrayed me. I have no hoard now, not even what is mine by right."*

Aris rested his cheek against her leg. "We'll rebuild it."

"It is the betrayal more than the treasures, though I'll miss those dearly." Smoke streamed from her nostrils. *"That is not the worst of it. They haven't hunted Perim."*

Bile scalded the back of his throat, but he swallowed it down. "Not good."

"I will find her when this is through," Kezari insisted.

"We will." Aris clenched his hands to still their shaking. "I cannot let her rule me."

"Mating has been good for you."

That surprised a chuckle out of him. "I suppose so."

Her head tilted. *"Why have you sought me out when you could be mating again?"*

Aris grinned. Elves weren't shy about sex, but dragons took things to a new level. "How do you know I wasn't coming up here for fresh air before waking Selia?"

"This weather is not pleasant for your form," she answered. *"Not conducive to sitting on towers."*

His humor faded. Her guess was correct—he did have a reason for coming up here. But she didn't know why. He'd grown accustomed to her presence at the back of his mind, sometimes a shadow and sometimes firmly connected. She had retreated to the farthest edges when he'd joined with Selia, granting them privacy, and she hadn't yet settled back into his thoughts.

That intrusion should have bothered him. But with each drip that passed, Aris drew closer to Kezari. She'd seen his darkest side, his deepest secrets, and accepted them without question. She shoved him beyond his limitations and into possibility. He couldn't mark the moment she'd become his friend, but she was.

For that reason, he hesitated. But there was more he needed to know despite how much he hated to request the answers. "Kezari…"

Her chest heaved at his back as she took a deep breath. *"Ask."*

"Why did you leave me in that cave for so long?"

"I thought that might be on your mind, now that you are well enough to consider it." Kezari's eye closed, and her head lowered. *"I am sorry, skizik. I should not have believed Perim's lies. I'd been hibernating, trying to connect to the Earth to find the source of my constant discomfort. It wasn't so bad then, but the changes consumed my attention. When she said you were barely an adult and needed training, I was almost…grateful."*

Though Aris flinched, he didn't interrupt.

"I spent weeks following the trails of Earth energy. Years, I suppose." Her snout tilted down until it almost brushed the roof of the tower. *"Convenient, I thought, for you to be training while I discovered the truth of what was happening. I never bothered to see you, fearing I would be pulled to bind before I knew what I was going to do. Would that I had thought of anyone besides myself."*

Aris rubbed a soothing hand along her foreleg as he processed her words. As much as he wanted to be angry, he found that he couldn't summon the emotion. Only a well of sadness for what might have been. "Your desire to save Earth belies any selfishness."

"I did not begin with thoughts of our former world, only worry about my own discomfort."

Aris sighed. "Much change begins with our own discomfort. It is what we do once we examine the source that defines us."

"You are full of wisdom, skizik," Kezari said, amusement slipping into her mental voice.

"Not really." Smiling slightly, he closed his eyes. "But I did spend hours alone on various expeditions. Do you know how much thinking you can do while tracking a newly discovered species of *daeri* across the northern planes to determine their migration patterns?"

Her soft snort sounded around them. *"New species of daeri?"*

He laughed at the interest in her tone. "Didn't you find time to hunt before you came back? You didn't seem grumpy enough to be hungry."

"One can never have enough daeri,*"* she grumbled in return. *"Now go back below. I hear your mate stirring. Perhaps you can ease more tension before we leave."*

Aris shook his head and chuckled at her words.

But then he complied.

24

Iren stared across the room at Eri where she perched on the edge of his bed. It was late, still several marks until morning, and they would both be in big trouble if their parents found out. He nibbled at his lower lip. Her plan had seemed so logical before he'd made up with his father. But in the quiet darkness of night, uneasiness crept into his stomach.

"Are you sure this is a good idea?"

Predictably, Eri didn't look at all worried. "We'll be seeing a lot of our rooms, but it'll be worth it."

"Your *onaial* will stop us," he argued.

"Nope." Eri grinned. "Lady Megelien said she blocked the strand. The goddess approves, so what could go wrong?"

"Ah, Eri, why did you say that?" The lump in his stomach grew. "Hasn't anyone ever told you how dangerous that phrase is?"

She swung her legs, bouncing her feet against the side of his bed with a thump. He really should know better than to listen to a six-year-old, but he couldn't help it. Eri was sweet, canny, and more persuasive than a little kid should be. She begged him with her eyes, and he did what she wanted. Of course, he usually liked her ideas. Unlike today.

"Not when I say it. We need to be there. I promise."

Great. Now her lower lip was starting to poke out. "Yeah, yeah. I already said I'd go."

"You got the cloaks?"

"Yeah." Iren slumped in his desk chair. "*Onaiala* is going to be furious. She hasn't finished working on these. They'll keep us invisible, though."

Eri slid to the floor and darted around the side of the bed. She crouched down until only her eyes peaked over the top. "You'd better get back in bed and pretend to sleep. Your parents will check on you in a few drips."

A few drips? His heart leaped, and he rushed to the bed as Eri's face disappeared over the side. Iren slipped between the covers and turned his back toward the door.

He squeezed his eyes shut, but he could hear a soft rustling from Eri's location, then a muffled thump beneath the edge of the bed. The mattress shook softly for a moment before all went quiet.

Just as he evened his breathing, the door clicked open and footsteps sounded across the floor, some heavier than others. Both parents, then. Slow breath in. Slow breath out. Iren kept his muscles lax as his mother's energy neared his back. The heavier footsteps continued as his father rounded to the other side.

"I wish we could wake him," his mother whispered.

"If you prefer—"

"He'll argue to come with us." She bent low and brushed a kiss across his forehead. "But the poison makes it unsafe. I just couldn't leave without kissing him goodbye."

His father's hand rested on his shoulder for a moment, and Iren almost opened his eyes to reassure them that he would be okay. They had to be worried about this mission. And here he was, planning to add to that stress without their knowledge. As his parents trudged out the door with heavy steps, guilt twisted the lump in his stomach until he thought he'd throw up.

Eri had better be right.

Selia's boots squished into the muddy path, and she gathered her cloak around her head to block out the drizzle falling through the trees. The mountains of Moranaia gave a whole new meaning to the season of rain. Rather than the flooding downpours of her homeland, the precipitation here was a near-constant annoyance. Thank the gods that the garden paths were largely stone, or the coming festival would be a mud bath.

It was a relief to step through the portal behind Kai and Kezari. The mists swirled around the group, but despite the foggy appearance of the Veil, it didn't have the same moisture. Or maybe it wasn't as noticeable after the rain. Selia pushed the hood of her cloak back with a sigh. Ahead, Kezari's skin morphed to golden scale, and she tipped her head back, a look of ecstasy on her face. But she managed to maintain her elven form.

Aris wrapped his hand around Selia's, and she cast him a quick smile. Then Kai pulled them through with a burst of energy. Almost at once, the mists faded, and bright light had Selia squinting as they exited the portal. Steamy heat enveloped her until she released Aris in order to tug her cloak free. One by one, they tucked their cloaks into gap in the ridge wall. Then Selia waved a hand over the space, hiding the contents from view.

"Are you certain you can transport us to the cave without draining yourself?" Kai asked.

Selia nodded, her hand slipping into her pocket for an energy crystal. Her body heated at the memory of how she'd recharged some of them, and a small smile crossed her lips. "I refilled these and grabbed a few extra."

"I could fly us." Kezari rolled her shoulders as though flexing invisible wings. "The wind here feels divine."

Kai opened his mouth and then closed it again, probably uncertain how to argue with a dragon without being eaten. But Aris saved him. "That would not be safe in the human world," her husband said, resting a hand on Kezari's shoulder. "They have technology that can fire into the sky."

Kezari scowled. "I can fly higher than arrows."

"Aris is correct," Kai finally said. "Humans have created machines that fly, and some of them come equipped with weapons. I'd rather not see how you fare against them. And vice versa. We have more important things to worry about."

Selia had no clue if dragons pouted in their natural forms, but Kezari's bottom lip took a definite turn downward in this one. Even so, she waved her hand regally toward Selia. "Let us proceed, then. This skin itches. I want to shift."

Before the dragon could change her mind, Selia tightened her grip on the energy crystal and connected to the power within. With a quick tug, she spun the magic into the travel spell. A thin line the height of a person appeared and widened, and as she formed the image of her destination in her mind, it filled the gap she'd built. But the cavern on the other side wasn't empty this time.

Kai cursed. "What is my father doing there? Let's move. Now."

Selia held the spell firm, channeling power from the crystal straight into the gate, as Kai, Kezari, and then Aris rushed through. The small portal flickered slightly, but it steadied a moment before Selia followed. Her head spun as she was wrenched across space. Shouldn't she have had to change crystals by now? Even as she settled on the other side, she examined the spell for flaws, but it had no obvious problems. The energy didn't sputter until just before she closed the spell.

What had changed? Suspicious, she reached out for Earth's well of power and gasped. Still difficult to access, but not as much trouble as it should be. The cracks in the wall must have widened, letting more energy through.

Aris froze at her side, Kezari standing in front of them as Kai strode closer to the small group in the center of the cavern. The youngest one was on the floor, writhing, a blood elf crouched over him with fangs extended. A Sidhe man with bright red hair paced anxiously while a second Sidhe male hovered at the writhing man's feet. Kai headed straight for the second Sidhe lord, and though his hair was pale, she could see some resemblance between the two.

Must be his father.

Selia's heart lurched, and she jerked another crystal from her pocket. But her view was blocked as Kezari grew in size, her body contorting in a swirl of energy that crashed like a gale against Selia's shields. She winced and shaded her eyes until the blur of motion ended. Once finished, the dragon stood in her natural form, though a quarter of her customary size.

At a brush against her hand, Selia glanced at Aris. He'd gone deathly pale, and his chest heaved rapidly with each breath. The cave. Ignoring the others, Selia stepped in

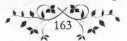

front of Aris and grabbed his face between her palms. Kezari would protect them. Aris having a breakdown could only make the situation worse.

"Stay with me, Aris."

"I'm trying." His throat bobbed. "Go help Kai. This may take a moment."

Selia brushed her lips against Aris's. "No. You can do this. Let yourself feel the cave. The life is different here, with a different rhythm. Do you sense the heartbeat? The creatures here need you."

His eyes glazed, and she feared she'd lost him.

Then green flared around his pupils as he pulled his head free from her hold.

The physical world ceased to matter.

Aris glided across the cavern floor, barely noticing Selia as he circled her to stand at Kezari's shoulder. He formed a loose link with the dragon, and the cry of stone joined the discordant song of the creatures living inside the cave. Nearer still, two lights beckoned, one of them pulsing with the darkest sliver of death.

Pressure built, ringing in his skull, and then snapped. A rough scream echoed through the chamber, but that hardly registered. His attention was on the sick energy within the light. He advanced toward it, his feet finding purchase without conscious effort. The Earth would cradle him no matter where he went.

"Don't merge too deeply, skizik."

He shrugged aside the dragon's words and kept walking.

Something tightened on his physical form, and he shook his arm to try to break free. A sharp tug, then. "Aris."

Sudden awareness washed over him at the frantic cry of his name, and he halted, blinking rapidly to clear his thoughts. The world returned to clarity. It was Selia clutching his arm, and the group he'd seen in the center of the cavern now stared at him, save the one stretched out on the floor. Gods. He hadn't been that pulled in by his magic since his first half-century of life.

"He is poisoned," Aris said, his voice rough to his own ears.

The blood elf hissed. "What do you know of this? If you think to harm Fen, you will have to reckon with me."

"You will not threaten one of my people, Vek." Kai stepped partially in front of Aris. "Your nephew knows me. I've spared him once already."

"I will not trust anyone who brings a dragon to undo the ancient pact." The anger Vek's expression didn't ease. "I don't care if you're the king of Moranaia. Clearly, you do not understand the intricacies of what is happening. Remove yourself, or I will remove you."

Kezari let out a warning rumble, and the air warmed with her anger.

Equally upset, the blond Sidhe lord leaned forward as though he wanted to spring. "I'll send you to your father in pieces if you threaten my son again."

"Enough!"

A crack of magic accompanied Selia's sharp command, and all three men froze.

Not voluntarily. Aris couldn't hold back a slight grin at the sight of his wife marching over, not even when the red-haired Sidhe lifted a ball of flame in his palm. The stranger met Selia's eyes for a moment, and then his hand lowered, the fire winking out. But he remained tense. Ready.

Selia undoubtedly was, too.

"Caolte," Selia said, nodding her head at the Sidhe man glaring at her. "Explain what is going on here. Since all these three can do is trade threats while Fen writhes in pain."

Even Caolte looked abashed. "Naomh and I were investigating the energy rift when Fen and Vek arrived. We…might have had some disagreement between us. Then a pulse from the rift struck, and Fen collapsed. We've been trying to determine what to do."

Beneath his feet, Aris sensed the hum of energy increasing. Slightly, but enough to give him cause for concern. "If the pulses are hurting him, you'd better get him out of here. There will be another soon."

Selia narrowed her eyes at the three men frozen in place. "I will release you, but if you begin arguing again, I make no promises."

A cool wash of power flowed around them, and her spell dissipated. She must have been feeling kind, for the slow dissolution gave the three time to regain control of their muscles. Naomh wobbled, his feet almost touching the ground before he righted himself, and Vek jumped up, glaring, but Kai tucked his hands behind his back and attempted to appear repentant. The wiser move when faced with a master mage who was thoroughly tired of one's attitude.

The blood elf snarled. "If you ever do that again, I will drain you—"

"I recommend you keep your fangs far from me," Selia said coldly. "I did not shirk my training when it comes to your kind."

Amazingly, Vek's mouth snapped closed, though anger still lined his face.

Another pulse of energy thrummed through Aris. "If you care for your friend, get him out. Now. Take him as far from here as you can manage. Once we have healed the rift, we can see what we can do for him."

"You have no intention of healing anything," Vek said. "Or at least your dragon doesn't."

Kezari's breath puffed out, filling the space with an acrid scent as her voice shoved into their heads. *The poison must be purged, but we both know that might widen the crack. I do not intend to dissolve our pact. However, I may not be able to control the results of what has been wrought. I didn't create this rift or the poison infusing it. I can only try to fix it.*

Vek shoved his shoulders back. "Give me a bit of your blood, and I will go seal the rift."

Impossible without trapping the poison inside, Kezari sent. Aris's blood chilled at the terrible finality in her tone. *That's too much to risk. The sickness would only gain strength behind the shield holding back the magic, and if your fix fails, the blight would pour free all at once, killing everything it touched. Besides, the wall is permeable in places to allow for the natural ebb and flow of magic. We don't know if the poison can seep through those thin areas."*

"Fen believes he can purify the blight since he helped Kien—"

"That boy will not live beyond a few days if the poison is not purged, and well you know it." Pieces of fallen stone rattled as Kezari lumbered forward. Her golden eyes stared at Vek as though he was her prey. *"This was no accident. It was punishment. When the wall shatters, he dies if the darkness is not removed."*

Vek's jaw clenched. "I cannot heal Fen."

The floor vibrated softly, although Aris wasn't sure anyone besides himself and Kezari detected it. "He might survive until we can return to help if you go now," Aris said.

Fen let out a low moan, and his uncle knelt beside him. The Unseelie's skin was paler than the snow coating the northern mountains as he studied his nephew's face. "Or he might not."

"Caolte and I will go with you," Naomh said softly.

Vek's expression went blank. "You? Why?"

"I bear some of the same talents as the dragon and her rider," the Sidhe lord answered, no sign of concern in his tone. Only the tense, high set of his shoulders gave his agitation away. "As well as a touch of the healing gift. I may be able to help."

"But you're a Seelie lord," Vek began. "I—"

"Talk it out later," Aris said as his head began to throb with the rising energy. "Selia, can you build another portal to help them get them farther away?"

Nodding, she extended her hand, and a different, more focused power built at her direction. Vek lifted Fen into his arms, and Naomh and Caolte shifted close. Kai barely had a chance to exchange a few words with his father about contacting someone named Maddy before the unusual group slipped through the transportation spell.

Selia let the portal drop, and the four of them were alone. Just in time for the next ragged wave of power.

25

This time, Selia didn't try to shield herself from the wave. She'd been caught off guard last time, and instinct had led her to protect herself. Now she was ready. She lifted the empty crystal in her left hand, and as the pulse of energy crashed into her, she channeled it into the stone. Unlike the energy fields themselves, these waves were pure power. Infinitely useable.

"What did you do?" Aris asked after the magic waned.

Selia shrugged. "I was being practical. Don't worry, though. I filtered against the poison."

She tucked the crystal in her pocket and joined Aris and Kai in the center of the cavern. Kezari advanced, too, her slow steps rattling the ground. The dragon lifted her head over Aris, practically settling it on his shoulder as she stared at them.

"I will smooth the path to the rift," Kezari sent.

Selia expected her to grow larger, closer to her natural size, but instead, she shrank until her body was the size of Iren's. Selia's lips twitched. She had a feeling it would be a terrible idea to call a dragon cute, but...in her small form, Kezari was adorable. Her little wings flapped rapidly as she arrowed toward the tunnels they'd used to reach the energy fissure.

Aris's eyes met Selia's, and for a brief moment, they shared a grin. Then they joined Kai in following Kezari. When Aris reached for her hand, she took it, startled to feel him trembling. His expression might not show it, but he was uneasy about being in the cave. She entwined her fingers with his and gave a comforting squeeze.

Kai glanced at them over his shoulder. "I wish I'd had a chance to speak with my father about Kezari's claim. I'm not certain what I'm supposed to do to guard the strands between worlds."

Selia smiled sweetly. "Perhaps in the future you will not waste time arguing."

"You're right." Kai shrugged one shoulder. "Though I admit that I'm surprised you reprimanded a Seelie noble and an Unseelie prince so...stringently."

Her steps hitched, but she forced herself to keep moving. She hadn't been thinking about status at the time, only their useless arrogance. She might very well have caused an incident between their peoples by immobilizing those two. Talk about a breach in etiquette. But blast it, Fen had been thrashing in pain while they'd exchanged barbs.

"I wasn't considering the ramifications." She winced. "I hope I haven't created another problem."

"Don't worry about it, Selia," Kai said. "We've dealt with worse."

With a sigh, she tried to ease the concern from her expression. It must have worked, for Kai stopped sending glances her way and concentrated on his steps. Or perhaps he worried more for the low ceiling in this tunnel. The walls had grown wider and smoother thanks to the steady thrum of power directed by Kezari, but she hadn't paid much heed to height.

Selia and Aris came to a halt beside Kai inside the small room with the shelf hidden behind stalactites. After getting scratched during the climb on their first trip, Selia wasn't relishing the thought of going in again. But the dragon flew closer, and the stone shifted away from her snout like a waterfall from a shielding spell, exposing the tunnel hidden by the stalactites. Even that began to widen as Selia watched in fascination.

But they would still have to crawl.

The dragon glanced over her shoulder. *"It would take too much energy for me to widen the tunnel enough for walking. I will do my best."*

Aris shivered against her arm, but if he made a return comment to Kezari, it was private. His gaze was pinned to the shifting stone, his expression drawn and pale. How would he bear going through the tunnel, not to mention the crevice they'd have to descend later?

Before their eyes, several stalactites and stalagmites appeared to melt and flow downward into a rough set of steps. Selia blinked in disorientation as the stone heaved and shifted before settling. Gods of Arneen. She could manipulate earth a little herself but nothing on this scale. As far as she could tell, it didn't even cause the dragon strain. Kezari hovered easily, her wings flapping steadily and her talons hanging lax as she studied her work.

Not that Selia was an expert at judging a dragon's body language.

Finally, Kezari flew back to them, hovering in front of Aris. *"This is the best I can do. Connect fully with me, Aris, and I will help you. Please stand guard, Selia."*

Aris's breath hissed through his nose as he peered at Selia. "If you need to immobilize me, I will not complain."

"I will not need to," she answered, her voice ringing with more confidence than she felt. "We can get through this."

His nod was slow in coming. "I suppose we'll see if you're right."

Perim understood little of what she'd seen in this strange world so far, but power she comprehended. As she pressed against the stone wall of a small building, another wave of energy flooded her senses, blinding her for a few precious heartbeats.

She was getting closer. She'd run for most of the day across a seeming island's worth of uneven, sometimes mountainous terrain, dodging unusual boxes on wheels and avoiding an endless series of strange habitations.

And humans. Like insects in summer, they swarmed everywhere.

Once her vision, and the energy, had cleared, she pushed away from the wall and started jogging once more. What a terrible, barren waste of a planet. She was no mage, but she used simple magic like any self-respecting fae. Here, it was difficult to light so much as a campfire without severe strain, except when one of those strange waves rushed through. And although there were many trees, they were much smaller. The air held an odd, chemical tang, and constant lights and noises ruined the serenity of many of the places she passed.

Who but humans could live in such a place? Even the island she hated was better.

Perim reached another road made of smooth, smelly stone. It held strange markings—white lines and yellow dashes. In some places, there were two center lines and in others, one line and a bunch of dashes. Were they magical symbols? Maps? So far, she hadn't been able to make sense of them, but if she grew desperate enough, she could capture a human for answers. Not that humans would provide much sport. She was too spoiled after Aris's resilience.

As she darted across the road, careful not to let her foot touch one of the lines—just in case—one of the rolling boxes flew around a corner. Perim yelped and jumped out of the way, barely in time to avoid being crushed. The wake from its passing shoved at her back, and a screeching sound chilled her heart.

She stumbled to a halt, glancing over her shoulder as a thin, clear panel moved downward on the box. The human inside shouted at her, but the words made as much sense as the device he controlled. Shrugging, she darted away without bothering to speak. He wouldn't understand, anyway.

Her laughter floated behind her, mingling with the human's incoherent remonstrations.

The closer Aris came to the hole in the cave wall, the harder his heart squeezed. Kezari had flown through first, and now Kai lowered himself to the floor and began to crawl through. Aris barely felt Selia's hand rubbing gently between his shoulder blades. Despite all of the mind-healer's work, this might be too much.

No. I can do this.

Aris sucked in a breath to center himself. Then he merged with Kezari. This time, he was prepared for the scope of the pain, the damage to the Earth that had almost swept him into madness when he'd accidentally connected with her before. He let it flow into him before pushing it to the back of his awareness. He sensed something deeper. More fundamental.

Suddenly, the earth beneath his feet became his blood and bone. He couldn't shape it as Kezari did, but he could become it—if he dared. A spasm passed through

his body. Caves were torment and despair. Why would he join with that? But this place was not the same location where he'd been held. The present and the future could not be judged so strongly by the past.

He let the stone speak to him. Through him. The rift in the energy field caused hurt. Each pulse a threat to a long, endless life. Minerals disturbed, water flow altered. Strangers traveling through, their bodies killing the living rock where they passed. Heedless.

Come. Please come.

Aris had crouched on his hands and knees before he realized it. He closed his eyes and crawled, shivering until the tunnel closed around him with pleased warmth. With each scuffle forward, the cave sent its welcome through him. He let it. As he followed the glow of a mage light partially blocked by Kai, some of the tension eased from his gut. He was not so broken, after all.

They emerged into a tiny chamber bristling with rock formations. Aris held out a hand for Selia and helped her to her feet. At her questioning look, he smiled. "Seems you were right."

But the crease between her brows didn't ease. "You haven't seen the next part."

Connected to Kezari as he was, he sensed her decision to shift before the others did. When the dragon's energy increased, Selia's focus transferred to Kezari. Thankfully. Aris hated seeing the worry in his wife's eyes, especially since it was warranted. He didn't know if the earth's comfort would overcome his aversion to a crevice worse than what he'd just crawled through.

In moments, Kezari stood before them in her elven form. Naked, predictably, but Aris didn't bother to mention it. Kai kept his gaze respectfully averted, no sign of discomfort on his face, and Selia let out a soft chuckle that the dragon either ignored or didn't notice. Kezari was too busy studying a narrow gap in the floor.

Without warning, bile rushed up Aris's throat and coated his tongue. That fissure looked like... *The chain shouldn't have reached the crevice, but it did. Aris's arms burned from their extended position, and the walls closed around him until he was certain there was no air. He panted. Thrashed. His back grew wet with his own blood. "Told you that you shouldn't have hit me," lilted down from above, a cheerful contrast to pure evil.*

Aris doubled over, resting his hands on his knees as he pulled in lungfuls of air. He wasn't there. He knew he wasn't there. Thanks to the healer, he could untangle himself from the memory. But nothing on Earth was going to get him through that gap without risking madness, not even the steady comfort of the cave still humming within him.

Then he heard a long, thin cry echoing from below—followed by a yelp of pain.

For one long moment, Aris's breath seized. "That sounds like Iren."

He and the others rushed toward the gap, and he plunged his senses down the tunnel.

Nothing.

But despite what his scan told him, whispers and sniffles echoed upward. With a wave, Selia sent the mage light into the darkness, but all Aris could see was the floor a couple of body lengths down.

To his right, Selia groaned. "The cloak."

Aris's brows twisted with confusion, but Kai cursed. "The one you based on Kien's design?"

Selia nodded, her lips thinning into a pale line. "Show yourself *now*, Iren," she called down into the tunnel.

After a bit of rustling, Iren's body wavered into view as the hood of his cloak dropped to his shoulders. Aris's heart lurched at the sight of the tears streaming down his son's pinched face, but an equal amount of anger surged alongside his fear. "What were you thinking?" he found himself demanding.

Not the most pressing question, unlike *Are you hurt?* and *How did you get here?* but it was all his lips seemed willing to form.

Selia fared better, thankfully. "Are you injured?"

"I hit my knee when I fell," Iren answered, his voice quivering with fear. "And my ankle hurts. And there's blood. It's not that I wasn't thinking. I just…"

Aris went cold at the sight of the dark stain blooming on the leg of Iren's pants, and his earlier question fled his mind. Tunnel or no, he had to get down there. "We'll talk about the rest later. I'm coming down."

"Allow me, *skizik*," Kezari said. "I can widen the gap after I see to your spawn."

"I could go," Kai offered.

Selia wrapped her fingers around Aris's wrist as though she wanted to hold him back. "Or I. Though I may not have much of the healing gift, I can—"

"No." The sick taste of fear filled his mouth once more, but Aris shook his head. "I can seal the wound."

Kai made an impatient gesture. "As can I."

Aris swung his legs into the hole and pinned Kai with a level look. "No."

He might never have descended the chasm for himself or even for Earth. But by the gods, he would help his own son. Carefully, he eased down the vertical tunnel bit by bit. Memories threatened, hovering at the edges of his consciousness no matter how hard he beat them back, and his breathing came fast and shallow. Aris closed his eyes and tried to pretend he was anywhere else.

Not even the earth's comfort could ease this.

After an eternity, his feet touched solid ground. Elation weakened his muscles, but he couldn't savor it. Iren needed him, and he would not fail.

Aris had barely shifted their son out of the way before Selia dropped down beside him at the base of the fissure. Her hands shook as she rushed to the wide spot in the tunnel where Aris bent over Iren's leg. Darting around him, she sank down at her son's other side and gripped Iren's face in her palms.

"Iren—"

"I know, I know," her son said in a rush. "I wanted to prove myself. And Eri said it was important."

That explained far too much. "Where is she?" Selia asked, trying to keep her tone level.

"Here," a small voice said as the hood of another cloak was lowered.

The child's face was milk-white, but Selia couldn't summon much sympathy at the moment. "You have gone too far, Eri."

"He wasn't supposed to get hurt!" Eri's hands twisted together. "I'm not sure what happened. There was no future strand for that."

All of Selia's worry left her mouth in a rush. "I can't believe you stole these cloaks from my room to cross worlds into certain danger. It seems I will have to separate you two, at least for the foreseeable future. That's *my* future strand," she snapped.

"*Onaiala...*" Iren pleaded.

"How am I supposed to keep you safe with all of the life energy your father is about to unleash?" Selia dropped her hands before she could squeeze his cheeks too hard. "Didn't you think of that? You can't justify this."

Eri lifted her little chin. "It was important for us to be here. I Saw it."

"And your father didn't?" Selia asked, eyebrow lifting.

"Lady Megelien—"

"Is not known to work through children at the expense of their safety." Selia studied the child's guilty expression. "I suspect there is more to this than I need to know. I'll leave that to your father."

Eri ducked her head. "Thank you, Lady Selia."

"I sealed the gash," Aris said, catching her attention. "But I can't heal the cracked bone in his ankle."

Kai crowded into the small tunnel, and Selia scooted out of his way. "If it is a small break, I can knit it a little. My healing gift is limited. Can you not do that with life magic?"

Aris shrugged. "I'm not certain. I can shift and adapt bodies, but I must have intimate knowledge of them. Unfortunately, I've never put that much study into anatomy. I'd far rather explore than modify or heal."

"Adapt bodies?" Iren asked, his eyes going round. Probably with excitement more than fear, if she knew her son. And she did. "I'll be able to do that?"

Aris's mouth tightened. "We'll see. Right now, we need to fix your ankle and then figure out how to protect you during what is to come."

"You won't need to," Eri whispered.

Usually, Selia loved the little girl, and in truth, she still did. But she wasn't particularly fond of her at the moment. One day, her overconfidence was going to get her in more trouble than she could handle. It certainly had Iren.

Here's hoping that trouble doesn't arrive today.

26

Selia half-expected to see the god Loki standing in front of the rift again, but the cavern was empty of all but the glowing red fissure when she and Kai led the way inside. Iren and Eri followed them in, and Selia directed the children to wait beside the tunnel opening as Aris and Kezari rounded the corner.

The dragon uttered a choked hiss and froze in her tracks, pain stark on her face as she studied the wound to Earth's energy field. "The Unseelie was a fool to consider sealing it up like this," she whispered.

Aris circled the pulsing rift, the red light painting him an eerie color. Selia tilted her head and examined it as well. More black threaded through, blocking the light, and she didn't have to be an earth mage to detect the sick hint of poison. If this was sealed within the energy field, it would sicken all who tried to use energy here, if not immediately then certainly over time.

Kien had used his death as a catalyst to turn his poison into something far deadlier than its original form. Before, he'd scattered nodes around the world, creating a framework of sickness that could be broken, if not easily. But this... This was a bomb. An explosion of this much tainted energy would kill many.

Lovely.

"Together, we can eliminate the poison," Kezari said to Aris. "But the walled off energy is going to break free. The damage is too extensive. Can you channel it while healing? Even hearing the Earth's cry, I did not expect it to be like this."

Aris frowned up at the rift. "I'll do my best. Perhaps if I channel it to Selia?"

Selia couldn't help but snort. "There aren't enough energy crystals in any world to hold this much power, and I have no ability to direct it into the living earth."

"Then I'll have to—"

"I can help," Iren blurted. He straightened from where he was leaning against the stone wall, resting his sore foot, and shoved his shoulders back. "Eri said we needed to be here, and I think this is why. I don't really know how to use the energy, but I can act as a conduit."

"No," Selia and Aris said in unison.

But Kezari peered at Iren with hope. "Your spawn might be an asset."

Aris spun to face the dragon. "Even you must admit that young should be guarded."

"What do you think will happen to him if you fail and this explodes?" Kezari asked.

A reasonable question, unfortunately. Still, Selia didn't want to concede the point. Perhaps she and Kai could escort the children to the portal first. It would cost a bit of her own reserves, but it would be worth the risk of draining herself to see Iren and Eri safe.

Before she could make the suggestion, a sputtering sound filled the cavern, and the red glow brightened—then flickered. Selia's scalp prickled and her arm hairs stood on end at the building power, erratic and strong. The waves were getting worse. *Clechtan.* She couldn't spare the time it would take to take the children back.

"Perhaps you could test whether Iren can handle a thread of your power," Selia said to Aris before she could change her mind.

His brows rose. "You jest."

"Not about this." She swallowed hard as the rift's light flickered. "This is growing unstable. We need to fix this now if we're going to do it at all. Surely you can feel the danger."

Aris's gaze flicked briefly to the crack and then to Iren. "I would rather see the end of this world than either of you."

"If we don't act, I fear you'll see the end of all three."

Another surge swept over them, and this close to the rift, Selia strengthened her shields. The other adults appeared to do the same, but the children cried out. As the power ebbed, Iren leaned against the wall next to a frighteningly pale Eri. Selia rushed over to examine them both. Her son looked more shaken than anything, but the little girl rubbed at her head as though it hurt.

"Eri?"

"It's a lot like the other poison," the girl whispered. "The one that almost killed me before my dad took me from Earth to Moranaia a few months ago. But not quite the same."

Selia's heartbeat drummed in her ears at the solemn expression on the child's face. "You risked your life to bring Iren here."

"I probably won't die." Eri summoned a slight smile. "But I don't want to be seriously hurt, either."

Well, that was a fine choice. Put Iren in danger or risk death for little Eri, a princess of Moranaia who was likely to be the greatest seer of her generation. Maybe any generation. Iren met Selia's apprehensive gaze without flinching, more like his father than he knew, but for a moment, all she could see was the baby the healer had first placed on her chest. She brushed an errant hair off his forehead and ran her fingers down his face to tweak his chin as she had when he was younger.

"*Onaiala,*" he said with a groan.

"You're still a child, Iren," Selia said. Then she took a deep breath. "But I believe you can do this. You are a clever, fast learner. My caution with you has always been your heedlessness, not your ability. Promise to follow your father's commands, even if you don't want to."

Aris stepped up beside her, the conflict evident on his face. "Selia, I'm not certain about this."

"I'm not, either." She forced a tremulous smile. "But you saw what that surge did. Loki said my task was to protect. I'll monitor the energy and step in if necessary. I can funnel it away from Iren."

They both knew she didn't have the same capacity for life magic that Aris or even Iren had, and this would be far beyond what she'd channeled for her husband in the past. Since she wouldn't be able to direct it straight into the earth, it would build within her until she burned out like an overfilled crystal. The best she'd be able to do was force it away from them before she died.

But she would do it for Iren.

"He doesn't need to know," she sent to her husband.

Aris's jaw hardened. *"I will always know. But you are right."*

Then he focused on their son and began to describe the basics of being a conduit.

Aris settled between Kezari's shoulder blades, no saddle between him and her scales. She'd widened one end of the chamber, unwilling to take on the task ahead without being in her full natural form, and shifted while he worked with Iren. Pride swelled in Aris's chest at the memory. His son was clever, indeed. He'd almost lost control several times as he struggled to channel the life energy he was fed, but he'd picked up the skill far faster than Aris had as a child. Selia had taught him well. If they survived this, Aris could train Iren to actually use the magic instead of merely directing it back into the natural world.

To the left of the rift, Kai sat, legs crossed and eyes closed as he fumbled with his power. If Aris scanned with his own abilities, he could see a few tendrils of something whipping around the other man, but it wasn't like the earth energy he knew. Kai had nodded when asked if he was ready, so they'd just have to trust that he'd figured it out.

They'd have to trust in a lot of things.

To the right, Selia stood behind Iren, ready to take on his burden if he faltered. If any of them faltered. Aris jerked his gaze away and caught sight of Eri, still leaning against the wall on the other side of the energy rift. For a moment, he could have sworn her eyes gleamed as she returned his stare, but she blinked, and the effect was gone.

A flicker of red captured his attention. Was it his imagination, or did the lightning-like cracks hovering in the air appear…longer? Deeper? The Unseelie and the dragons had been reckless to try to wall off this much energy. How had they not considered the possibility of a breech?

Kezari shifted beneath him. *"It would have succeeded had our peoples not grown complacent. We stopped actively maintaining the wall, so it is not as strong as it once was."*

"People?" he asked, poking at her in an attempt to lighten the mood.

"This language has no better word for a civilization comprised of sentient, non-bipedal entities," Kezari answered primly. Then she relented. *"Except perhaps 'civilizations.'"*

Aris chuckled softly and patted her neck. *"We'll work on it."*

She twisted her head to look at him, and the spines around her eyes shifted in a motion he'd come to associate with raised eyebrows. *"Are we waiting on something?"*

"I'm not sure," he confessed. *"I feel like there's…"*

Eri straightened, catching his attention once more. She pulled back her shoulders and nodded her head sharply. This time there was no mistaking the gleam.

"How about now?" he asked.

Kezari bared her teeth in a dragon's grin and faced the sputtering fissure. Aris closed his eyes and let himself settle into his power. The heartbeats that had fluttered at the back of his consciousness crescendoed like the pounding of drums at a winter solstice celebration, but the creatures here weren't ceremoniously summoning the sun back to life. They were fighting to fix their world the only way they could—by lending him their strength.

Fluttering and skittering sounds filled the cave as bats shifted their wings high above and insects darted around in their holes, just out of sight. There were rats and spiders, salamanders…all manner of creatures that generally fled before any people could find them. Even as they connected with Aris, they remained out of sight, wary of so many bodies. Particularly the dragon.

He fell deeper into himself. His dryad grandmother's blood flowed strong through his veins, and he tapped into the power held within. If he strained, he could count the strand of every root tunneling over their heads. Each tiny plant and bit of moss that grew where a hint of light reached now synched with the beat of his heart.

"What do you want me to do?" he sent to Kezari.

"I'm not certain yet."

The rustling from above increased as the bats picked up on his agitation. *"You said we could fix this."*

"We will," she answered, her mental voice placid. *"Merge. Explore. Find the discordant threads."*

Aris forced himself to relax. To let go. Kezari would not guide him wrong.

He connected fully with Kezari, and the stone around them returned to life the way it had earlier, before he'd dropped their connection to heal Iren. Rock groaned and flexed, though its physical form didn't move; even the minerals accumulating on the stalactites above his head hummed with the disturbance. The Earth held fathomless energy, but the earth was not accustomed to so much disorder, so much speedy evolution. Not here, at least, where only the occasional cave-in punctuated the steady drip of time.

Aris allowed his own power to flow into Kezari, then. She moved restlessly beneath him as the strength of it hit, but after only a moment, they managed to join their powers completely. Body and soul of the earth entwined. He basked in it for a couple of heartbeats.

Then he turned to the rift.

And he—they—knew.

A smile broke across Perim's face as she spotted the cave entrance. Finally, the source of the power. She'd had to cross two more of those strange roads and climb the side of the mountain, but it had been worth it. She took a few wary steps closer to the cave. No sign of life. But then an energy as familiar as her own washed over her, and she froze. Aris—but not Aris. He was greater. Different. She prodded the energy carefully and recoiled before he could notice. He'd joined with the dragon.

Finally, a bit of good fortune. She could honor her oath to Baza and rid herself of the final obstacle keeping her from true freedom. Then she would recreate herself, no one the wiser. Even if the Ljósálfar rejected her, she'd survive. Here on this strange planet if necessary.

Just one thing to take care of first.

Her smile widened as she shielded herself and started walking again.

Aris probed the edges of the rift, gathering as much information as he could. This cave wasn't the origin point of the spell walling off Earth's energy, but the fissure let him examine the handiwork anyway. How many Unseelie and dragons had joined together to create this piece of spell art? There were bits of earth magic twined with the other elements and a definite hint of strands similar to the Veil. Actually—

Yes, it connected to the Veil. Suddenly, he understood what Loki had meant, and he reached out to Kai. The other elf linked immediately, though his mental voice sounded confused. *"What's going on?"*

"Look," Aris said, sharing what he saw.

Silence while Kai examined it. Then a litany of mental curses. *"And I'm supposed to keep this from getting damaged?"*

"So it seems." Aris understood the other man's fear, but now wasn't the time to indulge it. *"I know you can't link magic the same way Kezari and I can, but maintain mental contact with me as you join with the strands."*

"I've followed them most of my life, but I—"

"Figure it out now." Inside, Aris winced with his next words. *"Do you want to get stuck here if the Veil is damaged? I assume you'd like to see your child born."*

A pause. *"Harsh but accurate. You're right. I don't have a choice."*

As Kai began to explore the rift further, Aris linked with Iren. This was different yet again, for his bond with his son was of blood and energy, not of mind or magic. But this time, he didn't set up a telepathic link, and he wouldn't unless he had to.

Unlike Iren, Kai could guard against any physical or emotional rebound. If there was pain, Aris would not share it with his son. Instead, he sent Iren a wave of reassurance before returning his attention to the fissure.

Small, red crackles danced along the lightning-like branches and sparked on the air. Something was about to happen, for good or ill, and Earth would not remain the same, no matter what. All he could do was try to tip the outcome in their favor.

Aris took a deep breath and loosened his awareness of his physical body. He felt more than heard Kezari's assent as they plunged into the rift and joined with it, not completely, but enough to purge the sickness marring it. His very existence thrummed with the force of the power.

Gods. So much energy. Too much—more than any person should have to handle. But he couldn't channel it through Iren and into the ground yet. All hint of poison had to be purged first. If he could manage the task.

Life. This scourge was made of death, and he would counter it with life.

He shoved against that dark stain with the essence of endless heartbeats. With the richness of fertile soil and living rock. Bit by bit, he chipped away at the poison with hope. He'd seen evil, and it did not have to win. It would not win. *Merge with life,* he offered the shattered heart of power. *Embrace it and be.*

Endless time passed, but finally the Earth heeded his call. Where poison had consumed, light poured through. But the power… His spirit ached from the strength of the magic that rushed into the spaces left in the wake of darkness, shattering through the ragged holes and deepening the cracks in the wall.

Aris channeled the magic down, toward the deepest heart of the Earth where it would merge with the existing energy field. *More than I can bear.* Grudgingly, he passed some to Iren, but his son was soon at capacity. If Aris couldn't handle it, someone else would suffer, either Iren or Selia.

No.

He doubled down, and pain shrieked through him. Body? Spirit? He didn't even know how much of it was his own. The earth trembled, and he sensed Kezari struggling to prevent the wall from shattering all at once. If they could trickle the power out slowly, in a controlled release like the floodgates of a dam, the final burst might not be too bad. Maybe.

Movement stirred on the edges of awareness. Who…? Eri and one other. That god. Loki? Bound in the magic as he was, Aris saw their glowing forms as they approached. Then they shoved their hands into the heart of the rift, and his world went white.

27

Selia was so focused on monitoring Iren's energy that she almost missed Loki's reappearance. He and Eri advanced on the rift, now flaring between red and white, the god holding the child's hand. Selia glanced at Kai to see if he noticed the pair, but his eyes were closed as he struggled with his own task.

What had they called Loki? The god of mischief?

"More like the god of cleaning up others' shit," Loki said, his voice echoing across the space. "Though I'll grant you I create my fair share of trouble."

Selia had no idea what to say to that. She looked between him and the child, whose focus was on the rift. "What are you doing here? With Eri?"

"Fixing things," he answered. "You know, I was once known for more than causing trouble. But call those in power on their failings one time, and you're forever the villain. I guarantee they'll never believe I did this."

He seemed to expect some response to that, but Selia didn't know what he was talking about. "I'll pass the message along."

"Tell them Lodurr still lives." He grinned. "Oh, and watch the entrance."

Before she could ask what he meant—about any of it—he and Eri plunged their hands into the ragged edges of the energy fissure. The impact of the resulting blast blinded her, and Selia threw herself around Iren as far too much power was released. All she could do was wrap her shields around them both and try to survive.

Pain flared in her side and back as she landed hard on the ground, her body cushioning Iren. Her shielding began to crumble, and she scrambled to reinforce the cracks. Then Iren linked with her, much as he did for teaching sessions, and joined his own power and protections to hers. She tried to open her eyes to check on the others but it was far too bright to see. Would any of them survive this?

Loki had said he was going to fix things, but he hadn't claimed he would spare *them*.

Kai had never linked with the strands quite like this before.

Or maybe he had on an instinctive level, as he'd always been the strongest guide at Braelyn. It was one of the reasons the previous Myern had allowed Kai to guide Lyr to Earth on his missions despite their friendship and youth. But grabbing a strand, examining it, was nothing like becoming part of it.

In this moment, joined to Earth's energy field and the very force linking the dimensions, he could create a strand to anywhere. Usually, he followed the line from Moranaia to Earth, then chose the appropriate sub-strand to the portal exit he wanted. Now he could make a direct line to anywhere.

That was far from all he could do, but right now, it was more than enough.

Locked with the rift as he was, he sensed Eri and Loki approaching. What in the…? Instinctively, he reinforced his hold on the strands. Just in time. They did something, joined in some way, and the world tipped into chaos.

Hold the strands as they are.

Kai didn't question if the words were his own or from an outside source. Instead, he did his best to obey.

Aris might have screamed, but he was too disconnected from himself to know. He struggled against the power swamping him and tried to pull his consciousness back to his body more fully. But it was agony when he did. Muscles clenched until they spasmed, lungs heaving for air. He sucked in a deep breath.

Part of him wanted to retreat once more from the anguish. But he'd lived through worse, and he would no longer back down. *"What did they do?"* he sent to Kezari.

"They are laying the groundwork," she answered, a hint of wonder in her voice. *"A base here. A link between Earth and Moranaia. The girl bears blood of both. She is the key."*

He cracked his eyes open as the blinding light began to settle. The jagged gashes of the rift were gone, replaced by an oblong column of glowing energy. Beneath it, a stalagmite grew upward, stretching toward the light. Aris was just able to make out Eri and Loki on the other side of the new fissure.

The little girl's dark hair drifted in tendrils around her placid face, no sign of distress in her demeanor. In contrast, Loki's hair and eyes flamed, his entire body tense as he poured himself into manipulating the energy. In Aris's magical sight, the god blazed as brightly as the rift itself. And was just as volatile.

"We should help," Kezari said.

Aris frowned. *"How?"*

"Step into the fissure, and I will show you," she answered. *"A working like this will require this kind of boundless energy."*

Kezari lifted her head, her long neck extending until her snout almost touched the rift. Aris unclenched his leg muscles from where they'd clamped around the base of her neck and forced himself to his feet. *This is madness.* But he balanced carefully between her shoulder blades and crept up the ridge of her neck toward the surging light.

Half way to the rift, Aris glanced across the chamber. Kai huddled in the same place, his skin ashen as he fought to hold onto the strands. Through their mental link, Aris caught nothing but resolve.

Selia and Iren, however, were curled up on the ground. Not moving.

Had Selia not sensed his regard and managed to meet his eyes, he would have leapt down from Kezari and cursed them all.

"We are not hurt," Selia sent. *"Whatever you are planning, do it. I love you."*

"I love you, too."

His attention shifted wholly to the rift, then, and he shivered. Stepping into this core of power was a foolish move, but it was the right one. He could better control what happened with the energy from the inside.

Aris took a deep breath, said a quick prayer, and leaped inside.

Selia's cry blended with Iren's when Aris disappeared into the column of light. What was he thinking? She'd expected him to insert a hand like Eri and Loki. But one moment, he was balanced on Kezari's snout, and the next, he was engulfed in the glow. She could barely see his body suspended in the center.

Watch the entrance.

The god's words rang through her head as though he'd just spoken them. Despite his apparent preoccupation, maybe he had. She shoved Iren behind her and spun to face the tunnel that lead into the chamber. Sure enough, a tall, thin woman stood in the dim shadows between the dark tunnel and the light cast by the rift. In her hand, a knife gleamed.

What in the world? Who would... A flickering gleam from the fissure lightened the woman's face, bringing a memory to life. But not one of Selia's. Laughing, blood dripping from a knife held high. Perim. This was Perim. What was she doing here?

Selia connected with Iren immediately. *"Get behind Kezari and stay out of sight. I mean it, Iren. That's the woman who tortured your father."*

Surprisingly, he didn't argue. But the whispered answer he gave as he darted out of view gave its own explanation why. *"I know."*

Gods, he must have picked up on Aris's memories somehow. Selia ached for Iren, for the things he must have seen were more than any child should have to deal with. Her hands clenched, that bittersweet pain morphing into anger. And the *drec* who'd caused it all wanted to do yet more harm.

Not on her watch.

Selia reached into her pocket for an energy crystal. There was enough magic swirling through the room to power an entire working group's spells, but she dared not use it. There was too much risk of unbalancing whatever the others were doing. She'd have to be careful with any spells she used, but she had little choice. Inona might have non-magical weapons tucked in every fold of her unusual Earth clothing, but Selia was no warrior.

At least the wretched woman's scowl was pinned to Loki's back and not on Selia. But as nice as it would be for Perim to be foolish enough to attack a god, Selia wasn't relying on it. She reinforced the layers of her protective shields as she eased toward the edge of the cavern. If Perim crossed into the room, Selia might be able to sneak behind her. Unlikely, but it was something.

Quickly, she scanned the woman's shields. Good. Only a few layers designed to repel basic attacks, a standard mirror shield at the end. Selia could counter that, even the one designed to reflect magic back.

Now what would be the best spell to use? Selia ran through her mental catalogue of the most painful ways to kill. *Inverting flesh. Teleporting away a few choice organs. Transfiguring blood into water.* The first would be too grisly with Iren present. The others… She heaved an inner sigh. They might give a moment's satisfaction, but they would render her no better than Perim.

Unfortunately, the only spells she knew that would render instant death might cause Aris trouble by unbalancing the magic flowing through the room. It was no easy matter to shut down the mind or the heart of a fae, and Selia was no healer to know the best way. Most of the methods she could perform required a massive amount of energy or the type of life magic her husband wielded.

She'd have to start with incapacitation.

Suddenly, the blond woman turned a smirking glance Selia's way. "Surely you didn't believe I hadn't noticed you?"

Freezing in place, Selia gathered the spell she'd used on Vek and Kai into her hand until her fingers tingled. "How did you get here?"

"A friend told me how to find my errant soulbonded." Perim shrugged. "What good fortune to find him so thoroughly indisposed."

"But not alone." Selia studied the woman. She was beautiful, her delicate features similar enough to Meli's that Aris's reaction to the Ljósálfar woman became clear, but Perim's eyes held a crazed glint the other's lacked. "Unlike you. You might have had an informant, but I don't believe you had a friend."

"Shut up." Perim lifted the knife and jiggled it. "Why should I care what you think when I have more important things to take care of? I can almost touch the red-haired one from here. Would you like me to begin with him? Or perhaps he isn't important enough to get Aris to come out to play."

Selia almost loosed the spell, but she hesitated. The other woman was too confident in the presence of so much power. Even with the rest of the group preoccupied, Perim was far outnumbered. She had to be hiding something, some weapon besides the knife. Perhaps a magical ability? None of Aris's memories included images of the woman doing magic, but that didn't mean she couldn't.

"You're Selia, aren't you?" Perim demanded with a sneer.

Selia lifted her brows. "What do you know of me?"

"Only what Aris whimpered or screamed when he was barely coherent."

That was more than enough. Selia cast her spell at the other woman, only to realize her mistake almost instantly. In her haste, she'd given Perim's shielding only a cursory examination—an apprentice's mistake. Her spell pierced the first couple of layers, but when it hit the third, part was absorbed and the rest rebounded.

The inner layer of Selia's own shielding held the counter for the original in case of that very thing. However, whatever piece the shield had absorbed altered the spell enough to slice through Selia's defenses as it bounced back. It captured control of her body, inhibiting her muscles so thoroughly that only her organs were able to move.

Her heart pounded in her frozen chest as though it wanted to break free. Panic threatened, but she couldn't let it consume. She'd created this spell, and whatever that shield had done to alter it, she could erase. If she had time. Perim advanced, a wicked smile twisting her lips, and wiggled the knife again.

As the woman began to circle her, disappearing periodically from view, Selia blocked her out. Instead, she delved into the components of her spell. The bulk of the immobilization portion was there—obviously. Ah, yes. That small fragment of Selia's power, the signature left by all mages, was missing, replaced by Perim's. A tiny but crucial change.

With deft mental fingers, Selia began to unwind the pieces the kept her muscles locked. Strand by strand, she pulled the components free from the other woman's energy. Something cool slid along her cheek. She ignored it. A pinch of pain along her arm almost distracted her, but she kept her focus firm.

Finally, she dissolved the enchantment and dispelled the remnants of Perim's energy. Her muscles went lax all at once, and she stumbled as her legs almost gave out beneath her. She threw her arms out to the sides to try to regain her balance but still almost went down.

Searing agony shrieked from her shoulder, heralded by an ominous crack. From somewhere, Iren cried out her name. As Selia dropped to her knees, she could only pray he didn't try to rescue her. *Miaran,* the pain… She couldn't move her left arm without almost blacking out.

She spun, tumbling onto her bottom with a thump that drew a scream of pain from her throat. Perim stood over her with a triumphant grin. Blood dripped from the tip of her knife and plopped onto the stone beneath them. For a moment, time suspended as they stared at one another.

Selia's shirt clung to her back, and a suspicious amount of wetness soaked the upper edge of her pants. She didn't have enough healing gift to probe the depths of the injury, but she suspected it was bad. If she was going to defeat Perim, she'd have to move fast.

"Iren," she sent. *"Contact your father. Now."*

"I can blast her from back here."

"Now," Selia ordered.

She darted forward and slammed her hand against Perim's ankle. Then Selia shoved her own surprise spell straight through the woman's shields.

28

Aris would never experience life quite this way again.

He could touch any lifeform. Alter or destroy it. But first, he would have to find it. He swam in a sea of life magic, and though he could pick out individuals here and there, like a single grain of salt, retrieving anything specific would be impossible. Only Kezari anchored him, but even she struggled with her merging.

"What do you want me to do now?" he asked her.

"A gate must be created." Her thoughts quieted briefly as she considered. *"The energy that was released here is reverberating through Earth. I suspect a great deal is about to change. We need a faster connection between Earth and Moranaia than the Veil and a safe place for our people to stay once they arrive."*

Cold washed over him. *"I can't set up something like that. Selia or Kai, maybe, but—"*

"The god and the girl will handle the gate," Kezari interrupted. *"It's the fortress we must construct. Hidden. This place will require constant guard. I will build the tunnels and chambers. You find a way to give them life. We'll never have this kind of access to raw energy again."*

He followed Kezari with his mind through the layers of earth to the very top of the mountain. Meticulously, she formed tubes for air and light, doorways and stairs, hallways and rooms. And he trailed behind, cajoling plants to life where he could. Moss and vines to obscure. Flowers in the entry, along with a few small fruit-bearing trees. In one large chamber where Kezari had brought in a fair amount of natural light with a crystal set into the tube above, he coaxed forth the beginning of several crops.

As Kezari directed her attention to the original entrances to this cave system, closing them permanently, uneasiness began to invade his consciousness. He didn't need to create life where she sealed the rocks. He should return to the fortress and do more work there. But he couldn't. Something was wrong. Some discordant energy amidst the flow.

His muscles clenched. All of the sudden, he felt exposed. His body was suspended in the column of light, and he couldn't see beyond it no matter how much he squinted. Were the others safe? Selia? Iren? Another hint of that dark power brushed him, and he let out a mental cry at the sensation.

Perim.

Impossible. She was on Moranaia, hiding on the dragons' isle. Could his connection to life energy stretch that far? His throat burned, and Aris swallowed down bile. He sensed Kezari's concern, but he was too paralyzed with fear to reassure her.

Then his son's voice broke into his mind. *'Onaiala is in trouble. She's hurt. That woman is here.''*

Fury and pain coalesced until Aris burned with it. The light flared around him, and he let the power build within him. *''I will do what I can.''*

''There's a lot of blood. Hurry.''

Blood.

Shuddering, Aris reached for Kezari. *''Selia is under attack. I must descend.''*

''Not unarmed, skizik.''

Connected as they were, he didn't have to ask what she meant. Aris held out his hand, fingers slightly cupped, as Kezari gathered the energy and concentrated it, forming metal into blade while he grew a hilt of living wood. The column sparked green as together they fired the sword—honed it.

When it finally settled against his palm, Aris tightened his fingers around the hilt and let the cool comfort of life ease the fear coating his mouth. Perim had done her best to destroy him, but she'd failed. And he would die a thousand times before he let her kill his beloved.

Perim screamed, and Selia almost released her out of instinct at the sound. Her stomach lurched. But even as revulsion swamped her, she continued pouring the jagged energy straight into the other woman. Like lightning striking water, the charge continued into Perim until it reached the shield Selia had cast to contain it.

The knife clattered to the floor and the woman toppled. Selia slammed her body over Perim's as the energy crystal sputtered out, and her own cry sounded at the pain in her shoulder. But training had taught Selia to disconnect temporarily from her body. She ignored the agony shrieking at her mind and shifted until she straddled Perim, her knees digging into the woman's shoulders.

Perim's head lolled against the stone, and her breath came in gasps. Selia stared down at Perim's cruel but beautiful face. So much pain caused by one person, and for what? Everyone knew you couldn't force a bond.

"Why?" Selia snapped as the woman blinked up at her.

"Escape," Perim whispered. "I didn't want to die there. I needed to control a dragon. Make it fly me free."

Selia's fingers balled into a fist. "I don't suppose you considered asking Aris and Kezari for help?"

"I will not be dependent on another. Can't count on anyone but yourself." Perim shifted beneath her. "Not even for a bond. I never would have kept him, you know. I would have killed him first."

Her vision whitened with fury, and for once, Selia didn't reach for her magic. Instead, she slammed her fist into the woman's nose with the force of seven years' worth of agony. Her cry of pain mingled with Perim's, and Selia wavered on the edge of consciousness as the wound in her shoulder tore with the motion. But it was worth it. So very worth it.

Should've teleported her gods-cursed heart to another dimension.

Selia shook out her hand and wondered if the blood was hers or Perim's. Didn't matter. The woman heaved beneath her, struggling, so Selia lifted herself up and slammed back down to knock the air from the other's lungs. Perim's breath rushed out, and she went still.

But Selia barely noticed. The light was blurring, Perim's face a swirling mass of blood and hatred. *Clechtan.* She couldn't lose consciousness now. Perim would kill her for sure and then try for Aris.

Or Iren.

Selia shoved her trembling fingers in her pocket and scrabbled for another energy crystal. She would empty herself accessing it, but it was all she had. If she died torturing someone, it would be better than letting this woman loose on the others.

Blood transmutation. That might be the easiest from her current position.

Gods forgive her soul.

As Aris shoved his body free of the rift, rock rose from below to meet his feet. He blinked to clear his vision, but his mind and spirit were still linked with the column behind him. Around the rift, Kezari was creating a framework for the portal from stone, but he was more concerned with his son. Aris could sense him nearby, but his sight kept blurring. Finally, Iren's pale face clarified as Aris descended to the floor of the cavern. His son practically vibrated with energy, life magic but other elements, too.

"I can't get a clear shot," Iren said, his voice ringing with pain. "I could do a fireball, but…"

A new kind of energy buzzed through the air, and Aris spun to face the source. Selia stooped over a prone Perim, but the surge of power obscured his physical sight after a couple of heartbeats. His beloved was about to cast a spell, and it had the taste of darkness.

"Selia!" Aris shouted.

Or he tried to. He had no clue which dimension the words rang into, and he didn't wait to find out. He hefted the glowing sword in his hand as he charged across the space between them. He might not have begun the bonding process with Perim, but stabbing her was going to hurt.

"You'll kill yourself," Perim gasped.

That voice had delivered years of cruelty, a torment beyond the physical. It had become his inner voice—but no more. He would fill the dark abyss of her influence with his own power even if he died in the process.

As his rage mounted, the real world became clearer. Just enough. He could see what was needed to end Perim's life. "Move back, Selia."

She shoved herself away, rolling from Perim with a cry of pain. As Perim scrambled up to her elbows, fear overcoming her usual mocking expression, Aris shoved the tip of his sword downward, straight into her heart.

Then he twisted. The blade was forged in life, but the opposite side was death. A verdict he had no qualms about delivering. He shoved his magic through the sword, the perfect conduit, until his vision went green from the glow. With another twist, he ordered the spark of life to return to the ether.

There must be no mistake. No way for her to escape death.

Aris did his best to shield himself, but the backlash was pure agony. He fell to his knees, buffeted by the storm Perim's death unleashed. His fingers tightened on the hilt of his sword, and he jerked it free. He would have no more connection to her, not even through the blade of a sword.

He sensed Kezari, then, wrapping her mind around his as she often did her wings around his body. The storm faded, and Perim's darkened spirit passed fully into the next life. He neither knew nor cared where her soul would end up. Judgement was for the gods. As he opened his eyes to focus on her lifeless face, he felt none of the satisfaction he'd dreamed of for all those years.

All that coursed through him was relief.

"*Onaial?*" Iren asked softly from behind him.

"I'm here," Aris said. An odd comment, but somehow fitting. "Guide me to your mother. My vision…"

Iren's hand wrapped around his arm as Aris shoved to his feet. Still bound to the rift, he tried to keep the power coursing through him from leeching over, but his son hissed out a breath and jerked free. "Sorry, I…" Iren stuttered. "Just circle the…the body here. She's on the other side."

A shiver passed through Aris at those words. The other side. He didn't care where Perim had gone, but he certainly cared about Selia. He followed Iren around Perim's corpse. Selia wavered in and out of his sight, a dark stain pooling beneath her huddled body.

Aris knelt beside her, settling his sword to the side. He would not touch her with Perim's blood, though the blade itself might be able to aid in the healing. He didn't need it. He rested his hand on her back. Selia's chest fluttered with breath—but barely. Without thought, he reached for the power his connection to the rift granted.

He grasped life. Wholeness.

Then he directed it into Selia.

Selia forced her eyes open as the power inside her waned. For a moment, she feared she'd taken damage to her vision, for the nearly blinding light had faded to a dim glow. But the world clarified quickly, settling into Aris's glowing face.

She gasped. His skin shimmered, and his eyes blazed green as he stared at her. It had been his power filling her, returning her torn flesh to its original life. What had happened? She'd been constructing her final spell against Perim when Aris had cried out for her to stop. After that, there was only darkness.

He wasn't himself. Normally, his forehead would be creased with worry lines, and he'd be demanding she tell him how she felt. But there was a fathomless weight to his regard, a hint that he wasn't quite...alone. Or perhaps he was only more aware, more powerful. With her second sight, his link to Earth's energy glowed like the sun.

Selia reached up a hand and cupped his cheek. Ever so slightly, he leaned into her touch, and his gaze softened. "I must..." he began, his voice low and rough. "The rift."

"Go," she whispered. "But bring yourself back to me. And only you next time."

She thought his lips curved upward, but he stood and bent to pick something up before she got a good look. As he strode away, Selia gathered her energy and shifted herself to a sitting position. Her head spun, but the sensation passed quickly. Just in time to see Aris approach...an archway formed of stalactites and stalagmites? That hadn't been here before she'd passed out. A set of steps led up to the bright white of the former rift, now anchored between the stone.

What was going on?

Selia could barely make out the forms of Eri and Loki on each side of the stairs, their hands still entwined with the light beside the base of the arch. Her body trembled as she shoved herself to her feet with the aid of a stalagmite. But her gaze stayed on Aris as she rose, even after he disappeared into the gate.

"You're okay!"

At Iren's cry, she turned to her son. He rushed toward her, his arms open, but she held up her hands. "I'm covered in blood, my love."

Iren's brow furrowed. "No, you're not."

Frowning, Selia glanced down. He was right. Her clothes were smeared with dirt, and both her pants and shirt bore several small tears. But no blood. She studied the back of her right hand, but there wasn't so much as a scar to show where she'd broken her skin punching Perim. That was almost a shame. She would've loved showing that trophy off.

Selia held out her arms and sighed with contentment when Iren threw himself against her for a hug. "I guess you're right."

29

Power wavered on the air and thrummed through the floor beneath Vek's feet. The electricity was out, so a ball of mage light illuminated the unusual group gathered in his living room. His skin prickled as his gaze landed on Naomh sitting on one side of the long couch. A Seelie Sidhe lord in his living room. Unbelievable.

Caolte leaned against the window frame, the Chattanooga skyline at his back. Young Maddy knelt beside Fen's prone form on the other end of the L-shaped couch, and her girlfriend, Anna, perched beside Naomh and nibbled on the tip of her finger as she stared at Fen. A veritable party of beings Vek never would have invited into his home.

But as needs must.

He paced in front of the window and behind the couch, finally stopping to lean on the back and study his nephew. Fen was deathly pale, his moans now silent. The girl was doing some kind of scan, and the energy had Vek's teeth grinding together. Better than Naomh's attempt, though, which had released so much Sidhe magic into the air that Vek had wanted to vomit.

He'd borne that indignity, and it hadn't even helped. Naomh hadn't been able to heal the poison—he'd tried while they waited for Maddy to pick them up. Perhaps his lack of connection to the environment had altered the results. He'd refused to set foot on the ground, hovering like an idiot where anyone could come along and see.

"If Maddy's attempt fails, perhaps Naomh should try again," Vek said. "He might be able to properly ground his magic now."

Naomh sneered. "A talented mage does not need to touch the soil to connect with its power."

"To keep to this foolish pact—"

"Your kind might have chosen to forgo your word, but we of the Seelie are nobler than that."

Vek let out a snort. "You're full of something, but nobility isn't it. Why do you respect a treaty the humans barely remember?"

"We gave an oath, and—"

"You didn't give anything," Vek interrupted, leaning forward. "Your ancestors promised the human sons of Mil that you wouldn't step foot on the surface, sure. Of Ireland. You ceded *Ireland,* not fucking Chattanooga on the other side of the world. Stop hovering like an idiot whenever we go outside."

A choked noise echoed from the window. Then Caolte burst out laughing, the sound so sudden and unexpected that Vek stared. "What?"

Caolte shook his head, a grin wreathing his face. "I pointed out something similar on our last visit to this region. Perhaps he'll listen for once."

Vek's brow lowered. "Really?"

"Maybe it's my Unseelie blood, but…" Caolte waved a hand. "I think it's foolishness at this point. Besides, from the feel of the energy increasing like the tide, I'd say things are about to change."

Naomh crossed his arms, his jaw clenching. Why did he cling so tightly to the old ways? Vek studied the Sidhe lord curiously. He obviously wasn't a stickler, or he wouldn't be here at all. Thousands of years before, the Sidhe had lost a war with the humans, Milesians, and sworn to remove themselves to the underhill realms a dimension away. The oldest wouldn't allow their feet to touch the surface, but they also wouldn't consider entering an Unseelie prince's living room.

Beside Fen, Maddy stirred, her eyelids fluttering open. "I can't fix it, either," she whispered.

Vek muttered a curse beneath his breath. "I don't understand. The energy fields are clear now. There was no mistaking that after the final wave."

"Maybe it wasn't connected to the rift," Maddy said with a frown. "He took Kien's blood, right? He could have done something to it before passing it along to Fen."

Silence fell. Then Anna's voice lilted across the quiet. "Water won't cure it."

Vek's attention swiveled to the half human in surprise. Her other blood had gotten stronger, augmented by the surge of energy that had swept through an hour or so before. Her features had taken on a sharper fae cast, and her aura hummed with the power of rapids and the depths of oceans. If she was anything to go by, there was going to be a problem. The magical races hadn't exactly been shy about sleeping around, so scores of humans could soon have latent fae blood surging to the forefront.

Caolte was correct—a great deal was going to change.

"We need to find a more experienced healer. One with more power." Maddy gave Naomh an apologetic glance. "No offense."

The Sidhe lord ran his fingers through his hair, his expression troubled. "None taken. You are correct to seek expert aid. My gift for healing is small."

Vek's shoulders slumped for a moment, but he forced himself to straighten as he peered at his nephew. He'd failed Fen enough over the years. That trend would not continue. "First, we'll see what happens when the others return. If they fixed the rift, they might yet heal Fen."

Of course, the geniuses had broken open the wall shielding the extra energy from Earth. They could've found another solution for the poison if he'd sealed it instead. Probably. There was no telling what damage that final wave had done across Earth. It had taken down the electricity here, and Maddy's cellphone had no signal, so they were cut off from outside news.

That release hadn't been the only consequence, either. Vek felt like he was standing in a cave, the water slowly rising from an unseen source. The life-dealer and the dragon must have channeled the bulk of the power into the natural energy field. Now the power his people had worked so hard to seal away would return to Earth, whether they were ready or not.

Here's hoping we don't all drown in it.

"It's time to disconnect, skizik.*"*

Aris floated. With each moment, the magic had become more a part of him. Did he breathe still? His body seemed a distant concept, one of billions of heartbeats forming a symphony inside of him. He could stay here and join with infinite life.

"Skizik."

Something pushed at his mind. Kezari. *"What?"*

"Disconnect, or we will remain here forever."

Lightness filled him at the thought. He could exist here in this place, free from pain. Explore this nexus of life. Such purity here. Who but the gods had ever experienced it in its fullness? Even connected now, Aris's comprehension was small. But if he had endless time to wander, perhaps he could attain such understanding.

Forever.

We will remain here forever.

Kezari's words replayed in his head, a discordant note amidst the hymn of life. We. *We* will remain. Linked as they were, he'd doom Kezari, too. She'd done so much to shield him. She'd saved him. He could not reward her with a living death.

And his family waited.

The song of the rift became a dirge. Infinite loneliness. There was no life without his family. What had he been thinking? Selia and Iren were worth foregoing this power. They were everything.

With a lurch, he struggled back toward his body. He wiggled his fingers, and the sword almost dropped from his right hand. He still held it? He circled his wrists and shrugged his shoulders. A deep ache tickled in the back of his mind and then bloomed to full life as he became aware of his body, stiff and sore from the force of the power he'd wielded. He groaned, but he let himself return.

Then something wrapped around his wrist and tugged.

He stumbled down the stairs, his legs so weak that he would have crumpled if not for Loki's hold. No mistaking the man for anything but a god now. His flaming hair stood on end and his eyes blazed as he gripped Aris's shoulders to keep him from falling.

"You were not supposed to want to stay."

Aris wavered in the god's hold. "I didn't want to. Not really."

One red eyebrow rose. "Could've fooled me, elf."

"I might have gotten a bit…lost."

How could he explain what it was like to merge with such power? How he'd abandoned himself, and his will, without even realizing? But there was a serious gleam in the god's eyes that suggested that he knew. Of course, he must. Heat crept up Aris's neck at the memory of Loki standing with his hand in the rift. Yes, he knew.

Aris gave a short nod. "Thank you for your aid."

"I do hope you won't get used to it," Loki answered, though a grin lightened the words. "Time for me to go. Enjoy the gift."

Between one blink and the next, the god was gone, taking his powerful energy with him. Aris's legs crumpled immediately, too weak to hold his weight. He'd been serious about not getting used to his help, it seemed.

Footsteps pounded against the stone. "Aris?"

"I'm fine, Selia," he answered. He leaned against one of the steps as he glanced around. "Only tired. The others?"

Eri stepped into his line of sight, pale and serious but otherwise unharmed. "The god shielded me."

He peered around the frame of the new portal as Selia and Iren reached him. Kezari's side, and thankfully, her belly moved with breath. Even so, he sought her through their connection. *"Were you injured?"*

"No." Her mental voice was slow, almost a whisper, but she didn't sound distressed. *"I only need rest."*

Good. That left Kai.

Aris peered into the shadows beside the portal where the other man had been. At first, he didn't see him, but after a moment, Aris made out the elf's crumpled form. *Miaran.* His fingers tightened around the sword hilt, drawing in power from the rift-forged blade, and he stumbled to his feet. He should have monitored their link better instead of lingering in the portal. If the other man was injured, it would be Aris's fault.

He forced himself to move, but the distance between them felt eternal. Fortunately, Selia caught sight of Kai and darted across the space far faster than Aris could currently manage. She bent over him, and her power hummed on the air as she scanned the fallen elf.

"He's alive," she said. "But in shock, I think."

Aris staggered, his hand shooting out for purchase. His palm found the side of a natural stone column, and he leaned against it to catch his breath. They needed to get Kai back to Moranaia, but there was no way Aris could carry him. If he didn't rest, he'd have to be hauled out of here, too.

"How are we going to get him to the healer?" he asked.

Selia stretched out a hand, and Kai rose silently from the cave floor. Iren rushed forward and helped his mother straighten the elf until he rested on his back in mid-air. Then she guided his prone form across the space, walking just behind him. Aris's brows lifted. Although her face was lined with exhaustion and sweat glistened on her skin, she didn't falter.

"It's going to be tough to get back without our guide, isn't it?" Iren followed his mother, a frown of concern focused on Kai. "And the old exit is gone."

The old exit. Aris scrubbed a hand across his face and studied the cavern. Hazily, he recalled working with Kezari to reform the mountain, but he'd been too concerned about the others to care what it looked like when he'd first emerged. The tunnel where they'd entered was gone. Instead, a staircase rose from the spot to spiral up the cavern wall.

Far above, alcoves branched into tunnels, and those led to a variety of rooms. A fortress, Kezari had said. Entranced by the Earth's power, he hadn't given it much thought as he'd filled those rooms with the beginnings of life. But if this portal worked as he believed, the fortified outpost would be a necessity. In a few years, it would be as elaborate as any underhill home.

"I think the rift goes directly to Moranaia," Aris said. "No Veil necessary."

Iren wrinkled his nose. "You were inside it, but you don't know for sure?"

"It is difficult for a fish to analyze the water or a bird to study the air," Aris tried to explain. "For a while, I simply…was. I lost sight of what the others were doing."

A surge of light sprang from the portal, and Aris straightened in alarm. Testing the energy, he found much more available than before. Earth was absorbing all they'd poured in and dispersing it until there was almost as much magic available as on Moranaia. He pulled it in greedily as several elves marched out of the gate.

They surrounded the small platform at the top of the stairs, ringing Eri in their midst, and Aris heaved himself forward in alarm. Then he examined the uniforms they wore. Dark leather, a grayish-brown shade worn only by the *loreln*, personal bodyguards to the royal family. They'd barely come to a halt before Prince Ralan himself strode through.

"Moranai Aldiaberen i Erinalia Moreln nai Moranaia," Ralan snapped at his daughter, and Aris couldn't help but wince on her behalf. The full title was never good. "I can't believe… This was not supposed to happen for…"

Eri wrapped her arms around her father's waist and burrowed against his side. "It was time."

"Our home isn't close to finished yet, and now there's a portal entrance sitting out in the open." Although his voice rang with exasperation, Ralan's fingers tangled carefully in Eri's hair. "How could it possibly be the right time? I'm lucky that we installed the local gate to Braelyn, or it would have taken a couple of marks to reach you."

"If I hadn't come here when I did…"

Ralan bent down and lifted Eri into his arms. "You may explain your actions in your room."

"I know, *Onaial*," she whispered.

"Let's go." Ralan's gaze flicked from Selia to Aris and back over to Kai. "All of you. Kezari will rest here and direct the guards I send through. Aris and Selia, you will need to go help Fen as best you can, but with the current state of Earth, I don't recommend transporting yourselves to the original portal. You're too unfamiliar with this world. If you come with me back to Braelyn, Delbin and Inona can guide you through."

Although the calmly spoken words were clearly an order, Aris hesitated. Leave Kezari on Earth while he traveled to Moranaia? Before he could protest, the dragon gave him a mental nudge. *"It will be a while before I can shift, skizik. I will be fine here. Go."*

Aris swallowed his protest. This solution made the most sense, and he *had* promised the Unseelie prince that he would try to help Fen. If Ralan had Seen the need for him to do so, then it must be important. Aris pulled in more energy and willed himself to walk forward. There would be no time to rest before their next task, so he might as well get used to being exhausted.

He clapped his hand on Iren's shoulder as he caught up. "You'll be staying in your room."

"I guessed as much." Iren rubbed at his eyes, the deep circles beneath standing out on his fair skin. "I think…I think I'm fine with that."

As they neared the stairs to the portal, Aris caught sight of Perim's body, abandoned near the wall of the cave. He gestured in her direction. "My captor has been brought to justice. I trust you'll see her buried?"

Ralan's nostrils flared. "I'll be certain of it."

Burial might not have been an insult to her people, but it was to his. Spirit and ash would not be released to ride the winds and merge with nature, though the worms would certainly be thankful for the feast. Provided they consumed her waste of flesh.

He turned his back on Perim, focusing on Selia as she directed Kai's still form to the waiting *loreln*. As soon as two of the guards took hold of Kai, the others filed through the portal ahead of Ralan and Eri. Then the prince and his daughter followed.

After the *loreln* and Kai were gone, Selia advanced. Aris squeezed Iren's shoulder and nudged him toward the portal. Then after one last word to Kezari, he strode through without looking back.

30

There was only a slight wrench as Selia followed the guards through the portal. She could have been crossing between estates less than a day away from one another, not passing across fathomless space. But she barely had time to marvel. As soon as she stepped through, cold rain soaked through her clothes and the light of morning had her squinting after the dimness of the cavern. It had been several marks before dawn when they'd left. Had so much time passed in that cave?

It had felt like next to nothing, yet eternal.

Selia glanced around the building site as she waited for Iren and Aris to follow her through. Only a few days had passed since construction had begun on the palace, so there was little to see. Underbrush had been cleared away and a few trees culled to make room. It appeared that Ralan had decided to use similar architecture to Braelyn, wrapping the structure around the largest of the trees, and there was already a framework at the base of one trunk.

There'd been a great deal of speculation about this new palace. Now, Selia had some idea why Ralan had ordered its creation. She spun around to face the stone arch situated in the center of the clearing as Iren emerged. It was all for this. Lyr might be in charge of diplomacy between Moranaia and the dimensions connected to Earth, but a direct gate that bypassed the Veil? All manner of problems could arise that would require quick decisions from the king, and the heir to the throne had more leeway to act in his stead.

Like setting up a colony on another planet. No small thing, that.

Aris finally shuffled through, the exhaustion on his face mirroring the heavy weight of her own body. He took her hand when he reached her side, and together they headed toward the smaller arch on the other side of the clearing. Ralan and the others had already passed through to Braelyn, although six of the *loreln* stood in clear view, guarding the area. Gods knew how many more perched in the trees.

She and Aris followed Iren through the gate and straight into chaos. The entryway of Lyr's estate was packed with people, enough that a couple of the guards stood beneath the arch next to the sacred tree. Arlyn, Lyr, and Meli gathered around Kai in the center of the room, while Ralan and Eri conferred with Cora next to the steps to the upper rooms. Several *sonal* and *loreln* waited at attention at regular intervals in case of danger.

Lial's voice cut across the noise as he tried to push through. "Out of the way."

Selia tugged Aris to get his attention and pointed toward Eradisel. He nodded, and together, they herded Iren to the side until they stood beside the trunk of the sacred tree. By the stairs, Ralan handed Eri to Cora and motioned for the *loreln* to follow him back into the portal to the new palace. Lyr commanded most of the *sonal* out of the room, leaving only two beside the gate.

"Stop crowding," Lial said as he shoved himself between Arlyn and Lyr.

Arlyn lowered herself to her knees beside Kai's head. "He's alive. Something they did when creating the portal must have drained him. I felt him slip into unconsciousness from here."

Lial nodded. "Probably shock. Get him upstairs, and I'll heal him. Why did you put him in the middle of the floor?"

"We weren't certain how far we should move him," Lyr said.

With a quick spell, Lial levitated Kai and strode toward the stairs. "Come along, Arlyn. And anyone else who feels the need to trail me like a woebegone child over a simple case of burnout."

Despite the healer's taunting words, Lyr, Meli, and Arlyn followed close behind him. "Might as well since I can't question Ralan about what's going on. What little I heard is insanity enough," Lyr said. At the base of the stairs, Lyr glanced back toward Selia. "Come with us, Iren. I'll ensure you remain in your room while your parents meet Delbin and Inona at the gate. And I will take that invisibility cloak."

"Yes, Myern." Iren jogged over to Lyr almost eagerly, and Selia smiled at the hint of relief in her son's voice. He was brave, but he was still just a boy. One who had seen more than enough adventure. "I'll do what I'm told. I promise."

They'd all have to take advantage of *that* while they could.

Selia and Aris slumped against one another for a moment as their son disappeared up the stairs. Suddenly, they were alone, save for the two guards stationed by the now-empty arch that held the local transportation gate. Even Cora had slipped out with Eri. Now silence held sway, and Selia was loathe to break it.

How was she ever going to rebuild enough energy to cross back to Earth and save Fen? Not that she had a choice. She was exhausted, her clothes torn and dirty. Gods knew what kind of mess her hair was—she didn't even want to touch it for fear of the tangles. But they'd promised to help the young blood elf, so help they would.

With a regretful sigh, she straightened. Aris swayed on his feet before he caught himself, and when he lifted his arms slightly for balance, the sword he held caught her eye. "Aren't you going to sheathe that?"

He scanned the blade almost absently. "There's no scabbard. I don't know where to put it."

"What about the one on your belt?" she asked, lifting a brow.

"On my…" His gaze slipped to his belt, and after a moment, he chuckled. "Well. Looks like Loki had one more bit of aid after all."

Selia studied the leather, bending down a bit to better see the engraving. A perfect replica of the rift as they'd first seen it was surrounded by a line of symbols she couldn't read. She trailed her fingers across the surface and shivered at the spark of contained power. She'd love to probe the spells embedded within, but there was no way she was messing with a god-created object without a great deal of preparation.

Shrugging, Aris twisted away enough to sheathe his sword. The life energy radiating from the blade disappeared, and with a panicked expression, he pulled it free once more. The energy around it returned to Selia's inner sight, and she smiled.

"That's a handy enchantment for when you don't want to announce the sword's power," she said.

"Yes, if a bit disconcerting." He sheathed the blade once more and took her hand. "Ready to go?"

She entwined her fingers with his. "Let's get this over with. Maybe then we can sleep."

As they trudged toward the front door, a wave of energy swept through her, a gift from the sacred tree. Selia sent a quick thanks to Eradisel. She wasn't restored to full power, of course, but she no longer felt like she would drop over from exhaustion.

A welcome gift, indeed.

After becoming a living part of the new portal, traversing the Veil was practically tame. For once, Aris was content to shirk further adventure. The trip was short, smoother than the last, and once they emerged, he let himself pause to take in a deep breath of the Earth air. This time, the sky had gone dim with the dusk, and the shadow of the ridge behind them stretched across the small clearing.

"That's the easiest the strands have been to follow in quite a long time," Inona said. "Maybe ever."

Selia glanced at the scout. "Kai was in charge of aligning the strands when the new portal was set. He knows this route better than anyone, so I suspect it's his doing."

"Probably."

Delbin shifted from Inona's side, striding a few paces away before holding up a glowing rectangle. The young elf frowned up at the thing and turned it in all different directions. What was he doing? Finally, he gave up and rejoined the group.

"No phone signal," Delbin said, glaring down at the device.

That didn't clarify things. "Is that a problem?" Aris asked.

"It is if you want to call someone to come pick you up so you don't have to trek across town." Delbin flipped the rectangle so that Aris could see the face. Beneath a series of colored squares, an image of Delbin and Inona smiled out at him. "See? Nothing."

Aris grimaced. "You're showing me that as though I have a clue what it is."

"Ah, right. You don't know much about this world." Delbin chuckled and tucked the device in his pocket. "It's a cell phone. Imagine a communication mirror that can capture images of the world and connect to libraries full of information. Of course, there are also cat memes, but that won't mean anything to you."

Aris shook his head. Selia had told him that the younger elf had spent much of his life with humans, and it showed. It would be a good thing, too. Aris had a feeling that Delbin would become a powerful liaison between their worlds, a link they might desperately need.

"With your communication…phone inoperable, I suppose we should get moving," Aris said.

"Great," Selia muttered. "More running."

Delbin shoved his hands into his back pockets. "Gotta agree with you on that. Hey, could you teleport us near that gas station we visited earlier? It's closer to Vek's house."

Aris wasn't certain what a gas station was, but Selia appeared to understand. Her tense expression lightened as she nodded. She gestured for them to gather closer to the ridge wall, out of sight of any humans who might get near. It seemed unlikely, since the only houses he could see were a fair distance away, but no need to take a risk.

After a quick step through Selia's temporary gate, they slipped into another forest. Aris jogged behind Delbin and Inona as they rushed between trees, a smooth stone road visible to their left. Earth was a fascinating place, full of unusual buildings and strange technology. Selia pointed out the things she'd already learned about and explained their purpose as they passed.

Power lines. Cars. Fascinating, indeed.

Night had long fallen by the time they approached a house situated on the side of a mountain. Dim light shone through the windows, and a vehicle sat unoccupied in the…driveway, he thought it was called. A few of those cars had passed by during their race here, but Delbin had been concerned by how few. The human world was busy, he'd said. The lack of life was unusual.

They rested for a moment before knocking on the door. Aris wasn't too winded, but Selia panted for air, and Delbin's face was pale and drawn. As they waited, Inona stared into the valley below with a frown on her face. Aris followed her line of sight but wasn't certain what bothered her. Moonlight gleamed on water and hinted at buildings below.

"There's no power," she said.

Delbin stepped to her side. "Damn. I was worried about that when I couldn't get a signal. The energy surge must have fried the cell towers, too, along with the entire power grid. I really, really hope that didn't spread too far."

"Why?" Aris asked. "Is this vital to humans?"

Delbin nodded. "They use electricity for everything. It's like magic contained,

and all of their devices require it. I have no idea how the surge will have affected technology like phones, either. I had this one with me on Moranaia, so it isn't a good indication. But if *everything* is broken, there's going to be panic once everyone figures it out. Chaos."

They'd focused so much on saving Earth from the rift's explosion that they hadn't considered any other effects of that final energy pulse. "Wonderful."

"Maybe the others will know more," Inona said.

The door jerked open before they reached it, and the blood elf stood in the entrance, his eyes a little crazed as he glared at them. "What took you so long?"

"Nice to see you, too, Vek," Delbin quipped.

"Now is not the time. Get in here and help my nephew."

So Naomh hadn't been able to heal Fen. Aris's brow furrowed as he followed the others into the house. A pair of mage lights hovered above, highlighting the unusual dwelling, but his focus was on the young blood elf stretched out on a long, narrow bed on the other end of the room. A red-haired woman with the look of the Sidhe knelt beside him, but Aris detected no energy flowing from her.

He strode across the room, intent on the task at hand, but Naomh leapt to his feet and blocked his path. "Where is my son?"

It took Aris a moment to figure out what the Sidhe lord was asking. "Kai? Back on Moranaia. The healer seems to believe he suffers from shock after using his abilities too much."

"I should go," Naomh said, flicking a glance at Caolte.

His brother nodded. "After you."

As the pair rushed toward the door, Aris continued toward Fen, Selia falling into step beside him. The Sidhe could take care of themselves. He had more important things to worry about—like how he was going to heal the poison inside Fen without Kezari there to help him.

At that thought, her voice broke into his head. *"I have not left you, but I do not have much energy to offer."*

"I'm not certain I can do this," he confessed.

"Nor am I, but not because of your ability." Her faint mental voice was tinged with worry. *"The rift's affliction was not quite the same."*

"I suppose we'll see."

The Sidhe woman glanced up at his approach, and the freckles on her pale face stood out as she studied him. "I hope you can do more than I can. Not that I dare do much."

"I hope so, too."

Aris lowered himself to his knees beside the woman and stretched his hands out over Fen. He closed his eyes, letting himself connect to the ebb and flow of life around them. The blood elf glowed brightly, his power low but impressive, yet the dark blotch hovering near his heart hadn't waned at all. In fact, it might have increased in size.

"Aris." Selia's hand settled on his shoulder. "I have an idea."

He glanced up at her. "Oh?"

"Since Kien had hoped to return to our world, he made certain his first attempt to poison Earth's power would not touch Moranaia. So the spell is vulnerable to Moranaian energy. I helped Arlyn construct the counter." Selia pulled a stone from her pocket. Unlike her typical crystals, this one was round and milky white instead of clear. "I brought this in case it was needed."

"You know I can't use that kind of stone."

She closed her fist around it. "I'll channel the power to you in a form you can utilize."

Aris considered the plan. He wouldn't trust just anyone to perform such a task, since most mages were inexperienced with his talent, but he'd worked with Selia many times. Not quite in this way but close enough. He nodded. "We'll try it."

He let his eyes slip closed as he reached a mental hand for Selia. They joined almost seamlessly, and after he gave his assent, she began to filter energy to him. He grasped it. Tested it. The power had the rich flavor of Moranaia—ancient trees and tall mountains, fertile plains and northern glaciers. He held it close but didn't absorb it, instead letting it merge slightly with his own gift.

Then he turned it toward the poison in Fen's heart.

31

Maddy nibbled on her fingernail before she jerked it free. Stupid habit. But the tension... As the man named Aris poured energy into Fen, Maddy's own heart ached as though she bore the poison. She'd even scanned herself to make sure she hadn't picked it up.

Nope. Just nerves.

Anna scooted closer until she sat a couple of inches from Fen's feet. Unlike Maddy, she made no attempt to stop biting her nails as she watched his face. Why did Anna care so much? Sure, Fen had saved Maddy's life, but it wasn't only that. The urgency riding Maddy lined her girlfriend's face.

Maybe it was because of the growing energy. Attempting to heal Fen had been a nightmare, a struggle to balance the power rising within her like the tide. She'd almost hurt him with her capricious healing magic more times than she would ever let Vek know. She flicked a glance at the Unseelie prince and shuddered.

Yep. Better he remained oblivious.

Suddenly, Fen sucked in a sharp breath, and his body jerked. Maddy lifted up on her knees and placed her hand on his forehead, not caringif it interfered with Aris's work. But it didn't seem to. As Vek leaned over the other side of the couch, a thunderous expression on his face, Fen's eyes popped open.

"What the hell?" he asked, his gaze darting wildly around the room.

"It's okay," Maddy said.

Vek bent closer. "Calm yourself, Fen."

Fen's breathing slowed, and sense returned to his eyes as he focused on their faces. He blinked up at them in confusion. "How did I end up here?"

"You collapsed in the cave," Vek explained. "Don't you remember? We carried you back."

Sucking in a breath, Fen shoved himself upright, almost butting heads with Maddy and forcing Aris back. Fen ran his hand through his hair and swung his legs over the side of the couch. "The rift. We need to go."

"It's over," Aris said, catching Fen's attention. "We fixed it. Sort of. And best I can tell, the poison is gone from you, too."

Maddy scanned Fen for herself. The dark stain over his heart was gone. His energy levels were low but otherwise normal. But… Her brows lowered as she studied him. She didn't detect anything *wrong*, but she wasn't sure he was quite okay, either. Maybe it was her own faulty healing gift.

More likely it was his lack of energy.

Without thinking, she lifted her wrist. "You need blood."

Fen's eyes widened. He stared at her wrist with an intense, hungry look that made her squirm. And not just because she was afraid of being bitten. "I can't believe you offered," he said roughly.

She wrinkled her nose. "I can't either. You need healing, though."

"I think I'll make it," he said, but a slow smile stretched his mouth.

"He'll take from me," Vek interrupted. His cold gaze caught at her until she jerked her arm away. "Fen needs powerful *royal* blood."

Heat rushed into her cheeks at the implication, but she lifted her chin. "Fine."

Fen scowled. "Dammit, Vek—"

"I believe it is time for our guests to depart," the Unseelie prince announced. "You have my thanks for your assistance, but my nephew needs quiet to recover."

Brows lowering, Fen straightened. "You are not locking me in here again."

"Not for long," Vek conceded. "But I will see you healed."

Despite Fen's protests, Maddy was ushered outside with the others in a shorter amount of time than she would have expected. That was…abrupt. What had bothered Vek so much about Maddy offering blood? He'd been fine, if a bit peeved at having guests, before that. Perhaps he'd been offended by her inferior half-Sidhe genes, but that didn't seem right.

"Not even the Unseelie are usually that inhospitable," Inona mumbled as they approached Maddy's car.

"At least I can give you a lift back to the portal," Maddy offered. Then she counted the number of people and sighed. "In two trips, unless we want to break the law."

Delbin settled his hand on the roof of the car. "Think it'll start? We did see a few vehicles, but there are no guarantees."

"Guess we'll find out."

As Anna slid into the passenger seat, Maddy settled behind the steering wheel. Bracing herself for problems, she slid her key into the ignition and turned. Then she let out a long, relieved breath when it sputtered to life. She lowered the window and stuck her head outside.

"Who wants to ride first?" she asked.

Aris and Selia exchanged glances before the woman spoke. "You needn't do that. I can transport us by magic since I know my destination."

Maddy's eyebrows rose. "Really?"

"The Sidhe can do such feats, as well," the woman said, a hint of confusion lining her face.

"In the underhill, maybe. There's not enough energy on..." Maddy's words trailed off as her magic stirred inside her. She stifled it again, just as she'd done while attempting to heal Fen, and chuckled uneasily. "There *wasn't* enough energy on Earth. I guess there is now."

Delbin stepped closer to the window. "You have the mirror, right? Call us if there's a problem. No telling what's going on with the electricity out."

"Yes, I do." Maddy smiled at her friend. "And I will."

The four Moranaian elves slipped away with a wave, and Maddy sat in the driveway long enough to watch the woman build a portal beside the house, out of sight of the road. Beside her, Anna gasped. "That's..."

"I know," Maddy said in awe. "I wonder if either of us could learn to do it."

Anna snorted. "You maybe. I don't even know what I am."

"We'll figure it out." As the elves disappeared, the portal winking out behind them, Maddy backed the car out of the driveway and started toward home. She reached across the console and gathered Anna's hand in hers. "I promise."

Though Lyr had sworn that Iren was in his room, Selia still peeked inside before going to her own. She relaxed to see him curled up on the bed, asleep without even getting under the covers, but then she recalled his earlier trick. Just in case, she tiptoed across the floor and did her best to remain quiet as she ducked down to look under the bed. Nothing that she could see.

Quickly, she scanned the room with her magic. No sign of the cloaks or of anyone hiding. And not only was Iren's breathing steady, but his energy was as well. She should've known to check that last time—and would have, had she not been so distracted. On the way out, she placed a charm on the door that would warn her if he left, much as she had used when he was a toddler.

Then she headed for her room. Aris had gone with Ralan through the new portal to retrieve Kezari, and then he planned to join her. For sleep—at least for now. That was all either of them would be able to do until they recovered.

Selia closed the door behind her and leaned against it, staring at the room she'd inhabited for a couple of months now. Only a few days had passed since Aris's return, but it could have been years. Her mind was jumbled from exhaustion, not to mention passing between day and night so often that not even the sun shining through the window entirely convinced her it was still afternoon. Her world had changed until the mundane seemed foreign.

The chime of her mirror distracted her from her wandering thoughts. Selia hurried to her desk and activated the link, ready to speak with whoever needed her so she could get some sleep. She smiled when Niasen's face filled the screen.

"Hello, sister," Selia said.

"Good day." Niasen returned the smile. "I hope you haven't gone to too much trouble trying to track down father."

Selia's stomach dropped as mortification rushed in. She'd forgotten. How many times had she been to Earth in the span of a day without even a thought for her missing father? Her cheeks heated. "I…no."

"He finally contacted me not long ago," Niasen said. If her sister noticed Selia's embarrassment, she was kind enough not to mention it. "He appeared a bit worn down but urged me not to worry."

Worn down? Selia's forehead wrinkled. "Do you think something happened to him?"

Niasen waved her hand. "No, nothing like that. He said there was difficulty with the energy there that caused him problems. He should be fine."

"Yes, I've heard the same." Experienced it, too, but that was a tale she wasn't sure she should share. "I am happy to hear that father contacted you."

Niasen's eyes narrowed. "Are *you* unwell, Selia?"

"Only drained," she answered honestly. "I've spent too much of my energy of late."

"Oh." Niasen's frown deepened, but she didn't push. "I'll leave you to rest, then."

Selia smiled. "Thank you. I'll contact you again soon."

"Of course."

Once her sister's image dropped from the mirror, Selia let her shoulders slump. Then she trudged over to the bed and dropped face-down across the covers. She would rest her eyes for a moment before she changed clothes. Only a moment.

Kezari's steps were slow, but she walked beside Aris into the gate at Braelyn. The shift to her elven form had been sluggish, and she'd thrown the barest covering over her body before they'd followed the prince through the portal. He'd never seen her look so tired, not even after she'd nursed him back to health after rescuing him.

They exited the front door into the late afternoon light. Her face tipped up toward the sky, and she took a deep breath. "Home."

"After you fought so hard to get to Earth, I half expected you to want to stay there," he teased.

Kezari snorted. "No. I wanted to save the planet, not live on it."

"Fair enough." Aris fell silent as they walked, but he couldn't contain the question for long. "What of our link? Once a full moon cycle has passed, I imagine you will wish to be rid of me. Our task is complete, and I can only bind you here when you could roam free."

She halted, staring at him with head tilted. "You have decided to end our bond?"

A few days before, he would have answered yes to that. Not anymore. "I do not wish to. However, I'm not certain how this works. Do you link only for a specific goal?"

"Some do. Others do not." Kezari lifted a shoulder. "I have grown to like you despite your odd ways. You are quite pleasant when you are sane, and your mate and youngling amuse me."

Aris chuckled. Leave it to Kezari to be so blunt. "Then linked we shall stay. I am considering moving from the observation tower, though, to keep a closer eye on said youngling."

"A solid plan," she said. "I believe it safe for me to sleep in my cave now. In fact, I will likely not emerge for several days while I recover."

"You deserve the rest."

Her lips curled up in an almost-elven smile. "We both do."

He wished her well, then watched as she shifted. Experienced now, he gathered his hair firmly behind his head when she lifted her wings and took off, a gale sweeping around her with the motion. A few green and brown strands still ended up across his face, but they were easy enough to push away.

He had a wife to return to—and a great deal of time to make up for.

Epilogue

Selia and Aris wound their way along the garden path, the soft sound of a flute lilting on the chilly air. She leaned into his side, and he wrapped his arm around her shoulders as they paused to watch the *omree* about to perform. Earlier, they'd cheered on Arlyn at the archery competition, and although her student had only placed fourth, Selia was proud. In a few more years, Arlyn would likely win despite her youth.

Selia had never been to such a large autumn festival, and she could now understand why many traveled from smaller estates to attend. Even Kai's half-brother Moren had joined them for a few marks that morning, a tense event since Moren hadn't met Kai's real father, Naomh, before. Kai had walked around looking confounded for a solid mark after his relatives had departed.

Iren shuffled beside them, a slight pout on his face at the proximity he was required to maintain. When the *omree's* song was over, Selia took pity on him and headed toward the tournament field for the sword-fighting competition. The renowned Kerel Liere nai Ebaia would be performing later, anyway, and Selia would far rather see her than anything else. Being at the Myern's estate while the heir to the throne was in residence had its benefits, for it was rare for Lady Kerel to stray far from the palace itself. According to rumor, she hoped to gain a permanent position as Ralan's lead *omree* once his new home was complete.

As they neared the field, they stumbled upon Ralan, Cora, and Eri. The children exchanged excited greetings and roamed over to the side to chatter. Cora smiled pleasantly, but Ralan frowned as he met Selia's gaze.

"Good day, Lady Selia," the prince said.

She exchanged a look with Aris at the stilted, formal words. "Is something wrong?" she asked.

Ralan winced, clearly growing uncomfortable. "I've been meaning to speak with you."

"But?" she asked, her heart pounding in her ears.

It was rarely a good thing when a seer wanted a word—and then delayed.

"I can't stop thinking about what happened. With the children." Was it her imagination, or had his face reddened? "That Iren encouraged Eri in this scheme makes me worry that playing with him increases her natural recklessness."

"Wait a moment." Selia stalked toward Ralan, sudden anger straightening her spine. "Are you suggesting that Iren was to blame? Eri acts on her own more often than not."

This time, there was no mistaking the prince's flush. "True. But I would expect Iren to resist her plans. He is older. I thought… Perhaps it is best that they don't spend as much time together."

"Don't be an ass," Selia snapped.

Her hand went immediately to her mouth as Aris made a choked sound beside her, but she refused to take the words back. She might have had a similar thought about separating the children when she'd found them in the cave, but that had been in the heat of the moment. No one else would criticize her son so casually.

"Selia," Ralan began.

She didn't give him the chance to finish whatever fool thing he was about to say. "You know as well as I do that Iren wasn't to blame. I am thankful they disobeyed. Both of them. I may not want a repeat, but without their actions, that wall would have shattered before we could get Aris down the fissure. Thousands would have died from the poison."

Unexpectedly, Cora laughed. "Told you."

Ralan's shoulders slumped, and he shoved at the long fall of his black hair. "You're right. But the thought of losing her…"

The anger drained out of Selia at his stark words. "That I understand."

"Thank you." A reluctant smile crossed his lips. "Glad to see you've joined the others in insulting me. I was beginning to think you didn't like me."

"Oh, I did," she said. He lifted his brows. "I do. Your comment about Iren notwithstanding."

Ralan chuckled. "Fair enough. I'll bid you good day, Selia. Enjoy the festival."

Selia shook her head as the prince walked away, his hand around Cora's. Eri waved at Iren and darted after them, and at the sight of the girl, Selia had to admit that she didn't envy Ralan and Cora for having to keep up with her. She wouldn't allow him to insult her child, but she had sympathy aplenty.

Aris settled his hands on Selia's waist and pulled her close. Smiling, she leaned up to kiss the slight cleft in his chin. "This celebration must seem tame after everything that has happened."

He grinned. "Not after seeing you tell off a prince. I'm proud of you."

"Shut up and kiss me," Selia said.

Aris bent down and captured her lips with his. Her heart soared, and in that moment, the past fell away.

Her world was right once more.

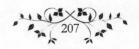

Awakening

Character Pronunciation Guide

Awakening

Main Characters:

Vek (vehk)
Dria (DREE-uh)

Secondary Characters:

Arafel (ehr-AH-fehl)
Fedah (fay-duh)
Gessen (GEHS-ehn)
Kethen (KETH-ehn)
Meren (MEHR-ehn)
Ralan (RAHL-ehn)
Retha (RETH-uh)
Quaea (QUAE-uh)
Torek (TOR-ehk)

1

As soon as Dria stepped through the portal, guards surrounded her. Gods, she hated being home. She forced her fingers to remain lax, though they wanted to curl around a fireball she could lob at the *drec* around her. She'd spent too many years during her youth dodging the *loreln*, bodyguards turned spies. They'd reported her every deed to her father, and at least one of them had shared information with those at court who'd loved to mock and torment her. Now when she left the palace for the Citadel where she trained, she dismissed the *loreln* upon arrival. Little was likely to happen to her there, the stronghold of the highest-ranking battle mages. But in the palace? Safety here was sadly less certain after the dark deeds of her brother Kien.

A great deal was less certain after Kien.

Head high, Dria gritted her teeth and ignored the trailing bodyguards as she strode into the vast entryway that led to the throne room. Clusters of nobles gathered in gossiping knots down the entire expanse, waiting for her father to begin receiving petitions, but she ignored them, too. It was safer that way. If one of them taunted her now, she'd zap them with a bolt of lightning, and then there'd be an uproar. Again.

Voices cut off mid-sentence as she passed, only to swell into frenzied whispers at her back. No change there. Yes, it was better not to listen, something she had learned during her teen years. There was no peace for a princess whose brothers had created the greatest court scandal in millennia. She might have few friends at the Citadel, but at least no one there treated her with suspicion or scorn.

Not anymore.

Why had her father summoned her? There would be no funeral rites for the disgraced Kien, and Teyark, her oldest brother, had bonded quietly and without ceremony months before. Perhaps the king was planning some fete for Ralan, her third and last brother. Everyone was surely thrilled by his return from his three-hundred-year snit on Earth.

Everyone but her. She had no desire to see Ralan, now or possibly ever.

As Dria ascended the pair of steps leading to the double doors, she gave no indication that she saw the nobles who shuffled off the tiny landing between her and her destination. Only the weak or the desperate waited on the platform right by the entrance. Those wanting to appear important pretended carelessness in the long hall behind her.

A pair of guards stood in front of the doors. Neyes and…someone new? The woman seemed familiar, but it didn't matter. Why bother learning her name? With luck, Dria would be gone within a mark's time. She barely resisted tapping her foot as Neyes pushed one of the great doors open.

As soon as she could manage without appearing hurried, Dria strode through the gap. Her steps slowed as she entered the throne room, but a quick glance revealed that her father wasn't there. The room was empty, and the tables from the morning meal had been cleared away despite the early hour.

She sent out a tendril of energy and found her father was in his study. She headed toward the door in the corner, but a hint of something off—something dark—brought her to a halt. Frowning, she swept her energy out in a more detailed scan. A chill trickled through her at the echo of death magic, the barest hint that someone less familiar with the place, and someone less skilled, might miss. Strongest in one spot…there.

Dria glanced down at the place her magic had carried her, and the ice inside her grew. In the smooth floor, a single flaw stood out. A chip in the stone.

The place where Kien had been beheaded by their father.

"*Feraien?*" one of the *loreln* whispered softly from behind her.

Dria stiffened, hating the title but unable to refute it. Until she worked her way up the ranks at the Citadel, "daughter of the king" was the best she was going to get. But it was a good reminder. Her older brother's death—and life—had marked their family, but she didn't have to let it rule her future. She would meet with her father quickly and return to her work.

If she worked hard, she might be promoted to third-in-command of her mage group within the next decade.

"I'm going," Dria said as she resumed her march toward the door in the back corner.

Let the *loreln* believe her to be rude and haughty. Everyone else here did, and she'd grown to appreciate the benefits of that opinion. They might whisper about her, it was true, but now that she was an adult who'd passed her mage test with ease, they also tended to leave her alone so long as she ignored them.

Dria entered the study without bothering to knock. Her father would have sensed the surge of power from the portal, and the guards would have notified him that she was here, particularly since she was late already. Sure enough, he was in the process of standing as the door closed behind her, leaving the *loreln* in the throne room. Her brows rose as she glanced around, confirming what her magic scan had already told her.

They were alone.

This must be something momentous if neither Teyark nor her mother were present. Enielle hated to miss anything concerning her children, and Teyark often acted as their father's assistant despite no longer being heir. The king's posture held a defensive, uncomfortable edge, but that wasn't new. He hadn't quite known what to do with her for centuries.

Dria stopped on the other side of his desk. The broad expanse of wood wasn't the only thing separating them, but it was easier to consider than the three hundred years of missed holidays and forgotten mirror communications. Not that it mattered. The father who had carried her on his shoulders around the throne room was long gone.

She inclined her head in a formal gesture and then waited as they studied each other in silence. The lines around King Alianar's eyes had deepened, and his once-black hair was now mostly gray. Her heart lurched at the change despite her less-than-charitable thoughts. The toll of grief hadn't been as obvious when they'd spoken through the mirror.

Or was it more than grief? Had anything else happened to effect such rapid change? Perhaps she *should* come home more often.

"Good morning, Dria," her father said tersely. "I am gratified that you have finally deigned to answer my summons."

She drew her shoulders back. "I had a mission to complete."

"According to Lady Fenae, you were reinforcing the cooling spell set into a minor lord's cellar. Hardly life or death, and not something you are suited to, besides."

He had her there. She'd hated that mission, which had taken her away from her combat practice, but they weren't exactly at war. Sometimes her group ended up doing less…urgent tasks. Work was work.

"Fire might be one of my strongest elements, but that doesn't mean I can't use others. I do have a little proficiency with water," she said. "And the task was important. The food stores were at risk, and if you must know—"

"Dria." Alianar sighed, and a touch of sadness darkened his expression. "I did not ask you here to start an argument, nor did I mean to insult what you do. However, it is obvious that you were avoiding me. We both know that the rest of your troop could have handled the task."

"You have been content to ignore me since my eighteenth birthday." Dria's nostrils flared at the memory of that ill-fated day. She'd expected a celebration. Instead, she'd been sent off to the Citadel. "I didn't think you would mind a delay."

"I made more than one mistake after Ralan fled and Kien's insanity was discovered. I should have believed Ralan when he told me that Kien was planning to murder him. I might have prevented years of grief for many." The king averted his gaze. "And I shouldn't have sent you away. I thought it best, considering how you were being treated, but if I could go back…"

"Save it," she snapped, though his words caught her by surprise. But, no. She would not settle her emotions on his favor again. "Just tell me why you wanted to meet with me so I can be gone."

Her father ran his hand through his hair in an uncharacteristic show of agitation. Uneasiness climbed her throat like bile, but she ignored it. He deserved to be upset by the past. And perhaps he agreed, for he didn't push the point.

"I have a mission for you," he finally said.

Dria's forehead wrinkled. That was the last thing she'd expected. "Excuse me?"

"You might have heard rumors that Ralan is constructing a secondary palace near the portal to the Veil, though few know the reasons why." The king's lips twisted. "I'll leave it to him to explain the bulk of it. Suffice it to say that there was a major incident on Earth two weeks ago."

Earth? Yes, she'd heard rumors, and some of them had concerned that distant world. Her friend Gessen had told her the bulk of the stories, since most avoided speaking about her family in her presence. According to the whispers, Kien had released some type of poison into the energy field—the vital well of power from which elves and other races of fae drew their magic. Some had heard that the poison was gone, but others contested that the palace was being built to deal with the situation.

But no one had mentioned an event two weeks ago.

"I've heard nothing reliable," she said. "What does it have to do with me?"

Her father gripped the edge of his desk and leaned forward. "A new portal was created, Dria. A direct gate between Earth and Moranaia, no Veil involved. In the process, one of our citizens and his dragon companion created a cavern system capable of holding a small outpost of guards. Between that and the new palace, we should be able to protect the portal."

"Dragon compan—no, never mind." If what her father said was true, dragons were the least of their problems. The Veil acted as a safeguard for their world, as those unable to navigate the relentless, endless mists would wander forever without finding their way to Moranaia. "A direct portal could be dangerous. I can see why you'd need guards, though I can't imagine the humans are thrilled with a fae settlement. I thought they didn't even believe in our kind."

His expression hardened. "The humans don't know. They can't know, regardless of what they believe. And that's where you come in."

Dria lifted her brows. "Me?"

"I need a mage who can set up the proper shielding and provide protection, and it needs to be someone I can trust."

She wanted to laugh. He'd spent too little time with her to be certain of her loyalties, so his claim of trust seemed foolhardy. Even if he was right—she wouldn't betray her people or her family—he had no solid reason to be positive of that. Besides, she was far from experienced enough for this kind of task, and there were plenty of trustworthy mages in his service.

"The best mages in the realm are at the Citadel," Dria said. "Including the Ogefa of the Taian branch, the Mage General. And you're going to assign this to me? I've only been out of training for a little under a century, and I've barely moved my way up the ranks of my own troop. If you think giving me a task like this will go over well, you've lost your mind."

"*Miaran,* Dria," her father cursed, his fingers going white on the edge of his desk. "I have to have someone I know will not talk. A single step can take us between worlds. Most are content here, but we both know our people are far from perfect. If anyone unscrupulous should hear of this before we protect it, they could create havoc on Earth. My own son—"

The king's lips pressed closed, but Dria didn't have to guess what he was thinking. Kien would have been the first to use the portal for evil. "Beyond that danger, you are still a member of the royal family," her father finally continued. "Your word holds more weight than even the Ogefa."

Her fists clenched. "No one would accept me as a leader at my age."

"You won't have to be in charge." Alianar shrugged. "Ralan is the nominal leader in my place. You have only to direct the mages if needed."

Ralan. *Of course* her other brother would be presiding over this potential disaster. Messing up her life once clearly wasn't enough for him. "Do I have a choice?"

The king sighed again, and she had to give him credit for looking regretful. "Not this time, Dria. Not this time."

Huddled in the corner of the booth, Vek spun the beer bottle absently between his fingers and glared at his nephew as he wove his way through the crowd, a tray balanced in his hands. *Be social,* Fen had said. *Learn to integrate.* Vek snorted. As though he would ever manage either of those things in a human eating establishment. He'd received a fair number of wary glances since the moment they'd arrived. It was an inevitable reaction to his predator's energy.

His nephew plunked the tray down on the table and slid into his place on the other side of the booth. A mischievous glint in his light blue eyes, Fen gestured toward a plate containing a pile of food in various shades of brown. "Chicken tenders and fries, Your Highness."

"Shove off," Vek muttered out of habit as he took his plate, but he couldn't get too angry at his nephew's sarcastic tone. They definitely shared a sense of humor.

The thick, breaded slices seemed most likely to be chicken. Vek lifted a piece and sniffed. A hint of pepper, but mostly bland. Ah well. He'd eaten worse. Shrugging, he took a bite, and…damn, it was actually good. He downed the whole piece before realizing that Fen was staring at him. Silently laughing, too, the ass.

"This world has its—"

"City," Fen interrupted, shooting a pointed look at the full table not too far from their booth. "Or town. Your English is slipping."

Vek's lips twitched. "Indeed. Sorry. This *city* has its advantages."

"This is why you need to get out more." Fen lifted his burger from his plate. "I mean, we've made a good start on the tan, but you'll enjoy your vacation more if you explore. Meet people."

Vacation, huh? It hadn't even been two weeks since the wall withholding most of Earth's energy had failed, releasing magic back into the world, but the effects were making themselves increasingly known. It was no pleasure for Vek to wander the human city of Chattanooga in search of those whose power was finally awakening. Well, he'd been looking for Unseelie descendants, at least. He had no interest in the trouble any other races might experience.

"I have become acquainted with three already," Vek said in a low voice. "But there was no need to form a friendship."

Thankfully. The three with latent Unseelie blood had been powerless enough that he had no cause for concern. None of them would be strong enough to do much more than light a candle with their new magic, provided they figured out how. If they felt an uncomfortable hum in the blood from the growing energy, that wasn't his problem, either.

So far, the awakening he'd worried about was a terrible disappointment—or it would be if he *wanted* humans performing magic. The increased energy had done little except create random blackouts and other technological failures around the globe, a phenomenon that human scientists were struggling to explain.

Oh, and it had empowered the fae who did know how to use magic. So far, they'd been smart enough to stay out of his way.

"Yo, Vek, the ladies by the bar are checking you out."

Why had he agreed to let his nephew stay with him? Not only would the Unseelie king be furious when he found out, but Fen was perpetually annoying. "So? Human women either stare or run, and I'm not in the mood to enjoy either."

Fen chuckled. "Not searching for love, then?"

"Absolutely not," Vek snapped. "I can find lovers whenever I wish, but I have no desire for love or mate bonds. Especially not with a human."

Fen lifted a brow. "I said they were checking you out, not putting on wedding dresses."

"Do I look like I have time for sex?" Vek waved his hand, and he scowled harder when his nephew smirked. But he could shut Fen up. "Besides, I'm babysitting. Were you older and not related to me, perhaps we could share. Alas, there are some kinks not even I enjoy."

That wiped away much of Fen's smug expression. "I'm twenty-three. A bit beyond babysitting age. And I never suggested sharing."

Was it the lighting, or had Fen's face reddened? Thanks to his half-human heritage, Fen wasn't quite as pale as Vek, but his blush showed just as spectacularly. "Have I embarrassed you, nephew?"

"It would serve you right if they were about to ambush you into a wedding," Fen muttered. "Maybe if you got married, you'd mellow out. Be less of an asshole."

Vek snorted. "Not likely."

The last thing Vek wanted to do was bring a mate into his life. He lived on the edge, never certain of his father's whims or the machinations of his power-hungry relatives, and it would not be fair to ask a woman to weather the maelstrom. The Unseelie Court was a brutal place for the weak and the unprepared. Besides, the desire to take blood from one's mate was strong for a *Felshreh*, and Vek's unique ability would make that...complicated.

And he doubted anything would improve his disposition.

Overhead, the lights flickered. A woman's yelp sounded from the bar area, and one of the men at the nearby table laughed nervously. "Gotta love those solar flares, right?" the human ventured.

Vek frowned. He hadn't detected a fluctuation in the energy fields, the true reason that electronic devices had become less reliable. Most people appeared to blame solar activity like Earth's scientists, but... A scan of the room revealed more than one uneasy glance being exchanged.

As the tart smell of fear hit his nose, Vek pushed his plate away and leaned back. "Sense anything?" he asked Fen, careful to keep his voice low.

His nephew shook his head. "Nope."

"Perhaps we should take a walk," Vek said carefully, hoping his tone would convey meaning. "Do some...sightseeing."

With a sigh, Fen dropped his half-eaten burger. "Probably."

Vek slid across the cracked leather seat, only to freeze when the electricity cut off with a soft pop and distant whine. He blinked, his eyes adjusting rapidly to the darkness. Beside them, the people at the closest table murmured amongst themselves, fear lifting their voices more with each passing moment.

"This ain't no solar storm," a human muttered. "Has to be a cyberattack."

The woman beside him shoved at his shoulder. "You're not reading conspiracy theories again, are you? The Earth is round, aliens aren't—"

"I know the Earth's not flat, and I don't care about aliens." The man's voice grew louder. "Y'all know this ain't normal."

Vek scanned the human with his magic. The man had fae blood, enough that it might bloom into something useful if he learned how to tap into it, but he wasn't Unseelie. Therefore? No one of consequence.

Dismissing the human from his thoughts, Vek braced his hand on the table to push himself out of the ancient booth. But before he could rise, two figures filled the space at the end of the seat. He glanced up, cursing to himself as soon as he recognized them.

"Quaea. Kethen," Vek said, keeping his expression as blank as possible. Quaea's presence he understood, as she was his father's preferred messenger, but not his cousin Kethen, who was in mourning. Were they here about Fen? "An interesting place to meet you."

"Not so." Kethen's shadowed gaze fastened on his face, his normal friendliness

absent. But of course, he hadn't acted quite the same since Kien's energy poisoning claimed his son's life. That death had resulted in the king ordering Vek to capture Fen, a sentence Vek hadn't *quite* carried out. "We were searching for you. Your father requests your presence."

Request? Hah. But at least they hadn't mentioned his nephew. If Vek didn't make a fuss, they might ignore Fen entirely. Seeming to sense what was at stake, Fen shrank into the shadows of the booth.

"He will tolerate no delay," Quaea added, her hand slipping to the hilt of her knife.

Vek gave a sharp nod, though inside, he seethed. "Of course."

2

Dria slammed the lid of her trunk closed without a care for the noise. Her displeasure was hardly a secret, unlike the scope of her mission. All her fellow mages knew was that the king had ordered her to work with her brother in the construction of the new palace. As far as she could tell, not even the Ogefa had been told the truth of the assignment.

With a huff, Dria spun away from the trunk to scan her room. No sign of her time here remained, save the still-rumpled covers on the bed. Such an infernal load of *drec* that she had to leave. Her gaze caught on the window, and she walked over to take in the view one last time before she had to depart. Better than staring at her barren room.

Tall grass waved as far as the eye could see, only the occasional golden stone building or odd tree interrupting the view. Gods, she was going to miss this. She'd fallen in love with the plains almost at once, and for a time, the rippling grass had been her only friend. The others had been hesitant about the princess in their midst. The whispers that had surrounded her family so soon after Kien's exile had only made it worse.

Even after three centuries, many of her colleagues were polite but distant. Did they still fear she'd turn out to be a homicidal criminal like her brother? Usually, she preferred to confront problems head on. In this case, though, she'd held back. Tangling with the others would prevent her from advancing up the ranks.

At a soft knock, Dria turned. "Enter."

Gessen slipped through the door, his familiar face pinched with worry. "Dree, are you unwell? You were supposed to meet me at the portal almost half a mark ago."

"Sorry," she said, a slight smile breaking free. With a flick of power, Dria levitated her trunk in front of her and started forward. "I must have lost track of time."

Though he quirked an eyebrow in disbelief, Gessen held the door open without comment as she crossed into the hallway. As usual, the quiet didn't last long. "I know there's something you're not telling me."

"Good guess, Gess," Dria answered with a smirk at the customary joke. "Truthfully, there's a great deal I can't tell you and even more that I don't know myself. *Ralan* is supposed to give me more details."

Gessen frowned, clearly not missing the bitterness in her tone. "Are you really that angry with your brother after all these years?"

"He broke his promise to me, and that's just the beginning." Her hands clenched. "Do you know he hasn't even contacted me since he returned to Moranaia? Even Teyark, busy as he tends to be, has made the effort to keep in touch. But the brother who'd claimed to be my best friend? No."

"That's—"

"I don't want to talk about him anymore. It will only make me angrier." They turned a corner in the sprawling complex, and she spent more time than strictly necessary ensuring that her trunk was situated properly. Anything for a distraction. "Any idea who the Ogefa will appoint to replace me?"

At his silence, Dria glanced his way. He winced—actually winced—as he answered. "Maybe...maybe me."

"Gess, that's wonderful!" A hint of happiness lightened her dark mood. "Did you think I would be upset? You've been hoping to find an opening for a year. If I can't be here, I'd rather my place in the troop be taken by a friend."

The tension eased from his expression. "Thanks."

After a few more steps, Dria directed her trunk through an archway and into the small portal chamber beyond. The Ogefa had wanted to send her to Braelyn through the formal gate situated by Eafere, the sacred tree of the deity Ea, but Dria had refused. She might be a princess, but she didn't need or want a send-off fit for royalty. She'd quietly bid farewell to Eafere and said a prayer to Ea, They of the Elements, before packing her things.

As the gate attendant activated the link, Dria turned to give Gessen a quick hug. He returned the embrace but let her go when she pushed back. "I don't know if my father will allow me to return to the Citadel or not," she said softly. "Perhaps the mage division of the army will have to do without me."

Gessen squeezed her upper arm. Gods, she was going to miss him. Only with him could she be herself and not what everyone expected her to be. "Let us hope not. You'll try to let me know when you arrive safely?"

"Yes," she answered. This time, her smile felt hollow. "Goodbye, Gess."

"Until next time."

Dria didn't bother to refute him, despite the sick feeling in her stomach that whispered that there wouldn't be a next time. She might not be a seer like her brother, but she knew when change was coming. And this had the taste of something monumental.

With a wave for Gessen, Dria directed her trunk through the portal and followed.

No use delaying the inevitable.

The cool dimness of the underhill both soothed and irritated Vek's skin as he followed Kethen and Quaea from the portal antechamber into the main hall of the palace. He'd been raised in the city at the base of the castle, not here, but the sameness of the environment gave comfort. Still, he'd grown accustomed to the heat and power of the sun, much superior to the massive crystal casting its dim light from the top of the cave.

No petitioners lined the hall to the throne room, a foreboding sign. The king was either dangerously furious or planning something he didn't want overheard. If Vek had to gamble, he'd pick both. It was probably why the king hadn't summoned him immediately after the wall restricting Earth's energy had shattered. Considering the Unseelie had worked with the dragons to seal away that energy thousands of years ago, the king's silence on the matter had been ominous.

At least Vek had made it out of the restaurant without either messenger noticing Fen, or he would have been dragged here, too. A fine mess *that* would have been, and a waste of months of strategizing, besides. Vek had fought hard to keep his nephew alive, and if the king found out that he'd helped Fen instead of delivering his death sentence, there'd be trouble. When it came to revelations like that, timing was everything.

A point that was all too clear as he eyed his cousin. Kethen's son Dereck had only been forty-seven when he'd fallen victim to the energy poisoning. The lad had tried to pull in power from one of the most afflicted areas, and the results had been disastrous. If Kethen knew that Vek hadn't killed Fen, he would be furious. But there was far more to Fen's actions than Kethen understood, information that Vek would share when the time was right.

"My kindest regards to your mate," Vek said in a low voice to Kethen. He might not want to tell his cousin the truth about Fen, but he still had great respect for his normally genial cousin. "And Divine be with you both."

"And with you," Kethen murmured.

"If you're quite finished?" Quaea opened the door to the throne room and, sneering, gestured Vek inside. He smiled at her as he passed, but it wasn't out of friendliness or pleasure. It was a promise. Though he had accompanied them willingly, mostly to keep Fen clear of Kethen's regard, they all knew Quaea would have forced him—or at least tried. And he would pay her back for her temerity one day.

Even if it took centuries to get around to it.

Both Quaea and Kethen remained outside as the door closed at his back. Without hesitation, Vek strode down the long purple carpet up to the dais where his father and his sister waited, their faces impassive as they stared down from their seats. *Slelen,* he cursed. If Ara was here, there was a good chance this was about Fen, after all. His sister periodically tried to claim parental rights, though she'd forfeited them before her baby's first cry had finished echoing.

At the foot of the dais, Vek knelt, but as a royal son, he kept his gaze on his father. It was easy to see their relation, since he had inherited the king's pale coloring. But his father wore his white hair long, the strands twisted into elaborate designs to suit his moods. The pattern was curiously sedate today considering the volatility Vek had expected from this meeting.

"I'm told you requested my presence, my liege?"

"Stand, Vekenayeth anh Torekthayed," the king intoned.

Vek complied, though he was careful to keep his posture on the relaxed side of formal. His father would pounce on any sign of tension or weakness. "Thank you for the honor."

And it *was* an honor that the king didn't leave him kneeling during the audience. Unusual. What was he planning?

"I appreciate your quick compliance to my request for your attendance," King Torek said, a slight smile crossing his pale lips. "It has been too long since I have seen you, my son."

Vek barely resisted the urge to point out that it had only been a couple of months. "Indeed."

"Your mother fares well?"

Damn him, why was his father asking that? The man had barely given Retha a moment's regard in millennia, and Vek had had to be circumspect about his closeness to her to keep it that way. "She is, my king. She and my stepfather will soon welcome their fourth child."

"Stepfather?" King Torek's lips tightened. "I didn't realize you were so close."

Shit.

"Not at all," Vek answered, hoping his tone revealed nothing. "I fear I have spent too long around humans of late and have adopted some of their strange classifications. It did seem a concise word to describe the unrelated husband of one's mother."

The explanation seemed to work, for the king's expression turned mild once more. "I suppose. Now, I imagine you expected me to demand an explanation, not to mention a bit of your blood, over the collapse of the wall our people helped build so long ago."

Vek nodded. "I confess that I did."

A hint of slyness entered his father's gaze. "I considered it. Not only did you ignore my directive to bring my grandson, Fen, here for judgment, but you allowed a group of Moranaians and a dragon to shatter a shield that prevented humans from accessing the bulk of Earth's magic. Now here we are, half-bloods stirring and Moranaia gaining power. Of course, if young Fen had not aided Prince Kien of Moranaia in damaging that magic, much of this might have been prevented. Interesting that you haven't presented my grandson for his punishment yet."

This…did not bode well, not with his father's apparent calm. Perhaps Kethen's role as messenger had been intended as a pointed statement. "My nephew helped defeat Kien and clean up his mess before I captured him. I held him in my home, but Fen had been injured in the conflict with Kien. I thought it best not to bring sickness here, so he remains my prisoner."

Had his father flinched? Vek peered at the king, but Ara's deceptively sweet voice broke his concentration. "I do hope my son is doing better."

"I believe he is completely recovered, but I was waiting a few days longer to be sure," Vek said, though he wanted to strangle his sister where she sat. Not for a moment did he believe that the concern lining her face was authentic. "I would have consulted the king within the week."

He wouldn't have brought Fen for punishment, nor had he confined his nephew on the king's behalf. But they didn't need to know that. Vek had always been loyal to his father—in his own way—but he was no fool.

"I should like to meet him," Ara said.

"Really?" Vek lifted a brow. "You've said quite the opposite for years."

Ara leaned forward. "I've heard rumors that he is a *Felshreh*. I hadn't thought it possible with his high percentage of human blood, but a son with our rare talent? You must bring him home, of course."

Gods above and below, his sister truly was vile. She'd known that Fen was a blood elf from the moment of his birth but had still cast him aside on Earth without regard for his well-being. She wanted something, and it wasn't a relationship with her son. But he had no time to uncover her current scheme.

"That will be up to our lord father to decide," Vek said, returning his attention to the king. "I would request to know if my nephew is to be treated as family and released from his punishment or if he is to be brought here a prisoner."

"I will grant him his freedom." King Torek smiled. "Provided he agrees to submit himself to your authority and tutelage. Ensure that he knows his place and can fit into our culture."

Relief and dread coursed through Vek in equal measure. It could have been far, far worse, but there was no guarantee that Fen would agree. "I will try, my liege."

"See that you do," his father said. But before Vek could request dismissal, the king's grin turned sly. "Oh, and I have one other task you must complete."

Not good. "Yes, lord father?"

"Kill the leader of this new Moranaian colony and wrest back the power they have stolen." The king's eyes narrowed. "And do it carefully, or you'll find more than one family member in peril."

Vek swallowed hard. So that was why the king had mentioned Vek's mother. "You want me to kill a high ranking Moranaian? We are not currently at war with their people, and I have heard no rumors any serious misdeeds."

King Torek's breath hissed out, and magic rippled around him, distorting his face for a heartbeat's time. "You question my orders?"

"I merely wanted clarification," Vek was quick to say. If his father was losing control of the shields he layered around himself, his mood was less stable than Vek had thought. "I had not heard of any stolen power and wanted to understand the ramifications. Their crime must be severe to court war with them."

"When they shattered the wall, they hoarded a large amount of the stored power for themselves." Resolve and fury lit the king's pale eyes. "You will return that energy to my control and ensure that the Moranaians pay for their crime. Do not skirt this duty, or many will suffer for it. Now go."

Vek bowed low and spun away to comply, though inside he seethed.

Yep. Not good at all.

Although Dria had feared a large group would be on the other side of the portal to greet her, only four people waited. Ralan, of course, but also a dark-haired woman, a child, and another man wearing the circlet of the Myern. Well, and a pair of guards on each side of the portal archway, but with all the rumors that had swirled about upheaval at Braelyn, that wasn't a surprise.

Her brother took a deep breath as though bracing himself and stepped forward. "It is good to see you, Dree. It is difficult to believe you're old enough to be out of training. Last time I—" His words cut off as he studied her. "What have you done with your hair?"

Resisting the urge to brush a dark red strand behind her ear, Dria lifted a brow. "What have you done with your manners?"

The woman snorted, and the Myern's lips twitched. Ralan had the grace to wince, at least, as the child giggled. "Forgive me," her brother said. "We've always shared the same hair color, so..."

"It was one of the first modifications I learned during my training," Dria said with a shrug. He didn't need to know that the switch from black to red had been intentional, a way to separate herself from her brothers. "I don't suppose you will introduce those who have been so kind as to greet me?"

"Of course. May I present—" The little girl darted forward, and Ralan muttered an oath she probably wasn't supposed to hear. "Eri, you promised to behave."

Dria braced for impact just in time as Eri launched herself against her, wrapping her small arms around Dria's waist. Stunned, she glanced down at the child hugging her with surprising strength. Who was she, and why was she reacting to Dria so strongly? Then Eri met Dria's eyes, and she knew. Few outside the royal family possessed irises in that shade of gold.

"This is Erinalia," Ralan said gruffly. "My daughter. Seems pointless to provide her full title while she's wrapped around you like a vine."

Gods. This sweet little girl was her niece. Thanks to a decree the king had made based on their aunt's prophecy, the first of his children to produce offspring was the official heir. Since Ralan had replaced Teyark in that role, it had been obvious that he'd returned from Earth with a child. But Dria had avoided any more details.

"It is a pleasure to meet you," Dria said, patting the child's back awkwardly.

But the girl didn't appear bothered by Dria's uncertainty. "I was hoping it wouldn't be much longer before I met you. If you had—"

"Enough, Eri," Ralan said. "Leave your aunt alone so I can complete the introductions."

Dria frowned. Her brother's tone had been sharper than necessary. What harm could one little girl cause? "Children are never a disruption."

The Myern stifled a cough behind his hand, and Ralan groaned. Taken aback by the odd reaction, Dria barely noticed when the girl darted to her father's side. Ralan had lived on Earth for a few centuries, so his poor manners made sense. But the Myern? Clearly, her brother was a bad influence.

Ralan shook his head, but he didn't bother to explain his behavior. Instead, he launched directly into the introductions. The woman's name was Cora, and apparently, she was her brother's soulbonded, though not the mother of the child. And Dria found she had been correct—the other man was the Myern of Braelyn.

"Thank you for hosting me in your home, Lord Lyrnis," Dria said politely. "Despite the brevity of my visit."

"Please, call me Lyr," the Myern said. "Our acquaintance might not be as brief as you assume if recent events are anything to go by."

That sounded problematic. Dria resisted the urge to shuffle her feet. "I assume I am only passing through. Setting up the shielding on the new colony is high priority, so I'd intended to go there directly."

The Myern shot Ralan a look, but her brother only shrugged. "Sort of true," Ralan said. "But the expedition leaves tomorrow, not right now. You'll go with the warriors Lyr has loaned me for the initial settlement."

A night spent near her brother? She would never be able to keep up the guise of civility for that long. "I mean no slight, for I am certain the Myern's hospitality is excellent, but I would rather go now. It will be easier to place the groundwork for the shielding when there are few others present to interfere with the energy."

"It may not be safe," Ralan argued. "There are only a handful of guards in place to prevent incursion on the portal. You would be virtually alone."

Pulling her shoulders back, Dria caught her brother's gaze and held it. "I'm a battle mage here under the king's command. Take me to the colony."

3

Vek leaned against the corner of his house and stared down at the city of Chattanooga nestled in the valley below. Inside, Fen played one of his video games—if Vek stretched his senses, he could hear the details of the cut-scene currently interrupting the action. A role-playing game, his nephew had called it. He spent hours killing fake monsters and rescuing artificial women. As if there wasn't enough mayhem in the real world.

His senses tingled as a wave of energy swept through him. A few moments later, the electricity wavered, and Fen's curse echoed through the wall as his game cut off. Despite the situation, Vek chuckled. *Hope he's saved recently.*

Vek needed to face Fen and explain the situation, but he couldn't. Not until he decided what to do. He had never outright defied the king, though he'd done his fair share of skirting the rules. But this? This was a tangled web he might not be able to unsnarl. The leader of the Moranaian colony would either be Ralan, a prince of Moranaia, or Aris, the man who'd subverted part of the wall holding back Earth's energy into something else—though what, Vek hadn't yet been able to divine.

And Vek owed a debt to both men.

Ralan had spared Fen even though his nephew had helped poison Earth's energy field, and Aris had healed the wound Fen had sustained while atoning for that error. Saving his nephew's life was a blood debt, and Vek never failed to repay those. There was no way he could bring himself to kill Ralan or Aris.

Aside from that, they'd acted in no way against the Unseelie. On the rare times Vek had used his talents against another on behalf of the king, it had been to prevent harm to his own people. He gained new abilities through taking others' blood, though there were limits. But if he wished, he could steal the darkest, most wicked magic and turn it to his own use. Vek refused to wield such a dangerous ability lightly—and never against allies.

But perhaps "allies" was a stretch when it came to the Moranaians.

They *had* destroyed the barrier restraining the bulk of Earth's magical energy, a necessary safeguard. Once ancient humans had learned to use magic, they'd torn their societies apart with power so intense it still echoed in their myths. If Vek's ancestors and the dragons hadn't stopped them, they would eventually have annihilated their entire race. The Moranaians had disregarded that protection recklessly.

But they were all about to learn if modern human society was more capable of handling the magic that had exploded into their world. It was only a matter of time until people began to use that power openly, and if they couldn't cope with that new truth, there would be panic and discord. Many of the fae races might suffer, including the Unseelie, and the wise would hasten to prepare. His father was right to be concerned about the results of the Moranaians' hasty actions.

Even so, not even Vek had expected an assassination order over the matter.

Behind him, the door clicked open. "Are you going to stop brooding and get your ass in here?"

Vek allowed himself a brief smile where his nephew couldn't see. Fen was getting better at detecting those of his bloodline. Good. But he hid his satisfaction before he turned. "How much progress did you lose?"

"It wouldn't let me save after the boss battle," Fen grumbled. "We'll see if there was an autosave after the power is back on. Seriously, though, what are you doing out here? Was the meeting that bad?"

Only when he'd brushed past his nephew and closed the door behind them, sealing the protective shielding on the house, did Vek speak. "It is wise not to discuss such business out in the open."

Fen waved a hand, and the mage lights lining the walls brightened, dispelling the gloom. "Fine. We're out of the open. Now tell me what happened. Are you supposed to take me back for execution or something?"

Vek strolled over to the large, L-shaped couch on the other side of the room and sat. "Not yet. If you cooperate."

"If I…" Eyebrows raised, Fen stared at him. "What else could I possibly do? I've tried my best to fix all of my mistakes."

Vek draped his arm over the back of the couch. "Well, if you want to be pardoned by the king, you'll have to work with me. Become my student and learn our ways."

Fen went so long without blinking that Vek feared he'd expired from shock. "Does that mean I would be accepted at court as one of your people? My people?"

"An eventual possibility."

"That's—"

"Not as great as you're imagining," Vek interjected. "Don't think of this with a child's hope when you make this decision. If your mother accepts you, it will be for her own agenda, and our way of life is not easy or pleasant."

Fen's lips twisted wryly. "I used to work for a guy who turned out to be a depraved torturer. You might like to appear dark and mysterious, but you're not evil."

"You've been around humans too long." Vek tried to tamp down the anger that association always caused, but he could tell from Fen's expression that he wasn't en-

tirely successful. "The Unseelie aren't evil, at least no more than any other race. But there are things that must be done in the darkness. We take that on and are villainized for it. Do you think anyone was grateful when we worked with the dragons to wall off so much of Earth's energy? No. But it was necessary to stop countless wars."

Fen lifted his hands. "Okay, okay. Sorry."

"What I meant was that other fae races will look at you differently, seeing only that you linger in the dark and missing the reason why. Your—" Mates, Vek almost said, but he stopped himself in time. Some things Fen had to discover on his own. Maddy and Anna were as young and unprepared as Fen, so hopefully it wouldn't be anytime soon. "You must learn to accept that."

Fen fell silent as he considered those words. "It wouldn't be much different," he finally said, his voice soft. "I'll always be remembered for my mistake in working with Kien. Might as well be true to myself in the process."

"Good." Vek leaned forward, resting his forearms on his knees. "Your first mission? Drive me over to the cave where the wall cracked. We need to figure out what the Moranaians are up to."

Though Ralan kept frowning at her over his shoulder, he led Dria through the portal to Earth with less argument than she'd expected. She barely got a glance at the new palace, a relatively humble building taking shape around the trees. She was too focused on the shock of cold that bit into her skin after they passed through the gate from Braelyn. This was far from the pleasant heat of the plains.

But she'd barely had time to wrap her cloak more tightly around herself before they crossed through another gateway and into the relative warmth of the cave. As they halted on a small platform, wide stairs leading down to the floor, Dria exerted a bit of power to keep her trunk in the air until she could find a level place to set it.

With the addition of the guards flanking the gate, the platform was cramped enough that Dria didn't argue when Ralan strode down the steps without preamble. Curious, she peered around as she followed. They hadn't been joking about this being a large cavern. Stalagmites speared up around the outer edges, though the center had been smoothed. Magic hummed inside the floor, a sign that the flatness wasn't quite natural, and the stairs spiraling up and around the cylindrical chamber were likewise marked by the energy.

"So," Dria said. "We're setting up a colony in a cave like the Seelie and Unseelie. Nice."

He lifted a brow at her sarcastic tone. "It was your choice to come alone, Dree."

Dria scowled. "Don't call me that."

"I knew this would likely be your reaction to me, but I had hoped a softer strand was still possible," Ralan answered, his shoulders slumping.

"I don't care what you See in the future strands, Ralan," she snapped. "You should have paid more attention in the past."

"I know." Her brother's gaze lowered. "It was unforgiveable that I didn't say goodbye. I was so angry at Father that—"

"You think a mere goodbye is at the heart of this?" Dria wanted to punch him. How could he be so oblivious? So self-centered? "You abandoned me without a thought. Did it never occur to you what life would be like for a fifteen-year-old at court when half her family creates such a horrific scandal? When one brother is caught dismembering the woman the other brother wanted to marry, the rest of the family doesn't go unscathed. Especially since you fled to Earth before the worst of it was discovered. That left Teyark, who was already overburdened as our father's heir...and me."

Ralan grimaced. "I never considered—"

"Of course you didn't," she interrupted. "Once you do, you can get back to me. I'm certain it will take a few decades to get through your selfish, stubborn brain."

His gaze shot to hers. "We shouldn't delay talking about this."

He'd once used his Sight to protect her, but he appeared blind to her life now. "How about you examine your precious strands and see how successful that would be, brother dear? You couldn't be bothered to do so before you deserted me."

Dria spun away, frustrated with herself for losing her temper. If he wanted to continue the conversation, he could do so by himself. She didn't owe him anything after the pain he'd put her through. Instead, she collected her trunk with a tendril of magic and marched up the staircase that curled up the side of the cavern. She would find an antechamber to stash her belongings in while she worked.

Eventually, Ralan's footsteps thudded along the stone behind her, but she didn't look back. She focused her attention on the hallway that led away from the first landing. The glow of the mage light hanging by the opening barely penetrated the darkness, but the entire structure was too regularly shaped to be anything but intentional.

Dria summoned light into her hand and cast it in front of her, pushing it down the hallway to illuminate the path. Doors of stone lined the tunnel at regular intervals, along with empty stone sconces shaped to hold mage globes. Whoever had used magic to create this complex didn't do much work in wood.

"There's a large room for you at the end of the hallway," Ralan said, his voice gruff with an emotion she didn't care to examine. "When the other mages arrive, they can stay in these rooms. It'll be easier for you to give them their orders that way."

She froze. "Orders?"

"You'll be the one in charge," Ralan answered, but this time, he sounded almost cheerful. "I'm technically the leader, but you're going to be the one running the place. I can't leave Cora and Eri for long periods of time."

Fury filled her so completely that she had to count the striations of color in the stone beneath her feet to calm down. Twice. "Father specifically stated that I would *not* be in charge, only responsible for helping the mages as needed."

"I'm delegating." Curse him, he was enjoying this. "You wanted to rise up the ranks, didn't you? Well, here you go."

Dria spun to face him, her tenuous hold on her temper snapping as she advanced on her brother. She barely resisted the urge to shove him. "No one is going to listen to me, and you know it. Your bonded and daughter will be fine for a few weeks, or you could bring them here. It should be safe enough once the shielding is solidified."

Though he'd been smiling, his humor fled. "No, I can't. Cora is pregnant, and her magic is bound to Moranaia. It could harm our child to leave with such a bond in place."

"With the portal, they're only a short distance away. Just step through from time to time and—"

"No," Ralan said firmly. "You are the leader here. Get used to it."

Dria huffed. "Why not Teyark? No one would dare to question him."

"He and his bonded, Corath, have finally found a surrogate to bear their child," Ralan said, shrugging. "I'm surprised you didn't know. It's not like you have a grudge that keeps you from contacting *him*. They'll have to remain close during the process."

Her cheeks heated. "I have not called home as often in the last couple of months, and I forgot to answer the message he left on my mirror."

The reason why hung in the air between them like her mage light—she'd been avoiding even the mention of Ralan.

"I need to go," her brother said abruptly. "Eri is about to talk her friend Iren into a jaunt to the fairy pond, and that is not something either of them is ready for."

"But—"

"If you follow the stairs to the top, you'll find a small, cloaked exit leading out to the surface. I wouldn't recommend you use it, however." Ralan grinned. "It's another planet out there, after all. But it's safe enough in here for a battle mage. I'll be back tomorrow."

Dria opened her mouth, either to argue with him or call him a few choice names, but he rushed down the hallway before she had a chance. Baffled, she stared after him even after he'd disappeared from view. After all that, he'd left her here so he could rush back to keep his child from going to a fairy pond? Seriously? She hadn't wanted to linger at Braelyn, but she'd expected to have the current situation explained in full.

At last, she shook her head and headed toward the door at the end of the hallway. This was going to be a disaster. By the gods, her brother was a seer. Had he not bothered to Look? Did he want her to fail?

Though maybe, just maybe, he knew she would pull this off.

🔥

Lord Naomh of the Seelie stared out the window at the verdant forest growing beneath an artificial sky. He'd been born here and was bound here, his magic layered into the spells that gave the underhill cavern life. His older brother, Meren, often bragged about inheriting the properties adjacent to the palace, as well as their father's place at court, but Naomh had received the best of their father's holdings. There was far more to this estate than his proud, ambitious brother knew.

But Meren had never been content to live beneath the surface, anyway.

Unfortunately, the sons of Míl, ancient predecessors of the modern Irish, had been clever at the end of their final war with the fae. In the treaty that ended the hostilities, they'd chosen to enforce the literal meaning of *fei talef*—underground— instead of the figurative "other dimension" that the fae had intended. After much negotiation, they had settled on a compromise: the fae would settle in closely connected dimensions beneath the surface of Earth while the humans ruled the surface.

The Milesians had no doubt feared what would happen if Naomh's ancestors had found another sunlit world as the Moranaians had. They would have regrouped and strengthened until they could return to demolish every trace of human civilization. Instead, the fae had poured the energy of centuries into creating underground domains like this one. And fighting amongst themselves, of course. The Seelie and Unseelie had become true enemies not long after, both sides blaming the other for the poor negotiation with the humans.

The Seelie had kept to their word not to set foot upon the surface, though it cost them. Over and over, it cost them. Naomh's price had been his Moranaian mate, who hadn't been bound by that oath—and Kai, the son he hadn't known about. If he could have touched the ground, he might have found his lover, for his connection to earth magic was strengthened by contact. Perhaps for once, he should have copied the Unseelie, the oath-breaking scum. They'd long ago decided that the treaty with the humans was useless and now roamed Earth's surface as they wished.

No wonder Meren was plotting something with them.

Naomh detected Caolte's energy before his younger brother entered the room. Quiet and seething, an ember waiting for its chance to flare. Born of an affair between Naomh's and Meren's father and an Unseelie woman, Caolte had long endured suspicion and scorn from many at court—including Meren. Naomh was only a few years older, so he and Caolte had grown close when the younger man had come here to train with their father as a child. They'd been inseparable ever since.

"Well?" Naomh asked as his brother halted behind him.

"As suspected, he was there," Caolte answered. "My sister trailed Meren all the way to a tavern on the outskirts of the main Unseelie settlement."

Naomh shook his head. Caolte's precocious half-sister was far too good at spying. "I'm surprised your mother allows Vren to take such risks at fifteen, though I confess I am grateful. Did she recognize his contact?"

"No, the person was well-cloaked," Caolte said, his voice rough with frustration. "But Vren heard enough to prove that Meren is negotiating with someone in the Unseelie court to circumvent our queen's orders. He wants to destroy the new Moranaian outpost and use that as a stepping stone to reclaim surface Earth."

Naomh spun away from the window, wanting for all the world to slam his fist into something. Anything. Caolte took a step back. "You are certain?" Naomh demanded.

"Positive." Caolte's lips thinned. "Whatever the Moranaians have unleashed under that mountain, Meren and the Unseelie are going to try to subvert it."

Naomh's chest tightened, and he shoved his long, pale hair back with an irritated flick. Would his son be at the outpost? With Kai's soulbonded pregnant, perhaps not. Naomh could inquire, but their relationship was…tenuous. Something that tended to happen when one was mistakenly captured by one's own father. But how could Naomh have known that Kai and his mate weren't Kien's allies, considering they'd been found in the madman's camp amidst countless severed body parts?

"Why would Meren not avoid the Moranaians entirely if all he wants is to return to Earth?" Naomh asked.

Caolte shrugged. "I assume because Lord Lyr slighted him, and that won't be easily forgiven."

"It's personal."

"Partially," Caolte said. "I believe Meren also hopes to gain power by taking control of whatever the Moranaians have. With Earth's magic growing, he only needs a little more influence to convince some of our people to return. The queen would have to yield if he gains enough power and support to overthrow her. Meren will hurt anyone who gets in his way."

"That he will." Naomh's hands fisted. He should have disposed of his brother years ago, but Meren had never quite given him a justifiable reason—at least not one that would satisfy the queen. But the bastard was treading on dangerous ground now. With Naomh's son and future grandchild among the Moranaians, a threat to their holdings would not be allowed.

"Should we warn Lyr or continue to observe?" Caolte asked.

"Until we learn more about Meren's plans, we wait." Naomh smiled as his brother tossed his flame-red hair out of his eyes with a scowl. Caolte never had been the patient type. "Wait and guard."

4

Night had already fallen by the time Vek and Fen arrived at the base of the mountain. As he stared toward the blessedly people-free summit, Vek shuddered at the memory of the countless cars Fen had woven their own vehicle around. How could the humans abide living and travelling in such numbers? Though this world was fascinating, he didn't foresee enduring such conditions for long.

"You're not still upset, are you?" Fen asked. "We didn't crash."

Vek lifted a brow. "You cut across three lanes of traffic."

Grinning, Fen shrugged. "I didn't want to miss the exit."

"If you had—"

"You can't even drive a car." Fen laughed. "Seriously, dude. Just admit when you don't know something."

Vek's teeth ground together at the unwelcome reminder. If he did decide to stay, he would have to learn to drive, and he would never live it down if he had to ask Fen to teach him. But that was a worry for later. With a rude gesture at his nephew, Vek started the long climb up. Better to get this over with.

The soles of his feet tingled with the energy emanating from below. Unlike the surges that still reverberated, this was power contained in the mountain itself. Fortunately, the increased energy was harder to detect without physically touching the ground, so it didn't appear to have been discovered by other fae yet. But once the surges settled down, it would no doubt be more obvious that this mountain held a massive amount of natural magic.

At the small clearing where the cave entrance had been, Vek halted. The Moranaians had closed it. Only a slight impression remained in the stone where the gap had once been. Though he was grateful to Ralan and Aris for their help with Fen, anger at their high-handedness began to overtake appreciation. That barrier had been built by the Unseelie, and the Moranaians had no right to shut him away from the remnants of it.

"I should have left you with the Moranaians and sealed that damn wall," Vek muttered.

Fen's brow furrowed. "Why do you care that they moved the entrance?"

"Moved?"

"Sure." Fen waved toward the summit. "It's up there now. Heavily shielded but easy enough for an earth mage to find. Double for me, considering how familiar I am with the area."

Yes, his nephew would know. Fen had worked with Kien setting up a web of poisoned energy in this region. Still, Vek hated being bested in knowledge by the younger man—practically a child, at that. If he'd stopped to think instead of reacting, he would have detected the entrance on his own.

Eventually.

"Let's go break in," Vek said, heading up the slope.

Though he chuckled beneath his breath, Fen followed without argument. Vek could sense the small shielded gap now that he was looking for it, but it was more of a strain than he liked. It had been far too many years since he'd taken blood from a powerful earth mage, and that lack was beginning to show. Too bad his ability to duplicate others' powers when he took their blood wasn't permanent, and asking his nephew for a refresh was out of the question.

After an annoyingly steep hike, they finally reached the hidden gap, just large enough for a single person to descend through. Vek paused, lifting an eyebrow at Fen. Breaths coming sharp and fast, his nephew bent with his hands resting against his knees. The lad was barely in his twenties, a solid millennium younger than Vek, and he couldn't handle a little hike?

"Perhaps I should have left you in the car," Vek said.

Fen shoved himself upright. "Hey, I was almost dead a week or so ago."

He peered at his nephew's pale face. "And you were fully healed. Or so I thought. Have you been hiding something from me?"

"No," Fen said. He even sounded sincere. "But I haven't been climbing in a while, and I haven't thought to feed in a few days."

"Dammit, why—"

"I haven't been low on energy." Fen raised his hands. "Promise. Maybe it's just this place."

Vek held out his wrist. "You should take some of my blood."

Grimacing, Fen shook his head. "That would overload me. Anyway, I haven't noticed you going out at night to feed, either. You sure you don't need some of mine?"

For a moment, Vek debated saying yes, but he resisted. He already possessed the dark, corrosive power of the Unseelie, an inborn magic that could eat through shields. He could drain energy from any whose blood he'd tasted or use his magic to seal and bind, and that didn't include the assortment of spells he'd picked up from his more unusual talent of mimicry. But Fen was powerful, unlike the last earth mage Vek had taken blood from, and an infusion like that could cause Vek more trouble than it was worth. Besides, his nephew's pallor suggested he couldn't afford to lose more energy.

"I am well enough," Vek said.

He focused on the shielding around the entrance before Fen could waste more time arguing. The intricate piece of work had the dragon's energy signature all through it, but he could tell from the frequency of the hum that she'd used Earth's power and not just her own. It would take hours to unravel, if he bothered with such a fool's errand. But he had a better idea.

"Fen," he mused. "Think you could create another small entrance a few paces away from this one? The shielding doesn't extend far into the surrounding stone."

His nephew paced the area, and relief filled Vek to see that his color had already returned to normal. Finally, Fen stopped an arm's span away and nodded. "Here. I should have plenty of energy for something that simple. I feel fine, really. Guess I've been sitting around playing video games too much."

Though doubt twisted Vek's stomach, there wasn't time to explore the problem further. They needed to get in and out quickly. "Do it. Quietly."

"I know how to break in to a place, Uncle."

Grinning, Fen extended a faint tendril of his power into the ground beneath them. After a few heartbeats' time, another gap opened in the earth.

They were in.

Dria ran her finger along the edge of the tall, freestanding mirror someone had placed on the far side of her room. Magic prickled against her skin and thrummed in her blood from the contact, and she smiled. This was a powerful artifact, the glass and frame imbued with multiple connections. After a quick probe, she discovered communication links to a wide array of places on Moranaia, a few here on Earth, and several more to various fae realms. Had Ralan enchanted this? One of the links led to Gessen's mirror, something far too specific to be random.

Perhaps her brother had some lingering care for her feelings, though how he knew about her friendship with Gessen, she had no idea. His visions? Court gossip?

It didn't matter. She would take it.

Her smile widened as she activated the connection and waited for Gessen to answer. She'd told her friend she would let him know when she was safely settled, but she hadn't expected it to be this easy. Maybe this assignment wouldn't be too bad. If nothing else, at least she wasn't completely disconnected from the only world she knew.

Her reflection disappeared, replaced by the image of Gessen's tense form. But his shoulders relaxed, and the confusion on his face morphed into pleasure as he realized who was calling. "Dria! I'd hoped you would find a way to send me a message. How did you set up a link already?"

She shrugged. "It was imbued into the mirror in my room."

"But how did—"

"My brother is a seer," Dria said with a snicker. "You never know what random stuff will happen when he's involved."

Gessen squinted. "Are you in a cave?"

"I can't tell you where I am, but I can say that you have always been the percep-tive type." She quirked her brow, and he grinned. "I made it to the secret location safely, as you can see, and will probably be here for some time. But you can attempt to call through the mirror when…"

Dria's words trailed off when her attention was snagged by a faint but somehow familiar energy signature elsewhere in the cave network. Someone was intruding. But how? She'd keyed herself into the spell guarding the entrance, and that hadn't been disturbed. No, it was as if the ground itself heralded something momentous. Or maybe the air. The fine hair on her arms prickled with the unusual sensation of a foreign presence.

"I have to go," she said, careful to keep her tone steady. "Something needs my attention."

Gessen frowned. "Something dangerous?"

"Nothing I can't handle," Dria answered with a confidence she absolutely felt. This was not the day to annoy her.

After Gessen bid farewell, Dria cut the connection and darted out the door. Quickly, she sent her magic ahead of her, sweeping her senses along the tunnel and into the central portal chamber. Nothing but the guards at the bottom. She directed a warning into their minds to be on alert and turned her attention toward the top.

This place had too many blasted rooms. Dria jogged up the long spiral staircase, examining each corridor and chamber that branched off along the way. At the end of the stairs, she navigated a large room intended for crop-growing that was situated before the entryway chamber.

Once beyond the tilled soil and mage lights, Dria halted as her seeking spell detected two men through the door on the far end. She probed the shielding around the hidden entrance once more. Undisturbed. After a bracing breath, she drew power into herself and reinforced her own protections. Then she sidled out of sight, duck-ing behind a column as she readied a containment spell.

Voices echoed into the room. "They couldn't have done that."

"It bears closer examination," another man said. "But I believe we will find I am correct."

As the grumbling timbre of the second voice flowed around her, Dria stiffened. An odd tickle, like the dance of leaves caught in an air spell, tumbled through her stomach, and her heart began to drum. She shook her head, trying to dispel the sus-picion taking root in her core. Not now.

Not. Now.

"Wouldn't it take a lot of planning to make a portal between worlds? You'd need someone to manipulate the threads of the Veil, someone who could channel that much power, and…I don't even know what else."

"A god, probably," the other man muttered.

Footsteps echoed closer. "Vek, that's—"

Dria spun around the column and released her containment spell at the approaching men. The one nearest froze, still as a statue, but the man to the right and just behind kept advancing as the spell shattered against his shielding.

Miaran.

Fury flushed color into his pale skin, and he snarled, revealing a hint of fang. A blood elf.

Shock hit her as the dancing in her stomach morphed into a tornado, but she was trained for shock. She grabbed for more power, manipulating it into a clear, solid wall in front of her. The blood elf must have detected the spell, for he halted a breath away from her impromptu shield.

Electricity crackled in her palms as she met his light brown eyes. "You will cease this intrusion at once," she demanded.

Gods, Dria hoped her voice didn't tremble. It was him. She'd suspected when she heard him speak, but feeling his energy brush against hers confirmed it. His power thrummed in time with hers, his very spirit a thread that could weave into her soul.

Her potential soulbonded.

Of course he would be a criminal. A threat. Did she have any other kind of luck?

If his snarl was anything to go by, he didn't feel the connection. "Release my nephew or suffer the consequences. Your hold on him goes beyond the bounds of politeness."

Dria laughed. "Politeness? You're jesting. You have entered Moranaian territory uninvited. Surely you didn't expect that to go unchallenged."

"Have I?" One pale eyebrow lifted. "Entered Moranaian lands? I thought I was in a cave on Earth. There was no shielding to prevent the creation of any tunnels. Seems a valid invitation to any earth mage exploring the area."

As a blood elf, he was most likely Unseelie. And she knew just how to needle him. "I've always heard that your kind prides itself on giving the harsh, blunt truth. Such prevarication is unworthy of your people."

His eyes narrowed. "Watch yourself."

"I could say the same to you." Dria analyzed his shield and adjusted the lightning's current slightly. Only then did she let the wall between them drop. "Who are you, and what is your purpose here?"

The stranger drew in a sharp breath. "Neither is your concern. I'll speak with the person in charge or no one."

What had the other man called him? Vek? The name sounded familiar, but she didn't have time to tease out the memory. "You won't have to go far. I'm the leader of this outpost."

Unfortunately—but he didn't need to know her reluctance.

A dubious frown pinched his forehead. "Really? Prince Ralan ceded control so readily? I don't believe you. The leader would have guards or some other retinue."

She allowed no sign her annoyance to show, though inside she seethed at the slight. "I am Princess Dria Moreln, Ralan's sister. He was happy enough to place me in charge, but you'll have to speak to him about his reasons. And as you can see, I do not require a retinue."

He fell silent, studying her face with an intensity that would have made a lesser woman squirm. Dria resisted the urge to do just that—but not because of intimidation. He was gorgeous in a way she couldn't describe. His unusually pale skin, white hair, and light, almost-taupe eyes combined with his dangerous predatory energy to send an unusual frisson of heat straight through her. But he wasn't her type at all.

Not that she'd encountered many blood elves to test that attraction.

The stranger eased closer. Their personal shields bumped, an almost-visible spark crackling between them. He sucked in a breath, and if possible, his skin grew paler. He jerked away, stumbling back a few steps. Sheer panic lit his eyes for a single heartbeat, a panic she empathized with all too well.

He recognized her. Their connection.

Vek opened his mouth as if to speak, but it was a moment before he managed words. "Forgive me, Princess Dria. I am Prince Vek of the Unseelie, here on behalf of my father. I sought to investigate the unusual energy I detected around this mountain."

Forthcoming of him, but it didn't answer the thing she most wanted to know. What did he think about their possible bond? From his fearful glance, it hadn't been welcome news.

"I invite you to come back tomorrow morning if you wish to speak with me about the matter," she said, her voice chill. "Make an appointment."

His lips turned down. "Tomorrow? I am here now."

"I am not prepared for an audience, Prince Vek of the Unseelie. Return politely and formally. Unless your mission isn't diplomatic?"

Though his nostrils flared, he didn't protest. "Release my nephew, and we will go."

She undid the spell, more than anxious for them to be gone. And more than ready for this awful day to be over. "There."

The other man stumbled forward, but he caught his balance quickly. "What—"

"Come, Fen." The blood elf turned his back on Dria and strode to his nephew. "I know you heard what we said. We'll return tomorrow."

"You're just going to…" Fen glanced between them, and his forehead wrinkled for a moment before smoothing once more. "Right. Tomorrow."

After one last enigmatic glance over his shoulder, Vek returned the way they had come. But the feel of his heavy gaze lingered after the two had disappeared from sight. Dria tracked them with her energy until they'd returned through the short tunnel they had created and sealed the hole behind them.

Only then could she take a deep breath again.

Vek stomped down the side of the hill, ignoring Fen's questioning glances as best he could. He didn't have any answers—not for himself, and not for his nephew.

The insanity of the king's decree had just magnified tenfold, and Fen didn't know a thing about it. His nephew wouldn't approve of killing the leader of the Moranaian colony, no matter who it was.

The leader who happened to be Vek's mate.

There weren't enough curse words in any language to cover this scenario. If he didn't comply with orders, or if he simply failed, there was no telling what would happen to his mother and siblings. Under normal circumstances, it would be a bit of honor lost, more jostling in the ranks of siblings and cousins and uncles and aunts as they used his misfortune for their benefit, but the king's pointed mention of his mother had been no coincidence. King Torek wanted the new energy source badly, only Divine knew why, and there was a chance he would be willing to hurt or even kill to obtain it.

Vek had killed for the king on a few occasions, but those had been for the greater good. Like the Unseelie lord who'd begun enslaving and abusing his people and hiding the evidence with magic. The man had been a powerful mage, and if he'd gone unchecked, he would have soon outpaced the most depraved dictators in history.

But the deed weighed heavily on Vek's heart. It wasn't regret, precisely, but it wasn't satisfaction, either.

He'd already doubted his ability to kill Ralan or Aris. Assassinating his mate, a woman who appeared innocent of any wrongdoing? He could never bear that. Yet he also couldn't stand the thought of harm befalling the rest of his family. Could he watch his pregnant mother be imprisoned? Beaten? And while Vek had remained distant from his three half-siblings to keep them from catching the king's attention, he couldn't abide them receiving any injury on his behalf.

Vek ground his teeth and picked up his pace.

"What's the hurry? Do you think the woman is going to chase us down the mountain?" Fen called, laughter in his tone. "She seemed happy to get rid of us, honestly."

"Not now, Fen."

For several more paces, Fen seemed to let the subject drop, but it turned out to be a momentary reprieve. "You're going to have to tell me what's going on. Especially if I'm supposed to be learning from you."

Vek slowed until his nephew walked beside him, but he didn't stop. Didn't look to see Fen's expression. The boy was correct, much as it galled him. This was too big to keep secret, since his nephew was at risk, too. The king would not grant his nephew leniency without Vek's cooperation with the assassination.

"We will speak at home," Vek answered.

It would undoubtedly affect the tentative if unusual friendship that had begun to form between them, but there was nothing to be done for it.

He should have known not to get attached.

5

Dria stopped in front of the trunk she'd placed only a half mark or so before, though it felt more like years. Decades. Even knowing how abruptly life could change, she wasn't certain how to process this shift. A soulbonded. It wasn't supposed to happen now. Ralan had sworn he'd had a vision of introducing them, but that hadn't occurred at all.

Had the future strands changed so much over the centuries? She'd assumed her chance was lost once her brother had fled, vowing never to return. She'd believed many opportunities gone with each broken promise. *I told you I'd find your bonded, Dree. I'll even introduce you,* Ralan had vowed. *I'll see you with the most ideal teacher. The most favorable assignments for your skills. And I'll protect you from the court intrigue you hate so much. You won't have to worry about the future with me around.*

Instead, his departure had dropped her straight into misery. Three years of torment at court and decades of cold loneliness at the Citadel.

Now there was her potential soulbonded. Prince Vek of the Unseelie. No wonder his name had sounded familiar. He'd visited their court a couple of times, but she'd been too young to meet him on his last trip. She'd heard plenty from Ralan, though. Her brother hadn't trusted Vek from their first meeting. Was it because he'd seen that Vek was a terrible soulbonded?

He definitely wasn't someone she could imagine her brother introducing her to. Had it all been a lie? Or had Ralan foreseen something else about her and Vek? Perhaps a dire future awaited them. After all, her brother hadn't said what would happen after the introduction. What if she had more than one soulbonded and Vek wasn't who he'd Seen at all? It was rare to have more than one chance but not impossible.

Sighing, Dria lifted the lid of the trunk and carefully shifted aside the formal overrobe folded on top. She'd created indentions in the stone to stack her belongings, but she wasn't enough of an artisan to make a hanging rack for the elaborately embroidered robe. Perhaps someone with that talent would be included on her team. Or she could ask the person who'd created these rooms in the first place. They clearly had skill and power aplenty.

She grabbed several of her simple working robes from the trunk and deposited the bundle on the nearest shelf. But as she turned back toward her trunk, her stomach rumbled. Oh, *clechtan*. Food. She'd used enough energy fixing the gap in the cavern's shielding to accelerate her hunger. Too bad she'd forgotten something so basic as nourishment. The group bringing the provisions wouldn't arrive until tomorrow, and her useless brother hadn't seen fit to remind her of that fact.

She would ask the guards beside the portal if they had extra food. If not, she would have to return to Moranaia. What a ridiculous situation. Ralan would mock her once she returned to Braelyn, and Lord Lyr would surely find her rude and indecisive. But it couldn't be helped.

Dria was almost to the bottom of the circular stairs when her cursed brother appeared. She stopped an arm's length away and glared. "Something you forgot to tell me?"

Ralan lifted a shoulder. "Quite a few things, I imagine. Come on. Surely you can bear my company long enough to have dinner at Braelyn?"

"Don't you already know my answer?" she demanded.

"I would if I bothered to Look." His expression took on a somber cast. "I've learned not to examine every detail, Dria. I try to stick to the major threads, and dinner isn't one of them."

She smiled sweetly. "I hope Father doesn't rely on you to plan formal feasts anymore, then."

Ralan made a rude face at her, but his eyes twinkled with humor. "Not as yet."

Her breath caught at the bit of banter, so reminiscent of earlier times. Happier ones. She marched down the remaining stairs and pushed past him, heading for the portal. His footsteps echoed behind her, but she forced herself to ignore him—if only for a moment. She couldn't fall back into their friendship, not after what he'd done.

Ralan loved Kenaren so much that he left his dear sister behind. Guess you're no better than the rest of us, after all.

You must be a freak like Kien. No wonder Prince Ralan ran away.

Everyone knows the king loves Ralan the most. Now he's stuck with a whiny, useless daughter. And Teyark, but he's too honorable to hate.

I hope your teacher isn't showing you any blood magic. Oh, maybe Ralan Saw you turning your fire on him. Kien liked to torture with his magic, so perhaps the royal mages all bear that flaw.

What's the matter, Dria? Your big brother not here to stand guard anymore?

Dria shook her head to clear her mind of the voices. Yes, she'd borne far too many years of mockery on her brothers' behalf.

"Dria?"

She smoothed her expression before she glanced back at her brother. "Yes?"

"You never said if you are joining me and the others for dinner."

Dria nodded, hiding her clenched fists in the folds of her robe. She rarely allowed herself to think of the past, but being around her brother dredged it up. "So

long as the Myern doesn't mind. I would not wish to impose upon him after my refusal."

Ralan surprised her by chuckling. "Trust me when I say that a slight change in dinner plans is one of the least odd things Lyr has had to deal with lately. And be warned. You may end up dining with a dragon."

She blinked. Then the mental image of a dragon crammed into an average dining room popped into her mind, and she laughed. "You're jesting."

He shook his head. "Believe it or not, no. No joke here. Her name is Kezari, and from all I've heard, she is the one largely responsible for reforming this cavern. But she will shift into elven form if she joins us."

Well. That explained Ralan's comment about strange happenings at the Myern's estate. If Lord Lyrnis had a dragon as guest, Dria's presence would be of little note. What was it about this day? First an Unseelie prince and now a dragon.

"Fine," she said. "Let's go."

The Myern's dining room was smaller than Dria had expected, but she hadn't visited many estates in this region. Instead of the larger stone structures of the palace or the Citadel, this building had been constructed around and between the massive trees. As such, the oval dining room with its walls full of windows was more intimate than she was accustomed to. Only a single long table filled the center.

Most of the chairs were taken already. Since dinner was about to be served, Ralan made quick work of introducing her to Lady Meli, the Myern's bonded, and his daughter, Arlyn. Beside Arlyn was her bonded, Kai, and then the mage teacher Selia and her husband, Aris. Dria had already met Cora and Eri, but there was also a boy named Iren next to Eri. The mage's son? She barely had time to make note before Ralan introduced Lord Lyr's mother, Lady Lynia, and the dragon, Kezari.

As she took her seat between Meli and Ralan, Dria tried not to stare at the dragon in the guise of an elf. Dark golden-blond hair streamed around the woman's thinly clad body, and she tilted her head at an odd, almost birdlike angle as she studied Dria in return. Even after Dria had shifted her attention to her empty plate, she could still sense Kezari's gaze pinning her from the far end of the table.

Hopefully, the dragon wasn't considering her for a snack.

Ralan leaned close. "Relax," he whispered.

His words had the opposite effect, but she refused to show it. Though tension coiled in her stomach until her hunger evaporated, she relaxed her hands in her lap and loosened her hunched shoulders. Instead of answering Ralan, she turned to the Myern's bonded as several members of the household streamed in with platters.

"It is a pleasure to meet you, Lady Meli," Dria said. "I appreciate your warm welcome on such short notice. I do hope my eagerness to get started on my work was not interpreted as a slight on your hospitality."

"Not at all," the lady answered with a smile. "I more than understand wishing to

complete an errand with all speed. And please, call me Meli, Princess. That is correct since your rank is higher, is it not? I'm still learning about your hierarchy."

Meli wasn't from Moranaia? Dria almost scanned the other woman to read her energy signature, but she resisted. It would be quite rude under these circumstances. "Technically, yes. But I would rather be called Dria."

"Very well," Meli said.

The Myern passed a platter to Meli, who stared down at the contents with a slight frown. Once she grabbed a piece and passed it down, Dria saw why. The oblong, golden brown lump looked like bread, but it smelled savory, like meat and spice. Curious. Meat pies were typically served in a dish, not in a loaf. Despite her confusion, Dria placed one on her plate anyway.

She passed the platter on to Ralan and received the next one from Meli. This one held...toasted *nesel* cuttings? She'd never had these any way except mashed and sweetened. Had cuisine shifted so much in this region? The plains elves had a few dishes that varied from those she'd had at court, but nothing quite this different. Who in the world would think to toast *nesel*?

But Dria dutifully took a serving and gave the plate to her brother. Never let it be said that she, unlike Ralan, had forgotten her manners. She might not want to be a princess, but she would act like one. No rude comments, even if the food was unusual—and some of her table companions even more so.

A princess could certainly dine with a dragon with aplomb.

As the others served themselves, the Myern caught Dria's gaze. "You will find that we are far less formal at our meal than you may be used to. I hope it does not cause you alarm."

Alarm? No. But it was disconcerting to be unceremonious with so many strangers. Still, Dria shook her head politely. "Of course not."

"We are quite blended here," Lyr continued. "My daughter is part human and only arrived a few months ago. Meli traveled from Alfheim not long after, Cora is from Galare, and of course Kezari is from the Isle of Dragons. Not to mention Ralan's long sojourn on Earth. But we manage to find a ready peace."

A part human woman, a Galaren, and one of the rare Ljósálfar, all at one table? Dria fought for composure at that revelation. "I will endeavor to keep that in mind."

Once the last of the food was served, Dria glanced around, trying to determine what she was supposed to eat first, but everyone else appeared equally confused. Finally, the Myern's daughter lifted a strip of *nesel* and took a bite. Her expression shifted from curious to exasperated, but at least she didn't look disgusted.

A strange, uncertain silence fell as the others followed Arlyn's lead. The toasted *nesel* wasn't horrible, exactly, but it was bland. And the meat bread might be edible, but the inside wasn't nearly as juicy as a pie. At least the flavor was good, if less spicy than she was accustomed to.

After a few bites, Arlyn set her bread down, her shoulders slumping. "It was a good attempt, but it isn't quite the same."

Her bonded, Kai, groaned. "That's it. I'm going through the portal."

"You can't bring Earth food back here," Lyr said calmly, though his expression was pained. "The time shift in the Veil does strange things to it, and there's a risk of contamination."

"We can use the new portal."

Dria's eyebrows lifted at that. He wanted to use the portal in the outpost to fetch food, of all things? "That is not advisable," she found herself saying.

Kai's nostrils flared. "Forgive me, Princess Dria, but—"

"I placed her in charge," Ralan interrupted. "If you haven't yet heard."

"And she's right," Arlyn said, giving Kai a sharp glance. "Pregnancy cravings are awful, but they don't justify the risk of exposing the outpost. I do appreciate your attempt to get me a hamburger and fries, though."

Comprehension flooded Dria. The woman was pregnant, and they'd tried to create Earth food for her. She found herself smiling at the sweetness of the gesture. "I'm sorry," Dria said.

"It's okay," the other woman answered. "It's not like you have the same ingredients to work with here."

On Ralan's other side, Cora murmured, "A burger would have been nice."

Ralan chuckled, and his bonded elbowed him in the side. "Sorry, love," he said, though he didn't sound particularly repentant.

Did he ever?

Finally, as the plates were being cleared, the dragon spoke to Dria. "You will want my aid in fortifying the outpost, yes?"

Despite the inquiry, Dria had the feeling it wasn't a question. "I am more than capable of building defenses against attack. I am a trained battle mage, and that includes a significant knowledge of shielding."

"I do not speak of that." Kezari tapped her fingers against the table. "There is more than magic needed. I am rested now. I would like to refine my work."

Her work. Of course. The dragon must have carved out the rooms in the cavern. "If you are volunteering to make the rooms more comfortable, I would be more than happy to accept."

Kezari inclined her head. "Yes. My *skizik* and his wife will aid also."

Dria blinked, uncertain what a *skizik* was or who they might be married to. On the other side of the table, Lady Selia chuckled. "She means my husband. The word refers to a dragon's rider or helper."

"I see," Dria answered. Even though she didn't. "It would be an honor to have a mage and teacher of your skill present."

Selia smiled gently. "I was there when the portal was created, so I might be able to provide insight. And my husband is a life mage. He helped Kezari construct the outpost."

A life mage? The ability to sense and manipulate the essence of life was a rare thing indeed.

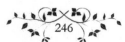

"Oh!" a small voice called from the end of the table, and Dria peeked around Ralan and Cora to see young Eri dancing in her seat. "I helped make the portal. Can I go, too?"

"No," Ralan said, his tone somehow hard, exasperated, and affectionate at the same time. A curious blend. "You are fortunate enough to be allowed at this dinner. Do not test your luck."

"It was a small strand, anyway," the girl muttered, returning her attention to her food.

Dria snapped her mouth closed before anyone noticed her gaping. Her niece was a seer like Ralan…and the child had helped establish a portal between dimensions. Good gods. Well, it explained the odd reaction Dria had received when she'd claimed that children were never a distraction. If Eri took after Ralan, she no doubt left a swath of trouble in her wake.

"We will go in the morning," the dragon said.

"I will return to the cavern after dinner," Dria answered. "There was already one incursion, and—"

"Vek will not return until tomorrow." Ralan waved his hand. "And I See no hint of any other trouble. You should rest here."

Dria ground her teeth together. If anyone else had suggested it, she might have cooperated. But she couldn't give him the satisfaction. "No. Your Sight is not infallible, and I have work to do at my assigned post."

Was it her imagination, or did he wince? But he merely nodded. "Very well. We'll go in waves. You tonight, Kezari, Selia, and Aris along with a few helpers in the morning, and then the guards and mages later in the day."

His capitulation was a small victory, but somehow, she didn't feel like she'd won.

🔥

Vek slumped onto the couch. Dread pervaded his senses, but he wasn't sure if it heralded doom or was a sign of his turmoil. Fen plopped down on the other section of the L-shaped couch, but he appeared more quizzical than upset.

"What in the hell is going on?" Fen asked.

"A great deal, unfortunately." Vek hated having to explain this. "My father demanded more than I take you on as a student when I spoke to him."

The room grew quiet as Vek tried to formulate the best explanation. Finally, Fen's brow quirked. "I don't suppose you're going to, you know, tell me? Sometime this millennium? You're likely to die of old age before I am, but I don't want to push it."

"Shut up," Vek said, glaring for good measure. Not that his nephew would care. "You aren't going to like this, but I suppose I should explain quickly. I'm supposed to infiltrate the new Moranaian enclave, kill the leader, and wrest the power they've gathered away from them."

"What?" Fen shook his head and then rubbed at his face. "That doesn't… Why?"

Vek's brow furrowed. "I…"

"It doesn't make sense," Fen said. "Why would the king of the Unseelie want to antagonize the Moranaians? There would be a war for sure. Damn, I can't believe you're even considering it. They saved my ass twice at least. Is that why you didn't want to tell me? Because I'd try to stop you?"

"Fen." Vek lifted his hands, palms outward. "Calm down. I know you wouldn't cooperate. And I can't…there are many reasons I can't complete this mission. If the Moranaians have done what I think with that energy and created a portal, there's no power to take, and the woman in charge of the colony…she's my mate."

That shut Fen up. Alas, though, not for long. "Unseelie mate? You mean like the Moranaian soulbonds? No one told me that was a thing. Not that any of you bastards, no offense, cared to teach me much of anything about our people."

"It hardly seemed relevant, considering your age," Vek said. Dammit, he'd hoped to put this discussion off for even longer. "Haven't you ever felt an inexplicable pull toward another? A strong connection, mind you, not mere interest."

"I…" Fen's voice trailed off, and his skin went pale. "You knew."

Vek smiled. "That Maddy and Anna could be mates to you? Yes. Snobbery wasn't the reason I wouldn't let you take Maddy's blood. Do not do so unless you are certain you wish to bind yourself to her. Or both of them. Whatever you choose."

"Shit."

"Pretty much all around," Vek agreed. "But you can worry about your love life later. I have to figure out how to tell my father that I can't complete this task without doom befalling my mother's family. You did ask a valuable question, Fen. Why does he want this? I knew he would be furious about the wall being destroyed, but it isn't cause for such a drastic move."

Fen snorted. "Yet you were going to do it until you realized the leader was your mate."

"I wasn't." Suddenly weary, Vek rubbed at his temples. "I didn't go there tonight with the intent to harm. It was reconnaissance only."

"If you say so."

Vek stood, unwilling to debate the matter. "I have much to think about. Tomorrow, we will meet with Princess Dria as planned, and then we will consider what to do next. For now, we should rest."

Before Fen could argue, Vek spun away and left the room, heading for the sanctuary of his sleeping chamber. It would be hours before he slept, but he did need to think. Something was going on, and he needed to figure out what.

Sooner rather than later.

6

Dria circled the portal in the middle of the cavern once more as she waited for her first visitors to arrive. She was tired enough that if she stood still, she might doze on her feet. She'd only realized after walking into her room that the stone beds hadn't been fitted with mattresses, so she'd spent an uncomfortable night tossing and turning atop a pile of her robes. Every time she had managed to drift to sleep, she'd been awakened by some strange sound or another. Why had she insisted on returning last night?

Because she was a prideful idiot, that was why.

She had dressed in her least wrinkled gown and an overrobe depicting the Citadel at sunset, and she had even coiled her shoulder-length hair into a court-worthy braid topped with a circlet. She looked the part of a princess, albeit a slightly rumpled one, but inside, she felt like an imposter. A hungry, grumpy, tired imposter.

The portal's light shifted, and she tamped down her frustration so she could greet her brother and the others. By the time she'd circled around to the base of the dais, Ralan, Selia, Aris, and Kezari had already stepped through. Her brother lifted a brow and then smirked at the sight of Dria's formal wear, but she pinched her lips tight and resisted making a comment. If he wanted to dress as though he were spending his day in his rooms instead of greeting a prince of a foreign nation, that was his choice.

Her own selection had nothing to do with Vek being her potential soulbonded. Much.

Dria shifted out of the way as the group descended, allowing more people to stream in behind them. Several people levitated trunks full of supplies through, and she directed them to the appropriate rooms as quickly as she could. All the while, she was annoyingly aware of the initial group that watched her every move. Particularly her brother.

He'd placed her in charge. Was he surprised that she'd taken initiative? Before trying to sleep, she'd toured the entire complex, deciding where to set everything up. She'd made note of storehouses and sleeping quarters, dining rooms and refreshing rooms. Ralan might have dumped the responsibility on her, but she would own it as though it was granted by the king himself.

Finally, she turned back to the others. "Forgive me for not giving a proper welcome. I'd like to get things set up right away."

Ralan's grin widened. "I knew you were the correct choice."

Dria chose to ignore those words lest she end up pummeling her brother in front of everyone. "How long until the mages and the rest of the warriors arrive?"

"The first of the guards should arrive around midday. The mages were supposed to be with them, but there has been a slight delay. They should be here by evening," Ralan answered.

"And I don't suppose you're going to tell me what I'm supposed to have them do?" Dria curled her toes inside her boots, a handy outlet for frustration that the others couldn't see. "Father wasn't specific."

Ralan shrugged. "Later. We should head up to greet Vek."

"How…" She shook her head. "Never mind."

Selia stepped forward. "If you'll forgive my interruption? We would be pleased to help organize while you are otherwise occupied."

It took effort for Dria not to bristle at the offer. Nothing but sincerity filled the other mage's eyes, but Dria couldn't help feeling intimidated. Selia was a well-respected teacher with several centuries more experience than Dria. A couple of Dria's peers had trained with her before coming to the Citadel.

"Unless you would rather we wait?" Selia asked softly.

Dria shoved aside that tiny thread of insecurity. "Of course not. We could use things like shelving, clothing racks, tables and other furniture, and decent mattresses. I formed a few shelves in my room with my limited earth magic, but I can't manipulate stone well enough to do more."

"I'm afraid I don't have the required talents to manufacture much of what you need," Selia admitted, no sign of embarrassment on her face. "But I will do what I can."

Kezari tipped her head back and peered at the staircase above as though she could see through to the chambers. Maybe she could. "I can form such things. I have seen them in your elven habitations. Soft things, though, I cannot do."

Selia smiled. "We will figure it out."

The mage's husband shifted on his feet with a considering frown. He seemed like a somber man, dark in a way Dria couldn't place. Haunted, maybe. He shoved his fingers through his brown and green hair in a restless motion, but his gaze was steady when it met hers.

"I will see about coaxing forth a garden in the space we created," he said.

"Come on," Ralan interrupted. "Or they'll be through the entrance before we are there to greet them."

"Then they'll wait," Dria snapped.

But she made haste to thank the others and head toward the stairs. She had a duty to greet her visitors, after all.

Vek wiped his palms surreptitiously against his pants as he stared at the entrance formed in the ground. It was foolish to be nervous, but his heart refused to heed reason. And Fen's curious glances did nothing to help. His nephew had asked more than once what Vek intended to do after this meeting, but he'd refused to answer. Namely because he didn't know.

He'd barely slept the night before, and none of his pacing or worrying had helped. Fen's question kept ringing through his head. Why? Why such a drastic measure? In all the centuries that Vek had worked for his father, the king had never threatened Vek's other family members. He'd never resorted to anything resembling bribery, and he hadn't needed to. The reason for the action had always been incentive enough.

What didn't the king want Vek to know?

"Something wrong?" Fen asked.

An army's worth of things were wrong, but Vek had no intention of discussing any of them. Not right now. "Just doing a final check of the shield. It should be clear."

Fen had to know he was lying, but for once, he didn't try to call him on it. Vek brushed past his nephew and lowered himself through the hole, bracing for the short drop. But the entrance's spell caught at him slightly, and he landed gently on his feet. More comfortable than their improvised entrance had been.

Vek shifted aside as Fen dropped through. Then they advanced through the small room and into the larger entry chamber where they'd encountered his mate. Ah, she'd been beautiful. Fiery, too. She might have caught him in that paralyzing spell if it hadn't been so similar to the one Selia had used on him not long ago. He'd been certain to perfect a counter spell to avoid the same scenario.

It was almost too bad. He could always go for a bit of friendly bondage. Well, without his nephew present, of course—that would be too strange even for him. Perhaps he should have left Fen at home this time, since it would be far easier for Vek to find out how amenable Dria might be to such things when he wasn't babysitting.

But no. Then he might be tempted to truly mate with her, and that would only compound their issues. Better to keep his distance entirely.

"Uncle?"

At Fen's soft question, Vek realized that his steps had slowed. Curse it. Ignoring his nephew's knowing look, he picked up the pace once more. He needed to focus. Instead of letting his thoughts drift to sex, he should be scanning the area for any threat. He might have been invited, but that didn't mean he'd be welcomed.

This time, the princess strode through the door rather than darting from around a column, and she wasn't alone—her brother was with her. But Vek barely acknowledged Ralan. Instead, he stopped in the center of the room and stared at Dria. Gods above and below. She'd worn court garb. He'd never been able to resist a powerful woman in formal clothing.

He was in so much trouble.

Beside him, Fen snickered, but Vek couldn't be bothered to tell him off. He was too enchanted by the glint of mage light on the princess's dark red hair and the shift and flow of her dress over her beautifully curved form. Her overrobe trailed behind her, and the golds and browns of the embroidery almost blended in against the cave floor. The garment seemed to be emblazoned with a nature scene. He'd love to see the design—once he'd peeled the robe from her delectable body.

And the way she held herself, so tall and proud. Princess Dria would take shit from no one, including him. Damn, that was sexy. He enjoyed women when he pleased—but more importantly, when they pleased. Far too many had been drawn to his darkness only to run away when given a chance to explore it. But Dria...she was a woman who would never flee.

As Dria and Ralan halted in front of them, Vek sent out a prayer of thanks for his years at the Unseelie court. Fen might have guessed why he'd stopped, but no one else would. Vek had long learned to keep his expression neutral and his body relaxed but confident. And above all? He'd mastered hiding his desires.

"We meet again," Ralan said, a hint of...something in his tone. Not quite anger, but Vek couldn't place it. "I'm given to understand that you were introduced to my sister yesterday?"

A curiously abrupt greeting from a Moranaian, but Ralan had always been an odd one. "Not formally."

Ralan's smile was tight but not exactly strained. "Then allow me to do the honors."

There was no mistaking the startled tilt of Dria's brows at those words, but she smoothed her expression quickly. Even so, there was tension in the hands she gripped in front of her waist. There was something going on between these two, some subtext that Vek couldn't define. Interesting...and possibly useful.

"Vek," Ralan said. "Allow me to introduce Moranai Feraien i Driathen Moreln nai Moranaia."

"A certain pleasure," Vek murmured.

He could have sworn she shivered.

Irritation flashed in Ralan's eyes for a moment, but he continued. "Dria, this is Prince Vekenayeth anh Torekthayed of the Unseelie."

She smiled. "I am gratified to meet you. Properly."

Ah, the politely worded rebuke of the Moranaian. He had a feeling she was a master. There was no censure on her face, but he had no doubt that she referred to his incursion the evening before. As well she should. He'd tried to defer the wrong-doing yesterday, but she had been correct in her assessment. Manipulating the truth was beneath him.

"Perhaps this might herald a new start between us," Vek said. He could use one after bungling their first meeting. "I am not an enemy of your people. Generally speaking."

She lifted a brow. "Sounds promising."

Though a litany of curses streamed through his head at his fumbling, Vek forced himself to smile. "I meant only that we are not formal allies. I'm afraid my Moranaian is not flawless."

Ralan frowned. "If you are here to—"

"You should go." Dria's lips thinned into a line as she scowled at her brother. "Since you've completed the introduction."

Pain flickered briefly across Ralan's face, but he nodded. Oh yes, Vek decided. There was absolutely some conflict between these two. An interesting development. When Vek had visited Moranaia a few centuries before, Ralan had spoken of his sister with affection and an ease that implied no disagreement. Not one like this.

"Fine," Ralan said. "But know that the strands are murky in this. Tread carefully."

Dria's eyes widened at that pronouncement, but she didn't call her brother back for further explanation when he departed. Vek might have been fascinated by that bit of foretelling himself if a cold wash of unease hadn't trickled down his spine at the words. He couldn't know for sure, but he didn't think the prince had been referring specifically to this meeting. There was more in play than that.

What a surprise.

Once Ralan was gone, Dria glanced between him and Fen. "Now. You stated yesterday that you are here on behalf of your father."

Vek could have sworn that he'd seen a spark of attraction in her eyes at their last meeting, but she was currently all business. Just as well—or so he tried to tell himself. "We detected an unusual concentration of energy in this location. I was in this cave before the wall restraining Earth's magic shattered, but I was not privy to the outcome."

"And why not?" Dria asked, a hint of chill to her tone. "If you were not entrusted to our secrets at the time, I'd say there was good cause."

Vek ground his teeth together. "I have worked with Ralan, Cora, Selia, and Aris. In fact, I owe them a debt of honor."

Before she could answer, Fen spoke up. "It's my fault. Poisoned energy made me ill, and my uncle was too concerned for my health to risk staying here. If not for me, he would have his answers already."

Her expression softened at that. "I see. Nevertheless, there's no reason why the Unseelie should be given access to our secrets."

"This is not Moranaia." Vek leaned closer. A mistake, as her sweet honeyed scent reached him again. Just like before, his traitorous body hardened, but he managed to hide his reaction. "Whether it is truly your domain is up for debate."

"Well, it isn't yours. The Unseelie have no claim here." Dria's throat worked, and her voice went breathy. "You have no claim."

Had interest flickered in her eyes? By force of will, he kept himself from taking a step back. Or forward. "Are you planning some action against me? I assure you I am more than prepared for any type of assault."

Vek could have sworn he heard Fen snort at the double meaning.

Dria's lips parted, her cheeks going pink. "I—"

"By the gods, Dree." Ralan's voice cut across the room from the direction of the doorway. "Bring him down to the portal. I wouldn't have introduced him if I found him untrustworthy."

At that, her skin filled with more color until her face almost matched her hair. But it wasn't entirely embarrassment. Oh, no. The bulk of it was fury, and that was more than warranted. Couldn't Ralan see how he undercut his sister's authority, or was he simply too blind to notice?

Dria glared over her shoulder at Ralan. "Interrupt me one more time, and I swear to all that is holy that I will suspend you over the central chamber in a week-long holding spell. I'm sure your bonded will understand. After all, she has to live with you."

Vek's lips twitched. "Don't be so hard on him, princess. He must have grown soft living amongst the humans."

Ralan's eyes narrowed, but it was worth it to see humor on Dria's face. "This is none of your business, Vek," Ralan said.

"He's the one I was talking to, not you." Dria huffed as she turned her back on her brother. "Tell me, Prince Vek. Can you give me any reason why I should trust you?"

"Honestly?" Vek shrugged, unwilling to lie even if he didn't volunteer the entire truth. "Not really."

Her brows rose. "Your negotiation tactics could use some work."

"Though there is one thing," he found himself saying. "You are mine." He captured her gaze and held it. "And I am yours."

Damn, he hadn't intended to say that.

Could the situation get any worse?

7

A maelstrom of emotions froze Dria in place. Surely to all the gods he hadn't just laid claim to her in the middle of a cave on the second day they'd met. Not in any binding way, but… She shook her head, but the motion didn't clear her confusion. Even Vek himself appeared stunned, his mouth hanging open as though *she* had been the one to drop that little blast spell between them.

"Have you lost your senses?" she hissed.

Vek twisted his fingers in his short white hair. "It is entirely possible."

His nephew laughed, his chuckles echoing around the large chamber until she wanted to scream. Dria refused to look back to see how her brother was reacting. *Miaran.* What was she supposed to do now? Whether he'd intended to or not, Vek's claim complicated matters. If she admitted their potential bond, she would have far less reason to openly mistrust him.

Soulbonds happened between people who were perfect complements, didn't they? To question his character would be to cast aspersions on her own. After all, how often did such links go wrong? She'd never heard of a bond being broken or denied, although she'd always been taught it was possible.

She could reject his words, but it would be a great dishonor to lie about such a thing—not to mention hurt any chance of a future relationship.

"You aren't Moranaian," she finally muttered, stalling.

A sardonic smile twisted his lips. "I believe we have indeed established that."

Gods, she wanted to hit him. "I've not heard of the Unseelie practicing the soulbond."

"We don't," he said, and her heart lurched. Then Vek eased closer, so near she could almost feel his body heat. "But we blood elves mate. Not many outside of our people know. You see? I've shown you a bit of trust by sharing a secret."

A lump formed in her throat as she stared into his pale eyes. His energy brushed against hers until she trembled, and there was no mistaking the edge of desire humming through his aura. "If you attempt to force some kind of link between us, I will not be pleased," she whispered.

Quick as thought, he traced a finger softly down her cheek. "Ah, dearest, my kind has no need of trickery. Our mates are willing participants in the process."

Though her mouth went dry, Dria brushed his hand away. She wouldn't be mesmerized. "A fine coincidence. So are ours. Shall I recite the bonding words to begin?"

He took a hasty step back at that, and she almost laughed. Vek might recognize the truth, but that didn't mean he intended to act on it. He was using the link to get past her defenses. Well, she could end that little game. Ralan obviously wanted her to show him the portal, and Vek was desperate enough to see it that he would flirt with her. She might as well guide him to the main chamber so he could satisfy his curiosity and then send him on his way.

Hopefully for good.

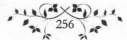

Still stunned, Vek trailed behind Dria through another empty room. What in the infinite hells of darkest creation had he been thinking? He didn't want a mate, even one as magnificent as Dria, but he'd almost called her bluff and told her to begin. She'd been visibly angry at his silence, but he hadn't been able to say a word lest he somehow end up begging.

Fen gave him a mental prod, and when Vek established the connection, he winced at the humor suffusing his nephew's surface thoughts. *"You're a fucking idiot,"* Fen sent.

"I am aware," Vek answered dryly. *"But I suppose your mind is always clear around your potential mates?"*

That certainly ended Fen's taunting. He cut off the connection with a snap so sharp Vek almost found himself chuckling despite the situation. The truth hurt—or so he'd always heard. But it was usually what the listener most needed to hear. Why else would it cause such pain and chaos?

In silence, Vek followed Dria as she marched along a short corridor and started down a flight of steps. If one could call the massive spiral to the floor of the cavern a mere flight. His mouth went dry as he peered over the side to examine the glowing archway below, but he couldn't bear to study the structure from this height. Instead, he eased closer to the wall and glanced down the corridors that branched off at each level.

Despite that, his unease grew with each step, although he wasn't typically afraid of heights. He lived in the underrealms, his very home built into a cave much like this one. And while the absence of railing here seemed a reckless oversight, it shouldn't account for his current state. He could always use a suspending spell if he tumbled over the side.

At the base of the staircase, Dria didn't so much as pause. But Vek's body seized so suddenly that Fen crashed into his back with an *oomph*.

"What the hell?" his nephew muttered.

Vek couldn't answer. He could barely even breathe. Panic and fury surged through him as his magic and his body were frozen, the hold so complete no simple spell could be to blame. Neither Selia nor Dria had done this.

Then his magic began to drain away, the power sucked from his blood until his very veins burned and his muscles chilled and spasmed.

They'd brought him down to kill him.

Someone cried out, but he couldn't move his eyes to see who. All he could focus on was Dria. She spun around, and surprise wiped away any traces of her anger. She stared for a moment before rushing forward, magic glowing in her hands. He wanted to tell her not to touch him. To back away. But he couldn't.

"Dria, stop," Ralan called from across the cavern. "That spell is not of Moranaian design."

She halted an arm's length away. Her forehead furrowed as she scanned his body, but she didn't try to use the magic gathered in her palms. "What *is* this?"

Another figure came into view—the dragon in her elven form. Vek would have scowled if it were possible. Of course she was involved in this. He should have known. But even as he had the thought, he noticed the confusion pulling down her brows. Could she be innocent of this treachery?

A furious hiss sounded from behind him. Fen. Fortunately, his nephew was wise enough not to step down beside him. "Release my uncle," Fen snapped. "You have broken the peace of this meeting. After I defended you all to him, too."

"Have we?" Aris stepped forward, a glowing green sword in hand. "There must be a reason Vek triggered this spell. Selia, did you—"

"This isn't something I set up," the woman in question said.

Vek's vision began to waver as the pain picked up in intensity. Fuck, it felt like his veins were being ripped out. He tried to shout. Scream. Beg. Anything to make it end.

Then it did.

Before Dria could decide what to do, Vek crumpled. His nephew managed to catch him in time to keep him from hitting his head on the stairs, but just barely. Grunting, Fen hauled Vek to safety, stretching him out beside the staircase before turning to face Dria. She'd never seen the younger man as anything but affable, but he was far from that now.

Not with fangs bared and earth magic rumbling around him like an earthquake threatening to break.

"What did you do?" he snarled.

Dria opened her mouth to explain, but she had no explanation for this. She'd probed the spell as best she could, searching for some hint on how to break it, but it hadn't been like anything she'd seen before. Similar in parts, but the power of the spell itself had been blinding, too intense to allow close scrutiny. "This isn't my fault."

A small army of stones rose to circle around Fen's head as he glared at her. "If my uncle dies—"

"Stand down, boy."

The rough, sardonic voice sliced through the air out of nowhere, and the rocks spinning around Fen dropped to the ground in a small skittering avalanche. Dria whipped around, widening her defenses to include the helpless Vek out of instinct, in time to see a man step out of the shadows near the cavern wall. She knew two things at once—he hadn't been there a moment before, and he was not one of the elves.

Flames crackled through his hair and glinted like suggestions in his eyes as he glided closer. He paused to nod at Aris and Selia, who stared in shocked recognition, and then smirked at Ralan before continuing in Dria's direction. Her skin prickled as his focus landed on her. Absolutely not an elf.

"You are correct. Although…" The stranger lifted a shoulder. "Well, we could spend hours detailing my lineage."

Dria swallowed against a mouth gone dry. "Who…?"

He laughed. "I am Loki, god of a great deal of shit. Doesn't matter."

"Is this your fault?" Fen called from behind Dria.

She wanted to advise him to remain silent, but she couldn't manage to form words herself.

"When Vekenayeth anh Torekthayed approaches the portal, it will be with pure intent or not at all," the god said. "Take him from this place until he knows the entire truth."

None of this made sense. She was on Earth. She'd always heard that human gods no longer walked amongst their people, at least not openly. Even Moranaian deities rarely did so.

"I don't know if I'd call myself a god *of* anyone in particular, including humans," Loki said as though she'd spoken aloud. "But that's not important. There is a great deal awakening, and not all of it is good. There's only so much crazy even I can deal with."

Vek's groan echoed from the staircase.

"Don't let him back in here until he has learned the truth from his father." The twin flames of Loki's gaze enthralled her, freezing her answer before it could form. "Beyond that, well…don't offer him blood until you've started the bond. And try not to wait too long."

No amount of training could peel her tongue from the roof of her mouth. The power pouring from the god before her was staggering, and she got the impression from his relaxed demeanor that he was toning it down. Unbelievable.

Then it was over.

He spun away, nodding at the others as he strolled toward the edge of the cavern—and disappeared. Staring at the spot, Dria sucked in a deep breath. That was… She clenched her hands until her nails bit into her palm. Intense didn't cover it.

And that wasn't even considering the questions the god's words had raised.

Finally, she was able to turn back to Vek and Fen, who sat on the stairs beside his uncle with a dazed look on his face. Fen blinked several times, though it was a moment before he appeared able to focus. It was almost as though he'd been physically stunned, but she hadn't sensed any form of attack magic.

"Guess I'd better haul his ass home somehow," Fen muttered. "I knew this was a bad idea."

Suspicion trickled into the wake of the god's passing. "Vek was here to cause trouble," Dria said.

"No," Fen insisted. But then he winced. "Not this time, anyway. The Unseelie King isn't happy about whatever you have going on down here."

Their earlier conversation flicked through her mind.

"Tell me, Prince Vek. Can you give me any reason why I should trust you?"

"Honestly?" Vek shrugged. "Not really."

He'd all but told her he had bad intentions, then distracted her with talk of their bond. Gods, she was a fool. Vek had been sent here to spy—at the least. There was doubtless more than that if a god had interfered, but she had a feeling Fen wouldn't give her more information. He'd probably said more than he should have already.

"Get out of here," Dria said through gritted teeth. "And tell him to stay away this time."

Naomh didn't wait for his brother to answer the knock. Meren deserved no courtesy for his treachery, and in any case, Naomh had done far worse than a bit of rudeness. Both of them had. Naomh shut the door as quietly as his ill temper allowed before marching toward Meren. The useless *eltor*. He sat draped in his favorite chair without a sign of concern on his face.

"Here without Caolte?" Meren asked in a mocking lilt. "I thought the bastard did nothing but follow at your heels and search for imaginary threats."

Though the words rankled, Naomh refused to be distracted. "You may speak to our brother about his activities later. You know perfectly well why I'm here. First, you worked with the Unseelie to murder perfectly innocent Neorans who could have been cured of the energy poisoning. Now, you think to strike the Moranaians?"

Meren waved a hand. "They'll stand in the way of any reasonable action we seek to take. If they retreat to their own domain, they'll remain unharmed."

"Have you grown so dishonorable that you'll fight against your own blood?" Naomh took a step forward, his hands clenching. If his brother couldn't see reason in this, he was beyond hope. "I have a son among the Moranaians. Your nephew—"

"I heard the rumors." Meren straightened in his seat. "But I wasn't certain you'd be fool enough to claim him. Bad enough that our father dishonored our mother by sleeping with that Unseelie woman, disgracing our blood with Caolte. Now you further weaken our heritage by breeding with a Moranaian. We are a noble house, Naomh. Not that you seem to remember."

Naomh kept his grip on his temper and his magic, but it wasn't a sure thing. Not for long. "Do you want our people to return to the surface badly enough to resort to this darkness?"

Meren shoved to his feet. "And are you a fool? Have you seen the queen recently? No, of course not. Very few have since she has been near death for months. In the meantime, her daughter botches every decision she attempts to make. Now, there are rumors of true power on Earth. Magic like the old days, and bloodlines awakening. Why should we remain here, our people withering and dying? Our queen dying?"

The vehemence in his brother's voice caught Naomh off guard, and for a moment, it almost swayed him. But the matter wasn't as simple as Meren made it seem. "There are honorable methods we might use to meet that goal."

"If you care to wait a few decades. Or centuries." Meren lifted a brow. "Haven't you enjoyed your little jaunts to the surface, after all? You might not have physically touched the ground, but you haven't exactly been innocent."

He wasn't wrong, much to Naomh's regret. Naomh had believed he could use the disgraced Prince Kien of the Moranaians to stop what he'd sensed was coming—the humans' discovery of the fae races. He'd hoped that he could find his missing soulbonded so long as he was free to roam without human interference, but the plot had spiraled out of control, threatening the existence of all Naomh had hoped to protect.

That was why he had to stop this.

"Leave off with the Unseelie," Naomh said. "They have no care with their methods."

Meren laughed. "And you do?"

Naomh winced. Yes, he'd helped Kien with the initial energy poisoning. It had been intended to keep the fae in the underhill, not harm them. But few could work with darkness to create good, not without getting caught in the miasma. How well he had learned.

"Harm Kai and you will regret it."

His brother only smirked. "Stand in my way, and you will, as well."

8

Pain was a worse alarm clock than the shrill device Fen insisted on using, though it pierced through Vek's head just the same. Groaning, he shoved his forearm against his eyes and took note of his condition. He was partially sitting, slumped against something soft. And his body felt as though it had been beaten by an entire family of angry cave trolls.

"Hey, don't move," Fen shouted from somewhere above.

Vek grunted some attempt at a reply.

He reached for his magic so that he could scan the room, but agony ripped through him, drawing out a curse. Drained. He was drained. How long had it been since he'd fed? Deepest depths, but he needed energy. Fast.

"Blood," he gasped.

Muttered curses rang out from above. Then he smelled the tinny scent of blood, but just before the blessed nourishment reached him, another odor clarified.

Illness.

"No," Vek mumbled. "You're sick."

His body shrieked in denial as the blood disappeared, but it was for the best. He was too weak to process disease. Voices tangled around him, but he didn't try to grasp the meaning. Elves didn't get sick. Why had Fen brought some human here instead of offering his own blood? And how many humans were there? There were three or four different people speaking.

The discussion subsided, and a few moments later, Vek smelled blood again. Not human, surely, not with that rich scent. Something nudged against his mouth, and he opened his lips to let the blood trickle through. It only took a few drops for clarity to return. A wrist. Leaning forward, Vek took a few long pulls until the power exploded through him.

With a groan, he closed the cut with his newly replenished magic and dropped his head back against the couch, only to wince at the feel of the frame through the cushion. But the poorly designed couch was the least of his problems. His muscles twitched and burned as energy poured into his starved body, and his head ached as new senses began to take shape.

Who had offered him the blood?

Feck. He was careful—very careful—of his sources. For good reason. He shoved his palms against his temples in a vain attempt to stem the flow of information. Three other people were in the room with him. Fen, Selia, and Aris. Outside, five birds perched on the nearest tree, multiple squirrels darted through the branches, and countless insects skittered through the underbrush. Flies. Mosquitoes. Dear gods, he could count them if he wished.

"Vek?" Fen asked tentatively.

With his new talent, Vek scanned his nephew and as feared, found a shadow of something wrong. But it was faint. Nothing like the illness he could have sworn he'd smelled. Had that been an illusion? Like most elves and fae, the magic in a *Felshreh's* body wiped out any diseases that tried to take hold. Fen might have had a human father, but he had more than enough power to keep from getting sick.

"What happened?" Vek asked, his voice sounding rough even to his own ears.

"The spell that god used on you fucked you up, that's what," Fen answered. "Selia was nice enough to make us a portal home so I didn't have to haul you down the mountain, and Aris gave you blood since you refused mine."

"That last part I figured out." Vek directed a grateful nod to Aris, though the other elf might regret giving aid if he discovered that Vek had gained his talent from the exchange. "But…a god?"

Selia answered. "Loki, he is called. He helped us set up the portal, and it appears he is protective of it. He forbade us to let you approach."

Vek frowned. He'd heard of Loki, of course. There were even rumors that some of the Unseelie might be descendants. But why would a god connected to Earth help the Moranaians against those who might be kin? Even if the tales were wrong, Loki seemed the type to side with the Unseelie over elves from another world.

"Did he say why?"

Fen lifted a shoulder. "Something about only letting you approach when your intentions are pure. Oh, and that your father hasn't told you everything you need to know."

Vek let out a long breath. No wonder he'd been escorted here by Selia and Aris. A kindness, sure, but also a guarantee that he was far from their little colony. Loki had apparently told them he wasn't trustworthy. And who knew what Fen had done or said? If—

Head snapping up, Vek connected with his nephew. *"You didn't tell Dria I'm supposed to kill her, did you?"*

"Hell, no," Fen answered, glaring. *"I'm not an idiot like you. I told them the Unseelie king was unhappy, but that's it. Give me some credit."*

"Perhaps we should go," Aris said quietly. "There is surely much these two must discuss, and I suspect we don't want to know the details."

Rude though it was, Vek nodded. "I am in your debt once more, but I'm afraid I must agree. This latest event has given me a great deal to consider. But know that I will not forget your assistance."

And he wouldn't. Despite their lack of trust in Vek, the Moranaians had offered aid at every turn. Whereas his own father had deceived him. It was one thing for his relatives to resort to trickery as they competed for influence, but another for the king himself to do it. King Torek had sent him into danger without full knowledge of the situation, a perilous lapse. But a Moranaian had saved him.

For the first time in Vek's life, he wanted to kill—or at least soundly throttle—his king.

"Yes, here," Dria directed as Kezari shifted rock like potter's clay. A pair of body-sized columns rose from the floor, as smooth as a time-worn stalagmite. "You're good. I've rarely seen a master earth mage work with such ease."

The dragon woman tilted her head. "They might if they lived in dens like ours. Even air dragons are handy at forming caves, though their work is less elegant."

If Dria hadn't been holding back anger, she might have laughed at the haughty arrogance of the dragon's tone. Kezari was an interesting one, that was for sure. Her facial expressions and body language didn't quite match her elven form, and even in the chilly cave, she wore the barest of dresses. On the climb up, Dria had figured out why, though. In close proximity, the dragon emitted an impressive amount of heat.

Kezari gestured at the columns. "Adequate?"

After a quick study, Dria nodded. "Perfect. Would it be too much trouble to place more of these in the other rooms while you are creating shelves?"

"I will do this while I wait for Aris and Selia," the dragon answered. "It is no trouble to be in this place where the energy still sings."

Now, that was an apt description. Dria hadn't known what to expect from Earth's energy, but not only had it been abundant, it also possessed both a deeply nuanced and yet buoyant air. Perhaps it was a result of the power being allowed freedom after so long behind a wall? Whatever the reason, it did very much seem to sing.

"Thank you, Kezari," Dria said. "I appreciate your help on such a menial task."

The dragon shrugged. "With the crisis over, I am not occupied with other duties."

Crisis over.

As Kezari departed, Dria considered those words. Perhaps the dragon's troubles were finished, but Dria couldn't say the same. Anger surged to the forefront again. She tried to ignore it, focusing on removing her formal overrobe instead. She hefted the garment over the first of the new columns and smoothed the fabric with trembling fingers.

She'd been a fool to bother wearing it.

Dria had told herself it would boost her confidence, but the choice had been more than that. Deep inside, she'd wanted to impress Vek. Gods, how pathetic. He'd been coming here to spy, and he would have used anything, including their potential bond, to ensure he met his goal. And somehow, some way, her brother had been in on it.

As though summoned, Ralan poked his head around the door. "The first of the guard contingent will be here shortly."

She gestured for him to enter. Though his brows rose, he complied, shutting the door behind him. "What are you really doing, Ralan? Is all of this some kind of test? A joke? Or has your allegiance changed in the centuries you've been gone?"

The friendly ease left his expression. "That is unwarranted. You've made it clear you are angry at me, but you have no right to call my loyalty into question."

"Don't I?" Dria stepped closer. "You told me Vek was trustworthy. Either you lied, or you're involved in whatever he is plotting."

Her brother didn't bother to look repentant. "If Loki hadn't stopped him, one of us would have. It was necessary. I had a vision, and—"

"Iron take your thrice-cursed visions," Dria shouted, her hold on her temper snapping. "They're just so convenient, aren't they? But they never work as promised. Oh, sure, Dree, I'll introduce you to your soulbonded. I promise. I'll tell father which teacher to pick for you. I promise. I'll direct you to an appointment that won't make you as miserable as you are here at court. I. Promise. Well, you can shove your promises in a hole and bury them like the dead, disgraced things they are."

His expression went slack with shock. "Dree…"

"Did you expect me to be happy that you abandoned me?" Her hands clenched. "Some protector you were. Once the strength of my gift became apparent, everyone assumed I'd turn out to be as twisted as our brother. People even said I'd driven you off with my perversity. You swore to look after me, but instead, you left me with that. At least until Father sent me away on my eighteenth birthday."

"Sent you away?" Ralan's brows lowered. "He was supposed to wait."

"What?" Dria asked.

"I didn't forget you," Ralan said softly. "I told Father before I left that he was to send you to the Citadel when you turned twenty-five. You were to continue working with your regular teacher until then."

Her shoulders hunched. "You mean the teacher who fled the rumors a few months after Kien was caught? I had a series of tutors after that, but none would stay for long."

Cursing, Ralan speared his fingers into his hair. "I'm sorry. The events surrounding my leaving must have changed the future strands. I didn't know. I…stopped using my Sight once I was on Earth, unless I had a vision. And I admit I did forget about introducing you to your soulbonded. I'd only had the vaguest idea of it, for the strand was so far in the future it could have been millennia. That promise was buried beneath my pain."

"You stopped using your Sight?" The idea seemed impossible considering how much he'd relied on his gift. "That can't be true."

His gaze met hers, and his eyes held so much agony and regret that her own heart ached with it. "Oh, but it is. If Father hadn't trapped me into spying on the strands concerning Kien and Kenaren, I never would have discovered their treachery. I wouldn't have argued with Father when he refused to believe me, and I wouldn't have fled. When I reached Earth, I swore to forego my talent, lest I See something else that would bring ruin. I've only resumed using my Sight in the last month or two."

Dria took a deep breath as she processed his words, and a new understanding awoke in her, one born of adult logic rather than childish hurts. Ralan might have forgotten his promises to her, but his world had been torn apart, too. He had loved Kenaren. Gods, he'd spent hours talking about the woman, and then he'd found out that she'd planned to murder him to be with Kien. But what had his leaving solved?

"You shouldn't have run away," she whispered.

"Ah, Dree." Ralan gripped her hand in his. "It was my only choice. Father couldn't accept the truth about Kien, and I didn't want to be murdered to prove him wrong. Now that I have Eri and another child on the way, I can even sympathize. Who wants to believe their own flesh and blood could be capable of such evil? Leaving was meant to be. If I hadn't gone, I wouldn't have Eri, and I might not have met Cora. But I am sorry you were hurt in the process."

Part of her wanted to let go of her anger—another wanted to cherish it. "I need time to think about this."

He tapped his finger on her nose, much as he had when she was a child. "You always do."

She couldn't help but laugh. "Sorry."

"Don't apologize for being yourself," Ralan answered, smiling. "About Vek…"

Hah. That was guaranteed to erase any hint of humor. "You were going to tell me why you wanted me to take him to the portal?"

"No." His smile widened into a grin. "I already did."

She poked him. "Saying you had a vision isn't exactly descriptive."

"You know very well I won't give the details," he said. "But it was important for his agenda to be found out now. Other strands are far more complex and dangerous."

"Sounds fabulous."

"Someday it might be," Ralan answered, a wealth of meaning in his words. But was he talking about her life or the world in general?

There were some things she knew better than to ask.

🔥

Vek tapped his fingers against his leg in time with the heartbeats nudging at his senses. "How did Aris come to be the one who gave me blood?"

Fen turned from his perusal of the Chattanooga skyline. "Instead of Selia? She offered first, and there was a bit of an argument about it. Something about Aris's past and how a cut might affect him. But he was determined. Turned paler than you'd believe, though."

"Did I dream the part about your offer of blood?"

Eyebrows drawing together, Fen shook his head. "No. I think you were delusional. I'm not sick. I'm as immune to human ailments as you are, and the energy poisoning was eradicated."

Vek heaved himself to his feet with a tired sigh, though his physical weaknesses had disappeared with his renewed energy. But there were more types of exhaustion than those of the body, as he'd had ample cause to learn.

Striding over to his nephew, Vek scanned him with every spell he knew, including his newfound life magic. Nothing obvious was wrong. Not a thing beyond that shadow he'd detected earlier. A nuanced darkness easily missed. It wasn't like the poison that Kien had lodged in Fen's heart, though, the evil that had caused illness and death among so many, including Kethen's son. This had a different tone.

"Mind cutting yourself again?" Vek asked. "I'd like to see if I can catch the scent now that I'm awake."

With a shrug, Fen slid the tip of one fang along his forearm and offered the small wound to Vek without visible signs of pain. Vek bent close and sniffed, letting each scent process through his senses. Adequate iron, vitamin, and magic levels, though perhaps a bit low on the latter. Nothing that… No. There.

The barest suggestion of illness—a physical one.

"You *are* sick."

Fen jerked back, closing the wound before glaring at Vek. "Can't be."

Vek frowned at his nephew. "Perhaps you should have smelled for yourself."

Fen flushed. "Is detecting diseases an acquired skill? Because I've never noticed anything like that in blood before. I just feed."

That gave Vek pause. When had he learned such a thing? It had been second nature for so many centuries that he honestly couldn't remember if he'd been taught or if he'd picked it up from someone's blood along the way. His kind might not drink blood as their sole nourishment like traditional vampires, but they did have to ingest it to gain magical energy. And since the body used energy to purge disease, taking in tainted blood would net less power.

"Hey, do you think it could be left over from drinking from a sick human?" Fen asked hopefully.

"I'm not sure," Vek answered. "I can't recall having checked another blood elf after they'd fed from the ill. How long did you say it had been since you last fed?"

His nephew's lips turned down. "Three or four days, I guess."

"Your body should have purged anything by now."

"Even with my human nature?" Fen rubbed at the spot on his arm where he'd made the cut. "Maybe it was a serious disease and my body is sluggish after the energy poisoning. I feel fine."

Though it was tempting to accept that explanation, his nephew's exhaustion after their climb up the mountain suggested otherwise. "You should see a healer just in case."

Fen shot him a dry look. "Like who? We don't need to give your father another excuse to kill me by showing up in the Unseelie court with a mystery illness to treat. Oh, and you just alienated the Moranaians. There's Maddy, but..."

"Her gift is not honed."

"Not just that." Fen blanched. "After what you told me about the whole mate thing, I don't know if... Maybe I should avoid her. If she and Anna could both be my mate, things could get awkward fast. Not a choice I want to make any time soon."

Vek chuckled softly. "You must be young if you've never been with more than one lover at a time. In the last couple of centuries alone, I've—"

"I didn't say that," Fen grumbled. "But we're talking mating. Isn't that usually two people?"

"Sweet, innocent child," Vek said. Mostly to see the annoyance on his nephew's face. "I've heard of matings between four people before, though it's rare."

"Damn."

Under different circumstances, Vek might have enjoyed Fen's shock enough to draw the moment out. Not today. "Perhaps we should ensure that you live to decide? Maddy might be inadequately trained, but she will be discreet. If nothing else, she might be able to identify the disease."

Fen's mouth settled into a thin, determined line. But finally, he nodded. "You win. I'll go see Maddy."

9

Dria and Ralan barely reached the portal in time to greet the guards arriving from Moranaia, but at least there was a new sense of peace between her and her brother. She wasn't sure if their past friendship would reform or if she could forgive him, but it was a start. Certainly more than she had thought possible before their argument.

The portal flickered, and then the warriors stepped through. There weren't mages among them; based on their armor, this group was more scout than soldier. In the close confines of the cave, the troop's composition was wise, something she might have suggested herself. But who had decided who would be stationed here? Ralan as prince and heir or Lyr as a general of the army? Either way, no one had bothered to consult her.

"How were these people chosen?" Dria whispered before the group descended the stairs.

Ralan gave her a knowing look. "Lyr decided before you were brought in to lead. Feel free to reassign anyone if you need to. But really, Lyr is an important ally in this. He's willing to provide this troop and knows his warriors well enough to choose the best. I wouldn't have debated him on the matter."

"I feel superfluous," she murmured.

"Don't," Ralan insisted. "Leaders delegate. Even Father would consult the nearest general for a mission like this. He'll certainly speak with the Mage General at the Citadel to pick the best mages."

Dria's heart thumped. "You've…you've put me in charge of a troop from the Citadel? Are you insane? I have no rank there."

Ralan grinned. "You have one now."

If the warriors hadn't neared, Dria would have cursed at her brother. Instead, she settled for a withering glare. Didn't he care what mayhem this could cause? She wasn't disliked at the Citadel, not in particular, but she hadn't earned a position of power, either. And among the mages, rank was deserved, not granted. When dealing with powerful magic, it had to be.

But Dria would worry about that later. Now, she fixed a neutral smile on her face and greeted the leader of the warriors in front of her. One of three in the group with Dökkálfar heritage, the woman's midnight skin blended well with the dim cave, as did the brown of her leather armor.

The woman tapped her chest and inclined her head. "Good evening, Feraien. I am Kera, Commander of this troop during the mission. Though I usually report to Lord Lyrnis as his third in command, I am to defer to you while I am here."

"It is a pleasure to meet you, Kera," Dria answered. "Since we will be working together closely, I invite you to call me Dria. I am leader first and princess last."

Kera nodded. "Very well. I will endeavor to remember."

Dria gestured toward the grand staircase curling up the cavern. "If you'll follow me, I'll show you to your quarters. Some of the rooms are still being prepared, but you should be able to choose according to preference."

"Thank you," Kera said.

Though the warrior's expression held nothing but politeness, Dria sensed a measuring weight to her gaze. No surprise there. Everyone knew the ages of the royal children, at least generally, and the woman had to be wondering why a mage who hadn't neared her fourth century would be giving the orders. But it could have been worse. Dria had half expected hostility, so a silent examination was nothing.

Stifling a sigh, she led the group toward the stairs. She'd get more than enough hostility when mages from the Citadel arrived.

So it began.

By the time Fen made it to The Magic Touch, the shop that Maddy was buying from Cora, it was almost lunch time. Though his stomach rumbled, he didn't duck into one of the restaurants near the shop. He'd promised Vek that he would go straight there if he was allowed to go alone, and he suspected his uncle would somehow know if he deviated.

The guy was as bad as any father. Not that Fen could remember his.

But Fen's promise meant Vek was able to return to the Unseelie realm right away. Fen had an uneasy feeling that whatever secret the king held would change everything. A germ of some sort was nothing next to that, not if Loki was concerned enough to interfere. Apparently, his uncle had agreed.

Fen peeked in the shop window before he approached the door. A couple of customers browsed inside, and a thin blond man rang up a purchase behind the back counter. No sign of Maddy. She had to be there, though. He'd texted her to ensure she was at work before driving to downtown Chattanooga.

Despite the seriousness of the situation, he almost wished she'd been busy. Maddy had a girlfriend—Anna. Fen would never in a million years be worthy of either of them, but knowing they could mate would make it much more difficult to resist flirting with her despite his shortcomings. But only a jerk would do that. She was in a committed, monogamous relationship. She might not even be bisexual like he was.

It would be just his luck to have a mating bond where the other people would never be interested.

"You okay, man?"

Fen turned at the seemingly concerned voice, but the human's eyes were filled with more than a little suspicion. Damn, he probably looked like a creep lingering by the store window. He forced himself to relax and let out a short chuckle.

"Yeah," Fen answered. "Trying to remember which of these display dresses my girlfriend was talking about. Don't want to screw up her birthday present."

The man laughed, most of the wariness fading. "Good luck."

"I think I've got it figured out."

Before the stranger could give him more grief, Fen strolled into the store and approached the counter without haste. A customer had just gathered his bag to leave, so it was only a short wait until the cashier was free.

Jase, his name tag read.

"Hey," Fen said, keeping his voice low. "I'm here to see Maddy."

"Yeah?" Jase's eyebrows lifted. "Does she know that?"

Fen couldn't blame the guy for being distrustful. Only a few weeks before, Maddy had been kidnapped by two of Kien's men. And Fen's former partners-in-crime, but Jase didn't know that. Probably. Fen had no idea what Maddy might have told him.

The door behind the counter swung open, and the woman in question hustled out, a dress held high in her hand so it wouldn't drag on the ground. She wore her long red hair pulled back with a loose clip, and she must have been in the sun lately since her freckles stood out sharply on her pale face.

Fuck, she was beautiful.

As soon as she caught sight of Fen, she smiled. Actually smiled as though she was pleased to see him. He couldn't fathom it. They'd first met when he'd pretended to rejoin Kien's group—at the same time she'd been held hostage. She knew he'd done terrible stuff. She had to. Why was she always so happy to see him? She'd even attempted to heal him after Kien's poison had taken root in his heart.

"Jase, would you show my friend to the break room?" Maddy asked softly. "I'll be in once I've finished helping this customer."

"Sure," the man answered, his earlier coldness gone.

Fen tried not to stare after Maddy as he followed Jase toward another door tucked into the wall. She practically glowed with light and life as she held the dress out for her customer to see. Had she always been this enchanting, or had the effect grown along with the magic available on Earth? Or perhaps he was seeing her differently now that he knew about their link.

Almost reluctantly, Fen trailed the other man into the small room. It held only a table and a small counter with a microwave on top. There was another door on that wall, probably leading to the stockroom. To all appearances, this was nothing more than a break room for the employees.

If you couldn't feel the multiple layers of heavy shielding.

Fen dropped into a chair, slumping against the back. Jase studied him from the door, and a tendril of energy brushed across Fen's magical protections. He smiled at the other man in acknowledgement and let him detect what he wanted him to know. He was no expert on the various fae races—yet another thing he needed to learn from his uncle—but he was fairly positive Jase had Ellyllon ancestry. The Welsh elves could be a persistent sort.

"Like what you see?" Fen asked, smirking.

He could already read the answer in the other man's scowl.

"Maddy is not an energy source, blood elf," Jase said. "Hurt her and I'll finish whatever scraps of you she leaves behind."

Ah, good. Jase was fully aware of Maddy's power. "I doubt she would leave scraps."

That teased out a reluctant grin from the other man. "That she wouldn't."

The door clicked open, and Maddy entered, sending Jase a pointed look. He nodded at Fen and left before she reached the table. Fen barely noticed. Maddy glimmered with power, her spirit so vibrant he was surprised it wasn't visible. Then he frowned. It was almost too vivid. How could she contain so much energy?

"What's up, Fen?" she asked.

Maddy took the seat beside him, and his thoughts fled as her scent washed over him. Honey and rain and plants newly budded. Fen clenched his fingers around the edge of the table to keep himself from reaching for her. It wouldn't do either of them any good.

"Fen?"

He scrubbed his hand through his hair. "Sorry. Look, I won't waste your time." More like *let's get this over with before I jump you.* "I need your help."

Her forehead furrowed as she scanned him with her gaze. And her energy. He shivered as it caressed him. "You're sick," she whispered.

"You can tell?" Fen peered at her, noticing again how dark her freckles appeared. Maybe she hadn't been in the sun. No, they only stood out because her already fair skin was so pale. "You are, too."

"No." Maddy's shoulders slumped. "Not now. But I was."

His heart squeezed. Hadn't it only been a couple of weeks since he'd seen her? "What are you talking about? You can't get sick. You're half Seelie Sidhe."

Maddy shrugged. "And you're half Unseelie blood elf. Yet here you are."

Silence landed like a bomb between them as they processed that truth. The fae didn't worry about physical sickness since their bodies cleared viruses before symptoms could be felt. Hell, most germs never made it past the heightened energy surrounding them. Their healers didn't even spend much time studying such things since illness was a non-issue.

If a virus had evolved to bypass their natural defenses...

"Did it clear on its own, or did you purge it with your gift?" Fen asked.

Maddy's jaw clenched. "Mostly on its own. I didn't have many symptoms, except for muscle aches and extreme exhaustion. My healing gift was unreliable as usual. But pulling in an uncomfortable amount of energy finally helped. That or my body cleared it like a human's would."

So that was why she glowed like an overcharged mage light. "I could—" His mouth snapped closed on the offer he'd almost made. Fuck. He couldn't take her blood to drain away some of the energy, not if Vek was to be believed. "That is, I should see what my uncle thinks. Once he returns from the Unseelie realm."

"Fen." Maddy arched an eyebrow. "I know you must have come here for me to heal you. No use pretending otherwise."

At least she hadn't noticed his almost-offer. "I did. You said it didn't work, though."

"Increased energy did," she pointed out. "Which I happen to have an excess of at the moment."

Damn. Fen took a deep breath as he tried to think of a reasonable explanation for refusing. Something besides the truth. "Vek said not to take your blood."

He winced as she shoved away from the table. Okay, that hadn't been the best choice. "To hell with your racist uncle, Fen. Who cares if I'm Seelie? I'm not poison."

"It's not that." Fen grabbed her wrist before she could march from the room. A mistake, he realized, as desire shot through him. "Some blood might affect me… differently. It's nothing personal, I promise. Vek wouldn't have asked you to heal me last time if he had anything against you."

Maddy's eyes narrowed. "I might be young for a Sidhe, but I'm a grown woman. Tell me what you're hiding, Fen, or you can walk out that door and never come back. I mean it."

She did, too. Resolve poured from her like the energy she barely managed to contain. Ah, he might as well reveal the truth. She would tell him to take a hike either way. "According to Vek, we could be mates. And taking your blood would seal the bond."

10

Head held high, Vek traversed the long hallway leading to his father's private sanctum. He wouldn't be in the throne room at this time of day, and Vek wouldn't request a formal meeting regardless. If there was subterfuge at play, it was better confronted away from all others. Especially Ara.

As Vek neared the door to his father's chamber, he slowed. Quaea stood guard, a sneer already on her face she studied him. She forgot her place, and he was in no mood to argue.

"The king is not receiving visitors," Quaea said as Vek stopped in front of her. "You may not enter."

"Move," he said. "That's an order from your prince."

Her smile only widened. "The king's command supersedes yours. Begone, or I will be forced to protect him."

Vek's patience shattered. Time to fulfill the unspoken promise he'd made when she'd brought him to his father the day before. Quick as thought, Vek grabbed command of her muscles with a single thrust of magic. His hand snapped out, his fingers digging into the side of her neck. Though it was reckless considering the painful cost he bore if he took blood too often, he had no time to do otherwise.

With a smile that revealed his fangs, he leaned close to her face. Unable to fight, she trembled in his grip.

"Dearest Quaea, shall I take your essence?" he asked. "By right, as a prince of the blood, I can do so without permission. Then you'll know the truth of the rumors, won't you?"

Her pulse raced beneath his hand. Few knew the extent of Vek's talent, the ability to glean another's magical ability by taking their blood, and in the vacuum of knowledge, tales abounded. He never bothered to disabuse anyone of their false impressions. In the Unseelie court, fear was a powerful influence.

Quaea's mind brushed his. *"I won't yield."*

Vek struck, sinking his fangs into her neck between one breath and the next. He only needed a sip to grab her energy and pull, but he let her blood flow into his mouth as he intentionally drained her of most of her power. Though it was more of either than he needed, he would leave no doubts about her place in this court. Only when she slipped into unconsciousness did he finally stop, closing the wound with his magic and dropping her body on the ground.

Perhaps she would learn not to defy him.

A tendril of pain flowed between his temples and through his skull as his mind sought to process his reforming channels. But as the ache faded, he took a moment to study what he had gained. He never received every talent his donor possessed, and sometimes he already knew the same skills. So it was with Quaea, save for two useful abilities: a spell for creating transportation gates and the key to unlock the door to his father's study.

Perfect. Without a backward glance, he cast the spell and shoved the door open.

"I don't know what to do, my king," the healer said before she registered Vek's intrusion.

Shocked, Vek halted in the center of the room. The ancient healer, older even than his father, bent over the king where he lay on a long sofa. But her wide, startled eyes were on Vek now. Fear clouded her gaze before she jerked to her feet and backed away.

"I will leave you," she whispered.

He barely noticed her as she shuffled away. His attention was on King Torek, the father he would have called immortal before today. The father whose skin was an ashen gray and whose face was lined with countless wrinkles. Vek knew the king wore a glamour, as many of their kind did, but enough to cover this? His father was so gaunt he could be near death.

"What is going on here?" Vek demanded, his voice harsher than he'd intended.

Just as well. The king would expect no concern from him.

His father pushed to a sitting position, though he slumped against the back of the sofa after the effort. "You shouldn't be here. I gave you a task, and it is not yet complete."

"I was stopped by a god." Vek swallowed against the lump in his throat. "Loki. He said you've been hiding things from me. Appears he was correct."

The king cursed. "You must find a way around him. The rest is not your concern."

Vek stared at his father. "That's it? You sent me off unprepared and expect me not to question?"

"Where's Quaea?"

"Likely being helped to her room by the healer," Vek said, unrepentant despite the alarm that pinched his father's face. "I claimed her blood, as the law allows. Perhaps I was too enthusiastic."

With a sharp inhale, the king leaned forward. "Sun's glare, Vek, you approach treason. You know very well she was ordered to let no one through."

Vek crossed his arms. "Did you tell her to bar me specifically?"

King Torek's lips thinned. "You weren't supposed to be here."

"But I am." Hidden from sight by his arm, Vek dug his left hand into a fist until his nails nearly broke the skin of his palm. Damn, his father was pale. With the new skill he'd gained from Aris, Vek followed the trail of life magic—and found a miasma of sickness. "Does Ara know? Is that why she was with you in the throne room?"

He didn't expect to receive an answer, but suddenly, the king let out a deep breath and fell back against the sofa again. "No one knows."

"This doesn't make sense. I have seen no signs of your weakness prior to to-day, and this level of illness seems unlikely to be sudden." Vek resisted the urge to rush forward. His father had never been the affectionate sort, and that was unlikely to have changed. "Besides, you're a full-blooded Unseelie *Felshreh*. You don't get sick."

"It has to be those Moranaians," King Torek muttered.

Vek frowned. "What are you talking about?"

"First, there was the energy poisoning that made it impossible for some to prop-erly regenerate magic. Caused by a rogue Moranaian." The king's brows drew down in a glare. "Then they shattered the barrier we created to hold back Earth's energy and to prevent the humans from annihilating themselves and us. They sent some-thing dark out with that power, and I'm probably not the only one affected."

Wait. His father thought this illness was deliberate? It couldn't possibly have taken root in him so rapidly. "The two can't be related."

King Torek's scowl only deepened. "I held a pillar of that wall, Vekenayeth. And the dragons the other. What coincidence that I should fall ill days after that pillar was shattered."

"I believe a life mage purified—"

"You'll side against me?" the king snapped.

"I did not intend to suggest such," Vek answered carefully. And hoped his father didn't notice the evasion. "I am merely sharing information. Earth's energy had been poisoned by Kien, it is true, but the initial spell was destroyed. Unfortunately, Kien used his death to cause a breach in the wall and imbued the weak point with a new poison. Perhaps it affected you before the Moranaians cleansed the energy as they allowed the barrier to fail."

His father's expression didn't soften. "The energy they stole? They hoard that power even as mine wanes. I used to be able to draw from that pillar at will instead of relying on blood donors. I could have purged this illness if I still had control."

The king had been able to pull from Earth's energy through the wall? Impossi-ble. Blood elves couldn't take from the world around them—or so he'd always been told. In fact, the closest his kind had come was to link to the Unseelie realm through blood spells, but that didn't allow a *Felshreh* to pull in energy. It aided in shielding and with transportation at best.

"That's why you want me to wrest control of the energy store away from them," Vek said.

"It should be mine by right," his father snarled. "For millennia, I have kept that power safe. Without it, our people will weaken. Our dimension is not as magic-rich as some, but the wall ensured that I could keep it adequate. We have to have it, Vek. You must find a way."

For a moment, Vek couldn't move. He could only stare at his father in shock. He was one of the strongest princes in the realm, considered by some to be next in line for the throne. He'd done countless tasks for his father. Endured quite a few challenges from rivals. And never—*never*—had the king given a single hint about any of this.

"Why are you telling me this now?" Vek finally asked.

"You must understand why your mission is vital." The king's gaze grew sly. "I know you've befriended the Moranaians. I'm no fool. But our realm is at stake. There's not enough energy to purge this disease from my body and maintain my life. If this spreads, many will die, because not even the healers know what to do. Just like poor Dereck. Do you want that to be the fate of everyone in our realm? I have no choice but to ensure that things are set right."

Vek's blood ran cold at the memory of what he'd seen in the Moranaians' cave—a portal, not a power source at all. It wouldn't be a matter of untethering an energy reserve and transporting it to the Unseelie realm. No, he would have to shatter a major portal between dimensions, and even if he managed it, there was no guarantee the remaining energy would be useable.

But something had gone wrong here. Terribly wrong.

He thought of his mother and his siblings—even Ara, as little as they got along. They were all at risk. Already Fen was ill, and he'd never even been to this realm. But he'd had contact with the poisoned energy. A great many fae had touched upon that same power. And if what his father said about their realm's lack of natural magic was true, it threatened their entire civilization.

"I'll see what I can do," Vek said.

Then he turned and left before the king could give any further commands. Vek would have to break enough of the orders he'd already received. He couldn't kill Dria or return a power source that didn't exist, but he would figure something out.

He always did.

Fen had to be seriously pissed. Or worse—hurt.

But still Maddy hovered in front of the safe, the mirror she'd grabbed from inside bundled against her chest. She'd rushed out with barely a word, mumbling something about the communication mirror. Ugh. She was a freaking coward. What was she supposed to say to a declaration like that, though?

Mates echoed in her head like an alarm.

Was that why she'd felt so drawn to Fen from the first moment she'd seen him? Guilt and wonder and fear twisted her stomach until she worried she might vomit. She couldn't betray her girlfriend. In fact, Maddy would swear she felt a deep pull to

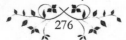

Anna, too. But Fen hadn't mentioned a connection to Anna. It might not even be possible.

Jase strode through the door, only to skid to a halt at the sight of her. "What's wrong?"

Swallowing bile, Maddy forced a smile to her lips and jiggled the mirror. "Nothing. Just grabbing this."

"And then staring at the safe?" he asked doubtfully.

"Sorry." Her chuckle had to sound off, but she wasn't going to attempt to explain. "I'll be out in a bit. I need to get back to Fen."

Maddy ignored Jase's worried stare as she ducked through the door to the break room. But when she entered, her heart thundered for a different reason. Fen slumped forward across the table, and a groan sounded from his direction. She rushed forward, but before she could react, he lifted his head slightly and smacked it against the surface.

"Stupid." Thunk. "Stupid." Thunk. "Stupid."

"Umm. Fen?"

She reached out a hand to nudge his shoulder, but he jerked upright before she could. Color rushed into his face, blending with the red mark from where he'd hit his head. Her lips twitched as she tried to hold back a grin. At least she wasn't the only one screwed up by the situation.

"I...ah...I didn't hear you come in."

Maddy did smile then. "I figured."

"Look, I wasn't trying to pressure you," Fen said, his words coming in a rush. "I wouldn't have said anything if you hadn't insisted. It's a mess. I'm a mess. But you deserve to know. I don't want you to think there's anything wrong with your blood. I'm sure it's phenomenal. I would love to... Well, that wouldn't be a good idea, but—"

"Fen." Maddy settled her finger against his lips and tried to ignore the zing of desire that shot through her. "Just stop before you hyperventilate."

He froze, and she noticed a fang peeking out over his lower lip. Hastily, she tugged her hand back. Well, why didn't she just wave temptation right under his nose? Bad enough that she'd run out of the room after his news. Now she was tormenting him.

"Sorry." With a wince, she rounded the table and resumed her earlier seat. "You caught me by surprise. I did want to get the mirror, but I shouldn't have left like that."

Fen glanced down at his hands. "I didn't exactly tell you gracefully."

"I honestly don't know what to do about it," Maddy said. "No clue. But I would hate to lose you as a friend."

His gaze darted to hers. "You consider me a friend?"

If not for the tension between them, she might have poked him. "Yeah. Somehow in the middle of all the insanity, I befriended you. And I have few enough of those to ditch one easily."

Fen stared at her. "I..."

"Why don't we figure out the rest of it later?" Maddy settled the bundle she held on the table and pulled the mirror from its velvety bag. "I want to call Cora. She can consult with the healer there."

"Might not want to mention me," Fen muttered. "Vek and I aren't exactly BFFs with them after trying to break into their outpost."

Maddy's mouth dropped open. "What?"

"It's a long story." Fen sighed. "How about I explain? Then you can decide if you're going to call Cora."

Maddy studied Fen's face for a moment and then nodded.

This she had to hear.

Dria paused beside Kera in the broad chamber where she'd first met Vek. The miserable lout. Stuffing those memories down, she turned to the warrior. "I would concentrate the bulk of the guards here. However, I'd like to have patrols all through the caverns at regular intervals. Kezari said that she hadn't had time to seal every off-shoot tunnel, and those could connect to other cave systems in these mountains. It's unlikely that anyone would widen those tiny tunnels to get through, but we shouldn't become complacent."

Kera nodded. "Indeed, Feraien—Dria."

Though the woman treated her with deference, Dria had a feeling there was something she wanted to say. Hopefully something besides *how did you get this assignment*, but there were no guarantees. "Did you have a suggestion, Kera?"

"I believe the area above the entrance is forest," the warrior answered, no emotion on her face. "Depending on how abandoned it is, I'm wondering if we might have someone camp above."

Dria's brows lowered in thought. It was an excellent idea, but it would be risky if they didn't do it right. "Does the Myern have any scouts well-acquainted with the human world?"

Kera smiled at that. "Several."

"I'll consult with him, then," Dria said. "It would do no good to have warriors stationed above if it turns out to be land claimed by hostile humans. That would draw too much attention. But if any of our people could blend in, it would be perfect."

"True." Kera nibbled on her lower lip. Then she snapped her fingers. "Ask about Delbin and Inona. If any pair would be perfect for the job, it's them."

Dria turned back toward the exit. "Thank you, Kera. I appreciate your input."

The warrior paced beside her in silence for a moment. "I admit you aren't what I expected."

"How so?" Dria asked evenly, though her steps slowed.

"Ralan is, well, Ralan, and when Teyark visited, he kept to himself a great deal. I wondered if you'd be like either of them." Kera lifted a shoulder. "But no one knows much about you. There were rumors centuries ago when you were at court, but few fare well in the tales told of childhood. Even so, I admit I worried you might be…difficult."

Dria smiled. "You feared I'd gained my position by way of royal tantrum."

"One might say that," Kera answered with a low chuckle.

Dria met the other's gaze squarely. "You have Ralan to thank for this. I was supposed to keep the mages on track for my father, and I was doubtful enough about that. Then when I arrived, my darling brother placed me in charge. I am well aware that I am young for this position. Not that I think I can't do it. I've worked most of my life for this."

"I understand." Something shifted on the warrior's face. A lessening of tension, perhaps, and maybe a bit of respect creeping in. "The Myern promoted me to third in command beneath the Captain of the Guard after the previous captain's death. Before that, I was the primary guard assigned to protect his formal study. A respected position but not next in line behind captain."

"Really?" Dria asked in surprise. "I'm guessing you received a fair amount of grief over that."

Kera grinned. "Some, but it wasn't my fault the others didn't prove to be as trustworthy."

Dria found herself returning the grin. Her brother's assessment of the Myern was correct—he had chosen perfectly. Unless something changed, it seemed she would work well with Kera. As they descended the staircase, they planned out the patrols with much more ease.

But she had a feeling things would not go so well with the mages.

11

Vek shoved through the door of the shop with barely a glance for the man at the counter. The half-fae whelp squawked some kind of protest, but Vek headed straight toward the room in the back. Energy built around the man, an admirably strong spell, in truth. Unfortunately for the half-fae, a human customer stepped between them, blocking his view.

Or perhaps fortunately. Vek wasn't in the mood to play.

The room's magical protections vibrated along his shields as he stormed in, but Vek was so full of energy after his encounter with Quaea that he could have diffused just about anything. But it wasn't necessary. As soon as Maddy glanced over from the table and recognized him, she altered the magic to accept his presence.

"Sorry, Maddy," the man from the front said from the doorway.

She shook her head. "Don't stress it, Jase. Vek is welcome here."

Vek came to a halt, staring at Maddy as the other man left. She actually sounded sincere about that. Odd. The Unseelie were more tolerated than welcomed by her kind. Double that for the royal blood elves. Didn't she know the power behind the honor she granted? He could use that in so many complex, political ways with her Seelie family, not to mention the danger that association with him could bring, and yet she tossed the words out casually.

Kids these days.

"Time to go home, Fen," Vek said. He would not take advantage of Maggie's offer.

His nephew straightened in his seat. "Don't you want to know what I found out?"

"Not now." Urgency gripped Vek's insides. He had to get to Dria. If the king was this upset, there was no telling what he would do. But Vek couldn't abandon Fen. "We need to go."

Maddy tucked a mirror into a shielded bag, but not before Vek scanned it. A communication mirror linked to Moranaia. His sense of urgency kicked up a notch. He'd sent Fen here to be healed. Why would Fen and Maddy have needed to contact

Moranaia at the same time his king had accused their people of wrongdoing?

"The situation is more complicated than you know," his nephew said. "You should sit—"

"You're fucking right it's more complicated," Vek snapped. "Come."

Fen shoved to his feet. "I may be your apprentice, but I'm not your child. *I'm* not a child. Listen, I'm not healed, and you need to know why."

Vek's teeth ground together. "We'll figure it out."

"Stop it." Her chair scraping the ground, Maddy stood. "You know, Fen claimed that you don't have anything against me personally, but I'm not sure I believe it. There's no need to be an asshole every time I'm around."

Fen snorted. "He's always an asshole."

Probably true, but now wasn't the time.

"I need to get back to Dria," Vek finally admitted. "Something is building. If you want to ride with us, Maddy, that's fine. But we're leaving."

Surprisingly, she nodded. Perhaps the little healer had more mettle than he gave her credit for. "Give me a second to put this in the safe. It can't sit out unguarded."

"Of course," Vek agreed. "Fen can pull the car around front to save time. I give my word not to leave without you."

Maddy looked over her shoulder as she headed toward another side door. "Nothing will save time in this traffic. Unless you have a spell for that?"

As she disappeared into the other room, Fen glared at him. "What the hell? You don't have to be so rude to her."

"What's the matter, Fen?" Vek drawled. "Getting protective? And she doesn't even know she's your..." His words trailed off as color flooded his nephew's face. "Fucking hell. You told her. Have you lost your mind?"

"I had to explain why I couldn't take her blood." Fen's shoulders hunched defensively. "Though I suppose I could have let her continue believing you're racist."

Vek shrugged. "I don't care what others think of me."

Absolutely true—for the most part.

"I'll keep that in mind next time," Fen grumbled.

With a smirk, Vek headed back to the main room. The half-fae glared at him over a customer's head, but Vek merely tipped his own head in acknowledgement and continued to the front door. As soon as Maddy joined them, they were off, rushing through the crowds wandering the charming downtown streets.

Unlike the first time Vek had traveled here, there was an almost frantic energy behind the tourists' steps. An uneasiness, like the proverbial calm before the storm. Even as he had the thought, a gentle wave of energy lapped around him, a reverberation as power ebbed and flowed around the planet like water displaced. The lights nearest them flickered, and nervous laughter sounded as half the block lost power for a moment. Oh yes, the humans sensed the changes.

It was only a matter of time before some began to take advantage.

By the time they reached Fen's car, the energy had smoothed out once more.

Vek slipped into the passenger seat, barely noticing when Maddy climbed into the back. His nerves twisted taut until he feared the slightest thing might make him snap. Was there truly danger to Dria, or did he need to dispel some of his energy? Either could bring its own problem.

"Okay," Fen said as he put the car in reverse and backed out. "So Maddy said she was sick with the same illness I have."

Vek spun in his seat to stare at Maddy. "What?"

She nodded. "Felt the way humans describe the flu, minus the sneezing and coughing. I could barely move. My healing gift wouldn't work, but increasing my energy input eventually wiped it out. I think."

Vek truly scanned her, then. Her energy levels were high, but the sight he'd gleaned from Aris revealed the physical weakness she still suffered. But the illness itself appeared to be gone. "You're certain it's the same? Fen hasn't shown any symptoms, aside from getting winded while mountain climbing."

"That's something we need to study," Maddy said. "But yes. I'm sure it's the same. I contacted Cora through the mirror, and she's going to send a message to the healer there. She'd already spoken to him about…"

Her gaze dropped as her voice trailed off. He shouldn't ask. He shouldn't care. But somehow, he did. "About what?"

Maddy lifted her chin. "None of the Seelie healers will train a half-blood like me, at least none that I've managed to speak with. Cora asked her healer if he would, but as far as I know, he hasn't decided yet."

Vek peered at her. "I suspect your gift isn't as simple as it seems. Perhaps the Seelie are afraid of revealing their lack of knowledge."

"Thank you," she said, her cheeks reddening.

"Hey," Fen interjected. "Maybe meeting your own mate shook loose some kindness, Vek."

As Maddy lifted her brows, Vek turned a glare on his nephew. "That was not to be general knowledge."

"Sometimes you have to trust," Fen said softly. "Maddy has helped us more than once. She deserves to be in on our secrets."

Vek tapped his fingers against the car door as he considered his nephew's words. They'd be easy enough to dismiss from one so young, but as much as Vek liked to needle him, he was the first to admit that Fen was hardly innocent. Far from it. He'd spent years working with a madman in an environment that relied on secrets, and that was after he'd been abandoned by his parents. Fen wasn't the trusting type.

Yet he trusted Maddy.

Truth was freedom, but there were layers upon layers that were best left undisturbed. Information should never be volunteered lightly, and Vek held his truths more tightly than most. He had to. Too many of his relatives vied for power, and the higher-ranking nobles at court weren't far behind. But in this case, his nephew was correct.

Gods knew Vek was short on ideas of how to solve this mess.

He twisted in his seat, draping his arm behind the headrest so he could see Maddy. "If you tell anyone else what I'm about to share, I'll drain you dry and incinerate your corpse, one of Fen's mates or not."

Maddy's mouth dropped open, and Fen cursed. "Shit, Vek, was that necessary?"

"This is serious," Vek answered, unwilling to yield on the matter. "I'm not being dramatic to say life-or-death. What I learned today…in the wrong hands, it would spell disaster. If you can't swear to your silence, Maddy, then Fen can drop you off somewhere else."

Vek ignored the hostility radiating off his nephew, his focus on Maddy. Face pale, she stared at him with wide eyes. But his earlier supposition proved correct—she had mettle. She sat up straighter, squared her shoulders, and nodded.

"I won't tell anyone," she said.

"Really?" Vek quirked a brow. "Even Anna?"

Maddy grimaced at that. "I don't keep secrets from my girlfriend. Not usually. But she's struggling enough with her newly awakened fae blood. If it's really that important, I swear I won't say anything."

"If?" Vek insisted.

She rolled her eyes. "I promise I will not reveal what you are about to tell me during this car ride unless you give me permission."

Energy flowed from her with the vow. Vek smiled grimly in acknowledgement before twisting back around in his seat. "Very well. My father, king of the Unseelie, is dying. Whatever this illness is, he has contracted it, too."

The car jerked as Fen took a curve too fast. Cursing, Vek glared at his nephew and gripped the small bar inlaid in the door. What did Fen care if the king was dying? He didn't know his grandfather. But his nephew's face was practically gray from the news.

"That's what he was hiding from you?" Fen asked, his voice sounding strangled.

"Yes," Vek answered, his own words sharp and clipped. "He was holding part of the wall. When it shattered, something happened to him. That's why he wanted me to kill the leader of the Moranaian colony and claim their power source. He thinks he needs it."

Maddy gasped. "Wait. Kill the leader?"

Tired despite the energy burning through his blood, Vek let his head drop back against the headrest and closed his eyes. "I'm not going to do it."

Fen's snicker lacked its usual verve. "Because she's his mate."

"No," Vek ground out. "Because it's wrong. And useless besides."

"But if the king didn't rescind the order, what are you going to do?" Fen asked. "Turn rebel?"

"I don't know what the hell I'm going to do." Vek sighed. "It would be a useless, foolish action in any case. There would be war, and for what? There is no energy source there. It's a gods-be-damned portal. Or maybe gods-be-caused."

"Loki," Fen said.

"Yes." Vek cast a glance back at Maddy. "The Norse god Loki seems to have an unusually strong interest in protecting the Moranaians, so my assumption is that he helped them. Creating a direct portal that bypasses the Veil is a major working. I have no better guess as to how they managed it."

"You weren't joking about this being serious," Maddy said.

One corner of Vek's mouth tipped up. "Jesting isn't my strong suit in any situation."

"You've got that right." Fen let out a short huff of laughter. "So why are we heading back to the cave if you don't even have a plan?"

An excellent question that Vek couldn't quite answer. He scraped his fingers against his scalp, the only outlet he had for the frustration and anxiety surging within him. There was no logical reason to think that Dria was in immediate danger, and she appeared to be capable of handling it in any case. But the desperation in his father's eyes—the hatred. There was every possibility he would send someone else in case Vek wasn't speedy enough doing the job.

"I'm not sure," Vek admitted. "But we're going."

He barely knew Dria, but he didn't have to. They belonged to one another, and he'd be drained before he allowed another to harm her.

Anyone who tried would find their own swift death.

Dria had just managed to sit down for a quick meal after bidding Selia, Aris, and Kezari farewell when she detected an energy surge at the portal. The mages? She'd received word that they would be arriving the next morning due to an unexpected delay, but there could have been yet another change. Sighing, she settled the cheese back beside her bread and stood.

No rest for the wicked.

As she headed to the portal, Dria checked the shields at the entrance and then the ones embedded into the walls of the cavern. No sign of disturbance there. She'd done several sweeps earlier, adding new layers to the shielding each time. One of her first additions had been designed to identify a shift in the earth, natural or otherwise, and that hadn't been triggered either.

Not that she wanted it to be. She'd meant it when she'd told Fen to take his uncle out of here and never return. She had no time for useless, betraying *drec* intent on causing her grief. Her fingers curled into her palms as she stomped down the stairs. Especially not if that *drec* was supposed to be her soulbonded.

As she neared the portal, an auburn-haired elf in a simple tunic and pants descended the stairs. The guards' lack of alarm told her they knew him, but Dria still scanned him as he neared. A hint of peace—and crankiness—greeted her seeking magic. A healer's energy, though the sense of aggravation wasn't generally so pronounced.

He halted in front of her and inclined his head. "Please forgive my intrusion, princess. I am Lial, the healer at Braelyn. Lyr urged me to wait until tomorrow, but I...disagreed with his assessment."

Lial. The name sounded familiar, but she couldn't pull forth why. The least of her concerns, really. "I'm afraid I was not expecting your arrival at all. I did not request a healer to be assigned here, although that might be a good idea."

"You misunderstand," Lial answered. "I'm not staying. But I received word from a couple of our allies that there might be a new illness developing among the elves."

Dria stared at him. "Elves don't get sick."

A scowl pinched his face. "Have you spent centuries learning every nuance of how our bodies function? No? Don't tell me what is possible. Only a few weeks ago, I spent hours treating Neorans who'd fallen ill from energy poisoning. I would in no way be surprised if some other form of the same problem has evolved."

"I see." She didn't, but she had a feeling that arguing with him would be useless. Was he naturally antagonistic, or had someone else caused this terrible mood? Either way, she didn't appreciate being the recipient of his bad humor. "If you would be so kind, could you explain what you are seeking from me regarding this matter?"

His eyes narrowed ever so slightly at her politely worded *what do you want?* but he answered the request. "I am here to check for any sign of disease among those at the outpost."

Simple enough. He would have saved them both time by saying so initially. "Fine," she said. "You can begin with me."

12

Half a mark later, the healer had cleared a good portion of the scouts who'd been near the bottom of the cavern. At least, Dria thought that was all the time that had passed. There were no water clocks here, and honestly, she had no clue if such devices would work the same on this world.

Earth. She'd been too busy to consider that she wasn't on Moranaia anymore. Beyond this cave, there were entire civilizations she knew little about. She might have learned about humans during her studies, but that had been three hundred years ago. Selia and Fen had described moving conveyances and other technologies before Selia had created a gate for him to carry Vek to his home. What other wonders would she not get the chance to see?

Suddenly, a nudge pinged against her senses, followed almost immediately by a tremble along the cavern's shields. Dria connected herself more deeply to the defenses she'd placed, only to bite back a curse. Vek, Fen, and a stranger. Wasn't it enough that she'd kicked him out twice already? Now he had to bring reinforcements?

Dria eyed the healer, but he appeared intent on his work. Even so, she sent a mental warning to Kera to have someone explain her disappearance if he asked. Then she darted toward the stairs, muttering to herself with every step up. She was a fit woman, but all this climbing had her legs and backside burning.

Another annoyance to place on her potential bonded's shoulders.

As she reached the top of the stairs, Dria released the spell barring entry to the top chamber. She knew Vek would sense it, and the shudder that went through her as his energy made contact with the shielding confirmed the suspicion. Cursing at her traitorous body, she strode with more determination toward her destination.

Not that she was eager to see him. The sooner she could get rid of him, the better. Maybe then she wouldn't do something foolish like attempt to bond with him. He might be the most attractive man she'd ever seen, but he was also one of the most lethal. Danger streamed from him as readily as the promise of sex.

Which was something she really shouldn't think about.

Dria braced herself against his pull before she entered the entry chamber, but it didn't help. His white hair settled in disarray around his harsh face as though he'd run his fingers through it, and his thin shirt clung to his defined chest, dampened with sweat. She couldn't stop herself from following the line of moisture down his shirt until it reached the waist of his pants, but she managed to tear her gaze away before she made a complete fool of herself ogling him.

Great gods of Arneen. Dria focused on his face and groaned inside at the slight smirk twisting his lips. Of course he'd noticed her lapse. Well, the bond was a powerful draw. That was all there was between them, and she had no intentions of cementing it. He was the type to break promises—and hearts. She'd had more than enough of that already.

Guards ringed the room, and Vek's companions stood beside him. But it was the prince himself she addressed. "I told your nephew that you weren't to return."

His smirk widened. "Do I seem the type to blindly obey?"

"I suppose not." No, he didn't. And gods help her, but that was one of the most attractive things about him. "Why are you here?"

The humor fled his expression. "We have…a situation. One I will only discuss in private. Though tell me, have there been any disturbances since I left?"

Left. Sure. No need to remind him that he'd been hauled out of here by his nephew, she supposed. "It would be none of your concern if I had."

Irritation flickered in his eyes. "There is more at stake than your opinion of me."

"You speak as though I have reason to listen to you," Dria snapped. "In case you've forgotten, a god told me you weren't to be trusted. I don't care what reinforcements you've brought. Continue to bother us, and I will transport you back to the Unseelie court myself. In pieces."

A choked laugh caught her attention, and she finally glanced over at Fen. "Holy hell, you two are a perfect pair," the younger man said. "But could you flirt later? He found out the truth from his father. Isn't that what you were told to wait for?"

Dria froze as the god's words played through her mind. *Don't let him back in until he has learned the truth from his father. Beyond that, well…don't offer him blood until you've started the bond. And try not to wait too long.* Heat flooded her face, and she prayed they'd assume it was from anger. It wouldn't even be untrue.

Not entirely.

That said, she might have to ignore a god on this one. Vek was the last man she would want to bond with, and she had no intention of giving him a single drop of her blood. Forever wasn't too long to wait, was it?

"Fine," Dria finally said. "Tell me what you discovered and then go."

It was Vek's turn to chuckle. "I think not."

For the briefest moment, Dria almost wished Ralan would rush in. Not to save *her*. No, she very much feared she might kill a prince of the Unseelie court in front of an entire room full of witnesses. To distract herself from murder, Dria studied the stranger standing next to Fen. Thin, tall, pale, red hair—and definite Seelie Sidhe energy.

"You didn't introduce me to your guest," Dria said.

"I'm Maddy." The woman took a step forward, a hesitant smile on her face. "I work for Cora, Prince Ralan's bonded. Well, I did. Jase and I are buying the shop from her now that she's staying on Moranaia."

Dria had no clue what Maddy meant. Perhaps if she'd spent more time talking to her brother and less time arguing, then she would have some idea if the woman's claim of friendship had merit.

"Maybe you should take us down to the portal," Vek said. "At this point, I'm certain nothing we say will convince you. But if I make it to the floor of the cavern without coming to harm, you'll know I'm now trustworthy."

She wouldn't wager a single energy crystal that he'd ever prove to be that, not completely, but it was the only reasonable test that made sense. He'd been stopped by a god before. If Vek had the same intentions, he would surely be halted again. And if he wasn't, there was still the possibility of killing him.

Honestly, she wasn't sure which result she most hoped for.

🔥

Vek might have loved the sight of Dria in formal wear, but he had to admit there was a definite advantage to being able to see the way her gown hugged her curves now that she'd ditched the overrobe. Too bad she hated him. Vehemently. Even if she'd done her own share of ogling when she'd entered the room. It erased any guilt he might have felt about staring at her ass as he followed her to the base of the stairs. Not that he was likely to have experienced much remorse. Life wasn't for regretting—it was for experiencing.

Ah, the experiences he'd love to have with Dria. Multiple, multiple experiences.

At least he managed to remove his gaze from her delectably rounded backside by the time they reached the cavern floor. Dria went first, striding forward and then spinning to watch as Vek followed. He didn't hesitate, nor did he brace himself in expectation. If the god found him unworthy again, so be it.

But though a low, taunting laugh echoed around him, nothing impeded his progress. Fen's loud sigh of relief sounded behind him, but Vek only smiled at a wide-eyed Dria. She had clearly expected Loki's interference again. It seemed Vek was forever disappointing her, and they'd only known each other for a day. He would without doubt do so again.

"I still don't trust you," Dria muttered as he neared.

Vek chuckled. "You're a wise woman. Though you're one of the least likely to receive harm by my hand."

The doubt on her face didn't ease—and he didn't blame her.

From the other side of the cavern, a man approached. Vek's attention shifted to the stranger, and he tensed as he scanned the man's energy. Healer. A powerful one, too. Ah, *slelen*, he'd wanted to taste a healer's blood for more years than he could count, but he'd never had cause enough to take the risk. If he did, he might feel obligated to take on others' pain, and he had more than enough of his own to deal with. But healers were always a temptation.

The man tossed a strand of red hair out of his eyes with an irritated flick, and his expression was pinched with annoyance as he stopped beside Dria. "Everyone below is clear."

A bit more gruff than healers tended to be. Vek approved.

"You're more than welcome to climb to the top to check the others." A slight grimace crossed Dria's face as she glanced upward. "It's a long way. Also, you might want to examine Kezari, Aris, and Selia if you haven't already. They were working here earlier."

"I did so before I left, and they are well." Then the healer pierced Vek with his gaze. "Vekenayeth anh Torekthayed. I did not expect to find you here."

Vek studied the man. "I'm afraid I do not recall our past meeting."

"We didn't meet," the healer answered. "I was visiting a friend at court during one of your trips to Moranaia. A prince of the Unseelie strays far to be here at such a time."

"At court," Dria whispered, and if Vek wasn't mistaken, that was embarrassment coloring her face. "Your name sounded familiar, but I should have recognized your face, as well. I can't believe I didn't know you at once, Lial."

The healer chuckled. "I'm not surprised, young cousin. We both so rarely journey to court. Possibly for similar reasons."

Despite his reassurance, Dria grimaced. "It was still a terrible lapse. I hope you'll forgive me for the insult."

Vek wanted to groan. Moranaians were worse than the Unseelie at worrying over slights. He had more cousins than he could identify without searching for a blood affinity. And even if he did recognize the relationship, he wouldn't know half of their names. His ancestors hadn't been known for their abstinence—in much of anything.

"I've had far worse," Lial said, shrugging.

Seemed likely considering the healer's disposition. The friendliness had already left his expression as he peered at first Vek and then the others in the group. Only a heartbeat passed before Lial's gaze narrowed on Fen, and the healer advanced on Vek's nephew with a muffled curse. Before Vek had time to do more than blink, a blue glow darted from the healer's hands to surround Fen.

Vek shuddered at the force of the power as the edge of it touched upon his senses. Peace. Life. If he could grasp that for himself, perhaps the world would turn aright. Or maybe not. Attempting to wield a healer's magic without adequate knowledge of the body was pure folly. Talents used without understanding were dangerous, something he'd experienced more than once as he'd tried to make sense of new abilities. He might risk himself to experiment, but he wouldn't wish to harm another in the process. It was yet another reason Vek had never tried to take a healer's blood.

He averted his gaze as the glow intensified. Maddy stood a bit behind Fen, her mouth slack at the display. Had she never watched a fully trained healer work? She might not have found someone to teach her, but surely she'd had a chance to observe. Then again, maybe not. The Seelie Sidhe were pretentious little fucks when they wanted to be—so, always.

When the light cut off, Vek's attention snapped back to the healer. "Well?"

Lial cast him an exasperated glance. "You are not my patient."

"He is my nephew and my apprentice," Vek ground out. "Do not test me."

"I don't care." Lial's expression turned so withering that even Vek gave pause. "Without my patient's permission, I will not—"

"Go ahead and tell him," Fen said. "He already knows I'm sick. If you have insight, I'd like to hear it. We all would."

Lial's lips thinned, but he nodded. "It's similar in flavor to the energy poisoning, but it isn't affecting your energy. It seems as though it has latched onto a virus. Maybe. Such things survive such a short time in our bodies that I've rarely encountered them long enough for deep study, unlike the bacteria I learned to purge from things like food. But with the poison augmenting it, the virus isn't being swept away as usual."

"I had it, too," Maddy said suddenly. "I tried to heal myself, but my gift... Well, the only thing that worked was pulling in a lot of power. But I haven't had much physical contact with Fen, not since I tried to heal him a while back. The virus would practically have to be airborne."

"But it isn't." The healer studied her for so long that Vek almost felt sorry for her. "We need to speak about your gift, Maddy. You are Cora's Maddy, correct?"

The Sidhe woman nodded.

"You should come back to Moranaia with me. You need to untangle your talents before you kill yourself or someone else."

Vek expected Maddy to blush, but instead she turned so pale her freckles stood out in stark relief. Still, she shook her head. "I have a business. A girlfriend. I can't just leave without a word."

Lial's lips twisted. "I didn't mean this instant. But if you value the lives around you, you'll make arrangements. In the meantime, I expect you to notify me through Cora if you discover anything else about this illness."

"What about me?" Fen asked. "Can you heal me?"

"I won't attempt it," Lial answered. "Not yet. You're a carrier, and as such, you could be useful to examine."

Anger surged through Vek at those words, and his every instinct screamed at him to grab the healer and force him to act. But logic won out over predator before he foolishly attempted the action. From the healer's sharp gaze, the man knew it, too. Bastard probably would have enjoyed turning Vek's insides liquid.

"Unacceptable," Vek said instead, a poor outlet for the rage making his over-full energy stores surge painfully inside of him.

Scowling, Lial waved a hand. "You're old enough to understand the sense in this. Keep him contained in this cave, and if he starts to show symptoms, we'll try to purge the virus. This may be something that only affects those with some human blood, but I would still prefer he be quarantined."

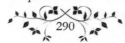

Vek almost told the healer about his father at that. The Unseelie king wasn't a half-blood, and he appeared to share the same illness. But that wasn't certain, and he didn't trust Lial enough to provide such sensitive information. He might be Dria's cousin, but he had no other reason not to betray the Unseelie at the first opportunity. Besides, he didn't know that Vek and Dria might become mates.

No. Not might. Could. Mating would be folly with a woman who hated him.

"I need to consult with Lyn—Lyr's mother," Lial said, his tone turning even sharper. "I'll see if she'll search the archives in case this has happened before. After I examine the others, in any case. Do not let your nephew leave, Vek, not unless you want to risk an outbreak. It might not be airborne, but I would not bet on that remaining the case. I'll advise the others not to travel through the portal until I know more."

The healer didn't bother to wait for agreement, spinning away and marching toward the stairs before Vek could formulate a reply. Reluctant admiration pulled a slight smile from Vek. The man was a serious force. It wasn't often he was out-ass-holed.

"He's kidding, right?" Fen asked.

Dria, curiously silent through the exchange, shook her head. "You're staying."

Vek caught her gaze. "That means I'm staying, too."

"Fine, so long as you keep out of my way," Dria said, though her nostrils flared. "I'm not going to have a plague on my watch, not if I can help it."

"I don't think that's a risk."

"You're not a healer," Dria snapped.

Great Divine. Would passion put that fluster in her face as readily as anger? Swallowing hard, he shoved the question aside. "I'm not, but I have…information. I'll not share it with Lial, but it's something you should know."

Dria frowned. "It had better not be another innuendo," she muttered.

"It isn't," Vek answered with a chuckle. "Though it is best delivered alone."

He could have sworn she bit back a smile at his quip.

"There's a room above where we can speak," she said. "We'll talk after I find a place for you both to sleep."

"What about me?" Maddy asked softly.

Dria shrugged. "Lial didn't say you had to stay, but I'm honestly not sure. If you'd like, you can wait down here until he returns so you can ask."

Maddy's forehead furrowed, and she bit her lower lip as her gaze drifted to Fen. "I…"

Fen caught her eyes and smiled. "Go. You can't disappear on Anna. Not again. I'll text you if I start to feel sick."

It was clear she didn't want to leave under these circumstances, but she was just as obviously torn. Though he didn't customarily concern himself with such things, Vek found himself wanting to help. An odd thing, that.

"I vow to collect you at once if you are needed," Vek said. "Provided the healer lets you go."

Finally, Maddy nodded. "Okay."

With a gesture for Fen, Vek headed toward the stairs. Dria studied him, a hint of surprise in her eyes before she covered it up, but then she drew her shoulders back and rushed ahead so she could lead the way. He had a feeling she would put his room as far from hers as she could, and the thought made him smile.

If they couldn't resist each other's pull, it wouldn't do any good.

13

Meyanen protect her, but she was about to be alone with Vek. Unfortunately, Dria feared it would take more than the god of love to stop the force that drew her to the contrary Unseelie. As she closed the door on the large chamber they'd set up for dining, she had the sudden urge to flee. But she stiffened her spine instead. Running would be cowardly, and she refused to be that.

Not to mention the smug satisfaction it would give Vek.

She headed for an empty table, but she didn't sit down on the long bench beside it. Instead, she leaned back against the edge and lifted a brow. "So, what's the great secret?"

Vek stopped an arm's length away. Uncomfortably close, but only because of her attraction to him. "You must promise—"

"To tell no one," she interrupted. "Yes, I guessed that. The only person I need to report to is Ralan, and if it's important enough, he'll already know. Just tell me."

A small smile crossed his lips, but only for a moment. "Very well." Despite his agreement, he hesitated, the silence stretching until annoyance curled within her. "It's my father. The king."

Dria blinked as he went quiet again. "If you don't think you can trust me…"

"It's not that." Vek rubbed his hand across his hair, and the lost look that flickered in his eyes had her heart twisting. "He's sick, too. Deathly so. When I returned to confront him about his plan, I discovered it. But he is no half-blood. He is a full-blooded *Felshreh* who has led the Unseelie for millennia, but now… I don't know what to make of this."

Miaran. No wonder he hadn't wanted to mention this to anyone else. Come to think of it, she wasn't sure why he was telling her. They had the potential to bond, but that nebulous link was the only thing between them. As a princess of another realm, the damage she could do with such knowledge was immense. Why was he trusting her?

He read the question on her face before she could speak it. "You are the leader here, and this affects your people more than you know." He paused. "But more than either of those things… You're in danger."

Dria straightened, drawing in energy with a thought. "Explain."

Vek didn't so much as twitch. "I was sent here to kill you."

Her own bonded. Naturally. Did she have any other kind of luck? With a flick of her fingers, she hovered a ball of flame above her palm. "I recommend explaining faster."

"I didn't say I was going to do it," Vek said, his tone so calm she found her own ire increasing. "I'm not now, and I wasn't on my last excursion. I might act the occasional assassin, but I am not a murderer."

Dria snorted. "What's the difference?"

Vek edged a little closer, his voice dropping low. "There's a great deal of difference. In this world, there is evil so profound that nothing short of death will stop it. Those like me who live in the shadows? Sometimes, we are that justice."

Dria's breath caught. "And who decides who must die?"

"I do." His jaw clenched. "Sometimes my father gives orders, but I've found my way around eliminating the undeserving."

Dria wasn't certain she believed him. He was too powerful, too assured, too… Too everything. He probably cut down whomever he wished and then celebrated at their funeral pyre. Scowling, she drew in more power until her hair crackled with it.

"Why does your father want me dead?"

Vek lifted his hands. "Not you specifically. The leader of the colony. He blames the Moranaians for his illness, and he demanded I return the energy you're hoarding here. He believes you've kept some of what was stored behind the wall for yourselves. Unfortunately, he doesn't realize there's a portal that would have to be destroyed to regain that magic."

No wonder her brother had been eager to drop this responsibility on her. But had he been eager to avoid this tangled conflict, or did he believe in her enough to be positive she could handle it? If the latter, he was correct—she would.

Dria leaned closer, letting the force of her magic slip along Vek's shields.

"I've changed my mind," she said. "Fen can stay, but you need to leave."

Vek's brows rose. "You think to force me away from my nephew?"

"You were ordered to assassinate me and steal our energy." She danced a flame between her fingers. "Even if you don't intend to do it, I can't risk the threat. You'll have to take your games elsewhere."

Eyes narrowing, he tipped his head toward hers, so close his breath fanned across her lips. "I. Am. Not. Leaving."

"Why should I let you stay?" she asked.

Or, rather, whispered. She cursed at herself for the breathless hitch to her voice, but his nearness dug into her resolve. Even so, she wouldn't retreat. She couldn't. If she yielded to him now, they would never have respect between them again.

"I need you," he answered, and her chest squeezed tight at the words. "It will be much more difficult to thwart my father without your help. You know, there's a risk to my people from this illness, as well. I have to find another method to solve the problem, and I'm not sure I can do it unless Moranaia stands with me."

Foolish heart. Of course he'd been talking about her as a leader, not a woman. It was better that way. Dria had no doubt he'd be phenomenal in bed, but he would be terrible as a bonded. He was too harsh.

Unfeeling.

"Fine. You may remain with Fen, though it isn't because I trust you," Dria said. "I'll do my best to help you deal with the illness. Then I want you to leave me alone. I know what you are now, and I'll have no part of it."

The hiss of his breath cut between them. "You have no idea what I am."

"I have no desire to."

Dria shoved past him, ready to be done with the conversation. With him. She let the fire in her hand wink out as she neared the door, though she kept her magic at the ready as she stomped away. Let him attack her from behind if that was his intent. She would relish a reason to strike his arrogant ass down.

But it wasn't his magic that caught her, and it wasn't an attack.

Vek reached her so swiftly that she almost couldn't track the movement, and his hand wrapped around her wrist before she could raise any defenses. He spun her around, shoving her against the wall beside the door. His odd, taupe eyes pinned her in place as he crowded her, and she didn't bother to struggle as he gathered both wrists above her head.

"You won't be done with me so easily."

Dria knew what he was going to do—and she let him.

His mouth crashed onto hers with such force her lip almost pinched against her teeth. Almost. Then he plundered, no gentle kisses to ease the way. Fire. She thought she'd held it before, but it was nothing next to this. Moaning, she strained against him, wanting her hands free so she could tug at him.

Vek shifted so close she could feel every bit of his hardness against her. Only then, when his body trapped hers, did he release her hands. She dug her fingers into his hair, pulling until she could meet him in the kiss. In that moment, it didn't matter if she liked him—she wanted him.

His breath came ragged as he pulled his mouth away from hers. "Dria..."

"I'm not afraid of you," she said on a gasp. "You're wasting your time trying to intimidate me this way."

"You would know if I wanted you to fear me," Vek murmured. "Though you have every reason to." He nipped at her bottom lip, letting the flat side of his fang slide across the delicate skin. "The slightest taste of your blood, and you would be mine."

Dria ran her finger along his ear, and he shivered. Smiling as he fell for the distraction, she found the weakness in his shielding. And pounced. Before he could blink, she cast the immobilization spell, and his muscles seized. But his eyes. Ah, his eyes promised such sweet retribution.

After she wiggled from his hold, she shifted him until he leaned against the wall. It would be no good to have the prince fall and break something, even if he did deserve it. Then she would have to explain to Lial what had happened, and that would be worse than any torture Vek could devise. Healers weren't the easily amused sort.

"Don't worry," Dria said before she opened the door. "It won't last long. Though I recommend you not threaten me like that again."

Her body was aflame with thwarted desire, but Dria couldn't help but grin all the way to her room. She had no idea how he'd get back at her.

But gods, she hoped it was spectacular.

He. Was. So. Fucked.

The door had barely snapped closed before Vek had the spell untangled. With as much energy as he had stored and the experience he'd had with such spells of late, it would have been a simple matter. But instead of rushing after her, he slid down the wall and leaned his head against the stone.

He. Was. So. Fucked.

Not literally, unfortunately. His aching body reminded him quite strongly of that fact. Metaphorically? That was something else. He'd sworn not to mate, not with the insanity of his life. But how could he resist Dria? She had a fire that drew him, a confidence that ignited him. What other person would dare cast a spell like that against him during an intimate moment?

She probably assumed he'd be enraged. Offended. Little did she know. Vek would never be happy with a woman who submitted without question. No, their mating would be a battle, and he'd never been able to resist a fight. He may not have wanted a link with another, but now he had found the right one. Provided he could figure out a way to keep her.

Despite what he'd said, he would never force a mating without permission. Vek wanted *her*, not an endless lifetime of anger and misery. Which meant he would have to avoid kissing her again. He was careful of his fangs, but accidents happened. She would be his by choice or not at all.

Dria might have believed he was kissing her for intimidation's sake, but she'd been wrong. Her confident authority did things to him, and her brush-off had erased his good sense. Not anymore. He would have to be on guard and control himself better. Because he had a feeling he would break before she did.

With a groan, Vek shoved himself to his feet and started back to the room she'd grudgingly granted him before their discussion. She might not have placed him as far away as absolutely possible, but he and Fen were still several levels removed from her chamber and from this one as well. He would check on his nephew and then... Well, he didn't know what he'd do then.

Vek wouldn't be able to sleep, not with so much energy coursing through him. He rubbed at the ache in his temples as he considered the problem. There was a reason he rarely fed twice in one day. Not only did he have more power than he could comfortably contain, but his mind felt stretched from the introduction of new talents. He would need to avoid taking blood for a couple of days, at the very least, or he'd suffer the effects.

Too much too soon would cause crippling pain.

Sensing that his nephew was alone, Vek gave the barest knock before pushing into the room. Fen sat cross-legged on his bed, his back against the cave wall, and nodded at Vek as he entered. His nephew didn't show any symptoms of illness, but if his expression was any indication, his spirits had suffered.

"There's always a cost," Fen said abruptly.

Vek sat on a stone bench formed from the cave floor, though the lingering hum of dragon magic prickled his skin even through his clothes. "Translation?"

"For the things we do. There's always a cost." Fen rubbed his palm across his pants leg. "I thought that if I worked with Kien and got my payback on the Unseelie family who'd abandoned me that I'd make the world better. Eventually. But that darkness tainted everything. It won't leave me no matter how much I change."

Vek leaned forward. "So you've given up already?"

"I don't know." Fen sighed. "You've gotta admit it's ironic. Kien pierced my heart with the same poison I helped him create, and now I'm sick with yet another version of it. Maybe my mother was right to ditch my sorry ass on Earth. Imagine the trouble I would cause with real training."

It was tempting to brush aside his nephew's words with half-true reassurances, but that wasn't what Fen needed. "It's fair that you have to deal with what you helped create. That is justice. Do not, however, mistake the echoes of the past as an indication of the future."

His nephew opened his mouth to protest, but Vek cut him off with a sharp gesture. "Fen, our natures are darker than many of the other fae, but there is reason for it. Some light can only be born in darkness. A fine line. You were left to process that on your own, far from any semblance of context. That you weren't irredeemably evil when I found you is a sign of your promise. And be assured that if I believed otherwise, I would kill you. That's my job."

Fen let out a choked laugh. "Damn. If you ever have kids, I hope you're not the one who has to comfort them."

Vek froze. Children. He'd never wanted a child, not after experiencing the way his father treated his various offspring. But if Vek joined with Dria, that concept was no longer an unpleasant one. How would she feel about the matter? How did he feel about it? He'd have to decide before they spoke more seriously about linking.

"I was joking," Fen said, humor returning to his eyes.

"It's no matter," Vek responded. "Though I fear you are correct in that regard. I suppose I'll be the one to chase away the threats. I'm rather good at it."

And he was. He had a lifetime of experience with scaring others away—friend and foe. Generally speaking, it was for the best. Now, here he was, cultivating allies and considering a mate. He really had lived long enough to see everything.

"If your kid is anything like you, it'll actually help." Fen grinned. "I think it somehow made me feel better. Guess I'm messed up in the head."

Vek stood, suddenly ready to be alone with his thoughts. "No more than I, little comfort though that may be. Stay on your guard, Fen. I'm going to attempt to create a gate to the house to gather a few things for us. Try not to get in trouble while I'm gone."

"Wait." Fen's eyes narrowed. "You've been able to create portals all this time? Then why have you—"

It was Vek who smirked this time. "Let's just say it's a newly acquired talent." Thanks to Quaea, but his nephew needn't know that. "I'll contact you telepathically once I return. Shouldn't take long."

Vek didn't give Fen time to argue. It would take a fair amount of energy mastering the transportation spell, but he'd be able to retrieve clean clothing for both of them. What else could he do with the excess energy that wouldn't annoy the Moranaians? Other than manipulating the stone furniture in his room, and he had no desire to do that.

They would simply have to deal with his portal experiment.

Dria spun the piece of dried-out cheese another half-turn along her plate and attempted to summon the urge to eat it. Satisfaction with besting Vek had faded into frustration, and no small amount of that was worry over the situation. Once her thoughts had settled, the news he'd delivered sank in. The king of the Unseelie was dangerously ill, possibly with the same thing afflicting Fen. The potential for catastrophe was immense.

And she'd sworn not to tell.

Miaran.

Well, she'd been granted leadership over this outpost, and that meant it was her duty to handle the problem. Fine. Dria might have been shocked by her abrupt placement into the role, but it was time to stop wallowing in any lingering doubt. She'd been trained to lead a troop of mages—this wasn't a great deal different.

So what was her next step? Dria gave the cheese another turn as her thoughts made their own circle. They needed to find out if others were ill. From what she'd been told, Fen had been connected to the poisoned energy at one time, and Maddy might have picked up a bit of that from him. Neither had been near the Unseelie king, to her knowledge, but the king had touched the energy bound behind the wall before the wall fell.

Had anyone else been connected? And when had the power behind the barrier become tainted?

At that thought, she hurried over to the communication mirror. She activated the link, and it was a blessedly brief amount of time before the Myern's image filled the surface.

If he was surprised to be contacted by her, he was too experienced to show it.

"Princess Dria," Lyr said smoothly. "It is a pleasure to see you. I hope my people were able to bring comfort to your accommodations."

"Yes, of course," Dria answered automatically, though urgency gripped her. "I appreciate your consideration."

"More will arrive with the mages," he said. "Is there anything in particular you would like to request?"

By rights, she should continue their polite banter before truly getting to her request, but she couldn't take the time. Hopefully Lord Lyr was familiar enough with Ralan that her lack of social niceties wouldn't disturb him. "As a matter of fact, yes. Several things."

Lyr nodded. "Of course. Please feel free to speak freely. My daughter is part-human, and your brother pesters me incessantly. I've even found accommodations for a dragon. I'll not be bothered, I assure you."

"I hope that is the case." Dria met his gaze through the glass. "I need a scout or two who can move with ease through the human world and is willing to risk exposure to the affliction that has befallen Fen. I trust Lial shared that information with you?"

"Yes." Lyr did frown then. "A concerning development."

"I would like to suggest that Selia and Lial work together to create something capable of detecting the presence of the illness. An object that can be carried, perhaps?" Dria pressed her lips together to avoid mentioning Vek. "I would prefer to rely upon our own people in this endeavor, and I am uncertain who besides Lial can identify the sickness. As for the scouts, Kera mentioned a pair named Delbin and Inona that might suit."

"An excellent suggestion. I'll consult them to see if they are willing to risk exposure to the illness for this mission. Once I know for sure, I'll send word," Lyr said. "And I will check with Selia and Lial, as well."

Dria smiled. "Thank you, Myern. I appreciate your haste in this matter."

As soon as Lyr bid her farewell, Dria cut the link. Only then did she allow the sigh to slip free. Her request might prove impossible, but if anyone could come up with a way to detect the disease, it would be Lial and Selia. Only if they failed would she ask Vek to assist her. Gods forbid.

Suddenly, his energy brushed against hers in an attempt to communicate telepathically. Surprised, her shield slipped, and he didn't hesitate to complete the connection. She cursed aloud as a shiver traced down her spine at the contact. With her luck, he knew it, too.

"I'm porting back to my house for some clothes," Vek said. *"Don't stride in here to kill me when you feel the power surge."*

"You're what?" Her lips thinned. *"You are supposed to stay here. Fen—"*

"Isn't going anywhere. Relax, Dria. I'm not leaving you." His laughter tickled the edges of her mind. *"I fear I have no talent for creating cloth, much less garments. You'll just have to survive without me for a while."*

Dria sent a shock of annoyance through the connection. *"I'll manage."*

Then he was gone, and the promised surge of power shivered across her skin.

She stared at the wall for more than a few drips of time. Not because she missed him—or was waiting for him to come back. Absolutely not. Besides, he would return soon enough. There was no way he was done annoying her.

If only she could decide whether she wanted him to be.

14

A chime from the communication mirror woke Dria, and with a groan, she sat up. It couldn't be dawn yet. She'd attuned a spell in the entrance at the top of the cave to alert her when the sun rose, since she didn't have another method of measuring time, and the simple alarm hadn't yet shrieked in her mind. But there was no telling how long had passed since she'd left Moranaia.

Another ring sounded from the mirror. Resigned, Dria swiped her fingers through her hair, smoothing the tangles with an enchantment, and rubbed the sleep out of her eyes. Then she stood, brushed the wrinkles from the robe she'd fallen asleep in, and marched over to the mirror to answer the summons.

The Myern's serious face filled the glass, erasing her reflection. "Good morning, Dria. Please forgive me for calling at such an early hour."

"These circumstances aren't precisely normal," Dria said. "Is something amiss?"

Lyr shook his head. "Not exactly. However, I would like to send my scout and her partner through in advance of the mages. Since the mages are arriving fairly early, I wanted to notify you now."

"Did Delbin and Inona agree?" Dria asked.

"They did." Lyr smiled. "You'll find them perfect, I believe. Inona is a scout of some experience who has traveled on Earth a great deal, and Delbin was exiled there for about a century. Mistakenly, of course. He knows Earth better than Moranaia. Lial and Selia haven't yet devised a method to detect the illness, but I thought you might appreciate the ability to have eyes on the surface sooner rather than later."

Dria had a feeling there was a great deal more unsaid about this pair, but she was willing to find out for herself. "You are correct."

"Very well, then. I'll send them through in…" A line formed between his brows. "Half a mark here, but I'm uncertain how you measure that there."

It was Dria's turn to smile. "It's no matter. I will be prepared."

Once they'd severed the connection, Dria sprang into action. In moments, she'd donned a new robe, braided her hair, and grabbed the loaf of bread still on the table before striding out the door. She ate as she walked, her thoughts on anything but food.

She had first considered having someone familiar with Earth camp near the hidden entrance, but it might be better to have the incoming pair scout the nearby cities instead. Some of that decision would depend on what she gleaned of their talents. Would the couple have any ability to discover more about the illness? And if Vek's father did indeed send forth others to attack the outpost, perhaps Inona and Delbin would catch word of their arrival in the area.

From what she'd seen of the Myern's previous choices, there was a fair chance that Inona and Delbin would have just the skills needed.

The cavern was quiet, although the lights ringing the walls hadn't been dimmed. Guards stood at their places beside the platform, but Dria didn't spot Kera. Or Fen and Vek. Even a traitorous potential bonded and his nephew had to sleep, it seemed. Thank the gods. If good fortune held, they would remain absent for her meeting with the mages. There was a chance that wouldn't go well, and she'd rather not have an audience.

Dria had just managed to swallow her last bite of bread when two figures stepped through the portal. The guards tensed for a heartbeat before they got a look at the pair. Then they gestured the newcomers forward.

The male had lightly tanned skin and blond hair a few shades darker than Vek's, but the woman's deeper gold tone and honey tresses looked more typical of plains elves. Dria guessed she wasn't a mage, though. Her Earth garb and wary, searching gaze marked her as a scout.

"Welcome," Dria said as they halted at the base of the steps.

"Thank you, princess," the woman answered. "I am Callian iy'dianore sonal i Inona Eman nai Braelyn, and this is…"

At her hesitation, the man smiled. "Delbin Rayac. I honestly don't know if I have a formal title at this point."

Yes, there had to be quite a story about these two. "I suppose it doesn't matter so much while we are on Earth," Dria said.

His smile widened. "The humans won't know the difference."

Dria couldn't hold back a chuckle. "Indeed."

"Hey, Vek," Delbin said as his gaze shifted to something behind Dria. Or someone.

The annoying man in question stepped up to Dria's side. So much for good fortune. "What are you two doing here?"

Inona's eyes narrowed. "We could ask the same."

"I assumed your leader told you about Fen," Vek said.

Sadness crossed Inona's face. "Yes. I was sorry to hear of the infection."

"I take it you no longer mistrust my nephew?" Vek smirked. "Though you have no such confidence in me."

Seemed reasonable to Dria.

"You have done nothing to earn my trust." Inona tipped up her chin. "But Fen faced death at Kien's hand to ensure the rest of our group escaped that cave. Cora might have been the one to close the gash on my throat, but I have not forgotten all who contributed to our survival. You weren't one of them."

Vek shrugged. "I didn't kill Fen as I'd been ordered to. See? I helped."

Inona scowled, but Dria found herself fighting back an unexpected smile. *No. Do not enjoy his dry sense of humor.* Delbin had no such inhibitions. Laughing, he clapped his hand on Vek's shoulder as though sharing a joke with an old friend.

"It's obvious you and Fen are related," Delbin said. "Tell him I'm hoping for the best for him if I don't get a chance to say so in person."

To his credit, Vek merely nodded, despite the way he'd tensed at Delbin's closeness. "I will do so."

Light surged from the portal, and the first of the mages stepped through. Dria wanted to curse. She'd thought she would have time to consult with Inona and Delbin on their coming mission before her next wave of duties, but apparently not.

Then she managed to identify the people who had already come out of the portal. "*Miaran.*"

Ah, well. At least they were too far away to have heard the curse.

"Why, princess," Vek whispered, his head tipped near enough for his breath to tickle her ear. "Am I mistaken, or did you neglect to address that to me for once?"

"Not now," Dria muttered. "I don't know who is responsible for this, but it can only mean trouble."

"What can?"

She shivered at the brush of air that came with the words and twisted her head to avoid the sensation. "That's my former troop."

Vek caught her gaze. "And?"

"I was in the lowest tier. I'd hoped to advance soon, but…" Dria swallowed. "Now I'm supposed to be their leader. Gods give me strength for this firestorm."

For a moment, she could have sworn that his eyes pinched in concern, but any hint of that emotion was buried in a dangerous, devious gleam. "Want me to drain them for you?"

Dria's mouth dropped open. Beside them, Inona let out a choked gasp, and Delbin's sudden cough sounded suspiciously like a laugh. But Dria couldn't take her eyes off Vek. Love of the gods. Was he serious? She honestly couldn't tell, and that reality sent twin bolts of fear and excitement straight through her heart.

"Careful," she murmured. "Or I might think you're being nice to me."

"I would be happy to be nice to you in many ways, dearest Dria."

Her breath hitched. *Clechtan*, she didn't have time for this. The final mage in the troop had just exited the portal, and Fedah, their troop's leader, was gesturing them to take formation behind her. Dria would not begin this meeting flushed and flustered because of an insufferable Unseelie prince.

"Did you eat before leaving Moranaia?" Dria asked Inona.

The scout shook her head. "We skipped the evening meal to make haste."

"Then perhaps Vek would be kind enough to escort you to the dining room."

Dria gave him a sweet smile. "I'm certain he remembers it."

His voice dropped to a low rumble. "Quite well."

Far from the anger she'd hoped the reminder would bring, desire lined his face. Her body heated as his gaze locked with hers, and she spun away from him. His laughter followed her as she approached the portal.

Dria didn't look back, but she could feel when he moved away. His absence bothered her almost as much as his presence, a sudden void where his warmth had been. Silly sentiment. He needled her constantly, not gave her comfort.

Didn't he?

Fedah and five other mages had already descended from the platform by the time Dria reached them. At the back of the initial group, Gessen sent her an encouraging smile, but it did nothing to ease the tension sending little sparks of anxiety tumbling in her gut. Not that any of these people would know. She'd faced far worse.

"Good day, Dria," Fedah said, her tone polite enough—if the listener hadn't trained with her long enough to detect the bite. "It is an…unexpected pleasure to see you again so soon."

Dria inclined her head. "Did the Ogefa not explain your mission?"

"Not as adequately as she could have." Fedah's lips thinned. "I learned upon our arrival at Braelyn that you are in charge here, not Prince Ralan. Well, I suppose it explains why you left my command so quickly despite our years of working together."

Ah, a hint of challenge already, reminding Dria of her previous appointment. But although Dria was nervous about potential conflicts, she had ceased being intimidated by Fedah a century or so prior. "This is not the Citadel. However, if my reassignment troubles you so deeply that you're grieved, you are more than welcome to return there."

The other woman's skin blotched red. "I did not claim grief."

"Good," Dria said, ignoring the insult. "Then after you get settled in your new room, you'll be prepared to join me to discuss the needed increase in protections for the outpost as well as improvements to our living conditions."

From the stormy expression on her former captain's face, Dria half expected to have her shields struck by lightning at any moment. But Fedah finally gave the barest nod. "Of course."

Dria scanned the expressions of the five mages at the front. Gessen appeared largely amused, although she caught a hint of worry in his eyes, and one of the other fairly new recruits, Bete, had a slight smile. Fedah's seconds, Pethan and Miria, were unreadable, and a third-tier mage, Kedep, had a frown that could have been confusion.

Any one of them could bring their own brand of trouble, intentionally or not.

"If you will follow me, I will show you to your rooms," Dria said.

At Fedah's reluctant consent, Dria ascended the base of the stairs. Hostility radiated from the woman behind her, an unwelcome reminder of the terrible situation. She'd likely made an enemy of her former captain, but she didn't let it bother her. In fact, after dealing with Vek, Dria had found this confrontation easier than she might have a few days ago.

Want me to drain them for you?

Dria smiled at the memory of his words. He probably *had* been joking, but the idea held more temptation now that she'd spoken to Fedah. But no. If it came down to it, Dria would challenge the woman to combat herself. There might be no other way to ease the resentment her sudden advancement had caused—not that it would disappear, no matter what Dria did. She would always be known as a rank-hopping princess at the Citadel now.

Vek had intended to ditch Delbin and Inona in the dining room and sneak back down to listen in on Dria's discussion with the mages, but Fen had walked in just behind them. His nephew had corralled him into staying, so now Vek sat a table with the other three and tried to conceal how much he wanted to be somewhere else. Specifically at the bottom of the cavern admiring how his future mate handled her former colleagues.

He hated to miss a good set-down.

"You're sure you want to get near me?" Fen asked for the third time.

Delbin shrugged. "I've risked worse. Chill."

"I'm not certain that cold would help the situation," Vek said.

Fen and Delbin broke out in laughter, but Inona appeared equally confused. "Probably Earth slang," she muttered.

"Yeah," Fen said as his laughter trailed off. "Sort of like telling someone to calm down."

"Reminds me of the way Vek lost his chill with Dria." Delbin smirked. "But I guess that was less about calm and more about—"

Inona nudged her shoulder into Delbin's.

But Vek stunned them all into silence by chuckling. "You're a brave man, Delbin Rayac."

The man in question grimaced. "Something like that."

"I'll end your speculation now," Vek said, concluding that truth would be to his benefit here. "Dria is my potential mate, and I have decided to claim her. Provided she agrees, of course."

Fen froze, his hand hovering over his bread. Then he gave his head a slow shake. "Good luck with that."

"She didn't seem particularly interested," Delbin said.

It was Vek's turn to wince. "I concede it may take a great deal of time."

Eyebrows drawing together, Inona studied Vek as she passed him a platter of cheese. "Do you know nothing about Princess Dria?"

He accepted the plate automatically, but he couldn't have said what he selected. His eyes were on Inona even as he handed the dish to Fen. "You sound as though you have crucial knowledge about my potential mate."

"Crucial might be overstating things." Inona smiled. "I've heard it rumored that she is cool and reserved…unless a person manages to bring out strong emotions. At court, she was either heralded as a frigid monster like Kien or an arrogant hothead like Ralan. Then again, the drama surrounding her brothers did her no favors during her teen years. She was fifteen when Ralan left and Kien was found torturing his brother's former lover."

"Fuck," Fen whispered.

Vek had to concur. Life at a royal at court was fraught with enough trouble without including two such tense events. He should know. His mother had been thrown out of court quite publicly after giving birth to one of Vek's siblings, a child who hadn't inherited the *Felshreh* traits from either her or the king. His father had been considering her for a marriage alliance based on Vek's strength, so the rumors spawned on that day had been vicious.

Of course, no one had been brave enough to repeat them in Vek's hearing after he'd almost ripped the throat out of the man who'd started the worst of them. His mother would never have tried to claim another man's child was the king's. She was no fool, and no spell on any world could trick a blood elf into misidentifying his own offspring.

The rumors at the Moranaian court after Ralan had fled to Earth must have been spectacular. And after Kien was revealed to be such a sick bastard? Brutal. Well, it did explain why Dria was all fight. If she'd cowered, she would have been eaten alive—both at court and later at the Citadel.

"Prince Vek?"

He startled, blinking as Inona came back into focus. Quickly, Vek grabbed the pitcher she'd been holding out for him. "Please forgive my inattention."

Surprise crossed her face. "It's…no matter."

"Hey, you do have manners," Fen quipped.

Vek shrugged. "When it pleases me."

It was more complicated than that, but they wouldn't appreciate hearing that he didn't waste civilities on people who served no greater purpose. Only the worthy earned the effort of courtesy, and Inona had proved herself to be such by offering him essential information about Dria. Divine knew her reasons, but Vek would accept the gift, nonetheless.

Now he had to figure out what to do with it.

Dria made certain to settle Gessen in his room last.

As soon as the door closed behind them, Dria spun to face her friend. "Nice warning you gave."

Gessen flushed. "I'm sorry. Our group wasn't the Ogefa's first choice, but the second-in-command of the other troop shattered his elbow. We were rushed out rather quickly to take their place."

"Fedah could have mentioned that," Dria grumbled. "It might have smoothed the situation for all of us to acknowledge that only an accident had placed her under my command."

"She has always had too much pride," Gessen said. Then he winced. "But don't tell her I said that."

Dria laughed, though she was grateful as much as amused. Few would speak bluntly in her presence, most too concerned with their own standing to risk it. A friendship like this was one to be treasured. "You know I won't."

His grin returned. "That I do. So are you going to tell me what's happening here?"

"Before I notify your captain?" Dria tapped her finger against her chin and then smiled. "Absolutely."

15

By lunch, Dria wanted nothing more than to curl up in bed and sleep, but she had far too much to do. She'd already chatted with Gessen, spent a couple of marks consulting with Delbin and Inona before sending them out on a mission, and then assigned the mages to their first tasks. There hadn't been any complaints about re-inforcing the protections on the various tunnels that connected to neighboring cave systems, but it was only a matter of time until the grumbling began. Fedah wouldn't hold her tongue for long.

A worry for later. Dria had her own task to complete, one she'd sworn to her aching thighs that she'd accomplish. The staircase spiraling around the cavern served its purpose, but it was an unwieldly way to travel. For one thing, it wasn't wide enough to accommodate more than two people side by side. Worse, it took forever to reach the top.

Dria settled her fist against her hip as she stared upward, trying to decide how to proceed. A direct local portal from the bottom to the upper chambers would be easy, but it wouldn't help anyone who wanted to access the rooms along the middle. She also needed to consider children, the elderly, and the injured. The outpost was inhabited by warriors now, but that might not always be the case. Better to prepare in advance for those unable to make such a climb.

A tingle of awareness shivered through her. Vek. His energy brushed against hers a moment before he spoke. "Analyzing the composition of Earth's caves?"

Dria released an exasperated sigh. "I wouldn't know how to identify the types of rocks and minerals available on Moranaia, much less this world."

"Then might I ask why you are staring at the cavern wall as though it holds life's mysteries?" he asked, humor coloring his tone.

She deigned to glare at him. "If you must know, I'm trying to decide how to improve transportation to the top. A direct portal wouldn't help anyone in the middle. I could make an entire portal system, but that would require the user to be able to connect with and control the spell to choose the proper destination. The best choice would be to create a moving platform. I'll have to wait for

Kezari to return, though. It's not something I have the ability to create."

"I see, he answered. "When is she supposed to return?"

"I'm not sure. Selia is working with Lial on a project, and I gather that Aris and Kezari are unlikely to return without her," she answered. Vek peered upward, much as she had earlier, and Dria grinned at the look of concentration he now wore. "Are *you* examining the composition of the cavern?"

Instead of getting annoyed, he smiled. "Yes, actually. I believe I could create a platform for you. I haven't used earth magic in a long time, so it's a little faded, but I should be able to manage the trick. It would be better than asking Fen, considering his illness, and then you won't have to wait for the dragon to return."

Dria studied Vek's face. There was something different about him. An openness that hadn't been there yesterday. But why? Was it some further trap? Some way to catch her unaware? He should have been furious after she'd used that spell on him in the dining room. He had to be planning some kind of retribution. After all, he didn't seem the type to ignore a dare, spoken or otherwise.

And what did it say about her that she felt a sliver of disappointment at his lack of response?

"Of course, I understand if you would prefer to wait." Ah, there it was. That hint of mischief and challenge in his eyes. "If you're afraid to spend too much time in my presence."

Gods. The cursed man did this kind of thing on purpose. He had to know how she would react. "Go ahead," Dria said. "If you're up to the challenge."

Truthfully, though, he needn't have pestered her into it. She'd never seen him perform any magic, nor had she been able to pinpoint his talents when she'd scanned him. In fact, Dria had never heard of him using magic openly like this. And what had he meant by the talent being faded? One could need refreshing on certain techniques, but an innate skill didn't simply go away when it wasn't used.

Vek stepped forward, moving closer to the wall, and her focus shifted to the flex of the muscles in his back as he lifted his arms, fingers splayed. Dria extended her own senses to watch how he performed the spell, even though her stomach twisted at the disorienting energy building around him. Instead of pulling from his environment, he uncurled his power from within like a rope unwinding.

No tether to the natural world. None.

She shuddered, withdrawing her awareness. Vek stood so motionless he could have been one of the stalagmites spearing up from the floor, a cave formation that moved worlds. But the tail of his power shifted the rock as his hands could not. From the wall in front of them, bits of stone separated from various places, small sections that wouldn't destabilize any one place, and began to warp and congeal. Then his magic shaped them into a platform, complete with hand-rails.

Before Dria could blink, the power was gone, gathered back behind his shielding as though it had never existed. Gods, her mouth was hanging open. Dria closed her

jaw with a snap and struggled not to show her amazement. What was he, exactly? She'd never seen magic work that way.

He spun to face her, and she gasped. His skin was so pale it was truly as white as his hair, and as he neared, Dria caught sight of his fangs. He couldn't replenish power from the environment. He'd used a great deal of magic and surely needed blood.

Her own blood surged—and heated. Suddenly, she wanted to be the one to offer it.

"Don't look at me like that," Vek said, his voice low and rough. "Don't."

"I wasn't…" She let out a long breath. She totally had been. "I'm sorry."

Vek trailed his knuckle along her cheek. "You'll offer the bonding pendant before I take your blood. That I vow."

Then the *drec* walked away.

Vek was going to pay for that display.

By the time he made it to Fen's room, his legs were shaking from lack of energy and from the long climb. Stupidity at its finest. He'd had to pour more power into creating the platform than intended, but he hadn't used that particular talent in so long that he'd almost lost his grip on the spell. Maintaining control had cost a great deal of energy. Too bad he hadn't kept hold of some of the excess he'd gained from nearly draining Quaea.

Fen lowered the book he held as Vek stumbled in. Dropping into a chair on the other side of the table from his nephew, Vek struggled to control his need. Not that it would do any good. In this state, he would have to take blood, or he would grow ill.

Closing the book with a snap, Fen's gaze focused on Vek. "What in the ever-loving hell happened to you?"

Vek grimaced. "I helped Dria with her work."

"Did you create another cave system or something?" Fen demanded. "You need blood. Now."

"Tell me something I don't know," Vek said. His nephew set his book on the table and started to lift his wrist toward his mouth, but Vek halted the motion with a snort. "You're sick, remember? But I couldn't take from you right now even if you weren't."

Fen lowered his arm to his lap. "What? Why?"

Vek took a deep breath. He'd never told anyone this. Never. In fact, only his mother and father knew, and they only because they'd had to help him learn how to handle the unusual gift. But he needed an ally, and Fen had proved his worth. They were kindred spirits, alike in more ways than Fen realized. This was a trust he wouldn't betray.

"There is more to my talent than people know," Vek said, each word dropping like a weight. "It is a benefit but also a great danger."

Fen's brows rose. "This isn't one of those 'now that I've told you, I'm going to have to kill you' scenarios, is it?"

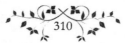

That surprised a chuckle out of Vek. "No. Not unless you make the mistake of breaking my trust. If you are uncertain of my regard for you, being given this truth should clarify matters. You will be one of three besides myself to know."

"I'm not sure what to say to that," Fen mumbled.

"Just listen." Vek leaned his head against the seat as exhaustion washed over him. Yes, he was going to pay for this folly. "Most have an innate talent, like your earth magic. Sometimes multiple abilities. And I suppose you could say that I'm the same. I possess many of the basic *Felshreh* spells, it is true, but the bulk of my talent is…unorthodox. Malleable, like clay. It is formed by the blood I take in."

Fen shook his head. "I'm not following you."

"Do you know how many bats there are in this cave system?"

"Uhh…"

"Of course not," Vek said. "But I could count their heartbeats if I wished. Because Aris gave me blood."

It only took a moment for Fen to puzzle it out. "You can use life magic now? Holy shit."

"Not as completely as Aris." Vek let his eyes drift closed. "But somewhat. My brain forms the channels based on the echoes in the blood."

"How are you not the most powerful man on any of the worlds?"

Vek cracked one eye open. "Who says I'm not?"

"Logic." Fen leaned closer, resting an elbow on the table. "If you could possess all of the talents of any fae in existence, none of this stuff would be a problem."

"That would be because I can't. Only echoes in the blood, remember? I get bits and pieces." Vek sighed. "The talent is far from limitless, and I have to be extremely careful who I take blood from. For one thing, the skills can jumble together in unpleasant ways if they are added too close together. If I'd taken too many types of earth magic, for instance, I would have made Dria a column of mud instead of a platform. And what I gain fades over time. A boon and a curse, depending. But the worst? If I take blood from those with strong talents too closely together, I'll suffer. Crippling pain, actually, as my mind struggles to incorporate it all. Which brings us to my current problem."

Fen frowned. "Which is?"

Vek caught his nephew's gaze. "Not only did I get Aris's blood, but I also took from Quaea when I confronted my father yesterday. If I don't find someone weak to take from this time, I'm going to be incapacitated for hours."

"Damn," Fen said. "How do you manage to keep yourself fed on a regular basis?"

"I can go a month or more without blood if I take plenty and then conserve my energy." Vek rubbed his fingers against the ache building at his temples. "Though after a week, my channels tend to settle well enough to prevent harm if I need blood again. It also helps if I feed from those with similar talents, so long as they won't

muddle. I might still get new abilities that way, but they are more likely to reinforce or overlap with old skills."

"Glad I'm not you. That's far too much trouble to go to for a meal." Fen snickered. "Why did you use all of your energy, then?"

A good question—and one he had no intention of fully answering. He'd known very well it was a terrible idea to help Dria. But for once, just once, it had been nice to have a problem he could fix without having to hurt or kill anyone. Not to mention the opportunity to surprise his mate…and show off.

"I was rustier with my earth magic than I'd realized," Vek conceded.

"Do you have enough power to teleport to the surface so you can find a human?" Fen asked. Then he snapped his fingers. "Wait, did you get that ability from Quaea? Lucky bastard."

"Didn't feel lucky when I struggled to use it. The first time I tried to cast the spell, I almost made a gate to the edge of the cliff outside my house, and even when I had it right, I nearly lost control of it mid-crossing. Ability doesn't equal knowledge of use." With a groan, Vek shoved himself to his feet. "I don't think I can get to the surface, so I'll have to do my best to find the weakest of the warriors here who will consent. I suspect it won't help, since Lyr sent only his best. Be prepared to guard my room until I emerge."

Fen's eyes widened. "That bad?"

"I suppose you glossed over the crippling pain part." Vek waved a hand before Fen could comment. "Don't worry about it. It won't be the first time I've made a mistake, nor will it be the last."

Then Vek strode from the room to amend his folly.

Her stomach rumbled with hunger and her muscles were lax with exhaustion by the time Dria directed the platform to the top of the cavern with a nudge of energy. Finally, the blasted thing lifted smoothly, not lurching or tilting as it had the previous five times. Thank the gods. She would have to show newcomers how to activate the spell, but it only required a press of energy rather than intimate knowledge of teleportation magic. Should be simple enough.

Smiling, Dria stepped off the platform onto the upper level. Then she froze. In the shadows beside the door to the dining room, Vek bent over one of the guards' wrists. A guard whose glazed eyes didn't focus on her as she jerked into action. Vek had beguiled one of her warriors without her permission—and possibly without the man in question's consent, either.

"Vek!"

Her wretched bonded didn't lift his head at once, but when he did, there was no sign of a wound on the wrist he held. The guard shook his head, reclaimed his arm, and nodded politely at Vek before ambling away. Vek merely lifted a brow.

"I can't believe you dared to feed on one of my people," Dria snarled as she halted a short distance away. Just enough to be able to resist shoving him. "My warriors are not—"

"I asked him first," Vek stated mildly. "Do you expect me to starve for energy?"

Dria sucked in a deep breath. "No. But you could go elsewhere. You made a portal last night."

"And could not today." Vek pressed his palm against his temple as his face pinched with a hint of…pain? "I must go. You'll have to deride me later."

Dria gaped as Vek stumbled past her. What was his problem? She stared at his departing back as he jogged down the stairs toward his room. Could he be coming down with Fen's illness? Taking the warrior's blood hadn't eased his pallor, and he'd acted as though his head hurt.

After a moment's hesitation, Dria headed after him. Not that she was likely to catch him at the speed he was moving. Her worry increased as Vek reached the landing to his floor and took off at a run down the hallway. She descended the stairs as rapidly as she dared. Something was absolutely wrong. She'd never seen him move with anything but deliberation.

Dria had just reached the landing when she sensed Fedah's presence at the edge of her mind. Stifling a curse, she opened a line of communication. *"What is it?"*

"One of these tubes opens into a chamber with a natural pool," the mage said. *"We'd thought to have Gessen purify it for bathing, but…"*

Dria's steps slowed. *"But what?"*

"Miria was able to shimmy through to check out the chamber in more detail. And she found footprints."

"Clechtan." Dria cast one last look down the hallway to Vek's room. He'd already disappeared inside, and she no longer had time to figure out his problem. It couldn't be worse than a potential intruder. *"I'll be right there."*

16

Vek barely managed to make it to his room and put a safeguard on the door before the full force of the pain hit. He didn't even try to reach the bed. He stumbled a couple of steps forward and dropped to his knees. As his muscles began to seize, he crumpled to his side.

He'd long ago trained himself to remain silent. Contained. Not even the slightest tendril of his pain would escape to alert any who might take advantage of his vulnerable state. In a royal court, it paid to be fanatical about safety. His pride trapped the agony until it magnified a hundredfold, reverberating through his mind and body.

Vek shoved his trembling hands against his head, though no amount of pressure would ease this. Nothing but time. Channels of power fought in his mind, but only he would be the loser.

As always, he prayed for an oblivion that would never come.

🔥

The tunnel Fedah had been checking was near the middle of the cavern, a small offshoot at the end of the hallway where the warriors slept. Dria had made note of it during her first exploration, even placing an extra shield across the waist-high gap. Now as she crawled through the narrow tunnel, she reconsidered the decision to leave it until later.

Unease teased at her belly, twisting her stomach and making her muscles ache. Behind her eyes, a dull throbbing pounded an anxious beat. Was this merely her concern over the footprints that had been found? Dria wasn't the prescient type, unlike her seer brother, so she doubted she detected some future doom.

But the sensation wouldn't leave.

By the time she pulled herself upright at the other end of the tube, nausea had crept up her throat, and her hands shook. Dria rubbed her palms against her robes and forced herself to focus on the small cavern. The chamber was just large enough for a broad pool of water, Fedah, Miria, a pair of mage lights, and a jungle of stalagmites, stalactites, and columns. Beneath her feet, the uneven stone was smeared with muck—as was she at this point.

This section clearly hadn't been altered by the dragon. It was too wild and natural. Carefully, Dria picked her way across the floor without touching any of the cave formations. The stalagmites she passed would be living here, and the oil from her hands would ruin them forever if she grabbed hold of them. It would take an earth mage of some skill to alter this area for their use without marring its wild perfection.

"Finally," Fedah said. "I was about to give up hope you'd get here."

Dria didn't bother to remind the other mage of the length of the tunnel. Doing so would acknowledge the barb, and there was nothing to be gained in doing that. "Where's the footprint Miria discovered?"

Miria gestured at the ground between herself and Fedah. "It's only half of one, but I believe it to be recent. Have any of the warriors ventured here?"

Studying the floor, Dria eased her way closer. She found no marks until she reached the place Miria had indicated. As the mage had stated, it wasn't a complete footprint, only one side of the foot. Smooth and easy to miss, save the indentions where the shoe had been stitched together. This wasn't the heavier, thicker leather of a soldier. Only a scout or a mage would wear this style.

"I doubt it," Dria finally said. "Kera might have sent a scout through here, but I'm sure she would have told me."

"Maybe," Fedah said.

Dria cut her with a glance. "I have nothing but faith in *Kera* to follow the chain of command."

Fedah gasped. "I did contact you about this discovery."

"At your leisure, I imagine." Dria scanned the ground once more, evaluating the probable direction of their intruder's movements. "What else did you find?"

"Nothing of concern," Fedah said.

But there was a sharpness to her tone that implied a definite *to you*.

With a quick thought, Dria activated her only tracking spell. Unlike Gessen, she was barely proficient with water or air-based spells, but she didn't want to take the time to call her friend down here. She directed the faint yellow glow to wrap around the footprint, and as soon as it had latched on, she sent it drifting across the cavern floor, seeking anything with a similar shape or energy signature. Once the magic had swept across everything in sight, it faded.

Except for a few minute traces of yellow leading between a pair of columns near the upper back corner.

"Have you investigated that far?" Dria asked.

Fedah shrugged. "Some things are better left for the leader."

Yes, Dria was going to have to deal with the captain soon. But not now. Rolling her shoulders, she shoved past Fedah and ascended the rocky floor toward the corner. Here and there, her magic illuminated hints of footprints in the muck. Suspicion built inside her as tautly as the ache between her shoulder blades.

Scouts wore soft leather shoes, the soles hardened but supple, but no scout would leave such visible marks. Any warrior worth their station would erase all signs, physically or with magic, before moving on. That meant this was either a trap or the person who had passed through here was inexperienced.

Dria swallowed the sharp taste of bile and increased the power in her shields before scanning the cavern with her magic. Nothing. No hint of power. No spells designed to entrap.

Nothing.

Perhaps a human had explored this cave system in the recent past? Dria had no clue what kind of footwear they used. She paused a few steps from the dark gap visible between the columns. The light from the mage globes in the main chamber didn't reach into the shadows, so she cast a small ball above her head and directed it forward.

A wall. There was nothing there but a cave wall. How could that be possible?

"Did you fare better than I?" Fedah called, her taunt echoing through the chamber.

Dria wanted to tell the woman exactly how she was going to fare if she didn't cease, but now wasn't the time. And in any case, Fedah had a right to her frustration. She never should have been placed as subordinate to someone who'd been her underling a few days before. Dria couldn't allow it to continue, but she did understand it.

Instead of answering, Dria approached the columns. A hint of yellow glowed softly at the base of the left one. She probed the area with her magic, analyzing the floor and the wall behind it. Only…there. A blank space, a gap easy to miss in the dim light. Before her magic reached the end of its range, she detected a widening in the fissure as though it opened into a larger space. It had to be where the intruder had slipped through.

She glanced back at Fedah and Miria. "I found something. Remain on guard, and if I do not return soon, sound the alarm."

Fedah's eyes widened. "There was nothing but a wall."

"I take it you don't have a great deal of experience with caves," Dria said.

"I was born and raised on the plains," the other mage snapped.

"Well, I wasn't." Dria smiled. "In case you've forgotten, the palace sits atop a mountain. And do you know what mountains have?"

"But as a royal—"

Dria laughed. "As a royal, I shouldn't have been in a cave. I did my share of exploring regardless. You can never count on a wall being just a wall."

She didn't wait for a rebuttal. The sad truth was she'd gone into the caves to avoid the more malicious gossips at court, and she'd been fascinated enough to return until her bodyguards told her father. If she hadn't been forbidden from endangering herself, she might have gained more experience. Caves had their own unique beauty that was difficult to resist.

Carefully, Dria eased around the column and into the fissure. Darkness closed around her, the tunnel ahead nearly black as her body blocked the light from her

mage globe. She'd need to rely on her other senses to guide her. If there was someone in the room on the other side, she would rather they not see her coming.

With each slow slide into the narrow space, her breath came more shallowly.
Even so, Dria sent her magic ahead of her, feeling out the dimensions and possible
inhabitants of the space beyond. Another small room, this one large enough for one
person to stand—maybe two if the people in question were close friends.

Was that another narrow fissure beyond the room? She probed as best she could,
but this type of magic wasn't her specialty. She could tell that there was no one living
inside. No energy signature, no shielding, no huddled form. Perhaps she could send
her mage globe ahead after all. Then she could examine the chamber visually before
determining her next move.

Crack.

Dria froze at the ominous sound. Her heart slammed in her chest, but she
brought up her best shield—the kind used to repel physical attacks in battle. Silence.
She let out a relieved sigh and eased herself back the way she'd come. If this cave was
unstable, it would be better to explore with an earth mage and a scout.

When the ceiling above the fissure gave, there was no other warning.

Instinctively, Dria crouched as stones tumbled around her. Stalactites pinged
against her shield, and she threw more energy into it to repel them. But this shield
was designed for large blows, not small ones. Cursing, she grabbed more energy from
the environment as dust and tiny stones peppered through, scratching her hands and
face.

Dria modified the solidity of the shield, but her energy began to drain beneath
the force of stone on top of her. Finally, she gave up on stopping the small incursions and focused on something far more important—survival.

If she lost control now, she'd be crushed.

Not exactly how she wanted to spend the rest of her day.

She needed help. But who... Vek. He could manipulate earth.

Before she could second guess herself, Dria reached for Vek's mind. He might
be angry at her for some reason, but he wouldn't let her die. Probably. It took a moment's effort to find him, despite their bond.

Doing so proved to be a mistake.

Dria connected. Pain flooded her mind and senses, the source of her earlier discomfort becoming clear before rational thought was crushed beneath the maelstrom.
Her shield wavered as she tried to pull away from him, and one section gave.

Help.

But her own pain saved her as a stone crashed through, pinning her ankle with
a force that shoved a scream from her lips. Her mind jerked free of Vek's, and she
used every ounce of her will to push the tumbling rocks away from her upper body
as her shield failed.

Silence descended.

But so did darkness.

Help.

The desperate cry echoed through Vek's mind, shattering his control. His cry rang through the room. A new pain, one not his own, slammed through his consciousness a heartbeat before Dria's mind disconnected from his, but he was already moving. Every muscle in his body shrieked in protest as he pushed himself to his knees.

Dria needed him. Now.

Vek wobbled to his feet and almost vomited from the effort. No. He couldn't be sick. He had to get to her. If she'd reached for him, there was a dire reason. The pain wouldn't kill him, but her loss would.

For a moment, he opened his mind to Fen and pushed in one word. *"Follow."*

Hopefully, Fen hadn't been too stunned by the pain that must have accompanied the thought. No time for shielding. No time for much of anything.

The cave swirled around Vek as he stumbled from his room and started down the stairs. His magic uncoiled in restless tendrils, providing information—but not always anything useful. He tripped on the next landing and almost tumbled as his energy snagged on a handful of bats nesting in a small hollow several levels above.

Where was Fen?

Vek tried—and almost failed—to focus his senses on Dria. Finally, he caught her energy. This level. He changed course, shuffling down the hallway until his left calf muscle seized and he dropped to his knees.

Dria's energy wavered, and fear propelled Vek to his feet. As he weaved down the corridor, a frenzied cry rushed to meet him. A woman's voice. But not his woman. He squinted, trying to get his eyes to cooperate well enough to identify her.

"Warriors, to the ready!"

What warriors? Ah, it didn't matter. He would kill anyone who kept him from reaching Dria, and Divine help the person who had hurt her. He would suffer a month's worth of agony to drain them dry and rip out their throat for good measure.

By the time he reached the end of the hallway, a woman was squirming free of a hole at the end. He almost grabbed her and sank his fangs in deep, but her panicked energy gave him pause. Friend or foe? Vek pressed his hands against his aching skull, trying to concentrate well enough to communicate.

"Dria," he managed.

"She's trapped," the woman answered. One of the mages by the cut of her robes. "Fedah is trying to move the rocks, but she has no talent for earth. My mental range is low, so I'm searching…"

Her words trailed off as Vek flexed his magic toward the stone wall. Pain cleaved his body like an axe, but the hole widened until he could slip through to the next chamber. He'd never make it if he had to crawl.

"Miaran," the woman breathed.

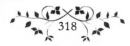

"Find. My. Nephew." The muscles in Vek's back spasmed, but he kept himself upright by force of will. "Fen. Now."

He could spare no more energy for words. The mage would obey or she wouldn't. Vek shoved his feet into motion, propelling himself through the tunnel as quickly as he could. Almost there. He would not lose her.

Dust floated on the air of the chamber, the worst of it in the back corner. Light flashed around another mage, though Vek couldn't tell if he was seeing the glow with his eyes or his senses. Everything was jumbled. But he staggered forward anyway.

The woman turned fearful eyes his way as he approached. "I don't know what happened."

Was this the former leader who had vexed Dria? "You."

She paled. "No, I swear it. I was angry, but I like Dria. I don't know what… She slipped through a crack behind the column that…that was here. There was a loud rumble, and then rocks began to fall. I can't get through."

Vek examined the tumbled stone as pain surged through him. Couldn't just move it. More might crash. Hell. He needed Fen. But the wavering flicker of Dria's energy drove Vek forward anyway. If he was careful, he could tunnel through and reach her.

More voices echoed behind him. One male, but not Fen.

"Stay back, Gessen," the woman beside him called.

Vek ignored them all as he sank to his knees. He was too busy fighting through the agonizing tempest of his mind as he sought control over his earth magic once more. His muscles spasmed, but he sent his uncertain power outward.

Forever. That was how long it took to shift one rock and crawl to the next. Re-shape. Slither forward. Shift. Wriggle. A few stones crashed behind him, but it didn't matter. He wasn't going back. Not without Dria.

Finally, he spotted the tip of her shoe between two rocks. Panic gave new life to his energy as he eased the stones from her lower body. Blood pooled beneath her, the scent twisting like a taunt within him, but he ignored his own discomfort. Only when he'd cleared the rocks that buried her to mid-thigh did he dare to glance up her body.

Alive.

Vek almost collapsed with relief to see her steady breathing. A pair of stones had wedged together above her head, blocking her from getting crushed, but a quick probe of magic revealed their unsteadiness. He had to get her out of here.

A small chamber lay not far beyond them. Could he pull her there? Should he? A trickle of dust and stone rained down on him, answering that question. Her spine hadn't been crushed, but even if it had, she'd have to be moved.

Vek crawled beyond her, shifting stones as he went. The tunnel was more intact on this end, so it didn't take long before he could turn and stretch out on his stomach. He reached forward and gripped Dria beneath her arms, tugging her with him as he wiggled backwards. Despite the cool air, sweat beaded on his brows and dampened his shirt, but still he drew her with him.

Slowly but surely.

By the time he settled them in the tiny chamber, his mind had gone fuzzy with exhaustion and pain. But he'd gotten her out. Now to determine the damage. His eyes had already adjusted to the darkness, so he cast the dimmest of mage globes, the light so faint it would barely be perceptible to many outside his race. Enough for him to see detail, though.

Abrasions lined Dria's face and arms, but the blood there was superficial. Not so for the blood coating her ankle. Her right leg had taken the worst of it, and Vek had a feeling more than one bone was broken. He had no talent to help that. But he could seal the gashes letting her life drip onto the rough stone floor.

If he could get his magic to operate properly.

His head pounded, and her sweet scent prodded him to drink. To replenish himself. But he would not do it. He would have her by choice or not at all. Vek lifted his hand toward her leg and grimaced when he noticed the dirt coating it. With a painful flex of earth magic, he forced the mud from his skin.

Then he gathered his power and got to work on her wounds.

It took forever, since the spell was intended for the small cuts he made during feeding. By the time he finished closing the worst of her gashes, his shoulders and arms were as hard as the stones he'd shifted. With a groan, he dropped to his side facing Dria. Spots danced in front of his eyes as he studied her pale face. He'd done his best.

Fen had better get his ass moving.

17

Pain was not one of Fen's favorite things, and he'd had more than his fair share of late. But that shock from Vek...that had been something else entirely. When Fen had returned to awareness after his uncle's message, he'd found himself slumped on the floor a few paces away from the chair where he'd been sitting.

Had he tried to obey the command? *Follow.* He must have, but the pain had overtaken him. Now, he ducked his head into Vek's room, but it was empty. Fuck. Where could his uncle have gone? A wealth of agony and fear had been embedded in the single word he'd sent.

Fen darted down the stairs, almost crashing into one of the mages rushing up from the opposite direction. He grabbed her shoulders to steady them both before releasing her. "Sorry. Have you seen—"

"Are you Fen?" the woman demanded. "I'm searching for the blood elf's nephew."

Fen's heartbeat thundered in his ears. "Yeah."

"Come with me. There was an accident."

The mage fled down the stairs before he could ask a single question. Though Fen wanted information, her haste prompted his feet into action. There was only one thing that he needed to know.

"Is my uncle injured?"

She tossed a look over her shoulder. "I do not know. He appeared ill when I encountered him, but he was not involved in the accident."

If his uncle had left his room while nearly incapacitated from taking that excess energy, the reason would have to be catastrophic—and only one thing came to mind. Dria. Vek's mate must have been hurt.

As Fen followed the mage down a corridor, three Moranaian warriors led by their captain, Kera, rushed up behind them. "There was some kind of cave-in," Kera explained. "Dria is trapped."

"Vek?"

Kera paused, a distant look in her eyes as though she spoke to another. "According to Fedah, he burrowed his way through to Dria, but the path collapsed behind him."

The mage turned into a tunnel carved unevenly into the wall. Sloppily done, but it held his uncle's energy signature. He must not have full control of himself, which meant he might have made the cave-in worse while reaching Dria. Not that Fen could blame him. He would do the same if it was his mate.

There wasn't much to the chamber where the tunnel emerged, only a small pool of water and a raw path curling to the left through an army of stalagmites. At the end of the trail, two mages worked to clear the pile of stones blocking their way. Fen hurried his steps before they caused a greater catastrophe.

"Step back," Fen urged once he'd reached the ruins of the stone wall. "Leave this type of work to an earth mage."

As they complied, Fen scanned the area with his magic and cursed. Vek's energy signature tunneled near the base, but near the ceiling, another person's power marred the stone. This hadn't been an accident, and it hadn't been set up by the mages who'd been trying to clear the area. This was an earth mage's trick.

It was a clever trap. One he'd used himself, in fact. Use the barest bit of energy to destabilize the ceiling, hold it steady with a spell, and enchant a trigger below. But who would have done such a thing, and why here, in a room that wasn't even part of the Moranaians' outpost?

"What were you doing in this area?" Fen asked the mage as he sent his magic in search of his uncle. Alive with Dria somewhere beyond. Safe for the moment, thankfully. "This isn't in the main cavern."

She bit her lip. "There were footprints. Dria traced them to a fissure in the wall."

"This is going to take me time to fix," Fen said. "There might be more traps. And I suspect I'll need energy before this is done."

"There's plenty to pull from on Earth now." Then her gaze shifted to his mouth where his fangs poked out. "Oh. Umm."

"I'll do it," the male mage said, stepping forward. "Dria is my friend."

The woman shook her head. "I've heard whispers that he is ill, Gessen. You can't possibly—"

"I can." Without hesitation, Gessen met Fen's gaze. "It is a personal choice, and it is one I make freely. I will provide if necessary."

Fen nodded, though he hoped he wouldn't have to accept the offer. "Thanks, man."

Damned illness. He didn't feel sick, precisely, but as he began the methodical work of repairing the cave, exhaustion already tugged at him.

He had to admit he wasn't exactly well, either.

Dria woke to the sound of her own sob. So much pain. Where was she? What...?

She shoved her hand against her mouth, but her palm slipped against her skin. She opened her eyes. Only the slightest glow lightened the darkness, not even enough for her to make out the source of the moisture on her palm. But with the flashes of memory that hit one after the other, her suspicions grew.

Blood.

Dria shifted her legs. Then screamed. Gods, had they been crushed? She couldn't feel her feet, but that might be the cold. No. No, something had crashed onto her ankle. Probably more rock had fallen after she'd lost consciousness. She might have held the shield if not for Vek's...

His agony. She could sense more to her physical pain. Something deeper, almost as though they were mentally connected. Or in close proximity. But that couldn't be right.

With gritted teeth, Dria gathered a bit of energy, though the effort had her shaking. No choice. Her breath hissed out as she bundled the power into a mage light and cast it above her. She barely maintained enough control to keep it aloft, but a muffled groan sounded from beside her at the glow.

A masculine groan.

Slowly, Dria turned her head to the side. Vek. His pale face twisted in pain, and his eyes were pinched closed. He lay curled on his side, knees drawn up. How had he gotten here? Had he been injured? But no. She'd felt his pain before that. What was wrong with him?

"Vek," she whispered.

His eyes popped open, though he squinted against the light. "Rest. I sense Fen near."

Dria licked her dry lips. "What...?"

"Cave-in. You called for me, so I came."

Words fled as she stared at him. She'd taunted him, teased him, argued with and confronted him. She'd all but told him he would make a terrible bonded. But at a single thought, he'd come for her. At great cost, too. The price was etched into every pained line creasing his face. It trembled in his hand as he reached forward to tuck a strand of her hair behind her ear.

But why?

Dria shifted against the cold stone, and her vision wavered as pain crashed through her. Vek flinched as she stifled another cry. Almost as though... Her blood chilled like the floor beneath her. Had he taken her blood? Had he bound them? Their pain blended, and...

"No," Vek said softly. "I used my magic to keep you from bleeding out, but I didn't taste your blood. We aren't joined. But..."

Pain echoed between them. Proximity might account for some of it—not all. "We don't even like each other."

Vek chuckled. "Speak for yourself."

He actually liked her? That was nonsense considering how much they argued, but she was too tired to debate the matter. Her eyelids grew heavy until she could barely keep them open. She had to admit, if only to herself, that seeing him beside her had brought relief.

Perhaps something more.

Only she would have to almost die in a cave-in to realize she might like someone.

Rock skittered against rock, the clatter striking Dria like the stones. Her whole body tensed, and another wave of agony ripped through her at the motion until she screamed. The scrape of moving rock resounded in her head until she was nothing but pain and panic.

Then Vek's hand settled against her cheek. "It's Fen. Be still, *ahmeeren*."

Ahh what? The odd word caught her attention. Was it Unseelie? As a princess and mage, she'd learned quite a few fae languages, but that one hadn't been offered. "What does that mean?"

"A simple endearment."

More pebbles rained down beside their feet, followed by the groan of shifting rock. Although the movement sent pain through her legs until Dria thought she would faint, she slid closer to Vek. Without a word, he rolled to his back and shifted his arm in invitation. One that she took.

The physical contact joined them into one giant bundle of agony as their individual problems became shared, but Dria settled her head against his chest. Somehow, he kept the panic at bay. Vek was a protector, but more than that, he was a fixer. He wouldn't rest until this situation was solved, even if he wasn't the one to repair it.

"What's another word in your language?" she asked to distract herself.

"*Felshreh*." His lips brushed against her hair as he spoke. "Means blood elf. It's what we call ourselves."

"Sounds almost Seelie." Warmth eased into her muscles, and she burrowed her face against his chest to breathe in his spicy-sweet scent. For the moment, she could forget he was dangerous. "Feels like I should be able to understand it."

His shoulder moved slightly beneath her head. "Similar base language."

Dust filled the room as one of the larger stones shifted. Dria yelped, and with a pained grunt, Vek wrapped his arms around her. Air flowed over her body, and the light brightened beyond her closed eyelids. But she didn't want to look. Didn't want to know if it was rescue or further danger.

"Shit."

Fen's voice.

"You sure you're both alive?"

Vek's breath ruffled her hair as he snorted. "Something resembling."

"I have no idea how I'm getting you out of here," Fen said.

"Gessen and I will levitate them." That was Fedah, and she even sounded concerned. "I'll take Dria to her room, and Gessen will return the blood elf to his."

"No," Vek snapped, his arms tightening. "Take us both to mine."

Dria cracked open her eyelids. "Bossy."

"Fen will guard us." Vek's mind brushed hers. *"I trust no other in this state."*

This time, she barely noticed the pain that echoed through his thoughts. But the vulnerability? *That* caught her. He'd actually let her see his fear of being helpless.

At another's mercy. Had he insisted on having his way, she would have refused. His comfort and safety? She couldn't deny that.

"To his room," she whispered.

It was going to be a long way up.

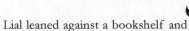

Lial leaned against a bookshelf and watched Lynia work. Gods, she was beautiful, with her brow scrunched in concentration and her magic flowing around the tomes stacked on the table. If anyone could find answers for him, it would be her.

In more ways than one.

Almost a mark had passed before she slumped against the back of the chair and rubbed at her forehead. "I found passing mention of disease in our ancient history, but there's nothing here to help you understand it."

On the other end of the table, Selia tapped an energy crystal against the table. "Maybe the illness afflicting Maddy and Fen isn't something that has struck the fae before."

"Anything is possible," Lynia said. "But I have my doubts. All of this began with Kien, and I did find record of his first spell being used before. Beyond that, history tends to circle. What we think of as new often isn't."

Lial almost slammed his fist against the side of the bookshelf but stopped himself in time. He had far too much to do to heal a broken hand. "If we can't find adequate information, I am uncertain we'll be able to create a tracking stone for the disease. I'd hoped the archives might give me something."

Lynia grimaced. "I'm sorry. I'll keep searching, but it could take time."

"Too bad I can't go with you when you heal Fen," Selia said. "I could shadow you as you work and create the stone then."

"*If* I can heal Fen." Lial took a deep breath in a useless attempt to calm down. "I've never faced anything like this, and as such, I will not risk putting you in such close proximity. If you caught the illness, too, then you would have to stay there."

Selia's shoulders slumped. "Away from Iren and Aris. I know."

"I'll do my best to— Oh, what now?"

Lial fell silent as he detected Ralan's mind shoving against his. Almost intruding but not quite. *"Your manners are still lacking,"* Lial sent as Selia and Lynia regarded him curiously.

"Kera just came through the gate to Earth," Ralan answered, ignoring the barb. *"Dria was injured, her legs pinned by stone. I know you're busy, but they need a skilled healer immediately."*

Lial sighed. *"On my way."*

"It appears I must be the one to leave," Lial explained to the women. "There is an emergency at the outpost."

Lynia's eyebrows rose. "How bad?"

"Not the disease, thank the gods." Lial tugged his long hair back and tied it firmly. "A leg injury, but one that requires immediate action."

"Be safe," she said softly.

Lial nodded. "I'll endeavor to do so."

18

By the time they reached his room, Vek thought his brain might turn in on itself, and now the beginnings of hunger stirred to join the turmoil. Surprisingly, Dria had managed to remain conscious, but it was no mercy. She moaned as the mage, Fedah, eased her body onto the bed. An echoing ache burned down his own legs until he wanted to scratch at them, but it would do no good. He should have let them take her to her own room as planned.

But he couldn't bear having her out of his sight.

"Be careful," the mage levitating Vek snapped. "You're hurting her."

"It's not like I can avoid it, Gessen," the other woman answered.

Vek studied the man's pale face as he worked. Although Gessen kept flicking glances at Dria, his hold on the levitation spell never wavered. With a gentle rush of magic, Vek was settled on the bed beside Dria. His mate whimpered as the mattress shifted, but she surprised him by gathering his hand in hers.

"Thank you," Dria whispered, though it was unclear who her gratitude was for.

The door opened, and the healer, Lial, rushed in. "Leave," he commanded the other occupants of the room. "Family or potential family only."

Gessen opened his mouth as if to argue, but Fedah gripped his upper arm and tugged. "She needs healing more than she needs us."

Vek twisted his head, intent on ordering Fen to go with them, but his stomach heaved with the motion. Then the healer blocked his view, and the expression he turned on Vek held a hard, almost scornful, anger. If Lial didn't mind that Fen had settled into a chair by the corner, Vek wasn't going to argue the point.

"Your folly hurts her," Lial said.

Vek scowled at the harsh words. "You know nothing about—"

"I know exactly what you are." The healer settled a finger between Vek's brows. "This is a pain that can easily be soothed by a competent healer. How many years have you suffered for pride?"

"Survival, not pride." The only healer his father had directed to help had been unable to fix the damage to Vek's channels, and he'd been unwilling to risk others learning of the weakness. "I could never open myself up to—"

"Ah, yes, the Unseelie code. Hide vulnerabilities and guard against betrayal." Lial snorted. "Spare me. You'll let me heal you now, or I will have you removed from this room. I can numb my cousin's nerves while I repair her bones, but it is not as easy to block what transfers through the beginnings of a bond. You will not distract either of us during this healing with your own stupidity."

Vek snarled, baring his teeth, but the healer merely lifted a brow. If he weren't in so much pain, he would rend Lial's arm from his body for daring to touch him. But then Dria's moan deepened, and Vek was forced to concede that the man had a point. The longer he waited, the more she suffered.

"Do not think to take advantage of what you find in my mind," Vek said.

"I have enough problems within my own," the healer muttered.

Then his power flooded through Vek's body in a rush.

Damn. Unseelie healers worked very differently than Lial. As the pain in Vek's head disappeared and his muscles loosened, Vek floated on an ocean of peace. The raw channels of his mind settled, their war of supremacy ended by the healer's hand. Incredible. He would never have dreamed it was possible.

But a discordant note slipped through as the power was withdrawn. Dria. A slow sting built in Vek's legs, but he was able to open his eyes and focus on Lial as the healer shifted his attention to Dria. This time, Vek could see the blue emanating from the healer's hands as he ran them across her legs. Then the light cut off, and Lial cursed.

"How bad?" Dria whispered.

"The left leg has a few breaks, but they are a simple fix." Lial frowned. "Your right ankle and foot…let's just say we are going to be here for a while. You may remain awake with the pain blocked, or I can use a sedation spell. Your choice."

Her eyebrows pinched together, but then she shook her head. "Awake."

"If that's what you prefer," Lial said, though his tone said he thought her daft.

Vek understood, though. She was the leader here, and he couldn't imagine choosing unconsciousness under those circumstances. He would never try to convince her otherwise. Instead, he shifted to the head of the bed so he could offer comfort while staying out of the healer's way. Even with the pain blocked, the procedure would be uncomfortable.

Lial pressed his hand against Dria's forehead, and the tension drained from her body as her pain eased. When the healer began work on her legs, Vek caught her gaze. "Want a distraction?"

Her lips twisted. "Dare I ask what you have in mind?"

His low laugh came more easily than he would have expected considering the day they'd both had. "Nothing fun under the circumstances. What happened in the tunnel?"

"I don't know," Dria said. "I was investigating footprints when a seemingly solid tunnel gave. My shield helped, but then I connected to you and…"

"You lost focus."

"Yes," she admitted.

Vek cursed beneath his breath. "Then I am partly to blame. If I'd had better control, I wouldn't have opened communication. But the way—" He snapped his mouth closed. They weren't alone, and although Fen and the healer knew something of his talent, it was something he would rather not explain to Dria with an audience. "There is much to discuss about that later."

Dria quirked a brow, but she obviously took the hint. "I understand."

Fen's chair squeaked as he stood and approached the bed. "You realize that was no accident, right? Someone set a trap."

That caught Vek's attention. "Explain."

"It's an interesting little trick," Fen said. "Make a weak spot in the cave ceiling, hold it up with a tiny bit of earth magic, and set a trigger somewhere unavoidable. It's not easy to detect if you aren't actively searching for it, especially if you aren't an earth mage."

Dria's lips pinched. "I don't think either Miria or Fedah have the ability to do that, but they were the ones who found the footprints first."

"It wasn't any of the mages who were down there," Fen said. "Energy signature didn't match."

Although it was good to narrow down the list of potential traitors, it left a crucial question. Who could have entered the heavily guarded cave system, and why had they set the trap outside the outpost? It didn't seem like a strategy his father would use. The king might send another assassin in through side tunnels, but he wouldn't have them create a snare that might never be triggered. There had to be a reason that spot had been chosen. Could there be a threat beyond that small chamber?

Dria must have been thinking something similar. "Did you seal what remained of the tunnel, Fen?"

His nephew's expression went blank. "I... Shit, no, I didn't. I was too focused on getting you both out of there."

"Go do that now," Dria ordered. "We can search it later. Do you have a shield that will detect if another earth mage tampers with your work?"

"Sure." Fen grimaced. "But I don't think I have the energy to cast it."

Vek held out his arm at once. "You shouldn't need much of my blood."

"But the contagion..."

"I'll risk it." Vek pinned his nephew with a look. "In fact, take enough to purge the disease if you'd like. Maddy said it worked for her."

The healer's voice trailed up from the end of the bed. "No."

Vek glared at him, but the effort was wasted. The other man's eyes were closed, his glowing hands wrapped around Dria's right foot. "There is too much at risk here already," Vek said. "I will not allow my nephew's health to suffer just to satisfy your research goals."

"I agree," Lial murmured. "But wait until I can monitor the process."

Well, that was an unexpected concession, one that made a fair amount of sense. "Fine. Take only a little, Fen."

Once his nephew had obeyed, Dria ordered him to meet the Moranaian mages beside the cave-in. Abruptly, they were alone—well, as alone as they could be with the healer a body's length away. Dria averted her eyes, her restless fingers twisting at the blanket beneath her hand. Occasionally, the blue light would flare, and she would wince.

"It feels so strange," she whispered.

Vek wanted to lean down and kiss her, but now that she was more aware, she surely wouldn't welcome his touch. "It is never an easy process to have one's bones rearranged."

A slight smile crossed her lips. "Had it happen often?"

"I've had my fair share of scrapes and breaks." Vek chuckled. "It must be difficult to believe, but some people aren't fond of me."

Finally, a true laugh. "You don't say?"

"Not everyone likes having their problems solved," Vek said. "Especially if they are the source of the trouble."

She surprised him by gripping his hand. "I'm usually one of them, but not today. Thank you for coming for me."

"We belong together," Vek said simply. "Where you are trapped, so too will I be. You just haven't accepted it yet."

Her fingers convulsed around his. "I barely know you."

Vek shrugged. "Not exactly true. Look in the mirror, *ahmeeren*. We are twins, you and I, at least in experience. Neglected royal children, always struggling to prove our worth."

"I never said—"

"You didn't have to," Vek interrupted. "Don't forget that I've met your family. I'm not certain if they are more or less dysfunctional than my own. Just perhaps more numerous."

A frown entered her golden eyes. "You never talk about them."

"It is generally safest not to." Vek glanced at the healer. Lial didn't appear to be paying attention, but his earlier interjection suggested otherwise. "Perhaps later."

"Fine." Dria blinked rapidly and rubbed at her eyes. "I think...I think I want to sleep. Naturally, I mean, not forced unconsciousness. Wake me when Fen and the others return."

Vek nodded. "I give my word."

With that, she closed her eyes and drifted into slumber as the healer reconstructed her very bones. Vek should have watched, taking in Lial's technique in case he ever had cause to drink a healer's blood, but he couldn't stop staring at Dria. She'd trusted him. She'd accepted his word and left herself vulnerable to his honesty.

Maybe there was hope.

Delbin laced his fingers through Inona's as they strolled down the street. The first thing he'd done after charging his cell phone was call Grunge, but the carnival where Delbin had hidden for the last few years of his exile had already moved farther east, beyond Knoxville. It was a shame, really. The fair was an excellent place to find the unexpected—like any fae displaying symptoms of disease.

At least Grunge hadn't yet noticed anyone falling ill, and he would now be on the lookout for any word of sickness. What he had seen, though, was an increasing oddness amongst the humans. As he walked through town, Delbin had to agree. He'd passed more than one person rubbing at their arms as though they had a rash. A few emanated a fair bit of power, though they appeared unaware of it.

Someone was going to take advantage of this, and then all hell would break loose.

All it would take was enough people using magic openly that it couldn't be dismissed as special effects. Talk about viral videos. Then all those people trying to convince themselves that the tingle inside was just their imagination and that the pressure building in their bodies couldn't be explained by any doctor... Yeah, shit would get real.

"How can they not notice?" Inona sent.

"Would you want to be the first person who insisted a myth was true?" Delbin asked. *"If they notice, they'll dismiss it so that others won't call them crazy. Hell, pagans have been getting mocked for years for saying that will-based magic is real. The average person will take time to accept this kind of power, at least until it's too obvious to ignore."*

They'd only made it another block before a woman's scream echoed from a nearby alley. As one, they broke into a jog and darted into the darkened alley without a second thought. Magic-based or not, this trouble would be resolved.

At the end, beside a dumpster overflowing with boxes, a woman blocked another lady in the corner. Delbin scanned them both and almost stumbled in surprise. That was a full-blooded Sidhe trapping a young half-blood. Before he and Inona were halfway there, the Sidhe lifted a ball of flame in her palm.

"Halt, or she will be the one to pay."

He and Inona skidded to a stop a few paces away. What the hell was going on here? The Sidhe woman wore the clothes of a high court Seelie, and they avoided the surface at all costs. They didn't hang out in alleys in Chattanooga threatening half-bloods.

"Not to butt in on an argument," Delbin began, "But have you lost your mind?"

The Sidhe's glance could have scalded him. "Begone. Do it quickly, and I might forget you said that."

"You are a long way from home," Inona remarked calmly.

"None of your affair."

The half-blood sank against the wall. Delbin peered at her. Had that been a spark striking where her hand met brick? "I don't know what's going on," the young woman said. "This lady said I had to go with her, but I'm not going anywhere with some weirdly dressed stranger."

Almost casually, the Sidhe tossed the ball of flame a few inches from the woman's head. It splattered against the wall as the younger woman shrieked and ducked.

Damn, she was serious. Inona must have thought so, too. As the Sidhe lifted another ball, his girlfriend's knife thudded into the woman's wrist.

"I hate having to throw a weapon," Inona muttered, tugging a second knife from her other pocket. "Good thing I have a spare."

The Sidhe woman screamed, and Delbin used the distraction to shove his power past her shielding. She was strong, so he only had a few moments. He wouldn't be able to seize complete control of her mind—but he wouldn't have to. After seeing the thoughts swirling through her head, he would be better served to wipe her memory of them entirely.

"Run," he shouted at the half-blood.

But he couldn't waste time seeing if she listened. All his concentration—and energy—was on erasing the Sidhe's recollection of their presence. He barely registered Inona as she darted forward to retrieve her knife. With a grunt, he took enough control to turn the Sidhe woman to face the wall. Then he sifted through her memories, removing as many as he could before she struggled free of him.

"Move it," he told Inona, gripping her arm and tugging her toward the street. "We need to get out of her sight now."

Inona didn't ask questions, thank the gods. They'd just exited the alley when he lost his hold on the woman's mind. Her pained scream rang out as the impact of her wound hit her consciousness, but there was no way in hell he was offering help this time. She could figure out for herself how she'd ended up with a gaping wound in her wrist.

As they rushed away, he scanned the area, but Delbin found no sign of the half-blood. Curse it all. He should have planted an order in her mind for her to stay close. A part-fae who'd just had a fireball lobbed at her head really shouldn't be running around without an explanation—and she would remember what they looked like.

"The girl headed to the right," Inona sent.

Delbin gave her a questioning look, but he turned left at the intersection. *"Not sure how you know that, but it doesn't matter. We have to get back to the outpost. Now."*

"She saw us. That could cause trouble."

"Not as much as that Sidhe lady is about to bring down on our heads." Delbin unlocked his new car with the click of a button. It was nice spending Ralan's money. *"They have their own cave network, and it isn't too far from ours. Best I could tell, she was trying to find a local half-blood with Sidhe heritage to manipulate into helping her navigate the human world. I think they want to recruit those whose powers are waking."*

Inona didn't answer until the car was moving. *"Why?"*

"I didn't catch a name, but someone wants the Seelie Sidhe to return to Earth. Someone important."

"So you're going to let the person they were trying to recruit go?"

Delbin's fingers tightened on the steering wheel. *"If it means warning the outpost of an imminent attack? Damned straight."*

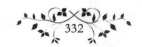

19

"That's the most I can do right now," the healer said. "I'll have to return tomorrow after I've had some rest."

A hint of fear rushed through Dria. "Tomorrow? But once you remove the pain block…"

Lial scowled. "You think I would leave you in agony? I localized the affected nerves and shut off the pain receptors until I release the hold. But do not mistake the lack of hurt for wellness. No walking. In fact, don't put any pressure on your feet at all."

"You're joking." Dria leaned up on her elbows. "I can't lie here in Vek's bed with an outpost to run."

"Works for me," Vek drawled.

Dria tossed him an annoyed glance. "Shut up. This is serious."

"It *is* serious, dearest cousin. Overwork yourself and you could be crippled."

Would he leave her impaired? It didn't seem in his nature. "But you healed the injury."

"Do you have any idea how much energy it takes to reconstruct shattered bone?" Lial demanded, and for the first time, she noticed how sallow his skin had become. "The fragments are in place and will begin to knit on their own. I will speed that healing in the morning, but I must have sleep. If you ruin the work I've already done, the cost will be yours."

After one last angry glare, Lial marched from the room. Dria stared after him. She'd unintentionally insulted him, but she honestly hadn't known how much effort went into healing bone. In over three hundred years, she'd never broken one. Truthfully, she'd never had more than a singe here and there from a spell gone wrong.

"Didn't anyone ever tell you not to anger the healer?" Vek joked.

"I suppose I do owe him an apology.," Dria said. "I just… What am I going to do? I can't be stuck here."

"You're sure?" Vek smirked. "I could find ways to entertain you."

Dria huffed. "Even if I was amenable, that kind of fun is difficult when you can't use your legs. I'd rather not explain to my cousin what I was doing when I shoved my feet against the bed."

"Only takes a bit of creativity, *ahmeeren*." Vek trailed a finger down her upper thigh. "If I tied your legs open from the knees and cushioned your calves with the right kind of spell…"

Dria's mouth went dry, and heat spread from her thigh to places much farther inland. "Sounds complicated."

He shrugged. "But worth it."

"I haven't even decided if I want to bond with you," Dria argued.

"Progress, then." His finger swept back toward her hip, and she almost moaned. "Yesterday, it would have been an automatic no."

Dria stared into his pale eyes. "You sound like you'd prefer a yes. I thought you didn't want a mate."

"I didn't." A wicked smile tugged at his lips. "Past tense. I've decided I want to keep you."

Her mouth dropped open, and chill replaced the passion that had been building. A potential bond was not something to take lightly. "Stop teasing me."

"Do I seem like the kind of man who would joke about such a thing?" Vek leaned close until his breath mingled with hers. "Contrary, strong, unafraid to stand up to me. Perfect. I like you, Dria. You'll have to learn to deal with it."

"Don't worry," Dria said, unable to hide the bitterness his words had invoked. A bitterness born of longing—and experience. "The feeling will pass. It always does."

"I am not your brother or your father." Vek brushed his lips against hers, the touch as soft as the finest wind spell. But far more deadly. "Fortunate considering all the things I plan to do with you if you'll give your consent. You restrained me with magic after our last kiss. Turnabout would only be fair."

Love of the gods. His draw was monumental, and it wasn't just the potential soulbond or simple desire. His darkness called to her, the part of her nature that wanted to tell the world to go immolate itself. She had a feeling he would stand with her against anything. *Miaran*, he'd probably help spark the fire that destroyed every enemy she'd ever had—and smile while he did so.

"I don't know what to do about you," Dria confessed.

Vek laughed. "Not the first time I've heard that."

An unexpected presence nudged at her mind, and Dria reinforced her shields. Then she recognized Delbin's energy signature and opened up enough to exchange words. *"Is something wrong?"*

"Depends on how much you savor a Sidhe invasion," Delbin answered. *"We're heading up the mountain now. Where should we meet you?"*

"Vek's room," she answered at once.

There was a long moment of silence. *"Okay, then."*

Dria winced. Yeah, that hadn't sounded good. *"I was injured, and… Never mind. Just come straight down."*

As soon as she disconnected from Delbin, Dria cringed down at herself. Impressions mattered. How could she be taken seriously as a leader while lying abed, her robe torn and mud-covered? Delbin and Inona didn't seem the types to hold it against her, but they weren't the only people who might need to speak with her. She didn't relish the subconscious doubts about her that might form.

"What is it?" Vek asked softly.

"Delbin and Inona are reporting in, and I…" Dria gestured downward. "I'm lying here a mess."

"I can help with that."

Vek bent down and gathered her close, one arm behind her back and the other beneath her knees. After a startled *oomph*, Dria hesitantly draped her arm across his shoulders and settled close. Her body burned at the feel of his chest brushing her side, and her heart ached at the tenderness of his hold.

"Why are you being so nice to me?" she whispered.

One eyebrow lifted. "Should I be cruel?"

"You're renowned for your coldness," Dria answered. "An enemy without mercy. You didn't even sound repentant about the people you've killed."

His shoulder shifted beneath her arm. "That's because I'm not. I only harm those who deserve the pain."

She dropped her head against him. "You never worry about being wrong?"

"I suppose that thought has occurred once or twice," Vek said, levity entering his tone. "Truthfully, though, I rarely kill without significant deliberation. I usually stick to maiming."

Dria surprised herself by laughing. "Lovely."

"You know very well that kindness doesn't always get the job done." Carefully, Vek settled her in a chair. With a burst of magic, he tugged over a stool to prop beneath her feet. "There are some people that no amount of benevolence will change."

"Like my brother," she muttered.

"Ralan?" Vek smirked. "Yeah, there's no helping him."

Dria snorted. "You know very well I meant Kien."

Vek's expression hardened, though his hands remained gentle as he tucked a blanket beneath her calves. "There's one I should have drained to the dregs."

"Did you know about Kien's madness?" Dria asked, studying his face.

"I suspected." Vek scowled. "But he was careful not to leave proof. It is no small matter to act against a prince of a powerful foreign nation."

"It's not much easier when it's a prince of your own land." Dria sighed. "But it is finally over now."

After a solemn nod, Vek strode to a chest set against the wall. Her eyebrows lifted when he peeled his shirt over his head and dropped it to the side. Surely, he wasn't going to strip in front of her? Then he lowered his hands to the button on his mud-coated, Earth-style pants.

Oh, *clechtan*. He was.

"What are you doing?"

Vek grinned. "Removing these disgusting clothes. I didn't think Moranaians were prudish."

"No, we aren't." Dria swallowed hard. "But it isn't polite to ogle without permission, either. I can't exactly leave."

"Feel free to stare, dearest Dria." The scoundrel winked. Actually winked. "I'm all yours."

Even so, she averted her eyes from the gorgeous, muscular planes of his back. Mostly. Dria couldn't resist flicking glances his way as he dropped his pants to the ground and kicked them off. Completely nude. Gods. He had a backside worthy of the finest painting. Her heart raced, and she wasn't certain if she wanted him to turn around or not. She might not be able to stand it.

The dratted man merely leaned over the trunk and grabbed out clean clothing. She almost drooled before she forced her attention resolutely to her own tattered robe. Unlike Vek, she couldn't change clothes. A glamour it would have to be. Well, at least she had enough energy for that low-level enchantment.

If she could keep her focus.

Vek was going to be the death of her.

If Princess Ara of the Unseelie knew anything, it was how to calculate—and she'd considered all sides of this risk.

Magic swathed her from head to toe, changing her appearance beneath the cloak she'd donned. She'd even underlaid several levels of glamour beneath the top layer in case any dared to look beneath. She could not be seen, not and survive.

As soon as she stepped from the Veil into the Seelie lord's underhill realm, Ara went still. He would no doubt have alarms, and she didn't want to be viewed as an intruder. Lord Naomh's cooperation was essential. According to her spies, he was at odds with Meren on a great many issues, and with Naomh's connection to the Moranaians, he might be powerful enough to help her stop what was coming.

It was too bad her father had gone mad.

First, the king had allied with the Seelie lord, Meren, to exterminate a colony of sickened Neorans who had reached out to Lord Lyr for help instead of their Seelie overlords. Now her father planned to strike at Moranaia and return the Unseelie to surface Earth. Did he honestly think that the Seelie Sidhe would co-rule the humans with him? Meren would betray him at the first opportunity. The plan made no sense.

She'd almost gone to her brother, Vek, but he hated her. Not without reason, in truth. Her mother had supplanted his in the king's favor, and their father had held Ara above Vek quite publicly for centuries. Then there'd been Fen. Poor, sweet Fen.

What they considered cold indifference to her son had actually been kindness. He might have exhibited some signs of *Felshreh* blood, but he'd still been half-human. Fen would have spent years being maligned, threatened, and challenged. He should have fared far better with his human father—if the human hadn't betrayed them all.

In the distance, Naomh and his brother Caolte appeared along the trail. If her father or Meren ever learned of this meeting, she would be a dead woman. Really, if her father had the slightest idea that she knew the truth behind his machinations, her life would be at risk. He hadn't trusted her with his secrets, not the way he did Vek.

How much did her brother know? He'd nearly drained Quaea, and Ara's spies had reported that he'd stormed from their father's room in a fury not long after. If they were closer, she might have asked him. His loyalty to the king was unquestioned, but they all knew Vek had his own methods of fulfilling his duties. She only hoped they didn't end up at war. He appeared to like the Moranaians. Perhaps he wouldn't work against them.

Ara straightened her spine and levelled her gaze on Lord Naomh as he stopped at the base of the small platform where she waited. *"Tarma,"* she said softly.

Caolte's eyes narrowed, but Naomh showed no reaction as he answered the formal request. "Come with us."

In silence, Ara walked between the brothers all the way to a large house in the center of the forested cavern. She'd used the Seelie version of the request for a formal, private meeting in case any had been near enough to overhear, but from the sidelong glances, she had a feeling both men suspected she was not one of them.

It didn't matter.

Once they'd directed her into a shielded room, Ara lowered the hood of the cloak she wore—along with the layers of glamour. Naomh remained impassive, but not Caolte. In a heartbeat, he had her pinned against the wall with an iron knife at her throat. She almost laughed. The *Felshreh* were immune to the effects of the metal, but perhaps it was all he'd had at hand.

"Explain your presence at once," Caolte demanded.

Divine, but he was a delicious one. If she had more time… Ara shook her head at the errant thought. "I come here at great risk to myself. Before I continue, I request your sworn word that I will receive no harm so long as I act in no way against you. I must also know if you bear loyalty to Lord Meren."

"Step back, Caolte," Naomh said. As soon as his brother obeyed, Naomh continued. "I give my word that I will deal you no harm so long as you act in peace. As for Meren…he has forfeited any loyalty from me."

She glanced at Caolte. Though he scowled, he also nodded. "I swear not to harm you…unless you threaten Naomh. Or myself. Meren can eat iron."

Ara had to admit that she admired his edge. "I'll feed it to him," Ara offered. "And once you hear what I have to tell you, that may be more than an idle threat."

Then she laid her father's plans bare.

20

She'd thought she was being discreet, but Vek had sensed Dria's every glance like a caress. With his back still to her, he smiled. She had to be aware of how much he loved to torment her. In fact, it might be the best way to claim her. Only when she confronted him with her needs would she finally own them.

There was a knock at the door. Vek straightened his tunic—much more comfortable than Earth clothes—as Dria called for Inona and Delbin to enter. The appreciative gleam in Dria's eyes disappeared as soon as she turned her attention to the door, but a hint of her desire drifted between them. The shadow of the bond they could have, provided they could overcome their obstacles.

Delbin rushed through the door first, a somber Inona at his heels. She closed the door behind them as Delbin skidded to the halt in front of Dria. He gave the barest nod to Vek before tapping his fist against his chest twice and bowing to the princess. His eyes widened as he noticed Dria's propped-up legs.

"Sorry about the rush," Delbin said. "The information I uncovered couldn't wait. Was there an attack?"

Dria grimaced. "Not precisely. There was a cave-in while I investigated footprints, but I'll be fine. What did you mean by a Sidhe invasion?"

"We caught a Seelie Sidhe threatening a half-blood." Delbin ran his hand through his hair. "When I took control to wipe her memories of us, I found out more than I'd expected. There's a high-ranking member of the Seelie court making his own little outpost in a connected cave system. They're trying to figure out the best way to eliminate us before claiming Earth."

Vek's forehead knotted. The Seelie were planning such a thing? They'd been the most stringent among the fae about holding to the old ways and living underhill. It seemed a rapid departure from the norm for their kind to be operating on the surface.

"How soon?" Dria asked.

"I don't know. They are trying to recruit a few half-bloods so they can orient themselves in the modern world. Although…" Delbin's gaze flicked to Vek. "I caught a stray thought about Unseelie impatience."

Dria's posture stiffened. "Unseelie?"

Fury rushed through Vek at that whispered question. So much for trust—and he wasn't just referring to Dria's suspicion. If others of his kind were involved in this, it meant the king had hidden a great deal more than his illness from Vek. Why would he order Vek to resolve this situation if he'd already been forming an alliance with the Seelie? The king must have been planning something with the Sidhe, for such a partnership could not have been created overnight.

His father had claimed to want the energy he believed the Moranaians had stored to heal himself and ensure that no one else sickened. But if Delbin's report was correct, the true goal held more sinister implications. The king might have grown dissatisfied with the amount of power he now possessed and decided to move against the humans.

Vek pulled his energy tight around himself when he caught the others' wary glances. He had no doubt what they must sense—the cold resolve of the predator. "I will take care of this."

He started toward the door, but Dria grabbed his wrist as he passed her chair. "Stop, Vek."

He halted at once. "You needn't speak your accusations. I am aware of what you must think."

"But you're probably wrong." Dria's fingers tightened. "I don't believe you're involved. Not this time."

Vek twisted to face her. Great divine, she meant it. His anger dulled beneath her steady regard. "After all that has passed between us? All that you know of me?"

"Yes, after that." Dria tipped her chin up. "You saved me in that tunnel at great cost to yourself. You've treated me with nothing but respect no matter how much I've pushed. I don't know what's going on, but I don't believe that you are involved."

He hadn't thought his heart could be disarmed until that moment. Not many people trusted the shadows. "Thank you, Dria. Later, you will know without a doubt what that means to me. But right now, I need to confront my father."

The door popped open again, and Fen rushed through. "We secured the area, but I did some investigating. I'd bet your hoard of gold that the earth mage who sabotaged the tunnel was one of our kind. Maybe even related."

Vek froze. There weren't many of his blood who could manipulate earth. He'd gained his ability by taking blood, but Fen had inherited his talent from Ara. "Your mother?" Vek snarled.

Fen's hands tightened into fists. "I wouldn't know. I can't remember meeting her, much less what her energy is like."

"*Athan ah shols angarn*," Vek cursed. He was an ass for not having considered that before asking. "Sorry, Fen. I'll go find out for myself."

Dria jerked at his arm. "I'd rather you remain close and search the caverns intrusions. We have no evidence that the person who left the footprints returned the way they came, since I only had a chance to cast the tracking magic in one direction before the accident. I've already directed Kera to scour every room, but you could scan for any familiar energy."

Frustration filled him as he stared down at her. "Dria…"

She gestured at the door. "Fen, Inona, and Delbin, go ahead and begin your search. Please."

Vek didn't have to look to see Fen's smirk, but all three left without argument. As soon as the door closed, Vek lifted a brow. "What is it?"

"Do you really think charging in and confronting the king will stop this?" Dria let out a humorless laugh. "And if *I'm* suggesting you avoid a confrontation, you know you should listen. It would be foolhardy."

She was right, tough though it was to admit. "I could challenge him. I never wanted to be king, but I'll do it if it means stopping this insanity. We've never been the type to try to rule over humans. It has to be the illness."

"Let's investigate first." Dria released his wrist, but he didn't step away. "Tomorrow, after I've been healed. If we can find their cavern, we might be able to glean more information."

Vek closed his eyes and tried to clear his thoughts of anger and betrayal. Yes, Dria was correct. Better results were usually achieved when more time was taken, and demanding answers from his father would yield nothing. But it could take a day or two, possibly longer, to locate their base. There were all kinds of problems with that.

"You intend to send your scouts?" Vek asked carefully.

Dria frowned. "No. We'll go. Just us and a warrior or two. I'll have to give it some thought."

"Why us?" He knelt beside her chair. "I assumed you would stay here since you're in charge. What are you thinking?"

"My father assigned me here because of my discretion," Dria answered, her nostrils flaring. "If Unseelie and Seelie nobility are involved in this, possibly royalty, then I'd better keep it as secret as possible. You're just as invested, and you can help with your earth powers."

Vek wanted to smooth the line from between her brows, but he was only going to add to her worries. "It's more complicated than that. If I have to use too much energy exploring the caves…"

"Why would—" Her mouth snapped closed, and her shoulders slumped. "Ah, right. You can't take my blood without… Well, it's something for me to think about along with the rest. Carry me to my room? I need to use my mirror to call my brother."

With a sigh, Vek lifted Dria gently from the chair and settled her close. He didn't like that she was injured, but the opportunity to hold her was an unexpected boon. They simply fit. As he carried her down the steps, he began to wonder what he wouldn't do for her.

Alarmingly, he couldn't think of an answer.

"I leave this up to your discretion," Ralan said through their mirror link.

Dria wanted to scream, but it would do no good. "That's it? You're a seer. You must have more guidance than that. Should I take more people to search for the Sidhe? Send someone else? My gut tells me to go with Vek, but it also led me into a cave-in. And I'll need to speak with our father for further orders once I've determined the extent of the threat."

Ralan leaned forward, a slight smile on his face. "Breathe, Dria. When I said it is up to your discretion, I meant all of it. Read between the lines. You know I'm not going to tell you what to do based on the future strands, but I'm more than happy to hint. So here's one. Follow your instincts, and don't worry about contacting Father. If you choose poorly, I'll bear the brunt. But I have every confidence that you won't."

"You used to have no problem telling me what to do," Dria grumbled.

Her brother laughed. "I suppose I still manage to from time to time, but past experiences have taught me to curb the impulse if there are better choices."

Dria sighed. Considering how their father had treated him, she could imagine. "Fine. But if I mess this up..."

"You won't," Ralan insisted. "I've always believed in you, Dree. Forgive me if I seem to have abandoned you there, but you're the only one I knew I could trust. I dare not risk contagion with Cora pregnant."

She lifted her brows. "You think it's going to start spreading."

Ralan averted his gaze. "There are many future strands at this time."

Dria had no problem catching the hint. "*Miaran.*"

"Do your best, Dree. It'll all become clear in the end." This time, the smile he gave her was tinged with sadness. "I do love you, you know. Despite all the ways I have failed you."

"I..." Dria took a deep breath. "I love you, too."

And she did—she wouldn't have been so angry otherwise.

"You know what you want to do concerning Vek," Ralan said as he lifted his hand toward the edge of his mirror. "Follow your gut."

Then he cut off the connection before she could argue. Probably wise. Despite his claim, she *didn't* know what she wanted to do. Her heart longed to give Vek her necklace, her body craved him, but her mind... Yeah, she didn't know anything. Logic told her a link between them would end in pain—but it also reminded her that Vek had cared for her better than anyone else before.

Dria glared at her reflection in the mirror Vek had positioned to face her chair. Leave it to her brother to hit upon the heart of her turmoil. Her instinct screamed that she and Vek must be the ones to explore the caverns, and it needed to be soon. But Vek had been correct about the problems that could ensue. If he ran out of energy, she would have to offer him blood. She would be forced by circumstances into a bond instead of joining with him by choice.

That wouldn't end well.

What had the god Loki said? *Don't offer him blood until you've started the bond. And try not to wait too long.* Had this been what he meant? If so, she would need to begin the bond before they left or risk… Maybe she didn't want to know what would happen if she ignored a god's pointed advice.

What would Vek be like as a bonded? She'd thought she'd had a good idea. Stubborn. Cold. Mocking. But there was more to him beneath the mask. An unwavering integrity, a belief in justice, and an innate goodness only a few ever saw. Some of his hardness was kindness, even if it was sometimes misguided.

He would challenge and support her, and he wouldn't back down from her darkest fears and secrets. He might never love her, but he would kill for her. And she… she might even do the same for him. Gods, *would* she kill for him? She'd trained for battle, but she hadn't yet faced it. Could she step in front of a threat to defend him?

A tiny voice inside whispered a terrifying *yes.*

No. They would do better together without strong feelings in the way. The Unseelie weren't known for their expressions of love, and her stomach churned at the thought of offering it herself. Family always disappointed, and a bonded would certainly be that.

But they could create a political alliance. A necessary joining—*that* she could stand. Could she get Vek to agree? He claimed that he wanted her, but she had no idea about his expectations. How did an Unseelie's mate act? Physical intimacy between them wouldn't be a problem, but how much would he require from her otherwise? Perhaps he would desire her adoration. Hah!

Dria would ask him later. It was well past dinner, a sad fact her stomach was beginning to make note of, and her body was heavy with exhaustion. Food and rest would help her heal, and recovery was of the utmost importance.

If she decided to bond, it wouldn't be from her bed.

At least not like that.

Insistent chimes jerked Kai from slumber. Disoriented, he blinked his eyes open and tried to get his bearings. All was silent now. Had it been a dream? Arlyn nestled against him, their fingers laced over her slightly rounded belly. With a smile, he cuddled her closer. They couldn't have been asleep long, but daybreak had to be near. She'd flay him if he woke her again for his own restless body's sake. Pregnancy had turned her into even less of a morning person.

Brinnnng.

Kai flinched at the sound. Fuck it all, was that his mirror? Who would be trying to contact him before the sun had risen? His father was one of the few people who used the thing, so this didn't bode well. Quickly, he eased away from Arlyn and hurried from the bed, grabbing his tunic and pants from the floor. As he tugged on his clothes, Arlyn shifted on the bed.

"Kai?"

"Mirror—" *Brinnnng.* "Chime."

"Better be someone bringing takeout," she mumbled.

Chuckling, he darted over to activate the mirror. At least he'd had the forethought to angle it away from the bed. Arlyn wouldn't have been thrilled to have the caller see her naked. Then his father's image filled the glass, and Kai was doubly grateful. Nudity might not be a big deal to him, but she'd been raised on Earth. She would have been embarrassed around Naomh for months if he'd seen.

"Did you forget how to calculate time changes?" Kai asked.

Naomh's lips twitched. "A pleasure to see you, my son."

Kai glanced down. Yeah, he'd put his tunic on inside out. "Forgive my disarray, Lord Naomh. It is not yet dawn here."

"I am aware," his father answered, his tone hardening. "You needn't address me so formally. And in any case, there is no time for banter. I have received news of impending trouble from a credible, high-ranking source."

Kai rubbed at his temples. "Shouldn't you be telling Lyr or Ralan this?"

Naomh's jaw clenched. "This involves family. Your uncle, Meren."

"Lord Meren of the Seelie court?"

At Naomh's nod, Kai cursed. He remembered all too well the interactions they'd had when Kai had been at their court on his last diplomatic mission. He wouldn't be surprised if Meren was responsible for at least one assassination attempt on him.

"It is best I don't give my opinion of Lord Meren," Kai said.

Surprisingly, Naomh smiled. "On that we agree. My brother has caused his fair share of trouble, and it is time he receives his due for it. His thirst for power has shifted to the human world, and he has allied with the Unseelie to invade now that magic is returning there."

A choked sound echoed from the bed. "What?" Arlyn asked.

"Is someone else there?" Naomh demanded, brows lowering.

"Yeah, my soulbonded," Kai said. "Who the hell else do you think would be in my bedroom in the middle of the night?"

Naomh leaned toward the mirror. "She must not spread word of this. I will deal with Meren, but if he hears about it before I can—"

"If this is a matter for family, then she should be included. As could Lyr, as you well know."

Out of the corner of his eye, Kai saw Arlyn grab her dress from the floor and tug it on. Her face pinched with anger, she stomped to his side. "My father has cut off all ties to Meren after your brother supported the murder of innocent, sick Neorans. He would not support Meren," Arlyn said.

Naomh studied them for a moment. "Very well. I will tell you what I can. I'll leave it to you to decide who needs to know."

21

When Vek returned, he came bearing food. Dria could have kissed him for that alone. She'd been considering how long she could wait before her stomach consumed itself, for she didn't want to disturb the *sonal* searching the caverns or the mages reinforcing the shielding. It was cursed inconvenient not to be able to walk.

"Thank the gods," Dria said as Vek lowered the plate of bread, cheese, and meat to her lap. Simple food, but it could have been a feast. "I was about to calculate how much energy a levitation spell would cost."

Vek laughed. "For the food or for yourself?"

"Myself," she answered. "I'm not particularly good at levitating objects I can't see."

"What an interesting sight that would have been."

Dria took a bite of bread, savoring it before she answered. "Yes, indeed."

"The others should return soon." His good humor fled as Vek settled into the chair beside hers. "I found nothing. Fen is doing a detailed sweep of any side tunnels he can find, and Inona and Delbin are searching the mountainside for other openings."

"Fedah and Kera have reported similar results." Dria sighed. "I spoke with Ralan. He hinted that my earlier idea was the best one."

"Do you trust the others to follow your commands in your absence?"

Dria shrugged. "It is to their benefit. And if not, I suppose we'll know who to remove from the outpost."

His lips pursed. "We?"

"Ah. Well." Dria took her time nibbling a chunk of cheese. His narrowed gaze remained on her the entire time. "I've been considering our other problem, and… I think we should bond. Mate. However you want to phrase it."

Vek stared at her so long she almost squirmed in her seat. "Why?"

"It would be a strong alliance. A powerful one."

He flinched. "No."

"But earlier, you said…" Heat rushed up her body and scalded her cheeks. "Never mind."

"You'll not dismiss this so easily." Vek wrapped his hand gently around her forearm. "I wouldn't expect a declaration of love, but I won't have a mate whose only motivation is a political alliance. I'm not even sure you like me. Binding yourself to me simply to take a trip through the caves? That's intolerable. Fen can go with you if that's your only reason. His earth magic is stronger than mine."

Was that hurt beneath the anger? She hadn't intended that. "I can't deny I want you. And somehow, I *have* started to like you. Gods know why, but I do."

One corner of his mouth lifted. "And yet?"

"And yet, I don't know what else I can offer you." Dria nibbled her lower lip. "I love my family, but the hurt they have dealt… Sometimes, I think I'm broken. I can form friendships, but anything deeper, anything romantic, eludes me. I might never be able to bring more to our bond than affection. But I've thought of little else besides joining since I saw you."

"*Ahmeeren,*" Vek said, his expression softening. "I'm uncertain I can give anything better, myself. But you make me want to."

Dria almost offered her necklace then and there, but experience had embedded pragmatism in her heart. "Would I have duties as your mate? I will not abandon my post here, nor am I keen to live among the Unseelie for any length of time."

"I'm not keen on it, either, at this point." Vek released her, only to dance his fingers along her forearm in a soft caress. "I'm done working for my father, and your duties will be what you make them. Rule this outpost. Take over Moranaia. Laze around my home on the surface. It's your choice, not mine."

She lifted her brow. "What are you going to do, then?"

"First, I have to find a way to solve this mess. And not just the invasion." Vek rubbed the flat of his palm against his forehead. "He threatened my pregnant mother, Dria. Not overtly, but he didn't have to. Even if he hadn't, I fear the illness will spread. Beyond that crisis? Everything has shifted for me. Between finding you and losing all respect for my father… I have no idea."

Dria set her plate on the side table so she could tilt her body toward his. "You haven't said much about your family. Are you close to your mother?"

"I once was, but the more interest my father showed in me, the more distant I had to become." Vek smiled sadly. "I dare not be close to my siblings, either, not with the work I do. But I watch over them nonetheless."

So many of his interactions with his nephew suddenly made sense. "Like you watched over Fen."

"I've obviously let him get closer than I have any others." Vek's gaze lowered. "What would I be if not a killer, Dria? A question I've long pondered."

She lowered her feet to the ground and almost stood, but a soft *tsk* from him reminded her that she couldn't. *Clechtan.* She wanted to offer comfort, though he hadn't asked for it. "Maybe it's time you find out," she said instead. "Bond with me, and we'll both find our way."

Dria tugged her medallion from beneath her shirt and was about to lift it over her head when a knock clattered on the door. Cursing, she sent out a mental probe. Lial? Gods, could her cousin have worse timing? He wasn't supposed to return until morning, and although it was getting late, it wasn't even time for bed.

"Enter," she called out as she let the pendant drop between her breasts.

When Lial strode through, she had to wonder if he'd slept at all. He was still pale, and twin shadows stood out beneath his eyes. His gaze flicked to her legs where they rested on the floor, and he scowled. "Dria—"

"I didn't put pressure on them," she rushed to say. "What are you doing here? You said morning."

"It is barely that on Moranaia," Lial grumbled. "Not what I'd had in mind, but Lyr told me of the pending invasion. I thought it best if you could walk."

Vek straightened in his seat. "Lyr warned you?"

"We only discovered the plot a mark or two ago," Dria said. "How would he know?"

"Lord Naomh of the Seelie Sidhe contacted Kai at some point before dawn." Lial knelt beside Dria and lifted her legs to the footstool. "His brother Meren is involved in the plot, and according to Naomh's source, a relative of the Unseelie king has been acting on the king's orders. They are determined to return to Earth no matter who stands in the way."

"Who is his source?" Vek demanded.

Lial shrugged. "He refused to say. Sworn to secrecy, it seems."

Dria studied her cousin as he examined her legs. "As much as I would like to be healed, are you sure you're up to this? You look like a drained mage who barely passed their final test."

"Yes, well, I'd already spent a fair amount of energy trying to create the disease-detecting device you requested, not to mention checking everyone in the cavern," Lial groused. But then his expression softened. "Though I do thank you for the concern. I've worked under worse conditions, Dria. I will survive."

Had it been anyone else, she would have argued, but it would be a waste of effort with Lial. "If you say so."

Without bothering to comment, the healer closed his eyes and turned his power on her injured limbs. The peace of it filled her until her own eyelids grew heavy, but the anger radiating from Vek kept her from resting. She forced her attention to her potential bonded, who sat with his hands clenched around the bottom edge of his seat.

"What is it?" she asked.

"A relative," Vek murmured. "I can think of several who might have earth powers. Then again, there's no way to know if our intruder is also the leader. It could be anyone, considering how prolific my family is. I'm a bit of an oddity for not having children yet."

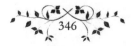

A sudden worry consumed her. "Do you not want them?"

"I do, but I long ago determined not to have them unless I mated." His lips thinned. "I'll not play my children and their mothers against one another the way my father does."

Well. For all of his faults, at least her own father hadn't done that. "Good," she said.

Desire glinted in his eyes. "It would be a pleasure to see you grow with my child."

Her body heated. "I—"

"Do *not* start," Lial interrupted. "Elevate her heartbeat while I'm working again, and you'll be leaving, Vek."

Her almost-bonded chuckled. "Sorry."

He didn't sound particularly regretful, but he did behave. Dria settled her head against the back of her chair and closed her eyes, pushing her thoughts toward anything but Vek and all the ways they could begin creating that child. Preservation rooms—that was what she should consider. Ice magic, imbedding layer after layer into stone and then locking it in place. Perfect for storing perishable food and lustful mages.

Lial's magic cut off, and a soft thump had her eyelids popping open. Concern surged through her at the sight of her cousin sitting on the floor, his head resting against his palm. "Lial?"

Fathomless exhaustion filled the glance he turned her way. "I only need a moment. The healing is complete, but I would appreciate it if you avoid crushing your bones again in the near future. At least it wasn't the spine."

Dria flexed her foot and flinched at the slight ache. "Is it supposed to hurt?"

"Trauma takes time to fully heal," Lial said. "Your body remembers, though the injury is gone. I recommend stretching before strenuous activities."

"What about my nephew?" Vek asked.

Lial didn't even bother to glare. "Do I look like I can take on a complicated disease at this time?"

"No." Vek sighed. "But his recovery would make things easier. I could take his blood to reinforce my earth magic. Though speaking of blood…will your healing hold if I take some of Dria's?"

Brow furrowed, she glanced between them. "Why would my blood hurt you?"

"I…" A vaguely guilty expression crossed Vek's face, sending worry through her. Vek never showed guilt for anything. "Many of my abilities come from others when I feed from them. But it isn't without cost. Too much at once causes extreme pain as my channels rearrange themselves."

Dria gaped at him. "You'll be a mage if you drink from me?"

Vek shook his head. "No, not exactly. Ability doesn't equal knowledge, and I don't receive every talent my donor has. Although the more I feed from you, the more I might pick up. If we bond, I hope you're up to the task of training me to use what you give."

"Your channels should be the same as they'd be after a week between feedings," Lial said before he stumbled to his feet. "If you'll excuse me, I'm going home to sleep."

"Would you like to stay here?" Dria asked.

"No, thank you," Lial answered. "I have too much to do on Moranaia. I'll make it."

After her cousin departed, Dria stared at the door for several moments. Learning about Vek's ability changed things, but not in the way he might fear. He'd trusted her, both with the knowledge and as a potential teacher. She turned to him, but his attention seemed focused on the water dripping from the stalactite in the corner. Did he expect rejection now that he'd revealed the truth? Did he expect fear? His gift was phenomenal, one she'd never heard of. She almost wanted to ask him to feed on her now so she could observe his channels rearranging.

"Vek?"

His expression held no clues to his thoughts when he glanced at her. "Yes?"

"Tell your nephew to report to Kera unless he finds something significant."

Vek's eyebrows rose. "Why?"

Dria sent her own orders to Inona and Kera before dropping her feet to the ground. She braced her hands on the armrests and stood, but aside from a slight ache in her muscles, her legs felt surprisingly good. Perfect timing. Vek jerked to his feet as she took a step, his arm outstretched in case she fell. But when she took his hand, it wasn't for balance.

"I thought you were an intelligent man," Dria said with a slight smile.

His fingers tightened on hers. "I'll need to hear you say it."

"Fine." Dria lifted the necklace from her neck and held it between them. "I've decided to take you for my own. *i'Tayah ay nac-mor kehy ler ehy anan taen.*"

Light flared from the heavy, round medallion that dangled from the chain, and a matching gleam mirrored in Vek's eyes. For a moment, he remained so still that she worried he wouldn't take it. Maybe he couldn't accept her. She had little enough to offer, save herself, and she was the only one who'd ever been satisfied with *that*.

But just as Dria was about to lower the necklace and step away, Vek's free hand closed over hers. The glow from the pendant exploded around them until she could barely see him place the chain around his neck. A million tiny threads built between them until his wonder, desire, and hope beat inside her own chest. She knew he would kiss her before his lips brushed hers.

She eased closer until her breasts brushed against him and lifted slightly to take the kiss deeper, but he pulled his mouth away. "What's wrong?" she whispered.

"I'll not take your blood by accident," Vek said, his expression intense. "Your style of bonding can be severed by priests, but I am not certain that is the case for the *Felshreh* mating link. I'll have your word you are sure of this."

Dria blinked in surprise. "I expected you to be more forceful once the bond had begun."

"You'll have all the force you want, *ahmeeren*, once you tell me what you want," Vek whispered silkily.

A shiver danced across her skin as she stared into his eyes. Gods, he was such a contradiction. He was as immovable as the Citadel, as dangerous as lightning, but he wouldn't take advantage. Then again, he had no need. Vek didn't have to lord his power over others to bolster his confidence, and that heated her blood more than anything.

"I promise I am certain," Dria said, her voice firm so he would have no doubt of her sincerity. "Now finish the bond before I go insane."

He wouldn't have a necklace of his own to offer, but she didn't care. Their second step would be sealed in blood, and she was more than ready to join bodies as the third. Now, preferably. Dria lifted her hand, extending her wrist for him, but Vek shook his head with a slow, wicked smile.

"I never thought to mate," he said. "So I'd rather savor the moment, if you don't mind."

Suddenly, he tugged her against him until air couldn't part their bodies. She expected his kiss, but once again, it didn't come. Instead, Vek ran his hands down her arms and manacled her wrists with his fingers, anchoring them at the small of her back. Her heart thumped a restless, excited beat as he bent his head and ran his tongue along the side of her neck.

She almost groaned when he didn't bite. "Vek…"

"Hush."

He nibbled kisses across her collarbone and then up her neck once more. Maddening man. Dria strained against him, but he only laughed. Before she could yell at him, he released her hands and lifted her by her bottom, his long strides carrying them quickly toward the bed.

"You'd better know a spell to rid us of clothing," he said.

Blessed gods, so she did. It took her a moment to remember the trick, but her diligence was soon rewarded by the feel of his flesh against hers. They both groaned as he lowered her to the bed and trailed his hands down her body. But she frowned when he leaned back and grabbed her foot.

"The healer said you'd want to stretch before strenuous exercise," Vek said, grinning as he ran his broad palms up her aching calf muscles, rubbing out the knots.

She gasped as heat surged inside her from the seemingly innocent contact. "I don't think that's what he meant."

Vek repeated the motion with her other leg. "Do you care?"

"Stop tormenting me."

Still grinning, he settled her leg onto the bed and crawled up her body, kissing and nibbling his way to her breasts. Dria whimpered and shoved her hands into his short hair. With a tug, she brought his mouth close to hers. He stared into her eyes, and in that moment, a lifetime's worth of understanding passed between them.

This moment had always been meant.

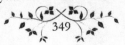

He brushed his lips against the corner of her mouth. "What's your rush?"

"We could be interrupted at any moment," Dria said. "And I want this bond complete, not barely formed."

"Anyone who dares to interrupt us at this moment will pay dearly." Balancing carefully above her, Vek lifted a hand and sent a bolt of power toward the door. She barely had time to admire his handiwork before he distracted her with another soft kiss. "But I'll not have you worried about it."

Then he set about torturing her with his mouth.

Nothing sounded sweeter than Dria's moans, not even the thrum of her pulse beneath his lips. Damn, but he wished he had more time than this. He'd asked why she hurried, but he was all too aware of the tasks that awaited them. So when she tugged at his hair again, he let her pull him up her body until he reached her breasts.

Her golden eyes sparked at him for the delay, and her red hair tumbled around her flushed cheeks until his body hardened almost painfully. But he would take all the time he could. Slowly, he stretched her hands above her head and held them there. Excitement surged from her through their bond, eroding his restraint.

Vek kept his eyes locked with hers as he lowered his head toward her breast-bone. Her gaze shifted to his fangs, and she shivered. A thread of apprehension trembled between them. He licked the spot where her pulse throbbed in invitation and sucked softly on her skin until she gasped.

"It won't hurt," he said. "I promise."

Her throat worked nervously, but she nodded. "Go ahead. Please."

Vek sent a tendril of numbing magic into her skin to reinforce the natural effects of his saliva. Then he sank his fangs softly into her flesh. *Slelen.* He hadn't been certain there was a Divine until this moment, but he felt it in every pulse of her heart as her blood filled his mouth. He trembled as power flared between them, more strands linking them than he could have imagined. Startled, he released her wrists.

Dria groaned and shifted restlessly beneath him, and her passion became his until he barely noticed the channels in his mind shifting and expanding. This. This was heaven. Then her hands gripped his back, the slight pain of her nails shocking him back to awareness. As her spirit filled all the blank places inside him, he forced himself to close the wound he'd made. She needed plenty of energy for what he had planned.

Resting his forehead on her heaving chest, he did a scan of his newly acquired abilities. Some he didn't understand, but...there. Vek smiled wickedly against her skin as he found the immobilization spell she'd used on him during their first kiss. Time for payback.

Vek lifted himself until he hovered above Dria. Gently, he brushed a coil of hair from his mate's face. Then he tugged her arms above her head again and locked them into place with the spell he'd gleaned from her blood. Her eyes widened as he

spread her legs and lifted them, another touch of magic keeping her from wriggling free. But the rest of her body he left unconstrained.

"What…"

He tipped her chin up and kissed her softly. "Tell me if I need to stop. I'll release you at a word."

"Gods, no," Dria said. "But kiss me for real this time. No gentle—"

With a growl, he followed her command, his mouth taking hers with all the passion he'd held back. The slight tang of blood hit his tongue as his fang caught her lip, but she strained against him, her breasts pressing against his chest. Thoughts blurred as he explored her body with his hands, their mouths locked together.

Then he entered her, and his world imploded.

Dria's scream was muffled against his mouth as his body joined with hers. She lifted her hips to meet him, and her hands itched to grip his waist with each thrust. It was maddening. Hot. She'd never been helpless like this, and it fired her blood.

But she couldn't yield to him so completely, not for long.

He'd said she could ask him to release the spell—and she trusted that he would—but that was no fun. Deftly, she unwound the magic holding her still, and before Vek could react, she rolled them over until she was on top. With a smirk, she ran her hands up his hard chest and then leaned forward to kiss him.

This time, his fang caught his own lip, and his sweet blood filled her mouth. Good gods. It shouldn't have given her energy, but the force of it charged through her, strengthening their forming bond. His hands dug into her hips as she began to move.

He tore his mouth away. "Fuck, Dria."

She let out a breathless chuckle. "That's the idea."

Then they both gave up on speaking as their worlds—their souls—fully merged.

22

Vek trailed his fingers along Dria's spine and marveled at the shiver of pleasure that tingled up his own back. Even knowing about mates, he'd never imagined being so closely bound to another person. Echoes of her thoughts hovered at the edge of his mind, and if he stretched, he could probably share some of her memories. Not that he would, at least not on purpose. She deserved her privacy.

"That was…" Her soft chuckle tickled his chest. "I don't have words for what that was."

He wrapped his arms around her and held her close. "Fortunately, we don't seem to need words any longer. Perhaps that will save us from arguments."

Dria snorted, though he could sense her amusement. "I doubt it."

"Alas, you're probably right."

They were alike enough in temperament that clashes were inevitable, but reconciliation would be delicious. Vek nuzzled the top of her hair until she slid down to rest against his side. For a moment, there was perfect peace, their bodies warm and content. No sounds except their steady breathing and the nearby drip of water filled the room. It seemed nothing would ever intrude.

Until Fen's presence tapped at the edge of Vek's shields.

Vek sighed. "Duty calls."

Dria tipped her head up to look at him. "How so?"

"Fen wants to talk," Vek answered. "Hold on."

Vek opened a link before his nephew became more insistent. *"What?"*

"Sorry," Fen sent. *"Kinda important. We didn't find anything in the cave, but I just got a text from Maddy."*

Vek frowned. *"A text?"*

"You know? A message on my phone?"

"I'm aware of what a text is, Fen," Vek snapped. *"What did it say? I'm assuming it's important if you're bothering me now."*

Fen hesitated. *"Well. There's someone on the Market Street Bridge threatening to electrocute anyone who comes near. Might be relevant to our interests since the person in question had lightning shooting from their hands."*

Vek's arm tightened around Dria's back. *"We'll be right out."*

"It seems there will be no mates' retreat for us," Vek said aloud. "Not even an hour's worth."

Dria pushed herself up with one arm. "Mates' retreat?"

"A few weeks where no one bothers a newly formed pair." Unable to resist, Vek ran one finger across her breast. "Maybe once the crisis has passed."

Dria swatted his hand away. "Don't start what you can't complete. What's going on now, and why wasn't I notified?"

With a resigned sigh, Vek swung his legs over the side of the bed. "It's not here. Fen received word from Maddy about an incident in the human city. It appears that someone is threatening people with lightning magic on one of their bridges."

"Iron in the heart," Dria cursed. "Is there no one above who can take care of such a thing?"

"Magical energy has increased, but magical knowledge hasn't." Vek scanned the empty floor. "Where did you send our clothes?"

Dria slid to the side of the bed and darted over to the chairs on the other side of the room. Oh yes, the Divine was real. Nothing else could be responsible for the full, perfect globes of his mate's ass. His body began to stir until he forced his attention away. Lightning. Innocent, clueless humans.

"Here," Dria called, right before she tossed his clothes at his head.

Vek snatched them from the air and tugged them on with haste. Unfortunately, he'd have to run upstairs to change if they were going to the surface. He wore the tunic and pants he preferred, not Earth clothes. And Dria had nothing suitable, as far as he knew.

"You're not going to blend in," he said.

Dria settled the folds of her dress around her legs. "You think I should go personally?"

He shrugged. "I plan to. This is the first time someone has overtly used magic where anyone can see. It may not be a coincidence if our adversaries are recruiting."

A line formed between her brows. "True. I... I haven't given much thought to going above. Looks like I'll just have to stand out."

After they pulled on their shoes and Dria retrieved a pouch from her trunk, they headed toward the door. Sensing Fen near his room, Vek started up the stairs, but he paused at Dria's groan. She stopped beside him, bending down to rub at her calf. If she hadn't been fond of the steps before, she certainly wouldn't be after her injury.

"I could carry you again," Vek offered.

"Tempting, but no," Dria replied. "Just a cramp. I guess you didn't do a good enough job earlier."

"Perhaps when we return, *ahmeeren*."

Dria grinned at him as she straightened, but the desire she sent along their bond

was far from humorous. This time, he was the one who cursed. Laughing softly, Dria darted up the stairs while he was distracted, but he followed more slowly. Thanks to his mate, climbing was a bit more…difficult.

He had a feeling that was going to be a persistent problem.

Fen, Inona, and Delbin were waiting in the hallway in front of Vek's room. Dria motioned them inside as Vek caught up to her, and she couldn't resist another smile at his aggrieved energy. Blasted man deserved to be tormented now and then. Maybe it would keep him humble.

Or something resembling.

As soon as Dria and Vek marched in, Delbin's and Inona's gazes landed almost instantly on the medallion visible on Vek's chest. Inona's eyes widened, and Delbin grinned. But neither of them mentioned it. Fen, on the other hand, was not so circumspect.

"Thank the gods," he said with a broad smile. "You're lucky she decided to put up with you. I wouldn't."

"For fuck's sake, Fen, you're my nephew." Vek scowled. "I would hope you didn't think of me that way."

Fen merely laughed. "You know what I meant. You're not exactly easy to deal with when you're annoyed. Which is a solid seventy-five percent of the time."

"That's all?" Dria asked, smirking.

Vek gave her a heated look. "I could adjust that ratio for you."

"Gag," Fen said. Then he pulled a rectangular object from his pocket and pressed his finger against the side, causing it to light up. "Maddy says they have a news crew filming from a nearby bridge, but the woman isn't budging despite the humans' presence."

Dria's brow furrowed. "How long will it take us to walk to this market bridge?"

"Quite a while, even at our run speed," Fen answered. "Probably more than an hour to drive, too. If we could even get through the traffic with one of the main bridges over the river blocked."

Inona tossed her long braid over her shoulder with a restless flick. "Selia could make a gate to Vek's house. Maybe that gas station where we stopped, but I don't think that was a great deal closer to the bridge."

"Not nearly close enough," Delbin said.

Dria tapped her fingers against her upper arm as she considered the problem. She could make a portal without too much difficulty, but she had to be familiar with the destination. Could she glean a proper image from one of the others' minds? If they'd misremembered something important, it would spell disaster. Mages were trained to make careful note of gate locations—most people didn't.

"Wait," Vek said suddenly. "What about The Magic Touch? The shop isn't far from Market Street, is it?"

Fen shook his head. "No, it's an easy walk."

"I could form a portal to her shielded room." Vek grimaced. "I'm not as fast at the spell as Dria or Selia, but I think I could manage."

Dria nodded. "If Maddy is amenable."

"Hang on," Fen answered.

He lifted the rectangle in front of his face, and a touch of energy flowed between his fingers and the small box. Then his thumbs tapped across the surface. Dria studied the shiny silver case beneath his fingers. It must be a communication device, but if she'd ever learned the name of it, she couldn't recall. A curious invention, but wouldn't a mirror be easier?

"What the hell did you just do?" Delbin asked as soon as Fen lowered the device.

Fen blinked. "I sent a text. The same way you've done on your own phone."

"No, that little surge. It wasn't like the spell I use to charge my phone." Delbin peeked over the other man's shoulder. "You have a full signal. Did you amplify it?"

"How else do you think I've been getting texts in a cave?" Fen asked, laughing. "I mean, it won't work if we go much lower, but we're pretty close to the top here. Just takes a little boost."

"Sonofa—"

A chime rang from the device, and Fen tapped at it again. "We're good to go. Maddy says you can cast the spell when you're ready."

"When Dria gives the go-ahead," Vek said.

"Orders first." Dria lowered her arms and straightened her spine. "Fen, you are not to leave. I want you to keep patrolling the outpost for more incursions involving earth magic, but try not to get too close to any of the guards. Just in case your illness worsens. Inona and Delbin, I want you to protect the surface entrance. I've already assigned the mages to scan the corridors and tunnels on a regular basis. Vek and I will do our own scouting of the tunnels once we've resolved this problem."

As the others scattered to their tasks, Vek rushed to change into Earth clothes, seemingly uncaring of any who might see. Dria didn't mind, considering she was the primary one to benefit. No one else even bothered to look at the wonderful sight on their way out of the room. Too bad she didn't have time to do more than ogle, but their troubles wouldn't wait.

When he rejoined her, she had to admit his soft, muscle-hugging shirt had its advantages. "Let me know if I start messing this spell up," Vek said. "I almost lost control of it last night."

"Sure." Dria wrinkled her nose. "Though I'm hoping you do better this time. Less work for me."

Laughing, Vek closed his eyes and lifted his arms. Dria switched to her mage sight, analyzing his power as it uncurled around him, the tail forming a door-shaped gash in the surrounding energy. He poured more magic in, but it was a rough attempt. The edges wavered as he struggled to transfer enough power from himself into the spell.

Without hesitation, Dria linked her mind with his, reinforcing the portal with her own energy. It flared and would have exploded if not for her experience, though he still held the main link. Patiently, she guided his mental hand until the vision of the location he sought became as real as the cave around them. Then together, they completed the portal link.

Dria blinked, and her vision returned to normal. Her hand was clasped in Vek's, and light glowed steadily from the gate they'd created. *Clechtan*, she hadn't meant to take over. But Vek only kissed her on the cheek with a whispered "thanks" and tugged her toward the room on the other side.

A slight wrench as they crossed the threshold, and they were on the surface of Earth.

Curious, Dria peered around the small room where they emerged. The table and chairs were fairly typical, if boring in design, but she didn't recognize the large, metallic box on top of one shelf. Why would someone put a window and numbers on the side of a box? And although the floor of the room was made of normal-looking wood, the walls were plain. Utilitarian, truth be told. Was this how humans lived?

Vek closed the portal a moment before the door in the wall opened. Maddy slipped through and closed it quickly behind her, fabric draped over her arm and a worry pinching her brow. Her odd, tall shoes clicked against the floor as she rushed over.

"We've got the news streaming on the back computer," Maddy said. "The reporter swears she spotted of a fireball, but I didn't see it on camera."

Dria huffed. "I didn't understand much of that besides 'fireball,' but it sounds serious."

"It's as though someone pointed a communication mirror at an event so you could see it, too." Maddy held up the bundle of fabric, shaking the folds loose. "I brought an Earth-style dress. Fen said you might want a bit of camouflage."

Shrugging, Dria pulled her robe over her head and draped it over the back of a chair. Maddy, her skin as red as her hair, averted her eyes as she held the dress out at arm's length. Vek chuckled, but Dria didn't bother to ask why. She could find out what Earth rule she might have broken while they walked. Perhaps nudity was frowned upon?

The fabric hugged her upper body and then fell in a loose drape from her waist to her knees. It was comfortable enough, if cut oddly. Maddy glanced back at her, but the brightness in her cheeks barely dimmed.

"I take it Moranaians don't believe in underwear," Maddy muttered. "Well, at least it's not cold outside."

Vek almost choked on his laugh. Dria elbowed him in the side and smiled at the half-Sidhe woman. "I'm sorry if I bothered you."

Maddy sighed. "Don't worry about it. Just trying to remind myself that I have a girlfriend. Besides, I don't think blood elves share their mates."

"It's been known to happen," Vek said lightly. "But not in this case."

The door opened, and a man stuck his head around the edge. "Whatever you're going to do, get to it. I saw a fireball that time."

Dria didn't stop to ask questions. She could find out what the others were talking about later. Right now, they had a battle to end.

23

Dria found it difficult to process her surroundings as she rushed with Vek down a tree-lined road. Countless points of light painted colors across the stone road they traversed, and windows glowed with yet more. Humans were everywhere—rushing along the walkway, sitting in self-propelled, wheeled conveyances, staring from the glass fronts of stores. And they were all peering fretfully toward the crackles of lightning flashing in the distance.

There were more strange objects than Dria could absorb, so she stopped trying. On the horizon, where two triangles of light joined, she spotted several unusual flashes, but she couldn't determine their origin. Vek hurried toward the odd sight without hesitation, so it must be relevant.

"Do you know where we're going?" Dria sent.

Vek nodded. *"The triangles in the distance are the aquarium. Two large buildings that house tanks full of sea creatures."*

"Why would you…" Dria shook her head. *"Never mind. The bridge is nearby?"*

"Just beyond," Vek answered. *"The flickering beams are probably spotlights set up by the humans. Difficult to tell. They also have devices that can record things and send the images to others. Their technology is worth exploring. I believe it could intersect in fascinating ways with magic, as Fen has begun to show me."*

Fear and curiosity twined in her gut. This place was nothing like Moranaia—and she loved it. Though she couldn't read the signs or understand the words the humans spoke, she hoped some day she could linger. To discover what the food tasted like in the restaurant they hurried past or to examine the inside of one of the moving conveyances. Even more, she would love to experiment with her magic on their technology. She'd enjoyed her training well enough, but it hadn't involved a great deal of innovation.

They dashed through a huge courtyard in front of the aquarium Vek had pointed out. Darting around decorative formations and the few humans who dared get this close to the trouble, Dria and Vek finally reached the main road to the bridge. Unfortunately, it was blocked by a line of conveyances and people wearing official-looking clothes. Metal flashed against their chests, and many of them pointed what might be weapons toward the bridge.

Not that she could see much of the actual bridge—the view was blocked by a massive wall of swirling energy.

A uniformed woman stopped them. She spoke, but Dria couldn't understand the words. "What did she say?" Dria asked.

Vek frowned. "She ordered us to turn back. You haven't learned human languages?"

"It wasn't a pressing need in the heart of Moranaia. What do you suggest?"

"Immobilization spell. I don't have the ability to control this many minds at once, and the situation doesn't warrant their deaths. They are doing their best to guard the city at great risk to themselves."

The woman's hand dropped to something strapped to her side, and she barked out a command. Vek answered, his voice low and soothing, as Dria gathered energy. Then she threw the spell outward, capturing the uniformed officials in the immobilization spell's grasp. Most of them were humans without command of magic, but a few must have had latent fae blood or natural magical talent. It would take more energy than she wanted to spare to hold them for long.

"Hurry."

Together, she and Vek dashed up the short stretch of road between the conveyances and the shield blocking further progress. Dria analyzed the obstacle and created a counter, a bubble of energy that would allow them both to pass through safely. She didn't know what weapons the humans held, but it seemed best to continue obscuring their vision in case they decided to use them. Once the magic started flying, the inexperienced wouldn't be able to discern friend from foe.

Dria pulled Vek through with her and immediately scanned the area visually and magically. She hadn't been able to get a clear view of the river beyond the shield, so the sheer size of it stunned her almost as much as the crackle of magic in the center of the long bridge. She'd expected the river to be significantly smaller.

Stone railings lined each side of the bridge, interspersed with columns gleaming with light. In the distance, lightning danced around something that looked like a large rock. *"Have you been here?"* she sent.

"Fen has driven over this bridge often on our travels," Vek said. *"In the center, there's a massive steel framework with concrete stones anchored on each side. I believe it's for balance if they need to raise the bridge."*

A flicker of fire streaked in a horizontal line near the stone, and lightning hit beside the origin point moments later. The glowing columns cast blotchy pools of light across the road beneath their feet and revealed a figure standing on one side of the bridge. A woman, Dria thought, but it was impossible to be sure at this distance.

"Are you better with fire or lightning?" Dria asked.

"I'll take fire," Vek answered. *"The energy has the feel of a Seelie Sidhe."*

"Can you mask your presence?"

"Easily, ahmeeren. You get their attention, and I'll sneak in behind."

At Dria's nod, Vek crouched low and crept away. True to his word, his energy signature dulled until few who weren't bonded with him could detect it, and his body blended into the shadows between street lights. Dria charged forward, pulling in as much energy as she could and casting her strongest shield around her body.

The figure near the center structure spun at the surge of power. Yes, a female Sidhe, one dressed like she'd just stepped out of the Seelie court. Could this be the woman Delbin had mentioned? Dria scanned her and then smiled. A mage of average talent. Perfect.

"Cease this madness," Dria called, using magic to amplify her words.

The woman jerked in surprise. "Stay out of this, Moranaian. Your time will come."

"You must know your actions are foolish. The humans are watching. Your magic has been revealed."

"That I doubt," the Sidhe woman answered with a sneer.

As Dria grew closer, another figure appeared at the top of the concrete slab that formed the top arch of the bridge's frame. Lightning snarled and tangled around her body, and tendrils flicked recklessly against the stone. Even a novice would be able to tell that the woman had lost control—if she'd ever had it.

The Sidhe mage lifted a ball of flame and tossed it toward Dria, but it was a wasted effort. With a flick of her hand, Dria gathered the abundant moisture in the air and solidified it into a globe before casting it toward the flame. She felt it hit, but she didn't stop to watch, instead using the distraction as a cover for her levitation spell.

She glanced down long enough to see Vek materialize behind the Sidhe woman, his fangs at her neck before she'd registered his presence. Dria had to trust he would handle the mage. Her attention was on the young woman shuddering at the top of the bridge. A half-blood, if she wasn't mistaken.

"Calm yourself," Dria said.

But the woman shook her head. *Clechtan*, she didn't understand. Sighing, Dria shifted her shielding to create a ground, a conduit for the lightning when it struck. Then she propelled herself forward until her feet touched the large stone slab. The woman flinched, and a spark whipped across the space between them before being swept away by Dria's shield.

Then Dria darted forward and slapped her palm against the woman's forehead.

The language spell surged between them, spearing pain through Dria's head. But she'd trained for pain. She let it wash over her until the bulk of it receded and her vision cleared. Just in time. With a cry, the woman began to crumple, and she might have fallen if Dria hadn't been there to steady her.

Lightning scattered around them as the half-blood gripped her temples and moaned. "What did you do to me?"

"I needed to know your language," Dria answered. The panic in the air was almost palpable. If the woman didn't calm down, she might summon an actual storm. "What's your name?"

"Tamara," she answered, wavering on her feet. "Are you with that bitch trying to kidnap me? I might be a freak, but I'm not going to be put on display."

"My soulbonded…husband, you might say? He is taking care of her." Dria was no empath, but she tried her best to send calming energy toward the other woman. "But you…I heard you're up here threatening people."

Tamara shuddered in Dria's grasp. "I wanted to jump, but I couldn't get up the nerve. Maybe it wouldn't even kill me. Or I'd electrocute a bunch of innocent people. I didn't know I could do this. I didn't know."

"Nothing is wrong with you," Dria said firmly. "Have you heard of elves?" The woman nodded. "Well, we're real, and I'd say one of your parents was some type of fae."

The lightning flared but then settled a little. "What?"

"Magic has come back to Earth, and many people with latent blood are awakening." Dria gestured toward the sky. "And now it will be evident to everyone thanks to your lack of care. Calm down, get off this bridge, and learn how to control your gift. I have a feeling you're going to need it."

A hint of anger crossed Tamara's face. "Who do you think you are?"

"Dria Moreln, Princess of Moranaia, and the mage who will knock you unconscious if you can't be contained." Despite her harsh words, Dria smiled. "But work with me, and I'll keep you safe from the woman trying to kidnap you."

"Need help?" Vek sent.

"Nope."

Forehead crinkling, Tamara studied her. "I don't know how to get control."

Dria gave her shoulders a gentle squeeze. "Then let's figure it out."

Vek pressed his knee into the Sidhe woman's back and tied her hands deftly with the silk cording he'd ripped from the sleeve of her fancy robe. He'd almost ripped her throat out after skimming the surface of her thoughts, but she was high ranking. A far better bargaining tool alive rather than dead.

He slid his fang against the top of his arm until a small amount of blood welled up and then smeared the liquid along the rope. With a surge of power, he activated his most powerful holding spell into the binding, a trick almost all *Felshreh* knew. If she wanted to be free again, she would only earn it with another drop of his blood.

He couldn't believe what he'd seen in her mind.

Kethen.

It was Kethen's face he'd discovered in her memory as he'd drained her to almost nothing. His cousin was the liaison between King Torek and the Seelie. Had Dereck's death driven hm to this? He'd been one of the few who didn't vie for power in the court. The amiable sort, always with a ready smile. Perhaps Vek had never understood Kethen—maybe his friendliness had hidden a deeper agenda. Still, he struggled to reconcile this plot with what he knew of his cousin's nature.

Dammit, he'd always liked Kethen. Now he'd probably have to kill him.

The lightning ceased its flickering. Sensing a surge of power from Dria, Vek hefted the Sidhe woman over his shoulder. Just in time. Dria and the young half-blood floated down until their feet settled onto the road.

"We need to go," Vek said. "The shield keeping out the police...the authorities...started to falter as soon as I drained this one. What about the half-blood?"

"Tamara is coming with us," Dria answered. He quirked a brow, but his mate's expression remained resolved. "She isn't a threat. I'll make a portal back to the shop, and we can figure it out from there."

Vek studied his mate. Something seemed off about the interaction, but he couldn't... Wait. "When did you learn English?"

"There's a spell for everything, love." Smirking, Dria patted his cheek. Then she tugged him under the concrete slab above them. "Maybe I'll teach you someday."

He found himself smiling as she formed the portal in moments. Far better than his clumsy attempt. The other woman, Tamara, gaped when the image of the shop clarified, and she balked when Dria tried to pull her through. Always willing to help his mate, Vek flashed his fangs until the half-blood yelped and darted into the gate.

The light of the shop was blinding after the dim glow of the bridge, but Vek's eyes adjusted quickly. As Dria rushed through the portal and closed it behind her, he shrugged his captive from his shoulders and dropped her into one of the chairs. Her head lolled, but she didn't wake. Probably wouldn't for a while, considering how much energy he'd drained from her.

Dria's adoptee, Tamara, leaned her hands against the back of one of the other chairs. She was quite young, even by human standards, and her blood radiated with the power of a strong Seelie noble. Lightning, hmm? Vek could narrow down her parentage quite a lot based on that alone.

Maddy hurried through a different door from the one she'd used earlier. "Well, this is going to start a riot."

The half-blood let out a squeak, and a charge built in the air. Dria settled her hand on the young woman's shoulder. "English, please, Maddy. Tamara doesn't understand Moranaian. Probably not any of the Sidhe dialects, either."

"Okay." Maddy's eyes narrowed. "Hey, you're the girl from the bridge." Then she noticed the Sidhe slumped at her table and paled. "Damn. Oh, damn. I know her. She's one of my father's contacts at court, Lady Egana."

Vek stiffened. "How well does he know her? Because her current plans include invading Earth, not buying jewelry from an exile."

"You'd better not be suggesting my father is a traitor," Maddy said, color flooding her skin. "She purchases diamonds. That's it."

"Lady? Court?" Tamara asked. "This is America, isn't it?"

Maddy studied the woman for a moment. "You didn't know, did you? That you have Sidhe blood."

The woman lifted her hands helplessly. "No clue."

"Why don't you two leave Tamara with me. I'll explain things to her." As fear lit the other woman's face, Maddy pulled out one of the chairs and sat. "I promise I won't hurt you. My name is Maddy. This store is called The Magic Touch, and we help any fae who need it. Mostly, we get them Earth clothes and convert gems into money, but I can hand out some explanations, too. Probably better than Vek and Dria can. After all, I'm also half-human."

Impatience scraped at Vek's insides as they waited for the woman to decide. But finally, she nodded and sank into the seat she'd been gripping. "Okay."

Dria darted to the center of the room and began to form the portal. As Vek bent to lift Lady Egana, he speared Tamara with a glance. "Do not betray us if you enjoy living."

With that bit of solid life advice administered, Vek turned and carried his captive through the gate.

24

It was a terrible time to have no dungeon.

Deciding to use one of the empty bedrooms along the warriors' corridor, Dria stepped onto the lift she'd designed, Vek following behind her with the captive still slung over his shoulder. With a burst of energy, she sent them smoothly downward a few levels. It might be lazy, but she was cursed tired. Not to mention hungry. She couldn't remember the last time she'd had more than a few bites of food in a row.

"Great job," Vek said when the platform came to a stop. "This is a brilliant design."

Kera emerged from the hallway as they stepped off. "You may have Selia attempting to emulate it at Braelyn. Such a thing would have been useful when the Myernere shattered her spine a few months ago."

Dria blinked. "Shattered?"

"There was an attack on her, and she suffered a serious fall," Kera explained, keeping pace with Dria and Vek. "She wouldn't have survived if not for Lial."

Interesting. That must have been the reason for her cousin's pinched expression when he'd commented about repairing bone. Dria could only imagine how complicated such a healing must have been. No wonder he'd all but ordered her not to break anything else.

Dria shoved open the door to a spare room, and Kera darted in to pull out a chair from the table so Vek had a place to put their captive. He dropped Lady Egana on the chair with a thud, and her head cracked against the high back so hard that Dria winced. But Vek didn't even show that little bit of sympathy as he accepted a bundle of thin rope from Kera. With quick, jerky movements, he positioned their captive's body upright enough to tie her bound arms to the wooden back and her legs to the base.

Not only that, however. As soon as he straightened, he slid a fang along his arm and smeared blood across the ropes at every knot. What in the worlds? Then his power surged, and her heart thumped. Blood magic. Gods above and below. It wasn't precisely forbidden, not entirely, but it wasn't an art that was encouraged, either. She'd studied a few of the allowed spells during her training. This…this was like none of them.

But she hadn't exactly trained with any Unseelie.

With her inner sight, she observed the magic as it took hold. Every fiber of the rope that had touched his blood tightened, clinging not just to its blood-soaked neighbors but also the untouched strands. They locked together, bound in a hold only Vek could break. A genius spell, one she'd have to see if she could reproduce. Hopefully, it didn't require being one of his kind.

The rope tightened across Lady Egana's flesh, and the woman stirred, a low moan slipping from her lips. Vek leaned close to her ear. "Awaken, traitor."

Her eyelids popped open. Fear lit in her gaze before she began to thrash, and a weak tendril of her magic tried to emerge. Dria had a feeling it would have been a wasted effort even if the woman had been at full strength rather than drained to almost nothing. Vek's bond wouldn't be easy to escape.

"I demand you release me at once," Lady Egana said, her voice ringing with the authority of a fae noble.

Dria lifted an eyebrow, and Vek laughed.

"Fine words from a person caught trying to kidnap someone from Earth," Dria said. "That has been illegal among the fae races for quite some time."

The woman sneered. "It was no abduction. I merely wanted to…encourage her to help us."

Vek pinned her with his gaze. "Don't bother. I've gleaned much from your thoughts already. What do you have to gain by this madness? You had all the power you could need in your own realm."

"In the underhill," Lady Egana snapped. "We might be in a dimension only slightly removed from Earth, but the surface there is far less hospitable. Some of your kind might enjoy being forced below into caves, but I do not. Many of the Seelie Sidhe agree with me. And no miniscule number of yours."

"So I have come to understand." Vek's expression darkened, and he circled the lady before stopping behind her right shoulder. "You'll tell me your secrets, or I will finish extracting them from your blood."

Dria studied the woman closely as her bonded rested his hand on Lady Egana's upper arm. She flinched, and the fear she'd tried to hide trembled in her lower lip. But still, she lifted her chin in defiance. "You break the will of your own king."

"I have no king," Vek said coldly. "Not anymore."

Lady Egana gasped, and Dria stared at him in surprise. What was he talking about? With any other man, she might have thought it a bluff. But no. Vek would never jest about such a thing. If he said it, he'd meant it. Whatever information he'd already pulled from the woman's mind must have been terrible for him to make such a bold statement.

"And you call me a traitor?" the lady cried.

"I am not the one breaking faith." Vek's fingers tightened on her arm. "My

father forgets his place. We are meant to be the shadows that stand for the light, not the darkness itself. Perhaps it is time he learns what that means."

Lady Egana paled. "You're rebelling for mere humans."

Vek bent low, his mouth near the woman's neck. "Were the Neorans human, then? My Moranaian allies were helping them. Word is that the damage from the energy poisoning was largely reversed by their healer. Perhaps if you hadn't gone through and slaughtered most of them before that help could arrive…?"

The lady's throat worked, and she tipped her head almost imperceptibly away from Vek. "Some losses are necessary. They should not have foregone the proper chain of command."

Dria pinched her lips together. This *drec* spoke of murder as if it was a right, not a travesty. "Queen Tatianella would not approve such an action."

"Perhaps not," Egana conceded. "However, her daughter is in charge while Tatianella…takes a little break. Queen Lera gives the orders now."

"Is my father aware of that?" Dria asked. She hadn't been, but she didn't spend enough time at home to keep up with politics. "I cannot imagine she has mentioned her current plans to him if so."

"I wouldn't know," the lady answered with a shrug.

"Does this plot go all the way to the queen?" Vek asked.

Another shrug. "I've told you all I will. My mental defenses are strong enough to withstand one pitiful blood elf."

Vek's chuckle held a cruel edge. "Too bad for you I'm not pitiful. I've tasted your blood and consumed your energy. I can slip into your thoughts as deeply as I wish. Might be painful for you, but so be it."

Lady Egana snorted. "Then why did you try to interrogate me?"

"Saves energy."

Before Dria could blink, Vek sank his fangs into the lady's neck once more. She jumped as Egana let out a choked screech—and then fell alarmingly silent. What was he doing? He'd said he could access the woman's thoughts since he'd already had her blood. Why bite her again?

His energy heightened until the room buzzed with it. Egana stared at nothing, her face going slack as a low, keening moan emerged. Dria reinforced her shields, even attempting to filter her bond with Vek to prevent being flooded with power. The woman's defenses must be strong to warrant this much force.

From her place by the door, Kera straightened. "What is he doing?" she whispered.

The concern in the scout's voice echoed Dria's own worry. She'd never seen a spell quite like this one. It was… Invasive didn't begin to cover it. "I don't know."

Should she stop him? Dria twisted her fingers in the folds of her dress and considered the best action. This was something her people would never approve. Gods, the woman would be lucky to have a mind left after the power of this spell. But Lady Egana had spoken of slaughtering an entire colony as though it was of no consequence. Now, she was helping plan an attack on this outpost. They had to know how to stop another massacre.

The woman's moans increased in pitch. Dria gripped her dress so tightly her fingers ached. No, this wasn't right. They might need information, but they didn't have to maim someone's mind to gain it.

Dria stepped forward to stop him, no matter the cost to herself, but Vek's energy retreated before she had the chance. *Miaran.* She was too late. Exchanging a wary glance with Kera, Dria eased close enough to touch her bonded. Egana's cries cut off, and Vek withdrew his fangs. Her gaze focused in on the two small holes. No blood? What had he been doing if not drinking?

"Vek…" Dria began.

He scowled. "I see you still have little trust in me."

"We do not torture people in my land. Not like—"

"You think I was torturing her?" Vek spun to face Dria, and the anger on his face gave her pause. But the hurt echoing along the bond? That pinched her heart. "If you must know, the spell causes pain but no permanent damage. That's why I bit her. The connection allowed me to save her mind. Not that it was *worth* saving. She would kill us without hesitation or regret."

Dria ground her teeth together. "No one is beyond help."

"Including Kien?" Vek asked harshly.

He had a point there. But… "His level of depravity isn't common."

"Not exactly rare, either."

Clechtan. Her bonded's hurt hadn't lessened—if anything, it was worse. "I'm sorry."

"We can discuss it later," Vek said, glancing over at their captive. "If her thoughts are accurate, we need to move. Their soldiers are under orders to attack the outpost if she doesn't return on time, and she's expected back tonight."

Dria sighed. "I was afraid of that. Were you able to determine the location?"

"Next hill over. They expanded existing tunnels between the two with the help of an earth mage." Vek's nostrils flared. "My cousin, apparently."

With a wince, Dria nodded. "Have to love family sometimes." Then she turned to Kera. "Do you have a scout you can spare to watch our backs?"

Kera's expression turned thoughtful. "I believe so."

"If you could have someone prepare us a few emergency provisions and send them with the scout to the area of the cave-in, that would be a great help," Dria said. "We'll await them there. But do not leave this one unguarded. I'll have Fedah join you for reinforcement."

"As you will it," Kera acknowledged with a smile.

Once Dria and Vek were in the hallway, he tugged at her arm. But she didn't stop her march toward the mages' corridor. "What?"

"Are you certain you still wish for me to go?" Vek snapped.

Dria cast him a haughty look. "Let go of me."

He released her arm at once. "You offered me insult, and now you're angry?"

"I'm not angry, despite your feelings flooding through our bond," Dria answered. "What I am is tired, hungry, and ready to get going. You were the one who didn't want to discuss the problem."

Vek's pace slowed. "Not with an audience."

Growling beneath her breath, Dria came to an abrupt halt. "Fine. There's no one else here at the moment. You're upset because I thought you were torturing our captive. Well, tell me, Vek. Have you ever tortured anyone in the name of a cause? Because all I've learned of your culture suggests that you probably have."

Some of his anger eased, but the hurt still echoed from his heart. "I can understand the reasoning behind your assumption, but we are joined. You've seen the very core of me, and so I'd hoped you wouldn't have to be told. To directly answer? No. I have never tormented another person for any reason, cause or not. I dispense punishment for deeds unjustly committed. I do not carry out atrocities with my own hand. Or mind. Or magic." He scrubbed at his face. "Great Divine."

Guilt churned in her gut. "You're right. It's just… When your own brother turns out to be a demented killer, you begin to doubt…"

Dria swallowed against the sudden knot in her throat.

You begin to doubt everything.

Understanding washed across his face and flowed along their bond. Suddenly, Vek cupped Dria's head in his hand and pulled her close, settling her against his chest. "Ah, *caramuin*. Would that I had Kien in front of me now."

She gave herself a moment to savor the embrace. A single drip of time to be with her bonded without obligations pulling her elsewhere. Then her stomach grumbled, and they both laughed. Smiling wryly, she pulled back.

"Would you gather some food while I retrieve Gessen?" she asked. "I'd like to speak with him about the mission before we go. He's the best of us at protective shielding during combat, and he'll want a moment to prepare."

His eyebrows went up. "If you believe we might end up fighting, why not take more people?"

"Then we're almost guaranteed a battle." Dria tapped her finger against his chin. "It's easy to make too much noise in a cave, and you'd have to form wider gaps in the tunnels to get us all through."

"The noise wouldn't be greater if they were Unseelie," Vek muttered.

Smiling, Dria gave him a quick kiss and headed toward Gessen's room. "Just remember," she tossed over her shoulder. "Get me something to eat on the walk down. I'd rather not rely on trail rations if I don't have to."

🔥

Dria halted outside the room where she'd sensed Gessen's presence. Air magic hummed beyond the door, but that wasn't what caused her hesitation. Would he feel differently about her now that she'd bonded to an Unseelie prince? They'd never been romantically involved, so there wouldn't be jealousy. But it was still a major life change that her best friend had essentially missed.

Before she could force her hand to move, Gessen's magic cut off, and the door opened. His brow lifted as he took in her appearance. "What are you doing hovering outside the door like an apprentice in trouble with the Ogefa?"

She winced. "I rather was, wasn't I?"

"It isn't like you," Gessen said. Then he smiled. "But at least you're healed. I went to check on you between tasks, but your shielding made it clear you were pleasantly occupied."

Though he said the words lightly, shame pooled in Dria's gut. She hadn't considered that Gessen might be worried about her. Truthfully, she'd forgotten his presence entirely. "Ah, yes. Vek and I…"

Gessen grabbed her arm and tugged her into the room, enclosing them in privacy. "You bonded. A bit fast, but if you're happy, I'm happy. Did you think I would be upset?"

"We usually talk about such things," Dria answered. "When you weren't certain if you wanted to partner with Caren, we discussed it for hours. And after my last failed relationship—"

"Those weren't soulbonds, Dree." Gessen chuckled. "It's more of a given."

Dria tipped her head back, pretending to care about the fissure in the cave's ceiling. "I'm not easy to be around at times," she finally whispered. "I had so many doubts I should have talked about, but there's a great deal happening right now. I didn't even remember to let you know I was feeling better."

"You're telling me now."

Stifling another grimace, she met his gaze once more. "I only recalled that I should because I have a mission for you. Some friend I am."

"Consider us even, since I didn't manage to get word to you that our troop was selected for this assignment." Gessen gestured toward the ceiling. "So what kind of mission do you have that's more important than shielding this gap?"

"Shielding us," Dria answered. "A group of Seelie and Unseelie is planning to attack from a base in an adjacent mountain. I'm forming a small, quick-moving group to find their camp before they know we're aware of their plan. Me, Vek, a scout chosen by Kera, and hopefully you."

His eyes widened. "Me?"

"I know you're new to the troop, but you are more than skilled enough," Dria said in a rush. "Though Miria would be adequate, you've always excelled at group protections. Unless you're worried about being under my command? I'm fairly new at this, myself."

"You wouldn't let harm befall me if you could prevent it." Gessen waved his hand dismissively. "I wasn't even thinking about that. Really, I can't decide if I'm more nervous or excited. It's a great honor to be chosen."

Dria laughed. "You might feel differently once you've climbed through the

muck with me and Vek. He has an unusual disposition for sure."

Gessen stiffened, a line pinching between his brows. "Is he cruel to you? Is that why your mood is so off?"

"Of course not." She shoved her friend in the shoulder. "You know I would have made him pay already if that were the case. But he *is* nicer to me than he is to anyone else. Just so you know."

"Still. If you ever need someone to help you hide the body, I'm your man." His grin resurfacing, Gessen opened the door and waited for her to precede him. "I'll go change and meet you in a moment. Mage robes might be comfortable, but they aren't exactly great for cave exploration."

Dria returned his smile, content to chat about less consequential matters as they hurried to the hallway that held their rooms. By the time they parted, a little of her tension had eased. There was a great deal of danger to face, but at least her friendship with Gessen stood firm. One less thing to worry about amidst disaster.

Naomh paused with his hand on the door and attempted to regain some sense of calm. His shoulder muscles were strung so tightly he thought they might snap, and the ground vibrated slightly under his feet. Even the wood beneath his fingers hummed from the force of his fury.

Meren had fled.

Just after Naomh had contacted Kai, Queen Lera called him to her private chambers. He'd known then that something had happened. Though his blood was as noble as his brother's, Naomh had never curried favor with the royal family the way Meren had. He hadn't been summoned by the queen, this one or the one before, in more centuries than he could count.

Meren believed that Tatianella's daughter was a fool, but he was wrong. Queen Lera had learned of his intention to go ahead with the plan she'd refused to approve, possibly starting a war with the Moranaians in the process. Livid though she might be, she was also shrewd. She'd recognized at once that Naomh would eliminate his brother quietly and without fuss.

If Meren had been here.

As calm as he was going to get, Naomh jerked open the door and strode from his brother's room. He shouldn't have spent so long waiting for Caolte to return—a wasted effort, besides. He might have reached Meren in time. But, then, perhaps Caolte had managed to track their traitorous brother. An excellent reason for his delayed reappearance.

Naomh rushed through the corridors as rapidly as he could, anxious to return home. He needed to consult with Caolte and formulate a plan to track Meren, provided his younger brother hadn't done so already. Stealth was one of Caolte's greatest strengths, his ability to blend into the shadows a legacy of his half-Unseelie mother. Or so Meren liked to claim. Naomh had never noticed a dearth of skulkers amongst the Seelie.

A point that became all too clear as Meren slid out of the shadow cast by one of the ancient statues standing guard over a decorative fountain.

"How kind of you to appear when I most need you," Naomh said, drawing to a halt an arm's length away.

Meren smiled. "You won't win at this. Too many are hungering for change."

"Ah, brother. You've already lost." Naomh drew power into himself. The queen had hoped for discretion, but his eldest brother's death was the most important point. "I'm surprised you linger here. You aren't the type to receive your punishment gracefully."

"And you underestimate me to your peril," Meren said.

Something glinted in Meren's hand, and Naomh reinforced his shields against physical attack. Then another form appeared at the end of the corridor. A flash of red, and—Caolte, his hair aflame. Their younger brother rarely lost control of his flame without good reason.

"Move back, Naomh," Caolte shouted.

Naomh jerked away from Meren. But not far enough. Instead of the magic Naomh had expected him to throw, Meren leaped across the short distance separating them—and slashed through Naomh's shields with an iron knife. Cursing, he danced back.

Flames crashed into the statue towering over Meren's head, and his brother laughed. "What's the matter? Threatened by mere metal?"

"All of our grandfather's line is," Naomh retorted. "Or should be."

Meren flexed his hand, and water curled from the fountain to wrap around Naomh. He reached for more magic, but his reserves had been so badly depleted that he couldn't grasp enough power to form his own counter spell. He had to get that knife. He might not be able to wield his magic now, but he could still cut.

Then a stream of mist shoved into his mouth, causing his lungs to seize.

His body fought for air, and panic took control. He grabbed at his throat, a futile gesture. Only his brother's death would break this spell.

Meren smiled again. "Yes, your grandfather's descendants are weak to iron." Another ball of flame blasted toward him, but a shield flickered into view. "I suppose you'll finally know the truth. We aren't of the same line."

With those words, he thrust the knife into Naomh's belly and twisted.

"Goodbye, *brother.*"

Then he disappeared.

25

Cursing, Caolte dashed across the remaining space as his brother crumpled to the ground. *Should've been faster. Should've been faster*, he chanted to himself as he knelt and turned Naomh over on his back. The one promise he'd given to their father—protect Naomh—and he'd failed to uphold it.

Now he understood the reason for the oath.

"Caolte," Naomh gasped, his gaze not quite focusing on Caolte's face.

"Take my power," he told his brother without hesitation.

As Caolte pushed as much energy as he could into Naomh's withered reserves, he unfastened his cloak and shoved the fabric against the gaping wound. But it wouldn't help. The iron left from the blade would prevent Naomh from using his small healing gift, and he would bleed out in minutes.

"Cauterize," Naomh whispered.

Caolte shook his head so stringently his neck crackled. "The pain alone might kill you, and the iron would be trapped inside."

Naomh's fingers wrapped around his wrist. "Hesitate and I die."

Ruya, Caolte cursed. His brother was right. He sent out an urgent call to the castle healer and reached for his fire. After fumbling with Naomh's wet tunic, he finally pulled the cloth away enough to reach bare skin.

He couldn't think about this—the agony he would cause or the fact that it might be too late. And especially not the lake of blood forming around them.

He took a deep breath and let his power go.

🔥

By the time Dria, Vek, and Gessen reached the tunnel to the underground pool, Dria had already polished off a large bread roll filled with meat and cheese and a handful of dried fruit. Mostly appeased, she brushed her hands against the pants she'd donned after parting from Gessen. Her friend marched behind her while Vek took point.

Her past and her future, two perfect bookends for her current reality.

Vek ran his hands along the smooth tunnel. "Fen must have evened this out when he came back down. I did a shite job if it."

"I'm surprised you could think clearly enough to move," Dria said.

"Fedah was, too. She said she'd never seen such severe brain shock," Gessen said, stepping up beside her to peer through the tunnel. "Should I begin shielding here?"

"No," Dria answered. "In the chamber beyond."

They trailed Vek through the gap as he used his earth magic to scan for traps. Dria didn't leave it to him, though. Fen might have taught him how to detect the spell that had caught her before, but that didn't mean others hadn't been added. She searched every shift and crack in the stone.

Once they emerged into the chamber, Dria advanced to Vek's side, Gessen now following. Near the pool of water that had initially drawn the mages to this place, a scout waited beside a small mound of bags. The young woman smiled, crinkling a dimple to life in her smoky gray skin. Her good humor seemed incongruous with the swords and knives strapped to her supple leather armor, but scouts tended to be unusual. Too much time in the woods?

"Good evening, Princess Dria," the woman said. "My name is Hyada. Kera thought I would be of use since I have a great deal of experience in caves. My mother was a pathfinder in the Dökkálfar capital before moving to Moranaia, and we've spent many pleasant hours exploring the caves near Braelyn. If there's anything unnatural here, I'll know."

"That definitely beats my limited experience," Dria said, returning her smile. "You kept the packs light?"

Hyada nodded. "A bundle of rope, extra food, a small stone mage light, and a moisture-repelling tunic. My armor is enchanted for such already, but I recommend you don the tunics before we proceed. You'll get cold when water begins to drip on your heads. It's inevitable near a pool this size."

"I imagine so," Dria agreed.

She tossed the closest bag to Gessen as Vek selected his own pack. Quickly, Dria removed the tunic from her own and slipped it over her head, tugging the attached hood over her hair. Warmth wrapped around her, the soft fabric proving surprisingly comfortable. Beneath the enchantment, the cool, damp feeling that had permeated her clothing faded.

Only after they'd slung their packs over their shoulders did Dria notice the long, slim box. She lifted an eyebrow at Hyada. "What is this?"

Hyada shrugged. "Prince Ralan sent it through while you were gone."

What was her brother up to now? Curious, Dria knelt and removed the lid. Nestled on top of a bundle of silken fabric, a folded card rested. She flicked it open and then almost laughed as she read the words. *This isn't for you, Dria. I asked Corath to make this for Vek. Move out of the way so your bonded can see it.* Of course, he'd known that she would be the one to open it, just as he must have Seen that they would bond. Pesky seer brother.

Shaking her head, Dria stood. "It's for you, Vek."

Her bonded froze. "Me?"

"According to Ralan's note."

Dria tapped her foot impatiently as Vek crouched down and stared at the top of the box. What in the gods' many names was he waiting for? Corath had been a renowned swordsmith even before he'd bonded with Teyark, and his enchanted blades were so sought-after that new commissions had to wait years. If Ralan had convinced their bond-brother to make this in haste, it must be important.

Fine. Sometimes family did have its benefits.

After an eternity, Vek peeled back the fabric to reveal the sword beneath. Dria caught her breath. Both the scabbard and hilt were a deep charcoal, but as she leaned over Vek's shoulder, her mage light glinted against red scrollwork traced into the cross guard. The designs trailed down the grip to the blood red stone embedded in the pommel.

"Are you just going to stare at it?" Dria asked.

Vek shook his head. "Why would he do this? I am already in his debt for helping Fen."

"Ah, bonded." With a sad smile, Dria rested her hand on his shoulder. "Not every gift has a hidden cost. Ralan used to do random stuff like this, often at the whim of his visions, and it seems he has resumed the tradition. Besides, you're his family now."

Vek grinned up at her. "Much as he must hate it."

"Looks like he doesn't dislike you as deeply as you fear," Dria said. "Or at the least, he doesn't want you dead."

Her bonded had no comment about that, she noticed.

Finally, he lifted the sword from the box. His fingers whitened around the scabbard as he slid the blade free, and Dria had to look away from the flare of red light that surged from tip to pommel. Only when the glow settled could she examine her bond-brother's handiwork. Gods, he'd somehow managed to darken the metal until it was almost as deep a charcoal color as the hilt. Thin red scrollwork vined up both sides of the blade.

"Is that..." Hyada whispered reverently.

"Made by Corath's own hand," Dria confirmed.

"Perhaps one day, I'll be lucky enough to commission one of my own." Hyada snorted. "Though I'll need a few more centuries to acquire that kind of wealth. I haven't been on my own for *that* long."

Dria had to concur with that. She might be a princess, but she would still have to work for her personal wealth. "Nor have I."

Vek remained silent, staring at the blade in his hand as though it might turn on him. She bit her lip. Had Ralan's gift offended him? The Unseelie were an unusual lot. She was about to ask when he abruptly pushed up the sleeve of his tunic and ran the sharp edge of the blade along the top of his arm, drawing blood.

Well, then.

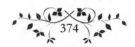

Few things stunned Vek to speechlessness, but this gift was one of them.

As he smeared his blood across the engravings, the spells imbued into the metal activated, and power surged upward and into his hand. An energy trap. The clever Moranaian had created a spell that would pull power from the blood of his enemies without need of ingestion. But only the energy. With this, he could replenish himself during battle without the fear of overloading his brain with acquired talents.

This sword was nearly priceless. Enchanted swords were rare since the perfect combination of magical artistry and swordsmithing ability was difficult to find, and each sword required an immense amount of physical and mental labor. That Corath of the Moranaians had created it so quickly was testament to his skill.

No matter what Dria said, Vek owed another debt to Ralan for this.

Still in awe, he closed the wound on his arm and used an enchantment to cleanse the blade now that it had been attuned. Then Dria helped him buckle the scabbard to his waist so he could sheathe the sword. Instantly, the glow winked out until the pommel appeared normal once more. But his link with the weapon remained.

"Your brother..." Vek finally said.

Dria laughed. "Yeah."

Vek bent down to close the box, and the note tumbled free to reveal more writing on the other side. He skimmed it and then chuckled. *You'll guard my sister's back as she does yours. You owe me nothing.* He held it out for Dria to read, and she nudged his shoulder playfully.

"I told you."

"Hah." Vek tapped his finger against her lips. "Enough of that. Now that I'm properly armed, I believe we have a mission to complete."

Her humor faded as her gaze took in Gessen and then Hyada. "Time to go. Shield up, Gess. Hyada will lead the way."

\#

Kai removed the end of the glass leaf from the flame and hurriedly bent to attach it to the ground beneath the little figurine's feet. But the piece of glass slipped from his fingers and shattered, a tiny shard slicing into his skin. Cursing vehemently, he used his slight healing gift to mend the small wound and then deactivated the flame spell.

The room went silent without the hiss of fire streaming above the edge of the containment cube. Fuck it all. Kai plopped down on the nearest stool and glared at the small statue on his workbench. He'd thought his hobby might calm him, but not even the peace of creating could ease the odd restlessness trembling through his body. He glanced down at his shaking hands.

Literally trembling.

What was wrong with him? Arlyn and the baby were fine. There was trouble on Earth, but for once, he didn't have to handle it. He'd recovered from the overuse

of his talents when making the portal to Earth. Hadn't he? That experience had an almost dream-like quality, a fantastical sheen more fiction than fact.

Kai shoved his hands through his hair, dislodging the knot that held the long strands back. It was no use trying to do anything worthwhile when he was like this. Glass working was a delicate process at the best of times, and mistakes could send him to the healer's tower. With all that Lial had to deal with, the healer would be less than amused if Kai injured himself by continuing to work when he knew better.

He'd just finished cleaning up the broken glass and dampening the furnace when he sensed Lyr's presence at the edge of his mind. *"Yes?"*

"Get to my study," Lyr said, the strain in his mental voice making Kai's heart leap. *"Now."*

Kai grabbed his cloak from beside the door and swung it on before darting into the chilly rain. *"What's wrong?"*

"I have Caolte on the mirror." Lyr hesitated. *"Your father is injured."*

Emotions tumbled inside Kai's gut. Fear. Regret. Anger. *"Be right there."*

Mud squelched beneath his boots as he hurried through the garden toward the main building. Was this why he'd felt so uneasy? Parent and child shared an unusual bond, a link of similar energy that connected them. It was slightly stronger with one's mother, whose magic surrounded and entwined with the child as they grew, but fathers were hardly left out. If Naomh had been present while Kai's mother was pregnant, he could have twined his energy with hers so the bond would be stronger.

Something Kai made certain to do for his own child as often as he could.

But even without that, a link was still there. *Clechtan,* he'd just started getting to know his father. They'd begun to tolerate each other enough to share a few stories, and Kai had allowed a reluctant hope that they might move beyond their rough start. Naomh had captured him by mistake, after all, and Kai would have detained anyone working with Kien himself. It wasn't like Naomh had known he had a son.

Thankful for the time-saving cleansing spell that stripped the muck from his clothes and shoes, Kai rushed through the door, almost colliding with Lynia at the door to the library. "Sorry," he said.

"Kai, what...?"

"I'll explain later," he answered, hurrying on before she could ask more questions.

It wouldn't be the first time he'd been considered rude.

By the time he reached the study doors, he was practically running. Arlyn headed toward him along the other hallway, joining him as he strode into the room. She sent reassurance along their bond, a silent support he'd come to depend on more with each passing day. Thank all the gods that she'd decided to put up with him.

Lyr stood before the tall mirror situated in front of the window near his desk. Kai made it across the oval room in record time and skidded to a stop beside his friend, Arlyn trailing at a more reasonable pace. He almost didn't notice her hand slipping into his a moment later. He was too busy staring at Caolte in shock.

Literal fire flickered and sparked around his head like a halo of doom, and his eyes glowed a deep red. It took a moment for Kai to recognize his father's study, since the tapestry that usually hung on the wall was a tattered, charred mess. Ash smudged his uncle's cheek, and his hands were a blackened mess. Caolte must have lost control of his flame.

"What happened, Caolte?" Kai asked.

"Meren," he snarled. "His plot to return to Earth was uncovered, and he stabbed Naomh with an iron blade before he fled."

Kai's mouth went dry. "My other uncle did this? I haven't met your eldest brother, but I—"

"He is not my brother." The flame above Caolte flared. "I'd just discovered from my own mother's people that Meren's mother lied about his parentage. She was already with child when she married Naomh's father, but she used a blood spell to conceal it. I'm not sure his supposed father ever knew."

Couldn't any aspect of his blood family be normal? Kai sighed. "Is my father...?"

"Alive, but barely." Another bit of the tapestry behind Caolte crumbled into dust. "The healers sealed the wound, but there are iron remnants that will slow his healing. He has been placed in a deep sleep. With time, he may recover."

Arlyn's fingers tightened around Kai's. "The iron conversion," she murmured.

Kai squeezed her hand in acknowledgement. "We'll be there as soon as we can. Arlyn knows a trick that might help." He lifted a brow at his uncle. "Try not to burn down the house in the meantime."

Caolte scowled, but the fire ringing his head dimmed. "Hurry. And watch out for Meren. He is not to be underestimated."

Abruptly, his uncle severed the connection. "Sorry, Lyr. I should have confirmed I have no other orders, but—"

"Go," Lyr said, a worried frown marring his brow. "And take your guards."

With a nod, Kai glanced down at Arlyn. "Ready, love?"

Her smile was tinged with sadness. "Whenever you need me."

26

His nephew had done a fine job of repairing the cave-in. Vek trailed his fingers along the stone he'd crawled through earlier that day. Difficult to believe such a short span of time had passed. He shared a knowing look with Dria, who'd been scowling at the narrow tunnel walls as though they'd collapsed on her intentionally. So much had changed since then.

In the small chamber beyond, Hyada crouched down to examine the floor near the spot where Vek and Dria had lain. Vek scanned the area with his earth magic but detected no sign of the trap Fen had taught him to find. He took special care with the fissure on the other side of the room, the only way forward at this point. Nothing suspicious.

"There's a footprint here," Hyada said. "Made within the last mark, I'd say. It appears to be from an adult female based on size and shape."

Not his cousin Kethen, then.

"Can you trace it through the fissure, or should I attempt a tracking spell?" Dria asked.

Hyada smiled. "Don't waste the energy. I can follow a trail like this without magic."

"I could also cast the spell if it later becomes necessary," Gessen interjected. Then he flushed. "Not that I meant to doubt you, Hyada. I just feel like I should be doing more than holding a shield."

Annoyance pinched Dria's face. "I know this is your first mission, but you don't have to be too eager. That shield is important. Although a bit of cloaking wouldn't go amiss."

Vek studied the young man, who nodded and got to work on concealing them from sight. His first mission, hmm? Perhaps he'd been the one who replaced Dria when she'd been sent here by the king. But despite that, they appeared to be friends. She wouldn't have requested Gessen join if there was animosity between them—or if the man was incompetent. An existing friendship would explain why the man had been so concerned when Dria was injured.

"Let's go," Dria said. "Switch to mental communication beyond this room."

As Hyada led them through a fissure so thin that Vek had to turn sideways to squeeze through, he resumed scanning with his earth magic. Nothing. They crawled through holes, ducked around mountains of stalagmites and columns, and climbed up countless stones. Twice, Dria and Gessen used magic to levitate the group to a lower level. But aside from the occasional footprint, there was no sign of life.

Vek tapped his fingers against the hilt of his sword. Life. Where was the life he should be sensing? Since taking Aris's blood, he'd grown accustomed to the steady hum of living beings existing around him. But aside from a few well-hidden insects, the area was clear of the typical inhabitants. Not even the countless bats that had beat at the edges of his consciousness since his arrival.

He sent a request to the others to pause. They complied, though Dria flicked a questioning glance over her shoulder. *What's wrong?*

I'm going to use a different type of talent, and I don't have a lot of practice with it.

Carefully, Vek unfurled his power. He flinched against the life-light of the others in his group until he managed to dim his sense of them. Then he sent his focus outward, bit by bit. At first, he found nothing, though a few creatures flickered into his inner sight down some of the side tunnels. It was as if this area had been cleared—and not naturally.

Vek followed their current path through a broad chamber and along a few more tunnels. Until he found it. Or, rather, them. A group of twenty...no, twenty-one, counting a straggler, were working their way closer. But he couldn't detect more details through their heavy shielding, not without exposing his presence.

He pulled back into himself with haste. *We need to move. There's a group of twenty-one people headed this way, and if we're fast, we can beat them to the large chamber I found. We can choose our ground to even the odds. Unless you want to go back?*

Dria nibbled at her lip for a moment before shaking her head. *No. They could catch up to us in one of the fissures, and then we'd be dead. Let's go. If we're to fall, we'll take the bulk of them with us.*

His lips curled upward at his mate's defiant tone. Ah, she was perfect. But he didn't have time to linger on the thought. As soon as Dria passed her orders to the others, they rushed forward as quickly as they could without creating too much noise. Then the words from Ralan's note entered Vek's mind, and his smile dropped.

You'll guard my sister's back as she does yours.

Apparently, they were about to put that to the test.

🔥

Dria scanned the twisting, oblong chamber where they'd have their battle. It wasn't the worst place to face combat, but it wasn't ideal, either. Still, there were so many places they could have been stuck, tight spots or rough climbs where they could be picked off by a skilled archer. It was only too bad that Vek hadn't been able to determine the talents of the approaching party. They could be largely warriors, or they could be all mages.

Far better to be the former.

"They will be here shortly. A small climb and another bend," Vek sent.

Dria nodded, tugging an energy crystal from her pouch and gripping it tight before ducking behind a thick column. This was it—her first battle. She took a deep breath and pushed down her nerves. She had trained for this.

They all had.

Hyada knelt beside an outcropping to the right of the hole where the group would emerge, and Gessen tucked himself into a hollow not far from Dria. She exchanged a smile with her friend, who was reinforcing the shields he'd placed around each of them, before checking on Vek. Her bonded stood in the center of the room with his sword drawn.

He'd ordered Gessen to remove the invisibility spell from him alone. Dria had argued against it, but nothing had been able to convince him to do otherwise. If his cousin was present, Vek wanted to confront him face-to-face. According to her bonded, Kethen had always been more reasonable than many of his kin. Only if negotiations failed would they fight.

Dria was absolutely preparing to fight.

A slight scuffing heralded the group's arrival. She pulled the first spark of lightning into her hand until her palm prickled, and Gessen's shield tightened around her. Gods, it would be better to have their entire troop here. Twenty would have been nothing to defeat together, but the odds were closer to even—depending on their competition.

The first person through had the pale coloring of Unseelie royalty, though he lacked the dangerous predator's energy of the blood elf. One of the less favored, considering what she knew about their court. Still, he entered like a king, only stumbling to an abrupt halt at the sight of Vek waiting in the very center. The three immediately behind him almost crashed into his back before managing to recover.

"Yield or fight, Kethen," Vek announced without preamble. "You know this is madness."

The Unseelie pulled his sword from its scabbard. Seemed he wasn't choosing yield.

"You're on the wrong side, Vek."

"On the contrary," Vek answered. "You've let grief cloud your mind. The Moranaian responsible for the energy poisoning that killed your son was brought to justice by his people. There is nothing to gain for you in this."

Kethen's skin mottled red. "You will not speak of Dereck again. Do you think I don't know that you spared Ara's wretched spawn? If Fen hadn't helped the Moranaian, my son would be here."

"Fen is only twenty-three, a powerful *Felshreh* left to drift by his mother. Trouble was almost inevitable." Vek's low, sad voice tugged at Dria's heart, but Kethen's angry expression didn't budge. "He made Kien promise not to poison the Unseelie realms, and once that promise was broken, Fen risked his own life to fix the damage that had been wrought. None of this should have happened, Kethen. Let us not compound that fateful mistake with a war."

"What has cowering in our caves gained us? Once the Unseelie rise to power, we can safeguard all the realms from the Moranaians." Kethen made a sharp gesture with his free hand, and the warriors behind him drew their swords. "Remain with these betrayers. I would rather kill them."

Dria analyzed Kethen's companions as they advanced. Warriors with moderate shielding, the easiest for mages to handle—at a distance. As Kethen charged Vek, Dria loosed her bolt at the woman behind and to his right, and the force of the blow sent the Seelie toppling until she crashed against the cave wall. Swallowing, Dria averted her gaze as the woman landed on the floor in a twisted, crumpled heap.

No time to dwell on the death she dealt.

More began to pour through the gap. Hyada sliced at the legs of the first two, knocking them over, and a couple more tripped over their fallen companions before shouting out a warning for the others. As the sound of metal crashing together filled the room, Dria released a second bolt at another person charging Vek.

Then the mages arrived.

Blow after blow rained down on Gessen's shields, and at least one earth mage must have been in the group because stalactites broke away from the ceiling to rain upon their heads. *Miaran.* Dria pulled more energy from the environment and cast a secondary shield against physical attacks, layering the added protection beneath her friend's. Even with that aid, the invisibility spell faded, leaving them open to view.

She flicked glances toward Vek between firebolts and lightning strikes. Already, his cousin Kethen lay bleeding on the cavern floor, and another opponent dropped as he twisted the sword in her heart. Red flared up the blade, and a wicked smile crossed her bonded's lips as he tossed a glowing ball from his free hand toward the cluster of mages.

An Unseelie spell. Fascinating.

The sizzle of electricity caught her attention, and Dria dodged to the right as a tendril of lightning made it through the shield. *"Okay, Gessen?"*

"They are strong," he sent back, and the panic in his mental voice had her heart pounding harder.

Of the twenty-one that Vek had sensed, only seven had been defeated. Five warriors circled Vek, three sparred with Hyada, and the five remaining mages were easing their way closer to Dria's position. She tossed a ball of flame at one's head and cursed when it slid along his shield. Had she miscounted? Where was the last one?

Vek stumbled and almost fell, though he managed to slice an opponent's leg in the process. He couldn't do this alone. But Hyada was trying to finish off her adversaries while dodging blows from the mages, and a glance at Gessen told Dria that his shielding would soon fall. They needed to defeat the warriors so that Vek could help with the mages.

Otherwise they would all lose.

Directing a series of bolts at the mages for cover, Dria darted across the space separating her from her bonded. *"Coming your way,"* she sent.

"Dria—"

"Shut up and enjoy."

One of the warriors on Vek's other side shouted out a warning, but the two blocking her path didn't have enough time to react. Without hesitation, Dria slapped her hands against their backs, bypassing their shielding to send lightning coursing through them. They barely had time to gurgle screams on the way down as she dropped them to the side.

"Try to turn us so I can see the mages," she said, standing back to back with her bonded.

"Got it."

The strongest level of Gessen's shielding dropped, and Dria darted a worried glance his way as she and Vek forced their opponents around. Four mages remained, and they were close enough to Gess that he'd been forced to go on the offensive.

Clechtan.

Where was Hyada? Dria formed a stream of water to extinguish an attack against Gessen even as she scanned the area. There. Crumpled between a column and the wall. But she wasn't dead. Her lifeforce pulsed strong.

Vek beheaded one of his opponents with a clean slice, and Dria distracted the second with a whip of lightning so her bonded could gut him. One left for him. Unfortunately, Gessen now had four mages circling him.

"Gessen is in trouble."

"Go," Vek replied. *"I can take this one. Then I'll help you."*

Dria pulled her stored energy from the crystal as she dashed toward the cluster of mages. Gessen shot water at their feet, making two of them slip on the cave floor, and then tossed spears of ice at their heads. But the mages' shield held stayed firm against the projectiles, if not the water on the ground.

What were they doing? Two were Seelie and two Unseelie. They must have found a way to interlock their unique talents to create a stronger shield. Dria scanned it for weakness and then smiled when she found the cracks between the layers. With a shove, she speared all the energy from her crystal through the slight gap.

Two of the mages, an Unseelie female and Seelie male, spun her way at once. Excellent. Hopefully, Gess had enough energy left to take care of the other two. "You just wasted most of your power," the woman said with a sneer.

"Don't worry," Dria said, dropping the crystal to pull another from her pouch. "I have more."

They didn't know she hadn't used her own stores, either. A wise mage never drained themselves if they had another choice.

The air heated and tingled as Dria exchanged fire—and lightning—with her opponents. A stream of fire made it through her shields, incinerating her sleeve and

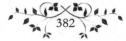

biting into her left arm. Though she cried out, she blocked the pain. That *drec* would pay first.

Suddenly, Vek slipped up behind the Unseelie woman and twisted his sword into her back. He tossed another crackling orb at the male, stunning him enough for Dria to blast him. Only two left now.

Dria spun to face them—just as Gessen screamed.

Her heart cracked at the sound, and she struggled to take in the sight that greeted her. A stalactite speared through his abdomen as a Seelie mage watched her friend with a satisfied smirk. Oh, gods.

Vek went for the other mage, but this one was hers.

"Go check on Hyada," Dria sent to her bonded. *"I'll kill the last one and then help Gess."*

Without waiting for a response, she slipped a knife from its sheath at her waist and charged across the space. The earth mage turned his head, eyes widening in surprise, but he didn't release his spell in time to stop her. With a cry, she shoved her knife into his side, twisting as she slapped her other hand on the man's neck.

Dria cracked the lightning through his heart before he took another breath.

Silence descended, the eerie stillness broken only by the thud of her opponent's body and Dria's harsh breaths. Then she rushed toward Gessen, hoping it hadn't been as bad as she'd thought.

Please…

But he was motionless and pale, only a low, keening moan proving he had any life. Dria knelt beside him and brushed her hand across his cheek. Gessen shifted and then screamed as it moved the stalactite pinning his gut.

"Dree," he whispered. "Love you. Best friend."

"I love you, too, Gess," she sputtered, trying to force the words around the tears choking her throat.

Her vision blotched with moisture, but nothing could block the sight of his last breath.

Then her head exploded with pain, and her world went black.

27

Vek had already checked Hyada's pulse when Dria's words truly hit.
I'll kill the last one…

Unless his senses had been muddled, there were two left. Had she misspoken or been mistaken? The former was understandable, but the latter…that would be deadly. As Hyada stirred, breaking free from unconsciousness, Vek straightened. He reached along his bond with Dria, but her choked cry sounded from across the cavern before he could warn her.

A cry that cut off far too abruptly.

He could tell through their link that she wasn't dead, but fear strangled his throat nonetheless as he spun back toward his mate. A burning rage nearly consumed the dread at the sight of Dria's body crumpled against his sister.

It hadn't been Kethen alone behind this treachery. Ara, too, had betrayed them.

"Let her go," Vek commanded as he strode forward.

"I recommend you stop," Ara answered, lifting a knife to Dria's throat. "I don't know if iron affects her, but a slice to the artery works against anyone."

Vek froze, the fury mounting. He didn't know if Dria was allergic to iron, either. Fucking hell. How could he not know something so vital and basic about his own mate? His hand gripped the hilt of his sword until his fingers ached.

What could he use against Ara without hurting Dria in the process? Many of his enchantments required physical contact, Ara would be able to counter his Unseelie spells, and he didn't have a strong enough grasp of the spells he'd gleaned from Dria. Nor the ones from Aris. A master life mage could jerk the lifeforce from a living being, but Vek hadn't yet determined if he had gained that ability. It would be far too easy to botch the magic while trying to find out.

"Why are you doing this?" Vek asked, hoping to stall. "We've never been friends, but we are far from enemies. My mate has nothing to do with any of it."

Ara laughed. "Tell that to the people she just killed."

"She did what she had to do."

"And I'm doing the same." Ara's grip tightened, the knife almost breaking Dria's skin. "She's coming with me. If you want your mate back, you'll follow. I'd recommend you use caution, however. Confronting Father will be no simple matter."

Red light rippled along his blade with his anger. "I will kill you for this."

"I expect you to try." Ara shrugged. "We'll see. Oh, and bring my son, will you? It is long past time we meet."

"Fen will not—"

"Bring him if you want your mate." Ara's expression hardened. "This isn't an idle request, brother. It is what must be."

Vek gritted his teeth. "Do you honestly think Dria will be a biddable captive?"

"I can always drain her," Ara answered. "Without killing her, of course."

He had to think of something. Anything. "Why does Father want her?"

"Father doesn't know what he wants," Ara said flatly as she eased herself and Dria toward the cavern wall. "Think over what I've told you very carefully, Vek, or all will be lost."

He drew power into his hand, forming the only spell he could think of. The immobilization spell. But before he could cast it, Ara loosed her own magic. Beneath his feet, the ground curled up like liquid, making him stumble, and then solidified up to his ankles. Cursing, he caught his balance, but the distraction was enough.

Ara parted the stone in front of her and pulled Dria through.

His curses rang out in a symphony of Unseelie, Moranaian, and even English as he used his magic to remove the stone from his feet. Not that it mattered. By the time he reached the cavern wall, Ara had already had time to activate the spell to return to the Unseelie realm. Sadly, she'd been too wise to attempt the spell in his sight, or he could have disrupted it.

Vek dropped his forehead against the rock, barely resisting the urge to slam his skull against it. He didn't need a pained and muddled mind. He would have Dria back, and everyone responsible for her abduction would die a slow, painful death. Starting with his *sremed* of a sister.

But he couldn't act too hastily.

Hyada's whisper echoed like a shout in the silence. "What happened?"

He couldn't hold back a snarl as he spun to glare at her across the cavern. "Dria was taken. Gessen is dead."

"Gods." Hyada leaned heavily against a column, her gray skin more ash than charcoal. "Something cracked into my temple. I don't remember…"

Vek used a touch of magic to clean his blade before sheathing it. "I'm not angry at you. I'd kill you now if I had any doubts about your loyalty."

"Thanks," Hyada muttered.

Ignoring the sarcasm, he nodded. "Of course. Now help me gather the dead. I'll incinerate them, except for Gessen."

Grimly, they stacked all twenty bodies in the center of the large chamber. Vek saved his cousin for last. In the end, he'd exchanged little more than a few blows with

Kethen, and that bothered him almost as much as having to kill him in the first place. His cousin had deserved a more impressive battle, no matter how far he had fallen from their people's values during his grief.

Vek had never hated his job so much as he did today.

Dria jerked awake, her consciousness returning like a mage globe activated in the dark. But it wasn't a warm glow that suffused her. Her head pounded with agony, and her muscles ached with rage contained. Whoever had hit her would pay with a bolt of lightning directly up their ass.

"Whatever you're considering, I wouldn't try it," a woman said from somewhere above her.

Cracking her eyes open, Dria examined her surroundings. She'd been strapped to a chair in a small, otherwise-empty room, and the unfamiliar woman stood in front of her. Her pale hair was braided back, and her tunic and pants were caked with dirt. The woman flashed her fangs as she lifted a knife toward Dria's face.

"If iron doesn't do the trick, I'll drain you," the woman warned. "But I'd rather not."

"I don't care about your preferences," Dria snapped.

The woman's lips thinned. "Calm yourself. I didn't bring you here to hurt you. I will if I have to, but that is not my goal."

"I don't suppose you're going to tell me what your goal is?"

"You'll see soon enough."

Dria considered her options. She could sit here meekly, waiting for the woman to get on with her plan, or she could find a way to escape. Preferably maiming or killing her captor in the process. The *drec* had been with the group that had killed Gessen, after all. Grief tried to swamp her, but she shoved it aside. Letting her guard down wouldn't bring him back.

And sitting here like a sacrifice would be the worst possible choice.

"Will you at least tell me who you are?" Dria asked, hoping to distract her.

"I am Ara," the woman answered. "Daughter of the king and sister to Vek. You would do well not to give me trouble."

"Do I look like a troublemaker?"

Ara simply lifted a brow.

Hah. Dria wouldn't have fallen for that, either.

"The blood of the unwilling tastes unpleasant." Ara's gaze dropped to the knife in her hand. "But there are multiple ways I can make you behave."

Carefully, Dria probed the rope around her hands. *Miaran.* The blood elf had used a similar enchantment to the one Vek had placed on the Sidhe woman's bindings, a spell that prevented the rope from being undone with magic. It would be nearly impossible to break, but *nearly* wasn't the same as *absolutely*. Perhaps she could exploit her link with Vek, since he shared kinship with Ara.

It was worth a try.

"So what now?" Dria demanded. "Are you going to haul me in front of the king, or am I just going to sit here for a while?"

Ara's eyes narrowed. "You make an obnoxious captive. No wonder you are the perfect mate for my brother."

"You could always let me go," Dria said.

"Perhaps eventually, if all goes as planned." Ara slid the flat of her iron blade across Dria's cheek. "And if you don't give me too much grief."

Someone knocked on the door, and Ara spun away, rushing to the door to crack it open. Dria ignored her whispered words and focused on the spell holding the rope. Escaping this would be a trick. Her connection to Vek helped her identify the almost-chinks and near-similarities in the blood binding her. What it didn't provide was a true weakness she could exploit.

But perhaps she was thinking about it the wrong way. No magic could unwind these knots, but nothing prevented her from cutting through them physically as far as she could tell. Ara obviously believed that iron was likely to cause Dria problems, so the woman wouldn't expect her to lunge toward the blade.

All Dria needed to do was wait for the right time.

It had taken longer than Vek liked to disentangle Gessen from the rock and bundle him respectfully in his cloak, but their fallen ally deserved honor. So Vek shoved down his panic, wiped the sweat from his brow, and hefted the man's body himself. Smoke and ash whirled around them, making Vek and Hyada cough, as he formed a portal back to the outpost.

As soon as the gate solidified, the opening filled with guards, their swords drawn. The sight of Vek didn't ease their wariness, but they did step back to allow Vek and Hyada to trudge through. One of the mages ringing the warriors cried out at the sight of Gessen, but Vek couldn't spare the time to care which one.

"We took out twenty," Vek said at once. "My sister has Dria, but our other opponents are dead. Send a group of soldiers and mages through to ensure that no one else is waiting to attack."

The two guards at the head of the group exchanged looks. "Our orders should come from Princess Dria."

"Are you going to dispatch a special request to the Unseelie court where she is currently being held so you can find out what she wants you to do?" Vek bit out. "Listen to me or don't. I'm going after my mate."

One of the mages rushed down the stairs. Fedah, he thought. "Oh, gods. Is that...?" she began, her question trailing off into horrified silence.

Vek settled Gessen's body on the floor of the cavern and tucked the cloak around him carefully. "Without his aid, we would all be dead. He held shielding against five aged and experienced mages. His funeral rites should be of the highest honor."

With that, he headed toward the stairs, doing his best to ignore the grief swirling through the cavern. If he let it swamp him, he would never be able to act. Not the way he needed to. Saving Dria was his greatest priority, and only his ability to feel her vibrant lifeforce through their bond kept him from panic.

Only once did he allow himself to look back. "I'll leave the gate open until I reach my nephew Fen's room. I must retrieve him for the coming mission. Send someone through if you wish or walk through the cave the long way."

Vek had made it halfway to Fen's room before he heard someone cry out Lial's name. A lost hope, that. The Moranaian healer was impressive, but not even he could repair the type of wound that had been dealt to Gessen. Nor could he bring back the dead.

Fen's mouth dropped open as soon as Vek shoved through his door. "Holy shit. What in the hell happened to you? You're covered in blood, and I know you're not a messy eater."

Normally, Vek might have tossed out a rude comment in return, but for once, he didn't have time to be an asshole. "They were coming to attack. Twenty to four. We defeated them at the cost of Gessen's life."

"Where's Dria?" Fen asked, his tone turning solemn.

The question brought a visceral reaction that Vek struggled to contain. He'd feared that Ara might be somewhat involved, but he'd never expected this level of betrayal. Fen was unlikely to be any happier about his mother's treachery. Vek's nails bit into his palms as he forced out the words. "Ara took her."

"My mother?" Fen leaped to his feet. "Fuck."

"She wants me to bring you with me." His vision went red around the edges. "Demanded, actually."

Someone pushed through the half-open door, and Vek snarled. But it was only the healer. Lial glanced between them both, his expression grim. "Let's see young Fen healed. Then you can go find my cousin."

With a sharp nod, Vek joined the healer by Fen's side. Dria wouldn't need rescuing, not if she could help it, but he was more than happy to assist her in cutting a swath through the Unseelie court. He could only hope he made it in time.

Nothing would stop his mate, save death.

And that was what worried him the most.

Arlyn sat back against her heels, frustration overcoming her at her continued failure. "I can't seem to get the iron to fully convert."

Kai rested his hand on her shoulder. "You've given it your best, love."

She had, but it wasn't quite enough. Staring down at Lord Naomh's pale, still form, Arlyn considered the problem. She'd poured a fair amount of energy into the iron flakes in the Sidhe man's wound, an action that typically changed the iron's properties enough to stop affecting those with allergies. But for some reason, what little energy Naomh possessed pushed outward, interfering just enough to prevent the iron's conversion.

"Why is he leaking energy?" she asked. "I know this method isn't absolute.

It only lasted a few weeks when iron was in my father's wound. But despite Lord Naomh's allergy, there's still enough magic streaming from him to keep me from completing the task at all."

Caolte knelt on his brother's other side. "He is bound to this place, his power part of what sustains and shields it. He has given me a key, but I can only reinforce. His energy constantly moves outward to support his realm."

Well, that explained the dull, worn state of the place. On the way in, Arlyn had noticed more than a few wilted flowers, and a tinge of orange and red had colored the trees' leaves. As they'd climbed the many staircases and tunnels deep into the estate's extensive basement, she'd seen loose bricks and tumbled stones. Even the room where they sat appeared dimmer and less vibrant.

"Lial might be able to help," Arlyn offered. "He fixed my father's iron-infested wound."

Caolte shook his head. "Naomh would not survive having his injury reopened, not now. His natural energy reserves were stripped bare, and his power stores are immense. He'll have to be placed into the Dreaming."

Even Kai's face scrunched in confusion. "The what?" he asked.

"Moranaians do not do this?" Caolte asked in surprise. "It is a trance. A heavy sleep, deeper even than this, that lasts for as long as it's needed. In such a state, this realm will be maintained while allowing him to regain his power over time. The iron will slow the process, but perhaps your healer will be able to aid him after a while."

"Sounds like Sleeping Beauty," Arlyn muttered.

"It could be the origin of that myth." Pain gleamed in Caolte's eyes as he stared at his brother. "The trick has long been used by ancient Sidhe nobles. Sometimes it is even done out of boredom when the centuries blur together. In this case, the cause is my own failure. The one oath I swore to my father, now broken."

"I don't understand how Meren could hide his true bloodline," Kai said. "Fathers resonate their energy with their children in the womb. Surely my grandfather would have discovered the trick."

Caolte's laugh was cold and gruff. "How could *you* question that? You were deceived into thinking another man was your father. People find what they expect. And in any case, I believe Oisin did know. It's likely why he had me swear to guard Naomh, his true heir."

Arlyn glanced up at Kai, whose face had reddened at his uncle's rebuke. "How did you find out the truth?" she asked before her bonded could say something he would later regret.

Caolte's nostrils flared. "I followed Ara."

28

Vek donned the bloodred finery of a *Felshreh* prince, an armor more visual than protective despite the enchantments woven into the cloth. The tunic was heavy with red embroidery—an interestingly close match to the engravings etched into his new blade—and his pants were loose and soft to allow unhindered motion. Even the rusty color of his sword belt blended in as though designed to match.

He met his nephew in the hallway. Vek nodded in approval at his nephew's appearance, for Fen had dressed in Vek's extra set of court clothes. By all that was Divine, his nephew had earned his place as a prince of the *Felshreh*, half-human or not. The Unseelie lived by strength, and Fen had more than proved he possessed an abundance of that.

"Where do we find the portal?" Fen asked, his voice unusually quiet.

Vek frowned at his nephew's reserved demeanor and pale skin. The healer had sworn that the illness had been purged, and Vek had confirmed it. But... "I will handle Ara if you are too unwell to go."

Fen glared. "I'm going. Where's the portal?"

"Nowhere external," Vek said with a sigh. He would have to trust that his nephew wasn't sick. "Those not of royal blood might need to devise a gate, but we of the *Felshreh* have another way. The key is held in our blood."

"Fucking hell..." Fen breathed.

"Connect with me and watch," Vek ordered.

His nephew would have to lose it over this revelation later.

He barely gave Fen enough time to follow as he grabbed the tiny corner of his mind that connected to home. It was a bond set up by the ancient ones, their blood imbued into the very stones at the heart of their underhill realm. Any of their descendants could return to their land if they heeded the call—a secret that was closely guarded. But few remembered to use it now, especially since it only took the caster back to the cave. Much less useful than the two-way portal they'd set up in more recent times.

Once he had hold of the link to the underhill, Vek picked his destination carefully. Not the comfortable estate he'd built beside the caves near the palace. That would be watched. But there was a small chamber near his home, one he'd been careful not to be seen leaving. With a tiny stretch of power, he connected to the spot and gave a tug.

Fen followed, but clumsily, stumbling before regaining his footing on the chamber floor. *"You've got to be kidding me,"* Fen sent.

"Later," Vek answered.

Not that he couldn't relate.

Vek wasted no time reaching for his bond with Dria, the link that had kept him sane since her abduction. He'd known she was alive, but the distance had prevented more information than that. Now her light filled him—a light tinged with grief, anger, and discomfort but one otherwise unmarred.

She latched onto him at once. *"Something isn't right here,"* she sent.

Vek paused. *"What do you mean?"*

"Your lovely sister hasn't done anything to me," Dria answered. *"Except keep me tied to a chair. I've been working the rope against a rough spot on the wood without much luck, but she hasn't been paying enough attention to notice."*

Vek's lips quirked. *"And that's a problem?"*

"She swears she doesn't intend to hurt me. Honestly, I think she's afraid." Dria's mental voice turned disgruntled. *"Not that it would stop me from incapacitating her if I could figure out this blood lock. I'd hoped she would get her knife close enough for me to cut through the rope, but she keeps running to the door to talk to someone."*

What could his sister be thinking? Connecting to Dria, hearing her voice, cleared his mind enough that Ara's warning trickled through his thoughts. *If you want your mate back, you'll follow. I'd recommend you use caution, however. Confronting Father will be no simple matter.* She hadn't said he'd be confronting her—a curious point that he'd missed at the time.

Why does Father want her?

Father doesn't know what he wants, Ara had answered. *Think over what I've told you very carefully, Vek, or all will be lost.*

Had Ara thought to use Dria to force him into a fight with his father? Surely, she knew that Vek would need little incentive. The king had grown unstable, and now everyone would be at risk. At this point, his mother and other siblings would be in danger even if he'd killed Dria and found a way to turn the portal back into the energy his father craved. If the king had gone mad, no one was safe.

Fen nudged him. "What are we waiting for?"

"Talking to Dria," Vek answered. "Be wary of your mother. She may be on our side, but there is no way to be positive. Her actions are irregular."

As Vek crept toward the opening to the small cave, he reconnected with Dria. *"The trick to the blood lock is iron. There's iron in blood, and it retains the energy of the Felshreh it once belonged to. Make it sing to your own power. If you are able?"*

"I'm not allergic," Dria answered, and her words sent relief cascading through

him. *"I'll work on it. If I succeed in getting out, I think I'll play along. Ralan said to follow my instincts, and instinct is screaming at me to wait until we're together to act."*

"Agreed, my love."

Vek sensed her surprise at the endearment, but he didn't take it back. He made it a habit not to lie, and in the short time they'd been together, his affection for her had grown stronger with each breath. He'd lived too many centuries not to know himself, and denying emotion did nothing but bring misery. Much of life's unpleasantness came from stifling the natural.

"I…"

"Later," Vek said. *"Fen and I are coming your way. Be prepared."*

Her thoughts slid from his, though their connection remained. Vek smiled. He had a feeling Dria wouldn't go back and change their link, not anymore. In spite of herself, she'd at least come to like him. Of that he'd received ample proof.

When they reached the short tunnel leading out into the city, Vek held up a hand for Fen to stop. *"Follow me carefully until we've bypassed the main palace gates. Then Divine help anyone who tries to step in our way."*

"Permission to fuck people up?"

"So long as they deserve it." Vek held Fen's gaze. *"You are a prince of the blood as surely as I, and that means you bow to no one except the king, provided we had one. Own it."*

Smiling at his nephew's surprise, Vek blended into the shadows. He had a mate to find.

Then they had a kingdom to topple.

Use the iron within, he'd said.

Grimacing, Dria tried to blow a loose strand of hair from her eyes. His directive made a certain amount of sense, but it wasn't as easy to enact as it sounded. Everyone, even elves with strong allergies, had iron in the blood. But it was attuned to life, its natural magnetic and conductive properties adapted to the person's body before birth.

Even knowing that, she'd never considered how individual that process could be. To her, blood was blood. Leave it to the *Felshreh* to discover otherwise. But how could she make iron that resonated with Ara's power turn to her own use? Could she reproduce part of the process?

If she directed enough energy through the blood, would the iron in it attune to her? Only one way to find out. As her captor's voice rose, Dria prepared. Then Ara ducked out the door, leaving the perfect opportunity. One quick shove of Dria's own energy, and the blood lock snapped with a harsh, mental click.

Shaking off the shock of the rebound, Dria loosened the physical knot with a simple spell and worked one hand free of the rope tying her wrists. She could see the side of Ara's arm through the crack in the door, and the woman's voice grew louder. Dria slipped the fingers of her free hand up her other sleeve and tugged open the tiny, shielded pocket sewn within. A wise mage also carried extra energy crystals in clever places.

"Search faster," Ara said as Dria palmed the crystal and crammed her hand back into the bindings.

Just in time. The woman marched back in, her expression blank but her impatient stride betraying her frustration. "I'm guessing my bonded isn't in a hurry to retrieve me?" Dria asked with a smirk.

Ara scowled. "I can't imagine why not."

"We haven't been together long." Dria lifted a shoulder. "He's good in bed, but I'm still not positive I like him. You could have done better with your choice of bait."

"With the way he reacted when I took you, I'd say you are wrong."

"Only because he sees me as his," Dria answered. "I can't imagine he has feelings for me."

Agreed, my love.

Dria shifted restlessly against her seat as his words ran through her mind. He must have been speaking casually, an idle endearment. Love didn't just…happen. Her own parents had been together off and on for millennia without settling into true love. She and Vek might share their souls, but love?

No.

Ara's expression grew distant for a moment. Then a smile twisted her lips. "He's marching into the palace now. Let's go see, shall we?"

Dria didn't bother to answer. Instead, she sat complacently as Ara untied the ropes wound around her chest and ankles, leaving her hands secured at the small of her back. Her captor's fingers brushed those bindings, and the woman went still. Had she noticed that Dria had broken through the blood lock, or would confidence keep her from checking? Ara pulled her to her feet without a word.

Then she studied Dria's face for a moment. "If you're planning trouble," Ara said, "Be sure you wait for the right time. I'd hate for you to waste your effort."

Ara knew. She had to.

But she nudged Dria forward without reactivating the lock. Did Vek's sister want her to escape? Ara wouldn't have survived in the Unseelie court for so long by being oblivious or foolish, and she would have known better than to leave a mage of Dria's strength improperly bound.

Be sure you wait for the right time.

Dria tightened her hand around the energy crystal and allowed the woman to direct her out the door and along a narrow stone corridor. She didn't need to put much effort into guessing where they were going—the throne room. Whether Ara had planned for an assassination or a battle to the death, Dria would be prepared.

Gods, but why did royal courts have to be such a pain in the ass?

Vek marched through the palace without hesitation, Fen at his left hand. No one tried to stop them. It wasn't entirely unusual that they proceeded without challenge, but there was a hint of surprise in the guards' eyes that gave Vek pause. Even the courtiers they passed appeared curious at the sight of two *Felshreh* princes in court garb advancing on the throne room.

Almost as though they hadn't been expected.

Fen drew the most attention—also no surprise. Every eye followed him. As they passed through the grand entryway leading to the throne room, whispers swelled behind them. Vek knew his nephew well enough now to sense his discomfort, but he had to give Fen credit. The young man betrayed no reaction to the brazen commentary.

Who is that?

He's a royal Felshreh.

Does Prince Vek have a son?

Wonder if he needs a bedmate?

I'd welcome either or both.

The last comment fascinated Vek the most, for it betrayed no knowledge that he was now mated. Everyone knew a mated *Felshreh* didn't stray, so if they'd seen Dria, they hadn't been told the connection.

"Everyone here seems a bit too…casual," Fen sent. *"Considering."*

"Don't worry, Fen. They'll learn you're taken soon enough. They'll stop scandalizing your delicate sensibilities once they know."

"I'm not…" His nephew's sigh was nearly inaudible in the noisy room. *"Fine, in a way I am taken, at least until Maddy and Anna inevitably reject me. But that wasn't my point. This doesn't look like a group of people waiting for a showdown. An orgy, maybe, but not a fight."*

Vek's lips twitched. *"Hardly an orgy. See? Delicate."*

"I do not have sensibilities," Fen grumbled. *"Some days, I think I barely have sense. Can't think of any other reason why I hang around you."*

"No way to argue that one." They neared the doors to the throne room, and Vek's hand settled casually on the hilt of his sword. *"You've always had questionable taste when it comes to mentors. In any case, I'd recommend getting used to the stares if we survive this. Power rules here, and you're wearing a target."*

"I knew I should have turned down the offer of fancy clothes."

Vek smiled. *"Keep that in mind for next time."*

The guards stepped forward to open the grand doors—just as a shout sounded from within. Vek stretched his senses. Dria was in there. He drew his sword and rushed forward, pushing the surprised warrior out of the way and forcing the door open with a flex of his power. The other guard unsheathed his sword, but Vek halted him with a single glance.

"Let all who wish to see this challenge witness it," Vek said.

The king held Vek's mate without cause, and that meant one thing. Vek could confront him without fear of reprisal.

29

The guard nudged Dria in the back, making her stumble. She gritted her teeth and held her energy crystal tighter as she regained her footing. It was the third time it had happened in the few minutes since the woman had joined them, and from the gleam in the guard's eyes, it was no accident.

This time, Ara cast an angry glance over her shoulder. "Hands off, Quaea. No need to take out your rancor on her."

"If she's mated to Vek, then she can't be worth much." The guard scowled. "He—"

"May be your king at some point in the future," Ara interrupted. "Stick to your oath and get over being bested. And we're almost there, so I recommend holding your tongue."

Well, wasn't that an interesting tidbit? Combined with all Ara had said before, this exchange was telling. Ara expected Vek to be king, and although she'd said "at some point," there had been a definite suggestion of "soon."

Of course, if that was her goal, this was an unusual way to go about it. Vek, king of the Unseelie. Dria's mouth went dry at the thought. That would make her queen, a position she'd never wanted. Not even as a young child still awed by the glitter of court life. Could she give up her place as a combat mage to sit in a throne room day after day, solving problem after problem? Worse, could she bear the constant scheming? The whispers?

Dria stifled a groan. She couldn't possibly make such a decision after being bonded for such a short time, but she might not have a choice. From what little she knew, the *Felshreh* took matings as seriously as her people did bondings. They could very well name her queen at the same time Vek was crowned.

But did Vek want to rule? She was bonded to the man and didn't even know the answer to such an important question. If she had to guess, she would have said no. He was ruthless when necessary and had no problem wielding power, but he didn't seek it. He'd never shown the slightest hint that following her lead bothered him. Then again, perhaps that would make him a good ruler. The best leaders had no need to wield authority like a cudgel.

Ara stopped beside a small but ornately carved door. "I trust you are ready to meet the king? I'm not sure how he'll take my surprise."

"Surprise?" Dria asked.

Ara smiled, opened the door, and strolled casually through.

The guard nudged Dria's back. "Move it. All you have to do is follow directions and try not to mess things up."

With each step forward, Dria grew more certain that Ara's intentions were not what they seemed. Unfortunately, she had no idea what they could be. She would have little to gain by Vek becoming king. Didn't the Unseelie royals jostle for power? It made no sense that she would cede it so readily.

"Pardon the interruption, my king," Ara said smoothly as she led Dria and Quaea across the massive throne room.

In front of the throne, a couple knelt, and Dria caught sight of the man's glare, quickly stifled when he realized who had spoken. Ara proceeded as though no one was present, and the king appeared to have forgotten the pair, as well, his attention shifting instantly to Dria.

Iron in the heart. The man was surrounded with so much magic that she couldn't fathom how his people didn't notice it. Had he always cloaked himself with heavy glamour? Dria didn't even have to delve through his shields to notice, a sign that a fae was concealing something with excess power. He must have built the layers over centuries for it to go unremarked.

The king could have been a harder, longer-haired version of Vek, provided the glamour could be believed. His white hair flowed around a night-black robe embroidered with red thread, the pattern uncannily like trails of blood making their way down the cloth. Even the circlet bound around his brow resembled dried blood. Not exactly subtle.

"What have you brought here?" he demanded.

Ara inclined her head. "Kethen failed where I have not. I captured the leader of the Moranaian colony."

The king leaped to his feet, startling a shout from the courtier kneeling at the base of the dais. "You," the king growled, ignoring the couple cowering beneath him. "You have the look of King Alianar. Are you one of his wretched spawn?"

Dria tipped up her chin. "I am."

Something crashed against the door, forcing it open. Just beyond, Vek stood, his sword already in hand. The king ignored the intrusion as he glared at her. "You continue your brother's perfidy. Kien took one child of our blood. Did you murder Kethen, as well?"

"It is impossible to murder someone who attacks you first," Dria said, using her clearest court voice to be heard over the people streaming in with Vek and Fen. Did her father know that the Unseelie ruler had turned so vehemently against their people? "And you may be assured that Kien was brought to justice by King Alianar's own hand. Anything that occurred afterward is your own doing."

Ara scowled at her, and Quaea tightened her hold on her arm until Dria almost winced. Apparently, she wasn't playing along with their plan. Too bad. She was a princess of Moranaia, not one of his subjects, and she would not be cowed.

Fury lit the king's expression, and for a heartbeat, she caught sight of his true face beneath the glamour. Aged and wrinkled, almost gray with weakness. As Vek had said, he was dying. And none of his subjects knew it.

Did Ara and Quaea?

"Remove her to the dungeon," the king ordered. "Place her beside Retha while I deal with my son."

Halfway across the massive throne room, Vek's steps slowed, so imperceptibly she might not have noticed if she hadn't felt his distress through their bond. An uneasy ache pinched her stomach. What had upset him?

It must have afflicted Ara, too. She whirled on her father, true surprise on her face. "Retha? Has she committed some crime?"

The king turned his gaze to Vek. "She whelped a traitor."

Oh, *miaran*. They must be talking about Vek's mother. This was not going to end well. Dria nudged her mind against Ara's and wasted no time speaking when the startled woman connected. *"How many guards here are loyal to the king no matter what he has done?"*

"Twelve are hidden in shielded alcoves," Ara answered. *"But there are countless more outside of this hall. I...I did not think he would harm Vek's mother."*

Dria watched her bonded as he neared. *"What was the point of this?"*

"My brother needed a legitimate reason to challenge the king. My father has been declining for longer than Vek knows, but lately, he has gone too far. Let's just say I found out that Kethen had no intention of bringing you back alive."

At least Dria's family wasn't the only one with serious problems.

The king's furious gaze shifted to Quaea. "Are you addled?" the king shouted, making both of them flinch. "I commanded you to take her to the dungeon."

"You will leave my mate where she is." Vek halted behind the couple still huddling at the base of the dais. "You two, begone."

Although they should have waited for the king's acknowledgement, the pair jumped to their feet and darted into the crowd. Wise. Everyone here could be in danger, even if a fair number of the courtiers disregarded the threat in order to bear witness.

"Your mate?" the king asked, his voice deceptively calm.

"In this court, she is Driathen an Enielle ceyl Vekenayeth," Vek proclaimed, and in that moment, Dria couldn't have looked away from the proud, determined expression on his face. "You hold my mate without cause. Release her at once or face my challenge."

The king snarled. "Without cause? Kethen—"

"*I* killed Kethen when he dared to attack me," Vek said. A murmur swept

through the crowd, and the energy surrounding the king pulsed. "Would you care to discuss what he was doing when he charged at me, Father?"

The king's hands clenched, but the outburst she'd expected didn't come. Instead, he glanced at Quaea. "Bring Retha."

Dria's guard released her and darted from the room.

Oh, yes. Things were only going to get worse.

Vek's blood burned and froze in turn. "My mother has nothing to do with this."

"I told you what would happen if you disobeyed me," King Torek stated. "Not only have you done so, but you mated with an enemy of the people and dressed a half-blood as a prince of the *Felshreh*. Don't think I didn't notice that slight."

"Fen has proved worthy of the blood," Vek retorted. "And the Moranaians are not our enemies. You are the one breaking our laws—"

"My will is your law," the king shouted.

Vek stared at his father, aghast. This had never been the way of their people. Although the king's word was final, there were countless ways to address grievances. Millennia of traditions set the foundation of their society and maintained a semblance of harmony among a people more prone to gray than black or white. Neglecting that could tip the balance to evil.

The swell of voices behind him suggested agreement with Vek's assessment, but he also caught sight of a few wayward glances. If he didn't act forcefully, the king could still turn the people to his favor. Fortunately, the truth made a fine bludgeon.

"That has never been wholly the case, as all here know." Vek gave Fen a warning look. *Be prepared.* "Did you think I would guard your secrets when you betrayed me? You hoarded power for millennia, siphoning from the energy our people blocked from Earth, and when the barrier shattered, you grew maddened by the loss of that power. You ordered me to murder a Moranaian princess in retaliation, and when I failed to comply, you sent Kethen with a group of Unseelie and Seelie to complete the vile task."

"Seelie?" someone hissed from behind him.

The king's voice cut off the whispers. "What of it? Our realm needs that power. Would you see your own family fall to the disease spreading among the fae?"

The side door opened, and Quaea entered, gripping his mother's arm tightly. His heart lurched, and in that moment, he wished he'd ripped out Quaea's throat when he'd had the chance. Her corpse would make a fine decoration for the fence surrounding his estate. But then her wide eyes met his, and she shook her head ever so slightly.

At the same time, Ara's voice broke into his mind. *"I didn't know he had her. Forgive me, Vek."*

"What have you done?"

"We have to stop him." Ara stared at the king, but she sidled closer to Dria, who stood with admirable calm. *"Should have decades ago."*

Decades? Unfortunately, he didn't have time to ask for clarification. Quaea had led his very pregnant mother to the king's side. Although Retha's pale skin had leached of all color, there was no sign of submission on her rebellious face. The murmurs—and the disquiet—grew around them. His father thought this action would bring Vek to heel, but he had to know that harming a woman with child would turn his people against him.

Didn't he?

"Challenge me, Vek, and I will ensure she is the first to sicken," King Torek said, a satisfied smirk on his lips.

Vek's fingers tightened around the hilt of his sword. "I thought you wanted more power to prevent such a thing? Or was it only so you could attempt to take over Earth?"

"It is none of your affair," the king answered.

The air vibrated with confusion and anger, but it had grown impossible to tell if the crowd was on his side or his father's. A dangerous situation, one they might not escape no matter whom the people ultimately followed. Vek met Dria's gaze, and she smiled at him. Smiled, for fuck's sake.

But then she surprised them all by stepping forward, the rope falling from her hands. Her grin widened as she caught the king's instant attention. "It seems you have captured my mate with your words and intent. As his mother's life is not bound by my actions, then I shall be the one to confront you. Leave the innocent aside and face a princess of Moranaia. Provided you have the courage."

Vek sucked in a surprised—and appreciative—breath. Had she seriously just challenged the king of the Unseelie, an experienced *Felshreh* who'd lived several millennia before she was even born? Many-faced Divine, she was exquisite.

Now he had to make sure she didn't end up dead.

30

Challenging the Unseelie king might not have been the smartest thing she'd ever done, but it was one of the best. There would be no way he could refuse without appearing weak, a fatal action in this court, and if he harmed Vek's mother before responding, his own people would rebel. From the fury lighting his eyes, she could tell he knew it, too.

Dria connected with Vek. *"Your sister said there are twelve—"*

"Guards, yes. That is customary. There may be interference from the crowd, as well."

"Make sure no one attacks me. I'm trusting you to guard my back."

His energy brushed hers like a caress. *"Forever."*

The king glared at Retha. "Remove yourself to the side, but do not leave if you value your baby's life." As Vek's mother got out of the way, the king straightened. "I, King Torek, accept your challenge. I hope your father will not be grieved when you die here."

Dria shrugged. "If I were you, I'd be more worried about my seer brother, Ralan. I hope your people aren't concerned with having good fortune. He would no doubt ensure the futures were unfavorable to them for centuries to come."

That garnered attention. The nobles exchanged worried frowns, and a few shrank back. Ralan's strength was well known, and it was never a good idea to anger a seer, regardless. Unfortunately, the king appeared undisturbed by the reminder, a sly smile on his lips.

"I'll deal with your brother," King Torek retorted. "The rest of you, *emeth.* My guards will stand as witness."

At the sharp command to leave, the Unseelie courtiers practically fell over each other to escape the room. While they fled, warriors stepped from the walls, the glamour shielding their alcoves fading. Six held unsheathed swords, and six trained arrows on either Dria or Vek. How lovely. Did the king intend this to be a fair fight? Vek would stop them, if not.

Aside from the guards, only Vek, Ara, Quaea, Retha, and Fen remained in place. Ara stared at Fen with a pained expression, Fen studied the guards, and Vek scowled at the king. Quaea hesitated before joining Retha in the corner of the massive room. She grabbed Vek's mother as though ensuring she remained, but Dria had a feeling the action was more protective than it appeared to be.

"Vek," Dria sent. *"What is your father's strongest talent? Any weaknesses?"*

"He is not elementally aligned, not strongly. Did you see the magic I tossed in the cave? Expect that from him. It's a uniquely Felshreh *spell, one designed to eat through shields and overpower an opponent. His weakness? That is not so clear. I think he has found a way to directly connect himself to this realm through the link he'd once used to transfer energy from Earth to here. If so, he could draw so much power the entire place could crumble on our heads."* Vek's gaze flicked to her face, and worry pinched his eyes and lowered his brow. *"Tegreh sil caramuin egem. I will cut out his heart mid-battle to save you, honor be damned. Divine help everyone here if you fall."*

Her heartbeat pounded in her ears at his vehement words. *I have my beloved in you.* He'd all but told her he loved her. Could she say the same to him? The fleeing courtiers and furious king faded to the edges of her awareness as she studied Vek's face. Just days before, they'd done nothing but argue, though a large part of that had been pride. Not only hers, either. Now, she couldn't imagine a day where they didn't battle wills.

Some fights were delicious, after all.

Vek smiled. *"I expect nothing from you, Dria. I want only for you to live."*

"Close the doors!"

The king's voice boomed through the throne room, ending the moment—and her chance to give voice to feelings she barely understood.

Miaran.

Dria tightened her fingers around the energy crystal as she took stock of her power stores. The battle in the cave had depleted her, though Gessen's sacrifice... She swallowed against the pain and shoved her friend's loss to the back of her mind for later. In the cave, not having to shield the group had helped. But once this crystal was drained, she would have to pull from her surroundings. Risky since the king was connected intimately to this place.

Too bad she couldn't form spears of rock and lob them at the king. She would love to shove one directly through his heart to avenge Gessen's death. King Torek might not have murdered her friend himself, but it had been done on his orders. Since she couldn't kill the mage responsible, well...sometimes revenge had to improvise.

"You are bold. I'll give you that." With a swish of his robe, King Torek stepped from the dais, gesturing for Dria to follow. "Face me across this hallowed room. Without your mate."

Glowering, Vek finally moved, though his fingers were so white from gripping his sword hilt that Dria suspected he was tempted to gut the king as he passed. If her bonded had been a lesser man, he would have, but Vek wouldn't shame her by suggesting she couldn't handle a battle like this.

Once he passed her, Fen trailing behind, Dria strode to her place in the center of the throne room. A hint of sweat beaded her brow and dampened her palms, but she ignored it. She'd trained for this. In fact, she'd had to defeat the Ogefa herself for her final test, and that was no small thing. All she needed to do was discover the king's weakness.

Then figure out how to exploit it.

With an extravagant twist of power, King Torek waved a hand, and his hair braided itself into an elaborate design behind his back. He sneered at her as he straightened his robe behind him. They must make an unusual sight, the king standing as perfect, still, and regal as a statue and the princess facing him in blood-and-dirt-smeared clothes, her hair a tangled snarl.

Why waste effort on appearances? There was a time for glamour, and this wasn't it. She could look nice later. Instead, she concentrated on her shielding, layering one after another to prepare for the magic Vek had mentioned. She designed them to be different consistencies and frequencies and set one to replicate itself if destroyed.

The king's energy brushed hers, probing. Dria allowed him to see a couple of the outer layers while she analyzed his defenses. Fairly standard—and much like Vek's. She held back a smile. She'd learned to slip past her bonded's shields. She could do the same for his father's.

"I will grant no mercy," King Torek announced. "You are young to die, but—"

"You go against custom," Vek said. "Challenges are not typically to the death. They haven't been for many centuries."

The king smiled. "Do you think I would dishonor my son's mate by granting her a lesser, more shameful loss?"

Pride and vanity. Those were his weaknesses. "I will remember that is your preference and kill you, then," Dria said, returning the smile.

There was no other preamble. Between one heartbeat and another, the king gathered energy in his palm and tossed it at her head. Dria ducked, easily dodging, but he didn't stick to one. As she spun and twisted to avoid the volley, she pulled energy from her crystal and cracked a bolt of lightning at his feet.

She heard a yelp, but it wasn't from the king. He repelled the blow without even disturbing the folds of his robe. Gods, if only she had unlimited power—a shame it came with madness to match. He would burn himself out channeling so much energy.

Perhaps she could hasten that. "You're a fool to try to rule Earth."

The king's eyes flashed. "What would your people do if they were bound into such a tiny space? The Moranaians have everything. All the land and energy you could want on the little world you found."

"Something stopping you from leading your people into the Veil to find a new place? You don't care about any of the other oaths you swore to the ancient humans, so I can't imagine why you haven't set off through the Veil like we did." Dria said as she tossed a fireball at a weak spot in his shield. It sputtered uselessly in the air around him. "The big, bad Unseelie. Lazy and complacent. But I suppose it might muss up your hair to go to that kind of effort."

Dria heard a choked sound from one of the spectators, but her focus was on the king. There. His glamour wavered, and he poured more power in to reinforce it. He really didn't want anyone to know what was beneath.

She would rip away the mask.

A blast from the king ate through three of her shields, but she reinforced them almost absently. Her attention was on the ebb and flow of magic surrounding the king. Ah, yes. He'd hidden his glamour between several layers of his shield. The illusion couldn't be buried too deeply, though, or it would become muddled.

Twisting and dodging, Dria forced her power through the weakest point in his outer shields, her focus on snaking through them rather than destroying them. The king's eyes narrowed, and a tendril of hair drifted across his cheek as he increased the pace of his blows.

But he didn't guess her intent until it was too late.

With a wicked smirk, Dria snapped the glamour, shattering the spell into the barest fragments. The illusion dropped, and instead of the youthful, regal king lording over the throne room, an old, emaciated man wavered in his place. Now, she could see the shake of his hands as he cast his magic at her.

The guards' shocked gasps were buried beneath the king's enraged snarl as he processed what she'd done. His attacks ceasing, King Torek stared at his hands before turning a hate-filled glance her way. If he hadn't wanted her dead before, there was no doubt of it now.

"She casts dark magic against me," the king cried.

Dria rolled her eyes. Had the *Unseelie* king seriously been the one to say that? "Are you the ruler of the light fairies now? Perhaps there are wings hidden by another glamour," she quipped.

The floor trembled beneath her feet as King Torek formed another glamour around himself. The idiot. Gods, Vek had been right. He would bring the whole place down around them if he had to, and he would be certain to uphold his image while doing it.

"Guards," King Torek snapped. "*Meregh.*"

Kill.

Every arrow trained on Dria, then, but they didn't fire. The leader stared at the king, her mouth working a few times before words would emerge. "My king, did you misspeak? This is a battle challenge. I—"

"You've sworn an oath to obey my commands." The king lifted a ball of energy in his hand. "Did you not see how she violated me with her darkness? *Meregh.*"

The exchange gave Dria just enough time to construct a hasty shield against physical attack, but it wouldn't endure long against twelve Unseelie warriors. If nothing else, they would overwhelm her. Unless she killed them first.

As the first arrows were loosed from bows, Dria cast a ring of fire around herself with the last power remaining in her crystal. The arrows incinerated, but she didn't have the power to maintain the flames for more than a few drips of time.

Hastily, she attempted to connect to the energy of this realm—only to be repelled by a shield placed around the heart of the cavern's power.

To think she might have won if it had been a fair fight.

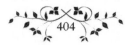

Vek cursed as the guards obeyed his father's command. He would have to hurry if they were going to escape this, and there was no guarantee the king wouldn't summon more warriors, besides. He spotted Quaea protecting his mother as he spun to face Fen. A small mercy that compensated, at least in part, for her other actions in all of this.

"Stop the guards by any means necessary," Vek told his nephew.

Fen nodded, already lifting his hand to direct his energy toward the floor. Stone wrapped around the feet of four guards on the right. "On it."

Vek caught Ara's gaze. "If you see an opening, kill our father. The fair part of the duel is clearly over."

She shook her head. "That would make me the strongest, and I have no wish to be queen. I'm ready to be done with this whole wretched place."

The fire around Dria began to falter. Vek had to hustle. "I don't care who rules. We'll sort it out later. You know as well as I do that there is no other way to stop him."

Vek darted from the dais, lopping off the head of one of the guards and shoving past his father. The king stumbled, the spell he held sputtering. No time to deal with him now. Dria's flame would drop at any moment, leaving her vulnerable to the archers.

And the swordsman dashing toward her through a weak point.

Bracing himself, Vek leapt through a gap in the weakening flames and reached Dria's side. Her energy stores had to be low, but she'd already singed the left side of the warrior who'd attacked her. The man screamed, faltering, and Vek awarded him a quick death with his sword. Power surged up the blade, filling his stores almost beyond capacity.

He turned to Dria, and his heart pounded at the tired, dazed look in her eyes. She needed energy, and he had it. Could he provide for her since they shared a mate bond? Vek dug his fangs into his wrist and held it out.

"Drink."

Her hesitant glance slid to his arm. "I'm not a blood elf."

"You got a charge from my blood when we bonded. If it doesn't work, you can use it to link to this place. It's how the *Felshreh* have bound themselves into the land."

A section of her flame wall winked out. Dria gripped his wrist, nose wrinkled, and did her best to drink deeply. Vek sensed a some of his energy stores shifting to her, and a satisfied smile crossed his lips as he captured his father's gaze through the faltering wall of flame. Even when the king bared his teeth in a clear threat, Vek stood firm.

Either Dria had a *Felshreh* in her heritage somewhere, or there was a greater magic to their bond than he'd known, because more of his power shifted to her. As she continued to feed, another guard crossed through the gap in the fire, requiring his attention. He lifted his free arm, spilling magic down the blade, and flicked the sword to toss the ball of power at his enemy. The woman's shields evaporated, but she was stronger than their previous opponent.

Dria released his wrist. "Guess you were on to something. Gross, but better than death."

He winked before spinning away to gut the approaching guard. Sealing his wound with magic, he stood back-to-back with Dria, much as they had in the cave. More warriors poured through the failing spell. As his mate sent lightning crackling into the opponents on her side, Vek swung, parried, and dodged until sweat tricked down his face to mingle with his enemies' blood.

Without his new blade, Vek never would have kept up, but with each blow landed, power surged through him. Blood was certainly plentiful here. When he could, Vek glanced toward King Torek, who shouted orders at the guards. But power built around the king as he gestured to his warriors.

He would return to the fray himself soon, yet Ara stood tall on the dais, her expression impassive. *"Kill him,"* Vek sent.

Of course, his sister didn't answer.

The king tugged one his men closer. "He's about to feed while his warriors to do the dirty work. Don't lower your guard against him."

"I wouldn't consider it," she answered. "I'm about to drop the flames."

"Good." Vek scanned with Aris's life magic. "Nine more out there. Either Fen hasn't killed any, or more have arrived."

"I'll take five. You can have the other four."

"We shall see, *ahmeeren.*"

Then the fire winked out, forcing them into chaos.

31

Vek's blood had filled her with an unusual surge of energy, its essence different than what she typically gathered from her surroundings. More vital. More primal. Fortunately, it was also useable. Dria gathered lightning in her palm and sent it toward the nearest guard.

She spotted the king bent over a guard, his fangs in the man's throat. He might be bound to this place, but he clearly couldn't pull from the environment as well as he wanted them to believe. Dria hurled the next bolt of lightning at the king's head, and the pair flinched as it cracked into the king's shields. Startled, King Torek shoved the man aside.

"You're wasting your time," the king snarled, swiping blood from his chin with an impatient hand.

"I'd say I have more time to waste than you do," Dria answered sweetly.

A wave of power swept through the room, shaking the walls and shattering one of the light globes in its sconce. The king threw another volley of energy balls, and Dria layered a new shield around herself and Vek to counter them. Several of the guards rushed them—those that could. Fen had bound more within columns of stone and was even now ripping the throat out of an archer with his fangs.

Her bond-nephew had not been idle. Unlike his mother. Ara stood on the dais and studied the battle as though memorizing it for a tale. Why didn't she—

A blast from the king made it through Dria's shield, and she cried out as it singed her side. Why didn't the woman help? She'd designed this entire encounter to see her father defeated, but she wouldn't even aid her son with the reinforcements.

Dria's world became the crash of Vek's sword at her back and the sting of power making it through her increasingly fragile shields. King Torek switched tactics, raining caustic magic from the ceiling, until Vek spun them around so he could repel the attack with his own power.

She barely had time to admire how he blended *Felshreh* energy with the flame ability he'd gained from her blood. She was too busy burning or electrocuting her opponents in turn. Dodge. Singe. Send a blast toward the king. Dodge again. How many more would rush in? Beyond the partially opened doors to the throne room, courtiers stared, but none of them had dared enter.

Or help.

As the last body surrounding them dropped, a scream rang out across the throne room. Dria twisted around to find the source as a massive bolt of the king's dark magic blasted directly into Quaea. Despite all of the carnage she'd seen, bile rose up Dria's throat as the woman's body splattered against the wall beside Vek's mother.

Vek's fury and fear surged around them like one of Dria's flames.

Almost faster than she could track, the king rushed across the room and jerked Retha from the corner. An eerie silence descended as he dragged her to the dais. Panic lined her eyes—the same shape as Vek's—and heaved in her panting breaths. She tugged at her arm, but his grip was too firm.

"Release me," she demanded, her shields surging around her. "Once my child is born, I will—"

"Your child won't be born if you don't shut up," the king snarled.

Vek lifted his sword. "That threat is profane."

"Perhaps the infant *could* be spared." King Torek swung Retha's awkward body in front of him, producing a knife from his sleeve and shoving the blade against her throat. "She's far enough along that the healers could save her babe, though probably not both of them. Surrender now, or we will find out."

"Our people will never support you after this," Vek said, his voice unwavering.

Unlike his fluctuating emotions, a tumult Dria could feel through their bond.

"I own this place. If they will not heed me, I will destroy it." The knife dug into Retha's throat. "How they haven't noticed how much weaker the magic has become after the wall crumbled is beyond me. We must break tradition, Vek, or we will all die. Do you think I want to do these things?"

Ara finally took a step forward. "The barrier has nothing to do with it. You siphoned the magic for your own purposes."

Shock suffused his features. "You are against me, Ara? You have been faithful to me in all things, even sending away your half-human son before he could cause trouble."

Dria heard a choked curse, but she dared not glance back at Fen. Some of Ara's actions made sense now. Her subterfuge in kidnapping Dria. The longing glances she'd directed at her son. There was more to her story than perhaps even Vek knew.

"Pregnant women are sacred," Ara said, her fists clenching at her sides. "No amount of power is worth this."

The king shrugged. "Perhaps you are not fit to succeed me after all."

Ara's chin lifted. "I never planned to."

While the king was distracted by his rebellious daughter, Dria connected to Vek. *"We need to strike together."*

"That's my mother, Dria," Vek answered. *"Do you know how many centuries I have worked to protect her? Yet here she is, being threatened by my father nonetheless."*

She squeezed his wrist gently, careful of his sword. *"You've harvested enough energy to level this place, and I have enough to do what I must. If we can crack his shields, we can immobilize him. I know you've mastered that spell."*

"The risk…"

"Do you honestly think he'll let her go if we yield?" Dria asked calmly. *"Look at his eyes. He is not well, and I don't think it has anything to do with the barrier falling. That level of aging can't be new."*

"What will it be, Vek?" King Torek demanded. "Are you as weak as your sister? Yield. Better yet, join me."

"Let's do it," Vek sent, opening his mind fully to hers.

She stepped inside his pain and grief, as he did hers. Together, they faced the king.

"I'm sure you can guess my answer," Vek said aloud.

The king's grip loosened, satisfaction already softening his features. "I should have trusted wisdom would win out."

And together, they speared their energy toward his shields.

That was where it all went wrong.

Combined, their strength was nearly unstoppable—provided they hit their target. At the last moment, the king sank his fangs into Retha's neck. Vek scrambled to pull his power back, but there was no time. The king established a link with his prey as the magic hit, deflecting it into her shields instead.

Vek's mother cried out and went limp. Merciless, the king drew at her blood and energy, pulling both free with ease now that her shielding had fallen. Vek's vision went red around the edges. His father would kill her and her child.

"Graem awn!"

The harsh crack of Ara's voice echoed through the room, and the sheer power of her words trembled through the stone. Beneath their father's feet, a fragment of the ancient floor liquified, the stone spiraling up his body so rapidly he barely had time to jerk his fangs from Retha's neck. Rock snaked between them and tightened around his chest. And crept ever closer to his neck.

"Grab her," Ara said through clenched teeth, her arms shaking as she struggled to hold the stone against the king's power.

With shaking hands, Vek sheathed his sword, heedless of the blood coating it. *"Cover me,"* he sent to Dria.

Then he sprinted onto the dais. As gently as he could, he pried his mother from his father's grip and lifted her in his arms.

His mother's heartbeat was slower than it should be. A quick probe revealed that her child was alive but weakening. He had to act now. Vek dropped to his knees beside Dria, and as his mate cast a shield around them, fire crackling in her hand, he tore a gash in his wrist and slapped it to his mother's mouth.

Thank the Divine she was *Felshreh*. She pulled at Vek's energy to save herself, and he gave.

Without reservation.

On the dais, Fen joined his mother, twining more stone around the king's lower body, and Ara directed the rock to solidify at the base of his throat. The king's glamour collapsed as she darted behind him and gripped his head.

Alarm rang in Vek's increasingly muddled mind. *"Don't take his blood. It's custom, but the illness…"*

"You needn't worry. I have far too much of his blood in my veins already," Ara said, her mind filled with cold resolve.

Head held high, Ara pulled the knife from her belt and slashed the king's throat. Blood sprayed from the wound, but it didn't stir Vek's hunger, not even as his own energy drained into his mother. Around them, the room pulsed and throbbed with the king's death.

Then stillness descended.

"King Torekthayed is dead," Ara announced. "He betrayed our kind in word and deed, and as such, I refuse to consume his blood. Our people support the light, not snuff it out."

Cloth rustled and footsteps sounded, but Vek didn't turn his head to look. His vision blurred, and his wrist dropped numbly from his mother's mouth. As courtiers circled the room, avoiding the fallen bodies of the guards, he leaned against Dria's leg.

The Unseelie nobles knelt, their heads bowed toward Ara. Together, they saluted, all but acknowledging her as their queen. Good. He didn't want to be in charge of this shit, anyway.

His mother began to stir in his arms, and the pull on his energy ceased. With a slight smile, he let his eyes drift closed.

Perhaps he wasn't just a killer after all.

The bodies heaped around them notwithstanding.

Her bonded slumped against her leg, his unexpected weight almost knocking Dria over. She managed to balance him just as Retha returned to consciousness. Then Vek's mother surged upright and almost toppled Dria again in the process. With a flex of magic, Dria steadied them all.

"Vek!" Retha gripped her son's face in her hands and darted a panicked look up at Dria. "What happened?"

Dria grimaced. "The king… You needed energy, so Vek provided it. Is your baby well?"

Retha shifted a hand to the swell of her belly, power flaring before she nodded. "Thanks to my son. Ah, Divine. If not for Vek…"

The woman began to sob, her hands trailing between her son's face and her stomach as though she couldn't tell where her attention should land. *Clechtan.* Dria had never been the best at offering comfort, and it wouldn't be any easier with her bonded unconscious against her legs. The last, at least, would be easier to remedy.

Dria bent down until she could run the top of her arm along Vek's fang. Even unconscious, he latched onto the small wound, but she couldn't let him feed for long. Not as low as her energy was. He'd barely come back to himself before she jerked her arm from his grasp.

"Did someone kill me?" he grumbled.

His mother wrapped her arms around him and cried into his neck. Heedless of the staring crowd and the bodies of their enemies heaped around them, Vek rubbed gentle circles on Retha's back and murmured soothing sounds into her ear. Finally, her tears eased.

Dria's muscles began to spasm as adrenaline wore off. She inspected the room, taking in the number of foes they'd killed, and suddenly wanted to crawl into Vek's arms right alongside his mother. With a shiver, Dria wiped her trembling hands against her hopelessly ruined clothes and tried to settle her queasy stomach.

Shock and revulsion were normal—the curse of the warrior—but that didn't make it easier.

Gods, she didn't want to break down here.

"You will always feel so, caramuin," Vek sent. *"We'll find our comfort together later."*

"Well done, brother," Ara said from her place on the dais. "I knew you would keep the interests of your people close."

Dria felt Vek's sigh against her legs. "I always do."

"By right of combat, I can claim my place as queen." Ara gestured at her father's body with the knife she still held. "But there may be some debate since the original challenge began with Princess Dria. Do either of you wish to attempt to claim the role?"

Vek's voice slipped into Dria's mind. *"What say you, love?"*

"If you want to be king, go for it," Dria answered at once. *"But I'll be lazing around your house on Earth once Ralan doesn't need my aid. I've had enough of this place."*

"I've found my taste for leadership has...waned."

Carefully, Vek helped his mother to her feet and then stood. Only Dria could feel what it cost him, his weakness masked from the crowd. "I accept your victory here, Ara," he said. "I have no desire to challenge it."

Dria stepped up beside him. "Nor do I."

Ara inclined her head, her cool gaze seeming to take in each courtier. "If any others would like to contest my rule, now is the time. And know that any who supported my father's actions will be dealt with harshly."

Not even a spell of silence could have quieted the room so thoroughly.

"Very well," Ara finally said. "By blood and blade, I am Queen Arafel an Verevethen. I name my son, Prince Feniarathen an Arafel, as my heir."

Dria peered curiously up at Ara. Who was she referring to? Then Vek coughed into his hand, his humor spilling across their bond, and comprehension hit. Fen. And based on the expression on her bond-nephew's face, he hadn't realized it, either. Didn't he know his full name?

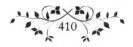

"Congratulations, Fen," Vek said, only the slightest hint of amusement evident in his voice.

Fen's eyes widened. "What in—"

"We shall speak in my private chambers after we have taken the time to clean up," Ara interrupted. "Your estate remains in your possession, Vek, as you are a loyal *Felshreh* prince. You may ready yourselves there until I summon you."

Vek inclined his head. "Of course, Queen Ara. Since Fen is my apprentice, I would ask that he remain with me for the time being."

Ara's mouth tightened as she studied her son. But finally, she conceded. "Very well. I will send for you once this mess has been scoured. You are dismissed."

After a bow toward the new queen, Dria's bonded said farewell to his mother and gestured for a bewildered Fen to follow. Then together, they strode from the throne room, the crowd parting for them with a few hushed whispers. Vek surprised her by taking her hand. After a moment's hesitation, Dria twined her fingers with his.

Such open affection wasn't usually shown at court, but she was beyond caring. Warmth curled around her heart, the only thing capable of combating the sick feeling rising from her stomach as her bloody boots squelched against the floor. What a tangle of emotions, sorrow not least among them. The *drec* might have deserved their fates, but they'd still been people with families who would mourn.

Doing what was necessary was forever a burden to the good.

32

They barely made it through the door of Vek's home before his nephew exploded. "What in the hell—"

"Not here, Fen." Vek nodded toward a door on the right side of the entryway. His steward, Pedek, slipped through with efficient stealth, his demeanor not faltering at the sight of the blood-covered trio. "We'll speak in my room once we've all bathed."

"Seriously?"

"You might not be covered in cave mud and two battles' worth of blood and guts, but we are. You can deal for half an hour," Vek said. Dria grimaced, but at least Fen shut up. "Pedek, please show my nephew and your prince to one of our finest guest rooms."

His steward bowed. "Of course, Prince Vek."

Vek made note to add an extra cask of gold to Pedek's next payment. He'd already earned enough to buy himself and his husband their own large home in the city, but they'd been considering adopting a child. The extra gold wouldn't go amiss.

The cold began to creep into his bones and the nausea to set in as he led Dria into his bedroom. He might not experience remorse for the wicked people he'd killed over the years, but that didn't mean the acts hadn't been without personal cost. The odd limbo of the warrior, the battle between conscience and necessity. He hadn't felt like eating or sleeping for a solid day after his last assignment, and that had been a single assassination. The number of lives he'd taken today…

Well, it was always easier to count the dead than to add up the number of people he'd probably saved. It never got better, not fully, and he hoped it never did.

Vek released Dria's hand and unsheathed his sword. Wincing at the sight of the blood congealed along the metal, he ran a cleaning spell across the sword and into the sheath before returning his blade to its scabbard. Then he glanced up and saw his mate shudder, her entire body shaking with it.

"The first battle is the worst," he murmured, brushing a stiffened strand of her hair behind her ear.

Dria nodded. "I know. I was prepared for that. In theory."

"Let's bathe," Vek said. "We can have a bonfire with our clothes later if it makes you feel better."

One corner of her mouth tipped up. "Maybe."

They undressed quickly, leaving a heap of blood-soaked cloth tangled on the stone floor, and then Vek took her hand and led her to his bathing room. To the right, there was a large soaking tub, but they wouldn't be wanting that yet. Instead, he hurried to a large alcove on the back wall and activated the release spell.

Water sprang from spigots in three of the walls and drained away through holes carved into the floor. Vek tugged Dria through the retaining magic that kept the liquid from splashing out of the alcove. Of all the things he'd commissioned for his home, this was absolutely one of the best. Easy to clean and large enough for three of four close friends.

Dria dropped his hand and darted beneath the spray. "Oh, gods."

Ever willing to help his mate, Vek gestured toward a ledge carved into the wall. "That shelf holds a variety of soaps."

He stepped into the stream of water beside hers. Divine knew how long he'd have to scrub to feel like himself again. He rinsed first, the liquid trailing down his body turning a sickly russet color against the tile floor. Then Vek picked a jar of soap at random and began scouring himself clean, starting with his hair. He hissed in a breath as his fingers found scratches and burns that adrenaline had kept him from feeling. All minor, at least.

Vek had just finished rinsing off again when he heard Dria's muffled yelp. His own ablutions forgotten, he crossed the short distance to her side. "What is it?"

Dria twisted so he could see her upper arm where a nasty welt blistered her skin. "I don't even know when I got this. There's a lesser one on my other arm and another on my hip. I didn't feel them before, but now..."

"They burn like the fire that created them." Vek pointed to one of his own scorch marks. "I know."

"For once, I'd welcome being fussed at by my cousin."

Vek smiled softly. "If it troubles you, we can consult the palace healer."

"I can wait." Dria bit her lower lip. "Would you... I scrubbed myself twice, but I still don't feel clean. Would you make sure I don't have anything left on my back?"

"Of course, *caramuin*," Vek answered. "Of course."

As Vek's hands trailed soap across her back, Dria's control snapped, and the emotions she'd held back escaped in one fell swoop. Gessen. Gods, Gessen. Though the burden of the lives she'd taken lay heavy on her heart, she would kill again to save others. But the loss of her friend...

Why had she dragged the newest member of the troop on that mission? She would never forgive herself for putting him in such a position. He'd trusted her to lead him, to ensure everyone's safety.

Best friend, he'd called her.

So much for that.

Tears poured down her cheeks, blending with the drops of water showering from above, and her shoulders shook from the force of her sobs. Vek slid his arms around her and pulled her against him. Then he simply nuzzled his face into her shoulder and held her as her grief took control.

"I killed him," Dria gasped through her tears. "Gessen was inexperienced. I—"

"As were you," Vek said firmly. "Do not weaken his memory by suggesting he was incapable of completing his assigned task."

Dria jerked in his hold as his words struck her heart. "That is unfair."

"Blaming yourself is equally unfair." His breath tickled the side of her neck, and she shivered. "If you had fallen, would you have wanted me to say it was because you hadn't been ready?"

In that moment, Dria wanted nothing more than to flay her bonded. Not because he was wrong—but because he was right.

She twisted in his arms, and Vek gathered her close until her chest was pressed firmly to his. Though his voice had sounded calm when he'd spoken, his eyes reflected the disquiet that echoed along their bond. She cupped his cheek, her thumb caressing his face. He had his own harsh emotions to deal with, but he'd comforted her anyway.

Her heart hammered, though Dria tried to ignore it. Gods, how easy it would be to love him. But to feel such an emotion would be to doom herself, for as soon as she let her guard down, he'd leave to tend to his duties here. Or worse, she'd get him killed like Gessen.

"You're my mate, Dria," Vek said, a frown marring his forehead. "Why are you looking at me as though you're about to bid farewell? I can feel your turmoil, so there's no use lying."

She let her hand drop back to his shoulder. "You call me beloved, but you barely know me. I barely know you. I didn't even realize you had an estate here, and that must come with duties to the crown. I have my own assignment I am unwilling to give up."

Vek peered into her eyes as though he could see her thoughts if he searched hard enough. "That's not the whole of it, but I'll let that rest for now. As to your words… We are bound soul to soul. We might change our appearances, our opinions, even our homes, but the core of us is a light that never fades or wanes. And it is the core of you that I love."

Her chest squeezed as she buried her face in the vee of his neck. "I don't know if I can ever give the words back."

Vek curled his arm up her back, snuggling her closer. "You don't have to."

How could Vek, of all people, be so kind and understanding? She'd been wrong during their first meeting. He wasn't cold, at least not to those who slipped beneath his guard. Now, it was his comfort seeping into her, filling her hurts. She might

struggle to express herself in words, but she sent the tumult of her emotions to him along their bond.

Warmth, reassurance, fear, grief, affection—and the stirring of something greater.

Vek leaned back until he could meet her gaze. "Dria."

Lifting up slightly, she brushed her lips against his. His body went hard, and before she could kiss him again, his mouth took hers. Consumed hers. Then they were both aflame, both ready to stave off the darkness with their own kind of light. Dria strained against him, her hands gripping his hair as he lifted her and leaned her against the smooth wall.

Her warrior—as she was his.

She held him close as he entered her. Emotion swirled between them, a power she couldn't contain. Vek released her mouth to trail kisses down her neck, and she tilted her head to give him better access. When the edge of his fang brushed the side of her neck, she shuddered and tightened around him.

"Please," she gasped.

Dria had never thought she'd crave being bitten, but this… She moaned when he complied, her mind fracturing with ecstasy. Not because they exchanged power, for they had little enough of that to spare. The connection itself was enough.

Eventually, the chill of the wall at her back broke through the haze of pleasure, and she shivered. Chuckling, Vek swung her under the spray of water until they were both drenched—but also warm. Dria wiggled until he released his hold on her thighs so that she could stand once more.

An unexpected smile crossed her lips as she lifted a jar of soap from the shelf. "We'd better finish up before your nephew rushes in to see if we're dead."

Vek's laugh echoed around the alcove. "He'll deal."

And for that moment, at least, everything seemed all right.

Fortunately, Pedek had left clean clothes for them in the adjoining dressing room. Perhaps two additional chests of gold were in order, Vek mused, as he watched Dria don a sensuous green robe that swirled around her every curve. She'd dried her red hair with an enchantment but otherwise left it loose. Barely tamed, as they both were.

Vek tugged on his shoes, straightened his tunic, and held out his arm for his mate. "I sense Fen pacing in our bedroom."

Dria smiled. "Can you blame him?"

"I suppose not," Vek conceded.

As soon as they entered the bedroom, Fen turned on them. "What in the hell took you so long?"

Vek's lips twitched. "You can probably figure it out if you give it a moment's thought."

Fen flushed. "Dammit, Vek, the queen is going to summon us any minute, I'm out here going crazy, and you're wasting time—"

"Shut up, Fen," Vek said sharply, his amusement cutting off at the rebuke. He might understand his nephew's turmoil, but he would not accept his criticism in this. "If my mate needs comfort, I'll give it, and I don't give a fuck if you, Ara, or a mani-festation of the Divine in its entirety awaits me. Leave off, or you will waste more of the time you find so precious."

Fen's mouth dropped open, and Dria's arm tightened around Vek's elbow, her surprise trickling through their bond. He let out a growl of frustration, one that had Fen stiffening as though Vek would strike him. How could these two misunderstand him so thoroughly? Dria couldn't believe he loved her, and his nephew seemed to think he would thrash him.

Foolishness.

"Sorry," Fen muttered.

Vek pressed his palm against his temple and rubbed. "Forget it. And stop acting like I'm going to carve you into pieces and use your limbs as decoration."

The color leeched from his nephew's face. "Kien would have."

Dria sucked in a sharp breath, and he winced. He should have considered his words more carefully, but his nephew hadn't appeared to be so sensitive before. What was his problem? Now he'd caused distress to Fen *and* Dria.

"Forgive me," Vek said. "That was ill-done."

Fen's eyebrows rose. "You're apologizing?"

"It happens from time to time. Enjoy it while you can."

The tension in Fen's shoulders slackened, but Vek didn't mistake that for a sign of defeat or weakness. "In this case, it's not your fault," Fen said. "What happened back there... My mother... I can't seem to get my head around anything right now."

"That she designated you as her heir?" Vek asked, careful to tread more lightly.

Fen scrubbed his hands through his hair. "I didn't even know she was talking about me, Vek. I've only ever had one name. One single syllable, in a world full of middle names and last names. None of this seems real."

That stunned Vek into silence. He'd known things had gone awry with his neph-ew and had never approved of the way Fen had been treated. He'd even looked out for him from afar, as much as he was able. But he'd never realized his nephew hadn't heard his own name.

"Your father didn't tell you?"

Pedek's knock interrupted any answer Fen might have given. Ara's summons, no doubt. "We'll finish this discussion later," Vek said. "Our new queen calls."

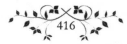

Lial forced his feet to keep moving, though he'd long ago lost the desire to do anything but sleep. Preferably for a week. But Gessen deserved full honors, so Lial's stride didn't falter as he led the guards carrying the mage's body down the path to Braelyn. They would settle Gessen in the Warrior's Hall until he could be transport-ed to the palace for the funeral. The king would no doubt give him recognition for guarding his daughter.

They were nearly to the estate when Kai hailed them from the direction of the portal. With a lifted hand, Lial stopped their small group. Kai and Arlyn approached, their gazes falling solemnly on the wooden board with Gessen's cloth-covered body atop. No mistaking what that signified.

"What...?" Kai began.

"One of the mages under Princess Dria's command was defeated in an attack," Lial explained.

"Fuck." Kai scowled. "Was Meren there?"

Lial rubbed his chin. "Lord Meren of the Seelie Sidhe?"

"He betrayed my father, injuring him so badly that Caolte placed him into a healing sleep." Kai shifted on his feet, indecision clear on his face. "According to my uncle, Meren was conspiring with Ara, the Unseelie princess. I almost went through the portal to warn Princess Dria, but with Arlyn pregnant and a possible illness on the loose..."

"*Clechtan,*" Lial cursed. "Dria was abducted by Ara. Vek and Fen went after her."

"Someone had better warn the outpost about Meren," Arlyn said. "He used iron against Lord Naomh. A blow to the gut. I tried to convert the metal so he could be healed more effectively, but I failed."

Lial winced. The stomach was a terrible place for a healer to have to work, worse if there was iron involved. He'd been able to purge Lyr of iron in his wound, but that had been a gash across his chest. Flushing debris clear of the vital organs would be nearly impossible. That Naomh lived was a testament to his healer's talent.

"I'll go back to the outpost," Lial said. "Hopefully, Vek and Ara will have returned."

Kai lifted a brow. "Did you say she was abducted? You seem remarkably calm about your cousin being in danger."

"You didn't see Vek." Lial smiled slightly. "They've bonded. Only a fool messes with a blood elf's mate, and Dria is no weakling besides. According to the mages who cleared the battle scene, she killed almost half of their opponents herself."

"How big of a force was it?" Kai asked.

"Twenty. All dead." Lial glanced at Gessen. "Only one casualty among our people."

A chill wind swept along the path, and a few drops of cold rain landed on Lial's exposed hands and cheek. Kai cast a shield above them to block the drizzle, but there was no stopping the frigid air. "I'll escort Gessen to the Warrior's Hall," Kai said. "If you want to return to the outpost now."

Want was too strong of a word, but Lial had long ago learned the vagaries of desire. "Thank you," he answered.

With a nod, Lial headed back toward the portal. Someday, he would rest.

33

An army of workers had cleaned the throne room while they'd been gone. Dria studied the floor as they crossed it, but she couldn't find the slightest scorch mark or fleck of dried blood. Now, only her group's footsteps marred the uneasy silence of their former battle arena.

Vek guided her and Fen through a door in the right corner, much like the one to her own father's study, but instead of a room, a corridor led to a flight of stairs and then another door. Only after several more hallways and turns did they end up in Ara's private office. But then, the Unseelie never had been as welcoming to their people as the Moranaian royals were to their own.

The new Unseelie queen didn't await them behind her desk, however. Instead, she stood beside one of the few windows lining the right wall. Dria blinked at the unexpected sight. The palace had been built into the side of the cavern, much as Vek's home had, so windows were few. She hadn't realized they'd curved around to an outer wall.

"You have much to explain," Vek said, not bothering with a greeting.

Ara smiled. "No deference for your ruler, brother dear?"

Dria studied her bonded's tense shoulders and angry scowl. Did he regret ceding his place as king? His words gave no indication of such. "You know as well as I do that I'm not the type to yield. You'll have to earn my respect the way our father did. Before."

"Before he lost his mind, you mean?" Ara's smile slipped. "Yes, Vek, I do know you won't yield. Why do you think I kidnapped your mate? Too bad the plan went awry. You were supposed to be king, and I was supposed to be free."

"No one made you intercede," Vek said.

"It had to be done." Ara stepped closer, her attention shifting to Fen. "I'm not what you think. I never have been."

Fen's hands clenched. "A cold bitch who left her kid to hunt for blood like an animal amidst the humans?" he snarled.

Both Vek and Ara appeared startled at that, and Dria recalled her bonded's face when his nephew had claimed not to know his full name. "You were alone?" Dria asked when the others seemed unable to speak.

That goaded Ara into speech. "Of course I didn't leave my child alone," she snapped. "He was to stay with his father until I could determine the reason for the king's unusual behavior. But Fen disappeared, only to be found causing trouble a few years ago."

Vek's guilt slammed into Dria through their bond, but there was no sign of it on his face as he glared at Ara. "Disappeared, Ara? We're *Felshreh*. If you can't track your own son through the blood, then you are either inept or a fool."

"I couldn't track him without causing suspicion, and I didn't want Fen to draw our father's attention." She averted her gaze. "And I...I thought you were watching out for him, Vek."

"I was." Vek's shoulders hunched. "But there was a solid decade where Father kept me busy, and I—"

"Enough," Fen shouted, anger flushing his skin. "Could you stop arguing about why you failed to take care of me? If you'd like to know the *actual* truth, my father died when I was four or five. I barely knew what I was and how to hide it, but I managed to get the blood I needed as I was tossed around foster homes. Eventually, I ended up scavenging for energy on the streets until Kien found me. So yeah, you screwed up, and I don't give a fuck why. Did you think calling me your heir would make up for that, *Mother?*"

Dria winced at his vehemence. She'd taken Fen for the light-hearted, joking type, but that was far from evident now. Even Vek's face registered surprise. But Ara...for a moment, naked grief gleamed from her eyes before she managed to shutter them.

"I named you my heir because that is what you are," Ara answered, her voice strained and taut. "You do not have to like or accept me, but you *are* my only child. However, you are welcome to repudiate the role. Divine knows I don't want to be queen."

Fen's lips thinned. "You could have rejected it the way Vek did."

"And cast the Unseelie court into a chaotic power grab?" She shook her head. "No. Meren schemes against us, much as he pretended to work with me, and there are still those who might wish to follow Meren's plan to overtake Earth. I do wish Vek would consider co-rule. If not, perhaps he might take your place as presumptive heir?"

Dria stiffened, her attention on Vek as his uncertainty hit her. Perhaps he had given up the crown for her. Would he decide to reach for it now, regardless of their bond? Tentatively, she connected with him. *"Don't let me hold you back."*

He sent her an irritated scowl before returning his attention to his sister. "I don't accept," Vek said aloud. "Nor will I work for you as I did our father. My mate has an outpost to run, and I tire of the endless bloodshed. I do not wish to rescind my place as a *Felshreh* prince, but I refuse to be owned by it, either."

Ara's shoulders slumped. "You have earned that much. Will you still train Fen?"

"Based on his anger, he may no longer wish for me to," Vek said tightly.

"Oh, hell," Fen grumbled, running his hands through his hair. "You think I want to have to get used to some other asshole? No thanks. Besides, *you* weren't my actual parent."

Dria stared at her bonded, her thoughts on his earlier words. *My mate has an outpost to run.* He'd answered matter-of-factly, no hesitation to his refusal. So why had she sensed his uncertainty? He couldn't truly be content living in a cave and training Fen while she set up an entire colony.

Could he?

"Then that is settled," Ara said. "Though it would be best to have my named heir present at court, you are young enough for your absence to go unremarked. There will be ample turmoil when I begin to purge our remaining traitors. Anything else?"

Vek frowned. "What did you mean about our father acting unusual when Fen was born? He claimed his illness was recent, caused by the destruction of the barrier. In any case, he was never an easy man. What was new about that?"

"You were rarely here." Ara's nostrils flared. "But I saw the increasingly odd decisions he made at court. Nothing around you, of course, since you rarely sat in for such things. He would take sides against tradition or end court abruptly to storm out of the room. He claimed to be unaffected by the energy poisoning, but I do not believe it."

Dria peered at Fen. How old was he? Early twenties, she would wager, though the tired, worried look in his eyes made him appear older. "It couldn't have been energy poisoning," Dria said. "That only started a few years ago. Didn't Fen help spread it?"

Her bond-nephew flinched. "Yes and no," he said. "Kien had obviously been experimenting with it for years. I…I set up the crystals that connected the spell to Earth."

"Father told me he held a pillar of the barrier," Vek said. "Perhaps the crack that caused the wall to fail was older than anyone realized, begun by Kien's experiments. Something for us to investigate."

Dria's stomach tightened at the reminder of her brother's perfidy. How many lives had he ruined with his sick selfishness? The list seemed endless.

"I don't know if there is anything to find at this point." Ara sighed. "I'd hoped he would improve once the energy poisoning was resolved, but it didn't happen. Not too long before that, he'd begun sending messages to Meren through Quaea. He had no idea that Quaea and I colluded, nor that I started delivering messages for Quaea until Meren believed I was part of the plot. The foolish Seelie told me more than he should have, though the deception became more difficult to hide when Kethen got involved."

Millennia would pass, Dria suspected, before Vek would share the hurt she sensed from him. "You should have come to me," he said in an even tone.

"You may act in your own interests and in your own ways, but in the end, you are always loyal when you give your word. I could not risk my deception getting back to Father." Ara glanced down. "And you've long made it clear you dislike me. My mother replaced yours, at least for a time, and you have never forgotten it."

Vek's eyebrows lifted. "You think I care about that? It might have bothered me as a boy, but that was centuries ago. And her dismissal from court turned out well. I'm glad my mother remarried, though I've worried for her, too. *You* were cold to *me* when we were younger. You still are."

"I only returned what I was given. You were hardly—" Ara's words cut off, and she squared her shoulders. "Forget it. We can discuss this later. Right now, we need to track Meren. He told me that he intended to kill his half-brothers and then strike at the Moranaians. He will not be pleased that the invasion of your mate's colony failed. And if he hasn't heard of our father's death, he will soon. He'll likely guess I deceived him."

The outpost. Dria wrapped her hand around Vek's wrist. "We need to go."

It didn't matter that her body ached and her energy stores were nearly depleted. If there was risk to her people, she would confront it. Preferably now.

🔥

Concern and anger swept Vek through the portal he'd formed to the cave in record time. They emerged so quickly that the energy let out a *pop* as it dispelled. He should have been relieved at how easily his sister had accepted his refusal to work for her, but he couldn't find that emotion in himself at the moment. Too much had happened that day for such a mundane feeling.

As soon as she got her bearings, Dria headed toward the door. "I need to find Fedah and Kera, then contact Lyr."

Vek nodded, though his earlier irritation at his mate lingered. "I'll join you in a moment."

Dria cast him an odd look, no doubt sensing his mood, but she bid him a speedy farewell. *Don't let me hold you back*, she'd said. As though any crown was worth more than her. Clearly, he would have to spend a great deal of time proving otherwise.

The door clicked shut, leaving him alone with Fen. Vek took a deep breath and faced his nephew—along with his own failings. "Why did you agree to work with me when all you should feel is hatred?"

Fen's eyes widened. "I never said I hated you."

"You should." Vek's teeth ground together. "Your abandonment was unintentional, but it happened. Had I a clue that I was the only one keeping track of you... Well, it doesn't matter, does it? You have a right to be angry. So why?"

"Because you're the closest thing to a father I can remember having," Fen blurted, a look of horror crossing his face at the declaration. "Shit, I didn't mean to say that. But it's true. Those times you checked on me when I was a teenager... I pretended not to care, but they meant everything to me. It's probably what kept me from copying Kien completely. Hell, maybe part of the reason I joined him was to get your attention. Out of all the people in my family, you're the only one who ever seemed to care."

Vek stared at his nephew, the odd urge to laugh almost overcoming him. Not out of humor, for there was nothing amusing about the fucked-up relationships in their family. "You had to scrounge for blood in the human world when you were barely old enough read. Ten years. How can you consider me anything like a father when I left you to that?"

And Divine, how the thought of it scraped at Vek's insides like glass.

"I never blamed you," Fen insisted. "Though hearing you and my mother discussing it brought back a lot of old feelings."

Old feelings. Vek had experienced the same, though the emotions were no doubt different. Guilt, shame, hope, love. In that moment, he confessed to himself what he'd always carefully hidden—he'd thought of Fen like a son, as well, one he'd been denied. It made no sense. But then again, few things in life did.

"I've been angry at Ara for two decades," Vek said softly. "I should have offered to raise you when you were born, but she'd already decided to leave you with your father. I suppose I've felt somewhat paternal toward you regardless."

Fen shook his head, a reluctant smile playing across his lips. "Then why have you always given me such a hard time?"

"Because I care." Vek lifted a brow. "Unless you would let a loved one ruin their life without a single comment?"

Fen laughed, and a new understanding seemed to pass between them without the need for words. "I don't think either of us can resist a chance to make our opinion known. Must run in the family."

"No doubt about that." Some of Vek's tension eased, and he allowed himself a small smile chuckle. "Let's go see how things have fared in our absence."

Dria encountered Fedah first, the mage no doubt drawn by the surge of Vek's magic. A look of pure relief washed over the other woman's face, and had they been on better terms, the mage might have hugged her. She settled on giving Dria's arm an encouraging squeeze.

Unfortunately, it was the arm most injured.

Pain seared through Dria, and she cried out, jerking away from the other woman's hold. Fedah paled. "I'm sorry if the familiarity—"

"It's fine," Dria insisted through clenched teeth. "I have a burn I need tended."

"Oh. Oh, I see." Wincing, Fedah lowered her hand. "I suppose it is fortunate that the healer returned not long ago. I believe he's in the dining room speaking to Kera."

Dria smiled. "The other person I need to see. Come. Along the way, you can tell me what you have done to secure the cavern in my absence."

"Your bonded directed us to tend to the battlefield, and although he has no authority here, it seemed the most reasonable course to take," Fedah said almost apologetically. "I hope we did not decide poorly in that matter. There was…only ash remaining, so there was little to do besides shield the tunnel to their outpost and set up traps along the return path."

"Ash?" Bile rose up Dria's throat. "But Gessen—"

"Wasn't there," Fedah said quickly. "Your bonded carried his body through. The healer was escorting Gessen's remains to Braelyn, but then Lial returned rather abruptly. He was about to share why when I detected your arrival."

Dria sighed, too tired to contemplate a climb up the stairs. She shuffled over to the lift and waited for Fedah to follow her onto the platform. Gods, she wanted to groan at the thought of using one more spell. But as she reached for her magic anyway, Fedah lifted a hand.

"Allow me." With a flex of her magic, the other mage activated the platform. "This was an excellent design. It was clever to use a spell that non-mages could trigger."

Dria's skin warmed in a pleased blush. "Thank you."

Perhaps her relationship with her former captain wasn't ruined after all.

Time would tell.

The platform slid to a smooth stop, ending the moment. It was a short walk to the dining room, which was empty except for Lial and Kera, who sat beside the healer while he ate a bowl of soup. Dria's own hunger stirred, but the sudden memory of battle stifled that at once. Unfortunately. Regardless of how she felt, she would have to force down food. She needed to regain her energy sooner rather than later.

Lial glanced up, and his spoon paused just above the bowl. "You're injured."

Dria jerked to a stop a few paces from the table. "How could you know that?"

"Do you know how many people have tried to hide pain from me?" A scowl darkened his face. "Don't bother denying it."

"A few burns and scratches, that's all." Dria shrugged. "We have much more to worry about."

Lial lowered his spoon and pushed aside his bowl. "No, we don't. If your mind is clouded by pain, you will be useless. Show me the worst of it."

There was no point in arguing with a healer, particularly not her cousin. Resigned, Dria tugged up the loose sleeve of her robe and held it out of the way as Lial approached. He took her arm in gentle hands and then hissed out a breath. After giving her a reproachful look, he closed his eyes, and his healing energy filled her. She relaxed as her pain faded away.

In a surprisingly short time, Lial pulled back. "Far from the worst burns I've seen."

"Thank you," Dria said, studying her cousin's wan face. "Especially considering how tired you obviously are. What are you doing here?"

Lial returned to his seat, but he didn't pick up his spoon. "Kai's father was injured gravely by Lord Meren of the Seelie."

"Kai's father, Allafon?" Dria sat beside him. "I thought the man was dead? I heard that Allafon was a traitor who had been killed a few months ago attempting to assassinate Lord Lyr. Did the man come back to life to insult the Seelie?"

"No, Allafon is dead." Lial glanced between them, a warning in his eyes. "I trust you will not carry rumors of this, for I do not know how widely Kai wants this known."

All three gave their assent.

"Allafon wasn't Kai's father," Lial said. "Kai's mother was a guide who helped people cross the Veil, and in the process, she met Lord Naomh. They were soulbonded, or at least they planned to complete the bond, but Enielle had a life on Moranaia. She was married to Allafon, after all, and had a grown son with him. She returned to dissolve her unhappy marriage and rejoin Naomh, but Allafon wouldn't let her go. He murdered her a few days after Kai's birth and raised him as his own. Naomh didn't know what had happened to her until he met Kai a few months ago."

Only Kera didn't seem surprised. But then, she'd been the Myern's guard. She no doubt knew a great many secrets.

"So how does this relate to Meren?" Dria asked.

"Naomh was known to have two brothers. Meren, who shared the same parents, and Caolte, who was born of an affair between their father and an Unseelie woman." Lial leaned his palms against the table. "But it seems Naomh's mother managed a spectacular deception. She was already pregnant when she married his father but found a way to hide it. Apparently, Meren tired of the lie. He told Naomh the truth just before he stabbed him. Caolte saved Naomh, but Meren disappeared."

"Gods, I thought our family drama was bad," Dria muttered. "Ara told us to beware of Meren because he would seek to attack us once he'd killed his half-brothers. I suppose he has attempted the first part of that plan."

Lial scowled. "Ara? Did you not kill her in order to escape?"

Dria grabbed a roll from the center of the table and tore off a bite. But she couldn't quite force herself to eat it. "She planned to lure Vek by abducting me. Then Vek would challenge the king for holding me. It was… Suffice it to say that the king is dead, and Ara, the new queen, is on our side."

Lial caught her gaze. "You might wish to tell me the whole of it later, and not just as your cousin. My talent for mind-healing is minor, but I can help a little."

"I think I can handle it," Dria answered. "Though I thank you. I will remember that."

Then they began to plan.

34

By the time Vek and Fen reached the others, they were deep in discussion about their next course of action. But for Vek, it was simple. "We set a trap," he said as he sat beside Dria.

"I take it you have a plan?" Dria asked.

"I'm assuming you haven't returned Lady Egana to her people for judgment?" he asked the others. Kera and Fedah shook their heads. "Good. Then we let it be known that she's willing to reveal all she knows to her queen and that we are arranging to hand her over."

Dria smiled. "He'll try to get to her."

"I believe so," Vek said. "We leave a few convenient gaps in our shielding, and I imagine he'll come to rescue her. Or kill her."

Lial shook his head. "The queen may already know of his crimes. You might want to consult with Kai."

Vek considered that for a moment, but then he shrugged. "I would wager she doesn't have a witness, and she likely doesn't know everything, besides. According to my sister, Meren already wants to strike at us. This will merely be one more reason."

"The rumor we create could even be true." Dria tapped her fingers restlessly against the table's surface. "We need to do something with the woman. A trap it is, then."

Lial's sigh rippled the soup in his bowl. "Just when I was about to return home. As sure as the sun rises, someone is going to need to be patched up. This outpost needs its own healer."

"Sleep in one of the spare rooms," Dria said.

Vek wasn't surprised when the healer surged to his feet. "You can summon me at my home. My first duty is to Braelyn."

Predictably, Dria didn't back down. She rose from her seat with a quiet determination that commanded respect. "That was not a suggestion. I still outrank you, cousin, and I refuse to allow you to leave in this condition. The marks of time you'd lose traveling would be better spent sleeping."

Lial leaned toward her. "I will—"

"Don't start giving your threats to me." Dria lifted a hand, and a tiny flame sparked in her palm. "Try to slip me a potion, and you can prepare to heal the scald marks on your own ass."

Divine, she was fabulous. Vek grinned as the healer stared at her, for once having no ready retort. But then he surprised Vek by throwing back his head and laughing.

"You're one of the few to ever call me on it," Lial finally said. "Though in this case, I hadn't been intending to threaten you. Well done, regardless."

Dria shrugged. "I wasn't seeking your approval."

"Nor do you need it," Lial said with a nod. "Do you have a communication mirror connected to Braelyn? I would like to contact Lyr and let him know the plan."

Kera stood up. "If you'll excuse the interruption, I'd like to offer my travel mirror. I'll show Lial to a spare room and let him use it there."

"That would be perfect," Dria answered. "Thank you."

As Lial followed Kera from the room, Vek eased closer to Dria. Fedah's gaze darted between them, landing on the hand Vek rested on his mate's back, and she smiled. "Would you like me to set up the trap?" the mage asked.

Dria didn't look at Vek, but he could feel her tension beneath his palm. "Please," she answered.

Fen shifted from Vek's side. "I'll help."

In short order, they were alone. Vek grinned at the memory of the last time they'd been by themselves in this room. He slid his hand up her back and gripped the nape of her neck. "Shall I kiss you against the wall again, *caramuin?*"

Her muscles shifted beneath his fingers as she swallowed. "I could immobilize you."

"Whatever works for you," Vek said, chuckling softly. "I trust you not to use me ill."

She let out a sharp, breathy chuckle. "Why are you flirting? I could tell you were angry with me earlier."

Vek trailed his thumb along the side of Dria's neck, making her shiver. "I was unhappy that you might consider yourself a burden. It is impossible for you to hold me back. In truth, you propel me forward, ever closer to the man I should be."

"No." Dria tugged herself free of his grip and faced him. "You don't need me for that."

He brushed a stray hair away from her eyes. "That's true, just as *you* don't technically need *me*. A good partner enhances what is already there. I knew that I no longer wanted to act as my father's enforcer, but I was uncertain if I could stop. You've helped me see that. So instead, I'll protect. My retribution will be reserved for those who would do my loved ones harm."

Dria huffed. "I don't need guarding. I'll confront anyone who bothers me directly."

"Of that, no one could have doubt." He allowed himself a small smile despite the seriousness of his words. "I can't think of a warrior I'd rather have at my side. Maybe together we can keep Fen from acting like an idiot."

That earned him the laugh he'd been hoping for. "Anything's possible. Why don't you grab a couple bowls of soup, and I'll fetch the bread? We can eat in our room and get some sleep."

Vek grabbed two spare bowls. "Which room?"

It was Dria's turn to grin. "I had your things moved to mine. Fen will also be on our hallway."

"Good," Vek answered, his body heating at her haughty tone. "Perhaps after dinner you will put on your formal robes. I'd love to take them off you the way I couldn't when we first met."

She merely laughed as she gathered the bread.

But he rather hoped she would comply.

Hours later, they lay together on the bed, their limbs entwined. Vek stroked his fingers idly through Dria's hair as she slept against his chest. She'd insisted on contacting Ralan and Lyr before they ate their dinner. By the time she had given her report and they'd scarfed down their food, Vek had been too impatient to care if his mate put on her formal robes.

Only a single mage light illuminated the room, and the cave echoed with the silence of near-dawn. But he couldn't sleep. Far too many images of the previous day's events filled his mind. Dria and Fen could have been killed. He could have lost everything with a single careless action on any of their parts. Hell, part of him still feared that he might. Despite their bond, his relationship with Dria was tenuous, her ultimate acceptance not guaranteed.

Unfortunately, only she could overcome her inner turmoil.

Vek willed his body to relax into some semblance of sleep. But as his thoughts began to drift, a new awareness trickled in. A discordant note. He strained his senses, searching for the source. He heard nothing beyond the dripping of water from the stalactite in the corner. No scent beyond the moisture-tinged minerals laced with the herbal smell of the bedding. Not even the air stirred.

He let his eyes drift open, but he didn't sit upright. Cautiously, he stretched out his magic, probing the shielding around their room. Undisturbed. But there was a place in the corner, a spot near the tiny pool where the drops from above gathered, that seemed…off. Darkness was his realm, and he would swear the shadows cast by the mage globe didn't bend the way they should.

Had they guarded the waters?

His arm tightened around Dria's waist, and he jostled her slightly. As soon as she stirred, he connected with her mind. *"Don't sit up. I think someone is in here."*

"The shields are undisturbed," she answered, instantly alert.

"What about the water?"

Her pain flowed between them. *"Gessen dealt with water, and he hadn't had a chance to... Yes, it's a weakness."*

The hair on Vek's arms prickled as the shadows wavered again. *"Did you see that?"*

"No." Her hand tensed and warmed against his chest as though she held back her fire. *"Your unease passes through our bond, but I can detect no reason for it."*

He knew then. It wasn't visual; it was Unseelie magic.

Had Ara found a way to betray him, after all? It wasn't her—he would know her by her blood—but the intruder had been supported by one of his kind.

"It's a cloaking spell," Vek sent. *"Possibly contained in a crystal or other object. It's made to help the wearer become the shadows. But if you're familiar enough with the darkness..."*

"Can you see through the disguise?"

"Not without alerting them." Vek kept his breathing slow and steady, although everything within him wanted to rip out their intruder's throat. Perhaps soon he would get that chance. *"Let them come to us and reveal their plan."*

Vek let his eyes drift nearly closed, narrowing his vision to the barest sliver. The intruder might already know he was awake, but if not, Vek had no intention of giving that away. Nor did Dria. Her chest rose and fell as deeply as it had when she'd slept, but her alert mind remained connected to his.

If not for an Unseelie's superior night vision, Vek never would have seen the black blade against the dark ceiling as his attacker lifted a knife high. Stifling a curse, Vek tried to shift Dria as he lifted his left hand to block the blow. Unfortunately, he only had enough time to slow it.

Vek hissed as the blade pierced his right side where Dria had lain. As she rolled to the other end of the bed, the flame in her hand lighting her face, Vek managed to snag his assailant's wrist. As he twisted the man's arm upward, Vek leaned forward and sank his fangs into flesh.

"Fecking *tralt*," his attacker snarled, jerking against Vek's hold despite the gash the motion caused.

Impure. Though his side burned, Vek smiled at the insult. The precious Seelie might think they were better, but they weren't. As he met Meren's eyes, Vek laughed in the noble's face and squeezed his wrist until the knife dropped from his hand. No, they weren't better.

Far too many used false righteousness to practice evil in the light.

"You're a fool to attack me," Vek said. "I can track you now."

With a surge of power, Meren broke Vek's grip. "I'll shield my blood as my mother did."

Vek smiled. "Don't let your guard down. Ever. And that will only work if you make it out of this room alive."

A whip of fire, thin and precise, flicked across the space between Dria and Meren and snapped against the latter's shields. The Seelie Sidhe danced back from Dria's blow with a chuckle as Vek tossed a ball of magic at the man. Instead of being deflected, the spell clung to the shield and began to eat at it. But slowly. Far too slowly.

"Did you think killing me would get you out of trouble?" Dria asked.

"I no longer care about trouble," Meren answered with a short laugh. "Let all the Seelie know my plan. It's time we fae return to Earth, and I'll war with Moranaia itself to see my goal met. Once I've eliminated you and this pathetic outpost, I'll—"

Crack!

The blast of Dria's lightning cut off his words, the thin tendril snapping against the weak point in his shield created by Vek's corrosive spell. Meren lost his satisfied smile as his defenses fractured. Power vibrated through the room, Dria at the center. Any moment, his mate would finish severing Meren's shields.

Then the fucker disappeared.

Had Vek been hit? Probably, considering the pain echoing in her side. But how badly? While Dria scanned the room with her strongest spells, she activated the mage globe over the bed. Then she braced herself to look.

Preparing herself didn't exactly help. His right side was coated in the blood streaming from a raw, gaping wound beneath his ribs. Despite all Dria had seen that day, her stomach heaved.

Not Vek. Gods, not Vek.

But if he felt the pain, he gave no sign. Vek levered himself upright, power gathering around his hands as he lurched to his feet. Dria scrambled forward, and her knee almost landed on the iron knife in the blankets. She brushed it aside as she rushed to help her bonded stand.

"You're bleeding," she admonished, reaching down to tear a strip of cloth from her nightgown—only to remember she was naked.

As she sent a mental summons to Lial, Dria grabbed a discarded tunic from the floor. Then she pushed it firmly against Vek's wound, drawing a hiss of pain from him.

"What are you doing?" he demanded.

"Saving you," she said. But he stared down at her, confusion and pain clear on his face. "Were you planning to stand here and die? The coward is surely gone, but I'd rather you stick around."

The power winked out in Vek's hands. "You're worried over this?"

"You aren't?"

"I've had far worse injuries than this." He wrapped his fingers around hers and tugged. "My body will already be repairing the wound. Look."

Dria didn't want to see, but as a hint of calm slowed the pounding of her heart, she eased the cloth away. At first, she couldn't identify a difference, but it soon became apparent that the bleeding had stopped. In fact, the hole might be a little smaller.

"We need to hunt Meren," Vek said.

But his voice had gone rough with pain, and his already pale skin had taken on a grayish cast. No matter what he said, something was wrong. Dria sent out a call for Kera and the mages. Meren could wait.

"We will once you are healed," Dria said.

Vek wavered on his feet. "I'll be fine."

Dria shoved the cloth back over his wound and placed his hand across it. "Hold this while I move the knife so you can lie down."

He argued, but she'd barely finished the task before he lost his balance and toppled onto the bed. Her heartbeat drummed in her ears at the increasing pallor of his skin and the dazed look in his eyes. Dria knelt on the bed beside him as the door slammed open and Kera rushed in, Lial and Fedah close behind.

"Guard us," Dria said to Kera and Fedah. "Search for every type of invisibility spell you know, especially those connected to water or shadow." Trusting them to do their jobs, she glanced up at Lial as he neared. "He said it was minor. I saw the wound closing myself, but something isn't right. Maybe because the knife was iron."

"No allergy," Vek whispered.

With a few quick tugs, Lial shifted Vek until he was stretched lengthwise along the bed. "Let me see."

The blue healer's light turned Vek's skin an even more sickly shade, and she shivered. Only moments must have passed, but it could have been an eternity. Finally, Lial spoke. "Perforated bowel and internal bleeding. If you've blood and energy to spare, give it."

Those stark words speared her heart. Trembling, Dria lowered her wrist to Vek's mouth and slid it against his fangs. His eyes had drifted shut, but he wasn't unconscious, for he actively drew at her blood—and her power. She settled beside him and rested her head on his left shoulder, content to let him take what he needed.

Beneath her ear, his heartbeat thrummed steadily, and hers slowed to match it. Everything matched him, a truth she hoped she hadn't discovered too late. Why was it always so difficult to share herself with others? It was easier by far to fight them, to confront them until they did what she expected and fled.

But Vek…he saw everything inside of her and accepted each piece.

Each and every shattered fragment.

35

Vek stirred beneath her, and his hand lifted slowly to tangle in her hair. "*Cara-muin?*"

Dria shifted onto her elbow and blinked sleepily down at his blurry face. Her wrist had fallen away at some point, and she must have drifted to sleep. Rubbing her eyes, she searched for Lial and found him in a chair near the bed, his head resting against the tall back.

When she caught his gaze, he smiled. "You did well to call me."

"I admit that for once I am happy to be ignored," Vek muttered.

She swiped her hair out of her face and struggled to form thoughts. It took far too long for her brain to catch up. Vek must have taken a great deal of her blood. "It was worse than he thought?"

"I would say so," Lial answered. "We may not suffer from diseases the way humans do, but no living thing does well when the contents of the intestines slip into the bloodstream."

Vek's chest heaved in a sigh. "That's never happened before."

Dria smiled at the exasperation in his tone. Her head began to clear, and she pushed herself to a sitting position so she could glance around the room. Kera and Fedah stood guard beside the outer door, and one of the mages studied the puddle of water in the corner. Vek's hand rested against her hip, and at the caress of his thumb, she stiffened.

She was still naked.

Ah, well. Her cousin was a healer. He would know very well why her nipples beaded and her skin flushed at her bonded's touch, even if she was too tired to act on her desire, but Lial wouldn't be shocked. Sure enough, with a slight smile, he rose and headed toward the door. He must have given the others an unusual look or silent mental command, for they filed out ahead of him.

At the door, he turned. "The protections were strengthened while you rested, but it might be wise to put another layer around your bed for greater warning. And try not to be too rough. Vek's wound is closed, but the area is still weak."

Vek chuckled as the door closed behind Lial, but Dria didn't laugh. Instead, she studied her bonded's tired face. He could have died, as she'd feared he would. Just like Gessen. But she wouldn't have regretted bonding with Vek. No, what she would have regretted the most was not sharing her love with him.

"I don't even know how it happened," she whispered.

Vek's brows quirked. "The attack?"

"No." She smiled. "Well, yes, but that's not what I was thinking about. I was more considering love."

His expression went blank. "Love."

"It makes no sense." Dria poked a finger into his ribs, though her smile remained. "You're contrary, stubborn, and difficult, and we argue as much as anything. But somehow, I still fell in love with you."

"You needn't say that because I nearly died," Vek admonished. "I told you I wouldn't leave you, and I meant it."

Dria snorted. "Not even you can promise not to die."

"True, I suppose." Finally, a small smile appeared. "But I'd probably haunt you. I imagine I would make an excellent ghost."

Laughing, Dria settled against his side. Her fingers drifted across the place where he'd been injured, but the skin was smooth now. And blessedly clean. "At least my cousin was kind enough to get rid of the blood. The spell might not be as emotionally satisfying as bathing, but it's more efficient. I've seen more than enough blood. Honestly, I'm considering changing my hair color again so I don't have to see red in the mirror."

Vek twined a strand around his finger. "If you want, though I admit I like the color. Very royal."

"Only if you're *Felshreh*, love," she said, and the endearment came surprisingly easily to her lips. It was just…right.

Her eyes started to drift closed, but then the blasted communication mirror let out a chime. By the tone, she could tell it was her brother. "I knew I shouldn't have agreed to lead this outpost," she grumbled. "It. Never. Ends."

Vek's laugh rumbled against her ear. "Now, *ahmeeren*, it might have been centuries before we encountered each other had you not traveled here."

"Shut up and get dressed," Dria said.

Perhaps if Ralan's message wasn't dire, she and Vek could tumble back into bed. But of course, there was a great deal to be done. Their shielding was inadequate against Unseelie magic, and with the fae races waking on Earth, she needed to ensure that the outpost was guarded against a greater variety of magics. And gods only knew what else might happen.

Dria grabbed the first clean clothes she found in her trunk—a simple training robe—and threw it on before striding toward the mirror. Vek had managed to find his own clothes, but he didn't join her, instead slumping into the seat Lial had abandoned. She couldn't help but feel envy at that. She might not be angry at her brother anymore, but she would rather not be talking to him this early in the morning, either.

With a sigh, she activated her side of the connection. Ralan's stark, weary face replaced her own reflection, and she blinked in surprise at how upset he appeared. "Is something wrong?"

"Besides knowing what I was sending you into but being unable to stop it?" Ralan snapped. Then he took a deep breath. "Sorry. I sent the sword, hoping it would help. Were you injured? The future strands don't indicate it, but I can't see the past and—"

"I'm fine, Ralan," Dria said firmly. A sternness that hid how much his words meant to her. "Vek was hurt by Meren, but Lial was here to heal him."

Vek joined her at the mirror. "Thank you for the sword. We wouldn't have escaped our battles mostly unscathed without it."

Some of the worry on Ralan's face faded. "You're welcome."

"I don't want to sound rude," Dria began, "but is there more to this call than checking on me? I'm too tired to hold my end of this connection for long. Not that I don't want to talk to you, but this distance..."

Ralan nodded. "I understand. I have a few orders for you, but that's all."

"From you or Father?"

"Technically Father but mostly me," Ralan answered with a smile. "I'm having a water mage sent from the Citadel. Shield every drop, or you'll risk Meren sneaking in again. It's his strongest element. Also, work with Vek to guard against Unseelie magic, and be prepared for Kezari to return to give aid when she gets tired of Aris fretting about disease."

"But we need to track Meren." Dria's hands tightened into fists at the memory of her bonded's injury. "He has much to answer for."

Ralan shook his head. "That's a task for Caolte. Kai's uncle. But it will be some time before he can bring Meren to justice. And that's provided that he... Never mind. You're to guard against Meren's return, but you shouldn't seek to engage. The purpose of the outpost is safety, and I'm not just talking about protecting the portal. There are those who will need your help."

Like the woman on the bridge, Dria thought.

"If we find Moranaian half-bloods, are we to bring them here?" she asked.

"Provided they are not a threat," Ralan answered wearily. "And if they are, I suppose we'll have to consider our next steps. I'll speak with Father on the matter and get back to you."

A wave of dizziness hit her, and her stomach rolled. "Anything else? I'm about to run out of energy."

"No orders. Just..." Ralan rubbed his palms against his temples. "I'm sorry about Gessen. I'd hoped that strand wouldn't happen, Dree."

She gave him a sad smile. "It wasn't your fault."

None of the things that had happened between them was his fault, not entirely,

and that realization filled her with an unexpected lightness. He'd had his own troubles to deal with and had done the best he could. After all, Ralan was a seer, not a god.

"I will make certain you will be able to attend Gessen's funeral," Ralan said.

"Thank you," Dria answered, and her head swam again. "I have to go. I love you."

Surprise crossed Ralan's face, but he smiled. "I love you, too, Dree."

As soon as the connection closed, Dria sagged against Vek. So much for a pleasant morning in bed—at this rate, she would need to sleep all day to be able to function. "I'd ask you to share blood again, but then I'd end up needing to feed you, too," she muttered.

Vek snickered. "After my injury? Probably."

A knock sounded on the door, and this time, they both groaned. Dria swept her magic outward to find an uneasy Fen on the other side. Gathering the last remnants of her energy, she trudged over to let her bond-nephew in. As soon as the door swung inward, he strode through.

"Maddy texted me," Fen said at once. "Things may be starting to heat up soon. According to the news, there are reports of witches doing real magic in places like Salem, and an entire town in Scotland swears they saw a dragon flying over the mountains. I wouldn't be surprised if we don't start hearing about dormant mythological creatures popping up around the world now that they have enough energy to awaken."

Dria huffed. "Well, they're going to have to wait until I have a nap. I don't have the energy to deal with any new problems right now."

Fen eyed them both. "You guys look like hell. I thought Lial healed Vek? That's what he said when I tried to come in earlier. Seemed like you were sleeping then."

"Thanks, Fen," Vek said dryly. "If you'd like to help, how about you give me a bit of blood and then fuck off?"

The younger man merely laughed. "Fine, fine. I'll go see if I can find out more from Maddy while you sleep. Or see if Delbin and Inona are back from their latest trip to the city."

"So long as you don't cause trouble," Vek said. "We've had more than enough of that."

"I suppose," Fen said with a grin. Then he held out his arm for his uncle.

While Vek fed, Dria stumbled over to the bed and dropped face-first into the pillow. She was already dozing by the time her bonded joined her, but she smiled when he tugged her against him. His warmth lulled her gently into sleep.

It was unusual to be standing in the Moranaian throne room as family instead of a visitor, but Vek had experienced stranger things. Based on some of the glances he'd received as he marched in beside Dria in formal *Felshreh* reds, his sword strapped to his back, a few of the courtiers here hadn't led such eventful lives. But he wasn't here for them. He never would be.

In front of the throne, Gessen had been laid out in state. Vek had no idea what the man's original rank had been, but the funeral rites would have suited a prince. The entire royal family stood on the dais, including Dria's mother, as the priest chanted to the gods. Vek didn't bother to listen. His attention was on his mate.

She gripped his hand in hers, but her face showed no sign of the turmoil he felt from her. Helplessness ate at him, for not even he could protect her from grief. But as the attendants lifted the bier holding Gessen, Vek shoved his own feelings aside. Dria needed him.

Her breath hitched as the royal family followed Gessen's parents in the long procession to the cliff where the pyre would be lit. There were no words he could give her in this moment, nor was there anything he could say that would ease the agony echoing between them as Gessen's mother called down the flame to start the fire.

Vek merely stood with his mate until the pyre was little more than ash.

Eventually, he followed her along the line of the ridge until they were alone. The mountain view was spectacular, but all he could look at was his mate's agonized face. She'd already spoken with Gessen's parents, and although they hadn't seemed to blame her, he was afraid that part of her would always blame herself. But he couldn't fix that for her, either.

"It doesn't seem real," Dria whispered.

"I know, love. The worst things never do."

"Hold me?" she asked, and Vek gathered her close, though she startled when her hands reached his sword. "I can't believe you came armed to a funeral."

He frowned. "Is this an honor not bestowed to fallen soldiers in your culture?"

"Not typically," Dria answered. "Perhaps no one wants to risk further bloodshed."

"Why do you think I strapped it to my back?" Vek chuckled into her hair. "Have you ever tried to draw a sword that way? It's not easy. But I thought his warrior's death should be honored the way my own kind would."

Dria shook her head against his chest. "I do love you. I'm not sure why sometimes, but there you have it."

"As I love you," he answered without hesitation.

"Thank you for withstanding the stares to be with me." She tilted back until she could meet his eyes. "It must have been awkward since you haven't been formally introduced as my bonded."

Vek shrugged. "You know I'd face far worse."

And he would.

Forever, he would.

Ascent

Character Pronunciation Guide

Ascent

Main Characters:

Anna (ANN-uh)
Fen (fehn)
Maddy (maddee)

Secondary Characters:

Dria (DREE-uh)
Lera (LEHR-uh)
Meli (MEHL-ee)
Meren (MEHR-ehn)
Shayan (SHAY-ehn)
Tatianella (tah-TEE-ah-NEHL-uh)
Torlahn (TOR-lahn)
Vek (vehk)

1

A muffled shriek sounded through the door just as Fen shoved his key in the lock. With a quick burst of magic, he scanned his uncle Vek's house for any sign of danger. The place should have been empty, but—no. Vek and Dria were there. Another shriek echoed through the wood, and the cry didn't sound like it was made in pleasure.

Vek might do many unusual things, but torturing his mate wasn't one of them.

After another sharp twist of the key, Fen finally got the damned lock to budge. He barged through the door, ready to mess up anyone who dared to attack his family, only to freeze. His keys dropped out of his hand with a clatter.

This was…not what he was expecting to see.

On the television on the far wall, a banshee darted around a decrepit building, and another piercing scream filled the room. Vek cursed, his fingers struggling to find the correct buttons on the game controller as the banshee headed straight for his avatar. Beside him, Dria let out a wicked laugh as her own character blasted the enemy with a stream of flame.

"Thank the gods for that mana potion," she said. "Too bad Lial can't mix one of those up in real life."

Fen's mouth dropped open. Those fuckers were playing his copy of the new *Death's Curse 3*. The very game he'd bought yesterday so he could continue his gaming marathon with Maddy and Anna. Not that he was going to tell his uncle that part. Vek teased Fen too much about his possible mates already, and that was without knowing how much Fen had been hanging out with them—despite neither woman having a clue about their potential three-person bond. He'd barely managed to tell Maddy that she could be his mate. He hadn't been brave enough to reveal the whole of it.

"What the hell?" Fen yelped. "I hadn't even opened that yet. That's bad gamer etiquette, Vek."

His uncle didn't even have the grace to look away from the screen. "You wanted me to introduce Dria to human technology."

"And you thought my new game would be the way to go? Seriously?" Fen snatched up his keys before slamming the door closed. "You could have picked literally anything else. There are at least ten other games that aren't shrink wrapped, for starters. Hell, there's a whole world of human technology out there."

"This game was on top." Vek shrugged before casting him a meaningful look. "I wanted her to relax and take her mind off her duties at the outpost. According to you, this is the best way." The banshee let out another scream, incinerating Vek's avatar. "Not sure I see the appeal."

"I'll avenge you," Dria said cheerfully.

But the hint of sadness around her eyes bellied her tone, and Vek's actions suddenly made sense. It had only been a couple of weeks since her friend Gessen had died defending her and Vek during an attempted invasion of the underground elven outpost. There hadn't been any further attacks, but that also meant there were no distractions.

"I didn't think you could leave the cave for very long," Fen said. "What if something happens?"

"We brought Fedah through so she would know where to build a portal if necessary," Dria answered.

Fen's steps slowed as he neared the couch. His uncle was unlikely to appreciate his suggestion, but he was going to offer it anyway. Because portals might be a quick way to travel, but they were a terrible way to notify someone of an emergency. And not even Delbin, the strongest telepath among them, could send a mental warning from the cave to Vek's house.

"You guys should get cell phones," Fen said as he sat down on the other side of the L-shaped couch.

Vek's eyes narrowed on the screen when Dria's character was defeated and both their avatars respawned. "Let's cut down the alley this time," Vek said to Dria.

Fen assessed the scene and grimaced at the mistake his uncle was about to make. Decrepit buildings? Check. Creepy ambient lighting? Double check. There was probably awesome loot down that alley, but there would also be about a million mobs. A pro could do it, but Vek? When it came to gaming, Vek had noob written all over him.

"I don't think that's a—"

A loud shriek made all three of them jump. Three banshees floated from behind a dark, graffiti-covered trash container, and a pair of vampires dropped from the roofs on each side. At the end of the alley, countless red eyes glowed through the gloom. They were so screwed.

Dria's avatar blasted light at the vampires, a bold move considering how much power those spells took. But she'd already accessed her inventory for a potion and downed it before Vek even got his character moving. His giant warrior barreled down the alley like a modern Leroy Jenkins.

The wolves at the end of the alley charged, and despite Dria's quick spell-casting, she and Vek were defeated in moments. As the spawn point popped up on the screen, Vek cursed and smacked his controller down beside him. Huffing, Dria dropped her head against the back of the couch.

"What were you trying to say before I got us killed?" Vek grumbled.

Fen smirked. "I was trying to warn you not to go down that alley. Gotta say, Dria has promise, but you may be hopeless. You hadn't even drawn your sword."

"I forgot the button." Vek glared at the controller as though it was supposed to do everything itself. "But that's not what I meant. You said something about a phone?"

"It seemed like a good idea, but now I'm not so sure." His uncle's scowl deepened, increasing Fen's amusement. Vek might know a great deal more about their heritage and blood magic abilities, but Fen was the master when it came to the human world. "There are a lot more buttons on a phone."

Straightening, Dria chuckled. "He's not that bad. He showed me how to game, after all."

Vek scrubbed his hand across his pale face. "Something like that. Why do you keep playing this stuff? The story isn't even accurate. The Bean Sidhe *do* deliver harsh news, but they don't go out attacking people like that. Honestly, many of them live perfectly normal lives outside—"

"Cut it, Captain Buzzkill." Fen's grin widened at his uncle's blank stare. "Stop ruining the fun. It's fiction. FIC. TION."

"Stressful fiction," Vek muttered. "Anyway, I am no idiot. I can learn to operate a cell phone."

Of course his uncle could, but that wouldn't stop Fen from pestering him. "Maybe," Fen drawled. "If you can get past all of the controls, it would be useful. I bet you could both learn the spell to boost a cell signal. Or I could help set something up throughout the cave system. A call or text would be much faster than creating a portal to come find you."

"Sounds good to me." Excitement lighting her eyes, Dria leaned forward. "How difficult is it to acquire one of these phones?"

Fen shrugged. "An hour or two, probably. Damned store is always slammed."

Dria's shoulders slumped. "We have to be back at the outpost soon. Kezari is traveling from Moranaia for a few hours to help fortify our protections against earth magic, and I believe she wants to scan for evidence of dragon magic after that report of a dragon sighting in the place called Scotland."

"Is she flying over there?" He'd met the dragon in passing a few times at the outpost, and she was…interesting. Though she was usually shifted into elven form when he saw her, he would never mistake her as one of the Moranaians. "Because Scotland is on another continent."

Dria's eyes widened, but she didn't comment on the distance. "I suppose that's a dragon problem."

"Well, I can't help with that," Fen said. "But I can run by the wireless store and grab a couple of phones for you. It'll cost me more to add a family plan, though.

Turning good hasn't been great for my bank account."

Vek waved a hand. "I will ensure you have ample wealth. Enough, I might add, to pay back those you have stolen from in the past."

Heat climbed up Fen's neck. He'd been joking, but obviously his uncle thought he'd lived a life of crime. Sure, he'd done some fucked up shit after he'd made the mistake of joining Kien's group, but he had never stolen anything he hadn't needed for survival. Even that had been when he was far younger.

"Not cool," Fen said softly before shoving to his feet. "You know what? You can get your own damned plan."

His uncle grimaced. "Forgive me if I caused offense."

"I've actually earned my own money for years, you know." Fen set his shoulders. "Odd jobs here and there. Selling gems I mined and shaped with my own talents. But if you'd like to throw money at random grocery stores in my hometown, I guess you could pay them back for the food I stole when I first hit the streets."

"Fen—"

"Sorry. Just…" Fen took a deep, calming breath. He'd been unusually sensitive since meeting his mother in person for the first time. He couldn't seem to stop himself. "Just drop it. It's been a long day, and I was *hoping* I could pop open my new game to relax."

After inviting Anna and Maddy over—but he sure as hell wasn't mentioning that.

His uncle's somber expression didn't fade at the weak attempt to lighten the mood, though he didn't press for more discussion or waste time on another apology. Instead, Vek lifted the controller and jiggled it at Fen. "Fine, then. Come show us how it's done."

With a slight smile, Fen complied. Dria wasn't the only one who needed a distraction. Besides, it wouldn't hurt to have a head start on the game before he faced the girls. He might even manage to win a match next time they did player vs. player. Anything was possible.

Maddy braided her long hair and then scrunched her nose at the result. How could her hair be both oily and frizzy at the same time? With a huff, she tugged the strands loose and grabbed the dry shampoo. Late summer in the South, that was why. She could go a week without washing the mess, and the humidity would still send little fly-aways sticking in the air like the spines of a red cactus.

Fifteen minutes later, she snapped the elastic band around the end of her braid, surveyed the results, and gave up. Most of the full-blooded fae she'd met were fastidious about their appearance, and Maddy had seen nothing to indicate that the Moranaian elves were any different. She was not going to negotiate with one of their healers while looking like she'd been electrocuted by a lightning spell gone wrong. A glamour it was. With a quick burst of magic, she smoothed the pesky stray pieces out of sight until the plait was as smooth and lovely as her full-blood Sidhe grand-mother's finest coiffure.

"What's taking so long?" Anna called from the other room.

After wiping her damp palms along her jeans, Maddy headed out of their small bathroom. Anna stood beside the bedroom door, and Maddy couldn't help but give her girlfriend an admiring glance. Anna's uniform might be serviceable, but it did little to hide her gorgeous curves. Too bad they both had things to do.

"Sorry," Maddy said, following her down the hallway. "I'm just nervous. I don't want to look awful when I talk to the healer."

"As if that's a possibility." Laughing, Anna skimmed her gaze down Maddy's body. "Yep. Beautiful as always."

Maddy grinned as they wove between the coffee table, couch, and dining room table to reach the front door. Their snug condo was just enough for the two of them. Barely. "It's a glamour. Not even the best hair products are a match for river air in the summer."

As if in agreement, the humidity closed around her in an unwelcome embrace when she stepped outside. Anna's chin-length hair outdid both product and glamour, though it hadn't always been so smooth. It had to be her newly awakened fae blood. Water didn't seem to react to her the same way, and enough energy swirled about her that Maddy worried it might be causing her problems. But Maddy hadn't pushed her to talk about it since Anna clearly wasn't ready.

There was no sign of turmoil on Anna's face as she slid into the passenger seat. "I hate that you have to go out of your way to take me to work," Anna said. "At least the repairs on my car won't be too much."

Maddy plopped her purse onto the center console. "I told you that my father would—"

"You know how I feel about that." Anna's bottom lip turned down in the way that never failed to make Maddy want to kiss her. Not the effect her girlfriend was going for, but that didn't seem to matter. "Maybe after we get married. Until then, your family shouldn't pay for everything. It doesn't seem right."

With a sigh, Maddy put the car in reverse and carefully backed out of the drive-way. It was an old argument, and one that wouldn't be won today. Even so, she was tempted to try. So what if they'd only lived together for ten months of the eighteen that they'd been together? If Anna wasn't so stressed about paying half the mortgage on the condo, she could work at the restaurant part time and write more. It wasn't *that* unusual to let a significant other offer support.

"Then maybe we should pick a date," Maddy finally said.

Silence stretched between them until Maddy's chest squeezed in alarm. She tried to figure out Anna's expression the best she could with a few quick glances, but the traffic was too heavy for her to make a study of it. "Anna?"

"You're still sure about getting married, right?"

Maddy's hands tightened around the steering wheel. If it wouldn't make Anna

late for work, she would have pulled over. "Of course. I can't believe you would even ask that."

"I know. I'm sorry. But…" Anna shifted against her seat belt. "You've been acting funny since you met Fen, and now that we've been spending time with him… Look, I know you love me, but are you having second thoughts?"

Maddy nibbled on her lip. She'd been trying to find a way to talk to Anna about Fen, but what could she say? His revelation had stunned her, and she hadn't figured out quite what to do about it. *According to Vek, we could be mates,* he'd said. *And taking your blood would seal the bond.*

How could she tell her beloved that?

Not even Maddy and Fen had talked about it since that day, though sometimes she was certain he was thinking about the unresolved truth hanging between them. How many times had he glanced away from her with a blush in the last couple of weeks? Though come to think of it, he'd stared at Anna with a strange expression, too, and quiet Anna had fumbled her words more than once in his presence.

"You don't exactly ignore him," Maddy pointed out. "And you tend to be attracted to guys less than I am."

Anna surprised her by nodding. "You're right. Whenever I'm around him, I feel…I don't know how to describe it. An odd pull, I guess. And I like him as a person."

"I do, too," Maddy agreed.

"But you don't seem like you're shaking off the feeling the way I do."

The stoplight turned red, and Maddy eased the car to a halt. For once, she was grateful for the delay, since it gave her the chance to meet Anna's gaze. "Absolutely nothing could change my love for you. I'm sorry if the last couple of months have made you doubt that. I can't imagine any relationship that didn't have you in it."

"I love you, too." Anna reached over to squeeze Maddy's thigh. "So it's sort of weird that we're both drawn to Fen. I'm sorry if I worried you, but I had to ask. I wouldn't want to be in a relationship without you, either."

A loud honk made them both jump. The light had turned. Maddy forced her attention back to the road and started the car forward. "We can puzzle it out later. I'd better get you to work on time so you can get your prep tasks done before the evening rush. Plus, I want to see how Tamara is doing at the shop before I call Moranaia."

"Probably a good idea."

It would be a nice procrastination tactic if nothing else. For two weeks, Maddy had avoided giving the Moranaian healer an answer to his offer to teach her, and there was a good chance he wouldn't like what she had to say once she did. Yes, her gift needed training. She couldn't use her healing magic without risking harm to the patient, and the Sidhe, her father's people, had no interest in teaching her since she was half human. But she couldn't relocate to another world for a few decades—or centuries—either. No way.

If the healer couldn't deal with that, she didn't know what she would do.

After she kissed Anna goodbye in the restaurant parking lot, she straightened her spine and backed the car out with all the confidence she could muster. It wouldn't stop her from finding a solution if Lial refused to accept her terms. She wouldn't let it.

2

Maddy snatched her purse from the center console and slung the strap over her shoulder as she rushed from the car. Thanks to protesters blocking part of the Market Street bridge, she was running later than expected. Not that she blamed them—they *did* deserve to know the truth about magic's return to Earth. The baffled local government might have tried to hide the women lobbing fireballs, lightning, and other bits of magic at each other on that very bridge, but the fight had been caught on film. There was no way to deflect something like that.

At least the news crew hadn't been able to get closer than a neighboring bridge during the initial incident, and the protection shield that had surrounded the fighting pair had obscured fine details like facial features. Otherwise, Maddy never would have gotten away with hiring Tamara, one of the two on the bridge. But the fight hadn't been Tamara's fault. The poor woman hadn't had a clue that she was half-Sidhe, and the full-blooded Sidhe who'd tried to abduct her had gotten what she deserved when Vek and Dria intervened.

As Maddy hurried along the side street that led to the back of the shop, she studied the area out of reflex. The crowds were thinner now that summer was nearing its close, both in the connecting alleys and the larger streets. Tourists poured in from surrounding areas for short getaways or trips to the aquarium in June and July, but there was typically a lull when school was solidly in session.

Too bad there wasn't a lull in the heat. A fine sheen of sweat covered her skin as she neared the back entrance to the shop, but her palms dampened further at the sight of a man emerging from the alley that ran beside the store. He had mahogany skin, closely cropped curly hair, and a frown, but none of that caused her heartrate to surge.

The strong, well-constructed shield of magic that surrounded him? Yeah, that could be a problem.

Maddy had been kidnapped in this very spot a few weeks ago by a pair of half-blood fae working for the rogue Moranaian prince Kien. This was *not* the place for a magic user to confront her. She might not have learned how to consistently fix illnesses, but she could kill. It would suck, she would probably hate herself, and she might go to jail—but she wasn't going to be kidnapped by anyone again.

She gathered healing magic in her palm and clenched her fingers around it. The power fluctuated, kicking her already pounding heart into overdrive, but she managed to wrestle it under control. She'd rarely used her abilities since energy had returned to Earth, and the amount of available power made holding onto magic now a real challenge.

Gods, I hope I can arrange that training.

"Excuse me," the man said.

Maddy stopped as far away as she could without being outright rude. "You'll want to head back to the main road. There's not much to see on this side street."

His frown deepened, though whether it was at her sharp, unfriendly tone or something else, she didn't know. "I'm not a tourist looking for the shops. You're Maddy, right?"

"Like I'm telling some rando in an alley." She tightened her hold on the energy in her hand before anxiety could shred her control. "You have a few seconds to explain what you want and go. Honestly, I don't even owe you that."

"Damn, that's harsh," the guy muttered. "But I guess it's deserved since I haven't introduced myself. My name's Anthony, and I promise I'm not here to cause you trouble. I might look—"

"You look fine, but that magic around you isn't exactly reassuring."

His mouth dropped open. "You're worried about my protection shield? Seriously? You got one, too. Might as well've grabbed your purse and rushed on by."

Maddy's skin heated. Dammit, she was overreacting, and not for the reason he thought. Nothing about the guy was threatening beyond the evidence that he possessed magic. His energy signature was as calm and easy as the breeze trying to waft in from the river, and he didn't have the vibe of any of the dangerous fae who sometimes came into the shop. It was this stupid back street, so close to where Kien's men had snatched her into their car at knifepoint.

"Sorry," Maddy said, still cautious but no longer afraid. "Last time someone approached me out here, it didn't go well."

Anthony grimaced. "Shit. Sounds like I'm the one who should be sorry. I know how those kinds of memories can be."

Though her curiosity stirred at the shadows that entered his eyes, Maddy didn't ask. She had enough of her own problems without delving into a stranger's. "So why are you out here looking for me?"

"I need help with a problem, and a couple of white guys directed me your way. They gave me a code. Something about clothing." His brow furrowed for a moment before he snapped his fingers. "Clothing is magic. As am I."

Maddy let her magic disperse—but not fully. "You're supposed to go into the shop."

"I did, but the woman inside said you weren't there." Anthony shrugged. "I was

told to talk to you. I didn't mean to scare you, but I was heading back to the parking lot when I saw you. You matched the description I was given, so I thought I'd take a chance."

Her nervousness eased, but the knot in her stomach didn't fade. That had nothing to do with the handsome man staring at her expectantly. "I have an appointment in…" Maddy checked her watch. "Ten minutes. If you can wait a while, we can talk, but you'll have to come back later if you're in a hurry."

He smiled. "I've got an hour, so sounds good if your meeting won't be too long."

"Shouldn't be." Maddy gestured toward the alley. "Let's head up to the front."

Thankfully, Anthony didn't seem to mind. The back entrance might be closer, but she wasn't letting anyone but employees or really good friends through that way. In fact, she would rather strangers not realize there was another entrance. Maybe she should change where she parked and avoid the other door entirely for a while.

The kidnapping had made her far too jumpy. It wasn't unreasonable to be cautious when walking alone in the city, but she wasn't usually rude without cause. The man could have been a fae tourist for all she knew. It was more common than most humans realized.

Anthony held the shop door open, and she entered with a grateful smile. Maddy waved at Tamara, who was ringing up a customer at the counter, and headed straight for the back corner. This time, she opened the door marked Staff Only and gestured for Anthony to precede her. If he sensed the shielding and refused to go in, that would tell its own story.

But although he appeared a touch uneasy—understandable—he entered the small break room without comment. There wasn't much in here, just a table, chairs, a tiny cabinet with a microwave, and another door leading to the stockroom. The true importance of the place only became obvious when she closed the door behind her and the shielding locked fully into place.

The protections here had been designed by her friend Cora, who had owned The Magic Touch before moving to Moranaia with Prince Ralan. The shields were clever, for although they mostly seemed to prevent anyone outside the room from scrying or overhearing by mundane means, they could also be used to barricade a dangerous or threatening fae inside. With enough power, the protections would keep anyone in or out. If she was going to trust an unknown fae man alone in her shop while she made the most important mirror call of her life, he would have to stay in this room. It might have been different if Jase were here, but Tamara had too little training to be put in charge of keeping them safe.

Anthony pivoted, his eyes going wide as his magic connected with the shields. "Maybe I should be the one worried."

Despite the nerves winding tighter at the thought of the mirror call, Maddy summoned her most reassuring smile. "The magic keeps us safe and ensures that our conversation is private. You knew the secret code. Don't you know what we do here?"

"You help newly arrived fae get what they need to blend into the human world."

Maddy nodded. "And as you might imagine, that involves some potentially dangerous fae. That's the reason for the shielding. But the well-intentioned never seem to mind."

He gave a quick grin. "Gotta say, I didn't think a clothing store could get so dangerous."

"There's more to blending in than clothes." Maddy skimmed her gaze along his perfectly modern T-shirt and jeans. "Which is something you don't seem to need."

He shrugged. "No weird-ass robes for me. I was born here."

"Then why—" Cheerful but insistent ringing sounded from her pocket, and she tugged her phone free to turn off the alarm. "I have to go. I promise I'll be back in a few minutes. On my honor as a Seelie Sidhe, you aren't in any danger in our safe room. Just give me ten or twenty minutes, and we can talk."

After a thankfully brief study, Anthony nodded. "I'll wait right here."

Maddy didn't have time to give him more reassurances. She exited into the main part of the shop so she could swing by the counter. The bell at the front jingled as their only customer carried her purchase out the door, and Tamara shot Maddy a nervous smile. Difficult to believe that such a sweet woman had been hurling deadly spells off the Market Street Bridge only a couple of weeks ago.

Crazy what fear would do.

Pausing at the end of the counter, Maddy leaned close. "If my new friend Anthony tries to leave, let him. I don't have the shielding fully engaged. But stay out here, and don't let anyone in that room. Even though he knew the passphrase, I have no idea if he's trustworthy."

Tamara gripped the edge of the counter. "You're leaving me alone with him?"

"My meeting, remember? I'll still be in the shop." Maddy patted Tamara's arm. "If you have to come into the stockroom, that's fine, but try to keep people from seeing inside it. I have my mirror angled where no one should spot anything, but you never know. And if there's any hint of danger, don't hesitate to interrupt. I'll adjust the shielding on the storage room."

"Ah...sure."

Maddy peered at the phone still in her hand and grimaced. "Gotta go."

She was late. One of the most important meetings of her life, and she was late.

Anna tried her best not to stare out the window instead of rolling silverware into napkins, but it was a battle hard won. Tuck. Fold. Wrap. Glance through the glass at the river flowing a few yards beyond the restaurant. Tuck. Fold. Wrap. Glance again. The pull was maddening, and it was only getting stronger.

How long would she be able to keep this up? She'd talked to Maddy about her newfound affinity for water after magic had returned to Earth, but she hadn't gone into as much detail as she could have. It was controllable, after all. Why worry Maddy about something that Anna could handle, especially since Maddy was finally close to getting the training she dearly needed?

But today, the pull of water promised to snatch that control away like a flooded river sweeping away a hapless car. Anna longed to walk into the depths of the river and never surface.

Not to die, though. That was the last thing on her mind. She suspected that no water would kill her, at least not freshwater. Anna hadn't tried to visit the ocean, but she had tortured herself with a trip to the aquarium after her powers had awakened. Excitement had grown within her as she'd ascended the long escalator to the top of the building containing the ocean exhibits, but although she'd felt a slight tug to the saltwater tanks, it was more mellow contentment thrumming within her rather than wild anticipation.

But the building with freshwater exhibits? She'd had to take an elevator down and leave the area entirely when she'd neared the larger tanks. Otherwise, she might have jumped in and made a fool of herself. That—that type of environment felt like home.

"You better hurry it up," Deanna, her manager, called from a few tables over. "I give it thirty minutes before we have to start seating your section. Y'all don't get your prep work done, it's always hell. Cory only has half the sweetener packs replaced."

"I'm sorry," Anna said earnestly, doing her best to concentrate on her work.

It wasn't the best job, but Deanna was a decent boss. Reasonable with hours, time off requests, and breaks, which worked well with Anna's writing. Deanna was also fairer about side tasks than some of the other places where Anna had worked. She'd already be done with the silverware if the river didn't keep distracting her. Why did the pull seem to be getting stronger?

Even when she didn't look, the power of it swished along with her blood and vibrated in her very muscles. Anna had heard that a woman in labor felt the undeniable urge to push, an instinct that was almost impossible to resist. Well, she had a similar drive, if a bit opposite. Instead of emerging, she itched to submerge herself in the quiet, underwater realm.

It was going to drive her insane.

If the intensity kept growing, she would have no choice but to talk to Maddy. Considering how little she understood about magic, it would be foolish not to, but she would do her best to maintain her control until Maddy got her needed training. It wouldn't take long for Maddy to get to a level where her healing magic wasn't a danger, right? She had to hope.

Maddy frowned into the mirror she'd propped beside her computer monitor. "He's not there yet?"

Her friend Cora, once the owner of The Magic Touch and now married—soulbound, they said there—to Prince Ralan of Moranaia, gave a sheepish grin. "And you were worried about being late. One of the warriors slipped in a patch of ice and broke his wrist, so Lial had to rush to the practice field. He sent word that he would be here in a few minutes. Is that okay?"

With a silent apology for poor Anthony waiting in the other room, Maddy nodded. "If it's only a few."

"How are things going there?" Cora asked. "Is Jase doing fine? And how is the new girl settling in?"

Maddy chuckled at the eager questions. For the most part, Cora hadn't seemed to mind moving to another world with Ralan, but it was obvious that she missed her friends on Earth, too. "The shop is fine, and we even made more than usual last month. Jase took a few days of vacation to go to Gatlinburg with his girlfriend, and Tamara is fitting in perfectly. She's still hesitant about her magic, but actually understanding what is happening to her solved most of her problems. You'd like her."

"I'm sure we'll meet once I can travel again," Cora said, rubbing her hand across her barely rounded belly.

"It's driving you crazy, isn't it?" Maddy asked.

"The baby?" Cora frowned. "No. Even the morning sickness is eased with Lial's potion."

Maddy rolled her eyes. "Of course not the baby. The being bound to Moranaia until the birth part."

"Oh." Cora's breath rushed out in a soft laugh. "Yeah, that's a problem. But she will only prosper if she's immersed in the magic of this world. I wouldn't risk losing her for anything."

"I know."

Cora was one of the more unique types of fae that Maddy had met. Instead of drawing magic automatically from her environment, Cora had to bind her power to a location to access it. When she'd bound herself to Moranaia, her child had been linked, also, even unborn. Cora's and Ralan's baby would have to remain on Moranaia until she was old enough to learn how to link to other locations, which meant Cora had to stay, too.

"Are you still doing okay with Eri?" Maddy grinned at her friend's pained expression. "Oh, come on. That bad? I thought you liked being a stepmother."

Cora sighed. "I do love being her mother, but there are days... Although she has been a lot more cautious about handing out prophecies, it happens more often than I'd like."

"I'm still not sure I believe that one little girl could be so frightening," Maddy said, not bothering to hide her laugh.

"Oh, just wait. If you come here, you'll..." Cora's voice trailed off as she glanced to the side. "Lial is here. We can chat later."

Just like that, Cora stepped aside, and the healer's face filled the mirror's frame. Maddy's levity vanished, her nerves returning in full force. She'd only met him once before, and that experience had been intimidating enough. He wielded his magic with

a confidence and mastery she would never possess. She would eat the damn communication mirror if *he* had nearly killed someone while trying to help them.

No matter how daunting it was to talk to him, though, she couldn't compromise on what she had to say, at least not much.

"Forgive my tardiness, Maddy," Lial said, inclining his head. "As you will learn, a healer's time is never quite their own. Breaks are easier to heal immediately, so the task couldn't wait."

"I hope the warrior is well."

His eyebrows lifted. "Did you think I would leave them otherwise? But yes, they are well."

Maddy groaned to herself. Only she could accidentally insult someone in a bad attempt to procrastinate. "Sorry, I—"

"It is no matter," Lial interrupted. "I assume you scheduled this meeting so that we can arrange your move to Moranaia for training?"

"Sort of." She twisted her fingers together in her lap where he couldn't see. "But maybe not exactly."

His expression hardened. "Clarify."

"I can't just move there." Her fingers began to hurt from the force of her grip, but it allowed her to keep her voice level—and hopefully confident. "But I do want to find a way to train with you if you are willing."

Up went his eyebrows once more. "You do realize how many centuries it takes to master this gift, don't you? I'm not certain how you expect to train properly from afar."

"I do know that I have to come there." Maddy sucked in a breath. This was it. Her chance to make her argument with the only person who had ever agreed to help her. If he couldn't accept her terms... She pulled in another deep breath for good measure. "But I don't want to *live* there."

His expression didn't soften. "Perhaps you should make the proposal you so clearly have in mind."

"I can't leave my girlfriend for who knows how long, especially not with her fae blood waking up. I won't leave her, in fact." Maddy lowered her shoulders and straightened her spine. "But I could travel to Moranaia for two or three days a week if Vek and Dria are willing to ensure that Anna is okay while I'm away. I'm worried about her."

A hint of concern entered Lial's gaze. "Do you think she might do herself harm?"

Maddy shook her head. "I don't think she's suicidal, but I can tell she's really struggling with being near the huge river that flows by our town."

"Is she willing to travel to Moranaia?" Lial asked. "With the new gate between our worlds, there should be little risk to her."

"She has a job. If she disappears, she'll be fired, and if she quits, we won't be able to pay the bills." At his blank look, she almost laughed. "Basic necessities are

not supplied here, and she can't exactly ask for a few days off to go to another world every week. My dad would help with money, but Anna won't accept it until we're married."

It took him a moment to process her words, his frown turning thoughtful as she waited in worried silence. Finally, he nodded. "I believe I understand. But has she considered that she might seek training here, even if her bloodline isn't Moranaian? Selia might be able to help."

"I'll mention that," Maddy answered. "But I also have the shop. I'm not going to dump the entire responsibility on my business partner after agreeing to go into business with him."

Another silence descended, and Lial pinched his lower lip, his gaze averted as he thought. Maddy glanced down at her hands, untangling her fingers when she saw how white they'd grown. Little prickles of pain danced along her skin as feeling returned, but she did her best to ignore it as she returned her attention to the healer.

Relief washed away the ache when he met her eyes again and smiled. "Very well, young Maddy. We'll try it your way for a while. It might take a great deal longer, but we'll do our best."

"Thank you," Maddy said, hoping her voice didn't quiver.

"We'll make the travel arrangements through Dria since you'll pass through the outpost's portal," Lial said. "If it is convenient for all involved, I'll have you come for a short initial visit tomorrow afternoon so that you might learn the area. We will do a couple of lessons, but for the most part, we will determine the pace and timing during that first visit."

Maddy let out a deep breath. "Sounds good."

And just like that, it was settled. She would get her training without giving up her world.

3

"Don't you have an outpost to run?" Fen grumbled as his phone rang. Again. He was about ready to chunk the damned thing through Vek's floor-to-ceiling window. "Look, you use the chat bubble icon to text and the telephone icon to call. Ugh, I knew this would be a mistake."

Fen's first error had been taking Vek and Dria with him to the phone store. After that, he should have let them return to the cave instead of offering lessons on how to use their devices. But no—he'd chosen mistake number two and tried to help. He could have been enjoying his afternoon rather than being tormented in the middle of his uncle's living room. At least Dria was a quick study.

The ringing stopped after Vek tapped his phone screen. Then he touched something else, frowned, and held out the phone. "The bubble didn't bring up the right thing."

Fen peered at the screen and groaned. "That…that was the internet button. It pulls up the browser, remember?"

"Ah, the mysterious internet," Vek drawled. "How will I ever learn its secrets?"

"You probably won't at this rate." Fen rubbed the heel of his palm against his temple. Getting through the phone store had been…an experience. "This is the third time you've accidentally called me."

"Is it?"

Wait. Was that a gleam of humor in his uncle's eyes? *Fuck me.* The bastard was trolling him. "You're doing it on purpose."

For the first time Fen could recall, Vek laughed—truly, fully laughed. From her spot on the couch, Dria glanced up from her own phone and grinned. "It took you long enough to figure it out. I was about to take pity on you."

Still chuckling, Vek turned his phone back around and deftly tapped at the screen. "Really, Fen. Adapt quickly or die quickly. How do you think I've lived this long?"

"Stubbornness and assholery?" Fen quipped.

"That, too." Vek shoved his phone in his pocket just as Fen's phone let out a chirp. "Dria, love, are you ready to head back? I know you didn't want to be gone this long."

Dria stood, slipping her own device into the pocket of the jeans she'd donned for their outing. "Probably a good idea."

As they gathered their things, Fen checked his phone's notifications. A text from Vek: *What was it you said earlier? Owned?*

Gods above and below. He'd created a monster.

"Ah, don't mope, Fen," his uncle said.

Another notification rang out before he could answer the taunt, and his heart gave a leap when Maddy's name flashed across the screen. Fen smacked the button so fast his finger stung. She hadn't texted him for twelve hours. Approximately.

I need to get with you. And Vek and Dria. Traveling to M from their place sometimes and have to figure out logistics. You guys free later tonight?

Fen read the text three times before he processed anything beyond "I need to get with you." Did the M stand for Moranaia? What did she mean by "sometimes?" Damn, he hoped she wasn't staying on Moranaia long term. The word "read" next to her text taunted him as he tried to formulate something resembling an answer.

"What's wrong?" Vek asked.

"Nothing," Fen answered quickly. "Maddy wants to know if we're free tonight. I think she might need to travel through the portal, but she left it vague."

Dria nodded. "Makes sense. Didn't Lial tell her to come to him for training?"

A fact Fen had tried not to think about. "Yeah."

"I can make a gate from her shop to the outpost if she'll tell us a good time," Dria said.

Fen sent Dria's offer to Maddy and waited a moment, but his answer remained at "delivered" instead of "read." Maybe the shop had gotten busy. "Guess we will see."

Dria shrugged. "You could go ahead and come with us. You don't have to sit around alone at Vek's house all the time, you know. You are always welcome at the outpost."

Fen shifted uneasily. She had told him that, and he could tell she meant it. But as things had settled down over the last couple of weeks, he'd felt increasingly out of place there. He'd been cured of his illness, no one was in danger, and he'd helped reinforce the cave's protective shields to the best of his abilities. He'd started avoiding his room at the outpost more and more in favor of Vek's place.

Truth be told, Fen felt a little adrift, but no one else could decide his future for him.

"I don't have any plans right now," Fen said. And he didn't. What was there for him to do besides play video games and fight off memories of his past misdeeds? He had to be close to becoming the brooding world champion. "I suppose I could go ahead and work on the cell signal spell while we wait on Maddy. It would be nice for all of our phones to work throughout the cave system, although I'm not sure if I can make the signal carry to some of the more remote spots like the bathing chamber."

The remaining humor faded from Vek's face as he studied Fen. Was his discontent that obvious? But Vek only nodded. "I can help if Dria's busy."

Perfect. Because suddenly, the last thing Fen wanted was to be alone.

Maddy paused in front of the door separating the storage and office area from the so-called break room. Connecting with the shields, she scanned the interior to see if Anthony still waited. Yep. His calm, steady energy signature pulsed near the table area. Seemed he was in a better emotional state than she was, at least if his energy was to be believed. She was a trembling mess of nerves after talking to Lial.

She ran her palms along her pants, took a few steadying breaths, and pushed into the room. Anthony popped up from his seat like a nobleman in a Regency novel—or a Southern boy with a traditional mama. As Maddy approached, he pulled out a chair for her and waited until she'd sat before he resumed his own seat. Yeah, she'd bet money on the traditional mama.

"Thanks," Maddy said. "I'm sorry about the wait."

"It's fine. I have another thirty minutes before I have to head to work."

"Third shift?" she asked, trying not to check the time on her phone. It had to be nearing four o'clock, so unless he worked retail, he had to have a night job.

He smiled. "Nah, I'm a nurse practitioner at one of the clinics that's open late. My coworker has to leave early, so I'm covering the last few hours for her."

"Nurse practitioner?" Maddy blinked. He looked young enough to be a freshman in college, not a professional. "Shouldn't you be wearing a lab coat or something?"

"I don't put that on until I get there," he answered. "We don't usually wear those on the street."

"Right." Maddy chuckled softly at herself. "Of course."

The entire situation felt surreal. She'd just made arrangements to learn how to use her healing abilities without killing anyone, and this man already worked as a healer using mundane means. At least she assumed so. Surely, no one had been foolish enough to recommend *her* to help with healing magic?

"Do you have a gift for that kind of magic?" she asked. "Because if you're here for advice on healing, I'm the wrong girl."

Anthony lifted a brow. "You mean using energy to heal? No, I don't do that. I have a bit of empathy, but that's it. I'm actually here on behalf of my coven. Nothing to do with my job."

"Your coven?" Maddy tapped her fingers restlessly against the table. There were more flavors of pagan in the south than a lot of people realized, but the fae she knew avoided them. Of all the humans, they were the most likely to sense real energy, even before Earth's magic had been restored. "Why would a fae man be in a human coven? Don't you fear discovery?"

"I might worry if we were a mostly human coven. A huge number of us are half-bloods, and considering what's happening when we try to do circles now, I'd say the rest are also part fae. I guess that's what drew us together in the first place."

Fae pagans. A little unusual, but it wasn't the strangest thing she'd ever heard. "So what I can I do for you?"

"I'm not sure." Anthony leaned back in his chair, and his eyebrows pinched together. "My friend and I ran across these strange white guys in town the other day. One of them was super pale and a little creepy, but the other one looked more like you, except blond. They weren't too interested in me. Ryan, though. The crazy-pale one chatted with Ryan for a while. Apparently, the man claimed he'd identified Ryan's Unseelie ancestry and offered to find someone to teach him to use his magic. I believe it. They matched what my dad told me about those particular fae, and Ryan has the right vibe."

Maddy didn't have to ask for names to guess who the men probably were. Vek and Fen. Vek was a blood elf, a prince of the Unseelie, and his white hair and skin stood out amongst the human population. But his nephew Fen had a human father—and thus more human coloring. Why would Anthony be here talking to her if Vek offered to help Ryan, though?

"Didn't Ryan know about his ancestry?" she asked. "Or was it a surprise?"

"He's aware. Unfortunately, he's also an idiot," Anthony muttered. "He panicked and said no. I guess I can see why, but he didn't even get contact info before he ran off. The younger guy told me to come here and ask for you if we had trouble. Said you helped fae integrate and gave me the password."

Maddy wrinkled her nose. "I'm guessing you did have trouble?"

"Well." He scrubbed his hand across his head. "We were about to do a prayer circle, but with so much energy available now, Olivia accidentally cast a solid circle. Literally. Damn thing was like glass. Then Ryan decided to go ahead and call in the elements, but the energy he tried to cast ate through the circle. We're all shook. I've done a little real magic here and there, but it has mostly been religion for us. Prayer and communion. Now we all have these growing abilities with no idea what to do with them."

His words didn't come as a surprise, but they did cause alarm. Maddy had heard rumors of real magic being performed in places like Salem, but there were so many crazy stories spreading that no one knew what to believe. How many other groups besides Anthony's were struggling with this? And what did he expect her to do? Hell. Too bad Cora wasn't here. She had far more experience dealing with complicated cases.

"I'm not really qualified to teach magic," Maddy said carefully.

Anthony nodded. "I'd already gotten that impression. But what about those guys I met? They obviously knew you, so I was hoping you had a way to get in touch with them. Getting Ryan assistance would be a start. Really, any connections you could help us make to area fae would be good. Only other full-blood I've met here

was weird as fuck. Walked up to me and Sparrow eating lunch by the river and kept touching her arm even though he was talking to us like we weren't shit. No way I was trusting him."

"And you trust me and my friends?" Maddy asked, watching his expression for any hint of deceit.

"About as well as I can," Anthony answered. Despite the slight doubt in his tone, his expression remained easy and open. "About as well as you can trust me, too, I guess. But I don't want to cause trouble. You know how much work you have to do in grad school? I don't have time to start crap."

Maddy considered her own upcoming training and winced. "I hear you on that."

Anthony smiled. "The blond guy who sent me here was more like the people in my coven than that creepy asshole we met at the river. This shop has been here a long time, too. I figured it was worth a shot to reach out before we blow ourselves up."

"I'm pretty sure I know exactly who you're talking about. Well, the two you met with your friend Ryan, anyway. No clue about the other person." Maddy pulled her phone out of her pocket and opened her note-taking app. *Ask Fen about Anthony*, she wrote. "Do you feel comfortable giving me your contact info? I could text you once I talk to them. Or maybe email if you'd rather do that?"

"Text would be fine," Anthony answered.

As soon as she'd typed in his number, they stood. Maddy held out her hand, and he gave it a firm shake. "I'll let you know. I'm actually hoping to see the two I think you met later tonight, so maybe I'll have some news soon."

"Thanks. I know it's weird, me showing up randomly like this, so I appreciate your help."

Maddy stifled a grin. He had no idea how *not* weird this encounter was considering all that had happened the last couple of months. Being kidnapped by a depraved madman was only the beginning. Besides, her instincts hadn't led her wrong yet, and everything within her said that Anthony was being honest.

"No problem," she said.

At least she hoped it wouldn't be.

Fen studied the small chamber that held the bathing pool. His gaze kept flicking to the far wall where a crevice had once collapsed, trapping Dria. It had been a harrowing experience to clear the stones without doing further damage to Dria or Vek, who had managed to reach her before running out of energy. After the emergency was over, they'd created a proper corridor out of the jagged passage with a sealed stone door on each side.

"Still worried about the tunnel?" Vek asked.

"You really should have closed up the whole wall," Fen answered. "Barrier spells can be broken, and the guy responsible for the last attack on the outpost hasn't been caught. Did you forget that he managed to sneak through a stream of

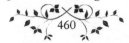

water to stab *you* in the middle of your shielded bedroom? Meren isn't the kind of person you want to leave a door cracked for."

"I have not forgotten his attack on me." Vek's jaw clenched. "If I get a chance to gut Meren, I'll take it. Unfortunately, he has proved far too adept at hiding his blood, but I'll find him eventually."

Fen grimaced in sympathy, though his amusement at Vek's struggle probably showed through. His uncle had always given him shit about his lack of skill with tracking people through blood. Fen had managed the trick a time or two, but his range was abysmal and accuracy questionable. But hey, he was learning. He might be *Felshreh*, a race of fae that gained their magic through blood, but that didn't mean tracking was an automatic talent, did it? No one expected a human to find chocolate on the other side of the world just because they'd tasted it once.

Though come to think of it, that would be a badass ability.

"Are you seriously smiling about our enemy running free?"

Fen coughed into his hand. "Ah. No. Sorry. My mind wandered."

With an annoyed look, Vek headed closer to the pool of water. Fen followed along the smooth path that he'd widened for ease of passage. Before, the stalagmites had crowded close, but he had used his earth magic to ease them back without "killing" them. Otherwise, people no doubt would have brushed the formations in passing, ending any chance of the stalagmites continuing to grow. Caves were beautiful ecosystems, and he'd be damned if he'd see another one harmed. Kien had always insisted it didn't matter, but—

Ruthlessly, Fen slammed the door on those memories. Fuck Kien. Hopefully, the bastard was rotting in whatever version of hell the Moranaians believed in. If Fen was really lucky, it wouldn't be the same one he'd inevitably be sent to when he died. Surely there was a limit on atonement. Most Earth religions spoke of redemption, but all too few of their followers granted it. Whichever deity or deities in charge of the shitshow called life would probably offer no better.

Vek poked him in the arm, drawing his attention. "What is wrong with you today?"

Fen shrugged. "Beats me. Lately, I've been…unsettled. I don't know how else to describe it. I can't get a handle on my emotions."

"If you need to talk—"

"Not yet. Maybe never," Fen said. Regret curled through him at the hint of hurt on his uncle's face, but he couldn't take back the vehement words. If he released everything that weighed him down, he'd crush the listener beneath the force. No one wanted or needed that kind of burden. "Nothing against you. I just don't know when or if I'll be ready."

Though displeasure lined his face, Vek nodded in understanding. "Let me know. In the meantime, perhaps we should determine if your spell is capable of working in this chamber."

Fen grasped the topic change like unexpected loot in *Death's Curse 3*. "I'm not

sure. There's a lot more stone between this room and the main portion of the out-post, and water can mess with the signal. Also, I don't want to risk interference with the shields keeping that door over there sealed up. I wish Olive was here."

"You need fruit for this spell?" Vek asked, his brow wrinkling.

That surprised a laugh out of Fen. "No. Olive is a friend of mine. It's a name. Well, her name is actually Olivia, but we started calling her the shorter version to pester her. She used to wear this green hat, and—"

"Get to the point, Fen."

"She's…I'd guess you'd say an artificer?" Fen frowned. That wasn't quite right, but it was all he had. "Olive is some percentage of fae, but I've never tried to break through her shielding enough to figure out how much or what. She's not someone you fuck with. Probably more so now that there's more magic available on Earth."

Vek scowled. "Is that what you call getting to the point?"

"What, you don't like context?" Fen ran a tendril of earth energy along the area around the pool as his uncle glared at him. Served him right for being an impatient jerk. The water shoved against his magic, eroding his power, but Fen managed to complete his scan. "Yep. I'll probably need her help with this room. She's the one who invented the spell, at least the version I know."

"So this Olive is an artificer of spells?"

"Yes and no." Fen smiled. "There's a whole underground of magical creatures, human-like or not, who've learned how to survive on Earth without anyone know-ing. Olive integrates technology with magic. I'm sure there are others doing it, too."

Vek crossed his arms across his chest. "I doubt Dria will allow a stranger to work on something so important inside the outpost. She will bring someone in who she trusts."

"I can vouch for Olive, but I get it." And he did. Who would trust someone *he* recommended? "Anyway, maybe it's better not to have a cell signal in the bathing pool. Telepathy isn't hindered, so if there's a problem, someone can use that to get your attention."

"Fen…"

"Come on," Fen said, spinning away from his uncle and marching back along the path. "We need to keep channeling the spell down to the bottom. Maddy said they'd come straight here after she picks Anna up from work, and I'd like to be done."

Anything was better than listening to Vek make excuses for Dria's lack of trust.

4

Anna glanced at her phone. 9:37. Where was Maddy? The shop closed at the same time as the restaurant, and Maddy usually finished her closing tasks well before Anna completed her checklist of duties. Now, the only person left inside was Deanna, who often did the bookkeeping for an hour or two after closing. The rare times that Maddy hadn't already been waiting, Anna had sat at one of the tables overlooking the parking lot or on the stairs up to the elevated building to wait. But tonight…tonight, she was restless.

The sidewalk was empty of people, her only company the twisted shadows of tree branches cast down by the quarter moon above. Her nose twitched from the tang of fish and water blown around her by the breeze. It would be a lovely evening for a swim, a break from the oppressive heat. She leaned against the fence bordering the sidewalk and peered at the riverbank.

Only a quick jump over the useless rail and a few steps down. Four or maybe five. That was all it would take to reach the water flowing in front of her. Her heart pounded, and her legs threatened to give beneath the weight of her desire. What would be so wrong about swimming—or at least wading on the edge? The water wouldn't hurt her. She wasn't some weak lady in an ancient tale who would be lost to the river forever with a single touch.

At least she hoped she wasn't.

Anna.

She jerked in surprise at the soft whisper that drifted across the wind. A female voice. Or had it been her imagination? She took a step back and glanced over her shoulder at the restaurant separated from the sidewalk by a small expanse of lawn. The door at the top of the stairs was still closed, and although she could see light from one of the interior windows beyond the screened-in porch, there was no sign of Deanna. Anna eased to the side and peeked around the building. The parking lot was likewise empty.

Anna.

She spun back to the water so quickly she almost tripped. What the hell? Squinting against the floodlights gleaming across the river, she studied the gently lapping surface. Nothing. No mysterious fog or strange figure rising from the depths. Only the swish of water and the rumble of cars from the highway. Was she losing her mind?

Her feet moved, practically of their own volition. Nothing. Was. Out. There. Sure, Anna wanted to touch water with an urgency she'd never felt before, but Vek could have been wrong when he'd named her a descendant of some kind of Welsh water fae. Her parents had taken her to the lake every summer when she was a kid, for God's sake. Wouldn't she have noticed a problem then?

Her stomach made contact with the metal fence, and she gripped the sturdy bars, longing to vault over and continue on her way.

"Anna!"

She stiffened at that all-too-real shout from Maddy. Anna blinked a few times, shaking free of the odd fog clouding her mind. Her gaze shifted downward, and she gasped to find one of her feet on the bottom rail of the fence. Fuck. She really had been about to climb over and stumble down the bank to the river. So much for being able to control herself. What was she going to tell Maddy?

Anna forced a smile to her face and hurried toward the parking lot. Maddy was already at the back corner of the restaurant, and the pinched fear on her face tore at Anna's heart. Her love had enough to worry about without this, too. So Anna shoved the call of the water to the back of her mind. It might insist on being answered eventually, but it wouldn't be now.

"Are you okay?" Maddy asked.

"Yeah, sorry." Anna gave Maddy a quick kiss on the lips and marched toward the car still idling in the parking lot. Her girlfriend caught up after only a few steps, her frown unbroken. "It's a beautiful night, so I thought I'd admire the river while I waited. Are *you* okay? You aren't usually this late."

Maddy grimaced. "It was a long day, capped off by a nice older lady who wanted a custom wardrobe of the extra-special kind. She was great to work with, but it took a while."

"Older lady?" Anna asked, her interest caught. The only custom clothes they made were for fae customers who needed to learn to wear Earth styles, and the races of fae that Anna had learned about were ancient indeed before they visibly aged.

Maddy waited until they were both in the car to answer. "A wood nymph. Her tree was cut down about a year ago, and she almost died. Can you believe someone would destroy a tree that was over three thousand years old? The return of magic awakened her, and now she wants to join the human world so she can track down the person responsible."

"And you helped her?" Anna's skin chilled. No telling what a tree nymph would consider proper retribution for killing her priceless tree. "Wouldn't that make you an accessory if she does something illegal?"

"Hell yeah, I helped her." Maddy rubbed Anna's thigh, but it only returned a

little of her warmth. It was beyond Anna how her beloved braved so many dangerous interactions. "I don't think selling her clothes makes me responsible for what
she does next. Maybe she's going to give the person a stern talking to. How would
I know?"

Anna's lips twisted. "I'd be more worried about a suspicious tree-related death
than a heated discussion. I wouldn't blame her, but I don't want you to get in trouble,
either."

"She was kind enough not to make any threats," Maddy said before letting out a
chuckle. "And I'm definitely not going to the police to report an angry tree nymph."

Put that way, it did sound ridiculous. If the authorities knew anything about
supernatural creatures, they weren't saying, but she'd never heard the police give credence to such things before. Anna had a feeling they had no clue what was causing
the power outages and energy surges any more than the average human did. Unless
any fae had joined their ranks, the government probably didn't know, either.

Uneasiness squeezed her throat. It was inevitable that they found out. Someone
was going to make a power play. If it wasn't Lord Meren of the Seelie Sidhe, who had
recently attempted to destroy the Moranaian outpost, then it would be some other
type of fae. How could they resist? When Earth had lost most of its magic millennia
ago, many of the magic-based creatures had fled to other dimensions. They would
surely want to reclaim their homes if they could. At the least, they would want their
own spaces.

"I didn't mean to worry you," Maddy said.

Anna sighed. "You didn't. Well, not directly. I just can't shake the thought that
things are about to change. Humans have ruled without much opposition for a long
time, and all of this… I don't see a way for it to go well for anyone. If the fae try to
ascend to power, humans are going to fight it. What will we choose, Maddy? We have
both inside of us."

"We choose the side that's doing what's right," Maddy answered, her voice firm.
Anna watched the streetlights flicker against her love's stubborn, resolute chin and
longed for the same optimistic confidence. "Right now, I'd trust the Moranaians over
my own people. Not that my father has any drive for power. But how many of the
Seelie agree with Lord Meren about humans being inferior creatures the fae should
rule? I've heard so many rumors about the Seelie court that it's hard to tell. They say
the real queen disappeared, either dead or ill, and the acting queen hasn't made her
intentions about Earth clear. The Moranaians, though… They've done nothing but
try to help."

"Cora and Vek aren't from Moranaia," Anna pointed out. She nibbled on her
lower lip. "Neither is Fen."

Maddy went silent for a moment. "Yeah. Hey, who would have guessed I'd put
more trust in a half-Unseelie blood elf than in my father's people?"

"Not me." Anna hesitated. "Any particular reason we're going to see Fen now
instead of going home, cuddling on the couch, and making love?"

Too bad the overhead light wasn't on. From the look on Maddy's face, she was probably blushing to match her hair, and that was always a sight to see. "It's not... I need to talk to Vek and Dria more than Fen. Lial agreed to let me go to Moranaia for training a few days a week, and I have to coordinate it with Dria."

Anna opened her mouth to ask why the trip couldn't have waited until morning, but she stopped herself before the question popped out. Yes, her feet hurt from running back and forth across the restaurant, and chances were good that she smelled like fish and chips. But Maddy had struggled with her gift for so long. She needed this training. Who could blame her for being in a rush to get things settled? Anna would, too, if she had magic that could kill someone.

"I'm glad your meeting went well," Anna said. "Have you talked to Jase about the shop?"

Maddy nodded. "I called him earlier. He's going to be back in the morning, and we'll shuffle around our days off to manage. Though I think we'll have to hire another part-timer. Want a new job?"

Work at The Magic Touch? Anna wrinkled her nose at the thought. Dealing with human customers was enough of a pain in the ass. Having to field questions from all manner of fae, too? No, thank you. She'd learned a lot about the magical races, but not enough to hazard that. She would far rather wait tables and write her book.

Besides, Maddy was the one who cared about fashion. Even this late, she looked bright and fresh in a cute summer dress and strappy sandals. Anna preferred jeans and soft T-shirts—bonus points if it was cool enough outside for a cozy cardigan. Helping people pick clothes sounded like a nightmare.

Maddy broke out in laughter. "I was just teasing. I know you don't want to work there."

"Thank God," Anna said, uncaring that her fervor was a little insulting.

"Do you want me to take you home?" Maddy asked.

The sudden shift in topic had Anna frowning. "Huh? Why?"

"You keep leaning your head against the seat as though you'd rather be sleeping." Maddy rubbed her thigh again. "I feel guilty dragging you out when you're so tired from work. But I couldn't wait. Lial wants me to come tomorrow for a couple of days so that we can work out how to proceed."

Anna did her best to hide her disappointment. "So soon?"

"I'm a little concerned about the speed myself," Maddy said softly, her usually bright expression dimming. "But all the extra energy on Earth has made my gift even more of a liability."

"Then you should go." She could hold out against the draw of water for another couple of days, right? "I don't mind tagging along to the outpost while you work out the details. Besides, I like spending time with Fen."

Even though it did cause her a little jealousy, if not in the way Maddy feared. Ever since Anna had overheard her telling Cora about the possible mate thing, Anna had been going silently crazy trying to figure out how to broach the topic. She'd al-

most managed it this morning, but she'd wimped out. But like her growing struggle with her water power, it couldn't go unaddressed much longer.

"If you're sure," Maddy asked softly.

"I'm fine," she answered. "Let's just hurry up with it."

She didn't say she wanted to talk, because that would have added to Maddy's worries. But Anna was done waiting to see if their problems would resolve themselves. They needed to sit down and discuss their issues before they had a stupid argument that could have been easily fixed in advance. If they were too tired after this meeting, she would insist they have a long conversation in the morning.

No more hiding.

Fen paced the length of yet another room he'd helped Vek create. Originally a large fissure beside the entry chamber at the top of the cavern enclave, the room served one purpose—a secure landing point for any portals the mages might create. Every inch of wall, floor, and ceiling was imbued with protective spells, and two guards were stationed at the door. With enemies on the loose, they could afford no lapses in security.

"No texts?" Dria asked.

He pressed the button on the phone he'd been gripping like a lifeline and scanned for any notifications. Nothing but the weather forecast and an offer from some shopping app he'd downloaded on a whim. "Not—"

A text box popped up as a ring sounded.

Ready when you are.

"Okay, they're in place."

Dria turned to the stone arch formed into the far wall and began to weave the spell. Impatient and more than a little nervous, Fen tapped his foot against the floor as light flooded the room, the spell far brighter than the handful of mage globes settled in sconces around the walls. Both of his potential mates were going to be here. Together. In the same place as his uncle and new aunt.

He'd admitted to Maddy that she could be his mate, but he'd chickened out before explaining that Anna could be, too. It wasn't like either would accept him, for fuck's sake, so it hadn't seemed to matter. Any time they'd been together since, he hadn't managed to find the right moment. But hey, if Maddy hadn't mentioned it to Anna, she wasn't likely to bring it up here. And his family wouldn't betray his confidence.

Of course, if he'd fessed up during any of the chances he'd had over the last two weeks, he wouldn't be standing here worrying now. Fact was, he hadn't wanted to lose the opportunity to get to know both women better, and it hadn't seemed worth causing strain in their relationship. They didn't deserve to have their lives messed up because of his sorry ass.

Before he could get too far in his litany of self-deprecation, the spell settled, and the women in question stepped through. Fen's mouth went dry, and his tongue froze.

He'd rarely found women he was so attracted to, though they were quite different from one another. Anna was several inches shorter than tall, willowy Maddy, plump and well-rounded where Maddy was lean. Her shoulder-length blond hair swung gently against her lightly tanned skin, while Maddy's bright red hair tumbled down her back in beachy waves.

Such a beautiful contrast—and he wanted them both.

"Hey, Fen," Maddy said, no sign of awkwardness on her face or in her tone.

Anna, on the other hand…

He could tell with a glance that something was wrong. She was generally quiet and reserved—the most he'd ever seen her do after winning a game was a fist pump and wiggle, while Maddy didn't hesitate to leap to her feet with a squeal—but Anna didn't usually appear somber. Had something happened? She averted her gaze before he could get a grasp on the emotions swirling in her eyes.

Maddy must have told her.

"Hey," Fen answered, though his throat wanted to close around the word.

If Maddy noticed, she was kind enough not to say anything. Instead, she glanced around. "Where's Vek?"

"He's headed up from the bathing pool," Dria answered for Fen. "We'll meet him in his old room. I've set it up as an informal meeting spot since it's more comfortable than the dining room."

When had she done that? Fen's room was next door to that one, and he'd seen no sign of such a transformation. Then again, he had spent more time at Vek's house lately. He might have a bedroom here, but the outpost wasn't his home—literally or figuratively. Aside from learning the Unseelie ways from Vek, Fen had no clue what he should be doing with himself. Whatever it was, it wasn't here. His constant lack of inclusion made that abundantly clear.

"Great," Maddy said cheerfully. "Let's go. We both just got off work, and Anna has been on her feet for hours. We could use a bit of comfort."

Dria led the way past the guards and out the door. Fen trailed behind, bleakness slowing his steps until Maddy gave him a questioning glance over her shoulder. He hurried to keep up, to hide his thoughts better. Why couldn't he shake free from this shitty mood? He'd been rejected repeatedly since his first foster home. Too uncanny. Too strange. Too difficult. He'd never let it affect him this much before. He could get through, just as he always did, but his emotions didn't seem to buy that truth.

It wasn't like things would get worse. He'd never been mated, so he couldn't exactly miss it. He was already hated by a fair number of fae after he'd helped a madman set up a spell to poison Earth's energy—and by extension, that of other fae realms. Fen was responsible for his own cousin's death, and gods knew how many other people had died or had their lives ruined because of his fuck-up. Helping to fix the mistake wouldn't change the past.

Fen was at the bottom of a crevice with nowhere to go but up, and that usually boosted his mood. His whole life, he'd tried to see low points as an opportunity to find another path—an adventure to begin. There was always a foothold in the stone, a way to advance, a new thing to learn. This time? He caught another strained look from Anna and sighed. This time, he might very well be stuck.

He followed the others into the room and stopped just over the threshold. The furniture that had been here before was gone, the space filled by a dining table on the left and a grouping of cozy-looking armchairs on the right. A series of maps had been affixed to the walls, and Fen wandered closer to examine them. A world map, one of Tennessee, another of the Chattanooga area, and even a topographic map of the region stretched nearly from one corner to the next.

"What's this all about?" Fen asked.

Dria smiled. "I had Delbin gather these. If I'm sending people out to search for danger, I should have a good understanding of the terrain. Of course, I found a map on my phone that allows me to zoom in on individual streets, so perhaps banners on the wall are unnecessary."

"It's still useful. You could place markers on the locations where strange things have been reported," Maddy said, stopping beside Fen to stare at the world map. "Like the dragon in Scotland. It's easier to see the whole picture like this."

"Fen did mention that Scotland is on the other side of the world, but I haven't had a chance to find it."

Fen tapped his finger against the country in question. "Right here."

The door opened, and Fen spun in time to see Vek enter. His uncle's brows rose in surprise as he took in the inhabitants of the room. "Finally bring your mates home to meet the family, Fen?"

Any thought of connections froze at the question.

What the fuck?

Beside him, Maddy sucked in a breath. Fen was too afraid to look at her or Anna to see their reactions to Vek's revelation, but he was more than willing to turn a death glare on his uncle. Vek had known both women would be there, the asshole. So much for not being betrayed by his family.

"Did you seriously just—"

"Mates?" Anna's incredulous voice cut across Fen's. "Plural?"

"Sure." Vek shrugged as though he hadn't upended Fen's world with a few casually spoken words. "You could both claim him if you wanted. Three-way bonds are rare, but they happen. I thought he talked to Maddy about this."

Dammit to every hell ever imagined. He'd told Vek exactly what he'd said. "You know very well—"

"Fen." Maddy's gaze hit him like a shove, and he couldn't bring himself to counter it. "If this is true, then why wouldn't you say something? That's sort of an important detail."

How could his uncle have betrayed him like this?

Fen studied the striations in the limestone beneath his feet as he tried to think of a way to explain, but shame crept up his throat. Choking. Ever-present. These

amazing women deserved far better than a screwed-up half-blood Unseelie prince who ruined everything he touched. They had to realize it. Gods knew Fen would never forget.

Without a word, he strode out of the room.

Maddy stared blankly at the door after Fen's exit. What did it mean that he hadn't denied his uncle's claim? Vek might be wrong, and Fen just didn't want to tell her. He'd been clear about respecting her relationship with Anna, even when he'd mentioned the mate thing. Despite their obvious mutual attraction, he had never pushed. When they'd spent time together as friends, he hadn't acted like he had any ulterior motives.

"That was not well done," Dria said softly to Vek.

"It is what was needed," Vek countered, his cool, confident tone sparking Maddy's anger. "He'll castigate himself until the sun burns out if someone doesn't intervene."

Maddy's brows lowered. What gave him the right to make that decision? Didn't he care about Fen's obvious hurt? Or the chaos this would cause with…

Her hands went cold and clammy. Anna. Her girlfriend hadn't known any of this. Oh, hell. Maddy sucked in a breath and finally dared to look. The surprise on Anna's face was easy to identify, but there was no hint of anger in the eyes that met Maddy's. Instead, she could have sworn Anna was…relieved?

That couldn't be right.

"I'm sorry, Anna," Maddy said in a rush. "Fen told me I could be his mate a couple of weeks ago, and I've been struggling with it since. I didn't want to upset you. I was going to talk to you about it, but we've been so busy. You have your new magic to deal with, and—"

"I know, love. It's okay," Anna said, her expression turning sheepish. "I… might have overheard you telling Cora about it. You didn't say anything about me, though."

Maddy's mouth dropped open. "You heard? That was over a week ago."

"I guess we've both been delaying a long-overdue talk."

"You're telling me." Maddy's chuckle held little humor. "Seems like Fen has been holding back, as well. He didn't say a word about being able to form a bond with you. I don't even know what that means. Are you and I already some kind of soul mates who didn't know how to link, or does that require Fen? Maybe he has to pick one of us. God, I'm so confused."

Vek took a few steps forward. "I can't answer the first, but I can the last. If Fen tastes your blood together, he could bind you all as one. A triad, I suppose."

"He didn't seem particularly interested," Anna muttered.

Maddy blinked. Was her girlfriend in favor of a polyamorous relationship? As far as she knew, Anna was rarely attracted to men at all. Would she actually consider this? Maddy herself had never really thought about long-term polyam relationships. She hadn't even begun to process how she felt about the possibility.

But Anna's lips were turned down in unmistakable disappointment.

"Anna?"

Dria marched over to Vek and jabbed his stomach, a sudden spark of lightning making him yelp. "Look what you've done, you ass. You could have tried talking to Fen in private."

Recovering from the jolt quickly, Vek curled his fingers around the nape of Dria's neck and bent close to whisper in her ear. Her expression didn't exactly clear of anger, but she no longer looked like she wanted to annihilate her mate. Maddy glanced away from the intimate scene and found herself studying Anna.

They'd been pulled together from the moment Maddy had sat down at Anna's table at the restaurant where she worked. Maddy had been having lunch with Jase, who had teased her mercilessly about the way she'd stared at their server. Thankfully, the draw had been mutual. They'd traded numbers that evening and went on three dates within a week. Anna had even accepted Maddy's half-Sidhe nature without having known that the fae really existed.

But then, neither had known about Anna's blood at the time.

Almost hesitantly, Anna eased closer, and Maddy reached out to take her hand. "What are you thinking?"

"Honestly, I'm not sure. Lots of things." Anna squeezed her fingers. "I'm mostly relieved, I guess. I've been... Well, I've been jealous, if you really want to know the truth."

Maddy's chest grew tight. "You know I wouldn't cheat on you or leave you for someone else. I'm a big girl. I can ignore my attraction to Fen."

"I know that." With a huff, Anna pressed the palm of her free hand between her brows and rubbed. "But I've been struggling to reconcile it all. I love you, but I was jealous that you could share a link with Fen that I couldn't. It makes no sense. I haven't known him long, but that didn't seem to make a difference with my emotions."

"Oh, Anna." Maddy tugged her girlfriend close and wrapped her in her arms. "I'm sorry. We'll figure it all out. Together."

They held each other, peace and love flowing through Maddy at the contact, but then Vek cleared his throat. With a grin, Maddy stepped back, though she reclaimed her girlfriend's hand. Vek and Dria must have come to some accord, since the latter now wore a slight smile.

"Perhaps I should check on Fen while you speak with Dria," Vek said.

Maddy frowned. "I need to talk to you, too."

Suddenly, Anna pulled her hand free. "Why don't you show me where Fen is? I'll calm him down and bring him back here."

"But…" Maddy studied her girlfriend's face and found stubborn resolve. For whatever reason, Anna really wanted to do this. "Never mind. If you're really okay with it, that would be helpful. I just know you get nervous about any kind of confrontation."

"I'll manage," Anna answered.

Vek smiled at them both, a pleased glint in his eyes that made Maddy want to shove him. Manipulative bastard. "If you'll come with me, I'll show you where he is and make myself scarce."

A maelstrom of emotions twirled through Maddy, a storm she couldn't define, as Anna followed Vek through the door. But she couldn't linger on that. It was getting late, and there was a lot to settle with Dria about her future trips to Moranaia. Actually, this might turn out for the best. Maddy could share her concerns for Anna while her girlfriend was with Fen.

Another thing they probably needed to talk about.

Fen settled between two stalagmites in the corner of the bathing room, the one place the cell signal still didn't reach. At least he'd found a spot that wasn't easy to see from the entrance. Though he could be tracked by anyone with even moderate skills, he was unlikely to be disturbed by accident. Unfortunately, it left him staring at the sealed door that kept the outpost safe from the rest of the cave system.

A small price to pay for the privacy.

Yeah, it was childish to hide in the corner sulking, but Fen couldn't bring himself to care. Fury, pain, and shame had almost overtaken him, and he'd be damned even more if he allowed himself to break down in front of the others. They didn't need to deal with the hot mess he'd become. Fuck, the only thing that would have been worse was if his mother had been there, too.

Fen closed his eyes and leaned his head back against the smooth stone, craving Earth's soothing touch. He worked with the element daily—had never stopped—but he didn't dare to truly merge with it anymore. The full depth of that connection was something else he'd lost to Kien. He couldn't bear to reach for Earth's heart after the poison he'd helped spread into its energy field.

How could he have let himself cross that line?

It wouldn't have occurred to him at the beginning of Kien's manipulation campaign. Their little group of neglected half-bloods had started with small things, and the first had been borne of shared hurt—the abandoned getting their revenge against those who had wronged them. But somehow, that had shifted to the weakness of humans and the malevolence of all other fae.

Your parents left you for your pathetic human blood, but so many of the fae are waiting to rule mankind. You think the Unseelie wouldn't kill anyone in their path? Even the "kindly" Seelie would slaughter entire countries if they so desired, and the very fact they've come to the surface often enough to produce you means they're considering a return. Disable the fae before they can do worse. Take control of the weaker humans. They'll be better for your more reasoned rule.

The others had been all in, barely hesitating even after Kien showed the extent of his madness. But fear, not eagerness, had kept Fen in line. Wasn't he a killer deep inside? He wasn't sure when that certainty had begun, but it was before he'd been forced to fight for his life at Kien's behest. That's what had ultimately earned his cooperation. If he, who couldn't even power his magic without blood, was a killer, then what atrocities would an Unseelie army commit?

But something else had countered that refrain, tempering his actions just enough to prevent his soul from become an irredeemable wreck. Memories. Sitting on a man's lap—his father?—while hearing stories of a noble people. The kind touch of one of his foster mothers. Vek finding him when he was an idiotic, headstrong teenager and attempting to talk sense into him. Too bad Fen had bluffed his uncle into believing he was fine and leaving him alone.

It was probably for Vek that Fen had insisted the poison not be directed toward the Unseelie despite his fear of being a killer. Not that it had mattered since Kien had poisoned them anyway. He should have known better than to trust.

Would this ever stop haunting him?

With a soft curse, Fen wrenched his thoughts away from the maudlin past before he slipped further into despair. He tried his best to relax against the stone wall as he'd once done so often when he was alone and needing comfort. But he expected no response from the Earth—not anymore.

To his surprise, the cave's welcome washed through him without conscious effort. Just like that. Unwittingly, Fen's muscles loosened, and his body eased into the rock until he could almost merge with it. He hadn't dared reach this far in years. What was going on? It was almost as though the Earth sensed his turmoil and sought him out, but that couldn't be right. Could it?

Whispers of the cave's past filled him. Sediments drifting in a languid sea, settling peacefully. Pressure. Endless pressure. Solidity. Water receding. Then almost-pain as the Earth shifted, folding stone until it reached into the sky. More water, this time trickling from above. Washing away bits and pieces, carving out holes in the mountain.

Upheaval that brought peace. Constant change that forever stayed the same.

Perhaps upheaval is necessary for life, young one.

Fen's eyes popped open, and he jerked his mind free of the earth-connection as the words resounded in his head. That hadn't been from Earth, and it sure as hell hadn't come from him. He peered around the area, studying it visually and with magic, but no one was there. His gaze landed on the door leading out of the outpost proper. But despite the suspicion that filled him, he couldn't find a single flaw in the shielding that would have allowed in an intruder's thoughts.

He settled back against the stone again, but the peace was shattered. Maybe he was losing his mind. He certainly had cause to. Every time his life stabilized, something else happened to throw it into flux. His brain couldn't even decide which problem to fixate on, though at least he'd been distracted from thinking about the bomb his uncle had just dropped on Fen's potential mates.

Naturally, that was when he sensed Vek's approach. So much for distractions.

Anger surged until Fen's senses blurred with it. Fortunately, his uncle stopped in the corridor leading into the room. Was he simply checking to make sure Fen was okay, or did he hesitate because he knew he'd dropped off the edge of the map straight into Dickville? Vek had to realize that Fen wanted to kick his ass.

A scuffing sound and a hint of soft, familiar energy near the entrance caught his attention, and Fen froze at the sight of Anna entering the chamber. She approached the bathing pool, her attention focused on the water, but after a quick shake of her head, she spun away and headed along the path that led to Fen's hiding place. Vek must have told her where to find him.

It figured.

Without a word, Anna sank down near him, her right knee almost touching his left. She glanced curiously around the chamber, a slight smile on her lips, and Fen's throat closed at the easy, casual look on her face. He wanted to ask her what she thought of his uncle's revelation. He longed to find out what she was feeling, but at the same time… Well, maybe it was better not to know.

She was just so *good*. It radiated from her, a purity that gleamed to his inner sight. She was the oak that grew resolutely beside the treacherous river. Her roots dug deep, pulling turbulent emotions from the world and cleansing them in her peace. Fen had been around her enough to know that she could undo him with a touch—if his darkness didn't hurt her first. Didn't she realize how risky it was to be around him?

"You shouldn't be here," he said gruffly.

Her smile widened. "Why? I have it on good authority that we could be mates. Yet here you are, moping in a cave instead of talking things through with me and Maddy."

"I needed to think." Fen huffed, though he was mostly frustrated at himself. Dammit, she was right. "I hadn't decided what to say, and then Vek had to get his nosy ass involved. This isn't something that should have been dropped on you like that."

"I'm not delicate," Anna countered, her smile disappearing. "People think I am, but they are wrong."

"I wasn't saying that you are." Oak trees were beautiful, but they were most known for being strong. Not that he was going to share that analogy with her at the moment. "But you and Maddy are together. You're solid. And I… Look, I'm bad news. Now that you both know the truth, you should go home and be happy. Forget about me."

Anna nearly choked on her laugh. "Sure. Forget about you."

"I'm serious," he grumbled. "We might have spent a little time together lately, but we haven't talked about my past. If Maddy told you any of it…"

She didn't even flinch. Instead, her gaze softened. "Everyone makes mistakes."

Why didn't she get it? Fen tipped his head back against the stone and closed his eyes. He couldn't watch her as he spoke, couldn't see the horror creep across her face. "I killed twelve people just a couple of weeks ago."

He heard her suck in a harsh breath, but he didn't dare look at her. Silence hummed around them, broken only by the occasional drip of water into the bathing pool. Fen expected her to flee at any moment, but her presence remained steady. He could barely resist the temptation to turn to her as he waited for a reaction.

Then her hand gripped his knee, her energy connecting with his as they finally touched. Even during the hours they'd spent together gaming, they'd never made physical contact, and the sensation… His entire body hardening at the beauty of her essence, he struggled to take in air. Anna wasn't really purity or innocence—she was grace. Dear gods. She had to sense the darkness of his soul as he felt her light. She had to realize that even her forgiveness could only go so far.

"Why, Fen?" she whispered.

It took him a solid minute to figure out what she was asking. "Dria challenged my grandfather, the king of the Unseelie, to a duel of honor. When she stripped away the glamour hiding his true nature, he ordered his soldiers to break protocol and attack. To help Vek, I entered the fight."

Her fingers tightened gently around his knee. "I would do the same if someone threatened Maddy or my parents. Well, okay, I would try. I'm no warrior."

Fen finally cracked his eyes open a sliver. Damn. She was undaunted. "I didn't even think about it, and I honestly don't feel a lot of remorse. How fucked up is that?"

Anna frowned. "I don't know what I'd feel, so I can't judge."

Seriously? It didn't bother her at all? Fen straightened, surprising her into pulling her hand away. "I dug my fangs into their throats and tore." He opened his mouth and pointed at one of the fangs in question. "These. Right here. I took their blood and sucked out their energy."

Her eyes widened and her skin paled, but she didn't run away screaming. "Unnecessarily graphic much? Dead is dead, Fen. I didn't need to hear how you killed them."

Fen let out a long, frustrated groan. "What is your deal? You act like you would consider mating with me, but you don't even know me. Not really. How can none of what I said bother you?"

"Mostly because I can tell you're saying it to bother me." Anna tipped her chin up, revealing the stubborn tenacity hidden beneath her apparent gentleness. "Stop trying to scare me away to save me or some other such noble bullshit. You *are* feeling guilty about the people you killed, or you wouldn't be talking about it. You wouldn't be using it to push me away. I have no idea if I want to mate with you or anyone, but *I'm* not the one afraid to consider the possibility. Clearly, you are."

Damn. He'd thought Maddy was direct. "I've seen a lot of bad stuff, and I'm not sure I'll ever feel comfortable sharing it. A mate deserves more."

"You think you're the only one who hides your problems?" Anna averted her gaze. "Sometimes I keep things from Maddy for her own good. Nothing so dark, but I think it's in our nature to protect our loved ones. And lately…"

Concern drummed loudly in his ears. "Are you okay?"

Anna stared at the pool of water, and he noticed then how her body angled toward it as though connected. Almost forcefully, she turned her face away and met his eyes. "I nearly climbed a fence so I could walk into the river tonight. I had my foot on the rung when Maddy showed up, but she has no idea. I can't tell her."

"What?" This time, it was Fen who gripped her knee. "Has something upset you? Gods, it isn't me, is it? Maddy would never leave you for—"

"No," Anna said, her hand resting across his. "I'm not suicidal, but I appreciate the concern. It's…it's the water. I'm so drawn to it, but I don't think it would hurt me. I don't want to find out otherwise, though."

"Why won't you tell Maddy? She would understand."

Anna's cheeks puffed out with her sigh. "We have talked about it a little, but I've held back the worst. I thought I had everything under control. But after tonight, I'm going to have to say something. I just… Fen, she has to get this training on Moranaia. Do you think she'll go if she's worried about me drowning in the river? I don't want her to miss this chance."

It was a fair point. When Fen had been sick with the energy poisoning Kien had released upon his death, Maddy had attempted to help, but only he and Maddy knew how iffy it had been. For whatever reason, she could barely control her healing magic. She truly did need that training.

"You have my number, right?" Fen asked, bracing himself for her reaction. "I'll help. Whatever happens with the mate thing, even if you and Maddy decide against bonding with me, I'll help. If the pull gets too strong, you can hang with me. Vek's house is up in the mountains. We'll play video games and avoid the river."

A smile broke across her face once more. "We'd better not start *Death's Curse 3* without Maddy, though, or she'll kill us."

"We can go buy another—"

Vek's mind slammed into his with almost painful abruptness. *"Get your ass back up here. We have a problem."*

Fen blinked. Truth be told, he hadn't been paying attention to his uncle's movements. When had he left the entrance to the bathing chamber? *"I don't want to talk to you."*

"I don't give a fuck. Get up here now. Bring Anna."

As quickly as it had appeared, Vek's presence was gone, and Fen focused on a bemused Anna. "My uncle just summoned me back to the top. Both of us, actually."

She frowned down at his hands. "But you don't have your phone."

"Telepathically," Fen explained. "Can't you communicate that way?"

"I…" Anna shrugged. "I don't know."

"Something to figure out later, I guess. We'd better go before Vek hauls us up there bodily."

Though she chuckled, Anna rose gracefully to her feet as Fen fumbled his own way to a standing position. Prickles danced down his legs and gathered in his soles, and he stomped lightly to help the blood return. He'd meditated with the Earth more deeply than he'd realized if his limbs had fallen asleep. Ah, well. His feet would just have to hurt.

Vek had sounded worried, and that was never a good sign.

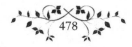

After disconnecting his consciousness from the stream, Meren stretched onto his back and let the cold water wash over him. His little expedition had drained his reserves, but it had been worth it. A smile crossed his lips as his body soaked in the energy swirling around him. The Moranaians thought they'd shielded their cavern, but they forever underestimated the tenacity of water.

It was true that he could no longer travel physically through the countless channels dripping and flowing through the stone. An inconvenience to be sure. But there was a spot where this stream flowed into the bathing chamber where he could push his thoughts close enough to pick up on conversations on the other side. As soon as he'd detected Fen drawing near, he'd sent his consciousness through the water to investigate.

So many of his plans failed that Meren had long ago learned to adapt. From secretly inciting a rebellion millennia ago in an attempt to overthrow the Seelie queen to manipulating the Unseelie king through a secret alliance with Ara, he'd often been required to wear away at his obstacles or go around them. He'd even fooled his so-called-brother Naomh into allowing Prince Kien to spread his poison through Earth's energy and into the connected magical realms, all while Meren secretly used the illness for his own purposes.

Each attempt toward one goal: to claim the Seelie throne.

Hopefully, he hadn't gone too far this time. Fen hadn't detected his presence despite searching for the source of the whisper Meren had planted in his head. Even so, Meren had been forced to divert a fair amount of energy from cloaking his blood to shielding himself from the female Gwragedd Annwn. It would be a miracle if Vek hadn't sensed him during the lapse, which meant he would have to hide far out of sight.

A small price for the knowledge he'd gained. So the boy had a possible mate now, and one who was drawn to the river. Meren had been trying for nearly two decades to find a way to get the young Unseelie under his control so he would have leverage over Ara, the princess-turned-queen who'd lied about being his ally.

She would pay for that slight, if not directly then through her son Fen. And if Meren was careful, well… A *Felshreh* earth mage and his Gwragedd Annwn mate would make powerful friends.

6

Maddy tapped one last note into her phone before turning it off and sticking it in her pocket. "Okay, I think I'm set for this visit. Tomorrow around mid-morning. You're sure it won't be a problem to keep an eye on Anna?"

"I see no problem—"

Dria stopped talking mid-sentence, her expression darkening, and Vek jerked to his feet. The scowl on his face combined with Dria's reaction had Maddy's heart pounding in her chest. There was a cruel, ruthless twist to Vek's lips that she'd never seen. She'd thought she'd witnessed his darker nature when the outpost was under threat, but those times were nothing compared to this. What was going on?

"Fen and Anna are on their way up," Vek said.

"How far away?" Dria asked as she twisted her shoulder-length red hair back and tied it. "Will we need a portal?"

Maddy's brows furrowed. "A portal to find Fen and Anna?"

"No," Vek answered, nostrils flaring. "Meren. I sensed him, but only for a moment. If I had to wager, I'd say he was in the camp his people had made in the adjacent mountain."

That couldn't be good. By all accounts, Meren had gone into hiding to escape the Seelie queen after he had tried to kill his own brother and then defied orders to send his minions to Earth's surface. Not to mention dodging the deadly intentions of Vek, the Unseelie, and the Moranaians. Could the guy be that much of an idiot? Unless he'd found a lot of new allies, it didn't make sense for him to hang around.

"Are you sure it was him?" Maddy asked.

"Of course it was him." Vek paused beside Dria's chair, his body practically vibrating with energy. "I have been waiting for him to lower the spell he uses to keep me from tracking him, and for a moment, he did. Blood never lies."

Maddy was no expert on blood magic, but she had no doubt that Vek was. If he was certain, then she had no reason not to believe him, stupid move on Meren's part or not. Any discussions about additional trips to Moranaia could be completed later.

"I've ordered several mages and warriors to meet us in the portal room." Dria stood. "I'll build a gate to the spot where we battled the invaders last time."

Vek ran his finger down his mate's cheek. "*Ahmeeren*, I wouldn't have you go back there so soon. I know Gessen's loss still grieves you."

"I'm hardly going to dishonor his memory by cowering," Dria said, though the sadness in her eyes caught at Maddy's heart. "It's the best place to go. Meren isn't likely to expect us to act so soon, even if it is a trap. Perhaps we can prevent him from rebuilding his group's numbers."

Maddy's phone vibrated against her hip, and she pulled it from her pocket to check the notifications. A text. While Vek and Dria debated strategy, Maddy unlocked her phone to read the message. Anthony's name popped up, and she frowned. Was he that impatient?

Sorry to bother you. One of my group members came in to the clinic sick. Could be a virus, but something was wrong with her energy. Not sure what to do. You said something about healing with magic?

"Fuck," Maddy blurted, almost dropping her phone.

Dria lifted a brow. "What's wrong?"

"That guy I mentioned before we started planning my trip to Moranaia..." Maddy caught Vek's gaze. "A man came into the shop today. He described an encounter he and his friend, someone named Ryan, had on the street, and it sounded like he'd met you. Anthony said a really pale guy told Ryan he had Unseelie blood, but his friend panicked. Fen, I assume, gave Anthony my information in case they had trouble. Well, they're having trouble."

Vek nodded. "I remember them. Is said trouble currently relevant? We must track Meren."

Fen and Anna hurried in before Maddy could answer. Surprisingly, they both appeared calm, aside from the annoyed look Fen turned on his uncle. "Our asses are now here," Fen said. "What gives?"

"I detected Meren," Vek announced.

"Ah, hell." Fen scrubbed at his face. "I guess my body count is about to rise."

Something about his expression saddened her, though he'd delivered the words matter-of-factly. Anna must have felt the same, because she halted beside Fen and settled her hand on his shoulder. An unnamable twist of emotion caught Maddy by surprise. She didn't think it was jealousy. No, it was more like isolation. Or maybe longing?

It definitely didn't blend well with the fear Anthony's text had lodged in her stomach.

"You needn't go with us," Vek said, his eyes narrowing on Fen's face. "Maddy was telling me of some trouble with Ryan, that kid with Unseelie blood we ran across in town."

Maddy lifted her phone, giving it a jiggle. "Not just that. Anthony texted me to say that someone in his coven is sick. Something is wrong with her energy."

Vek waved his hand. "He probably can't tell one human illness from another."

"Anthony is a nurse practitioner working on his doctorate," Maddy said. "He studies human illnesses for a living. He's also fae, and though I don't know his knowledge base, I wouldn't discount his ability to detect a problem with a person's energy."

Fen cursed. "Do you think it's related to the virus we had?"

"I don't know, but we need to find out."

"It's decided, then," Vek said. "You three investigate the possible disease while we track Meren."

"Not that I want to do more killing, but are you sure you won't need my help to stop Meren?" Fen stared at his uncle for so long that Maddy kept looking between the two to figure out why. She still hadn't divined the reason when Fen shook his head and continued. "You're sending me away on purpose."

Vek merely smiled. "Perhaps."

"Come on." Dria gestured toward the door. "I'll make you a portal before I create ours. Maddy can attune the connecting stone on the other end that will allow her to return without contacting me. It'll be more efficient than calling before each visit."

Maddy stood, slipping the phone into her pocket. "So long as you tell me what to do."

"Of course."

As Maddy trailed the others out of the room, her thoughts pinged between the possible return of a virus that could sicken the fae and her upcoming journey to Moranaia. Should she delay the trip in order to investigate the virus? It was tempting, but she would be better served on both counts by speaking with Lial. Without training, Maddy wouldn't be able to help if there was a problem.

Not unless she needed to kill someone.

As soon as the three of them exited the portal into the shop, Anna and Fen stepped out of the way so that Maddy could use the stone Dria had given her. Anna studied her girlfriend curiously. Despite living with a half-Sidhe woman, Anna hadn't seen a great deal of true magic. The hum of power danced along her skin with a pleasant tingle as Maddy held a palm-length, multifaceted crystal into the gateway that still showed the underground outpost. Light surged, and the hum turned into a vibration.

On the other side, Dria flicked her fingers, and the glow intensified until Anna had to pinch her eyes closed. She trembled with the force of the power, but it didn't hurt. The resonance was…she didn't know what it was. It echoed through her like the call of water, but she didn't feel the urge to step inside and lose herself. She was a calm lake rippling from the soft plop of a thrown stone.

The power cut off as Fen's hand settled on her shoulder. "Anna?"

She opened her eyes at his whisper. The gate was gone, and Maddy was shoving the crystal in her pocket. Anna spun to face Fen, dislodging his hand before her girlfriend could see it. Not that she felt guilty. Earlier, though, Maddy hadn't looked pleased to see her comforting Fen.

"That was interesting," Anna said with a tentative smile.

Fen's frown didn't ease.

Maddy glanced between them as she approached. "Something wrong?"

"No," Anna answered quickly. "I was surprised by the magic, and I think it worried Fen. That's the most powerful spell I've ever seen. Fen was checking on me. Sorry for freaking you out with my reaction, Fen."

Hell, she was rambling. Maybe she could even reference Fen a few more times to make it sound like she was obsessed. His brows had risen as she spoke, and at her groan, a wry smile twisted his lips. Ugh. She wasn't obsessed, but speaking with him in the cave had started something between them. Like the magic, she couldn't quite tell what.

"This is so awkward," Maddy muttered.

Surprisingly, the comment had Anna's shoulders drooping with relief, and a small laugh slipped out. "Yeah."

Fen rubbed the back of his neck. "Do you think this sort of thing would be less weird if we hadn't grown up on Earth? From the way Vek talks, bonds with multiple partners aren't that unusual. I mean, polyam is definitely a thing here, but…"

"It's not mainstream," Anna finished for him. "I couldn't say about the other, though. I don't know a thing about my fae ancestors. I was adopted as a baby, so my parents wouldn't have a clue, either."

Surprise crossed Fen's face. "You were adopted?"

"Yeah," Anna said. It had never been a big thing to her, so others' reactions usually amused her. But Fen's expression gave her pause. "Is there something wrong with that?"

"No, of course not," Fen rushed to answer. "I…I was a foster kid. Not adopted, though."

Silence fell between them. Maddy lowered her phone, her concerned gaze on Fen. Anna nibbled on her bottom lip. What could she say that wouldn't sound trite or assholish? From the pain barely banked in his eyes, it obviously bothered him. She'd never known that reality—that uncertainty of whether she belonged.

"The foster system sucks," Anna finally said. "So many kids get lost in it. If my parents hadn't known my birth mother, I have no idea what would have happened to me. My understanding is that they convinced her to let them adopt."

Fen averted his eyes. "I was five. After my father died… Let's just say it's not easy to be an orphaned blood elf."

Her heart pinched, and her hand tingled with the urge to reach out to him. Maddy's fingers had gone white around her phone, and when Anna met her gaze, understanding passed between them. They both wanted to comfort Fen, but neither of them had a clue how. Some experiences couldn't be healed, only eased.

A loud chirp from Maddy's phone made them all jump, and Fen laughed uneasily. "Perfect time for a subject change. Is it from Anthony?"

Fen's voice sounded nonchalant, and when he glanced up, his eyes were clear

of the pain she'd glimpsed earlier. But the resonance she felt from him didn't lie. No matter how he tried to appear, the agony of his past was merely shoved down, not gone. Maybe someday she would be able to help, but not now.

"Yeah," Maddy said softly. "He sent me his address. The clinic is closed, but his coven mate is with him."

Fen waved his hand toward the door. "Great. Let's go."

"Don't you think we should talk about this?" Maddy asked, settling her free hand on her hip.

"My past is over, and we have more import—"

"We *do* need to talk about that, I suspect, but that's not what I meant." Maddy shook her head. "I'm not sure we should go to this guy's house. He seemed perfectly nice, but it might be risky to meet somewhere private."

Anna frowned at that. She'd been willing to charge right along with Fen, but Maddy had a point. Good grief. When had Maddy become the hesitant one? "Could they come here?"

Maddy glanced at the screen of her phone. "It's almost eleven at night. I'm worried enough about how it will look for us to be seen leaving the shop at this hour, but having a couple of people show up this late... No, it isn't a good plan. There aren't many people downtown at this hour, but I still don't want to risk notice."

Fen let out a sharp bark of laughter. "You're worried about Anthony? I could subdue him in about two seconds. Give me ten, and I could drain him. I can't imagine his friend would be much more of a challenge considering the other shit I've dealt with."

"And I could stop his heart." An angry red stained Maddy's cheeks. "That's not the point. We can't possibly know what to expect. What if we're being set up by some of Meren's friends?"

"Then we'll be helping Vek and Dria by disposing of a few of the bastards."

"We need to—"

"Can we just get this over with?" Anna found herself snapping. "I've been on my feet for hours, and I'd like to go home and sleep. At this point, I'm about ready to strangle someone myself. Either we're going to go investigate or we aren't."

Maddy's and Fen's shocked expressions might have been comical under different circumstances. Then Maddy winced. "Sorry. Do you want me to take you to the house?"

Anna dug her fingers into her palms to keep from shouting at her girlfriend. For a couple of months, Maddy had been treating her like she couldn't handle her world. Like magic and magical creatures would somehow terrify or incapacitate her—even after Anna's own fae blood had awakened. It was ridiculous. How was she going to learn about herself or what she could do if everyone pretended like she was some fragile being incapable of understanding?

Having non-human blood had been a surprise, but she wasn't going to mope about it.

"You are *not* leaving me out," Anna said firmly. "Vek suggested that all three of us research this illness, and I'm going to hold up my end."

Maddy shifted her weight, crossing her arms. "But you don't know how to access your magic. Maybe you should come with me to Moranaia to seek your own training."

"Stop. It." Anna gritted her teeth so she wouldn't say more. Now wasn't the time. "I'm fine. Let's go find out what's going on with this guy, and we can talk about the rest later."

Maddy's cheeks puffed out before she released her breath with a soft pop. "Fine."

It was a small victory, but Anna would take it.

Dria tried not to stare at the spot where Gessen had been impaled by an enemy mage, but her eyes kept wandering there despite her intentions. The stalagmite that had shoved through her friend's heart was gone, no sign of blood marring the area where he'd fallen. Really, the only things that marked it were her memories and the cleanliness of the space.

The rest of the broad cavern was coated in soot from where Vek had burned the bodies of their fallen enemies. Neither he nor the mages and scouts who had swept in behind had bothered to sweep the mess away—a clear warning for their enemies if any more were to take this path. Dria couldn't help but approve. She wasn't as bloodthirsty as her evil brother Kien, but even she wouldn't have minded a few heads on spikes after what they'd done to Gessen.

"Are you certain you are ready for this, *ahmeeren*?" Vek asked softly.

Dria scowled. "I hope you aren't questioning my ability to lead this mission."

"No." Vek lifted his hands, palms outward. "But I can't help my concern for my mate."

Her irritation eased until she could offer him a smile. "I know. I suppose I *am* a little shaken. Why don't we move on from this chamber so we can get this over with?"

At his nod, Dria signaled for the first half of the mages and scouts to advance toward the opening at the far end. She'd never been beyond this area, although the members of their troop in the front had swept the entire cave system after the last attack on the outpost. As the rest of the group took formation behind them, Dria squared her shoulders and gathered a fire spell in her palm. A network of shielding held by several mages tightened around them as they made their way toward the enemy camp.

After far too many twists, turns, squeezes, and climbs, the advance troops reached the hallway leading to the broad natural chamber where the Seelie and Unseelie traitors had made their base. Dria sent out the order to halt, and the group froze as she scanned the area, then scanned it again. No spells or physical traps that she could detect.

"Do you sense anyone?" Dria sent Vek.

"No," Vek answered, his mental voice ringing confidently in her head. *"I can't sense Meren through the blood link, and my life magic reveals no lifeforms that shouldn't be here."*

"Maybe Meren is still here, masking his presence. Odd for him to come alone."

"I'm thinking…" His voice trailed off, sparking Dria's curiosity. Vek rarely hesitated. *"I want to try to close up this chamber. If he's here, he won't escape being trapped by a mountain of stone, and if he's not, we've still sealed up a weakness."*

"But?"

Vek frowned. *"It will take a great deal of my energy without Fen to help."*

"I'll see you fed, my love," Dria answered silkily, grinning when he trembled at the memory of the last time she'd let him take blood—in bed. *"Don't worry about that. Your plan is a good one. I've been uneasy about the vulnerability this place presents."*

"Fine, though I'll see you pay for getting me worked up with your innuendo."

Dria poked him in the side. *"I'm counting on it."*

He cast her one promise-filled look before striding through the troop waiting patiently in front of them. Though she wanted to call him back, urge him to be more cautious, Dria didn't. It would be as useful as telling fire not to burn to request he not do what he thought was necessary. What she herself would do, if the truth be told. Had she the power to shape earth, she would help cast the spell.

Instead, Dria followed him to the opening of the cavern chamber. Fedah and Nia stepped forward to flank her, ready to protect her with their magic. Dria gave each a grateful smile and halted just behind and to Vek's left as he directed a dim globe of light into the space. Over his shoulder, she glimpsed the large room beyond in the pale glow.

The stone hadn't been smoothed or shaped the way the central cavern of the outpost had, but then, it hadn't been created by a dragon and her life mage rider. Stalagmites and stalactites speared everywhere, only a few open spaces scattered through the cavern. It must have been unpleasant for those who'd tried to camp here, but Dria couldn't summon any sympathy for the bastards. Hopefully, they'd hated every moment of their stay.

A thin waterfall trickled into a pool on the distant side, and she stifled the pinch of regret at its destruction. Meren had used water to sneak into her and Vek's room a couple of weeks before, and Vek had almost died after being stabbed. Though they'd found a water mage to shield the water from future incursions, it wouldn't hurt to eliminate this waterfall and its potential usefulness.

Dria didn't flinch as the rock shifted before her eyes. She didn't feel anything except for satisfaction.

7

Anthony's house turned out to be a modest apartment not too far away from the university. Maddy studied his living room with curiosity as he led them over to the small, worn couch. A flat screen television sat atop a wood entertainment center, a video game console beneath it. Textbooks covered the coffee table, and the loveseat beside that had notebooks piled up on one side, highlighters huddled in a pile against the seat cushion. The only decoration was a carving of a leaf-covered face adorning the wall.

"Have a seat, guys. Sparrow is lying down in the other room," Anthony said. "I'll go get her."

"Sparrow?" Maddy asked before she could stop herself.

Anthony grinned. "Her Craft name. She's not as cool with giving out her real name as I am."

A Craft name. Maddy hadn't read a great deal about modern paganism, but that sounded familiar. Living in the Bible belt, she supposed having a code name made a certain amount of sense. "Whatever works."

As Anthony headed down a narrow hallway, Maddy lowered herself to the couch, Anna on one side and Fen on the other. Anna eased closer, brushing shoulders with Maddy, but Fen held himself apart. Was he bothered by their potential link? They hadn't discussed what had occurred when Anna had followed him earlier, though they'd had the chance on the car ride over. Maybe none of them wanted to find out what would happen once they did.

A moment later, Anthony led a woman about Maddy's age into the room. Her warm beige skin had a green tinge, and deep shadows curved beneath her brown eyes. Even her dark hair hung in lank clumps around her face. The woman—Sparrow, presumably—sniffled and then rubbed a tissue against her red nose.

Fen darted to his feet. "Here. You can sit by Maddy so she can examine you."

The woman halted. "Examine?"

"I'm in training to be a healer," Maddy said softly. A bit of a stretch, that claim, but it was technically true. "With magic, that is. I'm not allowed to use my talent to fix the problem yet, but I can scan you to find out what is wrong."

Lial hadn't given her that restriction, but Sparrow didn't need to know that. No one needed to know that.

After studying her for a moment, the woman sneezed again. Then she relaxed, nodded, and continued forward to claim the seat Fen had abandoned. "I guess Anthony told you to call me Sparrow."

"Yes," Maddy answered. "Is that okay?"

"Please." Sparrow nibbled on her lower lip. "I don't understand what's going on with me. As far as I know, my parents haven't had any weird things happening, but if Anthony is right about me having fae blood, you'd think they'd show it first."

Anthony leaned his hip against the back of the loveseat. "I was just telling you what I sensed. Anyway, genetics is weird. If each parent had a small percentage of fae genes that made it onto your X chromosomes, you might end up with more of those traits than either parent alone. Each egg and sperm get a different combo of genetic material, so even a sibling—"

"Cool," Sparrow interrupted. "But can we not? I'm freaked out enough without the scientific analysis."

"Sorry," Anthony mumbled.

Maddy did her best to look reassuring. "Mind if I go ahead and scan you? It might help answer your questions, but I'm not sure how comfortable you are with magic."

"Well, I got a lot more familiar with it at our last circle," Sparrow said, flicking a knowing look at Anthony. "We both did. As long as it doesn't hurt, scan away."

Maddy closed her eyes, trying to tune out the others. No easy feat with two potential mates and two strangers in the room, but she managed. As soon as her mind was clear, she stretched out her hands and extended her energy. Gently. Tentatively. She directed it toward Sparrow, brushing against the other's power with a soft mental hand.

Surprisingly, the woman's shields were formidable. Not dangerous, exactly, but it took Maddy a fair bit of time to weave around and through them until she could get to the heart of Sparrow's magic. Her shoulders drooped with exhaustion by the time she managed it, and she was so tired she didn't immediately notice the dark, sick pulse coating Sparrow's light like oil on feathers.

Maddy almost tugged herself free out of reflex, but she forced her energy to remain in place so she could probe the magic glowing green to her inner sight. Not the healthy green of life, either. This was the fearful color of the sky before a tornado. The tinge of a sick person's skin before they vomited.

And it settled near Sparrow's center, a splinter of evil much like the energy Fen had once borne in his heart before Aris had cured him.

How was this possible? Fen's splinter had been caused by Prince Kien. The madman had shoved his poisoned spell through her friend in a last attempt at revenge before his death. Later, another illness had taken root in Fen, this one affecting his

immune system despite having a magical origin. A disease, though elves and fae didn't catch diseases as humans did. None of them were sure whether the splinter had caused his illness or if it had been unrelated, but at least Lial had managed to heal the second one after Aris had cleansed the first.

Maddy scanned Sparrow again to be sure—but no. This little fragment of evil wasn't what was causing Sparrow to be sick. As Anthony had diagnosed, that was a cold virus. Enough of an anomaly among the fae, whose bodies used magic to cleanse away illnesses before they happened, but Maddy estimated that Sparrow had a minor portion of non-human blood. At that level, the occasional short-lived cold wasn't uncommon.

At least it hadn't been before magic had reappeared on Earth.

She returned herself fully to her body, and almost at once, the weight of her effort hit her. Maddy slumped back against Anna, who shifted to support her. Rubbing at her eyes, Maddy shoved aside her exhaustion and straightened with a grateful glance at her girlfriend.

"So, uh, where do you live?" Maddy asked, hoping her words didn't slur.

Sparrow stiffened. "Why do you need to know that?"

"I don't mean the exact location," Maddy rushed to add. "Just the general area. The last time I saw the sickness that's attacking your energy, it was in Fen."

At Maddy's gesture, Sparrow frowned over at Fen, who had gone still and solemn at the news. "He looks okay. And I still don't get what that has to do with where I live."

"I'm just trying to figure out how you came into contact with the same source. There's...there's a lot to explain, so bear with me." Maddy took a deep breath. "A few months back, an evil prince from the elven world of Moranaia was trying to poison Earth's energy. His plan ended when he was defeated on his home world, but he managed to send poison through to here. As far as I was aware, only Fen and one place on Earth were affected."

"An elven world," Sparrow whispered. "If not for the last few weeks, I'd think you were crazy as shit, girl."

Maddy laughed. "Trust me, I know."

His expression now blank, Fen pushed away from the wall where he stood. "You can't confirm the location unless you clear it with Dria."

Dammit. Maddy stifled a groan, but she couldn't deny the truth of Fen's words. No one in the human world was aware of the outpost, at least as far as they knew, and she couldn't do anything to risk that. Not without permission. Anyway, the only person capable of healing this type of poison was Aris, a mage who was able to channel and direct pure life energy, and he lived on Moranaia. Hopefully, she could speak to him and Lial about it during her visit.

"I guess it doesn't matter where you live, at least not at the moment," Maddy said. "I think I know someone who could help, but he's Moranaian. How about you stay here with Anthony, if it's cool with him, and he can let me know if you get worse. Or I guess you could text me yourself if there's a problem."

Anna rubbed Maddy's shoulder. "You're going out of town tomorrow, love."

"I'll give them my number," Fen said softly. "I could probably get a message through."

Sparrow's eyes shifted to Anthony as she sneezed again into her tissue. "I don't want to put anyone out. I can hunker in my room and avoid my roommates."

"No," Anthony said with a firm shake of his head. "I'd rather you stay here if you're okay with it. I'll be in class or at the clinic most of the time, anyway, but I'll be able to check on you when I'm not. You tested negative for the flu, but a cold virus might not act the way I'd expect with this weird energy thing. Makes me uneasy."

The two stared at each other for a long moment before Sparrow finally nodded. "If it's really no trouble."

"You're my friend, not trouble."

Another wave of exhaustion rushed through Maddy, and she almost slumped against Anna again. At Fen's frown of concern, though, she forced a smile and stood. "I don't think the virus will interact with the energy poisoning, but I'm glad you won't be alone. You should probably trade phone numbers with Fen before we leave, though. I'll see if I can get that helper I mentioned to come here, but it might be a day or two."

"Wait," Sparrow said, a hint of panic in her tone. "A cold is one thing, but you didn't tell me what this dark energy is going to do. Am I... Could it kill me?"

Maddy thought back to what she'd found during her examination. The poison hadn't been as severe as what she'd seen in Fen's heart, a tiny splinter compared to a log. And without the poison pulsing in the energies of the Earth, the effects didn't appear to be as dire.

"I don't think so," Maddy finally answered. "You're nowhere near as sick as Fen was. Just rest and try to stay calm. He went weeks with the same thing at a far more advanced state. We'll be able to help you."

Some of the fear eased out of Sparrow's face, but it didn't leave Maddy's heart. *Please don't let me be giving her false assurances,* Maddy prayed to any deity willing to listen. Though her words had probably been true, there were no guarantees. Was this the fate of the healer? The curse? It was a weighty thing to be someone's hope, and it would only get heavier as she advanced with her training. Hopefully, she'd be able to bear the burden.

And not kill people—that would be a good start.

❧

Holy hell, this entire situation was fucked.

Light flickered against Fen's closed eyelids, the flashes as chaotic and random as his life. His head rocked against the headrest, and the temptation to lie down in the back seat of Maddy's car pulled at him. Maybe he could curl up around the pain of existing. Of course, he'd long ago learned the futility of that. He would keep existing, and it would keep sucking.

Horrible enough that he'd inadvertently killed his own cousin with that ill-thought energy poisoning spell. Fen had deserved the splinter of darkness that Kien had hit him with, and he'd deserved to get sick again not long after. Sparrow? She was innocent. The poor woman hadn't even known she had fae blood, and now she bore the same poison that had afflicted him.

Would this shit ever end?

The car came to an abrupt stop, shocking Fen from his thoughts. He cracked open his eyes to see that Maddy had pulled the car into a driveway in front of a series of condos. He blinked and rubbed his face. Had something happened that he wasn't aware of? He'd assumed they would drop him off at Vek's house.

"What's going on?" he asked.

Maddy only glanced at him through the rearview mirror, but Anna turned in her seat, a serious expression on her face. "You're sleeping on our couch."

He stared at Anna. "What?"

"It's almost one in the morning, and Vek's house is up the side of a damned mountain on the other end of town," Maddy answered for her. "I'm too tired to drive that far. I asked Anna before we left, and she agreed. Unless it bothers you to stay over?"

Fen sat forward until he could rest his arms on the back of their seats. "I don't mind. But…"

"We've both worked all day," Maddy said, impatience and exhaustion warring in her tone. "Whatever you're going to say, just spit it out."

He winced. "Sorry. I worry about causing more…awkwardness. We haven't talked about what Vek so kindly revealed, and I can't help but notice how mad you seem about it."

Maddy's expression softened. "I'm not mad, Fen. Not really. But I admit I don't know what to do about it all. Right now, I want to get some sleep and see if my brain works better tomorrow. I'm too tired to sort out my emotions."

"Fair enough," Fen said.

"Hey, if you spend the night, we can talk about it in the morning before Maddy leaves," Anna said.

"Yeah," Fen answered, knowing there was a bitterness to his tone but unable to stop it.

It was going to be a special kind of hell sleeping a room away from his potential mates, especially with so much hanging between them. He'd probably spend the night staring at the ceiling. The discomfort would be worth it, though, since it would save Maddy from having to drive when she was clearly exhausted. It wouldn't be fair to ask her to do that, and calling for a rideshare would be rude after their offer. He didn't want either woman to think he disliked them.

Far, far from it.

With a tired sigh, Fen shoved the car door open and unfolded himself from the back. The thud of their doors closing echoed along the quiet street, making him

wince, but he followed the ladies into the house without comment. No need to disturb the neighbors further. They didn't deserve the same level of exhaustion he was sure to end up with.

While Maddy gave him a short tour of their small condo, Anna grabbed him a blanket and pillow. The living room was clean but a little cluttered, with books crammed into every conceivable inch of their bookcase, papers and pretty glass paperweights scattered across a tiny computer desk, and a couple of cups and plates on the coffee table. There were a few dishes in the kitchen sink, and in their room, the rumpled covers on their bed revealed their lack of care for the small details.

But it was a homey kind of disorder.

Anna had found bedding by the time they ducked out of the half-bath tucked next to the laundry closet. Grinning, she held out a pale pink and brown blanket. "Hope you're not the kind of guy who cares about colors."

Fen snorted. "Nah. The color of my blanket is pretty far down my list of fucks given."

He thought he caught the sound of a stifled laugh from Maddy, but when he glanced at her, her lips were merely twitching. "So what do you have to clear off that list to make it a big deal?"

"Honestly?" he asked as he took the blanket from Anna and unfolded it. "I'd say just about everything. People stress out about the strangest shit."

Anna chuckled. "So true."

Fen plopped down on the couch and shoved his pillow against the armrest. "Okay, you two go to bed. I'll be fine out here. Pink blanket and all."

It was true, even if he didn't sleep.

After Maddy and Anna bid him goodnight, Fen stretched out on the couch and tugged the blanket over his lower body, though it wasn't cold in the room. It was just comforting somehow. His nose twitched, and the scents imbued in the cloth hit him as he tucked it under his chin. It smelled like both women. Clearly, too. Maybe they cuddled on the couch beneath this very blanket.

Fen groaned low in his throat at that mental image, but he cut the sound off before the women could hear. Yeah, sleep wasn't likely with pictures like that running through his head, and that one had been fairly tame. It would be less so if he imagined himself sliding under the blanket with them and—

Shut the fuck up, brain.

Pinching his eyes closed, Fen forced himself to recount every unpleasant thing he could think of…and he was burdened with more than his fair share of those memories. Finally, his body began to calm, and he allowed his thoughts to drift. He could get through this. He would.

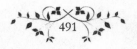

8

B*lood.*

Too much blood.

Fen tried to scream, but no sound came out. No, no, no, no, no.

No.

He threw himself across his father, his hand slapping across the ragged gash on the side of his father's neck. How had it happened? Fog clouded his mind, and his body trembled with cold and fear. How?

Maybe he'd done it.

But he never drank from his father's neck, and he didn't need much blood. Just a few drops now and then. Dad didn't care, but he was pretty clear about how much and how often Fen could take. It was one rule Fen had never broken.

But maybe…

He shoved his ear against his dad's chest, but there was no sign of a heartbeat. Already cold. Fen's vision wavered, and he bit his lip until his own blood filled his mouth. It didn't give him energy, though. Only more agony.

See what you've done?

Fen jerked his head up, looking frantically around the room for the source of the voice.

No one. Nothing.

Could've been his conscience, right? He'd done it.

He must have killed his own father.

Finally, Fen let loose the scream.

The wail of pain cut through Maddy's dreams and straight into her soul. With her own cry, she shoved herself upright and peered at Anna. Her girlfriend grumbled at being shifted aside, but she showed no sign of having screamed. Had it been part of a dream? She pushed back her tangled mass of hair and tried to clear her thoughts.

Another shout sounded from the direction of the living room. Male. What…? Maddy gasped and scrambled out of the bed as realization hit. Fen. She headed for the door, not stopping to explain when Anna stirred in the bed.

Maddy raced down the dim hall and into the slightly brighter living room, a bit of illumination flowing in from the kitchen. At the sight of Fen, though, her steps hitched. The blanket was tangled around his legs, and he thrashed his arms as if he was under attack. A low, keening moan filled the room as she sank to her knees at the side of the couch, just out of his reach.

"Fen," she said firmly.

He didn't seem to notice.

Hesitantly, Maddy placed her hand on his forehead and gave a slight shake. Fen jerked and punched out at the air—in the wrong direction, thankfully. Some terrible dream obviously held him, and she had no idea how to free him without causing him more distress.

Then Anna knelt down beside her. "What happened?" she whispered.

"A nightmare?"

"Fen!" Anna shouted, but when that only led to more thrashing, she placed her hand against his head, her fingers brushing Maddy's. "Try a trickle of healing magic?"

Maddy tensed at the doubt in her love's voice, though it was well-deserved. "That would probably make things worse."

There was a good chance Fen wouldn't suffer any harm from her magic, but she wasn't going to risk it over a nightmare. Stroking her hand across his hair, Maddy considered what to do. Was Fen a heavy sleeper, or was the dream that powerful? When the floor began to tremble beneath them, evidence of his earth magic, she suspected the latter.

Maddy grabbed his shoulders and shook him harder. The opposite of useful. Fen jerked out of her hold, his hand almost connecting with her face this time as he fought. Desperation took over. She threw her upper body across his chest, trapping his arms, and smashed her mouth to his.

It was almost a terrible mistake, and not only because of the consequences of the desire that surged through her. The edge of his fang slid across her lip, almost breaking the skin. Oh, fuck. If he took her blood, they'd be bound. Maddy pulled back as his hands gripped her upper arms, squeezing gently.

Fen had gone calm, and when she looked down, his wide eyes locked on hers. Desolation and desire swirled in his gaze, along with some unnamable emotions darker than anyone should experience. Then his grip slackened, and he turned his head to the side, severing the contact. The frozen silence that had hardened around them shattered, and the world rushed in.

"Are you okay?" Anna asked softly.

Maddy's heart pounded at her girlfriend's voice. She'd just kissed Fen with Anna right there. Right there. Anna didn't sound upset, but Maddy was afraid to find out for sure. She pushed herself back to her knees, forcing an *oof* from Fen as her right hand connected with his rib. This could go badly.

Very badly.

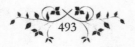

"Anna..." Maddy finally dared a glance at her girlfriend—and her heart pounded for a different reason. Instead of recrimination, Anna's expression was tinged with desire. "I probably should have thought that through a little better."

Fen sat up and then slumped against the back of the couch. "It's my fault."

"I hope you don't think I'm mad," Anna said. "I thought about doing the same thing. And you really shouldn't blame yourself for having a nightmare, Fen. It happens to everyone."

"I sure as hell hope *that* kind of nightmare doesn't happen to everyone." He tipped his head back and shoved his forearm against his eyes. "I haven't...I haven't had that one in years. Since before I got mixed up with Kien. I'd forgotten..."

The pain in his voice echoed in Maddy's heart, rebounding against his earlier cry of agony already caught within. "Do you want to talk about it?"

"Might as well." But he fell silent, the moment stretching until Maddy began to doubt she'd heard him correctly. Then his words whipped out like a lash. "I dreamed about killing my father."

Maddy sucked in a breath. "What?"

"There was so much blood," Fen whispered. "Everywhere. Under him. Over him. Pooling on the floor. I don't remember much when I'm awake, but the dreams..."

Anna settled on the couch beside him, a curious expression on her face. "Didn't you say you were five when your father died? How did it happen?"

"There was a jagged gash on this throat. I'm not sure how I did it, but I'd guess with my fangs. I didn't see enough in my dream to know."

Maddy frowned. "If you didn't see how it happened, how can you be so sure you were responsible?"

He dropped his arm to peer at her. "We were alone in the room. Who else would it have been?"

"Self-inflicted? An intruder? Literally anyone?" Anna said, reaching over to squeeze his knee. "Fen, you—"

"Maybe it's just a stupid nightmare," Fen interrupted. "My memory is really hazy from before I was seven. After that, I was too busy being tossed around foster homes while trying to get blood to try to remember. But when I was a teen, the dream hit. I honestly don't know what is real anymore."

Such a terrible, sad childhood. Maddy's chest squeezed tighter at the loneliness and pain that swirled around him. If he believed the dream could be true, it was no wonder he was so haunted. But she couldn't credit it. He'd made some hefty mistakes, but there was a surprising lack of malice in his nature despite it all. He wasn't the type to simply murder someone, especially not his father, and not at such a young age.

Maddy glanced at Anna, and understanding passed between them. With a slight nod, Anna slid over on the couch and settled her head against Fen's shoulder. He jerked in surprise, but he didn't move away. Then Maddy gathered the discarded blanket from the floor, plopped herself down on Fen's other side, and tossed the other side of the blanket to Anna.

After a brief hesitation, Fen curved his arms around their shoulders, settling them both more comfortably against him. "Thanks," he whispered. "Both of you."

Maddy linked hands with Anna over Fen's chest, and there they remained, providing comfort until the light of dawn peeked through the windows.

Anna rubbed at her tired eyes as she flicked on the electric kettle. This day called for her strongest tea, that was for sure. It was one of those rare times she regretted her sensitive stomach, because Maddy's dark brew coffee would be a welcome dose of caffeine. Instead, she sprinkled tea leaves into the infuser, dropped it into her cup, and started the coffee pot for Maddy while she waited for the water to boil.

Thankfully, the kettle was fast. As the tea steeped, Anna searched the pantry for something she could cook for breakfast. Baking would take too long, which was unfortunate. She could go for a nice blueberry muffin right now. Maddy was either in the shower still or packing for her trip, though, and it wouldn't be long until she was ready to leave. Maybe pancakes and bacon? Hopefully, Fen didn't have any dietary restrictions. He'd dozed off on the couch, so she couldn't go ask. She would just have to make him something else if she guessed wrong.

A short time later, Anna had drunk half a cup of tea and accumulated a respectable stack of pancakes. She opened the oven to check on her special-recipe bacon and was rewarded with the glorious smell that wafted out. This was her favorite part of being off work for the day. She could take her time and prepare a nice breakfast for herself and Maddy. And Fen, too, it seemed.

As though her thought summoned him, Fen wandered into the small kitchen. He ran his fingers through his sleep-disheveled hair, but it didn't exactly help. Anna couldn't stop the grin that broke across her face at his disordered look. His brow crooked upward, and he rubbed his hand over the back of his neck.

"What?" he asked.

"You're oddly cute when you're tired," Anna answered. "I mean, not the sleepy part exactly. It's just with your shirt all rumpled and your hair going crazy, you look a little…adorable."

Fen grimaced. "Like a puppy? Or maybe a kid."

Her gaze skimmed down his body, and her humor fled. His T-shirt might be wrinkled, but it outlined his muscles spectacularly. His jeans were slung low, too, revealing a hint of the vee leading to—Nope. She was not going to think about that. On the spectrum of bi-ness, Anna tended to prefer women over men, but dammit, Fen was just the type she was attracted to when she did go that way. Danger included, unfortunately.

"I promise that you don't make me think of either," Anna finally said.

This time, he was the one who grinned, a hint of wickedness in the curve. "Good."

Before Anna could say anything else, Maddy appeared at Fen's shoulder. "I smell coffee and bacon, so move it, blood boy."

Fen's mouth dropped, and twin spots of color darkened his cheeks before he

twisted to the side to let Maddy pass. "Blood boy? What the fuck, Maddy?"

She patted his cheek as she slid around him to enter the small galley kitchen, her laughing gaze connecting with Anna's. "Hey, it had a nice ring to it. That's your preferred form of nourishment, right?"

That was a good question, actually. One that Anna hadn't considered. She'd heard that Fen ingested blood to gather magical energy, but she didn't know if that was his food, too. "Well, crap. I hope I didn't make too many pancakes."

The statement erased the annoyance building on Fen's face. "I only need a small taste of blood to pull out the energy I need. If a *Felshreh* drains more blood than that, it's probably because they're pissed off. Otherwise, I eat food. You definitely didn't make too many pancakes. Or bacon, but there's never too much of that."

Anna grabbed her oven mitt and pulled the tray out. "Unless you're Jewish or Muslim. If you don't eat any, then one is too many."

"I wonder if either religion allows turkey bacon?" Maddy mused, ducking beneath the baking sheet as Anna turned to set it on the edge of the sink. "I hope they've found another yummy substitute if not. Hell, there should be good vegetarian bacon, too. Joy should be spread."

Fen chuckled, and Anna tossed her oven mitt teasingly at Maddy. Nowhere near her girlfriend's coffee cup, of course—Anna wasn't suicidal. "Only you would be contemplating bacon equality on three or four hours of sleep."

Maddy took a long sip of coffee and moaned. "Probably because of the lack of sleep. Not that it's a bad point."

"Hey, grab plates from the cabinet behind you, Fen," Anna directed. "And while I agree, I'd rather be eating bacon than talking about it."

"Fine, fine."

Smirking, Maddy grabbed syrup from the pantry and started sliding pancakes onto the plates Anna held out. Anna shook her head, but a smile claimed her lips as she placed bacon beside the pancakes and passed the plates to Fen to carry to the table until they each had a serving of food.

"Do you want coffee or tea?" Anna asked him.

"Coffee," he answered. "If you have creamer. Or at least a crapton of sugar and milk."

Maddy wrinkled her nose as she wove around them to get out of the kitchen. "Weakling."

Fen shrugged. "If my sweet tooth is wrong, I don't want to be right."

Contentment eased into Anna's heart as she took the milk out of the fridge. They needed to talk about their future, but she suddenly didn't want to. Serious discussion would disrupt the companionship flowing between them so effortlessly. Wasn't that an essential component of being together?

Finally, they settled around the small table. And as they ate, exchanging jokes between bites, no one brought up the issues between them.

It seemed they all felt the same.

9

As Fen stuck the last plate into the small dishwasher beside the sink, his pocket vibrated. He dried his hands on a dish towel and tugged out his phone. A text from Vek. *Come by the outpost with Maddy. We want to know what you learned about the disease.*

Fen groaned. Dammit, he'd planned to go back to Vek's house and see if he could get some real sleep. He was exhausted, and not just from lack of rest. That dream… No matter what he'd told Maddy and Anna, he was almost certain it was more memory than illusion. Unfortunately, his unconscious mind was never kind enough to reveal what had happened before or after. Though if he had killed his father, perhaps that was a blessing.

Fine, he wrote back. *But I'm crashing there after we talk. Got back really late last night.*

Three dots appeared for a second before Vek's reply. *Whatever.*

Shaking his head at his uncle's abrupt response, Fen closed the dishwasher and went to find Maddy. She'd wanted to double check her bag to make sure she'd packed everything she would need on Moranaia, so he'd offered to do the dishes while Anna rested. But when he walked into the living room, he found Maddy and Anna on the couch, kissing as though the world was about to end.

Fen froze, and a different kind of groan ripped from his throat. His body vibrated with the urge to be in the middle of them in that moment—well, not the *middle*, necessarily. Beside them, belonging in their circle. Worthy of sharing that kind of kiss. Part of him knew, just knew, it would be perfect. An acceptance he'd never known.

Maddy jerked back, her gaze darting instantly to his. "Fen?"

He scrubbed his hands across his face. "This is going to drive me insane."

"Sorry," Anna said, flushing. "She's leaving for a few days, and—"

"No need to apologize for kissing," Fen interrupted. "I'm not upset about that. It's my inability to join that's killing me. I should just stay away from you guys."

Maddy blinked. "Why?"

"Because I'm no good." He took in the sight of their joined hands. "And you two are solid."

"I knew we should have talked over breakfast," Anna muttered.

Maddy's phone blared an alarm, and she grimaced. "I have to go. It'll take time to get over to the shop so I can activate the portal back to the outpost."

"Yeah, Vek sent me a text. I'm supposed to go, too. I can make my own way if need be."

"You can ride with me."

Maddy let go of Anna and stood, but Anna grabbed her wrist. "Wait. We don't have time to talk this out, but we do have time to settle one question. How many of us want to at least explore the possibility of a three-person bond? Forget past histories and childhood bullshit. Who wants to try?"

Silence rang in the wake of Anna's words, seizing Fen's throat. His first instinct was to give a resounding yes, but despite her admonition, his past wrapped around him like a shroud. He was working hard to atone for his stupid, misguided actions. Would it ever be enough? Were his misdeeds the result of poor choices, or was there something tainted inside him? Vek said that the *Felshreh* often walked in the shadows, doing what was necessary to maintain good, even if that required a bit of darkness. But what if Fen was nothing but shadow? That had to be a possibility.

"I think..." Maddy started, biting her lip. "I think I do? We're all drawn to each other, and I don't believe it's only because of this mate thing. There's a lot to consider, though. Polyam relationships aren't exactly common around here."

"Yeah, it definitely won't help my search for a home church," Anna said. Then she smiled. "But belief is in the heart, anyway. I'd like to explore the possibilities."

Fen stared at them, their faces both turned expectantly to him. What was he supposed to say to that? "Have you two lost your minds?"

Fuck. That was not the best choice of things to say.

As Anna's eyes widened and Maddy scowled, Fen lifted his hands. "That's... not exactly what I meant. I just... I don't understand why you'd want to get mixed up with me."

Maddy snorted. "Like we aren't already? Look, lots of people make shitty choices. You can either mope about it or keep doing better. You saved my life trying to undo your mistakes, so I figure you're choosing the second."

An unexpectedly wicked grin crossed Anna's face. "And if you look like you're going the other way, we can kick your ass."

Good grief. Anna might be quiet, but she was fierce. The woman would probably try to drown him in the river if he stepped out of line—and that wasn't exactly a bad thing. Sure, he was responsible for his own actions and emotions, but it was reassuring to consider having two people who could tell him if he started being an idiot. Four, really, if he counted Vek and Dria. If he slipped back into past habits, they would let him know without hesitation.

"Okay," Fen finally said. "I have no idea how we'll work out the details, but I suppose we can figure out how to make it happen. Well, after we decide if we want it to happen. You know what I mean."

Both women smiled. Then Maddy grabbed her backpack from the floor and slung it over her shoulder. "I hope you're ready to head out," she said. "Because I really do have to go."

"Yeah, I'm good," Fen answered.

Maddy bent to kiss Anna goodbye, and Fen almost did the same. Almost. But no. They would all need to get to know each other better before he earned that level of intimacy. Instead, he winked at Anna as he followed Maddy to the door, and Anna returned her own wink and a grin.

Did he have two girlfriends now? It seemed that maybe he did.

He might not kill Vek after all.

Meren paced the confines of his small cottage and cursed every Unseelie who had ever been born. His most useful hiding spot, gone. He'd thought he would only have to conceal himself until Vek ceased his search. Unfortunately, he'd never heard that Vek had enough power over earth to plug up an entire cavern. Meren had barely escaped by teleporting away before the space had been filled.

At least he'd caught himself before activating the recall spell he still instinctively reached for when in danger—the one that returned him to his rooms in the Seelie palace. Wouldn't *that* have been a disaster? He had plans that would see his return to court necessary, but he wasn't ready to enact them yet. Being captured by the Royal Guard would in no way help.

If not for this hidden underhill enclave barely big enough for a cottage and storage building, he would be out in the open. Now that the Seelie queen had placed a price on his head, he couldn't return to the elaborate estate he'd inherited from his "father," either. If only he had his true father's holdings. Wouldn't *that* little revelation shake up the Seelie world?

All in good time.

He'd disabled Tatianella, and although her daughter acted as the Seelie's Queen Regent, Lera was weak. As long as he kept Tatianella under the influence of the new poison spell, Meren had plenty of time to undermine Lera's control in court. He'd already incapacitated Naomh, which meant his brother Caolte was out of the way tending him in their own underhill realm. Those two knew Meren best, so having them gone from court was a boon.

Being caught had been...a setback. As had his recent defeat by Vek and Dria, an alliance he hadn't seen coming. But he had time to rebuild. None of the Seelie knew the source of Tatianella's illness well enough to heal it, and Meren had done a good job of severing any alliance they'd once had with the Moranaians. There was plenty left of his plan to salvage.

It was time to secure that little *Felshreh* whelp. That continual failure was the most frustrating of all. He'd lost his grip on Fen as a child, and though he'd believed Fen properly subverted during his time with Kien, the useless bloodsucker had managed to wiggle out of that, too. Now Meren had sufficient incentive to get the kid

on his side, and with Ara the queen of the Unseelie and Fen her heir, the task was paramount.

He'd always planned to earn enough influence with—or blackmail material on— the Unseelie to gain their assistance in claiming his rightful inheritance. It would be far easier with the weight of the Unseelie throne behind him, and there were count- less ways to use Fen as leverage to force such an alliance.

It was almost time.

Meren halted in front of the grimy mirror hanging crookedly on the wall. With a wave of his hand, droplets coalesced on the glass before rolling down, carrying the dirt with them. His reflection showed the toll of his recent defeat, but reflections weren't reality. He wasn't the bedraggled mess staring back at him.

Nothing but a trick of the light.

He only needed a bath, a change of clothes, and the prodigious use of glamour before he would be ready to begin the hunt. Fen's mate was a creature of water. Who better to find her? Based on what he'd overheard, she was inexperienced enough to fall right into his plan.

Maddy stared at the gleaming portal situated atop a small dais in the center of the massive cavern. She'd been here once before when Fen was ill, but she'd spent more time watching the healer use his magic than studying the gate to Moranaia. Colors swirled within the stone arch, blues and greens predominant. Every once in a while, a flicker of flame red would catch her eye, only to disappear in the maelstrom. And she would be walking through it in a few minutes.

When Fen touched her on the shoulder, she jumped. Maddy tried not to laugh at her own nerves. Or maybe because of those nerves. "Sorry."

He smiled. "Don't be. I haven't gone through that one, either. Rumor has it that the god Loki helped create the portal, but no one has told me the full story."

"Nor are we likely to," Dria announced as she came to a halt next to him, Vek at her side. "Since you're casually recounting what you do know."

Maddy frowned as Fen's face flushed red and his lips tightened into a thin line. "I thought we'd determined that Maddy and Anna are trustworthy allies," he muttered.

"They are," Dria answered. "But still…"

Suddenly, Maddy wanted to do physical harm to the red-haired mage even though the action would probably be fatal. And not just because of the guards sta- tioned around the cavern. Dria had challenged the Unseelie king to combat and essentially won; an attack by Maddy would be no more trouble than swatting a slow-moving fly on a cool spring morning. Even so, her hands balled into fists as Fen stared at the ground, his embarrassment and anger surrounding him like a cloud. Had the mage intended to imply that Fen wasn't trustworthy? Because it was all too obvious that was how he'd taken it.

Maddy was still trying to decide if she dared to confront Dria when light flared from the portal and a pair stepped through. Two people? She squinted against the light. A woman with golden skin and hair wearing a dress far too thin for a chilly cave stopped on the dais beside a muscular elf with brown and green hair. Kezari and Aris? They'd expected the woman—dragon. Whatever. But as far as Maddy knew, she was supposed to arrive alone.

A theory borne out by Dria's words. "Aris? What are you doing here?"

Maddy could have sworn she heard Vek let out a low curse, but when she glanced his way, there was no sign of disturbance on his face. Then the prince smiled at Aris as though greeting a long-lost friend, and her curiosity grew. If the other man made Vek nervous, he was good at hiding it.

"I wanted to come with Kezari to help her…settle now that there have been a few more rumors about dragons," Aris said as he descended the short flight of stairs, the dragon woman glaring at his back when she followed. "Lial thought it would be fine since there has been no other sign of disease."

"I do not need tending, *skizik*."

"This is a strange world. If I know you, and I do, you'll fly off without regard for the customs here."

Kezari snorted. "There are legends of dragons still. It will not be such a shock."

Oh, damn. Maddy wasn't sure if she should laugh or groan. In a way, it was true, though. It wouldn't be a shock. It would be a straight-up bolt of lightning. "Yeah, not many people believe those stories anymore," Maddy found herself saying. "Trust me, you don't want to fly here in full view. You'll have people recording it and posting the images all over the world, and that's the least of it. The same radars that detect planes will find you, and the military might send out jets with missiles."

"You make no sense," Kezari said.

Crap, the dragon probably hadn't learned the meaning of the technical terms. "Lots of people will witness your flight, and a good number of those people will try to kill you."

"See?" Aris said. "Arlyn said something similar, but you thought she was over-stating the danger. We need a plan."

The portal flashed again, and another person marched through. A bronze-skinned woman in leather armor stopped in the center of the dais, her gaze landing almost instantly on Dria. The warrior tapped her chest three times and bowed. "I bid you good day, Feraien. Lord Lyr sent me to escort a guest to his estate?"

Maddy stiffened, and all at once, her backpack weighed down her shoulders as though she'd filled it with boulders instead of clothes. It was time. Could she do this? Could she just walk through that glow, straight onto another world? This was only supposed to be a short trip, but… Moranaia was a different planet, as far as she understood. Maybe another dimension. Who knew? Either way, it wasn't Earth. And once she accepted that reality, she had to think about training. Her stomach roiled.

Please don't let me vomit.

Fen eased closer, nudging her face upward with a knuckle beneath her chin. "Hey. You've got this. It's going to be okay."

She glanced into his light blue eyes, their pull as strong as the first time she'd met him. Deep inside, he still feared he was an irredeemable killer, but there was an innate kindness in him at odds with the dangerous energy of the *Felshreh*. How could Dria display such distrust in him? If she didn't see Fen's potential, then she wasn't looking deeply enough.

Goodness perverted was dangerous, but goodness redeemed was an unstoppable force.

"What if Lial says I'm hopeless?" Maddy whispered.

Fen smiled. "That bastard doesn't give up on anything. He'll make sure you're trained, out of stubbornness if nothing else."

Maddy lifted her brows. "Is he that unpleasant?"

"Not really," Fen said, shrugging. "I don't know how to describe him, but I wouldn't call him mean. Maybe grumpy. Then again, he did have to keep traveling to another world to heal us, so he had a good reason to be cranky."

Dria laughed. "No, he's usually like that. But it's mostly bluster. He won't treat you poorly. If I thought he would, I'd have the palace healer search for someone else."

For a moment, Maddy had forgotten that Dria was a princess, but those words were a stark reminder. Here, the mage might only lead this outpost, an important enough task, but on her home planet, she wielded a great deal more authority. Good thing Maddy hadn't punched her earlier when she'd been tempted. Assaulting a princess wouldn't have been the best start to her trip to another world.

"Thanks," Maddy managed to answer before the silence grew awkward.

Fortunately, they seemed to expect awkwardness since no one appeared to be offended.

Fen skimmed his knuckle softly beneath her chin, a subtle caress, before snatching his hand back. Why did he look so embarrassed? The idiot. Hadn't they already decided to explore the whole mate thing? Smiling, Maddy lifted up slightly and brushed her lips against his in a gentle, careful, fang-less kiss.

Heat flared through her, settling low and hot, but she pulled back instead of deepening the kiss. No matter how much she wanted to. Besides, Maddy had to struggle not to laugh at the stunned expression on Fen's face. She couldn't quite tell if he'd rather carry her to one of the bedrooms in the upper levels or turn tail and run. Maybe he didn't even know which it was.

With a grin, Maddy patted his cheek and spun away. She had an appointment with a cranky healer to keep.

10

Anna shifted in her seat, tucking one leg beneath her and biting her lip as she scanned the computer screen. Garbage. Half the stuff she'd written during her last session was awful, and the rest was decidedly meh. Her concentration was crap lately. Ugh. No one was going to believe her main character escaped the gun-wielding murderer by throwing her shoe at him. It wasn't even a stiletto, for God's sake. A ballet flat would only make the killer shoot her heroine faster.

With an annoyed huff, she selected the entire scene and hit the Cut button before pasting it into her Discarded Scenes folder. Sometimes, she could reuse bits of the things she'd deleted, but that one wasn't likely to see the light of day again. Or the light of her computer screen. Whatever. Although it might come in handy if she needed a way to kill someone off. A ballet flat. Honestly.

Anna reached for the glass of water she'd settled on her custom *Death's Curse 1* coaster, only to freeze as the water lapped toward her approaching hand. Her chest squeezed as she jerked her hand back. Although the liquid plopped back into the cup, it continued to ripple and slosh with each beat of her heart.

Was it picking up on her agitation? For all she knew, it had been doing that as she muttered angrily at her story. Anna hadn't had trouble making tea or taking a shower earlier, when she was tired and calm, so it was possible stronger emotion had to be involved. And she only felt an active pull to natural freshwater so far—a fortunate thing for the peace of said shower.

As her thoughts churned, the water followed suit. Anna tapped her foot anxiously against the base of her computer chair. What should she do? Let it calm or try to explore? She wasn't as bold as Maddy, and even Maddy hesitated to use her magic.

Although…

Water in a glass wasn't likely to be deadly, unlike a healing gift. Hadn't she been thinking last night that the others treated her like a child when it came to the magical world? If she wanted to be considered an equal, she was going to have to be bold about more than going over to someone's house. And why not? The idea of magic had always interested more than scared her, at least until she'd had to confront her own powers. But this was a safe location.

Maybe if she—

Her annoyingly chirpy ringtone eradicated the thought, and Anna cursed. That was the song she'd programmed in for work. She forced her attention away from the rippling water and stared down at the screen of her phone. For a moment, she was tempted to let it go to voicemail. She hadn't gotten much sleep, and she had too many other things to worry about—like water magic. But Deanna didn't call unless she really needed help, and Anna could use the extra money if there was an available shift.

With a sigh, she answered the call. "Hey, Deanna. How's it going?"

"Going all right, except that Maye had to call out of her lunch shift. Her daughter's down with a stomach virus." Deanna hesitated. "I really do hate to ask you, hon. You've seemed worn out lately. But do you think you could cover it?"

Anna glanced at the time. Going on ten a.m. She'd have to get ready quick, but she could probably make it. "Yeah, but I might be late if I can't find a rideshare. Maddy has her car, and mine's still in the shop."

Not to mention that Maddy was probably on another planet by now. They'd planned to have Tamara run the car back after the shop closed so nobody had to go out of their way.

As always Deanna seemed to understand. "Do your best, honey. It's fine."

As soon as she hung up, Anna saved her files, backed them up, and shut down the computer. It would be a mad rush to get to work, but that wasn't what she worried about. How strong was the river's call going to be today? Would it be worse now that she'd considered experimenting with her gift?

Well, she wouldn't know until she got there. Anna would just have to handle it.

Passing through the portal was nearly instantaneous, only a slight lurching in Maddy's stomach to show for crossing into another world. Although her escort kept walking toward another stone arch a short distance away, Maddy halted. Didn't the woman realize that they'd shifted between *worlds?* There was no way Maddy would keep going without checking out the area. This entire experience had to be savored, at least the first time.

Around them, massive trees rose into the sky, but the light was too dim to make out many details of the canopy. Was it just past dawn or nearing sunset? Great gods, how different was the time in this place? It hadn't even occurred to her to ask. But based on the person tapping globes to light the area, it must be closer to sunset. From morning on Earth to nearly night here. It was like jet lag.

Portal lag—now there was a new term. Sounded like a problem she'd have in an online video game.

Her guide glanced over her shoulder. "Are you unwell?"

There was nothing rude in the woman's tone, but her stance screamed impatience, from her half-turned position to the way she balanced on the balls of her feet as though ready to take off in a run. Geeze. What was the damn hurry? Sure, it was cold, but that didn't mean they had to rush. Shaking her head, Maddy rubbed her hands against the chill and started forward, doing her best to examine the area at the same time.

To her right, the glow from the mage globes illuminated the pale stone walls currently being constructed by a man and a woman with some kind of levitation spell. Maddy squinted, trying to make out the details. Were they building a structure around the tree trunks? Maybe the rapidly dimming forest distorted things, but it sure looked like it. Weird.

"We should finish this tomorrow," the man grumbled loudly.

"Stop complaining," the other mage snapped. "I want to complete this segment."

Maddy smiled at the exchange. If nothing else, elves and humans had one thing in common—annoying coworkers. Though as she waited for her escort to activate the other portal, her excitement finally dimmed enough to feel the cold wrapping around her, chilling her until her teeth began to chatter, and she suddenly wasn't sure which of the coworkers she'd call the annoying one. The guy probably just wanted to curl up in front of a nice fire with a cup of tea.

The stone arch filled with light, then settled into a very different scene. A room of warm-toned wood. A couple of well-dressed elves waiting patiently. Maddy didn't have much time to absorb what she saw before her guide motioned for her to go first. With a disappointed sigh, Maddy hurried through, bracing against the disorienting shift.

Her stomach didn't complain as much this time, thankfully. Blessed warmth flowed around her until she nearly moaned with relief, but she remembered herself at the last moment. No need to be the embarrassing half-human brought to court during her first meeting with her hosts. She blinked against the brighter glow, and the people she'd barely glimpsed came into full view.

Cora stood beside another woman, a lady with pale blond hair, a gentle smile, and the most gorgeously embroidered tunic Maddy had ever seen. Even the woman's pants had silver and gold embroidery down the side seams. But who could it be? She honestly hadn't given much thought to who would greet her. She'd been too nervous about working with Lial to care.

The guard stopped in front of Maddy, tapped her chest with her fist, and bowed. Both of the other woman inclined their heads in some silent signal Maddy didn't understand, but only Cora spoke. "Thank you. I'm sorry I had to pull you away from your other duties."

"It was no bother, Your Highness," the guide said, though Maddy would beg to differ based on the woman's demeanor.

Not that she would say so and risk getting the guide in trouble.

As her escort bid a hasty farewell, Maddy peered around the room. Well. Maybe they *had* been building that other structure around the trees, because this room was

wrapped around two. To her left, a massive tree trunk spanned the entire wall. In front of an elaborate doorway on her right, a staircase circled another, much smaller, tree. It didn't appear to be nailed into the trunk, though. She would bet money there was magic involved.

"I felt the same way."

At Cora's voice, Maddy returned her focus to her friend. "Huh?"

"That look of awe on your face." Cora grinned. "This place is amazing."

The lady beside her smiled. "I have to agree." Then she winced. "I'm sorry. I shouldn't have spoken."

Maddy's brow furrowed. There was clearly something going on that she didn't understand. "Why not?"

"I don't think any of us need to worry about Moranaian formalities," Cora said with a chuckle. "We're all certain to be terrible at them. To put guests at ease, members of the household usually wait until they are introduced before speaking so the guest doesn't feel awkward."

Maddy snorted. "I'm not sure that's working as intended. It's strange to have someone standing there staring."

With a laugh, Cora tucked a strand of her dark hair behind her ear. "I tend to agree. In any case, this is Meli, Myern Lyr's bonded. And Meli, this is my friend Maddy."

"It is a pleasure to meet you," Meli said. "My bonded sends his regrets for not being here himself and hopes you will not take offense. He had an emergency meeting with one of the ladies in command of the northern ridge."

Maddy almost grinned at the serious tone of the woman's words. She was used to the elevated manners of the fae thanks to her Sidhe father, but she hadn't participated in many formal occasions. If she hadn't learned a little about Moranaian culture, she would've feared they believed she was some kind of diva who expected the fanciest of greetings.

"I hope it's nothing serious," Maddy said.

"There was an ice storm, I think, but I haven't heard of any injuries." Meli's eyebrows drew together. "I haven't been here long, but I understand that such weather is typical for this season."

Maddy spared a glance for the windows bracketing the front doors, but she couldn't make out many details with the growing darkness. "Ice storm?"

"It hasn't reached here yet, but there might be one tomorrow," Cora explained. "There are spells stabilizing the tree limbs above any structures, and more spells guard the buildings in case those fail. Mostly, it will be unpleasant to navigate the outdoors."

Remembering the chill she'd already experienced, Maddy shivered. "Sounds like I picked a great time to train."

Both women grimaced in sympathy. "Especially since the healing tower is along an outside path," Cora said.

Damn. Hopefully, Cora would have some boots she could borrow—and maybe some warmer clothes. Maddy had packed a couple of sweaters but hadn't considered it might be cold enough for a coat. "Speaking of the healing tower... Am I meeting the healer there? I assumed he would be here when I arrived."

"He was finishing up with a patient," Cora explained. "Want me to show you the way?"

"Fine by me." Maddy shifted her backpack higher on her shoulder. "I'm ready when you are."

Lady Meli clasped her hands in front of her waist. "I'll bid you farewell here. I do hope you enjoy your time at Braelyn, and if you should have any need, please notify me or my bonded at once."

Maddy smiled at the softly spoken words. The other woman might not have been born here, but Maddy wouldn't have guessed it based on her calm demeanor. "Thank you. I will."

As the lady turned to go, Cora led the way toward the elaborate pair of doors to Maddy's right. Her steps slowed as they neared the exit, fear overtaking her feet, but she forced herself to catch up. This was the right thing to do. It might scare the hell out of her, but it was the best choice.

The only choice.

Fen flopped down in the chair and propped his feet on a nearby stool without regard for the others' opinions. He'd been more tired in his life, but that didn't make his current exhaustion any easier. Right now, all he wanted to do was sleep. If Aris and Kezari believed him to be rude for sprawling out, then so be it. But although Aris cast him a curious glance, the dragon woman didn't appear to notice at all. She was too busy pacing the sitting room.

"Why are you so agitated, Kezari?" Dria asked. "For all we know, the dragon sighting was only a rumor."

"If there are dragons here, they could help sway my Moranaian kin," the dragon said, her voice taking on a deeper, more resonant tone. "My own kind called me foolish for keeping my connection to Earth instead of stamping it out, and my leaders refused to believe me when I sensed the poison here. But if there are dragons who remained... They would still have that connection, unbroken. They would be more my kin than the dragons I grew up with on Moranaia."

Fen winced in sympathy. The others might not get the importance of that, but he knew all too well what it was like to feel like an outcast.

The dragon's friend seemed to understand. Aris placed his hands on her shoulders, stopping her restless pacing. "Then we will search for them properly. If they do not wish to be revealed to humans, your doing so would earn you no favor with them."

Kezari slumped. "That is so."

"Please, sit. We will help if we can," Vek said, waving toward the pair of empty chairs between his seat and Fen's. "But I must hear from my nephew first."

Although the dragon frowned, she pulled away from Aris to take the chair to Fen's right. The cool air of the chamber warmed perceptibly around him as she settled in. How the hell had Aris tolerated touching her skin if she emanated that much heat? But if it had hurt the Moranaian, he showed no sign of it as he sat between Kezari and Vek.

"My report won't take long," Fen hastened to say as the dragon's golden eyes pinned him. If he had more time, he would tell his uncle off for putting him between a dragon and her objective. "And it actually concerns Aris. I think."

Dria and Vek both leaned forward at that, but the elf in question only raised a brow. "Has your poison returned? I sense no sign of it."

Fen flushed at the reminder of their first meeting. So to speak. He'd been unconscious from Kien's energy poisoning at the time, at least until Aris had healed him. "Mine hasn't. But we went to check on a fae woman showing signs of illness. We thought it was that secondary sickness that happened after you cured me of the first one. It wasn't."

Dria's eyes narrowed. "Maddy scanned the woman?"

"Yes," Fen answered. "She said that it wasn't a disease, not like the one she and I both had. This was more like the dart of poisoned energy that Kien shoved in my heart."

Silence fell after that statement, heavy with implications.

"Shrapnel," Vek said flatly.

Aris and Kezari exchanged glances. "I do not know this word," the dragon said.

"It's like…" Fen frowned, trying to figure out how to explain it to people who didn't know about human bombs. "If you threw a fireball laced with metal fragments at someone. The fragments would fly free, doing more damage to the target and anything nearby. That's shrapnel."

"Ah, I see," Aris said. "You believe that the poisoned magic that Kien thrust into the wall holding back Earth's energy *and* into you might have had fragments attached that then hit others."

Fen crossed his ankles. "I don't know. Maybe."

"It is most the most logical explanation." Frowning, Vek shook his head. "Though I admit I could be wrong. If I am, though, then how did a stranger get infected? Are you certain it is the same? Maddy could have been mistaken."

"You'd have to ask her that," Fen said.

Vek pursed his lips. "I could check with my magi—"

His uncle's mouth snapped shut, a hint of red working its way up his neck and into his cheeks. Vek glanced toward Aris for only a second, but it was enough for realization to hit. Aris had given his uncle blood—and Vek gained abilities from those whose blood he'd consumed. Oh, damn. Vek had some use of life magic, a rare talent that could be abused in horrible ways. The other elf wouldn't be happy to know that the ability had been shared, no matter how accidentally.

Aris's eyes narrowed on Vek, and the barest pulse of the elf's magic flowed

around them. Unfortunately for Vek, the other man was no fool. "You did not bear life magic during our earlier encounter," Aris said smoothly, his words loaded with both threat and question.

Even so, Fen didn't expect Vek to answer. His uncle wasn't exactly a wimp, and he tended to hold his secrets close. He must have thought up some kind of bluff before this on the likely chance he'd see Aris again. After all, Vek lived in the outpost with Dria now that they'd mated, and Moranaians traveled through here constantly. He'd surely planned for this.

"I gained some of your abilities through your blood," Vek said.

A simple statement, simply delivered.

A bomb with its own kind of shrapnel.

"*Miaran dae fe onai*," Aris cursed, shooting to his feet. Iron in the heart—a mild insult if you weren't fae. "I saved you from death, and that is how you repay me? You took far more than I offered."

Fen stared at him in confusion. The other elf had gone pale, and a bead of sweat trickled down his temple. He looked like he was either going to pass out or incinerate Vek with his eyes. Hell, both outcomes weren't out of the question.

As Aris swayed on his feet, Kezari wrapped her fingers around his wrist. "Calm, *skizik*."

Vek lifted his hands, palms outward. "It wasn't intentional. In fact, I can't control it. This happens any time I take blood. And if you recall, I was unconscious when your blood was offered. I would have refused if given the chance."

Some of the panic left Aris's face, but he was still unnaturally pale even as he nodded. "That is true. I am uncertain, then, if I did you a favor or a disservice. I would not take away another person's choice."

"Well, it was preferable to death," Vek said dryly.

"Said by a man who has never had to decide between the two." Aris averted his gaze. "I've been held captive before. Let's just say that death isn't always the least favorable option."

The dragon half-growled. "You're not—"

"No, Kezari," Aris interrupted, resuming his seat. "I don't feel that way now, and I would rather not dwell on it. But as the blood elf has shown good faith in admitting what happened, so I thought I should explain my reaction." He turned back to Vek. "I assume you have a reason for sharing the truth?"

Fen glanced between them, only partially understanding the situation. Was Aris saying he'd been tortured? *You took far more than I offered.* Ah, hell. That sounded like more than the type of torment Kien had inflicted on his victims. Something far more intimate than the slice of a blade or a heated brand. But not all curiosity needed to be appeased.

"I will lose the talent over time unless I draw from you or another with your talent again, and I didn't gain all of the abilities of a life mage. But I received enough that I could use training," Vek said. "There are a few things I haven't worked out."

Aris's fingers tightened on the chair's armrests. "I imagine so. Perhaps we should go over them while your nephew rests. Then Kezari and I can go somewhere quiet and scan for her dragon kin."

Kezari folded her arms across her chest. "Fine. I suppose I can wait."

"I'll scout out a good spot, Kezari," Dria said. She winked at Fen and then waved toward the door. "Fen. You heard Aris. Go sleep. We all need to be clear-headed."

Fen didn't have to be told twice. After a quick goodbye, he rushed out of the room and straight into the chamber next door. It was just as he'd left it, complete with rumpled covers. No housekeepers here, not even for a so-called *Felshreh* prince. Best he could tell, being royalty was a pain in the ass.

And his mother expected him to be the king of the Unseelie someday. Hah.

Shoving that thought aside, Fen kicked off his shoes and pulled back the covers. No sign of any cave inhabitants in the blankets, but he wasn't going to take chances. He ran a quick refreshing spell through the linens and mattress, studiously ignoring the dust and anything else that slid onto the floor. With another burst of power, he opened a hole in the rock, directed the dirt inside, and sealed the mess into the stone.

As he settled beneath the newly cleaned covers and pulled his phone from his pocket to set it on the side table, the device chimed. A text from Anna: *Got called into work. Could you pick me up around 3?*

Fen frowned at the screen. He didn't exactly mind, but it was an unusual request from her. Besides, it was nearly eleven, and he might have to go with Vek to test Sparrow for the poison after his lesson with Aris. Could he get there in time?

I don't mind, Fen typed. *But I might be later than 3. I have to go out with Vek. Text me around that time?*

Her answer came quickly. *I can do that. I just…don't trust myself by the river. Accountability helps.*

That didn't sound good. *You'll be okay?*

Fen bit his lip as he waited for the three dots to resolve into a message.

Of course. Don't worry. I'll text near 3.

Despite her reply, he didn't exactly feel better. If she was that worried about being near the water, then he would sure as hell be there to pick her up from work, even if he had to leave Vek alone with Sparrow. Fen wasn't a healer or a life mage, anyway. His presence would be fairly useless.

But he wouldn't be useless to Anna.

11

Even in the dimming light, the view was phenomenal. Maddy could make out the outline of the valley at the edge of the ridge where they walked, the trees thin enough here to reveal the twilight sky. Lights twinkled below, presumably from houses. But she couldn't bring herself to ask how many elves lived there. They could have a massive, hidden city for all she knew.

Elves, elves everywhere.

Maddy snorted at her rambling thoughts. She was walking among strange trees on an entirely different world full of people she knew little about, but she couldn't fully enjoy it, no matter how much she tried. The closer she got to her meeting with the healer, the more her dread took over.

Steps slowing, Cora cast her a questioning look. "What's wrong?"

"I'm nervous, I guess." Maddy sighed. "To be honest, the healer intimidates me."

"He's nicer than people think. But don't tell him I said that."

Maddy laughed at her friend's wry tone. "Why not, if he's friendly?"

Cora grinned. "Because he gives me a potion that helps with morning sickness."

At the reminder, Maddy studied her friend's waist, but the dress she wore didn't reveal if she had a bump. "Are you okay?" Maddy asked, stopping on the path. "I mean, not just you and the baby. Is Ralan treating you well? Are you happy?"

"I am," Cora said, no hint of doubt in her tone. "And he is. I have no regrets about the way things turned out, except having to leave the shop. Not because I was attached, but… Well, I feel like I dumped the responsibility on you and Jase."

Maddy's forehead furrowed. "What? We wanted to buy The Magic Touch."

"Did you, really? Or did you think you had to?"

An unexpected question, but one that Maddy had no trouble answering. "I wanted to. I've always loved the place, and I was hoping I'd be able to buy it when your lack of aging got too obvious for you to stay. I thought it would be a few years longer, but the rush didn't bother me."

Cora sagged with relief. "Good. You think Jase feels the same?"

"I believe he does, though I guess you'd have to ask him to be sure." Maddy shrugged. "If he changes his mind, I'll buy out his portion, too. Maybe Anna and Fen would want to help out. Well, okay, not Anna. She hates retail."

As they began walking once more, Cora studied her. "So you're going to go there?"

Maddy didn't pretend not to understand. "We've agreed to give the relationship a try to see if it could work. I'm still a little uncertain, but it feels right."

"Just say the word if I need to singe Fen's ass. I've never been as sure of him as you are."

Maddy chuckled at her friend's vow, but her laughter faded as the trail opened up into a clearing. In the center, a round tower rose, lights gleaming from the windows. If any structure deserved to be called a healer's tower, it was this place. Peace emanated from the stone, drifting around the clearing like a gentle breeze. But there was no sign of the healer or anyone else at the door. Maybe he was still inside with his patient.

Cora paused again, a look of concentration briefly crossing her face. "He's around back. Come on, and I'll introduce you."

Maddy sighed with envy at her friend's ability to scan the area so easily, but she followed her across the clearing without commenting on it. Many fae were able to shield, use telepathy, and analyze their environment for certain energy signatures, but Maddy wasn't particularly great at any of those talents. She could uphold shielding, like the kind that Cora had cast around the shop, and even build her own with limited success, but she had little practice with the other two. Then again, being afraid your magic might kill someone tended to make a person hesitant to try new things.

They rounded the tower, and both women slowed at the sight of Lial, crouching near the base with a bowl in his hand. A mage light hovered overhead, and its glow cast streaks of blue across his auburn hair, tied at the nape, and his brownish cloak. With an annoyed glance, he held up a hand until they stopped.

What was he doing?

Maddy exchanged a confused look with Cora, but they stood silently in the chilly air as the healer stared at a shadowed spot at the base of the tower. Maddy pulled the cloak Cora had loaned her more tightly around her chest for warmth, but she didn't speak. Maybe Lial wasn't cranky or cruel—maybe the guy was crazy. Why else would he be staring at a damned wall in the cold twilight?

Then a soft mewling sound caught her attention. Almost kitten-like, but deeper and more resonant. Maddy peered at the shadowed area with more interest and was rewarded with the sight of a small, fur-covered head peeking out. The adult version followed as the animal's mother crept part of the way out of her hiding space, and Maddy caught her breath. It was almost a cat, but the animal's head was a little more dog-like, though with a smaller mouth. Taller, more rounded ears extended upward, and the long tail that whipped out from the darkness had a rounded tip that began to glow as it curled over the bowl in Lial's hands.

Well, that was different.

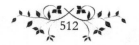

Slowly, the healer lowered the dish to the ground. Another baby stepped out to stand on the mother's other side, and the little ones held out their tails in a similar manner. But the lights on the tips flickered and pulsed until they let out soft cries of annoyance. With a soft chuff, the mother nudged them toward the bowl before bending her head to eat. After a brief hesitation, her children followed suit.

Only after the food was gone and the animals had returned to the hole did the healer stand and face them. But he didn't speak, only gesturing behind them until they turned and started back to the front of the tower. At the door, however, Cora didn't bother to hold back the questions.

"What was that, Lial? I've been here over a month, and I've never seen anything like that."

The healer smiled. "You wouldn't. The *camahr* hibernate during the hotter months. Truth be told, many of the wilder animals stay away from our habitations, so unless you hike into the forest, you'll not encounter them."

Curious, Maddy glanced around at the dim forest. Though she could hear a few bird calls and the occasional squeak or chitter, she didn't see the animals responsible. "It's sort of quiet for a forest, come to think of it."

"The season of Morne is close to an end, heralding the start of Neren. Early winter, you'd say. We have a fair number of ice storms before the snow sets in, so many of the animals hibernate or move to warmer climes." The healer waved toward the back of the tower. "I've hosted that *camahr* mother for several years now. She found the hole before I could have it repaired, so I had it reinforced instead. If I find favor, perhaps one of her kits will choose me as a companion."

Maddy's lips twitched, but she held back her smile. The fierce, grumpy healer wanted a pet? "You mean the way humans adopt cats and dogs?"

Lial chuckled. "Not exactly. It's more them adopting you. They make their own choices."

"Sounds like a cat on Earth," Cora muttered. "I haven't seen anyone here with a pet, though."

"It takes much time to cultivate the relationship. Decades, perhaps. Warriors move too often, in general, so there are fewer animal companions on the estate. More in the village, I'd say." The healer opened the door and waited expectantly until they followed him through. "Now, I suppose this is the time when Cora would introduce us, but we've already met. In a fashion. As our titles mean nothing to you, we can dispense with such formality."

"That would probably be good," Maddy said, though she struggled to focus on him instead of studying his workroom. She couldn't wait to examine the tools and equipment he used. "Just call me Maddy, Lord Lial. Or sir? Mister?"

His eyebrow lifted. "I am certainly no lord, not since my youth. Lial will do."

Not since his youth, huh? Maddy bit back a smile at the haughty statement. If he'd been born to nobility, it explained the arrogance that surrounded him like air. "Okay, Lial."

"Excellent," he said. "I will show you to your room. If that is well with you, Cora?"

Cora frowned. "If she's going to one of the guest towers, I can—"

"No. There's a chamber above mine where she can stay."

Maddy froze. She was supposed to sleep in the same tower as him, alone with someone she barely knew? That didn't seem safe. "Here?"

She half-expected the healer to scoff at her obvious worry, but he only considered her thoughtfully. "Forgive me, Maddy. I did not consider that your customs might be different. When possible, students stay close to their teachers for ease of shielding, especially at first. Learning to access and use your power brings it to the forefront, and that requires greater care. However, I assure you that the upper chamber has a door with a lock."

Maddy gripped the strap of her backpack as uncertainty overcame her. His words made sense, but the thought of being stuck at the top of a strange tower on another world wasn't exactly restful. She gave his workroom a quick glance, hoping for an alternative. To the left, there was a long workbench covered with jars of herbs and potions, to the back, a strange stone table took up the space next to a narrow spiral staircase, and to the right, a bed had been situated beneath a window.

"Could I sleep there?" she asked, gesturing toward the bed.

He grimaced. "In theory, you could, but I'm sometimes disturbed in the middle of the night by patients. And if someone was injured enough to need watching, they would require the bed."

If face-palming wouldn't have been as embarrassing as her request, she would have done it. Of course the bed was reserved for patients. Why the hell else would he have it? "Right. Sorry."

Cora caught Maddy's gaze. "I'll vouch for Lial. He's Ralan's cousin, you know, and I've never seen him act less than professional. Well, a grumpy professional. Besides, he's in love with—"

Lial's lips thinned, and Cora's face reddened at the words she hastily cut off. But surprisingly, he finished the sentence. "Lynia. Lyr's mother. Not that the emotion is likely to be returned. In any case, if you prefer to stay somewhere else, I can find out if a nearby guest tower is available. There is no need for you to be uncomfortable."

Damn. After seeing the hastily stifled pain in the healer's eyes at the mention of the woman he loved, she couldn't help but feel sorry for him. Anyway, she was being silly. Hadn't she arranged to come to Moranaia for the training he offered? It might be a little uncomfortable to stay in close quarters with a stranger, but *he* wasn't causing the discomfort. It was more the oddness of it all.

"I'll stay upstairs," Maddy said, straightening her shoulders.

Lial studied her a moment before nodding. "Very well. I'll show you to your room."

As the healer headed toward the staircase, Cora leaned close. "Are you sure?"

"Yes," Maddy answered at once. "But I trust you'll singe his ass, too, if he steps out of line."

At Cora's laugh, Lial glanced back over his shoulder. "Maddy?"

She smiled at Cora and then started forward. She could do this.

She absolutely *would* do this.

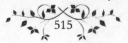

Queen Ara closed the door of her office behind her with a soft click that in no way echoed her mood. What a wretched mess of a job, one she'd never wanted. She'd planned for Vek to be stuck with the crown after their father was deposed, while she finally found some semblance of peace.

But no. Of course her brother hadn't cooperated. When had he ever?

Five hours. She'd spent five hours on that uncomfortable stone throne trying to sort through her peoples' problems. There'd been the mundane, naturally. Minor disputes and questions of property ownership. She'd sat with her father through enough court sessions to know the most effective way to handle those, but it was annoying to be the one responsible for those decisions instead of merely observing.

Then had come the darker, more pointed power plays. Ara was reasonably certain that she'd rid the court of the worst of her father's supporters, but the purge had shifted alliances enough that the remaining courtiers fought for prominence. Not to mention the implications she'd heard whispered, though never directly stated—prove herself as queen or be dethroned. A fate she wouldn't necessarily mind, except… She was one of the few who didn't want the throne, and that was a valuable asset for the Unseelie. The last thing her people needed was another power-hungry ruler. That kind of struggle for control could destroy them.

Rubbing at her lower back, Ara wandered over to her desk. Then she caught sight of the envelope propped casually on the surface, and she froze. It would appear innocuous to the average observer. The paper was plain, and the red wax seal had no insignia. But to her, that was its own tell, a sign she couldn't ignore.

Meren.

Ara snatched the envelope from her desk and broke the seal with a sharp motion, heedless of the slight tear her haste caused. The note within was the important part. With trembling fingers, she jerked the paper free and unfolded it. Only a few lines of Meren's elegant script filled the space. Lovely lettering from such a dark heart.

You neglect your son. Wouldn't it be terrible if your sacrifice was in vain?

She crumpled the paper in her hand. That *sremed* would pay for his threat, for threat it had been. Ara understood the seemingly innocent note well enough. Meren was planning something against Fen. But what? Her sacrifice had been to leave Fen with his human father so the former king, her father, couldn't use him or hurt him in his madness. She'd let everyone believe she wanted nothing to do with her own child, all to keep him safe. To keep him from being perverted to evil.

That sacrifice had almost been in vain already, when he'd fallen in with Kien. But

Fen was with Vek now, and though her brother was a difficult bastard, he had honor. He wouldn't let Fen return to his misguided ways. Would he?

Could Meren be warning her instead of threatening in an attempt to gain her favor now that she was queen? *You neglect your son.* If her trust in Vek was misplaced, Fen might be causing havoc on Earth even now. Unlikely, but she needed to check in on them both to ensure that all was well. If Meren was attempting to cause trouble, Vek and Fen needed to be warned, in any case.

Ara pressed a button hidden in the decorative stone carvings on the wall and slipped into the tiny corridor as soon as the secret door opened. She didn't know how to get directly to the outpost, but she'd made it her business to find Vek's Earth dwelling. It was a risk to leave the palace so soon into her reign, when her rule was barely established, but she couldn't find it within herself to care. No matter her intentions, she'd failed Fen since he was born.

She wouldn't do so again.

Anna wiped down her last table, pocketing the wad of bills her customers had left beneath the edge of the bread basket. Four dollars was a little low, but it wasn't too bad. The couple hadn't been much older than she was, and they'd told her their short, three-day jaunt to Chattanooga was the first vacation they'd been able to afford in three years. She couldn't begrudge them their frugality.

"You can go ahead and leave if you want," Deanna said as she stopped on the other side of the table. "It's only two, but I think we can handle the last hour since it's slower than I thought it'd be."

"Leave now?" Anna glanced quickly toward the river on the other side of the glass, then away. "I guess I could check with the friend who was going to pick me up."

Deanna shrugged. "You can wait out here or back in the office if you wanna. Just doesn't seem worth having an extra server on the clock."

So it was more cost than consideration. She could understand her manager's need to save money with fewer tourists coming in, but it wasn't great for Anna. Ah, well. She'd managed to resist the river for this long. What was an extra hour?

"I'll put my stuff away and clock out," Anna said.

"I appreciate you coming in today." Deanna smiled. "Really. You need anything, you just let me know."

Despite the tension coiling within, Anna returned the smile. "Thanks, Deanna. I will."

Anna tucked her supplies into the utility closet and clocked out on the back computer. Then she gathered the money from her apron and stuck it in her wallet before untying the apron and hanging it on a hook on the wall. With a sigh, she tugged her phone from her purse and sent Fen a quick text. If he couldn't get there early, she would call for a rideshare. It would be torture waiting out there by the water, but she'd managed before.

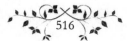

This would be no different.

Lyr's mirror chimed again before he'd even had time to sit. With a sigh, he rubbed his tired eyes. The weather this time of year wasn't as bad as the aptly named Season of Ice that preceded spring, but it was nonetheless unpleasant to deal with. Yesterday, patches of ice had formed overnight on the training field, and today, he'd had to send extra aid to the northern ridge to help a group of travelers stranded by the freezing storm.

What now?

But when he analyzed the energy signature from the incoming communication spell, his current aggravations shifted to the edges of his thoughts. Who would be contacting him from the Seelie royal court? Lyr had severed diplomatic relations with them after they'd sent an army through one of their colonies to slaughter those who had been overcome by energy poisoning, and he hadn't bothered to reengage after Meren, who'd been their liaison, had been outed as a traitor. This couldn't be good.

Lyr touched the edge of the frame, completing the link. Thankfully, decades of training and months of dealing with the unexpected allowed him to hide his shock at the image of Queen Lera's own form taking shape on the glass. For so long, the Seelie had pretended to seek Moranaian aid through Meren while preventing Lyr's chosen diplomat, Kai, from having any meaningful dialogue with the queen. That she was contacting him personally was indeed a bad sign.

"I bid you good evening, Queen Lera," Lyr said, careful to keep his tone polite and neutral. "I hope all is well with family and court."

They both knew this was unusual, but the queen showed no overt reaction to the friendly greeting. "Good evening, Lord Lyrnis. I and my court are indeed well, thank you. I trust your home and hearth are likewise?"

"We are."

Gods, he wanted to laugh at the ridiculousness of the situation. He'd last spoken to Lera over three hundred years ago during one of his visits to the king's court, and that had been the only time they'd interacted before or since. They'd both been emissaries for their parents then. Ah, how time had changed things.

"I hope you will forgive the presumptuous nature of my sudden, unexpected contact," she said, more frankly than he'd expected. "However, I am given to understand that Meren caused great harm to the relationship between my court and Moranaia. I thought it best to entrust this task to no other."

This task, hmm? Lyr studied the queen's coldly beautiful face, but she revealed no hint of her feelings or purpose. As third along the Callian branch, those whose strengths were combat and diplomacy, Lyr was in charge of most communications and treaties with other realms closely connected to Earth, although the king had the final word. Technically, there was nothing unusual about her contacting him first.

Yet his instincts said that something was amiss.

"I confess I do find some presumption in requesting our aid in any task," Lyr replied.

Her lips thinned the barest amount. "Please forgive my unclear statement. I meant that I did not wish to entrust this communication to another in my court, but I have no specific aid that I require from your people at this time. Rather, there is a point of some delicacy that must be discussed."

Lyr raised his eyebrow. "Have my people committed some offense against yours since your innocent slaughter of Neorans? Or perhaps you are distressed that we retrieved my daughter and her bonded from captivity in one of your noble's homes? I can assure you that the latter was settled with the noble in question."

"It concerns neither of those things, although I feel it imperative to assure you that the former was in no way directed or sanctioned by the crown." A hint of pink rushed into the queen's cheeks. "In this case, I wish to speak to you about the outpost you have formed on Earth."

They'd all known it was a matter of time before the other fae found the outpost, and it came as no surprise that the Seelie were the first to broach the matter after Meren's attack. Meren might be a traitor to the Seelie, but that didn't mean his discovery hadn't reached the ears of those who weren't. It appeared life was about to get more frustrating for Dria.

"In that case, I regret to inform you that I must pass this matter to Princess Dria. Her command of the outpost supersedes my authority in the matter."

Queen Lera drew back, surprise filtering across her face. "One so young?"

Lyr chuckled. "If I might offer advice, it would be to avoid such words in her hearing."

"Yes, of course." The queen reclaimed her reserved manner, though now Lyr could better see the cracks. "Then I must insist you connect us at your earliest opportunity."

Lyr replied to her demand with all of the polite evasions at his disposal—and he had a fair store of them. By the time they disconnected their link, he had no doubt that Queen Lera was cursing his name. He had no intention of flinging Dria into a pit of unreasonable demands without time to prepare. Since the queen had no link to Dria's communication mirror, he had ample time to give the princess fair warning. They would not act at the Seelie court's whim.

12

A sharp pinging sound jerked Fen from sleep. Groaning, he rubbed at his eyes and then fumbled for the phone on the side table. For a moment, he forgot where he was, but when his hand met only air, he realized he'd been reaching for the wrong damned table in the wrong damned room. He wasn't at Vek's house. He'd fallen asleep at the outpost.

Another chirp, and awareness hit.

Anna's text. How long had it been? Fen sat up—on the proper side of the bed this time—and snatched up his phone. Just after two o-fucking-clock. Sonofabitch. Why hadn't Vek woken him up yet? Surely he hadn't been talking to Aris for three hours. They'd never be able to reach Anthony's apartment in time for Fen to go pick Anna up from work at three.

He swiped his finger across the screen as he stood, reading Anna's text as he shoved his feet into his boots. *Out of work early. Should I grab a rideshare?*

Fen muttered a litany of curses as he sprinted toward the door. He barely re-membered to close it behind him before pushing into the sitting room next door. Dria, Vek, and Aris all looked up with varying expressions of concern, but he didn't see the dragon. Whatever. He didn't need a dragon's skills for this.

"I have to go," Fen blurted as he skidded to a stop. "I need to get back to your house for my car. Now."

Vek's brows lowered. "You were supposed to go with me to check on this en-ergy poisoning."

"I don't give a fuck about the energy poisoning or anything else. Anna needs my help."

"Did something happen?" Dria asked.

"Not yet." Fen's heart raced, a sense of doom coiling inside. "She's drawn to the water, remember? I'm supposed to pick her up, but I slept too long. I have to go. I'll text you Anthony's number, and you can figure out the rest."

Frowning, Vek studied him for a long moment. Too damned long. "She has resisted the water for a while now. Did she say there was danger?"

Fen let out a frustrated sigh. "Not exactly. But she's never reached out to me like this. It means something."

"Fen—"

"I promised Maddy I would keep her safe, and as I recall, you did, too." He tapped out a quick message to Anna—*On my way*—and hit send. "Help or don't. I don't care."

Dria shot to her feet. "Let's go to the shielded portal room. I'll make sure you get to the right place."

Fen and Dria were halfway to the door before Aris's voice reached them. "I've taught you everything you need, Vek. Though I did forget to caution you about one thing. Make sure Dria has a very strong birth control enchantment if you're not ready for children."

Dria stumbled to a halt, and even Fen had to pause at that. Fen glanced over his shoulder as Dria spun around, angry red rushing up her face. "What?"

If Fen hadn't been so near panic, the stunned look on his uncle's face would have made him laugh. As it was, he could barely summon a grin as Aris spoke again. "Life magic can be difficult to handle during sex. Especially…especially when there is love involved. Selia and I have learned how to deal with it, but I thought it prudent to warn you that you'll need to devise your own methods."

"I swear, Vek, if you've gotten me pregnant through my current enchantment, I will lightning bolt your balls," Dria said, and somehow, Fen's uncle went even paler than his normal white-as-fuck. "I don't want children for another decade at the earliest. Possibly a couple of centuries."

Vek shook his head. "If a life mage can do that, why are fertility rates so low among Moranaians? We Unseelie are far more fertile, especially the *Felshreh*. Though in this case, it might not be to my advantage to be so…"

"Lightning. To. The. Balls."

Dria's glare was so fierce that Fen took a step to the side. He would hate to be his uncle right now, that was for sure. And it seemed that Aris agreed. "I detected no sign of pregnancy," the mage said quickly. "Which is why I thought it prudent to tell you now. As to fertility rates… There are few with my talent, and we aren't exactly eager to spend our time with couples having sex. The magic must be used immediately to be effective, and—"

"As interesting is this is…" Fen dared to interrupt now that Dria no longer looked like she was going to incinerate anyone. "I have to go. You can discuss this without me."

"You're right that we'll be discussing this later," Dria muttered, but she spun around and started back toward the door, a hint of a stomp to her step.

They made good time to the magical lift Dria and Vek had installed to connect the floors that branched off the massive staircase circling the entire cavern. Fen gripped the stone railing as Dria activated the spell to carry them to the top and tried not to look over the side. It wasn't that he was afraid of heights, exactly. It was just that he didn't care to experience them. Especially not atop a stone platform held aloft by nothing but magic.

Magic had a habit of blowing up in your face when you least expected it. Literally, as he had reason to know. When the Moranaians had interrupted the web of poisoned energy—part of Kien's initial plan—the spell had backlashed into the last remaining crystal, and Fen had struggled to contain it. He'd wanted to destroy the damned thing, but by that point, he'd barely been able to control the surge of energy. Then Delbin had hurled a rock at Fen's hand, pushing it against the crystal and shattering the spell in a massive explosion.

Fen had never been that drained of energy, not even when he'd had to scrounge as a child.

And in that moment, he'd known he was done. With Kien and the whole idiotic plan to rule humans. With foolish childhood rebellions and the subsequent bad choices. Too bad Kien hadn't quite been done with him. Fen might have managed to escape after Delbin and Inona had captured the prince, but once Kien had freed himself and found his way back, he'd been more than happy to manipulate Fen into a position where he had no choice but to help the prince return through the portal to Moranaia. Maddy would have died otherwise, and Fen would never allow that.

"Do you truly believe the situation with Anna is dire, Fen?" Dria asked as they stepped off the platform.

Her words snapped him back to the present. Damn, she was even giving him that concerned grown-up look, the one meant to inspire teenagers to confess their every fear. He ground his teeth together, though he knew she intended no offense. "Maybe. Hopefully, I'm just overreacting."

Dria shrugged. "It will do no harm to leave now, especially if you text the information Vek needs to check on the human girl."

"Woman," Fen said sharply.

Opening the door to the portal room, Dria frowned over her shoulder. "What?"

"We might seem like children to you at your age, but on this world, we are adults in our own right. God knows I haven't been a kid for a long time." Fen followed her in, barely able to resist slamming the door behind them. "Try to remember it."

Dria studied him. "I've done something to upset you. You've been strange around me lately, and this only proves what I've suspected. Perhaps you would prefer your uncle had not—"

"I don't give a damn that you've mated." Fen glanced at his phone, and his heart leapt at the glaring lack of response from Anna. "And I like you fine. Look, can we talk about this later?"

"So long as we *do* talk about it."

Fortunately, Dria didn't wait for a response. Not that he had any illusions that she would forget about the conversation. No, his uncle's mate was one of the most tenacious people Fen had ever met, and that was saying something. As she began the spell to open the portal back to Vek's house, her forehead was still furrowed with a thoughtful frown.

Ah, well. One problem at a time.

A couple of steps and she would be in.

Laughter echoed from the restaurant parking lot, but the sound barely registered over the slap of the waves against the stones edging the riverbank. Anna glanced back the way she'd come. The sidewalk was empty, and a few bordering trees blocked her view of the restaurant. She'd thought the trees on each side of the path would prevent her from seeing the river—instead, she'd found a break in the fence where a couple of boulders made a decorative seating area. An even clearer shot to the water.

Dammit, where was Fen? Anna's phone vibrated in her pocket, but she couldn't make her hand take hold of it. Maybe he'd sent a message saying he wasn't coming. Maybe he couldn't. God knew she couldn't force her eyes away from the river rippling such a short distance away.

Enter now, Anna, and find your true heart.

If she'd been able, she would have snorted. She was pretty sure her heart was that thing beating frantically inside her chest each time she eased closer to the water. The poor, confused organ obviously didn't know what was going on any better than she did, either, because it tugged her in the most dangerous directions of late. What would the water do to clarify her feelings for Fen? Her uncertainty about her heritage? Her magic might rest in water, but liquid was hardly sentient.

Was it?

God, she had to know.

Had. To. Know.

Before she could stop herself, Anna stumbled down the slight incline and straight into the water. Cold. The shock of it soaked through her tennis shoes and wrapped around her feet, impeding movement until she found herself slipping the shoes off and chunking them back toward the shore where they splatted against the side of a boulder and rolled. She thought she heard a voice, but it didn't matter. Nothing mattered but the bliss lapping around her legs, caressing her like a lover.

Anna almost tugged off her shirt, but the call of the water was too strong to take the time. Instead, she plunged head first into the maelstrom and began to swim. Down. Ever down. She held her breath, afraid to test her lungs, but there was no way she could stop herself from heading toward the bottom.

Something good was down there.

Yes, the voice called. *Come to me, and I will take you in. You will be mine.*

What?

Anna slowed, peering through the murky water for the source of the words. She'd read what she could find about the fae Vek had claimed she descended from, and they had lived in lakes in Wales. Could some of her long-lost family have a home

in the vast Tennessee River? Was such a thing possible? If so, there had to be more than one. This voice was male, but a female had called for her yesterday.

Her lungs burned, and she swam harder toward…something.

We shall be together forever, little love.

Wait, forever?

Fear surged through her, overriding even the call of the water. She had a mate—possibly two mates. Now there was someone claiming they'd be together for eternity?

Hell, no.

The urge to suck in a breath filled her, and she began to claw toward the surface. She tried, at least.

Take a breath. The water will not harm you.

No. She couldn't.

But instinct overrode thought, and though she flailed against the action, she couldn't stop herself from pulling in a mouthful of the muddy water. Anna's hands went to her throat, and the river's current tossed her helpless form closer toward the bottom as she resigned herself to drowning.

Light glimmered, and pale kelp drifted in the murk.

Kelp? Couldn't be. No, it was hair.

Anna blinked, trying to separate delusion from reality. But whatever it was drifted away. Maybe she was near death. Except… Her chest moved. She was breathing.

Breathing water.

Fen didn't stop to plan—he kicked off his shoes and jumped in.

Why hadn't she turned when he called her name? He sucked in a breath, dove, and swam as though his life depended on it. Maybe it did. If he failed to protect Anna, he would let Maddy flay him at the first opportunity. There had to be torture equipment somewhere in the world.

Fuck, the current was strong, and it was impossible to see in this mess. Too much damned mud.

Mud?

With a burst of power, Fen connected to the particles of earth filling the water around him and forced them aside. The water sloshed harder until he almost lost focus, but the sudden visibility was exactly what he'd needed. As fish darted away from the unusual disturbance, he saw hope.

There—kicking feet. Anna.

Fen swam harder despite the brutal river current and the pain in his lungs, and sure enough, he drew up next to the figure until Anna's startled face came into view. Spots of darkness clouded his vision, and he began to lose his hold on the mud around them. Not much time to spare.

In one desperate, quick motion, he tugged her close, said a prayer to any listening deity, and swam upward with all his might.

There was nothing technically wrong with the little room at the top of the healer's tower. In fact, Maddy had a feeling she could stare out the window at the beautiful forest for hours, watching the last of the gorgeous, vibrant leaves fall from the trees that surrounded the building. The bed was small but comfortable, and the chair beside the window cradled her delightfully. She no longer questioned her safety, not after Lial had taught her to control the magical lock that barred the door to anyone, including him.

But she still couldn't shake the feeling that something was wrong.

Any minute, Cora would return to show her the way to dinner. And while Maddy was undeniably nervous about dining with elven nobility—and even royalty—that wasn't quite what twisted within her, either. This was different. Distant but somehow personal. Too bad she couldn't use her phone. Then she could call both Anna and Fen to ensure they were well. She could check with Jase to see if there were problems at the shop. Or what if it was her parents?

No, probably not. Her mother might be human, but her father was Sidhe. Maddy had made sure to tell him exactly where she'd gone, so if her mother was ill or injured, he would be able to find her. Unless he was hurt? It was far less likely but not impossible. But in that case, her mother would have contacted Anna, and Anna would have called Fen. She wasn't totally cut off. Plenty of people knew how to find her.

At the knock on the door, she flinched, then let out a nervous laugh. She'd worked herself right up, hadn't she? It was only being in a new place. Everyone at home was fine. She would go have dinner with Cora, and everything would be okay.

No worries here.

13

Emerging from the depths of the river was a shock after she'd acclimated to being underwater.

Anna flailed against Fen as her body resisted the sudden change, but his arms tightened as he tried to fight the river's current. Too bad she was more hinderance than help. Her lungs burned as they had within the river, but for an opposite reason this time. Instinct drove her to bend over Fen's arm as the water expelled from her lungs in a rush. Well, then. At least she hadn't essentially vomited murky river water all over him. Small mercies.

Now that she could breathe air again, her panic subsided, and she let herself drift with Fen as he treaded water. But before they could get far, a downed tree that hadn't quite breached the surface blocked their path. The current shoved them into the vee between two branches. Instead of fighting, Anna sighed with relief. The obstruction would keep them from washing away before she got her bearings.

She pulled back from Fen enough to tread water, one hand gripping the river-smoothed wood anchoring her side.

"Anna?" Fen said.

She glanced up into his worried face. "Fen."

"Are you okay?" He let out a snort. "Of course you're not okay. You almost drowned. We need to get you to the hospital."

Anna smiled. "No."

"You spit out enough water to fill the damned aquarium." Fen tugged her close enough for their lower bodies to brush and their kicking legs to tangle, though he didn't seem to notice. "What were you thinking? I called your name, but you still jumped in like it was a fucking swim meet. I can't believe—"

"Fen." She settled her free hand against his cheek, and he snapped his mouth shut. "I'm really okay. I…I guess I can breathe water."

His jaw muscle flexed beneath her hand. "You guess?"

"Fine." Anna pulled air into her lungs, almost like a dare. Smooth and easy, no hint of the burning pain she'd half-expected. "I can definitely breathe water. Then after we surfaced, it just…expelled itself. As you clearly saw. I don't even feel a hint of it now."

Fen's eyes narrowed, his gaze darting down to her chest as though he could see through to her lungs. Then his grip on her tightened, and she couldn't help a small shriek as he lifted her slightly until he could press his ear against her sternum. If it hadn't been so sweet, Anna would have laughed. He truly was worried about her health.

He struggled to stay afloat, but he didn't release her. Instead, he let her body slide back down along his, and a new awareness hit—one that bore little similarity to the refreshing cool of the water. Fen was no weightlifter, but his leanly muscled body was as hard as mountain stone. In more ways than one, she discovered as their lower bodies connected again.

Heat flared within her, and she didn't pull away. Was it the water that loosened her natural reserve? Anna wasn't prudish, but it usually took her ages to get physically close to someone. She hadn't even kissed Maddy until after their second official date.

Then again, Anna had been the one who'd suggested the three of them attempt a relationship. What better time to test her chemistry with Fen than now, when they were both so close? Anna released the downed tree limb so she could slide her arms around Fen's neck and then pressed herself more firmly against him. His breath caught, and the look he turned her way was amusingly surprised.

"I'm really not sure you're okay," he said.

Anna chuckled. God, he was adorable. "Why?"

"The way you're holding me." His hands slid from her waist to her ribcage, but the touch didn't feel more innocent. "Maybe you're delirious."

If she was, she suddenly didn't care.

"Are you delirious, too?" Anna asked, wiggling her hips slightly against his.

His cheeks reddened. "Sorry. I'm holding a wet, beautiful woman, so my body has its own ideas."

Unlike her, Fen wasn't the quiet type. Why had he turned shy now? And how had a guy so easily flustered by an erection managed to get involved with some kind of weird magical gang? Both questions she would have to ask him when she didn't have other things to think about. Like whether this spark between them had promise. Maybe Fen was a terrible kisser. Maybe they simply wouldn't be good together regardless.

"I really don't mind," she whispered.

Before she could second-guess herself, Anna brushed her mouth against his. Softly at first, prepared for him to pull away. But he didn't. Instead, Fen crushed her close, one hand gripping her T-shirt between her shoulder blades and the other slipping down to grip her ass.

He devoured her, and she let him.

Fen forgot he was supposed to be treading water until he sank enough for the water to tap against the bottom of his jaw. He resumed kicking, but Anna broke away with a chuckle. "I guess I should have kissed you on land."

He anchored his arm around the tree limb so he wouldn't sink again. "Not your fault I couldn't remember what I was doing. Mostly not your fault, anyway."

"So have you kissed Maddy like that yet?" Anna asked. Though she smiled at him, panic had his feet kicking harder. "I'm guessing not, since she hasn't mentioned it, but I'm curious."

Fen released her shirt and smoothed the fabric as best he could in the water. "Umm. No. Shit, is she going to be mad about this? I don't want her to think we waited for her to leave."

Anna tapped her finger playfully against his chest. "Then we'll both have to give her a kiss when she returns."

Honestly, he didn't know what to say to that. He wanted to do that very thing, of course, but the entire situation felt so tenuous. How could he trust that two people would find him worthy of love? Not even his family believed in him that much. But what if it could work? He stared into Anna's eyes, their kiss still heating her gaze, and for the first time, he let himself hope.

Fen brushed a scraggly, wet strand of hair off Anna's cheek and smiled. "Maybe we'll do that."

Though her grin widened, Anna released her hold on him and drifted back. "Well, come on. Let's get out of this water. Now that I know I can breathe in the river, it isn't nearly as scary."

"You don't think you'll be tempted to disappear beneath the waves?"

That dimmed her smile. "I…I guess I can't promise that. But I'll figure out something."

Fen studied her face, hoping for a hint of her thoughts, while he treaded water. "You know, you could just quit your job."

"I've already told Maddy I won't take her money until we're married." Her lips tightened. "So don't bother offering."

"Hell, I hadn't even considered that," Fen said truthfully. "I assumed you'd find something else. Listen, though. You have to start thinking like a fae, and part of that is being prepared to move quickly if things go downhill. It could be as small as a different job or apartment or as huge as inventing a new life entirely. Or as stupid as falling in with the wrong group because they offer you a fucking utopia of hope. Don't do that one."

"Fen—"

"I'm not looking for sympathy. It's an important point, one I didn't understand when I first met Kien. The trickiest fae make their offer seem like the only and best one. If it sounds like an infomercial, it probably is."

Anna coughed. "An infomercial?"

"Struggling to understand your magic? Sign up now and receive training for a

limited time. The clock's ticking," Fen said, doing his best imitation of an overeager salesman. "Call today, and we'll throw in a side of revenge and world domination. Offer ends at midnight."

She splashed water across his chest. "I don't believe you fell for something that obvious."

"No, but you know what I mean. You have to beware of people who offer help too easily."

Anna stilled, at least until the current forced her to resume swimming. "What about Maddy? I'd say that healer from Moranaia offered help fairly easily."

"Hah." Fen snorted. "You haven't met him, have you? Nothing is going to be simple with that guy."

A boat sped by, and the water grew choppy. The group of teenagers onboard laughed and shouted at them, waving and jumping like a bunch of little kids. Fen tightened his grip on the branch and kicked his feet faster to stay steady. The swim had turned out to be nice despite their strange conversation, but he and Anna really should head back. If they weren't careful, they would be run over by a dinner cruise or something.

"Come on," Anna said, echoing his thoughts. "I love being in the water, but I don't want to get hit by a boat."

They eased out from between the tree branches, and Anna turned in the water until she could float on her back. As she began to swim, Fen did his best to keep pace. Damn, she was fast. The current was strong, but she sliced across the water as though she was in a swimming pool. He considered turning to his back the way she was. But no. He'd never been particularly good at the backstroke, and he didn't have her unerring sense of direction. If he couldn't see the shore, he'd never find it.

Anna was already a couple of body-lengths ahead of him when pain seared his heel. Out of instinct, Fen yelped, but he didn't have time to do much more. Something gripped his ankle and tugged, and before he could kick loose, he was yanked downward. He sucked in a quick breath. Then he was under the water.

Fen's cry sliced through the peace that had filled Anna from her swim through the water. She tipped her head forward to try to see him, but she only caught the barest glimpse of his head disappearing beneath the waves. Her chest tightened in fear. What had happened?

She didn't wait to see if he would surface. Deftly, Anna turned herself in the water and dove. This time, she didn't hesitate to breathe in liquid. As the river filled her lungs, it gave her life. Power. She used it to propel herself after Fen.

Anna couldn't see well through the murk, but she could sense so much more. Fish. Plants. Another boat approaching, though far enough away not to be a concern. But most importantly, Fen—and the person trying to drag him under. With her eyes, she could just make out tendrils of blond hair drifting upward like the tentacles of a jellyfish, the strands tangling around Fen's legs as his attacker pulled him downward.

Convenient—if Fen knew about it.

Staring at his forehead, Anna did her best to send her thoughts to him. *"Their hair is floating up. Move your legs just right, and you can hurt them."*

Fen's head jerked up, and for a moment, he stopped flailing as his gaze connected with hers. *"Anna?"*

"Yes," she sent. *"Did you catch what I said?"*

Instead of answering, Fen shoved his knees together, drew them upward as much as he could, and twisted. A shout reverberated through the water, and the hand gripping Fen's ankle jerked away, moving instead to tug at the strands of hair Fen had trapped.

"Going to have to breathe soon," Fen said into her mind.

"Give another good pull on their hair, then let go. I'll help you swim for it."

As soon as Fen did as she suggested and then kicked free—with a solid thunk to his attacker's head—Anna slipped her shoulder under his arm and swam for it. With the force of her magic behind her kicks, they reached the surface almost instantly. This time, she barely noticed when her lungs expelled the water. She was too busy trying to get Fen far from his unknown assailant.

Anna didn't look behind her until they'd crawled up on shore. Fen flopped over to his back, panting heavily, as she scanned the water for any sign of another person. Nope. Nothing. She might have thought they'd been swept away and drowned, which was still a possibility, but she hadn't seen another person approach in the first place. Plus, she'd seen that drifting hair during her first dive down.

It had to be some kind of water fae.

"Is my heel bleeding?" Fen asked.

After one last look at the river, Anna crawled down until she could reach Fen's feet. Fortunately, there was no sign of blood. "No. A few red marks, but that's it."

"That's something, at least." Though his breathing had evened, his words were slow with exhaustion. "Think you could drive us back to Vek's house? No offense, but I'd like a place with some heavy shielding after that. I should report in, too."

She would have rather gone home, but he had a good point. If Maddy had placed a lot of magical protections on their condo, then Anna didn't know about them. Going to Vek's house made sense. They could try to sort out what had happened without worrying as much about safety, and the place was blessedly far from the river.

Anna stood up and wiped uselessly at her wet pants. "Sounds good. Except that we're soaked. We'll ruin your seats. And I'm pretty sure that if I walk by the restaurant like this, I'll be seen. I don't want to get fired."

Fen sat up, tossing his bedraggled hair from his eyes. "Maybe it's a good time to play with your magic. What goes up must come down. Or in this case flows out."

"You think I can force the water out?"

"Hey, it's worth a try."

Anna frowned at her clothes. The theory made a certain amount of sense, but

she'd never tried to use her magic on purpose. Stirring the water in the glass on her desk had been an accident. How could she do it intentionally?

"What if I cause a problem?" Anna whispered. "I could get us in trouble if I mess up badly."

Shrugging, Fen stood and gathered their scattered shoes. "Don't worry about it if you aren't ready. Vek has towels, and I can afford to get the car detailed if it's that bad. Take your time."

Anna took her shoes from him, and the wet, gross feel of the sides had her wrinkling her nose. It would only get worse when she tried to put them on. But maybe she *could* solve their problem. It only took a little courage. No big deal, right? If she could plunge under the surface to save Fen, she could try to dry them off afterward.

"If I start to lose it, toss me in the river. Or form a wall around me or something."

Fen straightened, one shoe still in hand. "What?"

"I'm going to try to get rid of the water."

"Anna—"

"Hush," she interrupted. "I've decided."

After taking a deep breath, Anna closed her eyes. It took her a moment to move beyond her self-consciousness, but once she did, she became aware of the water beading on her skin and weighing down her clothes. She fought to open her mind the way she had when she'd communicated mentally with Fen. After a few heartbeats, the water's resonance filled her like a heartbeat that thrummed in time with the lapping river.

She began at the top of her head and shoved the excess moisture downward. It flowed in rivulets toward the ground, leaving everything in the wake of her power dry. But it was almost too much. Before the natural moisture could leech from her hair and skin, she reined her magic in. Soon, she found a balance between forcing the water from her body and clothes and turning herself into a person-sized desert.

Once she was reasonably dry, Anna touched Fen's arm with her free hand and repeated the process. The only things she tried extra hard to dry were their phones. She pushed as much water from those as she could and hoped for the best.

Finally, she opened her eyes. Awareness of her surroundings returned as she blinked against the afternoon sunshine, and she glanced down to see that her clothes were for the most part dry. Not perfect—she could still see a few damp splotches on the thick fabric of her jeans, and Fen's shirt retained a hint of moisture when she rubbed the edge between her fingers. But who cared?

She'd done magic!

Anna couldn't stop the relieved laugh that slipped free. Before shyness overcame the thrill of victory, she leaned against Fen and gave him a quick kiss. But it wasn't long before she pulled away and bent to put her shoes on, leaving him staring at her with a bemused expression.

Until recently, she hadn't thought of herself as the spontaneous or bold type, but somehow the more she embraced her water nature, the more she'd begun to embrace her true desires. What was the point of doing otherwise? Like the river, life was an ever-changing force. It was time she learned to flow with it—even when she was standing on dry land.

14

Vek paced the entry chamber at the top of the cavern, his boots ringing hollowly throughout the vast space. His mate leaned against the wall beside the door to the heavily shielded gate room, but although she watched him, she didn't say a word. She didn't have to. She would be able to feel his worry and frustration through their mate link, just as she knew there was nothing she could say to ease his anxiety.

His feelings couldn't be related to Fen. Vek was nervous about the situation with Anna, especially because of the hasty way his nephew had charged off to save her, but he didn't anticipate anything dire from that. Fen was certainly capable of taking care of himself.

But Vek couldn't deny that he would feel much better when his nephew returned with a report.

Together, they could go find Anthony, who hadn't returned Vek's text. An ominous sign when potential dark energy afflicted the man's friend. Had something happened to her? To both of them? A prickly, jumpy feeling grew in Vek as more time passed. Something was wrong, but he had no way of knowing what.

Until the magical alarm he'd placed around his house shrieked a warning into his mind.

Vek halted a couple of paces away from Dria. "Someone is trying to enter my home."

"Which one?" Dria asked wryly.

"The Chattanooga house, not the estate in the Unseelie realm," he said. "Or here."

She waved a hand. "Obviously not here. Want me to come with you?"

Vek considered it but shook his head. "No. I'm not sure where Fen is. He might need your help. I believe Aris and Kezari also wanted to speak to you after they finish their search."

"Good point." Dria grabbed his arm and pulled him in for a quick kiss. "Come back safely or else."

Despite his worry, he laughed. "I'll keep that in mind."

Quickly, Vek entered the secured room and created a portal to his house. Dria preferred to set the end point in his living room, but as he'd grown more adept at the transportation spell, he'd started choosing his own destination—his bedroom. It felt safer to enter the enclosed space, which boasted one well-curtained window instead of an entire wall of glass like the public area of the house.

He'd spelled the whole building against prying eyes, but that didn't mean he felt comfortable appearing in the seeming open.

As soon as he marched through, Vek dispelled the portal and scanned each room of his house for incursion. No one inside. He closed his eyes and extended his senses carefully to the outside. There. Ah, fuck. Ara. What was his sister doing here of all places?

Vek hurried through the living room and unlocked the side door he used as an entrance. Then he slowed, sauntering toward Ara as he studied the back of her cloaked form. She had to sense him, but she didn't turn. Why had she come? It was dangerous to leave the Unseelie realm so soon after taking power.

He stopped beside her, and for a moment, they both stared at the view of Chattanooga where it nestled in the valley below. "Come inside," he finally said.

Ara nodded, settling the hood of her cloak more firmly around her face when it slipped. In silence, Vek headed back toward the door. She wouldn't speak until they were inside his home, their words and magics shielded beneath his wards. But as soon as he led her inside and closed the door, Ara tugged down her hood and glared at him.

"Where is Fen?" she demanded.

Vek blinked. "Couldn't you have contacted me through a mirror link to ask about your son? A bit risky showing up here, don't you think?"

"Don't chastise me," Ara said, her nostrils flaring. "I know very well the dangers of leaving the palace, but this is important. I received a threatening note from Meren. I believe he's after Fen."

His annoyance with her incursion vanished, replaced by fury. "Why would he do such a thing?"

Ara shook her head. "I'm not certain, but I can guess. He wants to use my son against me. Perhaps against both of us. I don't know his plan, but it can't be good."

"I assume you have a plan of your own we need to discuss." And Vek had a feeling neither he nor Fen would like it. "Or you would have merely sent me warning."

"There is nothing to discuss." Ara straightened. "Fen will be returning with me."

That, of course, was when the door opened, the man in question framed against the afternoon glow. Vek cursed under his breath. He could have handled this. Now, it was likely to turn into a disaster. Fabulous.

"Like hell I will," Fen snarled, barely remembering to let Anna through before he slammed the door behind them.

If not for his excellent hearing, he never would have had advanced warning of what they were planning. Or his mother, at least—he had no evidence yet that Vek agreed. Fen was so furious he was afraid to look at his uncle's expression and have his worst fears confirmed. If Vek betrayed him…treated him like a child with no control of his fate…

Anna's hand settled against Fen's back, and he took a deep breath to calm himself. Though he didn't sense any magic coming from Anna, her peace soothed him enough to allow rational thought. Ara and Vek were technically in charge, his mother as queen of their people and Vek as Fen's mentor, but they didn't control him. He was no longer a renegade, but he was no blind follower, either.

"I have to agree with Fen," Vek said calmly, and Fen finally dared to study his face. Thankfully, his uncle appeared more annoyed than anything. "Although my heart wishes to see him in a more secure environment, I am uncertain we have ample evidence to justify it."

Ara's lips pinched. "I am considering more than physical and magical protection. If he formally takes his place as my heir, he will have greater political recourse in the event that Meren does attack."

"That's debatable. With the court still in upheaval from our father's death, there could be people who would ally with Meren for their own benefit." Vek crossed his arms over his chest. "The outpost should provide ample protection, and Dria and I can keep him safe from Meren now that we have guarded against water based—"

"Stop it," Fen snapped. "If you insist on speaking around me, you can both fuck off."

And there it was—his mother's reasonable-adult-to-angry-child expression. Like she had any right to use it after leaving him with his human father and then losing track of him. Vek, at least, had the good grace to look abashed at the reminder. But then, his uncle knew him far better than the woman who had given birth to him.

"You are young yet," Ara said. "Not even a quarter-century. Meren is a couple thousand years older and capable of more than you can imagine. In case you didn't hear all of my earlier words, you should know that he is targeting you. You're in a great deal of danger."

Fen stared at her, so astounded he couldn't speak. Capable of more than he could imagine? Had she really just said that? He wanted to rage at her casual dismissal of all he'd been through, but doing so would only prove her point about his age. He wouldn't storm away this time. He was as done with that as he had been with Kien.

"I might remind you that Kien found me scrounging for blood on the streets," Fen said, as softly as he could manage. "I lived for several years knowing that with one false move, the bastard would spend days torturing me, then cutting off each limb one at a time and hanging it around his camp as decoration until there was nothing of me left. I am quite familiar with danger, and my imagination has enough filler for a million nightmares."

Ara's cheeks reddened. "That may be so, but this threat should not be taken lightly."

"Maybe…" Anna cleared her throat as all eyes turned her way. "Do you think that was him at the river, Fen?"

He might have cursed at that revelation if he hadn't felt her hand trembling against his back. Her voice sounded calm, but speaking up hadn't been easy. "I don't know. Did you see what the person looked like?"

"No, only the hair. Long and pale blond." Her forehead crinkled. "Except… the attacker's hand was fairly large. More like a man's. That's not definitive, though."

"Attacker?" Ara asked. "Someone tried to harm you beside the river?"

"We were, ah…in the water." Fen raised his eyebrow at Anna, uncertain he should reveal her troubles. She sighed but gave him a subtle nod. "I jumped in after Anna when the water's pull became too strong. Once we surfaced, we chatted for a moment. But as we were swimming back to shore, someone grabbed my foot and pulled me under. Anna helped me escape."

Vek's eyes narrowed. "It could have been him. Meren's power is water, a talent he used to sneak past our shielding and into our room. Perhaps Ara is correct. The Unseelie palace is heavily protected against the Seelie. You should go there while we track Meren down."

Fen sucked in a breath through his nose and let it out in a long stream. Unfortunately, it didn't help him find his calm. "Shall I grab a teddy bear and huddle in the nursery for safety, oh wise elders?" he asked with exaggerated formality. "If I'm good, perhaps I'll be given permission to have dinner with the adults."

"What in the hell is wrong with you?" Vek demanded as fury tightened Ara's face.

Ara stepped closer. "Feniarathen an Arafel, you will not use such a tone with me."

"Why not?" Fen lifted a shoulder. "You can say my full name, but you can't say much else about me. As far as I can remember, this is the second time in my life that I've seen you. Don't pretend I have a reason to care about your sudden desire to mother me."

"Fen." Vek gave a subtle shake of his head. "You shouldn't forget that Ara is also the queen."

"Yeah, yeah." Fen snorted, focusing his anger on Vek. "I have to stay in line, or I won't be allowed to return to my homeland. Gotta prove myself worthy. Can't cause a fuss. You know what? I don't care. No matter how hard I try to atone, you and Dria don't trust me. You, my mother, and the entire royal family…you'll never see me as anything but a fuck up. Hell, maybe you're right. But I can't play this game anymore. I need to find my own place on my own terms, and I am more than capable of doing so."

His mother could have carved out an entire cave system with the expression on her face. "You agreed to work with Vek. If you refuse—"

"Send out your assassins, then," Fen said. Anna sidled closer, her side brushing against his arm, but not even her peace could soothe him. This had been a long time coming. He and Vek had started to grow closer, but their budding camaraderie would never survive without respect. Nor could Fen ever feel he'd earned his place amongst the Unseelie if his position was given grudgingly. "I refuse to be treated like a potential liability. When Vek and Dria can stop eyeing me like I might turn bad and my mother can stop treating me like I'm still the baby she never raised, then I'll consider returning."

"You are my heir," Ara ground out.

Fen was half-surprised she didn't open a sinkhole beneath his feet. "Giving me a title won't make up for a childhood full of nightmares, and being overprotective now won't, either."

"He's right," Vek said suddenly—and with no hint of his usual sardonic humor. "At least on my part. I hadn't intended to treat him that way, but I can see that I have."

Fen peered into his uncle's shadowed gaze. "Then you'll understand why this is necessary. I need time, and I'm going to take it. But I'm not an idiot. Now that I've been warned about Meren, I'll take extra precautions. I know I can survive alone. It's time you know it, too."

He didn't wait for confirmation. Brushing past Vek and Ara, Fen strode out of the room and down the hall. He hadn't accumulated many belongings, so it didn't take long to pack his bag once he'd entered his bedroom. A few changes of clothes, his travel kit full of toiletries, a sack full of gemstones he'd coaxed from the earth when he had the chance—they were the only things he bothered to take with him everywhere he moved.

From the other room, he heard Vek's and Ara's raised voices, but he didn't bother to listen to the useless argument. It wouldn't change anything. He couldn't let it. He had to stand on his own, even if Meren killed him. Fen couldn't deny that the Seelie man was a threat, but cowering behind others would be its own horrible death.

A flash of movement caught his eye. Anna. Fen slung his bag over his shoulder and turned to face her. Gods, she probably thought he was insane. He'd just told off two of the most powerful people he knew and left a mentorship he truly needed. Could she see that not even learning more about his *Felshreh* bloodline was worth dealing with their scorn?

Her expression gave nothing away, but her words slashed at him. "If you need time away, then what about me and Maddy?"

Fen scraped his fingers through his hair. "I'm not running away, especially not from you. Sorry, Anna. I wasn't thinking about how you might take that. But those two…"

"Yeah," Anna said. Her tension easing, she slipped inside and closed the door behind her. "I get it. It seemed like a good idea to find out how alone you want your alone time, though. You said you wanted to find your own place. I'd offer you our couch until you do, but I'm not sure how you'd feel about it."

Suddenly, Fen wasn't sure, either. Maddy and Anna deserved an equal, not a scrounger who couldn't get his shit together. Relying on others had become too much of a habit. "If I did stay at your place, it would only be for a night. Depends on what I can find on short notice."

Anna drew close enough to take his hand. "It's like me not taking money from Maddy, isn't it?"

"Yeah." For the first time since he'd walked in to Ara's pronouncement, Fen smiled. "It's exactly like that."

She twined her fingers with his. "Come on, then. Let's go apartment hunting. If you want company?"

That, he found, was an offer he couldn't refuse.

15

After a rather unusual dinner, Maddy followed Lial along a series of trails situated between the trees. It was rather like a garden, but there were few things blooming at the moment. The area was beautiful, regardless. Here and there, ornamental benches or little decorative statues of wildlife she'd never seen peeked out of arbors or between carefully maintained bushes. Everything was designed to appear natural, but to someone who'd grown up around uncultivated woods, the subtle artifice stood out.

The forest as seen in fairytales. How apt.

"So tell me, Maddy," Lial began. "What did you think of dinner?"

"It was…" How did she describe its peculiarity without being rude? "It was an interesting experience."

Lial chuckled. "One could say that. Personally, I was thinking more absurd than interesting. A comedy worthy of a mid-winter festival."

"You mean it isn't usually so…"

"Colorful?" Lial turned between a pair of hedges and followed the trail to a small, round building. "It has been more so in recent months, though I rarely join the others enough to experience the scope of it. I'm surprised more people haven't started avoiding meals after some of the recent food experiments."

Maddy tried not to think about the unusual food and the stomach upset it had caused as she followed the healer into the building. A special training tower, he'd said. Magic here apparently didn't need many tools, since there was nothing inside except for a handful of cushions in the center of the floor and a table shoved up against the far wall. But power tickled across her skin as Lial closed the door and activated the shielding.

A safe place to practice, then.

"Do you know what tonight's dinner was supposed to be?" Lial asked, sitting on one of the center cushions.

Maddy shook her head as she followed suit. "Kai said pizza, but I have my doubts. The crust isn't supposed to be almost as thick as a bread loaf, the cheese was far too sharp, and the sauce…" She shuddered. "The vegetable they thought was close to a tomato isn't close enough."

Lial smiled. "We need a cook from Earth to work with ours, I suppose."

"Don't look at me." Maddy wrinkled her nose. "Anna's the domestic one. If she'd been here, I wouldn't have a stomachache."

"You are feeling ill? Good."

"Gee, thanks," Maddy muttered.

The healer had been reserved during dinner but not rude. Honestly, her heart had warmed to see how carefully he avoided speaking to Lady Lynia, though he'd tried to keep it casual so that others wouldn't notice. Everyone, of course, noticed. The lady in question had studied him more than once, varying degrees of annoyance and sadness pinching her face, and several of the others had exchanged amused glances and wry smiles when the healer wasn't looking.

After all that, Lial's return to brusqueness was a bit of a shock.

"I didn't mean it that way," the healer grumbled. "It will give you something within yourself to analyze. I want to examine your technique and see where things are going wrong."

Maddy rested her suddenly trembling hands in her lap. "I can scan myself without trouble and am getting fairly reliable about examining others. It's trying to fix the problem that's often a disaster."

Lial extended his hands and waited patiently until she settled her palms against his. "Then let us link, and you can attempt to fix the unrest in your stomach from the unfamiliar food. I will prevent your magic from doing harm if it begins to go awry."

"Okay."

She didn't dare ask how he would accomplish such a feat—she could only take it on faith if she hoped to keep her courage. After sucking in a deep breath, Maddy closed her eyes and opened her mind to the healer's presence. A shadow of his power washed across her, enough to ease the tension knotting her muscles but not so much that it felt like he was taking over. With that hint of peace, she could move forward with more confidence.

Maddy finally allowed her own power to unfurl, if only a little. Slowly, she ran her magic through her body, checking everywhere just in case. All perfect, save her elevated heartrate and aching stomach. Her pulse, she knew, was high from nerves and well within range, so she shifted her focus almost at once.

In theory, her stomach problems should have been easy to fix. The bread had contained more fiber than she was used to, and the cheese had a higher protein content, overwhelming her body's ability to break down the food quickly. Boosting the proper enzymes and drinking more water would do the trick. She could do that. No problem.

Hah.

Tentatively, Maddy directed her magic into her stomach, concentrating the energy on the task she had in mind—enzyme production. Almost immediately, pain

stabbed through her abdomen, and she swallowed down the bile that rose up her throat. With a frustrated groan, she released her hold on her magic and tried to breathe through the pain.

It lasted only a moment. Lial's power flared, and every trace of discomfort vanished.

It had only taken a fucking heartbeat for him to accomplish what she clearly couldn't.

"I believe I see the problem," the healer said. "It's your human blood interfering."

Stiffening, Maddy jerked her hands from his and glared at him. "That's rude."

His eyebrow shot up. "I was not offering insult. It was a true statement. As with Arlyn, there is a component of will magic twined with your Sidhe healing powers."

She'd met Arlyn at dinner but didn't know much about her except that she was the half-human daughter of Lord Lyr who'd found her way to Moranaia—and him—some months before. "I'm not sure what will magic is, and I'm not familiar enough with the lady in question to figure it out. Is she a healer?"

"No," Lial said. "A mage-in-training. That part is irrelevant. To answer the question you're truly asking, will magic is as simple and as difficult as it sounds. You direct your energy with the force of your will, much the same way a priest focuses prayers. As the mage Selia explained to me, humans have honed the talent in the absence of strong energy. You gather what you can, concentrate it, and send it to manifest your goal."

Maddy frowned. She'd heard pagans mention something like that when talking about their ritual circles. Combining their energy and prayers and focusing them on a specific task—a way to guide the universe in the direction a person wanted. Really, people in other religions often did something similar when they centered their prayers on common causes. She hadn't spent a lot of time thinking about it, though, and how often it did or didn't work.

"How does that mess me up?" she asked.

Lial smiled, but there was no hint of condescension on his face. "Have you studied anatomy? This is not a question formed in judgement. I need to know your knowledge base."

"I tried my hand at nursing school, but the classes brought back bad memories." Maddy pulled her hands from his and returned them to her lap. The low hum of his peaceful energy faded, but she hadn't wanted to unintentionally share her pain at the coming confession. "When I was a teenager, I almost killed a friend of mine from school. She had pneumonia, and I thought I could fix it. I sent my energy in and told it to repair, but the opposite happened. I still don't know what I did."

"Hmm." The healer pursed his lips. "I would wager you accidentally repaired the attacking virus. Knowledge of the body and of disease is vital for any healer, but for you, it is literal life-and-death. Entwined with will, your power needs exact directions. Today, you didn't specify which enzymes to boost, upsetting the delicate balance in your gut."

So simple but so complicated. "Looks like I have a lot of studying in my future."

"I'm certain Lynia would help you find suitable books, and if you can't read Moranaian as well as you speak it, I have a spell that can help." Lial sighed. "Otherwise, you must work on your confidence, first by letting go of the past. Healers make mistakes, Maddy. It is a terrible burden, our job, but one that does far more good than the opposite. You'll have to accept the risk and the responsibility or forego your healing gift."

The haunted look in his eyes told a story beyond his words. Lial understood. Truly understood. Maddy had received her fair share of sympathy and compassion from those few who had learned about what she'd almost done, but they'd never experienced quite what she had. Lial, though… He had walked that line of life and death and regret for far longer. No wonder his demeanor was prickly. There was always a cost, after all.

"I'll do my best," Maddy said.

And she would.

Defeated by veritable children. Not new, but just as appalling as the last time.

Meren gripped his hair in his fist and slipped the sharp blade beneath, slicing the long, tangled mass of it free. He shook his head and smiled at the lighter weight. Nobles in the Seelie court typically wore their hair long as a sign of status, but nothing would return to him the status he had lost. Nothing save his ascension to power.

Perhaps he would start a new style.

He had a feeling he would spend a great deal of time in the water, attempting to draw the woman to him, and he would not have his own hair be his downfall again. The woman had to be the key to Fen. If Meren could draw her to him beneath the waves and transport her away, it would be nearly impossible to trace, and that clearly required greater stealth. Then he could use her as a lure whenever it was convenient. He'd almost succeeded this time before Fen had arrived.

A diversion. That was what he needed. If he could find something to distract the young blood elf while the woman was near the river, Meren could grab her without interference. Unfortunately, Fen was under the protection of Vek, and the Unseelie prince would be able to sense Meren despite his cloaking spell if he got too close.

The plan would take much care, but Meren would succeed.

He was the son of a savvy king, after all, a secret he'd hidden for millennia. A few more months would be nothing for him.

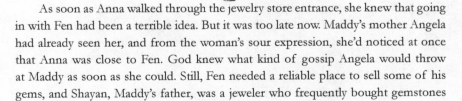

As soon as Anna walked through the jewelry store entrance, she knew that going in with Fen had been a terrible idea. But it was too late now. Maddy's mother Angela had already seen her, and from the woman's sour expression, she'd noticed at once that Anna was close to Fen. God knew what kind of gossip Angela would throw at Maddy as soon as she could. Still, Fen needed a reliable place to sell some of his gems, and Shayan, Maddy's father, was a jeweler who frequently bought gemstones

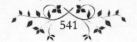

and precious metals from fae who needed assistance—provided he had the proper introduction.

Fortunately, Shayan came around the counter and rushed over to greet them before Angela could say anything. Despite the magic he used to conceal his true nature, Shayan looked every inch a Seelie Sidhe, from his tall, graceful form to the long, red-gold hair he wore pulled back from his handsome face. Anna had seen him a time or two without the glamour that added a hint of age to his appearance, and the man had practically glowed with light and life.

Why he stayed here with Maddy's unpleasant mother she couldn't imagine.

"Anna!" Shayan said, pulling her in for a quick hug. "It is a pleasure to see you. Have you finally brought Fen to meet us?"

"How did you know…" Fen began.

"Your name? An assumption, I confess." Shayan grinned. "Maddy called me before she left for Moranaia and said Anna might be hanging around a lad named Fen. An interesting situation you have there for certain."

Behind the counter, Angela stood, her eyes narrowing. Anna tugged Fen a little closer to Shayan and lowered her voice. "What did Maddy tell her mother?"

The Sidhe man's jovial expression slipped. "Not much. As touchy as Angela has been, Maddy didn't want to talk about it before she had to leave. Forgive me. I should have thought before I brought it up."

"No need to whisper," Angela called. "I know you've been keeping stuff from me."

Shayan winced sheepishly before he turned. "Beloved—"

"Anna left Maddy for a man, didn't she? This man."

A choked cough slipped from Fen before he covered his mouth with his fist, but Anna was too stunned to make a sound. Was it her imagination, or did Angela look…angry? The woman's pinched lips were curved down as she glared, and she'd dropped her clenched fists to her hips, leaving her elbows sticking out like spears. It didn't make sense. Angela hated Anna so much that she refused to invite her to most family events. Why wasn't she happy?

"Really, Shayan," Angela snapped. "How could you just greet her like that?"

Anna finally forced her mouth to actually function. "You have the wrong idea."

The other woman hurried around the counter. "I saw you holding hands before you walked in. Don't bother lying."

Damn. She hadn't thought about the glass storefront.

"No one is cheating on anyone," Fen said, settling his hand gently on Anna's shoulder. "Maddy knows all about it. She has even agreed—"

"To have her fiancée hanging all over some guy? I doubt it."

Anna needed to explain. She really did. But first, she had to get over the shock of Angela's behavior. The lady had been encouraging Maddy to ditch Anna for a man for as long as they'd been dating, and they'd all assumed it was because she couldn't handle her daughter being bi. What in the world was going on?

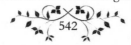

Shayan gestured wildly with his hands. "Angela, stop. The man is telling the truth. They're all...soulmates, I guess you would say. They're deciding if they want to form a triad."

A line formed between Angela's brows. "What?"

"Polyam," Fen supplied. Not-so-helpfully, judging by the color draining from the woman's face. "You know, polyamorous? A relationship with multiple partners? We can't get married legally, but we might end up mating the way my people do."

"The way your people..." Angela rubbed her fingers against her temples. "I can't believe this."

Anna sighed. "I'm sorry. I know you dislike me, but—"

"I have nothing against you specifically," the other woman said. "But more what your kind might do."

Even Shayan looked taken aback by that. "Her kind?" he asked.

"She's one of those feckless water fairies."

Anna's mouth dropped open. Even if Maddy had told her about that recently, it wouldn't explain why the woman had hated her all along. Angela must have known before Anna and Maddy did. Before the wall holding back Earth's energy had shattered. How would she be familiar with such a thing? As far as anyone knew, Angela was human.

Shayan hurried to his wife's side. "What are you saying, beloved? Are you ill?"

"No." Angela glared at her husband. "But I'm tired of pretending, and I'm tired of people thinking I'm awful. I might not be from a magical family, but that doesn't mean we haven't had dealings with the fae before. My grandparents were from Wales. I was raised on stories of the Gwragedd Annwn. I've always thought Anna had the look of them."

Anna had to remind herself to close her mouth. Good God. Maddy was never going to believe this. "What...what is so bad about the Gwragedd Annwn?"

"They leave," Angela snapped, pulling away from the comforting hand Shayan extended. "They take the best years of their lover's life and then abandon them. One of those bitches destroyed my uncle, leaving him to raise their little boy alone. He spent hours each day walking beside the lake where she'd disappeared. I watched my cousin almost drown trying to swim to his mother. Now here you are with some other man after hooking my Maddy, and I just can't believe this crap about being poly."

"Angela..." Shayan began.

"You deal with them," the woman said, spinning on her heel and marching toward the door behind the counter. "I'll come back out once they're gone."

A bewildered Shayan stared after his wife before shaking his head and hurrying to the door. He flipped the sign to closed and wedged an Out to Lunch sign in the corner of the door despite the fact that it was nearing dinner, but Anna didn't comment on the hour. It was dangerous to discuss fae business around humans, so it was best to discourage new customers while they spoke.

Even the Sidhe man's light had dimmed a little as he returned to their side. "I assume you needed something beyond a simple visit?" Shayan asked quietly.

If Fen was bothered by Angela's outburst, he showed no sign of it as he retrieved a small pouch from his backpack. "I'm an earth mage. I have several high-quality stones I've extracted and refined myself, and I'm seeking a fair price for them."

"Very well," Shayan said, his tone more subdued than Anna had ever heard it. "Come over to the counter, and I will examine them."

Anna didn't bother to go with them. Her heart hurt for Shayan, Maddy, and even Angela. All this time, none of them had known that Angela had previous experience with the fae. She'd been married to Shayan for decades and had accepted that he was Sidhe from the beginning, but it was clear that she hadn't told her husband about her history. Why would she have hidden it? Out of all the people in the world, Shayan would have understood. He was one of the few she could have told before Earth's magic had started to return.

What would Maddy say when she learned this new truth? It was one revelation Anna didn't want to deliver.

16

With no word from Anthony and no Fen to direct him, Vek had no choice but to return to the outpost without completing his task. As he formed the gate, frustration, fear, and a hint of anger clawed at his belly, and not all of the latter was directed toward Fen. What had Ara been thinking? She couldn't have screwed that up worse had it been her goal, but her nature had always been to command first and question later. Such tenacity worked well for a princess of the Unseelie court—not so much for the absent mother of a child who was just like her.

Not that either of them would admit to the similarity.

Vek stepped through the gate and into the outpost, barely pausing long enough to dispel the magic before connecting mentally with Dria. *"We have a problem."*

"I'll be right down."

Down? Vek scanned the cavern for his mate's presence, just in case she'd used the wrong word. But no. He discovered her energy on the surface above, near the secret entrance that guarded the way into the cave. He also detected Kezari, Delbin, and Inona on the outside. Either Kezari was scanning for a hint of dragon magic or helping with shielding. Each could cause a long delay with his mate's arrival.

He exited the portal chamber and strode through the massive entry room with its natural stone columns. Vek wasn't certain why the dragon had designed this space when she'd originally carved out the cave system for Moranaian use, but it was one of the few rooms that Dria hadn't ordered furnished. She would have been within her rights as the leader of the outpost to set up a formal receiving room instead of using Vek's old bedroom for meetings, but that wasn't his mate's style. She preferred to use the space for its own kind of natural shielding—if anyone broke past the protections on the entrance, they would find nothing unusual in this room.

By the time Vek made it to the other end, Dria was there to meet him. She didn't have to ask about his mental state. Without a word, she wrapped her arms around his waist. Sighing against her hair, Vek gathered her close and finally let himself process all that had happened. All that he'd messed up.

Once again, he'd failed to understand his nephew, and it might have ruined their relationship.

"Are you going to tell me the problem?" Dria asked. "I'm perfectly willing to annihilate someone if I have to."

Vek smiled slightly at her words. She would do it, too. "Not the best course of action, *ahmeeren*. It's Fen. I think I've driven him away for good. Or at least a long damned time."

Dria jerked back until she could meet his eyes. "What?"

"Ara showed up at the house and demanded that Fen return with her to keep him safe from Meren," Vek explained. "I was debating the merits of the plan with Ara, and Fen rightfully called me on it. He might be learning from me, but he isn't a child. I'm afraid I've unintentionally been treating him like one. Hell, he thinks we don't trust him."

"I haven't..." Dria wrinkled her nose. "*Clechtan*. I suppose I have acted overprotective at times. Maybe that's why he was angry with me before he left. What was it he said? 'We might seem like children to you at your age, but on this world, we are adults.'"

"Sounds like the sentiment he so forcefully shared with us before he left with Anna to go get his own place."

Vek's worry echoed in Dria's gaze. "Oh, no."

"I hope he'll talk to me," Vek said. "I have yet to hear from Anthony about the woman who is ill, and Fen didn't give me the man's address. I'm afraid I forgot while we were discussing Meren."

Dria nibbled on her lower lip. "You'd better try contacting Fen. He might be angry, but I suspect he'll answer. If he hasn't given up on you after all that happened when he was younger, I doubt he will start now."

Vek certainly hoped he wouldn't. They'd come to terms with Fen's accidental abandonment as a child, those years when Vek had been distracted by endless missions from the king. When he had finally located Fen as a teen, Vek had been appalled by the change from kind child to bitter, angry young man, and he'd only been able to mitigate his nephew's poor choices, not stop them. Now, he was supposed to be guiding him.

A fine failure Vek turned out to be at that. It was just as well that Dria wanted to wait a few centuries to have children—he would need that long to figure out how to raise one without it becoming a disaster.

Vek sighed. Time to start learning.

Maddy strolled along the twisting garden path and tried not to think about her failure of a lesson. Oh, she'd learned more about her gift, but who knew how long it would be before she could conquer it? With a sigh, she paused beside a carved stone column that cradled a mage light at the top. During the day, the piece probably looked like a decoration, much like the others she'd seen along the way—all in varying shapes and styles. The last had been created from metal, a vine curling upward like part of the greenery surrounding it; this one matched the bark of the trees directly behind it.

She'd been told that it was difficult to get lost so long as the estate was in sight. If nothing else, the tall, crystalline observation tower a short walk from the back of the main house was a beacon that was hard to miss, though that might not have been the case if the trees weren't losing their leaves. Everything about Moranaia was lush. Magical. Yet there was a sense of familiarity, too, in the forested mountains.

Her father had taught her that the Moranaians were among the first to leave Earth when the planet's natural magic had lessened. The Sidhe had departed later after making a poor treaty with the humans who invaded their ancestral home, Ireland, but they had ended up in a closely connected dimension beneath the surface of Earth. The Moranaians, though—they had traveled through the Veil to find another planet. She wasn't certain if they'd found others along the way, but she could understand why they'd chosen to stop on this one. There were enough almost-Earth things to provide a great deal of comfort.

Maybe a little unease, too. Maddy gathered her borrowed cloak closer to ward off the chill and slipped between a pair of trees, coming to an abrupt halt at the edge of a thin stream. She'd been warned to turn back if she reached the water. Though there were still guards stationed in the trees above, carefully camouflaged, their surveillance thinned beyond the river. She could get lost for certain in the less cultivated forest beyond.

Maddy spun around—and almost fell backwards into the water at the sight of the little girl illuminated by the mage globe at the edge of the path. Catching her footing just in time, Maddy paused to gather her composure. She'd been introduced to young Eri at dinner, but the child hadn't said much. What was she doing out here at night?

From what Maddy understood, the little girl had come to Moranaia from Earth not long ago herself. Prince Ralan had lived on Earth for centuries to avoid his evil brother Kien, but Ralan had returned with half-human Eri when the poison afflicting Earth's energy had made the child sick. Maybe Eri had wandered out and gotten lost in the darkened gardens.

Concerned, Maddy hurried over to the child. "Do you need help?"

The girl giggled. "Not as much as you do."

Despite the child's laugh, something in Eri's tone made Maddy uneasy, much as she had been before dinner. "I think I can find my way back."

"In another day and a half, right?" Eri announced.

"Huh?" The kid couldn't intend for her to wander the garden that long, surely. "I don't think I underst—"

"To *your* home, silly." The ambient light gleamed oddly in Eri's eyes, causing Maddy to huddle deeper into her cloak. "I don't expect for you to stay here."

There was nothing overtly wrong about the child's words, and yet… Maddy shivered as the child smiled up at her in the darkness. If it wouldn't have been com-

pletely cowardly, Maddy would have dashed down the nearest path. What was wrong with her? Eri was just a little kid.

"Erinalia!"

At the barked word, Maddy honest-to-God yelped. Only *afterward* did she see Ralan striding up the path toward his daughter. Maddy pressed her hands against her sternum to calm her racing heartbeat, and the cloak she gripped lifted enough with the motion to allow the cold air to dance around her ankles. A welcome distraction at this point.

Eri blinked up at her father. "Yes, *Onaial?*"

"I am your *onaial*, and you should remember it." Ralan scooped the little girl into his arms, his expression fierce despite her innocent smile. "If I have to confine you to your room, I will. Terrifying a guest is not okay."

The little girl lifted her chin. "I didn't say anything scary."

"There are kinder ways to deliver a prophecy than standing mysteriously in the middle of the gardens at night," the prince said, settling his daughter against his hip.

"Nuh uh, I was very good," Eri insisted. "I didn't give a single prophecy. Everyone knows she is only here for a short visit this time. I only wanted a chat before she leaves in a couple of mornings."

"And I will be taking you home now." Ralan met Maddy's gaze. "I'm sorry if my daughter disturbed you."

Maddy shook her head. "She didn't. I'm just jumpy being out here in the dark. No harm done."

All technically true, even if Maddy was downplaying how freaked out she was. The little girl was crafty. Despite the unusual delivery, Eri hadn't said anything new—until talking to her own father. Maddy and Lial hadn't decided on her departure time yet, only that it would be sometime in the next couple of days. The child oh-so-cleverly suggested it would be in two mornings. Though come to think of it, she'd been borderline specific with her "day and a half" comment, too.

"Ah, good," Ralan said, not appearing to notice Maddy's lingering discomfort. "Would you like to walk a bit of the way with us?"

Honestly, Maddy would rather return alone, but she couldn't think of a polite way to refuse. "Sure."

Ralan kept the conversation light as Maddy strolled beside him and his daughter, and Eri didn't say anything else creepy. But even after Maddy had bid them farewell and started down the path to the healer's tower, her unease remained. Was there a reason the child had hinted at a departure time, or was she making too much out of a simple conversation? She supposed only time would solve the mystery of that.

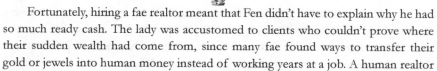

Fortunately, hiring a fae realtor meant that Fen didn't have to explain why he had so much ready cash. The lady was accustomed to clients who couldn't prove where their sudden wealth had come from, since many fae found ways to transfer their gold or jewels into human money instead of working years at a job. A human realtor

would have far more questions, the first being whether or not he was a criminal. Not that there weren't ways around that, too. Fen had seen far too many shifty dealings to believe otherwise.

"This place is for rent at the moment, but I believe the owner intends to sell in the next year or two. A good opportunity if you'd like to try and then buy."

There weren't many places he could get on short notice, but Fen had almost refused to see this one. Sure, it was fairly close to downtown and Maddy's shop, and the drive to Anna's work wouldn't be bad. But it also happened to overlook the river. Maybe he was wasting his time worrying about it, considering Anna and Maddy had their own place, but if they came over here, Anna might struggle.

"What do you think?" the realtor asked. "I know three bedrooms might be too many, but the other two I could get you into this close to the center are small studio apartments. If we go out farther, we might have more luck. You don't have your uncle's budget, so I'm a little more limited."

One side of Fen's mouth quirked up at that. Only the gods and a handful of ancient fae had his uncle's budget. "Let me look around one last time."

It was an interesting building situated on a fairly small lot in one of the neighborhoods that had popped up alongside the river. The bottom floor only held a garage and storage room, a good buffer between the ground and the upper rooms if it flooded. The living room where he currently stood had three broad windows overlooking the water, and the kitchen at the front of the building was large enough that three people could—that *he* would have plenty of room to cook for himself or guests. A nice space.

Fen's boots thudded softly against the hardwood floors as he bypassed the small downstairs bathroom and started up to the bedrooms. From a hallway at the top, there were four doors to choose from—two bedrooms on the right, a bathroom in the center, and the master bedroom to the left.

He turned left. Beside one of the tall windows overlooking the water, Anna stood, her gaze fixed on the river. But she spun to face him when he entered, and there was no sign of turmoil on her face. She smiled and held out her hand. Hesitantly, he took it, and his breath hitched when she twined her fingers with his.

"Do you like it?" Anna asked.

"The place is awesome," Fen answered. "But I'm not sure I should take it."

She tilted her head. "Why?"

How did he answer that without sounding like a hopeful fool? They'd all agreed to explore a possible relationship, but that was a long way away from a commitment. Besides, if they did end up together, he might move into their condo. "Ahh... I was thinking the proximity to the water might be a problem. If you and Maddy come visit me. Or stay the night. Not that I'm expecting that anytime soon, so no pressure."

Fuck. He totally sounded like a hopeful fool.

Her smile widened. "It's sweet of you to consider me. I think it's okay, though. I still feel the draw, but the view is also comforting. With you and Maddy here to keep

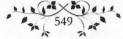

an eye on me, I don't believe I'm at risk of disappearing beneath the waves."

"I suppose I could dive in for you again," Fen said, finally returning her smile. "At least this place is a rental. If it is a problem, then I'm not stuck here."

"I bet you'll end up buying it." Anna gestured at the broad space. "This room is perfect. You could fit a huge bed in here and still have room for a dresser and side tables. And it has a great private bathroom with a massive tub and walk-in closet. Who wouldn't love that?"

Fen couldn't tell from her expression if she was intending to be suggestive, but his mind followed the possibilities she'd mentioned to their most pleasurable conclusion anyway. *Ungh.* He closed his eyes and fought his body's reaction to the mental image of that large bed. He and Anna and Maddy curled together in the center, exhausted from—

Not helping, brain.

Also not helping? Anna's hand caressing the line of his jaw.

"Fen."

He dared to open his eyes at her whispered call. Anna had shifted closer while he wasn't looking, so near he could lean down and kiss her. Hell. He was supposed to be picking a house, not seducing one of his mates. Not that he was trying, but still.

Anna's smile widened, and she eased up to brush her lips softly against his. "I can't tell if you're controlled or uncertain."

"Both, if you want to know the truth." His cheeks heated. "I've…only slept with a couple of people, and it was years ago. Before I joined Kien's group and saw how he used romantic partners against each other."

"You must have been young."

Fen shrugged. "Fourteen or fifteen, I guess. No one cares how early you have sex when you're living on the streets. I'm clean, though. Fae blood usually ensures that, but I had myself checked later just in case."

He didn't tell her that he'd only slept with each partner once, and both times had been quick and meaningless. He'd wanted to know about sex, but he'd never trusted anyone enough for intimacy. For the first time in his life, he wanted to see what that was like. Provided he didn't flub the whole possible relationship. His fear of that stopped him as much as anything.

Anna brushed her mouth against his again. "Well, I've never had sex with a man, though Maddy has. Then again, she hasn't been with more than one partner at a time, and I have. When she gets back, we'll all get to try something new."

Fen groaned. Gods above and below, she was going to kill him. But for once, it was a death he would meet with eager appreciation. Very, very eager.

17

After the moment they'd shared at Fen's new house, Anna had half-expected the rest of the evening to be awkward, but so far, that hadn't been the case. They'd grabbed burgers from a drive thru and brought them back to Anna's and Maddy's house to eat them. Avoiding heavier topics, they'd spoken of their interests and goals—which had led to Fen insisting she return to her writing while he worked on extra magical shielding against Meren. Not that she could have helped in any case. She could detect the tingle of increased energy, but she didn't know how to interpret it.

"Crap," Fen muttered as he reentered the room, his phone in hand. "I forgot to see if this thing still turns on after you pulled the water from it."

Anna spun in her seat. "Which might not have worked."

"Worked well enough on our clothes." Fen held down the button on the device and let out a relieved breath when it lit up. "See? I knew you did a good job. Okay, now that I've reinforced Maddy's shields with my own, I'm going to look online for furniture places. You should have plenty of time to work."

"Sounds good."

As if she could concentrate on her story after the events of the day. She'd pushed around water molecules with her mind, for fuck's sake. After breathing liquid like oxygen, no less. Add to that her growing interest in Fen and her longing for Maddy to return, and her mind was a muddled mess. But she might as well try to get something done.

Only fifteen minutes—and two sentences—had passed before Fen let out another oath. Sighing, Anna hit the save button and turned in her seat again. "What is it?"

"I missed a text from Vek," Fen said, glancing her way from where he sprawled on the couch. "He's going to think I'm still pissed."

Anna snorted. "Aren't you? I mean, you just rented your own place after a pretty big argument."

"Yes. No." Fen waved his phone in a frustrated gesture. "I'm upset at how he treats me sometimes, but I'm not as angry now that I've had time to cool down. That doesn't mean I've changed my mind, though. I do need to stand on my own."

"Then text him and tell him that?" Anna suggested, her thoughts being pulled back to the heroine's next move in her story. How could she—

"Yeah, I will."

Anna tried to ignore the rapid clicking coming from Fen's phone as he typed and instead forced her mind to the problem. So. Her main character couldn't get away from the murderer with a ballet flat, obviously. What else might be around her? Maybe if she ducked behind that Dumpster, there could be something unexpectedly useful next to the trash. Hmm. Pointy things that people might throw away…

"Hey, Anna?" Fen asked.

She stifled a groan. Didn't he know that a writer needed unbroken concentration to work? "What is it now, Fen?" she asked tightly.

"I know, I know," he said, regret lacing his tone. "I told you to work, and now I'm bothering you. But…could you see if you have a text from Anthony?"

Anna spun her seat around at that. "I didn't give him my number. Why?"

Fen frowned down at his phone and swiped a few times across the screen. "Vek hasn't heard back from him, and it's been hours now. I don't have any missed texts, either."

"That doesn't sound good." Despite the unlikelihood of a text, Anna checked her phone, but there was nothing new. "Maybe try calling?"

Fen nodded and did just that. Uneasiness built, making Anna's hands tremble as she saved her file and backed it up online. When Fen lowered his phone and shook his head, she started shutting down the computer. She didn't even have to ask what they needed to do next—drive over to Anthony's place.

"Come on." Anna grabbed the keys from the table and stepped into her shoes. "I remember where he lives. Let's go see if he needs help."

"We don't have Maddy to do any healing," Fen said, though he put on his shoes and followed her as he spoke.

Her heart twisted at the reminder, but she stifled her longing for her girlfriend the way she had all day. "Yeah. But if we can find them, you can call your uncle. Maddy said the life magic would work better, anyway."

"Good point."

They were on the road before Anna had time to consider what they would do if Anthony wasn't at his house. Search the hospitals in case Sparrow had gotten worse? Camp out on his doorstep? Really, they didn't have the right to do the latter, and the former might be a little stalkerish. They weren't family, and if Sparrow had decided to find treatment on her own, there wasn't a great deal they could do about it.

By the time they parked beneath a glowing streetlight by Anthony's apartment complex, it was after nine p.m. Anna covered a yawn as they headed up the sidewalk, despite the adrenaline coursing through her from their mad dash. It had been a long day, and her favorite thing to do when she was this exhausted was to curl up on the couch with a book and some mint tea before going to bed early. Instead, she was climbing the stairs to a pagan, part-fae man's apartment in search of a part-fae woman afflicted with poisoned energy and a wretched cold.

As one did.

Anna didn't dare ponder if life could get any stranger. Without a doubt, it absolutely could. So she knocked on said part-fae man's door and waited impatiently for him to answer. God help them if he didn't. Sparrow had seemed like a nice woman, and Anna worried about her.

The door opened just enough for Anthony to lean out and study the hallway behind them. Then without a word, he gestured almost frantically for them to enter. Anna exchanged a worried glance with Fen, who shrugged and hurried into the apartment. Well, she wasn't hanging around out here alone, waiting to see if there was some kind of problem.

As soon as Anna followed Fen into the room, Anthony shut the door behind them and turned the deadbolt. Alarm pounded in Anna's chest, and she sidled closer to Fen. She'd never been in a situation that required her to fight, but he had. Could she use her magic combatively? She would rather not get her ass kicked trying to find out.

"I'm not the kind of guy you want to trap," Fen said, menace clear in his voice.

"I have no intention of keeping you in here." Anthony tipped his head toward the door. "But I don't know what the hell has been going on out there."

Anna's forehead furrowed. "It's a peaceful night."

"You'd think."

For the first time, Anna noticed how tired the guy seemed. He slumped where he stood, and his eyes held the heavy-lidded look of someone ready to fall asleep at any moment. Even as she watched, he did a slow blink and then shook his head.

Fen must have thought the same. "You look terrible. Did Sparrow get worse?"

"Sort of." Anthony rubbed the heel of his palms against his eyebrows and released a long sigh. "Here's the situation. On the way to my car after work, that guy I mentioned approached me again. Weird shit has been happening ever since."

Anna scoured her memory but still couldn't figure out who he was talking about. "Which guy?"

"Hell, maybe I told your friend. I don't know. A few days before Sparrow got sick, this condescending white guy kept talking to us at lunch. I thought he was creeping on Sparrow since he kept touching her arm, so I told him to leave us alone. I think he was some kind of European fae. Norse elf or Seelie, maybe. I can't keep them all straight."

Beside her, Fen cursed, and Anna silently agreed with the sentiment. "Did he have long, blond hair?" she asked.

Anthony frowned. "The first time, yeah. Guess he got it cut before I saw him today. You think you know him?"

"Maybe," Anna answered. "But he had long hair when we saw him earlier."

Fen settled his arm around her waist, though his eyes were on Anthony. "What kind of weird shit has been happening? That might help us figure it out."

"First, the man came up to me in the parking lot and started insisting I take him to Sparrow. He seemed to know she was sick. Said only he could help her." Anthony shifted on his feet. "I told him hell no and got out of there. I drove every back road I could think of in case he was following me. Then not long after I walked in the door, something started slamming against the shielding I put up around the apartment."

He swayed slightly, and worry filled Anna, not just at the man's words but at his obvious exhaustion. "Why don't you sit down to tell us the rest? I can go make you tea or something if you have the stuff for it."

Anthony's eyebrows rose, and Fen let out a little chuckle-huff beside her. "You don't have to make me anything," Anthony said. "But I appreciate it. I'll take the seat, though."

She gave Fen a questioning look as they followed the other man to the living room, and Fen bent low until his mouth nearly touched her ear. "I didn't think Maddy was serious when she said you solve most things with a cozy blanket and a warm drink, but I guess that holds even when you're in someone else's house."

Anna poked her elbow into his side. "No teasing."

"No promises," Fen answered with a grin.

The hint of humor faded as she sat beside Fen on the couch. Poor Anthony. He lifted a laptop from the loveseat and set it gently on the coffee table before slumping against the cushions with a groan. Her fingers practically itched to toss a blanket over him so that he could take a nap.

"Sorry," Anthony said. "I only got a couple of hours sleep before I had to get up for work. At least there haven't been any more attacks since you got here."

"What kind of attacks?" Fen asked.

Anthony tapped his fingers against the arm of the loveseat. "The first ones tried to break my shields full-on, but Dad taught me too well for that. Then they shifted to…seeping through, I guess. That took a lot more effort than expected to fight, which is part of why I'm wiped. Oh, and Sparrow started feeling worse in the middle."

While Fen and Anthony delved into shielding comparisons, Anna considered connections. What linked all of the seemingly separate events? If Meren had encountered Anthony and Sparrow before their first meeting with Maddy, then the current situation wasn't as likely to be directed at Fen. But to attack Anthony today after the confrontation with her and Fen… Either Meren had discovered that their group had started talking to Anthony's, or Meren was trying to find more half-bloods to influence.

Unless there was something even more sinister going on? Maybe the guy was going around town hurting anyone who had a hint of fae blood. He'd attempted to take over the Moranaian outpost a couple of weeks ago, and part of the effort had included recruiting people like Tamara. This time instead of looking for allies, he could be trying to take out any who didn't fit his goal. That shifted from subtle influence to open action.

"Anna didn't have your number," Fen said, grabbing Anna's attention. "But why didn't you answer Vek?"

Anthony directed a pointed, incredulous look at Fen. "You think I'm going to give someone with an unknown number an invite while I'm under attack?"

Fen winced. "Sorry. I'm an idiot."

"It's been crazy." Anna rested a comforting hand on Fen's thigh. "And we're all tired. Why don't you two work on shielding while I check on Sparrow? We'll see about bringing Vek here tomorrow after we've slept."

Fen frowned. "Even though you made the suggestion, I still feel like I just asked you to make me a sandwich."

Chuckling, Anna stood. "I haven't learned to shield yet, so I can't help with that. And if anyone gets a sandwich, it'll be Sparrow. I might make a pot of tea if there are supplies, but for anything else, you're on your own."

She ignored Fen's lingering doubt and followed Anthony from the room. She half-listened as he pointed out where everything was in the kitchen before leading her to Sparrow. So Anna liked to nurture. Providing comfort wasn't a weakness, and she wasn't going to let anyone suggest otherwise.

Maddy scooted into the center of her bed and crossed her legs until she could cradle the mirror in her lap. This mirror was larger than the one Cora had given her to keep on Earth, but the beautifully engraved wooden frame was light and easy to grip as she leaned over and tilted the glass until she could see her pale face gleaming in the room's light. Damn, she looked as unsettled as she felt. She pinched her cheeks to force a little color to bloom beneath her freckles and curled the corners of her lips into a smile.

Not the most convincing display, but it would have to do.

She trickled a little power into the frame to activate it and waited. Then waited some more. Was something wrong at home? She didn't want to think about *that* possibility. Maybe the two mirrors were improperly linked? Maddy wasn't a mage, so she couldn't begin to understand how the spell worked. All she could do was trust that Cora's instructions were correct. Ugh.

Just as Maddy was about to disconnect the possibly broken link, light flared and the image in the glass shifted. The sight of Fen's furrowed brow and tilted head made her smile as he held his smaller mirror away from his body and moved it back and forth. Anna leaned in until the side of her head settled against Fen's shoulder, bringing her into view, too.

Maddy's fake smile widened into a real one despite her worry. "Oh, good! I was about to go track down Cora to see if this mirror was broken."

"Nah," Fen said. "Anna had to grab this one from the other room, and then I had to figure out how to activate it. Me and Anna both need lessons on this kind of magic, I guess."

Maddy took in the sight of Anna's pajama top, Fen's battered t-shirt, and the

dim light that surrounded the pair. "Sorry to call so late, but I guess I wasn't thinking about the time difference. I just wanted to see you."

"Oh, I should hand this over to Anna," Fen said.

"No, I meant both of you," Maddy said quickly, surprised to find it was true even though she had known Fen for far less time. "There's so much going on over there, and it makes me nervous. What are you guys doing, anyway? Did you get help for Sparrow?"

Fen frowned. "Not so much on the last one. Took us all day to track down Anthony. Apparently, someone was sending magic attacks at his apartment, but none happened while we were there. He wouldn't answer Vek's text under the circumstances, so we'll have to see about healing tomorrow. I helped him reinforce his shielding."

"How's Sparrow?"

Anna's image grew closer. "Her cold is a little worse, but I don't think the energy poisoning has changed. I set her up with some hot soup and peppermint tea."

It sounded like they had everything under control, but uneasiness still twined through Maddy. "What now?"

"I'm going to finish watching this show with Fen, and then I'm going to bed," Anna said. "We'll figure out the rest tomorrow."

Fen's eyes widened. "Alone. She's going to bed alone. I wouldn't…without you here, it doesn't seem right to…"

"Yeah, maybe we should wait until you get that big bed at your new place, too." Grinning, Anna nudged Fen, who almost bobbled out of the frame with the motion. For someone who'd made his fair share of sexual innuendos, Fen's current expression was priceless. "That's the other big news. Fen here told his mom and uncle to buzz off and went out on his own. He rented a nice house on the river."

"I didn't realize you had that kind of ready cash, Fen. Good for you." As soon as the flush of red filled his cheeks, Maddy realized her mistake. He thought she was commenting on his past. "And I was not calling you a criminal. I had to borrow money from my parents for a down payment, so I think it's great that you've saved that much."

He lifted a shoulder. "Your dad exchanged a few gemstones I'd harvested and refined for a bit of cash. That's all."

"You went by the shop?" Maddy couldn't help but wince. "I hope my mom wasn't rude to Anna."

Anna's breath hissed in. "Yeah, about that."

Then Maddy listened in shock as her girlfriend recounted the odd meeting. Her mother knew about the water fae? Damn. If that was true, then Maddy had to wonder what else her mother was aware of.

Not long after his head hit the pillow, the dream sucked Fen in.

How many days had it been? His mind was too muddled to grasp anything as solid as dates. Maybe weeks? He needed energy that he didn't dare get. He tried to lift his hand to rub his dry

mouth, but his arm barely moved. His foster mother had whispered something about the flu earlier. She couldn't know that wasn't the problem.

This was his third home in three years, and this had lasted the longest. They were nice here—had even adopted one of their other foster kids. Maybe they'd take Fen, too, if he wasn't a freak. No way he could ruin this by drinking someone's blood.

But. But what if he knocked over his water glass? Someone could get cut picking it up. If he rolled at the right time, he could accidentally get his face in the blood. It only took a drop, just a drop to unlock the other person's energy. No one would be hurt, and he could finally get out of bed.

Endless time passed. Fear began to pound beneath his breastbone as the hunger ate at him. Every muscle and tissue in his body ached, and his eyes grew heavy. Was this what dying felt like? Maybe it would be for the best. His mother's family didn't want him. His father was dead. He couldn't make it in this world. Only thing he was good at was school, and he was too sick to go to that.

You deserve to live, Fen.

The whisper echoed in his head. Over and over. Whose voice? A man. Familiar. His foster father? He couldn't open his eyes to see.

Take what you need. I'll help you

A hand brushed against his forehead, smoothing away his hair. Fen groaned at the gentle touch. Then a shock of cold hit his lips, followed by a trickle of water. Ice? He sucked at the slippery piece, pulling it into his mouth along with the finger holding it. Oh, no. Close to his fang. Way too close.

Live.

A quick movement, and the tinny taste of blood hit his tongue. Someone cried out, and the hand holding the ice was abruptly gone. But it was too late. Fen followed the unique energy signature in the blood to its owner—his foster mother—and pulled in the power his body needed.

He was too weak to be subtle, consuming more quickly than he usually did. His foster mother swayed where she stood and then tumbled backward, landing hard on her bottom. Health restored, Fen sat up to help her.

But the shocked horror on her face told her he'd be packing his bags soon enough.

Fen jerked upright, his entire body trembling and aching from the force of the dream. Well, that was a new one. He'd had plenty of nightmares about his father's death but not many about the time he'd fucked up his best chance at a home. He drew his knees up, wrapping his arms around them to stop his shaking. Why now? What had brought that event to mind?

At least he hadn't woken Anna this time.

With a sigh, Fen dropped his forehead to rest on his arm. He tried not to think about the week when he'd let himself get so starved of energy that his body had begun to shut down. He'd been almost nine and completely convinced he could solve any problem. Maybe, he'd reasoned, his father had been wrong about the need for blood to survive. If he didn't bite anyone, he wouldn't get caught and sent away.

Hah. There'd been no one to help him realize the folly of that.

Take what you need. I'll help you.

Fen straightened at the memory of that voice. He'd dismissed it as some kind of hallucination as his foster father had hauled him out of bed, ordered him to pack his handful of belongings, and herded him to the car within half an hour of his foster mother's cry. He'd mocked the whisper as he sat in a hard, plastic office chair, awaiting reassignment.

But he'd thought the voice sounded familiar then, and maybe he'd been right. An echo from his other nightmare drifted through his mind. *See what you've done?* Though years had passed, Fen would almost swear they were the same voice, but the tone and content were all wrong. The first had been accusatory, leading Fen to believe he'd killed his father, but the second had offered help and hope.

Were either of those true, or had it all blurred together in the landscape of his dreams? Even if he skimmed through his memories for more instances, he couldn't be sure. The mind could be tricky, and he'd fucked himself over too many times to easily trust in anything. Especially when he was this tired. Fen flopped back against the couch cushions and prayed he could fall back to sleep.

Into an oblivion free of dreams.

18

No matter how hard she tried, Maddy couldn't settle into sleep. It was so late at this point that there couldn't be many more hours until dawn, but she didn't understand the markings on the water clock well enough to say for sure. Honestly, though, years could have passed since the previous sunset. Gods knew her worry made her feel like they had.

Anna could soothe her out of this mood; she knew better than anyone how to help Maddy form sense out of confusion. Left to her own devices, Maddy would tumble her thoughts inside her head for hours—maybe even days. While they usually came out as smooth as the stones her father formed into jewelry, the process was a loud, obnoxious mess.

Now, worries about her mother collided against what she'd learned about the attacks on Anthony, and both ricocheted off the list of pros and cons of mating with Fen and Anna. Added to a handful of "tomorrow, I'll do more work with a powerful healer," the whole thing was giving her a massive headache.

Someone pounded on the door, and Maddy groaned. What now? She hurried over and pulled the door open a crack, only to be greeted by the healer's fierce scowl. "Would you mind sleeping sometime tonight?"

"I want to," Maddy grumbled. "But I can't get my mind to shut up."

Lial leaned a fist against the doorframe. "Right now, I don't care. If you don't stop pacing above my room, I'll put you under. Do you realize how precious rest is for a healer? You may not yet, but you'll know when you've drained yourself to nothing as I so often do. Right now, no one is injured, no one is giving birth, and no one is asking for a potion. So go to sleep."

"Tomorrow is my last day here for this trip." Maddy did her best to match his glower. If such a thing was possible. "Forgive me if I'm a little overwhelmed with all there is to do, and that's not even counting my concerns back home."

"When was it decided that tomorrow is your last day? We had discussed you remaining a large portion of the day after."

Maddy tucked her hair behind her ear. "Eri rather strongly suggested I would be going back after two mornings had passed. She told Ralan it wasn't an actual prophecy, but—"

"Well enough, young Maddy." Lial settled his hand against his face in what Maddy could only call a facepalm before crossing his arms. "That child… Let's just say I do not envy her father. But tell me. Do you wish to follow her suggestion?"

Maddy considered the question. There was no doubt she was curious about her mother's revelation, but that could wait. The situation with Anthony and Sparrow, on the other hand… Neither Fen nor Anna had given much detail about the attack on Anthony's house, and Maddy had been too distracted by the revelation about her mother to go back and ask. That combined with Eri's recommendation made her worried.

"Yes," Maddy finally answered.

"Fine." Lial's arms dropped back to his sides. "Then sleep or go outside. If nothing else, you can run over to the main estate and see if Lyr is awake and working. There's a high chance of it. If I'm right, he can contact Dria to arrange your journey home. But let me get some rest, or I'll be no good training you tomorrow."

"I don't get it," Maddy began, but her annoyance faded as she finally calmed down enough to notice the exhaustion beneath Lial's bluster. "This floor is pretty thick. How could I be disturbing you?"

"As your teacher, I am shielding you, and your energy is flaring." Lial pinched the bridge of his nose. "It isn't as pronounced when you're out of the tower, but right now, it feels like darts of your energy are falling from the ceiling. Very sharp, very piercing darts."

"I'm sorry," Maddy said. "Sometimes, I really do struggle to clear my head. And I don't think the time change between worlds has helped."

Lial pushed away from the doorframe. "It was not an idle suggestion to see if Lyr is awake. He seemed more pensive than usual at dinner, which is a sure sign he'll be up working to fix whatever is bothering him. And I must beg forgiveness for my poor humor. Before you arrived, I worked with the healer of Oria on spine regeneration techniques and helped stop a woman from going into early labor. And while you were walking in the garden, I repaired a broken leg. I'd hoped to regenerate some of my energy before your lessons tomorrow."

After hearing all that he'd done, guilt clawed at her for her own grumpiness. "I'll walk over to the estate, then. I'm not going to get stopped by a guard, am I? Are there any places I should avoid?"

"The edge of the cliff." If not for the glint of humor in Lial's eyes, she might have thought he was mocking her. "Recall that it borders the path, quite closely in a few spots. I would rather not have to heal you on top of everything else today."

Hah. Maddy didn't particularly want to disturb his sleep again, either. "Noted. But what about guards?"

"They are aware that you are allowed entry here." His lips twitched. "You are unlikely to be shot by an arrow."

Maddy laughed. "Good to know."

She followed the healer down the stairs, pausing in his room to bid him good-night, and grimaced at the sight of his tangled bedding. No wonder he'd finally lost his temper. As quietly as she could, Maddy took the spiral staircase to the lower floor. Earlier, Lial had shown her some of the herbs he used to concoct potions and salves, making it easier to identify some of the homey, savory scents that filled the air of the workroom. He'd also explained the purpose of the weird stone platform on the back wall—an operating table. Well, sort of. The stone was easy to sterilize with magic, and there were little runnels on the side that allowed blood to flow down to a basin until it could be disposed of.

Creepy but effective.

Maddy grabbed her cloak off the hook by the door and bundled up. Fortunately, she hadn't bothered to undress after dinner, so she was out in the cold night in a matter of moments. That seemed…less fortunate when the icy rain began to pelt down halfway to her destination. By the time she reached the front doors of the estate, she was soaked through, even with the enchantments Cora had told her were imbued in the cloak.

Despite that, Maddy stared at the doors for a good minute before reaching out to open one of them. She hadn't seen a single person along the faintly lit path, and no guards were stationed at the front, unless they were hidden. Shouldn't an important lord's manor have protections? She couldn't shake the feeling that she would be detained at any moment.

When she finally slipped inside, warmth wrapped around her—along with a brush of magic that pulled the water from her clothes and body. Well, that was handy. When she smoothed the cloak back from her head, she found that even her hair had been treated kindly, no straggling bits of frizz daring to stand against the force of that magic.

If she had the ability, she would coat her entire house with that kind of power.

To the left, a pair of guards stood beside the stone portal, and another warrior protected the archway beside the massive tree trunk. It was the latter who came forward to assist her, his expression impassive. "May I help you, honored guest?"

"She is coming to speak with me," a voice announced from the other side of the room.

The guard inclined his head as Maddy turned to face the Myern of Braelyn, who waited with a slight smile beside the base of the stairs that spiraled to the upper floor. She swallowed against her sudden nerves. The man's emerald eyes were kind, and the handful of times he'd spoken to her at dinner, he had been nothing but courteous. But he also possessed an aura of leashed power and authority that made her edgy. She was a stranger here, and if she stepped out of line, he could order her punishment with the flick of his regal hand.

No doubt even her death.

"At least that is what Lial indicated," Lord Lyr said, his right eyebrow quirking ever-so-slightly upward. "Have you decided to return to the healer's tower?"

"Ah, no." Maddy's fingers tightened around the fabric of her cloak. Damn, she hated being so uncertain. "I mean, no, my lord. I did come to speak with you."

He smiled. "Come, then. And please, call me Lyr. Save the formalities for taunting Ralan."

That comment drew a surprised laugh from her, and she found herself relaxing as she followed Lyr down a gently curving and exquisitely designed hallway. The wood paneling alone was carved with so much detail that she could have been walking through a museum display, and instead of boring sconces, globes of light hung from tree branches. Or...no. Not real branches. She squinted, almost reaching up to touch one of the fixtures. It had been carved from the same piece of wood as the paneling.

"Your home is lovely," Maddy said, proceeding through the door Lyr held open for her.

This room appeared to be a large, oval office. Between the tall windows along the sides, bookshelves stretched to the ceiling, and the far end of the room held a desk on a slight dais backed by an arc of broad windows. The view had to be amazing during the day.

"Thank you," Lyr said, gesturing toward a grouping of chairs in the center, nestled beneath a handful of skylights. "Although I confess I cannot claim responsibility for it. Neither I nor my father changed the estate a great deal from our ancestors' designs."

With that reminder of the age of the place, Maddy sat gingerly on one of the seats. What would it be like to take charge of properties that were thousands of years old? It couldn't be easy. "This is the original house? How do you maintain it?"

Lyr took the chair across from hers. "Lots and lots of magic, though most of that is done through latent spells that are renewed every few decades. As to the first question, only a few parts are the original structure. The early Moranaians warred with the dragons not long after arrival, so a fair bit of the place was burned. But I imagine ancient wars aren't what's disturbing you?"

"How much did Lial tell you?" Maddy asked. "Assuming he contacted you telepathically, of course. As far as I know, you aren't a seer like Prince Ralan."

The Myern visibly shuddered. "May the nine Gods of Arneen forfend, I am not. My understanding from Lial is that a certain headstrong little girl made a pointed suggestion regarding your plans. Is that correct?"

"Yes."

In the warmth of the room, Maddy released the tie on her cloak and let it fall across the back of the chair. Although Lyr eyed her Earth clothes with curiosity, he didn't say anything. Hopefully, it wasn't considered rude to remove outerwear without asking, but she was already sweating lightly with nerves. No need to be sweltering on top of it.

"She made a point of telling Ralan that she wasn't delivering a prophecy." Maddy swallowed against a sudden lump in her throat. "In fact, you could take her words as casually spoken. But the entire encounter was eerie. It was late enough not to be a natural random encounter with a child so young, unless you have vastly different ideas about bed times."

Lyr smiled wryly. "Yes and no. As you can see, we sleep far less as adults, mostly depending on how much magical energy we have expended. But since children are still growing, they rest much as human young do."

"Then lurking on the path at the far end of the garden hours after dinner definitely wasn't typical." Maddy began to relax a little at the sympathy on the Myern's face. Perhaps he, too, had been taken unaware by the child before. "Mentioning to her father that she wanted to chat with me before I left in two mornings' time didn't seem like an accident, either."

"Ralan is a seer. If he didn't refute her words, there could be a reason."

Maddy nodded. "I thought so, too. Lial urged me to speak to you about arranging passage back. But I don't think it's urgent. He mostly wanted to get rid of me so he could sleep."

"And he did so none too politely, I imagine," Lyr said.

"You've got that right," Maddy replied dryly. "His grumpiness is an art form."

Lyr's lips twitched. "Indeed."

"So would you rather I come back tomorrow to contact Dria? I think I'm calm enough to sleep a little, and you must be wanting rest at some point. There's not much left of the night."

"I'm up early rather than late. It is less than two marks until the dawn. Had I remained in here all night, I fear my soulbonded would have hunted me down." His expression softened at the mention of Lady Meli, but only for a moment. "In any case, I must contact Dria anyway about another matter. You should seek your rest, and I will update you tomorrow."

Well, then. If ever there was a polite dismissal, that was it. "Thank you for your help."

"It is no trouble."

Maddy refastened her cloak and stood. After exchanging a polite farewell with the Myern, she retraced their earlier steps through the hallway and out the front door. She shivered against the increasing cold and hurried along the path as quickly as she could with the patches of ice beginning to form. If nothing else, at least she had one thing settled.

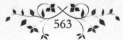

Dria had just twined herself around Vek when her mirror chimed. *Clechtan.* She dropped her forehead on her mate's shoulder and groaned. "Remind me why I accepted the leadership of this outpost."

"Your annoying brother?" Vek asked, his soft chuckle vibrating between them.

"Never mind," Dria muttered. "Don't remind me."

It was too late, of course, but she tried not to think about her brother all the same. Though they'd reconciled, she was still aggrieved at him for dropping this task on her. But it was hers now, for good or ill. With a sigh, Dria shoved away from Vek as the mirror rang again, and his humor disappeared at the loss of contact.

She wasn't exactly amused herself.

Who was trying to reach her at this hour? Fen would have texted the phone shoved in the pocket of her robe, and Dria's relatives would have calculated the time difference before calling. Concern began to replace irritation as she hurried toward the mirror. With a quick surge of magic, she activated the link.

Dria tried very hard not to wince when Lyr's image filled the mirror, but she could tell she failed by the wry twist of his lips. She didn't bother to explain that it wasn't personal—he knew better than anyone how renowned he was becoming for being the unwitting harbinger of trouble.

"Good evening, Lord Lyr," Dria said politely. "I admit I did not expect to hear from you at such a late hour. Is all well with your household?"

Lyr nodded, but his expression turned serious. "For once, my household is perfectly fine. However, two matters of import have converged, and I thought it best to go ahead and contact you."

"Two matters of immediate concern?" Dria asked.

"If you're wondering about an invasion, then no," Lyr answered, but despite his calm tone, her stomach dropped. "The most pressing is certain to be unpleasant, however. Queen Lera contacted me to demand information about the outpost. I informed her that I have no authority over such, and she insisted I pass her request for communication to you."

Dria felt the warmth of Vek's chest against her back as he stepped close behind her. "I thought the Seelie had too many problems in their own court to worry about us," he said.

A shock of pleasure filled Dria at how easily her mate said "us," almost as though he'd been a Moranaian born. Not that she would show it. "I will speak with her as soon as I can, although she may want to send an emissary. Since I do not wish for outsiders to see the portal, it seems I must create a formal receiving area near the upper entrance. Will you be able to accommodate extra requests for furnishings?"

"I believe so." Lyr's lips quirked slightly upward. "And if not, I'll foist the task onto Ralan. It would be a pleasure."

Dria let out a soft laugh. If she hadn't known the two men were friends, she might have worried. Who *didn't* want to give her brother a little grief after all his prophesies? Besides, he was technically in charge of the entire expedition to Earth and should have a more active role.

"Dare I ask about the other matter?" Dria finally ventured.

That brought a frown back to the Myern's face. "It doesn't appear to be serious. Maddy has set her return time at approximately one Moranaian day from now."

Dria might have glossed over his words, but the way he delivered the news bothered her. "Doesn't appear?"

"Her choice was made after a pointed suggestion from your niece."

Vek tensed against her back. "A prophecy?" he grumbled.

"Not officially, but be on your guard for anything out of the ordinary." Lyr sighed. "I would like to think Eri is being subtle because she has learned her lesson, but I also wouldn't count on it."

"We'll do what we can."

Fabulous. An imperious demand from the Seelie queen, a sick part-fae woman, an enemy after Fen, and a child seer acting out of the ordinary. Their two weeks of calm were at an end.

19

To say that the drive to Anthony's house was awkward would be an understatement. Fortunately, Fen was mostly able to ignore his uncle in the seat beside him. Traffic was heavy, and Anna kept Vek engaged in something resembling polite conversation. She knew how worried Fen was about all of this. If Vek brought up Fen's decision to go out on his own, there would definitely be a fight.

"How often have you been to the Seelie court?" Anna asked.

"Perhaps twice," Vek answered. "Our two peoples have never gotten along, but it has been a long time since we've had a war. I worked with Queen Tatianella to smooth over a couple of larger squabbles before they could become such."

Anna leaned forward, and the curiosity on her face pulled Fen's eyes to the rearview mirror until he forced himself to look away. "Maddy told me a month or two ago that her father was concerned about the lack of word on the queen's health. But apparently some fae put themselves into a deep sleep sometimes? Do the Unseelie do that?"

Vek snorted. "We would not reveal it if we did. But I suppose it is a sound method for dealing with boredom. After a couple of centuries away, you'd have a whole new world."

According to rumor, Naomh had been placed into such a sleep after Meren attacked him, but Fen hadn't been present for any of that. As far as he was concerned, it would have to be one hell of a deep sleep. Who would want to spend that long reliving awful dreams? Though granted, it might work fine for those who didn't have nightmares of their dead and bloody parent or other terrible moments in life.

"What do you do for your work here, Anna?" Vek asked.

"My passion is writing, but…" Anna hesitated, and a quick glance in the mirror showed her abashed expression. "Right now, I work in a restaurant waiting tables. I suppose you would think of me as a servant."

Oh, hell. Maddy might have laughed and told Vek to take a flying leap, but Anna seriously looked worried about gaining his uncle's approval. If Vek said something assholish to Anna, Fen would throttle him. He would drop him through a hole in the ground and seal the damned thing. He would tell Dria. Anything to get retribution.

Fen pulled into an empty parking spot in the visitor section of the apartment complex and slammed the gearshift into park. But before he could interject, Vek responded.

"I've never been inclined to think poorly of those who do service work. Each task in life must be completed by someone, and it sounds like you provide great value to your society. I do hope they compensate you accordingly." Vek shot Fen a challenging glance. "I can't imagine anyone would believe I would feel otherwise. I've paid my own steward enough gold to buy a home among the nobles."

"Lucky," Anna muttered from the back seat.

Fen had to agree.

"I bet you pay your artists well, too," Anna said. "I haven't decided if I should bother to publish the book I'm writing once I'm done. There's so much competition."

Vek turned in his seat at that. "You write, Anna? Perhaps you should consider releasing your tales amongst the fae now that you know of us. We do indeed pay for artistic labor."

"I don't even want to think about how brutal the critics must be," Anna said with a laugh.

For a moment, Fen let himself imagine what that kind of life would be like. Anna could set up an office upstairs in his new place and write while Maddy was at the shop. Maybe he could have a table in the corner where he shaped some of the raw stones he found in the area. And then...

He sighed. He honestly wasn't sure what else he might do. Sell rocks? He hadn't decided if he would accept his place in the Unseelie court, and he had no idea what would be required of him if he did. It might be hard to mesh his duties as a prince with the life of an artisan.

"As much as I dread this, we should go inside," Vek said, interrupting Fen's thoughts.

He glanced at his uncle in surprise. Vek was actually nervous? "Should I be worried? I'm not sure I've ever heard you mention dread like this."

Vek's smile held a decidedly self-mocking edge. "Uncertainty happens to us all. I wager you wouldn't be comfortable attempting to use a new magic you haven't mastered on a stranger."

That was true enough. "Why didn't Aris come?"

"Exposure to an illness would mean he couldn't return to Selia and Iren until he was cleared," Vek replied. "He was away from them for long enough during his captivity, so I bid him and Kezari to return to Moranaia."

It sucked, but the decision made sense. With a nod, Fen opened his car door and exited, prompting the others to do the same.

"Let me help," he suggested as the three of them converged on the sidewalk.

"Kien created the spell, but I helped connect it to Earth and was the only one who could contain it when the enspelled crystals started to fail."

"And I can try to see if there's a connection to water," Anna offered. "I wouldn't know what to do about it, but it's something."

Vek studied them, his gaze flicking from Fen to Anna and back again. "I am not hesitant because of your skill. I would not see you reinfected, Fen, nor would I want Anna to sicken."

"I understand." Fen met his uncle's eyes. "But that isn't your decision. You are no less valuable than we are. The risk doesn't have to be yours alone."

After a deep sigh, Vek relented. "Very well. Let's go do what we can."

Satisfaction filled Fen at the victory. Yes, standing up for himself had been the right decision. The argument, the rush to find a new home, the energy expended to shield both his new house and Anna's and Maddy's condo—all had been worth it. He'd thought it necessary to convince Vek of his worthiness, but it turned out that Fen had needed the prompting himself.

Now it was time to make use of his growing confidence.

Maddy couldn't decide if her timing had been awesome or terrible. The potential ice storm had roared into reality a couple of hours after she'd finally gone to sleep, and injuries had started to trickle in not long after. It had to be some kind of cosmic payback for something she'd done, though when or what she couldn't say. But as an almost viciously good-humored Lial had pounded on her door a couple of hours after dawn, she'd become convinced her past actions must have been terrible.

Despite her exhaustion, though, the storm had given her more than enough opportunities to watch a trained healer in action. So far, she had assisted Lial as he'd healed a deep gash made by an icicle, three twisted ankles, frostbitten toes, and a concussion inflicted by a falling branch in the wilder area of the forest.

But she hadn't done any healing herself.

They'd just finished a hasty lunch of meat, cheese, and bread at the battered table in the corner of Lial's bedroom when Maddy heard the door slam below. A man called out Lial's name, and the healer let out a sigh. His moment of cheer while waking her had long since dissipated, leaving exhausted resignation in its wake.

"Do you ever get a lull in work? For more than a few hours, I mean."

"Sometimes, but thankfully not often." At her raised brow, Lial smiled slightly. "I haven't minded as much lately. The work keeps me from lingering on my own unhappy thoughts."

He didn't say more, and Maddy didn't ask. She didn't know him well enough to pry, and in any case, she could guess. He was in love with the Myern's mother, who according to rumor had lost her soulbonded. A terrible blow, and one that made it likely she wouldn't want another relationship for a long time. If ever.

Saddened by the conversation, Maddy followed Lial down the spiral staircase. The healer helped a woman in leather armor to sit on the bed against the wall. Another guard of some kind, presumably the man who had called out, lingered anxiously to the side.

"What happened?" Lial asked.

The woman took a shaky breath and gestured toward her left arm. Even that small movement had her wincing. "I think I tore something in my shoulder. My foot slipped while I was climbing down from the tree, and all my weight ended up being supported by my left side."

Lial said nothing, but a sheen of blue light covered her shoulder as he ran his hand just above her armor. After a moment, he nodded. "Several strained muscles, a couple of torn ligaments, and a partial dislocation. I'll block the pain."

"It isn't too bad," the guard said, receiving a snort from Lial in reply.

Maddy studied the woman. That level of damage to the shoulder had to hurt, but she hadn't done more than wince. No exclamations of pain or muttered curses. But the look of pure relief on her face as the healer's magic hit was a revelation. Lial glanced up, and whatever he saw on Maddy's face made him smile.

As he had a few times that morning, the healer established a communication link with her. *The scouts often sustain injuries out in the field, though rarely serious. They are accustomed enough to discomfort and pain that you can't assume they aren't hurting more deeply than they appear or even claim. I imagine warriors on Earth are similar.*

"Good to know."

"Come," Lial said. *"I will heal the worst of the damage, and then I would like to see you try."*

"Me?"

Lial quirked a brow. *"Is there some other reason you are here?"*

Maddy's cheeks heated, but she didn't comment. They both knew her question had been foolish, and Lial was not inclined to coddle her fears. Not that he'd been dismissive. Instead, he seemed to sense that she needed someone to kick her ass into gear.

As he began his portion of the healing, Maddy sidled closer. She knew from their earlier work together that he wouldn't be bothered by her own scan, so she sent her own magic out to examine the soldier's injuries and Lial's method of healing them. His work was phenomenal. There was no part of any wound his magic missed, not that she could tell. As she watched, he knit the torn ligament back together with ease.

When he stopped, only the strained muscles were left untreated. "Do you mind if my student completes the final portion of your healing? With my supervision, of course."

The scout eyed Maddy for a moment before nodding. "If you trust her work, then I will do the same."

Maddy took a deep breath, surprised by the depth of the excitement blending with her nerves. This was it. She could discover once and for all if she could be taught how to use her recalcitrant gift. If she was a lost cause, Lial would let her know—and he wouldn't let her hurt anyone in the process.

She crossed the short distance to the healer's side and extended her hand over the guard's shoulder. Maddy sent her power out in a soft flicker of light green, less steady and certain than Lial's. But it was hers, and she was going to let herself use it. She had to trust that Lial would watch her actions carefully.

Maddy's eyes slipped closed as she yielded to her inner sight. She couldn't name the muscles or their general function, but she could see the damage done near the shoulder blade and up higher near the top. What was the best method to deal with it? Lial had told her that she would either need to know the anatomy of the injury minutely or be able to force the repair with her will.

The second choice was her only option with this one.

After gathering her power, Maddy commanded her magic to correct any tears or strains. The scout's body jerked as energy poured in faster than it should have, and Maddy struggled to pull her magic back before it did harm. Dammit, dammit, dammit. She was going to screw this up. Already, one of the strained muscles had stretched further instead of rebounded.

Then Lial's magic surrounded hers. *"Stop. Your fear of failure causes you to make mistakes. How can you direct your will when your will is claiming you've already lost?"*

"But—"

"You are not using your full power. When you do, it will not be this pale shadow of green but a true light."

Her forehead furrowed. He wanted to talk about her magic's color? *"That doesn't seem relevant."*

"Think on it," he snapped. *"In the meantime, follow."*

For a second, she didn't understand what he meant, but then she noticed how his magic formed around hers, providing a path for her to trace. Painstakingly, he guided her to each tiny tear in the muscle, directing her on how to heal them. Alone, he would have been finished long ago, but she sensed no impatience with the delay despite his grumpy demeanor.

By the time they finished, Maddy wanted to cry with both relief and despair, but she couldn't. She had to observe with apparent calm while Lial removed the pain block on the scout's shoulder and tested her range of motion. She had to pretend like she hadn't almost hurt the poor woman.

How could she not claim she'd already lost?

Her patient paused to thank her before leaving, but Maddy could only wince. "You're welcome, though I need to apologize for my clumsiness at the task."

Shrugging her newly healed shoulder, the scout smiled. "I'm the one who slipped climbing down the tree I've been stationed at for several years, am I not? I've trained for centuries, and yet accidents still happen. The only thing that matters is that my shoulder is well."

Maddy stared after the elf as she thanked Lial and then departed with the other guard. Talk about a casually delivered bomb—and an accurate one. Why was she being so hard on herself when she'd barely started to learn? Every person who'd come to the healing tower that day had succumbed to the unexpected, and it hadn't mattered how old they were. There was no shame in that.

"Perhaps I should send her a reward for your epiphany," Lial grumbled.

Maddy blinked. "What?"

"I can practically see your thoughts, and if I'm not mistaken, they are correct." He sat on the stool beside his workstation, and his shoulders slumped with the exhaustion he'd hidden from his patients. "Self-recrimination causes you a great deal of trouble."

"It seems inevitable sometimes," Maddy said, sighing. "I definitely didn't do the right thing in that situation, and I honestly don't know what would have happened if I couldn't have pulled the energy back."

The healer frowned. "Your healing gift is different, but I do not believe that should be a hindrance to learning its use."

"Different how?"

"It is very…active. Vibrant." His gaze grew distant. "The one time I've seen that, the healer in question joined the military. He was an excellent combat healer, able to send his power across distances I could not. I must be close. Nearly touching. I have a feeling that is not the case for you, and combined with your will magic, you'll need to take care. But I believe we are both up to the task."

Distance healing? The military? Maddy had never thought about either possibility. She wasn't a natural nurturer like Anna, although Maddy didn't mind easing hurt when she saw it, and she'd never visualized herself as a full-time healer like Lial, even after training. Still, she didn't think she would want to join the army. It was a noble career but not one she was well-suited for.

But she didn't have to be in the military to help in combat situations. What if she'd been in the group that had stopped Meren's allies from invading the outpost? Fully trained, Maddy might have been able to save Dria's friend Gessen. There were enough similar skirmishes that her abilities could come in handy.

The role of emergency battle healer might end up being all-too-perfect.

Being involved in this kind of magic without Maddy present was strange, especially since Anna felt like a poor substitute. Chances were good that she wouldn't be any help, but at least she might learn something. And who knew? Maybe she would notice a detail the other two didn't. If nothing else, she could offer comfort. So she'd positioned herself at the foot of the bed while Fen and Vek took the other two sides, ready to do what she could.

"Are you sure you can do this without the healer I met?" Sparrow asked, giving Vek a nervous glance. "Maybe we should hold off. I'm not coughing much today, so the other problem might be resolving, too."

Vek shook his head. "It is not. I can see the darkened shard of energy with little effort."

Anna smoothed the blanket around Sparrow's feet and smiled when the motion attracted the other's gaze. "Don't let Vek scare you. He's really a nice guy."

"A nice—" Wisely, Fen cut off whatever he was about to say when their patient turned her worried look his way. "Ah. Yeah. My uncle is a great person. And he was trained by the life mage who healed me."

Sparrow's eyes narrowed. "I thought this other mage was the one you were summoning? No offense intended, but it sounds like your uncle just learned this skill."

"I did," Vek said without hesitation. "But our friend has a family to return to, including a young son he would not want to risk infecting. I do understand your doubt, but I am your best option. Unless you know other fae with the required skill?"

With a huff, Sparrow shook her head. "Not really. I'm sorry if I sound ungrateful. This is just so new and weird."

Anna squeezed the other woman's foot softly through the blanket. "I found out I have water powers less than a month ago, so I understand. When it comes to the strange, sometimes you have to face it and embrace it."

The door opened, and Anthony entered. He'd been finishing up one of his online courses when they'd arrived, and his absence hadn't helped his friend's worries. Based on the way Sparrow's expression brightened at the sight of him, Anna wondered if this incident had sparked another kind of interest between them. None of her business, though.

"Hey, I'll sit over in the corner and make sure you're okay," Anthony said. "You know I won't let anyone do anything bad."

Finally, Sparrow relaxed against the pillows and closed her eyes. "Fine. Let's get this over with."

Vek and Fen exchanged wry smiles, their current disagreement apparently forgotten for the moment, and began their work. Anna let her own eyes close and did her best to open her senses. She detected Fen easily—his energy had become familiar to her over the last couple of weeks. But when it came to his uncle, she struggled against the wave of the power he wielded, the force of it muffling the spirit of the user.

Did it really matter? Instead of trying to identify the origin point, Anna let her senses drift over Sparrow as the powerful magic swept through her. Anna couldn't see anything wrong near the other woman's heart. At least not at first. Whatever darkness the others understood was beyond her skills, and yet... Here and there, she thought she saw a few flecks of something odd, pulsing outward through the blood.

Quickly, she connected with Fen. *"I can't see the core of the poison. Can you?"*

"Unfortunately, yes," he answered, his mental voice full of bitter anger. *"It's the same shit. Vek hasn't needed my help so far, though."*

"I thought...I thought I saw weird specks in her blood."

Fen went silent for a moment. *"I told him. Are you sure it is related?"*

"I barely know what I'm doing, so no."

"Vek will check just in case."

A moment after Fen gave that assurance, the life magic swept through Sparrow's veins with sudden intensity, and Anna had to withdraw from her scan before the force overwhelmed her like a tsunami. As soon as Vek finished, she looked again, and as far as she could tell, the dark flakes were gone.

Anna blinked her eyes a few times to clear her senses. She'd never considered how much of the body was made of water, so she hadn't expected to see a great deal. Now she had to wonder how many times she'd been drawn to care for people after sensing something off with their health.

She didn't know if she had the ability to fix anything. But how neat would it be if she detected illnesses that Maddy could treat? They could start a magical medical practice. Maddy the Healer and Anna the Disease Sonar. She sucked her lips against her teeth to keep from laughing while the others finished their work.

It was a fun line of thought, but it was probably silly. For one thing, Anna had no clue if she'd really sensed anything or if it had been her imagination. Planning out a healing side-show was probably a bit much. Though maybe she could turn it into a short story.

The power from the other two faded, and Sparrow opened her eyes. She appeared far less tired and weak, but as they studied her, she started to cough. Anthony appeared at the corner of the bed, and a frown wrinkled his face.

"I was hoping this might resolve her cold."

Anna grimaced. From Sparrow's expression, it seemed she'd thought the same. Would they be upset? Anna hoped not, because she liked them both and wouldn't mind becoming friends. She needed more people in her life who understood what it was like to have fae blood.

"Unfortunately, I am no healer," Vek said. "I was able to clear out poisoned energy, but I don't know how to look for human-type illnesses. In any case, the type of magic I used might not affect something organic. Viruses are unpleasant, I hear, but they are part of nature."

"Balls," Sparrow muttered darkly.

Anna gave her a sympathetic smile. "Hey, I could always make you some more tea."

20

Anna's foot tapped restlessly against the stone floor as she stared at the shimmering portal. Any minute now, her beloved would walk through. Hopefully. According to Dria, Maddy was running late, and if she didn't hurry, Anna would have to leave before Maddy got here. It was just after ten in the morning, and the lunch shift would start soon. Dria had been kind enough to open the portal to the shop so that Anna wouldn't have to drive out to the outpost and hike up the mountain, but it would be for nothing if Maddy didn't move it.

Besides, the tension between Vek and Fen was starting to drive Anna insane. They'd compared notes after healing Sparrow yesterday, but otherwise, the drive to Vek's house afterward had been just as awkward as the trip to Anthony's place. Fen hadn't wanted to talk about it after dropping his uncle off, even though they'd had plenty of time while hunting down furniture and household goods. They had parted after dinner so that Fen could work on shielding his new house, and when he'd stumbled back to her place to stay on the couch, he'd gone to sleep without mentioning his uncle. Now, they were pretending not to cast annoyed glances each other's way.

Maybe between them, Anna and Maddy could get the two to talk.

Finally, the portal flashed, and all thoughts of Fen and his uncle faded to the background as Maddy stepped through. She'd barely made it off the small dais before Anna rushed her. With a happy cry, Anna tugged her girlfriend close. Her hand wrapped around Maddy's braid as their lips met and tangled.

Anna wanted to sigh and moan at the same time. Home. Maddy tasted like home after an adventure—familiar comfort with a hint of something new. Honey and apples and spices Anna couldn't name, but Maddy all the same.

"Ah, fuck me," she heard Fen mutter.

With a chuckle, she and Maddy pulled apart, and Maddy's eyes gleamed with the same humor Anna felt. Poor Fen. Too bad he didn't know that trying out his new bed was pretty high on Anna's to-do list now that their girlfriend was back. He would just have to live with the torture until Maddy was ready, though.

"So how did it go?" Anna asked, taking Maddy's hands in hers.

"Fine." Maddy's nose wrinkled. "There's a lot for me to learn, but I didn't have any disasters. I think I can do this."

Pleasure and relief clogged in Anna's throat. Her own discomfort had definitely been worth it, and she'd even confronted her trouble with magic regardless of the disquiet it caused. "I'm glad."

Maddy squeezed her hands. "Something happened here, didn't it? Are you okay?"

"Things did get a little weird," Fen said, easing to a stop beside Anna.

She could have kissed him for the rescue. She didn't want to hit Maddy with her little river experience right after she'd stepped through the portal. Though Maddy's eyes narrowed thoughtfully, she didn't question them about it. Maybe she could tell it was something better left until they were alone.

The last thing Fen wanted to deal with was Vek blocking his entry to the gate room. Anna and Maddy had followed Dria inside, but his uncle had shifted to prevent him from following. Dammit. He was *not* in the mood for another confrontation.

"A word," Vek said.

Fen considered ignoring the command, but with a sigh, he paused beside his uncle. "What?"

"Don't worry," Vek said flatly. "I'm not giving you an order. This is more of a request."

Despite his uncle's low, even tone, Fen found himself studying Vek, too. His demeanor was even more ridiculously serious than usual. Had something happened? "You want to ask *me* for something?"

"In a manner of speaking." Vek leaned close. "I want to set up the kind of blood-link transport used by the *Felshreh*, similar to the one we used to return to the Unseelie realm after your mother took Dria. I found a proper chamber for it. Would you like to help? You would be able to use that portal, then, too."

"Help?" Fen's chest ached from the force of the hope he tried to restrain. Surely, his uncle hadn't thought this through. "I don't think Dria will approve of giving me that kind of access. The Moranaians wouldn't be happy, either."

"You think I give a fuck?" Vek scowled. "I do not need their permission to act. This is my home, too."

Fen didn't bother to hide his snort. "Right."

Before Vek could counter, Dria slipped through the door. "Are you going with Maddy and Anna, Fen?"

"As soon as Vek finishes telling me about the plan he doesn't give a fuck if you approve of."

Fen grinned at his uncle, who mouthed *traitor* before lifting his hands in a conciliatory gesture. "You know about this, *ahmeeren*," Vek said to Dria. "The blood gate."

Dria flat-out laughed. "I guessed as much when I overheard your bluster. You gave your word that you would obey the rules of my outpost, so I am certain you wouldn't dare to challenge them. Or me."

Instead of offering reassurances, Vek tugged Dria up against his side. "I'll be happy to challenge you, my love. I'll provide you more challenge than—"

"Please don't give me nightmares," Fen interrupted before his uncle could take that statement from innuendo to gross. "I have enough trauma to relive without those kinds of mental images."

Vek let go of Dria, and his eyes pinched with pain at the reminder of Fen's misspent youth. "Forgive me."

"Oh, chill." Fen shook his head. "I was mostly joking, but I would enjoy a change of subject. Please."

"Fine. Come back this evening if you want to help with the portal. Send word if you don't."

For a brief moment, they'd returned to their usual banter, but now, Vek's face held the remote formality it had worn since their disagreement. Suddenly, Fen hated the strain that had returned to their relationship. Was it because of Fen's unintentional reminder of the past, or was it because he had insisted on standing alone? As Vek strode away without another word, Fen suspected it was both. Unfortunately, there wasn't much to be done about the problem, at least nothing that time wouldn't repair.

"Vek told me you have a friend who can interface human technology with magic," Dria said, her considering gaze on his face. "He dismissed the idea, but I'm intrigued."

Fen's lips twisted. "If you're saying that from guilt or pity, don't bother."

"I'm not," Dria insisted. "Though it's true that your argument with Vek made me evaluate some of my own words and actions. For what it's worth, I'm sorry. I know what it's like to be dismissed for being younger than what people anticipate or prefer. I shouldn't judge you based on Moranaian expectations."

He studied her face for any sign of deception and came up empty. "Thanks."

Anna leaned out the door. "Hey, can we go? I'm going to be late to work."

"We'll talk about your artificer friend later," Dria said. "I hope?"

The whole conversation was so unexpected he almost didn't know how to answer. "Ah, sure."

Fen followed Dria into the portal room, barely noticing the open gate back to Maddy's shop. The sudden inclusion was everything he'd wanted, but he couldn't trust it to hold, either. For that matter, maybe he couldn't trust himself. If he messed this up, it would be ages before he had another chance.

No problem, right?

The consultation room at the shop looked the same as always, the table, chairs, and counter seemingly untouched since she'd left, yet it seemed almost foreign to Maddy as she closed the portal behind them. After gently curving walls and spiral

stairs, the hard angles here jarred her senses, and she'd gotten used to how even the most basic items on Moranaia bore a decorative touch. She and Jase should consider a change in aesthetics.

"So what's the plan for today?" Maddy asked, glancing between Anna and Fen. "Should I drive Anna to work?"

"I can't," Fen answered. "I have to get back to my new place for another furniture delivery. Nothing like the between-noon-and-five window to ruin the day's plans."

Anna slipped her arm around Maddy's waist. "How about you go with Fen? I'll take your car to work and then meet you both at his new place after. You haven't had a chance to see it."

Maddy stared at her girlfriend, noting her eager smile and bright, open gaze. Anna didn't just tolerate the idea of her going with Fen—she wanted it. Hell, Maddy wouldn't be surprised if her girlfriend wasn't half in love with him already, and the idea of that brought a warm and fuzzy yet anxious feeling to Maddy's gut. What if she decided she didn't want a three-person mating but Anna did?

Some of the turmoil must have shown on her face, for Anna's smile softened. "Hey, there's no hidden meaning to that, and I wasn't trying to pressure you."

"I know," Maddy said automatically, though she didn't. Not completely. "I'm just tired. It was dawn on Moranaia when I left, and I didn't sleep much last night, either. I would love to see Fen's place, so long as I'm welcome."

Fen squeezed her shoulder lightly as she met his gaze. "Any time, Maddy."

For a moment, everything was perfect. With Anna's arm around her waist and Fen's hand on her shoulder, her world felt complete. Like she could conquer anything so long as they were together. But worry had her stiffening in their hold. What if it didn't work out? She might lose them both if it didn't. Bucking the norm to be together was a challenge for all of them.

Sensing Maddy's turmoil, Anna tightened her hold, but Fen jerked his hand away and stepped back. Maddy wanted to tell him that it wasn't him. Or Anna. Or any one thing alone. It was everything, but she didn't know how to explain her confusion without sounding like she wanted to give up on their possible bond. So she let Fen retreat, if only until she could find the words.

"Let's go then," Maddy said. "Before you're both late for your commitments."

"Crap," Anna muttered, letting go of Maddy. "Work."

Maddy brushed her girlfriend's hair behind her ear. "Hurry or Deanna will get mad. We'll see you at Fen's place."

"Sounds good." Anna gave Maddy another quick kiss before darting over to Fen to repeat the action. "Don't try out the bed without me."

Surprisingly, Fen's cheeks flushed. "Umm."

With a grin, Anna rushed out the side door leading to the stock room, and silence descended in her wake. What had Maddy's life become that she could watch her girlfriend kiss the man Maddy had fought her attraction to without a flicker of guilt

or jealousy? Maybe a little discomfort, but that was more social conditioning than anything. That and the desire to join them.

"You don't have to go with me if you don't want to," Fen said softly.

"Of course, I do." Maddy nudged him with her arm on the way to the door. "Especially if you have a couch I can take a nap on. Or is that what's being delivered?"

Fen smiled, though not as widely as he usually did. "Nope, you're in luck. The couch and T.V. were yesterday evening. I even snagged my game system from Vek's place."

"I bet he'll be ticked when he realizes," Maddy said. "Considering what you told me about his new love of *Death's Curse 3*."

"Hey, he's way richer than I am. He can buy his own."

Though Fen's tone had been light enough, he kept his gaze averted as they headed out to his car, and he didn't say much during the short drive to his new house. Was he having second thoughts about going out on his own? Pestering him for more information wouldn't help, though. She was no Anna, able to coax out a person's woes with ease. No, Maddy would have to wait until he was ready to talk.

Fen pulled into a small neighborhood beside the river, and Maddy frowned at the series of cute houses they passed as they drew ever closer to the water. "Umm, Fen. Not to be rude, but…"

"Isn't this bad for Anna?" Fen finished with a sigh. "Yeah, that was my worry. But she was with me when I was looking and said it was fine. We'd still better keep an eye on her when you're visiting."

Maddy blinked at that, turning to glance out the passenger window before he could see her surprise. Visiting. Why had that word caught her off guard? She hadn't consciously thought about them living together since they hadn't decided if the relationship would work, but her mind must have headed that direction without her. And it even made sense. If they all stayed together, they would need a bigger house than Maddy's and Anna's little condo.

If.

She had to admit that she loved the house as soon as she saw it. It wasn't a veritable mansion like his uncle's home in the mountains, but it had a cute garden tucked against the side and a private garage on the bottom floor. As soon as Fen parked inside, Maddy was out the door and peeking into the large storage room that made up the rest of the bottom floor. A good feature in case of flooding, so long as they—he—built tall shelving and kept true valuables upstairs.

Maddy wandered back into the garage and smiled at Fen, still staring at her from beside the car. She hadn't noticed when he'd turned it off or closed the door, but he must have been watching her study the place like an appraiser. He probably thought she'd come unhinged.

Maybe she had.

Fen said little as she explored the next floor, from the living room overlooking

the river to the huge kitchen that Anna must have adored. But at the bottom of the stairs to the third floor, he hesitated, a tense, guilty expression flickering across his face. Was he hiding something questionable up there?

"Do you have an unusual fetish you're afraid to talk to me about?"

Fen's mouth dropped open. "What? No. I mean, no offense to anyone who does. But what the hell, Maddy? Why—"

"You don't seem to want me to go up there." Maddy couldn't help but laugh at his shocked face. "And you have this *I don't want to tell you something* look going on."

"I do. Or don't. Just…" He rubbed the back of his neck. "Look, I kissed Anna, and I don't mean that quick peck at the shop. We didn't go any further than that, but I don't know how you'll feel about it."

"Oh."

Maddy took a moment to let that revelation settle. She'd thought it might happen, but the confirmation still came as a bit of a surprise. Did it bother her? The mental image of Anna in Fen's arms flashed in her head, along with a variety of conflicting emotions. Not anger, though. Her body went hot, desire fighting with envy. She'd spent all that time worrying about what Anna would think, and here her girlfriend had shared a true kiss with him first. Maddy wasn't sure whether to be amused or jealous.

In the end, humor won out. Fen's forehead furrowed as she started chuckling, and his bewildered expression made her laugh harder. How ridiculous were they? A bunch of goofballs circling each other, trying to either avoid or embrace the obvious depending on the day. Fen thought he was unworthy, Anna believed Maddy disliked the idea, and Maddy couldn't grasp the concept of actually having both people that she wanted.

"Maddy?"

"God, we're all idiots." Her laughter faded, but her grin didn't. Poor Fen looked so confused, and he was about to get more so. "Come here."

He shook his head. "What?"

Before he figured out her intentions, Maddy stepped into his space, easing her body against his as she wrapped her arms around his neck. "We had a tiny kiss once, but I deserve equal treatment to Anna. I expect an equally fabulous kiss. Then, I'm going to take a nap on your comfy couch, and you and Anna can give me a tour of the upstairs later. Got it?"

For once, Fen seemed incapable of speaking. But that didn't stop him from taking action. His mouth met hers, softly at first. Tentatively. Then he ran his tongue along the seam of her lips until she opened for him, and they both caught fire. Maddy had to force herself to be careful of his fangs. His kiss was hard and hot, so much so that she nearly forgot herself more than once.

The side of her tongue slid against his fang, almost near enough to scrape, and Fen wrenched himself away. "Dammit. Too close. I've gotta say my sympathy for my uncle has grown."

Maddy blinked. "Vek? You're thinking about your uncle *now?*"

"Only of how careful he had to be with Dria before she agreed to mate." Fen ran his finger down the side of her neck, and she shivered. "Like him, I will not force anyone into a mate bond. It wouldn't be right."

"Fair enough." Maddy patted Fen on the cheek. "Guess that means it's time for the nap."

She was no longer as tired as she had been, not after that kick to the system, but she marched through the living room to the couch anyway. It was situated on the wall perpendicular to the windows, so Maddy stretched out where she could see outside. Maybe watching the clouds stream by would slow her racing heart. It was worth a try.

21

The lunch rush was almost over when the strange man came in.

Anna paused, the plate she held bobbing until the hamburger almost toppled off. Her customer yelped, and Anna glanced down in time to save the food. Offering profuse apologies and silently kissing her tip goodbye, she settled the plate carefully on the table and left the lady to her meal.

Her heartbeat pounding in her ears, Anna did her best to appear unbothered as she refilled a couple of drinks at the next table. There was no specific reason to be on edge, but there was an energy about the guy that thrummed against her water magic. She couldn't decide if it made her want to flee or move closer.

Anna set the pitcher of soda on the server station and took a deep breath to settle her nerves. An effort ruined by Deanna's light tap against her forearm. "Hey, the gentleman who just came in asked for your table. I know you were hoping to get out of here early, but Cassie already had one more than you."

Anna tried not to be too obvious about looking at the guy's table, but he offered her a smile when she inadvertently made eye contact. "Why would he ask for me? I've never seen him before."

"Huh." Deanna frowned. "Well, he gives you any trouble, let me know. I'm not going to stand for any creeps around here."

"Thanks."

Anna really, really didn't want to go over there, even though the man seemed relatively normal. His button-down shirt and creased slacks stood out a little amidst the tees and shorts of the late-summer vacation crowd, but not so much that she would normally be disturbed. He could be a businessman who'd strayed from downtown for a change of scenery. His energy, though… It couldn't be a coincidence that someone who ruffled her magical feathers had asked for her table.

Though her legs grew heavy with dread, Anna carried a glass of water and a napkin-wrapped silverware set to his table. Somehow, she managed to place both down without her trembling becoming obvious, or at least she thought she had until the stranger flashed her a mocking grin. She ground her teeth together and resisted the urge to yank out his short, white-blonde hair. Forget being a business type. This guy acted more like displaced nobility than something as mundane as an executive.

"Could I get you something else to drink while you look at the menu?" Anna asked in a voice honed by years of dealing with shitty customers.

"I'll not ingest hu—" The man coughed into his hand. "Forgive me. Water will suffice. Unless you have freshly squeezed juice made from the current harvest?"

Anna blinked. "Ah, no. I'm sorry."

He waved his hand in a dismissive gesture. "Tell me of your current food offerings, then."

Her stomach dropped at his unusual phrasing—yet more confirmation that something was not right with this guy. And Meren was still on the loose. If he had really been the one who'd attacked Fen in the river, he would have seen her, too. Good Lord. Surely, she didn't have the villain ordering lunch at her table?

"Well, we have fresh cod on special. Otherwise, the menu describes our various dishes better than I can. Is there anything in particular that you were wondering about?"

"Yes, indeed." One minute, the man sat like a king addressing a servant, and the next, he'd leaned forward, his fingers gripping her forearm. "I'm wondering about you."

Anna froze, her skin prickling with tiny needles of warning. "I am not on the menu."

Something like disgust filled his eyes before he quickly masked it. "Naturally not."

"Let go," Anna demanded.

The dangerous energy around him intensified, and the unusual tingle of awareness his touch created made her want to vomit from its force. Her mind hazed over, her thoughts becoming as muddy as the river water.

"You mistake my intentions," the man answered, letting go of her arm quickly, which reassured her. It was absurd to think he was a threat. They were in a public place, and he'd just been trying to get her attention. "I have neither violence nor seduction in mind. We are kindred, you and I. Children of water, if you will."

Anna tried to make sense of his words through her jumbled thoughts. Could he be implying that he was one of her people? Being a water fae would match his odd behavior and clothing, wouldn't it? It might also explain the zing of energy she'd felt when he touched her arm. How would he know about her, though? Could her presence in the river have caught his attention? There was so much about her heritage she didn't understand. For all she knew, her people had already been looking for strangers with their bloodline.

"Ah, I see that you understand." His grin returned, minus the mocking. "Good."

Another voice broke through Anna's confusion. "You bothering one of my servers? I saw your hand on her, and that kind of behavior is not allowed here."

Deanna. Anna's fingers twisted together as she fought the urge to scream. While she appreciated her manager looking out for her, it couldn't have come at a worse time. The man might have important information about her ancestry. They might even share some kind of kinship, if only in magic. None of which she could say to Deanna.

"He was just—"

The scrape of the stranger's chair interrupted Anna's words as he stood. "Leaving. I find I am no longer hungry."

"Good," Deanna said, eyeing him for a moment before hurrying over to an annoyed-looking family of five.

The man leaned close to Anna, his fingers gripping her elbow in a slight hold. "If you wish to know more of your power, meet me at the park just down the river, and speak of this to no one. There should be enough people to ensure your safety. I'll be waiting on one of the benches after your shift ends. If you don't show up, I will not seek you out again, but you will lose your chance to learn about your heritage."

And with that pronouncement, the stranger released her and strode from the room with the arrogance of a king departing a ball, no doubt in his mind that his subjects stared after him in awe. Anna had to admit that she was doing just that, but it wasn't often that one encountered fae nobility while waiting tables.

Maddy excluded, of course.

She shook her head. Why was she assuming the guy was noble? The stories of the fae depicted them as being sly and arrogant, so his behavior didn't necessarily mean anything. Most of the fae Anna knew actually *were* nobility or royalty, and they didn't act like that. Either way, Anna had to consider his offer. Her first thought was to call Maddy, but he'd said to tell no one. Maybe her people were secretive.

Anna wanted to know more about her fae ancestors and the magic they wielded. She could breathe water and dry out her clothes. What else? Could he explain why the river had called to her with such intensity and if that pull would return? That information would be more valuable than anything.

Out of habit, Anna cleared plates and brought out refills, but her mind wasn't on her work. Thank God she'd been here long enough to operate on autopilot with relative success. It gave her the freedom to ponder the stranger's offer before the end of her shift. A crazy decision, but it was the only one she could make. She had to find out what he knew.

What was the worst that could happen?

Meren had no doubt that she would come.

She'd been far more resistant to glamour and coercion than he'd expected, but even if the suggestion Meren had tried to slip through her shielding failed to take root, her curiosity would lead her to him. Unfortunately, though, he still hadn't decided what he preferred to do with her.

Murder wouldn't serve his cause, at least not yet. He wasn't ready to leave that kind of serious message. Killing was…messy. It had taken far too long to scrub the blood from his clothes after the last two times he'd stabbed people, and neither of the wretches had even had the good grace to die from the effort. No, Meren would rather wait until he could recruit another assassin before he decided young Anna or anyone else needed to die.

He could kidnap her, but that was another last resort action. He only had one safehold left. Why risk having it overrun by the Unseelie if Vek and the boy had some way to track the girl? Not to mention dealing with her whining. Humans always whined, given enough time. They had a bad habit of wanting things like food.

But subversion…that would be delicious.

Meren wasn't certain Anna would be a suitable candidate, but their little afternoon meeting would give him a good idea about that. If she was as foolish as the average human, she would follow wherever he led for crumbs of information. And who knew? The Gwragedd Annwn were powerful water fae. She might end up trainable enough to be of some use.

Propping his arm along the back of the bench, Meren smiled. All he had to was wait.

A warm hand settled on the curve of Maddy's waist. She jumped, and if the touch hadn't awakened her, the slamming of her heart would have. Who was it this time? One of her less-adept captors—or Kien? Her body trembled, but she couldn't lie there without knowing. She had to see. She opened her eyes slowly, and only then did full awareness kick in. Fen crouched beside her, frowning down at her from beside the couch in the middle of his new living room. She sank into the cushions in relief.

"Sorry, Maddy," he murmured softly, rubbing her waist in a comforting motion. "I called your name, but you didn't stir. Hell, you slept through a team of movers carrying my new bedroom suite upstairs. Your phone pinged, though, and I thought you might have set an alarm."

Maddy took a deep breath in and let it out slowly. Poor Fen. It wasn't his fault she'd been dreaming of the cave where she'd been imprisoned by Kien, and she wasn't going to tell him, either. Fen hadn't been part of that plot, but he'd been forced to pretend he was in order to infiltrate the camp. He bore enough guilt without knowing how much the experience still haunted her.

"Sometimes, I sleep deep," Maddy answered in a rough voice.

She rubbed at her eyes and cleared her throat before she sat up. Fen pulled his hand away, but he didn't move from his crouch. As she slid her feet to the floor beside him, their knees touched, and she shivered with awareness from the contact. She had the sudden urge to leap against him, so strong she almost gave in even if it would have knocked him to the floor. Something in her craved reassurance that she was alive, and she did not want to risk sleeping with him out of that mad impulse. It wouldn't be right without Anna, at least not the first time.

Still frowning, Fen rubbed his fingers against the scruff lining his jaw. Sexy, although it would feel rough against her face if she leaned in and—

"Stop looking at me like that, Maddy." Fen stood so abruptly that she almost yelped, but the sound caught in her throat when she saw the evidence of how her glance affected him, now level with her eyes. "Dammit. I'm going to go make a late lunch. Want something?"

She couldn't help it—she had to quirk her eyebrow at a wicked angle.

Fen groaned. "I'm talking about something to eat."

Maddy's lips twitched. "Really?"

"Do. You. Want. A. Sandwich?" he ground out, making her laugh.

"Okay, okay, I'll stop tormenting you." Maddy grinned. "A sandwich would be good. I didn't even think about food before I fell asleep."

"Yeah. I'll just…"

Maddy had to fight hard not to let her amusement show as Fen backed toward the kitchen, a flush spreading up his neck. She'd seen him make his fair share of suggestive jokes to others when it didn't matter, but now that it did, he was adorably flustered at the slightest provocation. Would he blush when they were all in bed together?

She suddenly—desperately—wanted to see. Anna had better hurry herself home after work. Then they could all find out.

Maddy was half-finished with the sandwich Fen brought her when she remembered his comment about her phone. She hadn't set an alarm, so it must have been a text. Still chewing, she grabbed the device from the side table and swiped it open. But the text that she found from Anna almost made her choke.

Met a man who might be one of my people. I'm going to chat with him in the park near the restaurant. He said not to speak about it, but texting isn't exactly speech, right? You and Fen should come down here. But just watch unless I'm in danger. I need to know about my magic.

"Fuck," Maddy blurted, almost dropping her sandwich. "Hope you don't have any more deliveries scheduled, because we need to go. Now."

Fen, who had just started toward the kitchen, paused to frown over his shoulder. "What? Why?"

"Anna texted and said she's meeting some guy who offered her info about her heritage." Maddy slapped her plate down on the side table and stood. "That was half an hour ago."

In moments, they were in the car, speeding toward the park Anna had mentioned. If something happened, it would be Maddy's fault for not checking her phone sooner, but she'd been distracted by her dream. And Fen, of course. The hard set of his jaw and glaring eyes told her he was probably blaming himself as thoroughly as she was.

Fen's thumbs tapped out an anxious beat on the steering wheel, and Maddy squeezed his thigh in comfort. Really, they were both wrong. Blame might seem inevitable, but it was also disabling. How could they have known that Anna would make such a rash decision? Missing texts happened—at least that was what Maddy told herself.

Now to get her heart to listen.

Anna had no clue if pepper spray would affect one of the fae, but she couldn't bring herself to enter the park completely defenseless. She kept her right finger against the trigger, the canister chill against her inner wrist where it wouldn't be obvious. In her left hand, she held her phone so she could mash the emergency call button on the lock screen if necessary. Her mind insisted she was silly and paranoid, but her instincts screamed that she shouldn't take any chances. She'd even dared to send a text.

On the farthest bench along the trail—and the one closest to the water—the stranger sat. Anna swallowed her nerves and marched resolutely toward him. They wouldn't be alone in the park. A father watched his two young children play on the small playground situated in the field behind the benches, and a lady stood on the riverbank, throwing breadcrumbs out for the ducks.

The man didn't mean her any harm, her inner voice insisted.

But for some reason, she had to prevent her steps from slowing of their own accord.

The afternoon sunshine gleamed against the fae man's hair as he glanced her way, and the smile that crossed his face had Anna tightening her hold on the pepper spray canister. The smile should have been pleasant—in fact, she was fairly confident the man intended it to be. But there was a hardness to the edges of his lips and a dark glint in his eyes that revealed more to the seemingly happy curve.

No. There's nothing there but friendliness.

Even as that thought rang in her head, Anna was careful to sit as far away from him on the bench as she could without being completely rude, and she settled her hand with the pepper spray against the large hobo-style bag she wore crossways over her chest so that the canister was hidden in the opening above the zipper. If he noticed, his closed—and decidedly regal—expression gave nothing away.

"I see you made the smart choice," the stranger said softly.

"Maybe." Anna lifted her chin. "But I probably shouldn't have come in the first place. I don't even know your name."

The man's smile widening. "Easily solved. I am Lord Rianehd a Orsed, and although I am not of the Gwragedd Annwn, I am a Sidhe water mage. I sensed your uncontrolled power when I was passing through, and such a thing is a danger to all. I thought it best to offer aid."

Not one of her people.

Sidhe.

Meren was Sidhe.

The shrieking alarm of that reminder blared through her mind and cut through the muddy mess of her thoughts. Holy shit. Had he messed with her head somehow?

Enchanted her? Anna's pulse leaped, but she did her best not to let her reaction show. For a moment, she considered pepper spraying him in case he sensed that whatever spell he might have placed on her had been broken, but that could make the situation worse.

This man called himself Rianehd, not Meren. But Meren had found allies before. This could be a trap to lure her away. That was how she would have written it in one of her stories, and Anna had fallen right in like the poor girl with the ballet flat.

"Are you overcome with my generosity?" Rianehd asked sharply.

Crap. How could she play along without getting herself in more trouble? She had to answer. "I'm guessing you want something in return."

His eyebrows rose. "I have asked for nothing."

Hah. Because there were so many fairy tales where the fae offered help out of pure altruism. Anna barely resisted rolling her eyes. "Yet. But you might as well get it over with. I've heard enough stories of the fae to know it's coming."

Lord Rianehd studied her for a moment before nodding. "Very well, then. If you must know, there are secrets of the water magic I have yet to unlock, and it is my hope that I might help you become proficient enough to find your own people, the true masters of water. Then you can return the favor by teaching me a few new tricks."

There was a certain logic to that, but something about his assertion didn't ring true. Really, if he was a powerful lord, why couldn't he seek out some of the full-blooded Gwragedd Annwn himself? Had he tried and been refused? Or maybe he was bullshitting her to try to get close to her.

She would bet on the last one.

"I need time to consider your offer," Anna said.

Surprise flashed across his face before his expression returned to neutral, a change so quick she almost missed it. Oh, no. He had to realize she wasn't under his influence anymore. "I suppose I can grant that boon, although I must tell you that I will not remain in this area long."

A limited time offer. Fen's comment about infomercials sprang into her head. She'd been amused by it then, but the reality was far from funny. Rianehd definitely had intentions far more sinister than selling her a cheap gadget—and she didn't want to know what those intentions were.

Anna forced a shrug. "Then I'll find someone else."

He couldn't hide his surprise this time. "You would give up this opportunity for the sake of hoarding the knowledge you gain? I ask for little enough."

"Do you?" The guy obviously thought humans were total fools. "I don't know enough to say whether or not you're asking for something small, and I'm not making promises based on information I don't have. I might be nice, but I'm not gullible."

If she'd been fast enough, Anna would have snapped a picture of the Sidhe lord as a mixture of shock, anger, and affront passed across his face, stronger than before. Then she would've titled the image *His Highness Denied* and hung the thing

on her wall to laugh at. Alas, the moment was gone too soon, his expression smooth and confident once more.

"Would you like a sample of what I could teach you?" he asked, a sly lilt to his voice.

Had there been the slightest spark of sexual interest in his eyes, Anna would have left at once, but there was no indication the statement was laced with the innuendo some men would have intended. "I'm not agreeing to anything."

Lord Rianehd lifted a hand almost casually, and the river sloshed with more force against the bank. "I will grant you this bit of knowledge freely and without condition. Water is a force of emotion, and both have the power to sustain or destroy. Water connects all living beings, but it also carves through solid rock. If you cannot gain control of your emotions, you will never succeed at using your magic. Think on that next time you are in the water. Otherwise, the element will rule you absolutely."

From the way the river slapped against the shore, Anna had to assume that the Sidhe lord was less calm than he appeared. "Somewhat useful, but more inspirational poster than practical advice. I doubt I can do much with that."

"More than you think." Lord Rianehd stood, brushing the wrinkles from his slacks with a regal flick. "I will give you the time you so obviously require, but I warn you I have little patience. Tomorrow evening, I will return to this spot. If you wish to negotiate a deal, meet me here after sunset. Alone."

"Again, you insist on me being alone. Is there a reason? Maybe you have something to hide."

He smirked. "Don't we Sidhe always have something to hide? Be here or not. It makes no difference to me."

But as Lord Rianehd walked away, his shoulders appeared knotted with tension, and his stride was not as easy as his casual smirk suggested it should be. For whatever reason, this future meeting made a huge difference to him, and Anna had the uncomfortable feeling she needed to discover why.

This was absolutely going to be dangerous. Darn it. Anna didn't mind tagging along on adventures, but she didn't want to be the star of one. Though it would be nice if she could figure out how to get revenge for that bit of mind control the asshole had used. After all, she wouldn't be in this situation without it.

As soon as the helpers from Lyr's estate finished affixing the large mirror to the cave wall of the new receiving room, Dria stepped forward to attune herself to the enchantment. Behind her, mage globes illuminated the rich furnishings she'd opted to install—a large rug enchanted against dirt and water with a grouping of nice but not-too-comfortable chairs arranged carefully in a loose circle. On the wall opposite, she'd had Vek raise a small dais out of stone, but she hadn't yet decided if she wanted to place anything resembling a throne there.

The room was a work in progress, but it would do.

Dria activated the link she sought as soon as she was alone. She'd dressed carefully in formal clothing, despite the awkwardness of wearing the long, trailing over-robe in a cave, and had even donned her tiara for good measure. Lera had a few centuries on her, but she would not be intimidated.

Almost at once, the link completed, and Queen Lera's image appeared on the other side. Just as frosty and perfect as Dria remembered from their few meetings. Why did Lera echo her pale blonde hair and fair complexion with the lightest colors possible? The other woman's personality wasn't nearly as cold, or at least it hadn't been the one time she had spoken freely with Dria after a long day at the Moranaian court.

"Forgive my abrupt contact, Queen Regent Lera," Dria said, trying to hide her annoyance. She didn't dislike the lady, but she had too much work already to deal with her. "I understand from Lord Lyr that you wished to speak to me regarding the outpost?"

Lera's eyes widened, probably at the directness of the question. Maybe Vek was rubbing off on Dria, because she couldn't find the patience for pleasantries. She expected some amount of affront, but Lera surprised her by inclining her head without comment about the lapse.

"It has always been understood that your people would not establish a permanent residence on Earth after your departure."

Dria smiled. "And it has also been understood that your people would make no move of aggression against ours, yet one of your nobles launched an attack against us. He also attempted to murder my mate, an Unseelie prince."

At least embarrassment brought color to Lera's features. "Meren is a criminal, wanted by the crown for multiple crimes. We are not to blame."

"Nor did we plan the circumstances that led to this outpost." Dria lifted a brow. "Is there an actual request you wish to make of me?"

Lera's nostrils flared, but her tone remained calm. "I would like to send an emissary to your outpost in case Meren attempts to attack once more. His retrieval is of utmost importance to the crown, especially considering his former rank in our court."

Now that was interesting. For Lera to reveal so much, she had to want his return badly. "Is there some incentive you can offer? It is a great imposition to host a dignitary in these rough accommodations."

"Rough?" Lera's gaze flicked briefly to the furnishings behind Dria. "It seems no hardship."

"This is the first room at the beginning of the cave system," Dria said smoothly, though she had no intention of mentioning the many levels down to the portal. "I cannot promise a comfortable place to sleep."

Queen Lera considered her for a moment before drawing herself up straighter. "As Queen Regent, I am prepared to offer the Moranaians a future boon, so long as it is in no way taxing or dangerous to my people. Two such favors if you actively help my emissary bring Meren back to my court alive."

Miaran. Dria had already expected this request, but she'd never thought Lera would make such a rich offer. It would be foolish not to accept. "I agree."

Now to keep Vek from killing Meren before the Seelie had to fulfill their end of the deal.

22

Fen wasn't certain he believed in any particular divine being, but he prayed anyway as he sped through afternoon traffic. Why in the hell would she have gone to meet a stranger knowing that Meren was out there looking for revenge? She'd been with Fen when his mother had delivered her warning, and that had been less than an hour after Anna had watched someone—likely Meren—attempt to drown Fen in the river.

Why did people connected to Fen always have to suffer? His fingers tightened on the steering wheel. This time, it wouldn't be directly related to something he had done, at least as far as he knew. Kien and Meren had worked together grudgingly and rarely, neither trusting the other. Fen had never even met the haughty Sidhe lord, and if he had, the man wouldn't have known Fen by anything other than his alias, Tom. But that didn't stop Fen from being sucked into the shitstorm anyway.

"I'm worried, too," Maddy said. "But you look like you're about to have a panic attack. Is there something I don't know?"

Dammit, they hadn't even had a chance to talk about everything that had happened while they were apart. "Yeah. While you were gone, Anna got a bit carried away and jumped into the river. I went in after her, but she turned out to be fine. Then someone tried to pull me under. We think it was Meren, but he got away before that could be confirmed."

"There was an attack, and no one called to tell me?" Maddy's glare arrowed through him, though he only caught a glimpse of it before he returned his attention to the road. "You've got to be kidding me. That's not the kind of thing you leave out."

Fen grimaced. "It wasn't on purpose. I had to tell Vek and Ara to fuck off, and then I met your parents for the first time. Not to mention searching for a house and furniture with no notice and trying heal Sparrow. It got lost in the shuffle."

"You just...forgot that someone tried to kill you?"

"The whole thing was over in a matter of moments, and I wasn't hurt." Fen dared another glance her way and was heartened to see that she no longer appeared capable of murder. "With no more sign of Meren, it didn't seem like there was anything to do except stay on guard. Even if I had remembered when we spoke, there wouldn't have been a point in you coming back. Still, I'm sorry."

"Fine. I won't yell at you about it. Just don't let it happen again." Maddy fell silent for a moment. "Do you think Anna would really meet with Meren after that?"

"I hope not," Fen answered. "I really hope it's a coincidence."

It took all of Fen's willpower to slow down as he swung the car into the parking lot, when what he wanted to do was tear ass through the turn and speed over all the empty parking spaces. But kids played on the playground, and people jogged the nearby paths. He couldn't risk hurting anyone. So he took a deep breath and directed the car as calmly as possible into a spot near the sidewalk.

"Do you see her?" Maddy asked as he scanned the area.

Fen almost answered no, but before he could get the word out, Anna came into view on the trail near the water. "There."

He pointed, and Maddy followed the line of his finger. "Thank goodness."

Maddy leapt from the car, slamming the door behind her. Fen turned off the ignition, grabbed the keys, and followed suit, but despite his haste on the road, he didn't run toward Anna as well. Instead, he glanced around the park, hoping to see the mysterious stranger his girlfriend had come to meet.

Despite what he'd told Maddy, Fen was almost certain this was no coincidence. Meren was out there somewhere, waiting to pounce, and although the threat the Sidhe man had sent Fen's mother hadn't mentioned Maddy or Anna, that didn't mean they were safe. No one connected with Fen was safe if that bastard was out to get him, so a stranger luring Anna into a meeting was more than suspect.

Fen cursed beneath his breath. Really, he should leave Maddy and Anna alone for their own good. Make some excuse and bolt. Then they wouldn't have to stress about his shit catching up with any of them like this. His chest squeezed, and his steps slowed as he watched Maddy pull Anna close for a kiss. Foregoing the mate bond would be the wisest choice.

But he never had been wise—maybe that was why he wouldn't walk away.

He'd done his best so far to atone for his mistakes, and he always would. But it was past time for him to climb out of that gutter where he thought he belonged. He might never deserve to have two amazing mates, but *they* deserved someone who would spend his life trying to be worthy. If someone like Meren tried to jerk Fen back into the darkness, they wouldn't find the task an easy one. He didn't have to stay where he'd fallen.

The women pulled apart, and they both looked his way, silently beckoning him to join them. Despite the threat, the tension emptied from his body as though a drain had been opened at the welcome in his mates' eyes. No, he couldn't live in the past. Not anymore. Whatever it took, whoever he had to defeat, Fen would move forward with them.

If they let him.

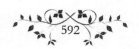

It felt perfectly natural to stand there holding Anna's hands, yet Fen's absence bothered Maddy, too. Yeah, she and Anna would be fine—if a little heartbroken—if Fen decided he didn't want to be with them. That was a given. But that didn't mean Maddy would be at her happiest. She would forever know that *more* could have filled her life. More love. More belonging. More everything.

Maddy held out her hand, and after frowning their way for a moment, Fen hurried to cross the space between them. He skidded to a halt beside them, his gaze stuck on her outstretched hand. Would he do it? Would he join them? Finally, he settled his palm against hers, and her shoulders went lax with relief.

Before anyone could say a word, Anna grabbed Fen's other hand. "Didn't my text say not to approach? What are you two doing out here?"

"Us? What were you thinking?" Fen blurted. "With Meren trying to—"

"It wasn't him," Anna was quick to interrupt. "The person in the river had insanely long hair, but this guy's was short."

That might have been enough to convince Anna, but Maddy knew better. "The Sidhe use glamour constantly, love. That could have been an illusion."

Anna went pale. "I should have thought of that considering how often you use magic to hide your bad hair days."

"Didn't Anthony say that the man bothering him had just had a haircut?" Fen asked. "If that was Meren, too..."

Maddy frowned. Fen hadn't mentioned a connection to Anthony. They clearly needed to sit down and talk through everything that had happened. In a safer place, of course.

"I realize that now, but I wasn't thinking clearly at the time. It felt like a dream. I think he used magic to control me." Anna shuddered, and Maddy grew alarmed at the fear in her love's eyes. "Though maybe our friend has a new ally. This man gave me a different name, one I've never heard."

"Don't speak it here," Maddy warned. Names had power, a lesson she'd been taught since childhood. If he was still close, he might feel the pull of it. "Let's go back to Fen's place. If that's okay, Fen?"

Without a word, he gave a gentle tug on each of their hands, drawing them up against him in an epic hug. "More than."

Maddy wrapped her arm around Fen's waist, her arm brushing Anna's as their girlfriend did the same, and settled her left ear against Fen's chest. She and Anna shared a smile, content to enjoy the moment. Something had shifted, but she couldn't say what. Only that it was good.

If the rest of the night went as she hoped, it might even be great.

For the first few minutes of the car ride, Anna was able to brood in silence. Not that time to ponder was the best thing in the world, considering the varied ways her

body was knotting up with delayed reaction. How had the stranger gained control over her mind so easily? The only good thing out of the whole situation was that she hadn't been entirely under his influence.

Really, her mind hadn't been clear—truly clear—from the time Riane-hd-or-Meren had walked in the door, but the full force hadn't hit her until he'd touched her. It must have been that odd zing when he grabbed her arm. How could she have thought their kinship for water might have caused it? Though *she* hadn't really been the one who'd considered that angle, had she?

Being controlled sucked.

"Stop beating yourself up," Maddy finally said. "Before I regret riding back with you instead of Fen."

"I'm not upset at myself, exactly. Mostly the situation." Anna's fingernails dug into the steering wheel. "But I admit Fen would have been better company."

"Maybe," Maddy retorted, reaching over to tuck a strand of Anna's hair behind her ear. "But I thought we could use a few minutes alone. We haven't had a chance to talk about how things went with Fen while I was gone."

Latching on to the change of subject, Anna relaxed. "Great. I'm not sure what it is about Fen, but I love being around him. I mean, he has his downsides, of course, but I think…I think my feelings could really deepen."

Maddy's hand settled on Anna's shoulder. "I thought about you both while I was gone. Is that strange? I don't want you to think I'd like to replace you or anything."

"I don't."

Anna followed Fen's car into the driveway and parked while he continued into the garage. They wouldn't have long before the moment ended, and Anna wanted to meet Maddy's eyes while she could. Her girlfriend's gaze was as soft and loving as ever, though a hint of worry marred it.

"Have you…" Maddy swallowed. "Have you decided on what you want?"

"Yes, I have." Anna lifted her left hand to cover Maddy's. "I want both of you. I think we should do this. What about you? I've had a brief polyam relationship before, but you haven't. It can be an adjustment to have two equal partners instead of just one."

Maddy took a quick breath and let it out in a huff. "I know. I wouldn't be able to put one of you above the other, and that's huge. But…I believe I'm there, Anna. We should go for it."

Anna leaned forward and brushed her lips against Maddy's. "Think we'll be able to convince Fen anytime this decade?"

Maddy laughed. "Here's hoping."

Someone tapped against the window, and Anna turned to offer a reassuring smile at Fen, who peered in anxiously from the other side. The poor guy had no clue they'd been talking about him, but he would soon enough. Well, after they discussed the mystery stranger.

Fun times.

They were all silent as they climbed the staircase to the second-floor living room. Anna plopped down on the couch, Maddy settling on the other side. Fen hesitated for a moment, and if the thought of the Meren-or-Rianehd discussion hadn't soured her mood, Anna would have been amused by the way he glanced between the two and then at the empty space between.

"Yes, I left that for you," Maddy said impatiently. "Are you going to sit?"

One corner of Fen's mouth lifted. "I don't know. It seems like I'm coming between you. You guys can still cuddle when I'm here."

Maddy chuckled. "Sure. But I was sort of hoping we could all get a cuddle, and it would be awkward as hell with you on the outside since you're the biggest and tallest. I am *not* going to let you sit on my lap so you can touch Anna, too."

"Same," Anna said, and the mental image eased some of her bad mood. "So how about we lay things out really quick? If Maddy and I want to snuggle, kiss, or have sex with just the two of us, we do, but the same goes between you and Maddy or you and me. Or we can all be together at the same time. Anyone who feels like they aren't getting enough attention should say so, because if we try to keep some kind of scoreboard, we'll all go nuts. Sound fair?"

Predictably, Maddy nodded first. Fen would need at least another minute or two to angst over it. "Talking about issues," Maddy said. "Revolutionary."

That jogged Fen out of his mope enough for him to finally sit down between them. "Okay, okay. I worry too much. But I was thinking earlier... If we do this, I'm making it my life's mission to be worthy of you both."

Anna smiled as Maddy settled against Fen's side and tapped her finger against his leg. "Don't act like a martyr, Fen. Me and Anna aren't angels looking for a supplicant."

As Fen finally curved his arm around Maddy's shoulders, Anna tucked herself beneath his other shoulder. "Yep. Not much angelic thinking here. Anyway, we all make mistakes. I might have just met with the guy trying to kill you. A can of mace against an ancient Sidhe lord. Brilliant, right?"

Fen's chest vibrated against her cheek. "You had mace?"

"Hey, better than nothing." Anna rested her hand on his waist and then shivered when Maddy's hand settled over hers. "I was thinking about the whole thing on the drive over. He tried to control me, but it didn't entirely succeed. I managed to fight through the haze enough to send a text and to think of the mace. For the most part, it's like most of my resistance fled."

"Sounds like a glamour that didn't quite work," Maddy said. "They aren't always just for looks. My father tried to teach me to use them in case I ever got in trouble, but I never could master them. Best I can do reliably is mask the appearance of something."

"What name did the guy give you?" Fen asked, his voice rumbling against her ear.

Anna furrowed her brow in thought. "Something like...REE-ahh-ned ar-sed?"

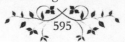

"Arse?" Fen laughed. "He had 'arse' in his name?"

But Maddy sat bolt upright, her face going pale. "Was it 'a Orsed'?"

"Yes!" Anna answered, and a sick feeling rose up her throat at Maddy's look of horror. "Is that bad?"

Maddy swallowed. "Orsed was the name of the Seelie king just before Queen Tatianella, his only child. At least as far as anyone knows. But '*a* Orsed' means 'child of Orsed.' Whoever you spoke to is claiming to be the son of a king. In fact, your stranger's given name sounds uncomfortably like a mixture of the Sidhe words for 'unknown or hidden king.'"

Crap.

Fen groaned. "That can't be good. As much as I hate to admit it, we should go talk to Vek. His old ass might know something about a hidden son."

Anna pulled away from Fen, shifting so she could see both his and Maddy's expressions clearly. "Okay. But I have a question first."

"Can't it wait?" Maddy asked impatiently. "I should call my father before we head to the outpost. This is important."

Anna frowned at her. "If this guy is thousands of years old, then he's been in hiding a hell of a long time. I don't think a few minutes' delay is going to make much of a difference."

Maddy's shoulder's slumped, but she nodded.

"Fen." Anna took a bracing breath and plunged forward before she could second-guess herself. "The *Felshreh* mate bond… Does it allow mates to sense each other? Communicate silently and such?"

For a moment, the only sound filling the room came from the speed boat zooming down the river outside the window, and worry seeped in to replace bravery. But finally, Fen nodded. "Yeah. Vek used it to track Dria when she was kidnapped, and I know they sense each other's moods and stuff. It seemed to give Dria a limited ability to pull power from Vek, but I don't know if she would be able to find him through the link since she's not *Felshreh*. Umm. Why?"

"We've been circling around this a lot, but…" Anna twisted her fingers together. "I think we should do it. Mate. Well, if we're all on board. Why wait when it could give us an advantage?"

Fen stood, knocking Maddy's hand from his leg, and paced across the room. Anna winced. She didn't dare look at Maddy to see how she was reacting, considering Fen shoved his fingers through his hair and twisted as he marched back toward them. Her girlfriend probably wasn't taking his obvious distress any better.

Had she ruined everything?

23

The words welled up before Fen could stop them. "No. No fucking way."

Anna flinched, and anger flashed across Maddy's face as she jerked to her feet. "You don't have to be such an asshole about it."

"I didn't…" Fen tugged at his hair, the pinch in his scalp helping to dispel the panic circling in his head. "I'm sorry. It's not mating with you that's the problem. It's the circumstances. I am *not* going to do this because it's expedient. Vek once told me that he worried Dria chose to mate out of necessity, and I refuse to spend my life wondering the same."

Maddy's eyes narrowed. "Anyone can tell that Dria adores your uncle."

"She didn't at first." Fen dropped his hands from his hair and stepped closer. "They were going to have to search the cave system for intruders when Vek was low on energy, and if he'd taken Dria's blood to gain power, he would have bound them before she could start her people's bonding process. I'm not sure he's ever admitted to Dria how much it bothered him to mate under those conditions. Do you think I want to do the same?"

"It's not the same at all," Maddy snapped. "We've been getting closer to each other for a while now, little as any of us wanted to admit it. You're such an idiot. I was already—"

"Stop it!" Anna stood, and the pain filling her eyes made Fen's heart tumble. "We don't need to argue, okay? If Fen's not ready, then he's not."

Maddy sniffed. "We should go."

How could he be so perfect at botching things? Fen extended his arm when Maddy started forward and prayed she wouldn't shove him out of the way and keep going. "Please, don't. I'm sorry. I didn't realize that either of you were close to deciding, so it caught me by surprise. It's *not* that I'm not ready. But if you're just wanting a safety net in case one of us gets kidnapped…"

"Do you want me to knock him unconscious?" Maddy muttered to Anna. "Because I know I can do that fairly reliably."

No hint of Anna's emotions showed on her face as she studied Fen. "Nah. He'd probably just assume he deserved it."

Fen had to snicker at that.

Yeah, she'd gotten to know him really well.

Anna eased closer to him until she could reach out and touch his chest. If she wanted to. "You know, Fen, it would be useful to be able to sense each other, if Maddy and I even get that benefit. No denying that. But I'd already decided I wanted a formal bond with you both. You fit. We fit. The timing doesn't make a difference to me."

"This isn't a small commitment," Fen said bluntly. "Not even Vek knows if it can be broken completely. He told me that in one of the triads he'd seen, the link remained between the remaining two after the third person died. And none of us knows how long we'll live since we're all part human. The two of you obviously do well together, but either of you could be stuck with me for centuries if the other died."

Maddy shrugged. "And you could be stuck with me. I'm grumpy before coffee, annoyingly cheerful at random intervals, and possibly unable to use my magic without killing people."

"I don't know what's going to happen with my water powers," Anna added. "Or if I have family somewhere who would teach me. I'm a homebody who would rather stay home than go out around people, and there's a lot I don't know about the fae world. None of that changes how I feel."

Fen wanted to believe that, but it was a struggle. "I've never been anything but an annoyance," he found himself murmuring. "Someone convenient and ready to use but not valued. It's hard to imagine being chosen. Desired. Before you and Vek, the only person who wanted me around was Kien, and we know how that turned out."

Anna's mouth curved into a soft smile. "Do I look like a murderous maniac to you?"

"We all have issues, Fen," Maddy said as she stomped the rest of the way to Anna's side. "But if you compare me to that sick fuck again in any shape, form, or fashion, I will kick your ass."

"I hadn't meant to in the first place," Fen said, wincing. "It's obviously not the same situation, but—"

"If you really want to rise above the stuff that has happened to you, start acting instead of reacting. Find these traitorous little thoughts and stomp them out." For the first time, Maddy's expression softened. "I've had to do a lot of that myself. All of us have."

As the depth of that statement sank in, Fen flushed. He really had been self-absorbed, hadn't he? Anna was wrestling with the discovery of her fae blood and all that entailed, and Maddy had just traveled to another world to try to train a gift she'd almost killed people with. Yet here he was, angsting about the same shit all over again when he'd already decided to move forward with his life. Too bad decision didn't automatically create habit.

"You're right," he said.

Getting over bad things didn't mean ignoring them, and it didn't mean they'd gone away. It was a matter of changing focus—of not letting the past win. The acknowledgement of that fact rushed through him, unlocking the parts of himself he'd been too afraid to reveal. Dammit, he wasn't tainted. He might walk the line between light and dark, but in the twilight, there was magic.

Fen took Maddy's and Anna's hands and pulled them closer as he had in the park. Fen lowered his head until their foreheads touched, a triangle almost formed. "I'm ready to do this if you are. You have to be sure about forever."

"I am. Obviously," Anna said, and her chuckle flowed between them. "Hope you wash dishes."

Maddy laughed. "Between me and Fen, we can surely cover it. I'm in. But what are we supposed to do?"

Frowning, Fen eased back. "I have to take a taste of your blood, but I'm not sure if there's any particular order? Or maybe together? I guess I could call Vek and ask him, but after telling him I could figure stuff out on my own..."

"Hold on," Anna said, darting away to the kitchen and opening several of the drawers. "I know we bought knives, but I'm not sure where you put them."

Fen laughed. "I have fangs, love."

"But if Maddy and I cut our palms and mingle the blood, it might work better."

"You've watched too many movies." Fen wrinkled his nose. "The palm is a terrible place to cut yourself. It's one of the most sensitive places on your body. How about you give me your hands, and I'll find a good spot on the top."

Not exactly where he would prefer to take blood from either woman, but in this case, it would be the fairest. Unfortunately, he had a moment's worry that the reality of his nature might prove to be a deal-breaker. Maddy stared down at her hand and nibbled anxiously on her lower lip, and Anna seemed to be crossing the space separating them at the speed of a sloth.

All he could do was wait. If this were to work, both women would have to decide freely.

Maddy hated pain, so the thought of having a fang slice the top of her hand wasn't pleasant. But surprisingly, that wasn't bothering her the most. It just seemed so...unromantic. She and Anna hadn't intended to have a fancy wedding, but still. There ought to be something splashier than a quick cut in the middle of Fen's barely furnished house to mark the occasion.

"This isn't right," Maddy said.

Anna groaned. "Seriously? I thought we'd finally decided."

"I'm not talking about mating itself." Maddy gestured between them. "Just look at us. You're still wearing your work uniform, I'm a rumpled mess since I'd barely woken from a nap before we left to get you, and Fen looks so flustered I'm surprised he didn't run away. It doesn't seem particularly special, that's all."

Fen grimaced, and Anna darted a glance down at her clothes before frowning back at Maddy. "You have a point," Anna said. "But unless we drive across town to our condo, I'm not sure how to solve it. I don't have clothes here."

"Neither one of you needs to change a thing," Fen said, and his voice had taken on a gruff tone Maddy had never heard from him before. He walked over to Anna and took her hand. Then they both approached Maddy. "Seriously. You're adorable with your hair a little mussed, and I'm sure we'd both be happy to help Anna ditch her work clothes for a while. Upstairs. Honestly, it might be a good idea to sleep together first. In case…"

"We're bad in bed together?" Though her body heated at Fen's suggestion, Maddy forced a light smile for his sake. "I don't think that's a possibility, but testing the theory is fine by me."

"Same." Anna wiggled her eyebrows. "No need to be shy, Fen."

That delightful flush crept up his neck, a telltale sign that despite his past, Fen wasn't as jaded as he seemed. "I've already told Anna this, but… I've only slept with two people, and that was years ago."

Maddy smiled. "Okay. Well, I've never been with more than one person at a time, and Anna hasn't had sex with a guy. I imagine we'll figure it out anyway. Less talking, more doing."

Anna laughed, a flustered Fen shoved his fingers back through his hair, and all was perfect. Or maybe it would be once they got upstairs.

Once they reached the bedroom, Anna took a wicked satisfaction in stripping off her uncomfortable work uniform in the late afternoon sunshine streaming through the window. Two pairs of eyes tracked her every movement, heightening her desire. To be wanted by two amazing people was a powerful drug. Fen with his hard edges and soft heart, and Maddy with her wry humor and boundless light.

There was no place Anna would rather be.

She reached for Maddy first, giving her girlfriend a soft kiss before tugging her shirt over her head and throwing it wide. Fen sucked in a breath, and Anna smiled. "Want me to do the same for you?"

Fen laughed, some of his tension easing, and pulled his shirt off himself. "I can manage this, at least."

Anna shared a smile with Maddy. "I'm sure you can manage far more."

In moments, they'd shed the rest of their clothes and stumbled toward the bed. "They make bigger beds than king size," Fen said, "but I haven't had time to order one."

"Good enough for now," Anna murmured, dropping back on the soft surface with a happy sigh and scooting up toward the head of the bed. "So long as you two are here."

Maddy crawled up the bed on Anna's left as Fen stretched out on her right. Anna knotted her fingers in Fen's hair and tugged him close for a kiss as Maddy took

Anna's nipple in her mouth just the way they both preferred. Anna moaned. This was going to be perfect. So perfect.

For the first time in a while, Fen let himself live in the moment—no regret, or fear, or hesitation. He lost himself in Anna, her mouth hot beneath his and her soft belly smooth beneath his palm as he caressed her. Then Maddy reached over to wrap her hand around his dick, and the lazy moment of discovery flared into pure heat.

They tumbled together on the bed until Fen couldn't have said who was bringing pleasure to whom. It didn't even matter. The past and future faded into nothing but that moment and the bond between them that couldn't be denied, whether he took their blood or not.

Fen licked a trail up Maddy's back as she kissed Anna. "I have to get inside one of you. Now. How do we decide…"

Maddy rolled to her back and parted her legs. "You make love to Anna while she makes love to me."

Anna frowned. "But—"

Maddy settled a finger on Anna's mouth, cutting off her words. "You connect us, somehow. It just feels right."

Though Fen's body was more than ready, he couldn't help but worry. "Anna hasn't been with a man, though."

"Oh, Fen." Anna chuckled as she crawled between Maddy's legs, but the look she sent him was hot. "Women use toys when they play together, you know. You aren't going to hurt me."

Every remaining ounce of thought fled Fen's brain at those words. As Anna bent to take Maddy into her mouth with deft experience, he had to pray that she was right. Because he very much feared that he wouldn't be able to stop now.

Still, his hands shook as he gripped Anna's hips to position her, and he entered her so slowly he thought he might die. Gods, she was like home.

Perfection. Absolute perfection.

Pleasure exploded through Maddy when Fen began to move, shifting Anna closer with each thrust. Over Anna's back, Maddy met his eyes, and joy crashed through to mingle with the heat, an unstoppable swell that sent her over.

Crying out, she gripped Anna's hair lightly with her left hand and put her right against Anna's shoulder. As heat began to build in Maddy again, her girlfriend slipped three fingers inside, bringing Maddy close to the edge.

But this would be a cataclysm.

"My hand," Maddy gasped at Fen. "Take our blood now."

"Yes," Anna cried, and Maddy moaned.

He hesitated so long that she thought he wouldn't do it. But finally, he braced himself with his arm and bent low over Anna. His breath tickled the side of Maddy's hand where it met Anna's back, and then he brushed his lips against her skin.

"I don't want to hurt—"

"Do it, Fen," Maddy snapped. "For fuck's sake."

Anna laughed against her at the choice of words, but they both gasped as Fen's fangs drew blood. It didn't hurt, exactly, but the sensation was unusual. A tingling sort of pressure that suggested he must have only scratched. Or if there was pain, it was lost to sensation. Pleasure. Wonder. A blending so complete she couldn't imagine life without it.

Once again, Maddy flew.

There was no describing the magic and joy flowing between them as Fen took Anna's blood along with Maddy's. Anna's eyes slipped closed as the links began to form, tenuous but true. Like a drop of dye dissolving in water. Instinctively, she gathered the tendrils and twined them together, ensuring she and Maddy were as strongly mated as either of them were to Fen.

He reached around Anna to caress her, and she followed Maddy over the edge. It only took Fen a moment to join them. Ah, it was just as perfect as she'd known it would be. Could there be a better wedding than this?

As Fen collapsed on the bed and pulled Anna and Maddy into a loose, gasping heap against him, she didn't think so.

24

Something sharp poked Fen in the side, and a distant, annoying ringing sound broke through his hazy mind. He cracked one eye open and smiled to see Maddy leaning over him in the dim light. It had to be near sunset, but he didn't even care. After round two—and both women insisting on taking a drop of his blood—they'd all fallen into a blissful sleep. But he was rested enough now for round three if either or both of his mates were interested.

"Your phone is ringing, Fen," Maddy said, her eyes dancing with laughter.

He reached up to tweak her nipple, and she yelped. "I have voicemail."

The poke repeated in his side. "This is the third time, sleepy," Anna said from behind him. "I don't think they're giving up."

"Figures," Fen grumbled.

He managed to separate himself from his mates and stumble from the bed, but it was a hard-won battle. Whoever was calling had better have something damned important to say, because short of an alien invasion, he really didn't give a fuck. Muttering beneath his breath, he found his pants where he'd thrown them on the floor and tugged his phone free.

Vek. He should have known.

"What do you want, Vek?" Fen snapped as soon as the phone was at his ear.

"Were you *sleeping?*" his uncle demanded. "I thought you were going to return to the outpost so we could work on the blood portal, but you decided to take a nap instead? If you want me to treat you like an adult—"

"I was napping with Maddy and Anna, if you must know." Maddy's chuckle rang out from the bed, and Fen smiled. "As we were celebrating fully mating. Is there anything else you require to excuse my absence? I'm sure the ladies would be happy to write me a note, though maybe not with as many details as your pervy ass would prefer."

Vek let out a choked sound. "I am *not* a pervert, and I don't want details. You could have left it at the first sentence. Damn."

Even though his uncle couldn't see it, Fen's grin widened into a smirk. "That wouldn't have been nearly as satisfying, though."

"Shut up, Fen," Vek said. "And tell me if you're coming over to the outpost today or not."

Fen sighed at the reminder of the world that awaited him outside of the bedroom. He didn't want to go, but there was the mysterious maybe-Meren guy from the park to talk to Vek about. "Give me an hour."

"Fine. But I won't call to wake you up again if you decide on another nap."

Laughing, Fen hung up the phone and turned back to the bed. Maddy was curled up against Anna, but they both stared at him with amused expressions as he started toward them. "I could probably spare a few minutes if I shower really quickly after," he muttered.

But Anna shook her head. "Nope. Girl time."

"If your uncle still wants you to go to the outpost after hearing that we've mated, it must be important," Maddy said. "And girl time does sound nice."

Fen groaned, even knowing he did need to leave. "I really wish I hadn't answered my phone."

"We need to get some spare clothes and stuff anyway," Anna said. Then she frowned. "Which…I guess we'll have to decide where to live."

"Later." Maddy smoothed Anna's brow with a soft finger. "We'll figure it out."

"If you talk about it while I'm gone, consider me team whatever," Fen added from the bathroom door. "There's more space here, but I don't really get attached to places. I'll be happy to move anywhere."

It took all of Fen's willpower to leave the bedroom and jump in the shower. A really, really cold shower. This new portal had better be worth it.

Aside from the gentle hiss of water coming from the bathroom, the house was quiet as Anna stared out the bedroom window at the river glimmering in the moonlight. Her body felt fabulous—a touch sore but mostly relaxed and satiated—but the water brought out the uneasiness that had haunted her for weeks. If what the stranger had said at the park was true, that emotions were tied to her power, then her anxiety really made no sense.

She couldn't remember being so happy, aside from the feelings the water stirred.

Fen had already gone, and she and Maddy had cuddled a bit longer before scraping themselves out of bed. For speed, Anna had grabbed one of Fen's spare shirts from his dresser and run over to the other shower so she and Maddy could clean off without getting distracted with each other. But of course, Maddy took far longer with so much hair to wash, leaving Anna nothing to do but ponder the river.

Maybe the uneasiness wasn't hers at all. Frowning, Anna pressed her palm to the glass. Was the river hurting? Could she have relatives down there in danger? What was it? She had a feeling it was important to find out, but exploring the river with Meren on the loose was risky, especially if he did turn out to be the guy she met in the park.

Anna shivered. He could have used her against Fen and the others so easily. Then again, maybe he'd left her an opportunity. He'd invited her to meet him tomorrow evening, hadn't he? That would be a handy chance for a little trap if they were clever. As the thought took form, she found her phone and sent a quick text to Fen. He could discuss it with Dria and Vek, and Anna could talk it over with Maddy.

Though chances were good that none of them would like it.

Vek himself opened the gate to the shielded room at the top of the outpost, though he glared as soon as Fen walked through. But then his uncle turned his dark expression toward the door, and it became clear that Fen wasn't the greatest source of his agitation. What could be going on now?

"Something out there I should know about?" Fen asked.

Vek's scowl deepened. "Fucking Seelie."

"If there's a Seelie orgy out there, I'm going back through the portal," Fen quipped. "Except for Maddy and her father, I haven't had the greatest experience with that bunch. I'd rather not see their kinks, too."

"You know perfectly well…" Vek closed his eyes for a moment as if for patience. "There is not an orgy in the receiving room. That would almost be preferable to the pompous little shit of a Seelie noble acting as emissary. I dearly want to smash my fist into his face."

Fen frowned as he struggled to keep up. As far as he knew, the Seelie didn't even know about the outpost. "How did that happen? *When* did that happen?"

"Within the last day. The queen contacted Lord Lyr, who referred the issue to Dria." Vek pinched the bridge of his nose. "They must want Meren badly. In return for our assistance capturing him and allowing the emissary to take him back to the Seelie court, Dria has been promised two favors. Open-ended favors, mind you. So long as it isn't injurious to the Seelie."

Holy shit. That was a rare move. Nearly unprecedented. "We might have a lead on that."

"Really?" Vek asked.

"Someone who might have been Meren approached Anna. We were all going to talk to you about it after I finish helping with the blood gate."

Vek's brows lowered thoughtfully. "We'll need Dria, but she is greeting the emissary. Can this wait?"

Fen nodded. "The guy isn't supposed to meet with Anna again until tomorrow evening."

"Fabulous," Vek said. "Then how about you help me carve out a room up here for the emissary? We don't want him in sight of the portal, and if we make a tunnel from this room, he'll never notice it's new. We'll just have to seal the route to this room behind us."

Fen paused to consider his energy stores. He hadn't drawn any power from

Maddy and Anna while mating, but he was fairly confident he still had enough magic to complete this task and then the shield with Vek.

"Let's do it."

Maddy shoved a few changes of clothes into her spare backpack, the other still a world away on Moranaia. She'd decided to leave her things there since she would be traveling back and forth for training, and now she would be hauling yet more to Fen's house. She might have found it funny if she weren't so tired.

Not because of mating—that brought her more joy. How cool was it to be able to sense Anna in the kitchen, packing a few of her favorite things? And if Maddy paused to concentrate, she could detect Fen's direction. Eventually, she had no doubt she'd be able to glean more information even at a distance. Although such a level of closeness could have been odd, it instead made her feel more comfortable than she could ever remember being.

It was just that current events had been…a lot. She'd struggled with her first healing lesson on Moranaia, only to come back to Fen and Anna in danger. What if Maddy hadn't been there? Anna had fought through mind control enough to text Maddy, but that could have been partly habit. Anna might not have thought about contacting Fen while she was being controlled. There was no way to know, but the timing of everything was eerily perfect.

Was this why Eri had suggested she return today?

"Hey, what's wrong?" Anna asked from the door, surprising Maddy.

Crap, she thought, as she pressed her hand against her sternum. *That'll teach me to stop paying attention to Anna's energy.*

"Aside from you startling me?" Maddy asked with a half-hearted laugh. "I'm just worried about all the stuff that's up in the air. I need to call my parents. My dad won't care about our mating, but I'm less certain of my mom considering what she told you. Then there's the mystery surrounding that guy who tried to control you. And Anthony and Sparrow. We really should make sure they are okay. Oh, and we have to decide where we're going to live."

Anna pushed away from the doorframe and crossed the space between them. "How about we take it one thing at a time?"

"I'm honestly not sure what to tackle first," Maddy confessed. "Anthony hasn't answered the text I sent earlier, but I guess if they thought Sparrow's poisoned energy returned, he would call."

"Then that's one we don't have to think about now. And we might get more info about Lord Rianehd from your father, so those two can go together." Anna took Maddy's hand gently in hers. "Unless you'd like to talk about living arrangements first?"

Maddy sighed. "We both know Fen's new house is perfect for all of us, as long you're really okay being so close to the water, and he said he was happy with whatever. I hate to sell this place, though. It has a lot of good memories."

"Maybe we shouldn't," Anna said thoughtfully. "You never know when an extra apartment could come in handy, and you have enough in savings to afford the mortgage and any upkeep."

True enough. Her father earned a great deal of money selling jewelry, and he'd set up an account for Maddy at an early age in case something happened to him. But she didn't rely on it. For one thing, her fae blood meant an extended lifespan, complete with the need to relocate every few decades and reinvent her life. She'd done her best to add more to her funds than she took away so she wouldn't have to stress about money when it was time to move on. Did she want to expend some of that cushion on the condo even if she wasn't living there?

"Oh!" Anna's slight frown morphed into a surprised smile. "Here's an idea. What if we leave a few basic furnishings and rent the place out? It could be a safe vacation condo for the fae or something. Or a place for allies to gather instead of drawing attention to our homes."

Maddy let out a relieved breath. Finally, a solution for one of the problems spinning in her head. "Good idea. Something like that would have been handy when Ralan was searching for his brother, Kien. Hey, instead of an Air BnB, we can have a Fae BnB."

"Sounds like a great way to share some of the happiness this place has given us."

"We can see what Fen thinks, and if he agrees, I'll talk to my dad about setting up a business." Maddy squeezed Anna's hand. "Thanks, my love."

Maddy's phone buzzed in her pocket, and she tugged it out to find a message from Anthony. Finally. *Sparrow said if you want to check her again, that's fine. I don't think she was too sure about your friend's uncle. Can you swing by after nine? I know it's late, but she has to work.*

"You feel like going by Anthony's place later?" Maddy asked Anna. "He said Sparrow is willing to see me, but it won't be until nine-ish."

Anna smiled. "Why don't we go by your parents' house on the way? It's Sunday, so the shop is already closed."

"Without Fen?" Maddy typed a quick answer to Anthony and shoved the phone back into her pocket. "It doesn't seem right to announce our mating with just two of us there."

"I know, but…" Anna bit her lip. "Your mom is likely to be upset, considering how she reacted at the shop. Maybe fewer people would make it better?"

Maddy shook her head. "Together. Let's finish packing what we want to take tonight, and if Fen's done in time, we'll go together. If not, we'll wait until tomorrow."

"Okay," Anna said with a nod. "But I'll have to call my parents since they're out of town."

"True."

After Anna gave her a kiss and left, Maddy flopped back on the bed and stared at the ceiling, trying not to let her thoughts return to all that could go wrong. Instead, she inventoried the furniture and made a list of what she would prefer to take instead

of leave. Though she supposed she would have to talk to Anna and Fen so they could agree on a plan for the new place.

It was about to become theirs and not just his.

25

Fen followed Vek through a gap in the cave wall, the narrow gash disappearing in the shadows at the end of the hallway where Fen had his room. He'd explored the entire cave system with his magic at this point, so the spot wasn't new to him. Unlike the thin, snaking corridor his uncle had created beyond the natural opening. He must have added this before the Seelie envoy's arrival.

Bemused, Fen slipped sideways through a tight spot and inched along until it opened into an area just large enough for him and Vek to stand side by side. "Nice handiwork."

Vek scowled. "But heavy on the energy. Why do you think I wanted you to help carve out that other room? Now I won't have to take much from Dria."

"I thought your mate was more than willing to donate."

"Oh, she is." Vek's expression turned even darker. "But not during sex. She's afraid I'll lose control of the life magic after Aris's warning."

Fen shouldn't laugh. He really, really shouldn't.

So of course, he did.

"Sucks for you," Fen joked. Then he laughed harder. "Or not."

Vek flashed his fangs. "Shut the fuck up, Fen."

"Oh, no, not me, too," Fen was able to get out. "Put those fangs away before I end up pregnant."

If Vek had ever planned to do Fen harm, he surely would've done it now. But then his uncle's expression turned mocking. "You don't have to worry about life magic yourself, but you do have two mates now. Both women. And the *Felshreh* tend to be fertile if precautions aren't taken. I'm sure you remembered that earlier."

That cut through Fen's humor, and his laugh turned into a choked groan that had his uncle smirking. Not that Fen cared. Damn. None of them had considered birth control the first or second time, which meant both women could end up pregnant. Sonofa… He'd barely started getting his own shit together. Having two infants dependent on him at the same time was scarier than any danger he'd ever faced.

And he'd spent years evading Kien's torture sessions.

Vek slapped him on the shoulder. "Relax. I was only joking."

"It…might be an actual concern."

"Well, hell," Vek said. "I didn't intend my jest to hit you so harshly. For what it's worth, I think you would make a good father, and you have family and allies to help. Your mother hasn't even truly disowned you, you know."

Fen hadn't known, but at the moment, he didn't exactly care. "Great. Can we get this stupid spell over with so I can return to Maddy and Anna? They might want to think about this lovely bit of news themselves."

With a shrug, Vek slid the pad of his thumb across his fang until a bead of blood welled up. Fen watched carefully as his uncle wiped the drop of blood across a jagged section of the stone wall, activating a spell he must have already imbued inside. A piece of the wall swung inward, and Fen peeked over Vek's shoulder at the small chamber.

Smaller than Fen had expected, honestly. Three or four people could stand comfortably in the cylindrical room—a couple more if they were really friendly. A handful of mage lights were embedded in the walls, illuminating the space well enough to make it seem less stuffy. The floor was level beneath his feet as he followed Vek inside, and no rough edges poked his ass when he sat on the ground.

"You've been practicing your earth magic," Fen said as the stone door slid closed.

Vek lowered himself to the floor. "I had to do something with all that spare time now that I don't have you around to pester me."

"Yeah, sure." Fen's lips twisted at the guilt trip. "Because we spent every moment together before I decided to go out on my own a whole two days ago. And really, I spent almost no time alone at your house while you enjoyed having a new mate. Practically had to chase you off."

A surprised bark of laughter slipped from Vek's lips. "Point taken. And for what they are worth, you do have my apologies. I hadn't intended to neglect you or to make you feel like a child these last couple of weeks. It might take Ara longer to accept your words, but I get it. Maybe you are still angry at me, but there is no need for us to be at odds. You were right to seek your own home and your own life. However, there are still things I must teach you. Learning has no age limit."

"Fair enough. I hadn't intended to give up on learning about my heritage." Fen sighed. "And I do accept your apology. I was more hurt than angry. Can't promise you won't piss me off again, but we'll see."

Vek smiled wryly. "I can't promise that, either."

"Also fair." His tension easing, Fen glanced around the room. "I assume this blood portal is one of those things you want to teach me."

"Partially." Vek shrugged. "More than that, you should be included. Where I have a home, so do you. If Dria decides to return to Moranaia, we'll set up a gate there, too. But I don't see that happening in the near future."

Fen barely registered the last part of his uncle's statement. He was too busy fighting back the rush of warmth—and guilt—that filled him at the first part. Frustration really had made him be a little too hard on Vek, though the cause behind their argument was true. He should have seen how many of his uncle's actions were born of love, not condescension. Maybe a simple discussion would have solved their problem instead of an argument.

"Are you paying attention, Fen?" his uncle asked, frowning.

"Ah, yeah. I just..."

Vek waved his hand. "Never mind. Let's get this over with so we can return to our mates. The initial spell is easy enough, once you know the trick of it, but it's also one that should be well guarded. And I'm not referring only to the knowledge of it. We'll have to layer a great many protections through it since anyone with enough of our blood and enough skill could crack through the base spell otherwise. I'll begin with shielding."

Fen's head spun with worries about possible fatherhood and doubts about his recent reactions to Vek, but he pushed his inner turmoil to the back of his mind, at least as much as he could. "Okay. Show me what to do."

After connecting psychically with Vek, Fen closed his eyes and settled into his role as an observer. First, his uncle pulled forth a dark energy Fen had only seen him use in combat. The dull bundle of power sat above Vek's palm, hissing as it strained to be set free. This was void magic, designed to eat through shields and destroy defenses. What good would that do in a shield?

"Have you learned to use this type of energy?" Vek asked absently, his focus on his task.

"No, but I think I followed what you did."

Fen held out his hand and closed his eyes, searching for the place in his mind he'd seen his uncle access. It took him a moment, but as soon as he found the channel, he activated it. Power filled his hand in a rush, until he instinctively cupped his other palm around the bundle to try to contain it. He cursed as his personal protective shields crumbled beneath the caustic magic. He hadn't even considered the possibility of that.

Vek's magic swirled around Fen's, steadying the power. "Sorry. You'll need to learn how to integrate void magic into your shields, but this task should be helpful for that."

Fen watched as Vek merged the energy balls and wove another strand of magic through and around it. Studying the second type had Fen's eyebrows lifting. The other stream did consist of the same type of void energy, but it was blended with Vek's energy signature combined with a hint of blood magic. What was the point?

He quickly found out.

Without warning, Vek expanded the ball outward, somehow passing it through them without doing damage as he merged the power into the walls. "Void is excellent for hiding things from view, so long as you control it instead of letting it own you. It takes practice."

Fen chuckled. "It was a bit of a fail for me."

"Not at all." Vek's smile held none of its usual mocking glint. "You pulled out a reasonably steady amount of it. You'll have it perfected in a few more lessons, perhaps even without my help. You mastered earth magic alone."

True enough, but Fen hadn't had a choice in that. As long as he could remember, the Earth had called to him in gentle whispers he'd been helpless to resist. He'd started trying to use that magic early, and his skills had grown along with him in ways he would never be able to teach. Except for gleaning magic from blood, his *Felshreh* abilities hadn't been that natural.

"I hope you're right," Fen merely said. "That shit's dangerous."

Vek nodded. "Very. While I've every confidence you could figure it out for yourself, I would rest easier if you work with me to master it. Or someone else trustworthy."

"I don't want to stop training with you," Fen muttered. "You're going to be sore about this for a while, aren't you?"

"Perhaps only a decade," Vek answered, chuckling. Then he gathered more energy between his hands. "Now. This wasn't part of the original spell you saw in the Unseelie caverns, but it is a type of elemental shielding that seems prudent. Can you tell what it is?"

Tentatively, Fen probed the magic his uncle held and discovered an interesting mixture. Water, earth, fire, air, and spirit were all blended and merged until the ball of energy contained each permutation. The cool slide of mud, the creeping hint of lava, the brush of mist against skin, the burning ache of passion—no element stood alone, except when it did. He'd never seen anything quite like it.

"I'm not sure I can do that," Fen admitted.

"I picked this up from a mage I drank from a few years ago, so maybe not." With a deft surge of power, Vek expanded the ball out and joined it with the edges of the void spell. "We'll test your abilities later and see if you'll need an alternative. I'll have to find one myself once the borrowed skill fades."

Fen didn't bother to comment, too busy watching as Vek layered shield after shield into the walls and floors of the room. Surely, this many spells would need frequent renewing. Magic untended often seeped back into the earth, losing its potency. Countless types of energy entwined to create this level of shielding? They would have to pour power into this place yearly, if not more often.

"How are we going to maintain this?" Fen asked after his uncle finished the last shield. "What has kept the one in the Unseelie stronghold from sputtering out?"

"I've contributed blood and energy to the effort over the centuries, but in this case, I have a different idea." Vek tapped his knuckle against the stone floor. "And it has to do with earth magic."

Fen blinked. "Neither of us can draw power that way."

"True," Vek agreed. "But I've been thinking about your connection to Earth. You might not pull energy from it, but you do resonate with this cave system in a

way I've never seen. From what I've gathered, that's how Kien exploited you. Didn't you create a focal point for his poison spell? Crystals that the Moranaians learned to shatter."

Fen rubbed at the goosebumps popping up along his arms. This couldn't be going where it sounded like it was going. "If you are thinking I'll—"

"Don't say something you'll regret," Vek snapped. "You know very well I wouldn't ask you to poison the outpost."

"No, I..."

Bile scalded the back of Fen's throat as the unexpected memories flooded his mind.

"You agreed to help me of your own free will." Kien smirked. "Tom."

The bastard knew that wasn't his real name, but Fen was beyond challenging the mocking tone. The alias was all he had left to protect the ruins of his old life. "But you never said that punishing the full-blooded bastards who abandoned us here would hurt the Earth. If we have enough magic to rule over humans with the fae gone, why would we—"

"I didn't recruit you for your planning abilities." Kien wiggled his knife toward the cave wall. "Pick a stone capable of holding the spell, or you'll join all the others who have betrayed me. Perhaps I could use your blood to create the connection without having to deal with your whining."

Fuck. Kien would do it, too. He would carve Fen up and find a way to use his blood to make the situation worse. How did he always get himself involved in this shit? The only way out now would be death, and gods knew what a sicko like Kien could do with the energy he gleaned from killing a blood elf like Fen.

He had to cooperate.

Maybe he could find a way to mitigate the worst of it. At this point, he had no other choice but to try. "Forgive me," Fen said around the lump in his throat. "I wasn't trying to back out. I was hoping to have your word that my blood relatives will only be weakened, not killed."

Kien's eyebrow rose. "You beg for mercy for the ones who abandoned you?"

Not all of them had, but Kien didn't know that Fen's uncle had found him a few months before and tried to talk sense into him. "No. It is prudence. Weakened or not, the Unseelie assholes would hunt me down for sure if someone dies."

"Very well. You have my word." Kien tapped the flat edge of his knife against his palm. "Now go harvest any crystals we'll need."

Fen's stomach roiled harder with each step closer to the cave wall. The Earth groaned beneath his feet in protest, almost as though it knew what it would be used for. Betrayal. This was the worst betrayal he could ever commit against the element that had always welcomed him unconditionally. How much would the land suffer for this poisoned energy?

How many lives would be ruined because of him?

If there was any sort of divine being out there, it had surely abandoned him, and for all he'd done, he deserved it. Oh, how he deserved it. As Fen settled his hand against the cave wall, a tear trickled down his cheek. At least Kien couldn't see his face from this angle. Fen had to hang on as long as he could until he found a way to undo this.

And he would never manipulate the Earth at another's bidding again.

After working, mating, and packing boxes, Anna's body was heavy with exhaustion, but a strange restlessness had her tapping her hands against her knees as she sat beside Maddy on Anthony's couch. It wasn't the healing energy she could sense flowing between Maddy's hands and Sparrow, and if there was anything wrong, Anthony didn't seem to notice it. He was calmly studying on the loveseat. What the hell was her problem?

Maddy's magic cut off as she leaned back. "You're clear. I guess Vek knew what he was doing after all."

"I just wish the actual cold had gone away with the poison," Sparrow said with a sniffle.

Anna ached at the uncertainty that crossed her love's face, but at least there wasn't the same level of pain Maddy usually displayed when she couldn't heal someone. She still showed a touch of fear and regret, but not the agony of before.

"I'm afraid I don't have enough training for that," Maddy replied. "Sorry. I'll have to learn a lot more about how viruses affect the body first."

Anthony glanced up from his notes. "Need any textbooks? I have a few old ones the bookstore wouldn't buy back."

As Maddy and Anthony started talking about the price and type of texts he had, Anna's unease grew. She scanned the room for any sign of trouble, but calm blanketed this place—everywhere but inside her. She reached for Maddy, gripping her hand. Too tightly, if her expression was anything to go by.

"What's wrong?" Maddy whispered.

"I don't know." Anna forced her fingers to relax. "Something is off, but I don't think it's here."

Maddy's lips turned down, and Sparrow and Anthony both went quiet. "Could it be that Rianehd guy again?" Maddy asked.

"No. The energy isn't the same."

Abruptly, the discomfort surged into pain—emotional, not physical. Anna shoved her palm against her forehead and rubbed. The resonance reminded her of Fen, but it might have been her imagination. Had he gotten her text and freaked out? Her plan to confront Rianehd was daring but sound. Or could there be danger? God, she hoped it was her imagination.

"Do you…"

"Fen," Maddy said, apprehension pinching her face. "I thought it was my own nerves before. We…we need to go."

Anthony and Sparrow exchanged confused glances, but Anthony set his notebook aside and hurried toward the door without asking any questions. "I hope everything is okay," he said as he held the door for them. "And keep in touch? It would be cool to have friends with similar interests, you know?"

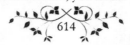

Though nausea was creeping in, Anna did her best to smile. "Same here. Sorry to rush off."

"No worries," he said. "Y'all go help Fen."

Hopefully, they could. Whatever was happening in the outpost, it didn't seem good.

26

"Fen!" Vek's voice sliced through the memory, jolting Fen back in the present. "Snap out of it, or I'll use the shock spell Dria showed me."

Shakily, Fen settled his arms onto knees he hadn't remembered raising and then lowered his forehead to rest atop them as he searched for his equilibrium. What the hell had happened to him? He'd had plenty of nightmares over the years, but he'd never been drawn into a memory so vividly. His heart pounded, and acrid fear coated his mouth.

"Or I could always break your video game system."

"I already went back and got it," Fen said, his voice rough and low. "What kind of dumb as fuck threat is that, anyway?"

Vek huffed. "I wasn't going for the truth. I wanted results, which I would say I got since you're talking now."

"Typical."

But Fen found himself smiling slightly despite it all. It *was* typical, and normalcy helped to steady the weird tumult that had claimed him. With a groan, he lifted his head to face his uncle's worry—and maybe censure. They had serious work, and he'd just disrupted it.

"Stop with the 'someone is about to hit me' look, Fen." Vek slumped, his expression wearier than it had been after hours of performing magic. "I should have considered that you would react poorly to such an idea. Your work with earth magic is always so seamless that it didn't occur to me that you still had issues."

Fen slid his palms against the cave floor and sighed at the trickle of warmth that filled him. "I once vowed to work for the Earth's benefit, but I betrayed that when I was caught up in Kien's plan. I've spent hours in communion, seeking atonement, and I believe that has mostly been granted. I'm able to work with my element, though I don't dare to delve too deep. But I am the one who harvested the crystals that Kien used for his poison. Me. I have never asked to be granted such a precious piece of the Earth again. These days, I only claim gemstones I happen to find. If you're thinking to use a crystal to anchor this spell, it would require calling forth something special."

His uncle nodded, no sign of disappointment in his demeanor. "Then we'll use the old method. Dria might be able to contribute energy since I am linked to her, but if not, it should cause little hardship for me to renew the spells myself when needed."

Not *no* hardship, of course. That would have been a lie, and they both knew it. This type of *Felshreh*-exclusive transportation gate would get more use than the one in the Unseelie realm since Fen couldn't cast the other type of portals Vek, Dria, and the other mages used at the top of the outpost. His uncle might claim that this effort was in the name of security, but Fen suspected it was for Fen to have easy access. And he couldn't even get up the nerve to help set up an energy renewal method.

Dammit. No. Kien had taken much from him, and the rest Fen had thrown away. This was another thing he could reclaim, if he dared to reach out. Maybe he would be rebuffed, but the cave had granted him its memories a couple of days before when he'd been moping in the bathing room. That could have been a sign. If the Earth hated him, he wouldn't be able to work with it with such ease.

"Let me try," Fen said.

Scowling again, Vek leaned forward. "After that? I don't think so."

"I thought you were going to stop treating me like a child," Fen retorted despite his uncle's dark expression. "Now that the surprise is over, I believe I can do this. Allow me the chance."

Vek studied him for far too long, but Fen didn't flinch. He was tired of cowering, evading, and denying. He'd made it through the dark memory, and he would make it through all the others. Now, he had a purpose—mates to care for and an Earth to protect from future poison. Everyone needed a starting point for their ascent.

This could be his.

Finally, Vek nodded. "If I have to shock you with Dria's spell—"

"It'll be straight to the balls," Fen finished for him. "Considering how often Dria threatens you with that, I'm guessing that's how you learned the spell in the first place."

"I assure you she has a better use for my balls." Vek smirked. "Now stop being an asshole and get to work."

Tuning out his uncle, Fen closed his eyes and let himself sink downward until he merged with the cave. A shallow link, at first, but one he gradually strengthened. Bit by bit, until he was lost in the story of the mountain's creation once more. He cycled through the minerals he detected, most of them useless for his purposes. But...fluorite. It held energy well, and there was an abundance of it in the area.

If the Earth would grant it.

Fen took in a deep breath and held it for a second before releasing the air in one long rush. Breathe in. Breathe out. He could do this. As he had once done so easily, he let himself go completely until there was nothing but the heartbeat of the ground beating in his chest. The slow, immortal spirit of Earth wrapped around and through him.

This is what I need, Fen sent out. *And this is why.*

It might have been moments before he received his answer, or entire continents might have formed around him. It didn't matter. Slowly—so slowly—the cave answered his call. Beneath his hands, the ground hummed and warmed as bits of fluorite ascended like wood bobbing up in the water.

As the floor became bumpy beneath his hands, Fen opened his eyes. In a rough circle between him and Vek, a solid patch of fluorite had risen. He barely had time to marvel at it before Vek was directing him on how to link earth energy through the fluorite to the shielding and then the transportation spell itself. The Earth had answered.

Following Vek's command, Fen slid his fang across his forearm, just enough to draw blood, and spilled the precious liquid onto the stones for the last part of the spell. He didn't feel the pain. Honestly, he was too numb with shock to do more than participate by rote.

The Earth had answered.

Maddy and Anna reached the shop in record time, and for once, Maddy didn't care what anyone on the street might think about people entering well after business hours. She barely remembered to set the security system behind them before leading the way to the break room that held the embedded gate to the outpost.

In moments, Maddy had the spell activated and waved Anna through before following. It didn't matter that the turmoil she'd sensed from Fen had faded—they had to find him now. Unfortunately, she'd forgotten the guard stationed at the door that exited into the rest of the outpost. She and Anna came to an abrupt stop when the woman drew her sword and took a step forward.

"Halt," the warrior commanded.

"We're here to find Fen," Maddy hurried to explain, though she was careful to keep her hands lax, palms outward, at her sides. "Dria keyed me into this gate herself after my last visit."

The guard didn't yield. "I'm afraid I'll have to check on your claim."

Maddy wanted to groan with frustration, but it wouldn't do any good. The woman was just doing her job, and it was Maddy's bad luck to arrive when a guard she hadn't met was on shift. "Fine. But please hurry."

Thankfully, the warrior didn't have to. Dria rushed through the door and waved the guard off. "I sensed your gate activate. What's wrong? Fen didn't tell me you were coming by tonight."

"We weren't," Anna said, her hand wrapping around Maddy's. "Until we felt Fen in distress. Where is he?"

Dria cast a quick, meaningful look back at the guard. "The other room. Come on."

Even though Dria didn't appear to be upset, Maddy's anxiety cranked up at the vague answer as they followed the mage into the large room beyond the door. Maddy

slowed in surprise to see that a carpet lined the walkway between the natural stone columns. There was even a sitting area with chairs and a massive mirror over to the side. Hadn't this room been empty when they'd last visited?

But she didn't stop to ask. Instead, Maddy followed Dria and Anna out to the spiral staircase that connected the various floors of the cavern. Only when they descended a few levels and slipped into the more informal meeting room did Maddy lose patience.

"What's going on?"

Dria lifted her shoulders. "I have no idea. Vek and Fen left to create some kind of *Felshreh*-specific spell some time ago, but neither one has contacted me. As far as I know, everything is fine."

"Then why the secrecy up there?" Anna asked, gesturing toward the ceiling.

"Vek doesn't want anyone to know the details about his spell with Fen," Dria answered. "Seems kind of pointless since only a *Felshreh* can activate it, anyway, but you know how the Unseelie are."

Maddy tapped her toes inside her shoes. "We're Fen's mates. Surely, we're allowed to approach."

"I don't see why." Dria stared at her with an unflinching gaze. "I'm Vek's mate and the leader of the outpost, but I've been asked to stay clear, too."

Anna slipped her hand into Maddy's. "But something is wrong."

"Not to be rude," Dria began, "but are you certain? Vek would have called for me."

The door swung open, and the two men in question stumbled through, both surprisingly pale even for them. Fen froze, alarm filling his gaze, as Vek closed the door with a trembling hand. Anna let go of Maddy and rushed forward, reaching Fen's side before Maddy could react.

"What's going on?" Fen asked.

Maddy almost wanted to laugh. "You're asking us that?"

"We were going to meet at my house. Or our house now, maybe." Fen rubbed his knuckle against the bridge of his nose. "I'm too tired to figure it out."

"You were upset," Anna said as she slipped her arm around his waist.

Fen lowered his own arm over Anna's shoulders. "You felt that?"

Vek snickered. "They're your mates, idiot. I should have sent Dria a warning."

Maddy barely gave Vek a glance. She was too busy trying to get her legs to work, but her body felt frozen by the aftereffects of fear. What was wrong with her?

"I'm fine, loves," Fen said softly. "I had a panic attack, but it wasn't Vek's fault. Just the price of having shitty memories to relive."

The pain in his words gave Maddy the energy to move. Uncaring about her audience, she dashed across the space between her and her mates. Anna and Fen pulled her in, and they stood together, absorbing and sharing the pain until it settled into something dull and distant.

"I was afraid my text upset you," Anna said softly as they finally separated.

"What would have upset him?" Maddy asked, confused. Nothing bad had happened to her or Anna while they'd been parted. "He already said he didn't care which house we chose."

Anna blanched. "Oh, no. I was going to talk to you about it after we packed, but I got distracted by checking on Sparrow and then rushing here. I'm sorry."

"Hell," Fen muttered. "I haven't even seen the text, but I get the feeling we're going to want to sit down for this discussion."

Uneasiness curled through Maddy at the worried look on Anna's face. This wasn't going to be something simple. Would they ever find a semblance of normal?

With the spell completed and the euphoria of victory fading, Fen would have rather collapsed in his bed next door than have a discussion. Hell, he hadn't even noticed Maddy's and Anna's energies nearby, despite the worry radiating off of them. But he was aware of them now, and there was no way he could sleep without finding out what was wrong. Not with the thread of guilt he'd heard in Anna's voice. So once again, he found himself stretching out in one of the meeting room chairs when he would prefer to be in bed.

This time, though, Maddy sat on the arm of his seat and extended her wrist. "Take some of my blood before you pass out."

"You don't have to give me energy," Fen murmured.

Maddy rolled her eyes. "You obviously need it, and I don't care. It's not like you haven't bitten me before."

His body heated at the memory of the last time he'd tasted her blood. Hell. He couldn't look at her while he did this, or he would never get his dick under control. But he couldn't resist trailing his fingers gently down her arm before cradling her wrist in his hands. With a quick brush of magic, he cast the spell to numb her skin. Then he pressed the tip of his fang against her flesh until the slightest drop welled up for him to taste.

Sweet sunshine, just like Maddy. Fen smiled against her wrist as he drew in a little of her energy. Far from enough to replenish what he needed, but his exhaustion eased with the influx. Quickly, he sealed the tiny wound, but he twined his fingers with hers instead of letting her go. She tugged her hand free, only to slide into his lap so she wouldn't be uncomfortable on the arm of the chair.

Fen searched for Anna, half-hoping she would join the pile even though the chair wasn't large enough, but she smiled hesitantly at them from the seat to their left. What could she have texted him to have her so worried? He pulled his phone from his pocket as Vek and Dria sat in the other two chairs. Based on Vek's sudden strength, Dria must have been giving him some of hers.

Damn, he really was tired—he couldn't even summon the energy to make a joke at his uncle's expense.

Fen unlocked his phone and scrolled through his missed notifications until he found Anna's text. He read it once. Then a few more times. She couldn't be serious.

Use herself as bait? His first instinct was to tell her no, but she was his mate, not his kid. She would do what she decided was best.

"I'm not sure about this," he finally said.

The others gave him curious glances, since they hadn't seen the text, but Anna's nose wrinkled in reaction to his words. "I'm not either, but it makes sense."

"In a spy movie or suspense novel." Fen let Maddy snatch the phone from his hand to read the message for herself. "Does that happen in real life?"

Maddy's fingers tightened around his phone. "I don't think we should find out. Honestly, Anna, you've been writing too many mysteries lately. If this guy is Meren—"

"Meren?" Vek barked, leaning forward in his seat. Menace poured off of him like the void magic had earlier, raising the hair on Fen's arms even though the anger wasn't directed at him. "You have seen him?"

Anna didn't flinch as she met Vek's gaze. "A man approached me at work earlier and offered to tell me information about my bloodline if I met him at the park. He used some kind of spell on me to get me to cooperate, so I followed through. He introduced himself as Lord Rianehd. Rianehd...Orsah? Orsad? I can't remember exactly."

A curious blend of surprise and anger worked across Vek's face. "Orsed, I would wager. *The ancient line* or *ancient one* is what it would mean in the Seelie Sidhe tongue, and it was the given name of Queen Tatianella's father. Rianehd a Orsed, he said?"

"That's it," Anna said. "I'm fairly confident."

"Then Meren or not, we may have a problem." Vek tapped his fingers against the arm of his chair. "Someone willing to call himself 'The Unknown King of the Ancient Line' can't be good news, especially not if he's claiming to be the literal son of King Orsed."

Maddy shuddered, and Fen tightened his arm around her waist in reassurance. She was the only one of them with Seelie Sidhe blood, so she was most likely to be affected by turmoil in their court. Then again, Meren had some kind of plan for Fen, and the maybe-Meren stranger was toying with Anna. Who knew?

"I still can't believe I fell under his control," Anna whispered.

Vek flicked out a hand. "It can happen to anyone who doesn't know the proper shielding, and that skill can be learned. Why do you think he might be Meren?"

Anna shrugged. "He used water magic and claimed to be a Sidhe lord? It didn't occur to me at the restaurant because this guy's hair was short, and the person who attacked Fen in the river had very long hair. Apparently, lunch-rush me forgot the existence of scissors. And magic."

"I would wager on Meren," Fen said. Vek nodded, but beside him, Dria's brow was furrowed in thought. "It seems like too much of a coincidence that this stranger approached my mate not long after someone tried to drown me. After my mother's warning, it makes the most sense."

Dria stood, and the command that settled across her features warned Fen that he wouldn't like what she had to say. "Anna's idea of being bait has merit. If we observe the meeting, we'll be able to confirm if it's Meren."

Nope. He didn't like it at all. Especially because she was right.

She hadn't anticipated such quick agreement—if any.

Anna swallowed hard as a heavy silence descended in the wake of the mage's words. Fen's expression was both frustrated and thoughtful, much like his uncle's, but Maddy… Maddy leapt from Fen's lap so abruptly that he barely had time to move his arm, her furious gaze on Dria.

"If you think—"

Anna reached out and grabbed her mate's wrist, cutting off whatever she'd been about to say. "Stop, Maddy. Please don't argue."

Maddy stared at her. "You don't even know how to use your magic. You'd be helpless."

"Will any of us be safer just sitting around waiting for Meren's next move?"

A haunted look crossed Maddy's face, twisting Anna's heart. "I don't want to lose you. I might be a healer, but—"

"If we plan things well, I won't need healing. That's why this makes sense. We'll be able to control more of the variables." Anna nibbled at her lower lip. "Though I admit I didn't expect you to be the only one to argue."

As Maddy turned her frown on Fen, who hadn't jumped in with the protest Anna had assumed he would give, Anna glanced at Dria and then Vek. They were the most experienced out of their group, and Vek seemed familiar with the dynamics of the Seelie and Unseelie courts. Were they both in agreement about this plan?

"There is much risk in this," Vek said. "Neither Meren nor any other ancient Sidhe lord would fail to search the area before approaching Anna. I am fairly confident I can hide myself from detection, but can the rest of you say the same?"

Under other circumstances, Anna would have laughed at the look Dria gave him. "*Really*, Vek?"

"Not you, *ahmeeren*," Vek hastened to say. "I was attempting to be polite."

Dria's lips twitched. "Sure. Everyone knows that's a strength of yours."

"I hate to pass up an obvious joke." Fen straightened in his seat. "But it's a good point. Meren doesn't seem to have trouble finding me despite my shielding, and none of us know if he would recognize Maddy. If nothing else, it would be prudent to get Vek to take a look at our shields before we leave."

"I could screen us all," Dria said.

Part of Anna wanted to accept that offer, but it didn't feel right. The outpost had already been attacked by Meren once. What did they know about his plans? His target might not even be her or Fen. They couldn't afford to dismiss any possibility.

"Shouldn't you concentrate on keeping the outpost safe?" Anna asked. "None of us know for sure if Meren and Rianehd are the same person or if this is a trap of some kind. These guys could be working together to draw everyone away from the outpost."

"*Slelen*," Vek snarled. Anna didn't know the word, but his tone made it clear it wasn't a nice one. "That is true. Meren knows I would be able to detect him if his shielding drops, so it would be all too convenient if I were drawn away."

"There's also the Seelie emissary. You can't just disappear while he's here," Fen added, drawing a confused look from Maddy. "And if this is Meren, I highly doubt Vek will be able to resist killing him. We can bring him back alive."

Maddy shook her head. "One of my people is here?"

Dria's scowl might have been amusing if Anna hadn't been low-key terrified. "Queen Regent Lera discovered the outpost somehow and asked to send an emissary to help search for Meren. I don't know why, but she badly wants him returned to her court alive. You're right that Vek wouldn't be a good help with that goal."

"Letting my nephew and his young mates confront a Seelie Sidhe lord who claims he's a king is intolerable," Vek said, his expression as stony as the cave wall. "Despite the risk to the outpost, I'm not certain I can do it."

Fen rose, taking his place beside Maddy. "You won't be *letting* us do anything. I might not have learned all the Unseelie ways, but I have mastered my earth power. I haven't been a helpless child in a long time. Didn't you just promise to stop treating me like one? You know as well as I do that our reasoning is sound. Assure our shields are strong and help us come up with a plan while you guard the outpost."

Anna stood beside Maddy. *"What do you think, love?"*

Maddy looked startled at the unexpected mental communication, but it didn't take her long to answer. *"I hate this plan. Which means it's probably what we should do."*

Though Vek's continued anger had Anna smoothing imaginary wrinkles from her pants and trying not to shift nervously on her feet, she was determined to stand with her mates. Even Maddy was grudgingly on board. She would probably argue about every detail, but she would be with them all the way. Always.

Dria smiled at the show of unity, but it took Vek a few more moments to soften. Finally, though, he flicked his hands outward in a sharp gesture. "If you're determined to do this, then we might as well make sure you have the most solid plan possible. And not because I don't trust you. Strategy often benefits from multiple minds, so long as all are trustworthy and acting in accord."

Laughing, Fen returned to his seat. "You think we can pull off that last one?"

Vek smirked. "I suppose we'll have to do our best."

Not exactly reassuring. Anna had a feeling it was going to be a long night.

27

Perfect warmth enveloped Fen, and he nuzzled his cheek into the soft fall of Maddy's hair with a contented sigh. It had to be midmorning at least, but he didn't give a damn. Neither of his mates had to work today, so until they had to prepare for the coming confrontation, he was going to soak up every moment of joy he could. Especially since it had been the middle of the night before they returned from the outpost.

And spent who-knew-how-long making love after that.

Anna wiggled against his back, and Maddy shifted until she was lying more flat than on her side. Smiling, Fen stroked his hand down her torso, hoping to wake her in one of his favorite ways. But when his palm slid over her lower stomach, he froze. Vek's warning. After the blood gate spell and all the planning, he'd forgotten.

Fen shot upright in the bed, not considering the confused tangle of women he would leave behind. He barely heard Anna's surprised yelp beneath the sound of his heartbeat preparing to rupture his eardrums. Stupid, stupid, stupid to have forgotten, especially since they'd never discussed whether they wanted children.

"Fuck," he muttered.

Maddy chuckled. "That's not the tone of voice I'd expect for that kind of request."

"No, I didn't mean…"

Fen sighed. He might as well get it over with. If they were pissed, it would be best to find out now. They couldn't decide to *un*mate, so uncertainty and stress would make them all miserable.

He didn't have to look to know that it was Anna who rubbed a soothing hand between his shoulder blades, though her question confirmed it. "Did you have a bad dream?"

"No." He gathered his nerve and scooted around in the bed until he could look squarely at them both. Or maybe triangle-ly. Hell, he had to be losing his mind. "I remembered something Vek mentioned."

Shoving her long hair out of her face, Maddy sat up. "Spill it."

"It's…umm…" Dammit, he could already feel the flush creeping up his neck. "Birth control. Vek said the *Felshreh* tend to be fertile if we don't take precautions. I meant to bring it up, but by the time we got back…"

Maddy chuckled. "Calm down, Fen. I've had an IUD for years. I thought about having it removed when Anna and I became exclusive, but I haven't gotten around to it."

"And I'm on hormonal birth control for my cycles," Anna said, her smile soft. "We should be good."

Relief knocked the tension from his muscles in a rush. "Thank any gods listening."

Anna's eyebrows twisted together. "Are you against having children? I guess that's something we should have talked about."

"Not in general." Fen rubbed at his temples. "But I'd like to get my life in order a little better first. Not to mention all three of us learning to be a solid unit."

"We're kind of in the same place," Maddy said. "We'd thought that in five or ten years, we would find a donor and have Anna carry our first child since her lifespan and mine… Well, now we have no idea how long she might live, so I guess we can all reevaluate that when the time is right."

The gleam in Anna's eyes warned him, but his cheeks still burned hotter at her words. "At least we don't have to hunt for a sperm donor anymore."

Both women burst out laughing, and he didn't blame them. No doubt his expression was priceless. Fen could throw out innuendo all day when it wasn't related to him—or near to his heart. But this kind of openness had his instincts screaming danger, even when it didn't make sense. The three of them, they belonged to each other now. How long would it take his instincts to adapt?

"Ah, sorry, Fen," Anna said. "We didn't mean to make you uncomfortable."

Maddy tugged at his hand, and he let himself be drawn forward until he was settled between them. "I know."

Anna and Maddy snuggled up against him, their hands twining across his stomach. Fen took a deep breath and released it, along with the awkward insecurity that had filled him. They were going to be fine. Once they solved their current dilemma with Meren and/or Rianehd, Maddy, Anna, and he would settle into their new life.

Maybe in a few decades, he would believe he deserved it.

They only had one stop to make before heading to the park, and Maddy was dreading it. Although she wanted to delay telling her parents about her new bond, she needed to talk to her father about this Rianehd guy before Anna went to meet him. Not only that, really. She had to ask her mother if she had more information about Anna's heritage—or any other fae.

As they walked up the sidewalk to her parents' front door, Maddy frowned up at the sky. Dark clouds were piling up to the northwest, a sure sign that it would rain within a couple of hours. Would all their planning be for nothing? If a thunderstorm chased off Lord Rianehd after all of this, she might sit down and cry.

Okay, probably not. But still.

Maddy didn't bother to knock, though she had to pause to let Fen and Anna through her father's shielding. It wouldn't exactly hurt them since they didn't have ill-intent, but it was designed to make any uninvited fae feel really damned uncomfortable, like the magical equivalent of an appliance buzzing and whining constantly. Her father didn't have many true friends among his own kind anymore, and he didn't want any acquaintances to hang around bothering her mother.

"Back here," her dad called as soon as they'd stepped into the entryway and closed the door behind them.

Following his voice and energy signature, Maddy led her mates through the rarely used formal dining room and into the den beyond. Instantly, her shoulders relaxed and her nerves eased as the light cinnamon scent of her mom's favorite candles wrapped around her. In the back corner, her dad sat at the large U-shaped workstation that had been there as long as she could remember. He'd once considered building an outside workshop, but he'd ultimately decided that he didn't want to be separate from his family when inspiration struck.

Maddy smiled to see him bent over his desk-mounted magnifying glass, engraving a gold ring with magic and one of the *peresten* tools he'd commissioned from Moranaia countless years before she was born. In fact, all of his tools were made with the same metal since he couldn't work with steel. No wonder Moranaian was one of the languages he'd thought to spell-gift her as a teenager.

But Maddy's smile dropped when she scanned the rest of the room. The couch and recliners were empty, and the comfy reading chair in front of the tall back windows was also unoccupied. "Where's Mom?"

"Finishing up some bookkeeping in the office," her father answered absently. "Thought you'd be a few more minutes."

That made enough sense that a little of Maddy's dread eased. Her mom was an accountant—it was how she'd met Shayan, in fact—and had handled the jewelry shop's books for basically forever. Most fae assumed that Shayan had left the Seelie court to be with Angela, but the truth was funnier. He'd decided to leave court life behind on his own but had almost gotten in trouble for tax evasion after cluelessly opening a jewelry store without understanding the laws. Her mom had saved his ass with a well-timed lesson on human finances, and then they had fallen in love.

Maddy and Anna sat on the couch, but Fen wandered over to her father's workbench, stopping a few feet away. She should have considered that Fen would be interested, since he harvested gemstones from the earth when possible. Maybe he would take up jewelry making with her dad, who'd been a little bummed when Maddy showed no interest. But she hadn't inherited any metal or gemstone shaping abilities from him, and she'd never wanted to try the wide variety of human methods.

Her dad chuckled. "It would bother me less if you directly observed, Fen. No need to hover over there in the corner of my vision."

Fen didn't need a second invitation. Happiness filled Maddy at the sight of her mate standing beside her father, both of them intent on the tiny piece of metal Shayan worked on with a low hum of magic. Contentment practically infused the room, so fully that Anna rested her head against Maddy's shoulder and closed her eyes.

Maddy would die if she lost any of this—any of them. At that thought, she had to force herself not to stiffen and alert Anna. She breathed in deeply and held her emotions close. So close to her core that maybe her mates wouldn't be able to sense her sudden dread. What if their confrontation went terribly wrong? She'd struggled to use her healing gift even under Lial's guidance. She could kill one of her own mates out of ignorance if they were injured.

Before her brain could run too far down that awful path, her mother walked through the door beside her father's worktable. Angela froze at the sight of Fen standing by her husband, but when she saw Anna leaning against Maddy, her mouth dropped open. Maddy's stomach plummeted. Her father hadn't warned her mom that they were coming.

"Shayan," Angela snapped.

He didn't even look away from his work. "Forgive me, beloved. Did I forget to mention we were having guests? Fascinating what can slip one's mind."

Ohhh boy. This must be one of their rare true arguments. Her father was fairly easy-going, so everyday quarrels passed quickly between her parents. But when they had large disagreements, Maddy got a glimpse of what her father must have been like in the Seelie court—reserved, chill, and scrupulously polite. Chances were good he was still upset that her mother hadn't told him about her knowledge of the Gwragedd Annwn.

Her mom averted her gaze. "You aren't usually cruel when you're angry."

Great. She found a visit from them hurtful. Maddy eased Anna off her shoulder and stood. "We should go."

"No." Her father glanced up. "Please don't. Your mother meant no slight. I *did* know she was worried about speaking to you, and I failed to give her warning on purpose. But no cruelty was intended."

"I've been nervous about this for months," Angela bit out. "Maybe years."

Shayan made one last change to the ring he held and then set it down beside two others on a lined tray. Maddy frowned at him. Why was he working in the middle of an argument? It really wasn't like him. But he took care to put his tools in their box, fold the mounted magnifying glass back into its neutral position, and flick off the bright lamp that illuminated his work before he stood and faced her mother. Poor Fen was stuck awkwardly beside him, probably unwilling to cut between him and Angela to escape.

"You might have been less so had you told me of your family's encounter with the Gwragedd Annwn," her father said. "They are an honorable people but not perfect, as some of the myths well attest."

Anna jerked to her feet. "Do you know them?" she blurted. Then she slapped her palm across her mouth at the interruption. "Sorry."

Maddy couldn't help but smile at the muffled apology coming from behind her mate's hand. "Don't be sorry. This discussion should have happened ages ago."

Even her mother nodded at that. "It should have. I swore I wouldn't talk about it, but it's a silly secret to keep from you. I haven't spoken to my cousin for twenty years, and he didn't believe the stories even though the Gwragedd Annwn woman was his own mother. She obviously didn't care about him since she left."

"That's not necessarily true, beloved." Shayan crossed the space separating him from Angela and took her hands in his. "The Gwragedd Annwn rarely enter relationships with humans, but when they do, they are required by their king to demand certain conditions. If those terms are broken, they must leave, whether they want to or not."

Her mom's lips pursed. "Yeah, yeah. I've read the myths. The guy strikes her three times, even accidentally, and she returns to her lake home. My uncle swore he never hit his wife."

"We can't know the agreements made between them. I doubt he told the rest of the family everything, even if he was wholly innocent." Shayan smiled over at Maddy and Anna. "And yes, I have met a few of the Gwragedd Annwn, though none are close friends. There used to be a small colony in Nickajack Lake. They moved in after the dam was built, but I'm not sure they stayed."

Anna rocked up and down on her feet like she was preparing to race off. "Would it be safe for me to check it out?"

"I imagine so," Shayan answered. "Doubly so with your mates with you. The Gwragedd Annwn are a peaceful people, known to be hospitable when they allow themselves to be seen."

Maddy tried to process the conversation between her parents, but she couldn't make sense of it. Based on what her mates had told her about their other encounter with her mother, she'd gathered that Angela's uncle had married one of the Gwragedd Annwn and something bad had happened. Something about her cousin almost drowning? But it made no sense that her mother had knowingly married a Sidhe man without saying a word about her family's history.

"There are lots of unpleasant stories about the Sidhe, but you still married Dad," Maddy pointed out. "Why didn't you assume the worst about him, too? Are you waiting for him to turn into a mythological bad guy?"

Shayan froze, and Maddy could tell from his expression that he dearly wanted to know the answer, too. Her mother winced. For a moment, it looked like she wasn't going to reply, and Maddy had a real worry that her parents might have their first major problem—the kind that ended relationships.

"It wasn't a human who saved my cousin from drowning," Angela said softly, pulling her hands from Shayan's to rub her arms. "I was only five, but I still remember the gleam of his long red hair and the point of his ears poking out from the soaked strands. He smiled at me as he lowered my gasping cousin to the shore, bowed low, and walked away. Just disappeared between a couple of trees. The Gwragedd Annwn didn't seem to have pointy ears, and he didn't disappear into the water. I suspected he wasn't one of them. Then my parents moved us to America and insisted I not mention my uncle's 'fanciful' stories. The memory of the rescue faded."

Shayan's lips parted. "Angela—"

"I thought you looked familiar when you entered my office." Her mother's smile was wry. "But I didn't make the connection until we were already engaged. I'm still not sure I'm right. Maybe I was afraid to confirm it, and I had promised my family not to talk about what had happened. What if the reminder of the event chased you away? The Gwragedd Annwn leave. I didn't want to risk the Sidhe being the same."

Tears prickled Maddy's eyes as her father pulled her mother close. "I would never leave you," he said, the words nearly muffled against Angela's hair.

"I know that now," Angela said. "I'm sorry I was afraid."

When her parents parted from their embrace, their usual ease had returned. Maddy let out a relieved sigh. Their love had been such a constant in her life that she'd never really considered it being shaken. They shared such a deep bond. Apparently a longer-lasting one than she'd known.

Angela's gaze darted between Fen and Anna before settling on Maddy. Her mother gave her a hesitant smile. "So. You're in a relationship with two people?"

Maddy stiffened out of reflex. "We've mated in the way of Fen's people."

Bracing herself for disapproval, Maddy pushed her shoulders back and kept her eyes trained on her mother's. No matter what she'd learned about her mother's past, it was tough to imagine Angela ever being okay with this.

"Oh, Maddy," her mother began, her sad tone making Maddy's hands clench, "I've done a poor job with you lately. I haven't handled things well at all."

"What, me being bisexual?"

Angela shook her head emphatically. "No, not that. I admit I had a slight preference toward you marrying a man, but only because I'd be more likely to have grandchildren. And the discrimination is awful when you're dating your own gender. The whispers and looks. The lost jobs and uncertain housing. The threat of getting disowned by your family. It's a little better than it was when I was your age, but...well, a mother worries. I'm sorry."

Maddy blinked at those words. Getting disowned? She might have been upset at her mother's strange behavior, but Maddy had never believed it would go that far. Then she noticed her mother's downcast eyes and the way she nibbled on her lower lip, a sure sign she was uncertain about something. Shayan rubbed his hand across her mother's back as though to offer comfort.

Finally, it clicked, and Maddy gasped. "You had a girlfriend?"

"A couple of years before I met your father. It was the family scandal at the time."

"I…" Maddy honestly didn't know what to say to that. A quick glance at her father showed him to be unsurprised, at least, so this wasn't a complete secret. Still. "Why didn't you tell me?"

Her mother grimaced. "I thought it was better for you to decide for yourself without thinking you had to be like me."

"That doesn't make sense." Maddy shook her head. "If you're bi, then you know it's not something influenced by the power of suggestion. It just…is. Unless you randomly decided to date a girl even though you weren't attracted?"

"Absolutely not!" Her mother flushed. "There were a lot of changes in the sixties, but my parents weren't exactly on board. To say they weren't supportive is an understatement. I learned to repress a lot of things from them. They never knew the truth about Shayan being Sidhe, either. They mocked my uncle enough for me to know better than that."

Maddy stared at her mom as this new revelation sank in. Sometimes, she forgot that her mother was older than she appeared, her lifespan extended by a fruit the Seelie queen had granted Shayan. But that didn't make the last year or so any less difficult. As soon as she'd gotten serious with Anna, her mother had started acting strange. Pointed Maddy-only invites to family events. Suggestions of men she could date. It had seemed so out-of-character, and apparently, it was. More so than Maddy would have guessed.

"Discriminating against Anna because she might be one of the water fae isn't any better than treating us badly because we're bi," Maddy said.

Angela's shoulders slumped. "I know. I was wrong, but I can learn to be better."

"I need time to think about this, Mom," she said. "I'm not exactly mad. I just…I don't know what I am."

"I understand." Her mother's focus shifted to Anna. "And I owe you an apology, Anna. If I hadn't held on so tightly to the past, I could have given you a chance from the beginning. I hope you'll forgive me."

Naturally, Anna smiled. Because that was who she was. "Of course."

Such an odd conversation. It certainly wasn't what Maddy had expected—nor was the sly look gathering on her father's face. Damn, she hoped he didn't have some big secret to impart. She was so not on board for another revelation.

Fen couldn't concentrate on the awkward-as-hell conversation, even though he really, really should have. Instead, he kept getting distracted by the rings set in a careful row in the small tray on Shayan's desk. They were spectacular works of artistry, resonant with energy, and he practically vibrated with the desire to see their creation from start to finish. Even observing the fine detail work around the edges of one ring had been an amazing experience.

"I'm glad to see your approval," Shayan said.

Fen glanced up to see that the other man had returned to his previous place beside the workbench, his wife looking on in confusion. Maddy and Anna appeared equally baffled, and Fen wished then that he'd been paying attention. Had Shayan said something upsetting before leaving his wife's side? He could have announced his imminent departure for the Seelie realm for all Fen knew.

"It's amazing work," he finally replied. "I taught myself to harvest and refine stones, but I'm not sure if I could work with gold like that. Is it a form of earth magic?"

Shayan nodded. "It is. Perhaps when your current troubles have been overcome, we can see if you possess the talent. I would be happy to help, though I must warn you that the offer isn't entirely altruistic. I could use some new creations to sell at the shop, and having someone who can assist with jewelry repair would be a fine thing, indeed."

Taken aback, Fen could only stare at the other man. He'd never had a near-stranger offer him an honest job like that. As though he was someone worthwhile to hire. Even if he didn't possess the talent, the trust was blessing enough. "Thank you. I would be happy to consider it."

"Good." Shayan gathered the rings into his palm and smiled down at them. "You sense the energy I imbued in these, so there's hope for you. Follow me."

Fen lifted a brow, but when the Sidhe man headed toward Maddy and Anna, he followed. Shayan stopped across from Maddy and Anna, so Fen ranged himself at Maddy's right. He had a feeling those rings were intended for them—a suspicion confirmed by Shayan's smile as he extended his palm in front of Maddy.

Light sparked around the rings, and energy swirled around them. Then the glow settled, and Shayan handed each of them one of the bands. Though Fen had watched the other man engrave the last few tiny leaves that circled the top and bottom edges of the band, he hadn't paid much attention to the stones settled smoothly around the entire perimeter.

The design was impossible.

Fen spun the ring in his fingers, counting the stones. Eleven. Fluorite, bloodstone, aquamarine, pearl, amethyst, citrine, emerald, kyanite, lapis, clear quartz, and rose quartz—each blended smoothly into the other until they could have been one piece. It was so well-done that he couldn't feel a single bump, and he detected no bonding agent or glass when he scanned it with his magic.

"How did you...?"

"A technique I've honed over the centuries." Shayan grinned. "And one I never use on the jewelry I sell in the shop. It takes a great deal of time, so these are quite rare. I'd already started Maddy's and Anna's when Maddy told me about meeting you, Fen. I was afraid I wouldn't get the third finished."

"That was a couple of months ago, and you hadn't even met Fen." Maddy held hers up for a closer look. "Yet there's something for each of us in the stones you chose. Thank you, *Adai*."

The way her voice caught on the Seelie word for "Dad" had Fen's throat clogging with emotion. Damn, but he couldn't help but envy her a little for her obvious

connection to her parents, even the mother she disagreed with. There was no question that they were close in a way he would never manage.

But as he met her eyes and then Anna's, love and belonging shot between them, and past hurts faded into the background. They would create their own close family, and someday, when they were ready, they would show their own children this kind of love. He would see to it.

Together, they slipped on their rings, and Fen's chest tightened at the perfection of it. A subtle hum vibrated along his skin and seeped into his shields, clarifying his link to the other women and reinforcing it. Their bond had already been solidifying this way without the rings, but the sudden focus of it was glorious.

"Will the effect remain if we take off our rings?" Fen asked.

"Of course," Shayan said. "My enchantments didn't create your link. They only helped steady it. Oh, and there is also a spell to heighten psychic powers and ease communication through shielding."

Frowning down at her finger, Anna shook her head. "How did you get our sizes right? You barely know me and Fen."

Shayan shrugged. "Magic."

Fen chuckled at the consternation on Anna's face. "I think he means that literally, not as an evasion."

She blushed, her smile wry as she glanced at Shayan. "Sorry. I'm still not used to thinking about magic as a real thing. I barely know anything about my own powers, but if I can find that colony you were talking about, maybe they can teach me."

"They might provide clarity and explanations, but water is as much emotion and instinct as anything," Shayan said. "Or so I've heard."

Before Anna could ask the question Fen could see building in her furrowed brow, Angela approached, her steps slow and hesitant. He hoped she wasn't about to cause Maddy more grief, because cussing out one of his new in-laws wouldn't be a good way to start their relationship. Not because he couldn't sympathize with some of her faulty reasoning—gods knew he has his own—but because he couldn't bear to see Maddy hurt.

Fortunately, she gave a tenuous smile and held out her hand. "Could I see the rings?"

Maddy only hesitated for a moment, but as soon as she extended her hand, Fen and Anna followed suit. Angela examined them each in turn. By the time she got to Anna's, she was sniffling, tears running down her cheeks. Suddenly, she pulled Maddy into a blubbering hug that made Fen both uncomfortable and happy.

"We should have an actual wedding," Angela said, her voice muffled against Maddy's shoulder.

Despite the tears Fen could see in Maddy's eyes, she chuckled. "Well, that would be a disaster. A guest list full of Seelie, Unseelie, and humans? And hey, if Anna finds some relatives, we might be able to throw some Welsh water fae in the mix. What could possibly go wrong?"

Angela pulled back to frown at Maddy. "We'll only invite people who can behave."

Fen had his doubts about the feasibility of that, but it would make for a much smaller crowd. Like, what, two people? But poor Angela didn't know that Fen's mother was the queen of the Unseelie or that Maddy's Seelie relatives would probably rather eat iron than inhabit the same space as Unseelie royalty. The inevitable battle would traumatize any human family for generations. But who was he to point that out to an excited mother?

He might be many things, but an idiot wasn't one of them—usually.

28

Rain plopped halfheartedly against Anna's umbrella as she marched down the sidewalk, doing her best not to check over her shoulder for the car. They hadn't wanted to arrive together in case Rianehd was watching, but Maddy and Fen had parked close enough to keep an eye on her as she walked toward the park. As soon as she reached the gates, they would seek their own positions.

This was such a terrible idea. When they'd told Shayan about the man who called himself Rianehd a Orsed, his face had taken on such an expression of deadly fury that Anna had been ready to flee. *A rumor,* Shayan had said, *that started during an attempted coup millennia ago when the old king died and Queen Tatianella ascended the throne. No one ever stepped forward claiming the title, but the rumor almost tore the Seelie court apart.*

Whether this was the person behind the original lie or an opportunist who knew the story, it was certain that he wouldn't be a random passerby who decided to help Anna out of pure altruism. According to Vek, this was exactly the kind of thing Meren would do in order to gain the power he desired, but any random fae asshole could have decided to do the same thing. It wasn't likely, but it wasn't impossible, either.

Twilight was slipping steadily to night, and that along with the rain left the park completely empty. Her Sidhe "friend" wasn't sitting on the bench where they'd originally met, but she hadn't expected him to be. Not until full night. Whatever his intentions, she didn't think he would want witnesses to this conversation.

What would he do when she rejected his offer? That was the biggest risk to this reconnaissance mission. He might disappear as he'd promised during their last meeting, or he might try to force her cooperation. The second possibility was why Fen and Maddy guarded her from the sidelines. All they had to do was distract the Sidhe lord long enough for Anna to get away, and then all three of them could escape and report back to the outpost.

That was the goal, anyway.

Anna stared down at the wet metal bench and sighed. If she had a clue what she was doing, it could be dry in seconds. Though maybe she could push the rain aside the way she'd shoved the river water from their phone and clothes. It wouldn't create a rain-free forcefield or anything, but her umbrella was good enough at that. A dry ass was better than nothing.

After a quick look around to make sure she was still alone, Anna extended her hand, palm down. Her arm trembled as she held the umbrella over the bench, preventing more rain from landing as she worked, but it wasn't from the weight. Nerves assailed her until she took a steadying breath. If emotions were key, then she had to calm them.

Finally, she felt ready. Anna let her draw to the water rush through her and shivered at the force, so strong beside the river with the rain pouring down. But she could resist. With a surge of her will, she shoved at the puddles until they rolled like tiny waves off the bench. Then she sank down on the dry metal and slumped in relief as she stifled the water's lure once more.

How awful was she at this that clearing a place to sit was a big production?

It was in that moment of doubt that he arrived, of course. One moment, the path was clear, and the next, the tall regal Sidhe man appeared. Had she even blinked? Maybe he could transport himself, too. She wouldn't take it for granted that he couldn't, so it was best to make mental note of the possibility.

With a wave of his hand, the other side of the bench cleared of water. He held no umbrella, but the rain didn't dare to mar a single strand of his hair or blotch the fine fabric of his clothes. This time, he wore what had to be Sidhe finery, his tunic embroidered with silver thread and even jewels. No pretending to be from Earth today. That had her heart slamming in her chest as much as his casual use of power.

"You made a nice showing of it," Lord Rianehd said, an indulgent tone to his voice like a teacher speaking to a small child. "But you have much to learn before you would even count as a novice in my court."

Anna forced herself to smile. "And here I thought the Sidhe were masters of flattery."

"Would it work on you?" He chuckled. "No, I can see from your expression that it would not. Let us cease these games. Will you accept my tutelage or did you foolishly decide to refuse?"

His voice was cool and unyielding, any hint of charm gone. Were Maddy and Fen in place, or had Rianehd arrived too quickly? Time to stall. He didn't look prepared to give up when she said no.

"What are the terms?" she asked.

Lord Rianehd's eyebrow rose. "So you agree?"

"I won't agree to anything unless I've heard all of the terms and find them acceptable." She hadn't thought it possible, but his face hardened even more. "I might be partly human, but I know better than that."

He stared at her coldly, his gaze so intense that she couldn't help but shiver. Then her ring warmed against her finger, and Lord Rianehd twitched as though someone had smacked him. It wasn't a coincidence—his focus went instantly to her ring. Rage broke through the chill of his demeanor as he leapt to his feet.

"What is this?" he demanded. "Do you seek to betray me with one of the Cairdai bloodline?"

It took Anna a moment to guess what he could be talking about. Maddy's last name was Carden, so maybe Cairdai was Shayan's Sidhe name? They sounded similar enough. "I'm afraid I don't know what you mean."

Lord Rianehd gestured at her hand. "Don't bother to lie. Such an artifact is not granted unless one is in high standing with that clan, and I know you didn't have it yesterday. My magic would not have worked otherwise. Which one of them gave you the ring?"

My magic would not have worked otherwise...

Her stomach squeezed until she thought she would throw up. That confirmed that he had cast some kind of glamour on her, and he had probably just attempted to do so again. "How do you know I didn't buy it in some store?"

"Because most humans don't possess the wealth of a small nation," he snapped. "I know of very few outside of fae royalty who could afford that kind of craftmanship."

Oh, hell. Couldn't Shayan have warned her about this? Of course, he might have done so if they'd told him they were going to confront Rianehd. He probably hadn't thought that anyone she knew would recognize his work. Now what?

"It was a gift from my new wife," Anna said, trying to think fast. "I'm not sure where she got it, and I wouldn't tell you if I did. I mean, it really isn't any of your business. I'm not quizzing you about the source of the jewels on your tunic."

His eyes narrowed. "If you are betraying me, I would say it is my business. I am displeased that you returned here with ill-intent."

"I didn't." Which was strictly true. Trying to figure out if Rianehd was the same guy who'd tried to kill her new mate was hardly that. "The timing is pure coincidence."

"Then you decided to accept my offer?"

How quickly would he kill her if she punched him in the face? Because he was clearly trying to evade her question about terms at this point, and she was sick of it. "I have yet to hear your conditions."

The rain plopped harder against her umbrella. Was it a natural phenomenon or something magical? The Sidhe lord didn't appear any angrier, but looks could be deceiving. "You are clever for a human. What conditions would you accept?"

Hah. There was a fine trick. Ask her a leading question and see how much freedom she would unknowingly give away. Anna pretended to consider the matter, but really, there was only one answer. A fact made all too clear when Fen's voice slipped into her mind.

"It's Meren," Fen said. *"He hacked off his hair, but it's definitely him. Try to get away without a fuss. I'm in the parking lot, and Maddy is hiding in the stand of trees on the other side of the park."*

Maybe if she puked on the guy it would scare him away? Considering how her stomach felt right now, it was a real possibility. As Anna stood, she had to force herself not to wipe her damp palms against her pants. "I'm afraid there aren't any. I had my doubts, and this conversation has confirmed them. I will not work with you. I'm not going to change my mind, so there's no need to contact me again."

A sudden sheet of rain slashed down, cutting beneath her umbrella with sharp little slices that stung her exposed skin. "You have made a poor decision," Meren said, his soft voice somehow reaching her through the driving rain.

Yep. She was going to die.

Fucking hell. Why had they thought they could do this? Fen did his best to stay in the shadows between streetlights as he dashed from behind the cover of the cars. Rain poured down in furious waves, almost knocking him off of his feet a couple of times. Unnatural, just like the asshole hovering over Anna with murder in his gaze.

Meren knocked the umbrella out of Anna's hand and grabbed her arm, and suddenly, Fen didn't give a damn who saw the coming battle. With a surge of power, he parted the ground beneath Meren's feet and smiled as the bastard toppled in. Meren caught himself on the edge, of course, but seeing him struggling to lift himself out of the hole was its own satisfaction.

With a yelp, Anna leaped back and glanced over her shoulder at Fen. *"What are you doing?"*

"Hopefully ripping Meren's throat out."

She shook her head in denial. *"No, Fen. I know you don't want to kill. Besides, we're not here to fight. We're supposed to get away unless we have a clear shot at capturing him."*

Fen didn't want to be a killer, but he couldn't stand the thought of Meren hurting one of his mates. Apparently, he would be no better than Vek at bringing the bastard in alive. *"We'll see."*

Though he was soaked to the skin from the driving rain and exhausted from using so much of his precious energy stores to open the earth, Fen ran the rest of the distance to Anna before Meren levered himself from the hole. *Too bad I didn't take more energy from Maddy. I could've crushed the bastard.* A foolish oversight to let himself be so distracted by his new mates to properly feed, but there wasn't anything he could do about it now.

As Fen skidded to a halt beside Anna, Meren finished freeing himself, shifting to stand beside the hole as if it didn't exist.

"Why, Tom," Meren began smoothly, the anger on his face dissipating like sugar in water—though his was an artificial sweetener. "A pleasure to truly meet you. We've just missed each other so many times, you know. You were leaving on an errand the one day I visited Kien's enclave."

The world slowed around him, muddling Meren's words and blurring the raindrops easing their way toward the ground. That voice. That. Fucking. Voice.

See what you've done?

You deserve to live, Fen.

Take what you need. I'll help you.

Perhaps upheaval is necessary for life.

"You," Fen growled, seeing nothing in that moment but Meren's smirking face. "How long have you been manipulating me?"

"I can't imagine what you mean, Tom."

Fen's fingernails dug into his palm. "Enough bullshit. You know that isn't my name. You've been messing with me my whole life."

"Perhaps." Meren's smirk widened, but he made no other movement. "I sensed the surge of energy when you murdered your father, but humans arrived before I could decide what to do with you. Haul you back to your mother or train you to do my bidding? Both would have had advantages. You really do have a habit of attacking people, hmm? I hope poor Anna here is aware that you're a killer."

Rage almost blinded Fen, but shame nearly felled him. How could he refute that truth? There was no telling how many people his stupidity had harmed. And hadn't he killed to defend his uncle just a couple of weeks ago? "I could add you to my tally."

Meren laughed. "I highly doubt it, whelp. I am far more ancient and powerful than Kien was."

If doubts hadn't been circling in Fen's head, he might have laughed, too. Nothing like a metaphysical dick-measuring contest with a dead man to round out the evening's confrontation. "Let me guess. He was working for you, and you were the mastermind."

"Hardly." Meren flicked his fingers. "He was too evil to trust, though I admit I didn't mind using his darkness to my advantage. His goal might have been to return to Moranaia for revenge, but his methods aligned with my objectives. Like keeping you where I could find you."

Fen shook his head. "Why?"

"A talented *Felshreh* abandoned by his people? You're powerful and ruthless, a definite asset to any group," Meren said. "We would work well together. We're both willing to do whatever it takes to be granted our rightful place. All we must do is return our peoples to prominence on Earth. Imagine the kind of world we could establish now that magic has returned."

Fen's stomach flipped. Hadn't Kien once made a similar claim? Sure, Kien's offer might have included a little more "rule over humans and get revenge on the fae" than Meren's, but the heart of it was the same. This bullshit wouldn't end any better this time.

"I'm not the ruthless killer you think I am," Fen bit out.

"Really?" Meren chuckled. "You were planning to kill me for talking to your girlfriend, weren't you?"

Gods, he had been. His heart pinched to remember Anna's plea and his casual dismissal of it. Meren hadn't actually hurt her, his threat implied but not delivered.

And even though this encounter had obviously been designed to bring Fen out into the open, Meren hadn't done anything but talk. Fen had been the aggressor.

Maybe he hadn't changed as much as he thought.

Anna's mind brushed against his. *"Fen. Don't let him mess with your head."*

Her words steadied him until he could focus, and for the first time since that voice had scratched his mind, the world around Fen resumed its normal pace. The rain slammed against his back, and Anna's hand gripped his. When had she reached for him? He'd been so lost to his own turmoil that he hadn't noticed.

Fen's sharp gaze caught a flash of red—a color his kind could detect in the darkest night—several feet behind Meren, and it was all he could do not to react. Maddy was approaching. He almost wished he could slip back into a daze to avoid his rising fear.

"And you claim you want me as an ally?" Fen forced a mocking smile to his lips. "Pulling me toward the bottom of the river was an interesting invitation. Not to mention trying to kill my uncle. Bad form."

"I merely intended to take you to my home for a private word," Meren said, his pleasant tone growing strained. "And you truly wish to defend the uncle who forgot about you for so many years? Perhaps if he had been there, you wouldn't have killed your father. An accident on your part, I'm sure."

What was Meren's game? If he'd truly wanted Fen to cooperate with him, he would have made more of an effort over the years. But in every memory Fen had of that voice, it had been trying to misdirect him. Maybe even concerning his father's death? It had certainly done him a disservice at his most stable foster home.

Now Meren was trying to coax Fen to join his wicked crew like the villain in a movie, preying on the doubts he'd helped to embed in Fen's mind. Suddenly, Meren's probable intent began to take shape. Pervert to his side an Unseelie princess's child—who also happened to be the only heir Ara or Vek had produced—and either weaken the Unseelie throne or exert influence on it.

He didn't want to eliminate Fen. He wanted to use him.

"You killed my father," Fen said flatly.

Hell, he sounded like characters in at least three movies he could think of off the top of his head, but it didn't make the claim ring any less true. Nor did the pleased expression that crossed Meren's face.

"Clever lad," Meren said. "Though *I* didn't do it. I prefer not to touch human blood if I can avoid it."

Rage clouded Fen's mind until he shook with it. Deep inside, he'd always blamed himself. Murderer. Wretch. Unworthy. It might not have formed his earliest foundation, but those bricks had been placed right on top of that groundwork to create the crumbling base of his fucked-up wall. And not a damned bit of it had been his fault.

Only Anna's hand kept him tethered to the sidewalk. To reality. Beneath them, the earth trembled in a low hum, an unending cry of Fen's pain. "I will find a way to make you pay," Fen said.

"Go ahead and try." Meren stretched his arms wide. "Water always wins over earth in the end. Your inexperience makes the possibility of your victory laughable."

The ground shook harder, and Fen did his best to tamp his power down. He wouldn't wreck the town. Meren wasn't worth it.

Behind the Seelie bastard, Maddy eased closer. She was as pale as a full-blooded *Felshreh*, and her hand shook around the hilt of the knife she'd brought for self-protection. Still, she advanced. Fen had to do something before she got close enough for Meren to sense. She'd hurt others in defense of herself before, but she was a healer at heart. It would crush her if she ended up killing Meren.

Fen would far rather take this blow—if he had the chance.

29

Emotion clogged Anna's throat and fired in her blood, dangerous and heady. The pelting rain no longer stung her skin—now, it invigorated. Meren couldn't wield her own element against her, not in this moment. He'd hurt her mate. Running from this encounter wasn't an option now. He was a hurricane beyond the bounds of nature's control, and that was an abomination she couldn't stand.

She told herself to let go of Fen's hand before she let the water in, but she couldn't. Without her to anchor him against the force of her power, he might go adrift. But what about Maddy? Anna met her gaze and found solid resolve. Maddy wouldn't be set off course. Whatever Anna's instincts led her to do, Maddy would stand firm.

Anna lifted her right hand and allowed the water to crash through her. She pulled it in, ruthless. The center of a new hurricane. Around them, the rain suspended its fall, hovering in the air as though it had been frozen. Meren's eyes widening, he raised his own hand to pull at the water, but she kept it in her grip.

Flecks of dirt and rock lifted into the air as her power blended with Fen's. Anna made no effort to stop it. Let Fen do what he would with his element—she had faith he would control it. Or she did until the mass of water and earth swirled into a condensed ball in her hand, leaving the air so dry it could have been a desert.

"What are you doing, girl?" Meren cried.

She couldn't have answered even if she'd wanted to.

Her palm chilled as the water-and-earth mixture compressed in her hand, but the air around her began to grow hotter, evaporating the rain in an ever-widening ring around them. Then that moisture was sucked in, too.

Oh, God. She was going to lose command of this.

With a cry, Fen let go of her other hand. The ball began to harden into ice, and her ears popped from the increased pressure. Anna shoved her left palm over the top of the bundle, but instead of containing the spell, it concentrated it. A few feet away, the river began to roll like the ocean toward the bank, seeking her call.

Meren's shout was stark with fear. "You have to stop. Now. You're going to kill us all."

In that moment, she no longer gave a damn what any of them had done. Meren was right. Unfortunately, he didn't offer any helpful suggestions to solve the problem. Should she try to unwind it? Would that discharge the water in some kind of deadly explosion, complete with rocky shrapnel?

Direct and release.

The voice rang in her head with the authority of lightning, impossible to deny. Anna could only spare a warning look for Maddy before she released the bundle toward Meren under the direction of that implacable voice. The icy ball blasted across the space, striking the Sidhe mage in the stomach and tossing him backward even as the force knocked Anna flat.

Her head cracked against the sidewalk, and her vision darkened into pain.

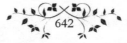

By the time Maddy understood Anna's warning, it was too late to avoid the impact. She danced to the side as quickly as she could, but Meren still collided into her with bone-jarring force. The world twisted and spun as they tumbled across the grass. Maddy cried out as pain seared through her from multiple places, and she could only pray she hadn't stabbed herself with her own knife.

Finally, they stopped, and her breath heaved in panic. A rock dug into her stomach. Her right side was a bundle of pain where it was pinned beneath Meren's weight. She did her best to catalogue any other injuries, but it was nearly impossible to tell what was what.

Then the rain crashed down around them in an abrupt flood, adding misery to pain.

"Maddy!"

She couldn't have said if Fen's cry had been aloud or in her mind. Telepathy wasn't a strong talent of hers. "Alive," she tried to call, but she couldn't get enough air for anything but a whisper.

Maddy searched for her link with Fen and did her best to follow it back to him. Then she pushed her thoughts toward him the best she could. *"I'm alive. Don't think I'm badly hurt, but damn, am I going to bruise."*

"Anna hit her head, and I'm so sore I can barely move," Fen answered, his voice in Maddy's mind unmistakable this time. *"Can you get out from under Meren? Fuck, I don't know which of you to help."*

Maddy had no doubts about that. *"Help Anna."*

Doing her best to ignore Fen's panic, Maddy wiggled herself to the left, wincing as the stone dug into her stomach. Meren groaned, and only then did she realize that her fingers were still wrapped tightly around the knife beneath his still form. Shit, had he landed on the blade? From the angle of the hilt in her hand, it was inevitable, which meant that wasn't rain and mud clinging wetly to her fingers.

A sick feeling rose up her throat. She wasn't supposed to hurt people. How was she going to free herself if moving dug the knife more deeply into Meren? Even if she let go of the hilt, shifting him around could do more damage. It was one thing to defend herself but another to harm a barely conscious man, enemy or not.

Maddy was about to call out for Fen's help when a surge of power froze her mental voice. Water rushed around her in a swirl, a vast pool she could in no way blame on the rain. Light flashed, blinding her, and then she was falling.

This time, when they landed, her world went dark.

Fen had just managed to slide a little closer to Anna when a burst of light nearly blinded him. He shoved his forearm against his stinging eyes and braced himself for whatever fuckery was about to happen next. Tornadoes? Tsunamis? A mass of fae having an epic dance-off? He wouldn't rule anything out at this point.

When there was only darkness beyond the shield of his arm, Fen finally dared to look. But he wished immediately that he hadn't. The clearing where he'd spotted Maddy and Meren was empty, only a hint of trampled grass visible in the faint glow of the nearby streetlight.

The bastard had taken Maddy.

Fen braced his hand against the ground and struggled to get himself to his knees. Damn, he hurt. What kind of spell had Anna conjured? Her magic had grabbed at his power like a flooding river snatching up hapless debris, draining him until he could barely move. And the concussive force of the ball she'd thrown? He'd definitely never seen anything like that.

How was he supposed to help anyone when he couldn't even stand up? Maddy was in danger, and Anna was unconscious. Fen squinted at the shadows around Anna's head, but the unmistakable scent of blood hit his senses before he could process the splotch beneath her.

He wobble-crawled the remaining distance between them, only to lose his balance and tumble face-first into the mud. He wasn't a strong enough telepath to reach Vek from this far away, and his phone was either broken or ruined in the pocket he was lying on. Fucking fabulous. Unless someone decided to take a walk in the rain, they were screwed.

Fen managed to roll to his side as Anna moaned. She shifted slightly, and relief flooded him like the rain. She was waking. He lifted his hand to brush the hair out of her eyes but only reached her waist before his strength gave out. So. Screwed.

A glow emanated from the area near the river, but Fen couldn't see over Anna well enough to discern the source, not without lifting his head. Yeah, that wasn't happening, no matter how much he needed to see what was going on. What if it was Meren, returning to kill them? Or maybe Maddy had found a way back? He was too damned weak to see.

His energy was gone. Just gone. Like Maddy. Like the rain. Like everything that made sense. And unless he took some of Anna's blood so he could regenerate, the situation wasn't getting any better.

Not something he could—or would—do with Anna injured and unable to consent.

The light grew brighter. Closer? Almost like an approaching lantern. But when the woman finally entered his sight, he couldn't discern the source of the glow. It seemed to surround her.

Fen squinted against the glare as the woman knelt at Anna's side. Thankfully, the luminescence faded until he could make out the swirls and ripples of the stranger's clothes—almost a diving suit in form but covered in strips of fabric in shades of brown, green, and blue. Underwater camouflage?

Her aquamarine eyes flashed beneath her short-cropped blond hair, and the delicate structure of her face was set in harsh, cutting lines. "She should not have been here."

Fen opened his mouth to speak, but no sound came out. Not that he could refute her words. Why had they ever thought this was a good plan? None of them should have approached Meren without more knowledge of the situation.

Anna's hand twitched, her fingers jumping as though someone was testing her reflexes, but she made no other movement. Only the steady rise and fall of her waist beneath his palm tamped down the panic rising against his weakness. She was alive. If they could get through this, they could go save Maddy.

He had to believe.

The strange woman clasped Anna's head gently in her hands. "Poor little granddaughter, so unprepared."

The action should have made Fen uneasy, but the lady examined Anna with such a tender expression that he couldn't summon the emotion. "You are…"

"Be quiet and save your energy," the woman said. "I am Torlahn of the Gwragedd Annwn. Your mate will come to no harm at my hands."

Light flared around the woman again, and this time there was no mistaking that it came from within her. Fen blinked against the glare as Torlahn traced her hands above Anna's body, finally settling once more upon her head. Another flash, and Anna cried out, her abdomen heaving against his palm. What was the woman doing to her?

Fen tried to slide himself closer, but most of his energy went to breathing. If he could just make the strange woman get her hand near him, he could sink his fangs in and draw out some energy. He didn't want to without permission, but to save Anna… Had to save Anna.

"Do not think to steal what you need from me," the woman snapped. "I am helping her. If you cannot see that, then you are a fool."

"But she—"

"Fen." Anna's voice was soft, but there was awareness to it. "I'm okay. Better than okay."

He glanced from the woman back to Anna's face, and his mouth dropped open. The color had returned to her skin, and she met his eyes easily, no hint of muddled

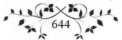

thinking in her regard. Beneath her, the puddles of rainwater were gone, only a dry, rusty dust remaining where her blood had been. What the hell?

Anna sat up, gently shifting his hand from her waist in the process. "She healed me."

And so she had.

Fen could only stare at Anna in awe. Her eyes shone aquamarine, and she practically glowed with power, much like the woman who had emerged from the water.

"You look…"

"Her blood has fully awakened. A dangerous time," the woman said. "She should return with me."

"No." Fen sucked in a breath. "Maddy."

Anna scanned the area, her expression shifting from worry to panic in only a moment. "Where is she?"

"Meren."

Dammit. Things would be a lot easier if he could gasp out more than a couple of words at a time.

Only then did Anna seem to notice the state he was in. "Fen. Crap, I accidentally drained you. Take from me."

She settled her wrist against his lips, but he couldn't bring himself to open his mouth. He didn't have enough power to numb her skin. If he accepted her offer, his bite would cause pain, and he couldn't bear the thought of that.

"Will hurt," he mumbled against her skin.

Fortunately, Torlahn solved that problem with a quick bit of her healing magic. Moments later, he brushed his fangs against Anna's skin as lightly as he could, only enough to create a small scratch. The salty-sweet tang of her blood hit his tongue, making him shiver as he established a temporary link and took some of her energy. But not too much.

When he disconnected from her magic and pushed her wrist away, Anna frowned at him. "I can tell that wasn't enough."

A flash of memory hit him—his foster mother tumbling to the floor. Taking blood when this weak was dangerous. "You should save your power. We have to go after Maddy, as soon as we figure out where she might have been taken. I'll see if Vek has any to spare when we get back to—" Fen glanced at Torlahn, her rapt attention reminding him to watch his words. "When we get back to his place."

For the first time, Anna really seemed to see the Gwragedd Annwn woman who had saved her. "My power… You did more than heal me, didn't you?"

Torlahn shrugged. "I eased your blood forward in its ascent. You fight against it, granddaughter, and that courts disaster."

"You had no right," Anna said sharply.

"There was already a crack in the dam," the woman retorted. "One you almost shattered by trying to use your power. Should I have let you flood your world rather than facilitate the inevitable transition?"

Fen wasn't entirely sure what the hell Torlahn was talking about, but Anna's falling expression suggested she understood. "No," Anna said. "But I don't know what to do with this."

Torlahn stood. "You will come with me. We will discuss your heritage, past and future, and I will ensure you are trained."

"Wait." Anna nibbled on her lower lip. "Did you mean granddaughter literally?"

The other woman smiled. "Follow me, and you will find out."

Cold seeped into Maddy's bones, and she shifted against the unyielding stone beneath her belly. A faint thread of alarm coursed through her, though she had no clue why. At least for a brief, blessed moment. One masculine moan later, her memory flooded back.

The park. Anna's spell. The harsh impact when Meren crashed into her, tumbling them both across the grass. Then the awful realization that she'd stabbed him.

Maddy forced her eyes open as she catalogued her body's position. She wasn't pinned anymore, and she couldn't see anyone between her and the beautifully painted wall in her immediate view. They must have ended up somewhere nice—even the stone floor taking up most of her sight had been placed with immaculate care. She could see a pattern, but the lines where the rock connected didn't pinch into her cheek.

Another moan filled the room, and Maddy turned her head to find the source. Sure enough, she spotted Meren's pale face to her right. He must have rolled off of her after they'd fallen through whatever portal had carried them here.

He didn't look like he was in any shape to have kidnapped her. His skin was so colorless he could have been mistaken for Vek, and a hint of blue tinged his lips. Based on his groans, he was obviously alive—but not by much. Could she do anything to help? *Should* she?

Meren was their enemy. Hadn't she drawn her knife to protect herself from him? Maddy had been fully prepared to defend herself and her mates as she'd crept toward him in the park, but now she found herself scanning his body for a wound as she sat up. What madness would it be to heal him? What horror to watch him die?

It is a grave burden, our job, but one that does far more good than the opposite.

Lial hadn't been talking about this situation, but his words echoed in her mind as she focused on the knife sticking up from Meren's side, blood trickling around the blade to drip steadily against the stone. Yes, she wanted to do more good than harm. Meren might be an asshole who deserved what he got, but she didn't have to be the one who dealt the final blow.

Intentionally.

Maddy winced at that harsh truth. What would she have done if he'd attempted to hurt her? She'd planned to render him unconscious with her magic if the meeting went wrong, but she'd brought the knife as backup. Now, she doubted that she would've been able to strike to kill. Not even against a guy who would eliminate them all without a thought.

Well, if she couldn't stand to watch someone die, she could make sure he was properly contained. Maddy scrambled to her feet and rushed over to a massive wooden wardrobe taking up part of the wall. After a quick search, she located a leather belt that was thin and supple enough to be tied in a knot. It would have to do.

Careful of the knife jutting from his side, Maddy settled Meren's arms in front of him and bound his wrists together tightly. It wouldn't be very effective if he woke fully, but she wasn't relying on the fragile bonds to keep him biddable. They were more to keep him secure if the sedation spell started to wear off while she was working.

She'd sworn never to let herself be abducted again, yet here she was, sitting cross-legged beside his wounded form. Though it was a stretch to call him her captor. How had they come to this place? It seemed likely he'd activated a return spell when only half-aware. Frowning, she glanced around the sumptuous room, each furnishing, painting, and tapestry its own work of art. This looked less like a prison and more like a noble's home or even the Seelie palace, though that was unlikely with Meren on the run.

With a shrug, Maddy cupped her hands over the man's wound, not quite touching the knife that stuck up between her palms. Did it really matter where she was when she killed or saved the guy? No. All she should focus on at this point was controlling the power that Lial had barely started teaching her to contain. Lial had told her that she needed to be as specific with her magic as possible to get the best results, but she hadn't exactly had time to study anatomy.

After ensuring Meren was sedated, Maddy let her magic gather between her hands, and for the first time, a few little sparks of yellow danced with her usual green in a miniscule reflection of Lial's blue light. What in the...? She closed her eyes to avoid the distraction. Reflecting on the changes to her magic wouldn't get the bastard healed any faster.

Instead, she forced her awareness outward. Then into the wound that throbbed to her inner sight. Such a mess of torn muscle and sliced intestines. Landing on the knife had sent it deep; the blade had severed veins and lodged into the base of the kidney. If she pulled the knife out, Meren would bleed out in less than an hour.

Despite her resolve to be better, temptation rushed through her in a sickening wave. *One tug, and so many people might be spared.* She wouldn't have to turn him over to the queen and risk the politics of a Seelie court trial. Didn't the rich and powerful always wiggle their way out of trouble? It happened far too often. Not to mention that if Meren died, she wouldn't have to worry that he might attack Fen or Anna.

They were completely alone. Who would ever know?

Maddy's stomach heaved.

She would know.

Justice wasn't hers to deliver, and since she didn't know why the queen wanted Meren brought back alive, she'd better not be hasty. Letting him die might make matters worse. Better to heal him and keep him secured—and unconscious—until

she could locate the proper authorities. If nothing else, Fen and Anna would find her and help.

Silencing that wicked whisper for good, she concentrated on the task at hand. Unlike some of the body's systems, this was pretty straightforward. She could see the places that needed to be knit back together. No hormones or delicate bacteria to balance. No war to wage with a disease she might accidentally augment. All she had to do was will her magic to repair, keep her power in check, and trust that it would work.

But trust, of course, was the problem—one she didn't know if she could overcome.

30

Frustration and despair crashed through Anna as she stared at the fae lady standing so regally in front of her. This might be her best chance to learn more about her heritage, but she couldn't take it. Not with Maddy in danger.

"You know perfectly well I won't be going with you," Anna said tightly.

Torlahn lifted a haughty brow. "You think not?"

"My mate just disappeared with the madman who tried to kill Fen." Anna stiffened her spine. "As much as I would like to learn about my people, I will not do so at the expense of my family. It is wrong of you to suggest otherwise."

The Gwragedd Annwn woman studied her silently for a moment and then nodded. "That is true, but I worry about your awakened power. I guided you in dispelling the energy you unwittingly gathered from the water. I will not be with you if the same happens again."

They all knew it was a risk—not even Fen could hide the worry shadowing his gaze. Anna had pulled in far more water than she should have, and the result had cost them. Wasn't it her fault that Maddy had gotten tangled up with Meren in the blast? Maybe Maddy would still be here if that hadn't happened.

But there was no way Anna was going to stay behind and wait for Fen to track down their mate. It simply wasn't a possibility.

"You could come with us," Anna ventured.

The other woman started shaking her head before Anna had finished speaking. "I'm afraid I cannot. I have almost traveled too far already, and I dare not go farther without dispensation from the king."

Anna liked to think of herself as a patient person, but she was nearly at the end of that finite state. "Then can you teach me a little about my power? I could use a crash course on grounding that kind of magic."

Torlahn's lips thinned, but she nodded again. "There are a few tricks, but I warn you that they might not be enough."

"They'll have to do."

Although she wanted to rush, Anna forced herself to pay close attention as the woman led her through a series of exercises. First, connecting to the earth beneath her feet. Then, letting her power trickle downward in a steady flow until it disappeared into the ground like a hidden stream. It was a wonderful feeling—until her body grew heavy with exhaustion.

"Pull some back," Torlahn said. "The water within you needn't flow one way like a river toward the ocean. You can draw in energy, too."

Anna took a deep breath and tugged at the power she'd released until it poured back into her. Fascinating. Could she do this in any area with water? With any*one*? She let her magic settle, neither pushing nor pulling, and opened her eyes.

"I accidentally sucked out Fen's magic earlier," Anna began. "Could I return it to him the same way I just did with the Earth?"

Fen shook his head. "I'm *Felshreh*. Without a blood link…"

"It might be possible." Torlahn's forehead furrowed as she stared at him. "Blood *is* mostly water. An experiment you'll have to conduct between you."

"Later." Anna's heart pinched at leaving the woman who might be her grandmother, a link she'd never thought to find, but they had to save Maddy. "I hope you will not refuse to talk to me again in the future. I know the fae have rules, and you sounded certain that I would have to go with you."

With a soft smile, Torlahn touched Anna's arm. Just the barest brush of her fingers, but peace eased through Anna all the same. "Return here when you are ready and speak my name into the water. I will come."

Before Anna could think of the proper response, the woman rushed back toward the water and dove in without a splash. Then she was gone as though she'd never been there. If not for the steady rush of power Anna still felt, she might have thought that Torlahn's presence had been a hallucination. But there was no denying that she'd been healed.

"What now?" Anna asked.

"Let's return to the outpost." Fen twined his fingers with hers, and his worry slammed into her until she caught her breath. "Maybe Vek can track Meren now. I fucking can't."

Anna caressed the back of his hand with her thumb in a slow, calming gesture. "That's a long drive. Maddy's father would be closer, and he's one of the Seelie Sidhe."

"Not if I take us through the new gate I constructed with Vek."

Anna blinked. "Did you forget I'm not *Felshreh*? Dria said it was only for your kind."

Fen turned to face her, his eyes fierce embers. She'd never seen him like this, although his intensity didn't bring fear. No, it was an echo of her own resolve. She didn't know how, but they would bring Maddy home.

"I didn't forget." Fen gathered both of her hands in his and brought them to his lips. "We're mates. I have taken your blood, and you have sipped some of mine. I think that if we merge minds, I might be able to pull you with me through the blood portal, and if it doesn't work, you can drive to the shop and wait for Dria to create a gate."

"What if this is the wrong choice?" Anna asked softly. "If Vek can't help, we'll waste a lot of time."

Fen's eyes practically blazed over the top of her hands. "It isn't. Vek won't let me down in this. I feel it in my soul."

His conviction resonated within Anna until she felt it, too. She nodded and closed her eyes, letting the link between them deepen until their thoughts began to merge. Then there was no her.

Only them.

When the knife tipped against the edge of Maddy's hand, she flinched in surprise. It seemed like she'd been healing for hours, easing the blade free bit by bit as she repaired the organs and blood vessels in its wake. Still, she was only half done. The knife was free enough that the hilt was overbalancing it, but there was a lot left to check.

Even though it would allow more blood to pour free, Maddy plucked the knife from the wound and set it aside. If the damned thing kept tilting, it would cut into undamaged flesh, and then she would have more work to do. Sweat already trickled down her face and between her shoulder blades from exertion as it was.

She settled to her task once more, trying to ignore the growing weakness in her body as she expended her energy. It was working. She was healing instead of hurting, and she'd only come close to losing control once. Maybe she wasn't hopeless at this.

But before Maddy had knit much more of the injury, a crash sounded behind her. Startled, she glanced over her shoulder in time to see a group of Seelie Sidhe soldiers pour through an open door with swords drawn. She lifted her hands out of reflex, her magic sputtering out without her conscious command.

A good thing, really. She could kill as well as heal, and she would never have forgiven herself for accidentally hurting one of the guards—provided these were the good guys.

They swept around her and Meren in a circle, and a woman in golden armor settled her sword at Maddy's throat. Afraid to even blink, Maddy stared at the elaborate engravings on the soldier's leg-guards and tried to calm her pounding heart.

"State your name and purpose," the warrior demanded.

What should she say? If Meren had brought her to one of his bases, then the less information she gave, the better. But if this was the palace, then these were the queen's guards. Telling them everything would be the most prudent.

The soldier eased the blade a touch closer, almost breaking the skin. "You have been found in the company of a known traitor. Your silence does you no service."

The queen's guard. If a sword hadn't been at her throat, Maddy would have sagged in relief. "I am Maddy Carden. Well, I guess that would be Maddy a Shayan of the Cairdai? Not that my father's family will claim a half-blood like me."

Perfect. Now she was rambling.

The sword didn't ease, and the legs in front of her didn't shift an inch. "And your purpose here? Even if you are of the blood, you have not been given permission to enter the inner palace."

Being right about her location usually would have brought more satisfaction, but not this time. Her father had petitioned to introduce Maddy to the court several years ago, but the request had never been granted or denied. That meant she was technically trespassing, even though she hadn't arrived by choice.

Worry began to edge out relief. "I'm not here by my own power. I was defending myself and my mates from Meren when he crashed into me. Then I woke up here."

"Look at me," the warrior commanded.

Carefully, Maddy tilted her head back, fighting the urge to swallow with the blade pressing into her throat. The soldier's harsh expression did nothing to ease the fear coating Maddy's mouth. Couldn't the woman see her innocence?

"Do you deny healing Meren a Nuall, traitor to the crown?"

Oh, fuck. She hadn't even though about that aspect of her actions. "No. He fell on my knife. But I wasn't trying to help a criminal. I just couldn't sit and—"

"Silence," the solider snapped. A general, actually, based on the symbol Maddy could see engraved upon the breastplate. Double fuck. "Maddy a Shayan, you are under arrest for illegal entry into the palace's inner sanctum and for aiding a wanted criminal. You may save your pleas for the queen and the court."

There were so many things Maddy wanted to say in her own defense, but she could see from the general's harsh gaze that they would do no good. Unfortunately, there was one point she couldn't resist making. "I didn't finish the healing. He still needs help."

The general's lip curled in scorn. "Your lover's health is no longer your concern."

"My *what?*" Maddy almost gagged at that conclusion. "You've got to be kidding. Why would I have tied him up if we were together?"

"I have no reason to believe anything you say, half-blood. I will leave it to the queen to judge."

Before Maddy knew it, her arms were bound behind her back with enchanted chains, and a thick hood was shoved over her head, blocking her sight. Her magic cut off, severed from her control by the bindings, and a sword tip nudged her back.

Her muscles trembled with terror as she stumbled forward between the guards. The only reality in her world was the stone floor beneath her feet, the blade at her back, and the hands on her arms guiding her movements. By the time they started down an endless flight of stairs—one laborious step at a time—she almost wished they'd just stabbed her and been done with it.

She hadn't been this afraid when Kien's minions had kidnapped her, and they'd been the bad guys. But as the hands holding her shoved her forward into nothingness and slammed a door behind her, Maddy thought her heart was going to pound itself to pieces. Was she alone? She couldn't use her magic to scan the area, and there were no physical clues she could discern.

Maybe they'd left her in a cell, bound and helpless. No telling how long she would stay that way, either.

She was so very, very screwed.

It took longer than Fen liked to follow the link to the blood gate, but it wasn't a magic he'd used before beyond that one time with his uncle. But the combination of the blood link and his connection to the fluorite he'd brought forth did the trick. With the last surge of his magic, he held Anna close and pulled them both through.

Only Anna's hold kept him from crumpling to the cave floor in an ignoble heap. They swayed together until he was certain he was going to fall anyway, taking her with him. Instead, she helped him lean against the wall until he could slide into a more dignified cross-legged position.

His head spun, and he closed his eyes so he wouldn't throw up. "That's going to take more practice."

"Don't give me that," Anna said. "I told you that you didn't take enough energy. Does my water worry you that much?"

Fen's hair caught against a rough edge in the stone as he shook his head, but he didn't have the energy to care about the nip of pain. "Didn't want to weaken you. I'm dangerous when I'm low."

She knelt beside him. "What's that supposed to mean?"

"I've accidentally pulled too much before." Too exhausted to explain, he sent her a quick mental image of his foster mother on the floor. "Ends badly."

"Oh, Fen." She caressed the side of his face, and her lips pressed softly against his. He reached for her hand, tugging until she settled against his side. "You were a kid, right? You won't do the same thing now. Stop torturing yourself and take more energy."

"Waiting for Vek."

Her hurt reached him through the mate link, and his own heart twisted. "So you won't let me take care of you?"

Fen pulled her more closely against him. "It's not... Save yours for helping Maddy."

Fortunately, she seemed to understand what he meant, since he couldn't make a solid sentence to save his life. Again. As Anna settled her head against his shoulder, Fen used the last of his precious magic to call for Vek in the off chance his uncle hadn't detected his arrival. What had they added into the shielding again...?

The sharp taste of familiar blood hit his tongue, and only then did he realize that he'd drifted almost to sleep. Vek. Without hesitation, Fen took the power he required, halting as soon as he sensed it would weaken his uncle to take more.

Vek hadn't had to stop him.

That revelation rang in Fen's head as he opened his eyes. Danger, weakness, fear for Maddy—none of that had mattered. He'd followed his instincts, and it hadn't ended in disaster. His uncle stared down at him, perplexed but not harmed. No one was drained or unconscious on the floor.

Maybe he could trust himself.

"What's going on?" Vek demanded, clearly not noticing Fen's epiphany. "Where's Maddy?"

Fen rubbed his eyes. Now wasn't the time for self-reflection. "She disappeared with Meren after Anna did some kind of water spell. A Gwragedd Annwn lady showed up to help Anna, and then we decided to come here."

It was a truly shit explanation, but Vek nodded anyway. "I sensed Meren not long ago and was preparing to go after him. I need only trace his blood for the exact location."

As awareness fully settled in, Fen scanned his uncle and noted the red leather armor and sword belted to his side. *The* sword—the one specifically designed to harvest energy from the blood of those Vek struck, a powerful artifact his uncle didn't bear casually. Good. If they caught Meren, the asshole would pay.

Anna stood, brushing dirt from her pants before she straightened, and Fen followed suit. Now that the haze was clear from his thoughts, urgency was taking its place. What was happening to Maddy? Had Meren hurt her? Surely Fen would know if she'd been killed. Would he sense something like that through their bond?

"Do it," Fen said. "We need to go."

Vek's gaze grew distant as he began to follow the link, and it was all Fen could do not to tap his foot and demand answers as the silence lengthened. His thumb found the ring on his left finger, the symbol of their bonding, and he spun it impatiently as he waited for his uncle to speak. To give them a target.

The ring. It was supposed to deepen their connection and ease communication. Could he and Anna use theirs to contact Maddy?

"Impossible," Vek whispered, and for a second, Fen thought he was somehow answering the question about their rings. Until his uncle continued. "The bastard wouldn't be that stupid. And yet I've never tracked wrong before."

Anna took a step forward. "Where are they?"

"The inner palace of the Seelie Sidhe." Vek's hands clenched at his side. "The restricted portion where high-ranking nobles and royalty live. Unless he's planning a coup now…"

Fen frowned. "He wasn't in any kind of shape for that. Last I saw, he was unconscious. Anna's blast took him down hard."

Vek cursed, low and viciously. "He had a recall spell, I wager. One designed to take him to safety if incapacitated."

"That doesn't sound like safety," Anna said.

"Maybe he forgot to change it after his betrayal was discovered?" Fen spun the ring faster as he tried to beat back hope. "If so, Maddy is likely okay."

Vek sighed. "I'll have to approach the Seelie court to check."

"You?" Fen scowled at his uncle. "Are you trying to take over shit for me again? Because Anna and I can find a way to—"

"Get arrested by the royal guard for intruding?" Vek asked, his tone turning incredulous. "I understand pride, but this level of stupidity is baffling. Why refuse needed help for your own ego?"

Though his uncle had a point, Fen ground his teeth in frustration. "She's our mate."

"Technically, you've renounced your place as heir to the Unseelie throne, and as such, your position is nebulous. You could barge into the Seelie court as prince and heir, but without that exalted position, you will not be granted entry. Force the issue, and they'll throw you in prison." Vek lifted a brow. "Are you ready to claim your full heritage? Because that is what you will need to demand audience with the queen."

Fen's stomach dropped. How could he claim anything when he obviously didn't know the rules of either court? Honestly, he would have marched up to the palace and asked about Maddy, consequences be damned. But then, he had two conceptions about castles: people liked to go to foreign countries to visit them, and the one the Unseelie inhabited was weird as fuck.

"There has to be another way," Fen said, uncaring that his voice broke on the words. "I'll try to contact Maddy for more information. Our rings…"

"Oh, yeah." Anna's expression brightened. "Let's try that. Maddy's father did say they should help us speak over distances."

Vek's lips thinned in displeasure, but he gestured toward the chamber entrance. "Fine. Let's go to the meeting room, and you can give it a try. But consider my earlier words, Fen. You can't live in limbo forever."

As if Fen could avoid thinking about his position among the Unseelie. It haunted him all the way through the cavern tunnels. Could he rise from a homeless, troublemaking failure to the heir to the throne? He'd learned to trust in himself somewhat, but that much? By the time they reached the meeting room, he still didn't have an answer.

31

The guards hadn't abused her, but Maddy had no doubt she looked like they'd beaten her anyway. She'd refused to simply stand there awaiting her mysterious fate, and so she'd spent the last eternity exploring the room—sometimes with her face. Her nose still throbbed from where she'd run into something that might have been an unlit wall sconce.

Her cheek had discovered bars straight ahead from where she'd entered, but best she could tell through the stifling hood, no air passed around the rails. If the little opening had once been a window, it was probably blocked off. Now, she eased sideways along the wall, moving slowly in case she encountered more obstacles. So far, there hadn't been any furniture. For that matter, her feet hadn't caught on a pallet or bedroll. No bucket, tray, or toilet.

Maddy reached the corner she thought was nearest to the door and stopped to suck in a calming breath. She rubbed her fingers against the unnaturally smooth stone behind her. Aside from the sconce and the bars, she'd found nothing to hang on to, literally or figuratively. Would they simply kill her here and then wash the blood away without a thought? This didn't seem to be the kind of cell a person would stay in long term.

The royal guards didn't mess around.

Her arms were numb enough from her bindings that it took her a minute to realize that her ring finger had heated up. Maddy rubbed her finger against the gemstones and jolted at the hint of power that filled her. It wasn't her magic—that was blocked by the chains—but it connected to something deeper.

Anna and Fen.

Maddy concentrated on the indelible power of that bond, picturing her mates as she pressed her thumb as hard as she could against the ring. Worry and hope filled her first, followed closely by fear and doubt. Yep. Anna and Fen. Despite it all, she found herself smiling against the rough fabric.

"Are you okay?" Anna asked.

"Well…"

Then Fen. *"Did Meren hurt you?"*

Pain slammed into Maddy's head as she struggled to hold their mental connection through her bindings. The spell's talons hovered over their link, ready to grab at any moment.

"No," she tried to explain. *"But the Seelie royal guard is holding me prisoner. They think I'm working with Meren. Oh, and apparently, I trespassed. Like I wanted to be brought here."*

Stunned silence.

"Why would they think—"

"Prisoner? Like torture? Please tell me you're in a nice room or something."

Maddy winced at Anna's question as her mates' words tangled in her head. *"No torture."* Except sensory deprivation, but no need to mention that now. *"But I wouldn't call the room nice. I'm not really sure what's going on."*

"I can feel your hurt," Fen said.

"It's hard to hold the link." No need to talk about the pain she'd inflicted on herself by running into stuff. *"Call my father. Not sure his rank's high enough, but I'm going to need the help."*

"Maddy…"

She rolled the side of her head against the wall to try to ease the building agony, the only thing she could do without hands to rub at the ache. *"I can't hold this any longer."*

Fen's and Anna's voices wove together with their last words. *"We love you."*

Maddy's tears dampened her hood as the connection faded, and her sobs sucked at the oxygen inside until her head spun.

With each endless moment, the chance of seeing them again dimmed in her heart.

Anna glared at Dria's back as the woman dug through a trunk while muttering curses. She wanted to be on the move, but instead, Vek and Dria were playing dress up. Did it really matter what they wore while Maddy was in the Seelie queen's dungeon, her fate uncertain?

Dria straightened, a bundle of blue fabric in her hands. "Thank the gods. I have it."

"Great," Anna said, doing her best to stifle her temper. "I'll hurry up and change."

Dria's lips twitched, but she shook out the cloth to reveal a robe embroidered with swirls of periwinkle and baby blue—an idealized version of water for sure. "I'm not trying to slow you down, Anna. In the Seelie and Unseelie courts, appearance plays greatly into power. Or at least the perception of it. They will not listen to someone who shows up in human clothing."

With a sigh, Anna shucked her T-shirt and pants before reaching for the robe. It was lighter than it appeared, but she still needed Dria to help get all the fabric over her head and settled around her. As Dria searched the trunk again for accessories, Anna glanced in the mirror at the wrinkled robe engulfing her and grimaced.

The mage had a good point about perception. Wasn't the same true among humans, after all? Across time, entire class structures had been defined—or at least revealed—by clothing style or fabric choice. That wasn't the only factor, though. Mannerisms, customs, attitude… Anna could wear a fancy robe, but could she assert herself in front of a room of powerful and ancient fae?

Probably not. But she would try for Maddy.

Dria wrapped a silver and gold chain around Anna's waist, smoothed out the wrinkles in the fabric with magic, and affixed a circlet above Anna's brow. After the mage stepped back, Anna blinked at yet another image of herself. She looked like a princess, and as Fen's mate, she supposed his people would see her as one. Too bad her inner self didn't match.

"For the most part, only the power-hungry feel equal to leadership, you know," Dria said quietly. "Fae and human. Ruler and subject. All of us look in a mirror and wonder if we have what it takes. Maybe not every day, but more often than you might believe. We're all just people in the end."

Anna turned to the other woman in surprise. "Was I that obvious?"

"Yes and no." Dria shrugged. "I guessed based on your expression."

"It was a good one."

The mage smiled and gestured toward the door. "Vek said that Fen is almost armored. Let's head up to the portal room."

Lifting the hem of her robe, Anna pointed at her sneakers. "What about shoes?"

"The fabric is long enough to hide them," Dria said. "Why not keep the comfort of your current footwear?"

Bemused, Anna followed the mage from the room. Moranaians must not have many fairy tales involving shoes, unlike humans. Who could imagine a modern fairy godmother sending Cinderella out in sneakers? Though it would make any potential escapes more reliable—and less trackable than a glass slipper.

Vek and Fen reached the lift at the same time as Dria and Anna, and it was all Anna could do to make it onto the platform without tripping and toppling over the rail as she stared at Fen. She'd never seen him dressed in anything remotely formal. Certainly not armor. The dark red leather might have been simple in design, but it lent him an air of danger barely restrained.

Damn, it was a good look.

"Ralan should have commissioned another of those swords for you," Vek grumbled as he and Fen followed them onto the stone platform. "I am sure his brother's bonded would have been willing to help."

Anna frowned. Fen was wearing a sword, though the hilt wasn't as fancy as the one Vek had strapped to his belt. "What do you mean?"

"Mine is enchanted to gather energy from the blood of those I strike," Vek explained. "Fen's is not. If there is battle, he will not be able to gather power as easily. I would give him this one if it wasn't bound to my blood."

"Don't you think strolling into the Seelie court with a steel blade will be state-ment enough?" Fen asked. "You might as well have handed me a personal invitation to war, hand-addressed to the queen."

"Not quite. Still—"

Dria activated the spell, and the platform slid smoothly upward. "His path isn't yours, Vek. There's a reason my brother didn't do as you suggest."

Anna lost track of the conversation as she studied her mate's expression. As the lift rose, he closed his eyes, and his fingers gripped the rail until his knuckles whit-ened. Was he afraid of heights or nervous about what was to come? He appeared more certain as they hurried along the corridor to the portal room, but it was difficult to tell.

"What's wrong?" she sent.

"Magical elevators freak me out almost as much as being the Unseelie heir." Fen gave her a quick, wry smile as they followed Vek and Dria into the small room. *"I'm still not sure about this. Are you? Unless my mother has more children, we might be stuck ruling one day."*

Anna shuddered at the thought, but it wasn't a problem she could deal with today. *"Let's save Maddy first. Then we'll figure it out."*

Fen's smile widened. *"That's the plan I'm going on."*

We'll solve this mess, Anna resolved as she took Fen's hand and prepared to step through the portal to a different world. *Even if I have to be a queen.*

Maddy almost blacked out twice before she calmed herself enough to breathe steadily. She could pull in air through the hood so long as she didn't panic and fill the thing with carbon dioxide. The thing wasn't airtight, after all. Unfortunately, it took far longer than she would have liked to convince herself of that fact.

Once she'd stifled her panic enough to take it from hyperventilation to a burn-ing, buzzing ache that pulsed through her veins with each racing heartbeat, Maddy continued her exploration. Her right shoulder slid easily along the smooth stone, but she still crept forward at a ridiculously slow pace. She had no desire to discover another wall fixture the hard way.

After another lifetime had passed, her shoulder nudged into a bump in the stone, and she did her best to feel out the details with her arm. A doorframe, maybe? A few more steps confirmed that theory—a doorknob bit into her right hip. Maddy's heartbeat surged, but she tried not to hope. Even so, she turned until she could get one of her hands around the knob. She took a deep breath and attempted to twist.

She'd known it would be locked, but she slumped in defeat anyway when it didn't budge. That foolish spark of hope had apparently wanted the outcome to be otherwise. Unfortunately, her captors weren't idiots. They wouldn't have shoved her in here and then left the door unlocked.

Maddy was so busy chiding herself that she barely heard the footsteps in time to shuffle away from the door. It swung open so quickly that her clothes fluttered against her body. A hint of light flickered against the hood, and Maddy shuddered with fear. Had touching the entrance caused some kind of alarm spell to activate? Without her magic, she couldn't probe for something like that, so it was possible.

What was happening?

Only when the warm hand gripped her upper arm did Maddy realize how chilled she'd become, but her captor's heat brought it into sharp relief. Who had hold of her this time? One of the guards? Another prisoner? Meren? Shivering from cold and fear, she jerked back against the stranger's hold.

"You dare to resist?" a low female voice hissed. "You are under our authority now."

"Whose authority? As far as I can tell, you're nothing but a hand."

The stranger released Maddy, but only to remove the hood and brighten the mage globes. For a moment, Maddy was too stunned by the light to struggle against the woman's renewed hold. The glow was so intense she could barely look at the general's golden armor without pain.

"Feel better, little traitor?"

The Sidhe general was just doing her job, but that didn't stop the sudden surge of anger that rushed through Maddy. "You have judged me without reason."

"And I have no *reason* to do otherwise," the warrior quipped. "Come. As soon as the palace healer has Meren stable, you will both be answering to the court and queen."

Maddy stifled a frustrated groan as she was led down an endless corridor that seemed to cross the length of the entire palace. Their healer was finishing the work she'd begun, yet *she* was being hauled in front of the queen for helping Meren? What kind of bullshit was that? She wanted to yell the question at the general, but she didn't dare.

The calmer she stayed, the more likely she was to survive—hopefully.

A guard shifted from his position beside the base of a staircase to open a broad metal door over to the side, and the general hauled Maddy through. This room was stone like the first chamber, but there was one major difference—manacles attached at waist-height all along the walls.

Two hard-faced warriors grabbed Maddy and turned her so that the hands secured behind her back were even with the manacles. She expected them to remove the thin chain that blocked her magic, but they didn't. Instead, one of the guards snapped the cold shackles around her wrists above the other chain.

"Consider how you will defend yourself," the general said. "While I arrange your trial."

Maddy stared helplessly after the woman as she marched from the room. A quick trial with the queen of the Seelie wasn't a good thing, not when the speed was measured in hours. That meant they considered the situation dire. She had to convince the queen that she hadn't been involved with Meren's plot—whatever it was. And she apparently didn't have long to formulate a defense.

32

Night would have been the best possible time to arrive in the Unseelie realm without causing a stir, so naturally, the gate opened upon a bustling walkway filled with light—or at least as much as the artificial sun crystal set in the ceiling managed to cast upon the city below. Fen pushed his shoulders back and tried to ignore the weight of the leather armor he'd donned. His armor, too, not something borrowed from his uncle. Vek had had the set commissioned after their last trip to the Unseelie court, a show of faith Fen wasn't sure he deserved.

On the other side of the portal, people stopped to stare, and Fen could just make out a handful of guards advancing from the distance. Their arrival would not go unnoticed, especially considering the steel sword he carried. Dammit. He'd hoped for a quiet meeting with his mother. So much for that.

"Are you certain you don't want me to accompany you?" Vek murmured, too quietly for his voice to travel through the gate.

Fen cut an annoyed glance his uncle's way. "You know I would never be respected if I relied on your strength. But I do appreciate the offer."

Vek nodded. "Remember…the *Felshreh* bow to no one save the monarch."

It would be nice to possess the confidence his uncle had grown up with, but since Fen didn't, he would just have to improvise. He'd bluffed his way through those hellish years with Kien. Now it was time to pretend himself through this. Fake it 'til you make it—except with a legion of power-hungry Unseelie relatives nearby, ready to gut you for a chance at the throne.

Such fun.

Though most of Dria's attention was on maintaining the portal, she glanced over. "Tell the Seelie queen I'll be sending her emissary back now that she has Meren. If you didn't have to stop to speak with your mother along the way, I'd toss the annoying Sidhe through with you."

"Will do," Fen answered, smiling at her last muttered threat.

Fen held out his arm for Anna, who wrapped her trembling hand around his elbow as if to anchor herself. "Let's go save Maddy," she whispered.

There was no more time to second-guess. The guards were almost at the Unseelie side of the portal, and an ever-growing crowd gathered along the path to the castle. Fen took a deep breath and advanced, not slowing even when they passed through the gate into the other realm. Voices swelled around them as Dria closed the portal behind them, but Fen and Anna kept moving.

The guards' steps slowed at the sight of Fen's armor, a color and design worn only by the royal *Felshreh*. The five of them exchanged uncertain looks as they blocked the path, and the one who stepped forward to speak appeared ready to bolt. Poor, miserable bastard. He must not have been around when Vek and Fen had come through a month prior.

But then, the new queen had been forced to replace a fair number of the royal guard who had died supporting her father in his madness.

"Forgive me, my lord," the warrior began hesitantly. "But your choice of portal location was…unorthodox. Are you from a distant branch of the royal family?"

A nice, polite way to ask if Fen was a poor relation, wasn't it?

Well, Fen didn't have time to banter. "I am Feniarathen an Arafel. You will move at once."

Though he'd felt foolish practicing the pronunciation of his own damned name while Vek had gathered his armor, Fen was suddenly grateful for the time spent. The troop parted, two moving to each side of the path. Only the one who'd broken away to challenge Fen and Anna had remained.

"Forgive me, my prince," the guard said. "We will provide you escort to the palace."

Curious. Had Ara given her army orders in the event of his arrival?

It seemed likely considering the change in the troop's demeanor, their suspicious expressions now hardened into resolve. The leader barked a sharp command, and the warriors turned to face the palace. As soon as Fen and Anna started walking, their new entourage sprang into action. Though there weren't enough of them to truly stop a crowd, having two armed soldiers on each side and another marching just behind his right shoulder encouraged people to move without need of threat.

Anna's hand tightened around his arm. *"This is a bit much."*

She had to hate being drawn into this mess. His heartbeat picked up its already frantic pace. *"I hope you don't regret our mating."*

"Never," she answered, and he could feel that she meant it.

But knowing didn't stop fear.

As they strode through the gates of the palace, they reached a new level of scrutiny—courtiers. But this time, Fen was recognized, and the whispers began in earnest. He did his best to keep his head held high, but he wasn't so sure he managed not to blush.

"Isn't that Vek's nephew? Crystal above, but the Felshreh are attractive."

"And the queen named him heir on his last visit."

"I'd rather make him king of my bedchamber."

"Who's the woman? Please tell me he hasn't already mated like Prince Vek."

"*Listen, Fen,*" Anna sent, her mental voice somehow both amused and annoyed. "*You've united the male and female Unseelie nobles with your hotness. At least until they find out you have two mates. Will Maddy and I have to threaten them daily?*"

Yep. The tips of his ears were definitely burning. "*No. Once mated, the Felshreh do not stray. Not that I would cheat even without an actual blood link.*"

The aggravation slipping across their bond faded, replaced by satisfaction—and love. Although worry and embarrassment twisted inside of him with every step, that sense of love carried Fen through the rest of the whispering hordes and straight up the long aisle leading to the dais at the end of the throne room where his mother sat. He wanted to turn around, then, at the unyielding expression on her face. When last they'd spoken, Fen had renounced his title.

What would Ara do now that he'd returned?

Fen halted at the end of the aisle, and silence descended on the throne room. If the proverbial pin dropped, it would sound like an explosion. Was it any wonder? The last confrontation that had happened in this room had led to the king being challenged and killed after he'd broken Unseelie laws. In fact, Fen had killed twelve of the traitor's guards himself.

He kept his eyes on the queen and tried not to wonder if there were ghosts.

There was probably some formality he was missing. What had Vek done that day? Bowed? Knelt? The memory was lost to the frenzy of battle and the horror of shedding yet more blood. But even if he knew, Fen wasn't sure he could bring himself to bow to the woman whose abandonment had brought him so much pain.

Fen inclined his head and hoped it would suffice. "Mother."

Gasps echoed behind him, and the queen's eyes widened. Fuck. He probably wasn't supposed to speak first. He didn't exactly care, but they needed this to go well if they had any hope of gaining Unseelie support to save Maddy. So he pinched his lips closed and waited, praying any slight would be glossed over.

Thankfully, his mother didn't make an issue of it. "Welcome home, Feniarathen an Arafel. I assume you have a reason for returning at such a busy time without the mentor under whose authority you last departed."

He caught the question in her words: where the hell was Vek? How could he give his mother a suitably vague but adequate answer? All around them, the courtiers stared, making Fen regret leaving his uncle behind. He was not trained for this. He fought for composure as the weight of this meeting settled over him. How could he claim himself heir when he couldn't handle a formal meeting?

Anna gave Fen's arm a subtle squeeze, and he wanted nothing more than to turn and rush his mate away from all this.

But he couldn't.

"That mentorship might need to be reevaluated," Fen finally stated.

Ara's eyebrow rose. "At odds with my brother already?"

A few light chuckles echoed from behind him, but Fen didn't bother to seek out the sources. "Not at all. However, I have mated. That makes me a little too old for a guardian, don't you think?"

This time, he caught a couple of groans from the crowd, but they quickly ceased when the queen stood. "Mated? To this woman?"

"Yes," Fen answered, irritation rising within him when Anna's hand twitched against his arm at his mother's sharp tone. "And one other."

Ara's nostrils flared as she processed his words. "I see we have much to discuss."

"In private," Fen said firmly.

"Is that so?" His mother's gaze skimmed across the crowd before a tiny, sly smile touched her lips—there and then gone. "If you wish to formally accept your role as my heir, then you should announce it before all. Afterward, we might retire for a private conference."

Oh, she was good. Though she hadn't said it directly, it was surely obvious to everyone in that room that the queen had no intention of meeting privately with him unless he obeyed her "suggestion" to claim his place. Shouldn't he have expected as much? His mother had never let anything like family or feelings stand in the way of what she wanted.

For the first time since they'd entered the throne room, Fen met Anna's eyes. Her smile held a tremble, but her chin tilted upward in steady resolve. *"I am with you either way."*

His breath caught at her words, and he brushed his fingers tenderly across her cheek, the wonder of her filling him with awe. He might not have deserved her or Maddy in the past, but by any divinity out there, he would start doing so now.

Sensing his decision, Anna let go of his arm, and Fen turned to face the staring nobles. He didn't know a damned one of their names, but he would still rule them—sort of. His ways were not fully theirs and never would be. Never. Acceptance of that fact washed through him, and none too few of the nearest nobles looked uneasy at the smile he couldn't quite stop.

Fair chance his mother was going to regret this.

Too bad.

"A few months ago, I could have been brought here a prisoner. The king might have killed me as a traitor." Ah, the indrawn breaths and startled glances. Lovely. "Technically, he would have been right."

"Feniarathen—"

"I'm only telling the truth." He barely bothered to cast an annoyed glance his mother's way. "They know it. We all know it. I worked with Prince Kien, an exile of Moranaia, and I foolishly believed he would keep his word to spare the Unseelie from his plans. The poison was not supposed to reach here, but it did. My own cousin died from it."

The whispers started, then, but Fen ignored them.

"I absolved my crime by working with Prince Vek to correct that mistake, and after being abandoned by my family for nearly my entire life, I have begun to work with my uncle to learn the Unseelie ways." A few nobles looked at his mother after that slight, but if she was as furious as he suspected, she didn't say so. "Queen Ara has named me her heir, and I have decided to accept that place. But know this. I've never been particularly good at doing what I'm supposed to, nor do I ignore the outside world in favor of tradition. I'll make changes without apology. I won't play your little games. But most of all, I refuse to take anyone's shit."

Really, Fen? he berated himself. God, he was terrible at giving speeches. What kind of prince used the word "shit" in a formal announcement? But it didn't seem to faze the Unseelie gathered in the throne room. Though they didn't cheer or throw themselves prostrate like courtiers in some movie, they did lower themselves to one knee, heads bowing—if a touch reluctantly.

Huh. They hadn't laughed.

Close enough to a victory.

The Sidhe guards were not the inexperienced goons Maddy had dealt with when she'd been kidnapped by Kien's group. Here, they didn't rely on fear alone to keep her in place—there were actual iron shackles for that. Iron, in the heart of a fae castle. While it was a myth that the Sidhe were universally harmed by the metal, no small number were affected to varying degrees. The warrior keeping watch over her must have been, since he'd worn silk gloves when he'd bound her to the wall.

For those who were allergic, iron usually interfered with magic, but whoever had embedded the short set of chains into the wall must have been immune. Even with her magic blocked, the hum of the shields warding others from the metal's effects buzzed against her skin. Only the roughened inner portion that touched her wrist was left unguarded.

Maddy leaned the top portion of her back against the wall, then pushed away as pain surged down her arms. She hadn't been given any kind of stool or chair, and the chains were too short to sit on the floor. There was no way to get comfortable like this.

Which was probably part of the point.

The door opened, and someone else was hauled through. Meren. Her hands clenched against her back at the sight of him, though he looked worse for wear. They weren't treating him as nicely as they had her, either. Relatively speaking. The general herself marched him in with her sword at his back, two more warriors holding him up on each side.

He looked like he could barely stand, but they shoved him roughly against the wall perpendicular to hers and chained him anyway. If her hands weren't behind her back, she could have reached out to touch him, but she'd rather kick him in the balls than check on his health now that the knife wound was somewhat repaired. Though it would have been a cheap shot. He slumped back against the wall despite

the pain she knew it caused, and his chest heaved as though he fought for every breath.

Their healer must not have put much work into it—not that she could blame them.

The general glared at Maddy. "Do not think to attempt escape. You will be judged by queen and court soon enough."

"Faster than the human justice systems, I hope," Maddy muttered. "If your other prisoner passes out, which seems likely, then he'll break his arms. And eventually, we'll have to eat and drink. Are you going to feed us by hand?"

"You will be properly attended." Though affront colored the general's words, she gestured at one of the other warriors. "Ensure he remains upright."

As their leader spun on her heel and marched out, the guard tasked with supporting Meren shot Maddy an annoyed look while the other two warriors took their places beside the door. Maddy pretended not to notice the anger radiating off the first guard. She would probably be frustrated at having to hold the bastard up, too.

But it was the right thing to do.

She had no idea how much time had passed when Meren finally opened his eyes. He rolled his head enough to glance in her direction, though she wasn't sure he'd seen her until he spoke. "Why did you help me?"

"Some of us aren't assholes," Maddy snapped.

"Ah, the crudeness of the human-born tongue." His mouth curled into a mocking smile. "Forever lacking in polish."

Could she stab him again? There had to be a knife somewhere. "What do you have against humans, anyway? Some ancient grudge? My Sidhe father doesn't hold a grudge about a war fought thousands of years ago. Do you?"

"A grudge?" Meren's expression went blank. "No. I may dislike my ancestors' decision to consign us to the underhills based on a worthless treaty, but I hold no anger toward humans. That half of your bloodline is beneath my regard, useful only as a means to increase my own power. Grudges are in no way involved."

Great. The guy was a racist. Faulty logic and misunderstandings had a chance of being smoothed out, but it was harder to sway someone blinded by a sense of superiority. No evidence would prove humans his equal, not even saving his life. He would simply take it as his due.

"Perfect heritage or not, you still have to face the same queen I do."

"I'll find a way to free myself." Meren shrugged, the action making the guard tighten his hold. "Water has a way of escaping any barrier."

He didn't say anything about freeing *her*, but Maddy wouldn't have run even if it was an option. She wasn't going to be a fugitive for something she hadn't done. "Too bad you didn't free yourself to somewhere besides the Seelie palace the *first* time. Not that I wanted to be dragged anywhere with you."

"It was not intentional," Meren ground out.

Maddy stayed silent, hoping he would confirm her suspicions about what had happened. No such luck, though. Whatever messed up spell had gotten them in this situation, he wasn't sharing any details. It was just as well. If she had to hear too much more of his smug, smarmy voice, she wouldn't be able to resist kicking him in the balls.

No telling how the guards would react to that.

33

Being in the heart of the Unseelie palace was beyond surreal, but Anna did her best not to let it show. Not with so many curious—and sometimes hostile—eyes on her as she and Fen followed the queen out a side door. But even after they reached the isolation of the twisting hallways beyond, she didn't lower her guard. Fen's mother hadn't seemed pleased by his choice of mates, so Anna couldn't assume she had an ally there.

Finally, they reached a small but richly decorated office with a spectacular view of the underground city beyond the palace. Not that Anna had the time or inclination to study either. The place might be beautiful, but right now, it felt more like a prison keeping her from Maddy. They didn't have time for some stupid, lengthy discussion.

Fen apparently agreed. As soon as his mother shut the door behind them, he lifted his hand as though to stop her. "You can argue with me later. We have a bigger problem to deal with."

Queen Ara raised one regal brow. "Being my heir does not grant you the right to insolence."

"I'm guessing you didn't pay attention to my speech, then?" Anna tightened her hand around his arm in warning, and Fen took a deep breath. "Listen. We both know I have a good reason my anger with you, and we both know I'm never going to be a model prince. Feel free to produce another heir to replace me. I don't care. Right now, my other mate is being held captive by the Seelie Sidhe, and I need the weight of my title to help free her."

Although the queen's expression had gone blank when Fen had started speaking, his last words had a rush of color flooding her cheeks. "Your other mate is a criminal?"

For the first time, Anna couldn't hold back. "No! Maddy is as law-abiding as they come."

Anna half-expected the queen to send her from the room at the very least, but something like admiration moved in her eyes instead. "I see you are not mere decoration. Good. Perhaps you two should explain what is going on. I assume you have formed a triad?"

"Yes," Anna said before launching into a quick description of Meren's current actions. "And Maddy got pulled into Meren's transport spell when my magic accidentally shoved him into her. We were able to contact Maddy telepathically for a few minutes, and they think she's with Meren."

"I should have killed him years ago," Ara said, her breath hissing out in anger. "But I imagine your mate will be released without our intervention despite their incorrect supposition. The Seelie might wipe her memory of the fae, but they wouldn't harm a human."

Fen freed his arm from Anna's hold and lifted his left hand to let the light glint against his ring. "See this? It was a gift from Maddy's father, Shayan of the Cairdai. He's full-blooded Sidhe."

Ara's mouth dropped open, and she strode forward to grip Fen's hand, turning it this way and that to examine the ring. Anna found herself glancing at her own band, smooth and perfect. It was a gorgeous piece, and she couldn't deny that it had helped them reach Maddy telepathically. But why did it have other fae in such awe?

"No one commands the work of the Cairdai family," Ara said, unknowingly answering Anna's question. "And it is granted rarely. They are a powerful force in the Seelie court, so I cannot imagine your Maddy will come to harm."

Some of the tension drained from Fen's stance, but Anna was not reassured. "They refused to help her find training for her magic, so I wouldn't be too sure of that."

She hated to see her mate's shoulders draw up again, but they had to consider every angle.

"That's right," Fen said, running his free hand through his hair. "We can't count on her family for anything. What rank are Anna and Maddy as my mates?"

The queen's eyes narrowed. "Whatever I grant them. Is that not standard to human monarchies?"

"I wouldn't know. I didn't grow up with one, and I never paid attention to anything but the basics when it came to other countries." He shrugged. "Lady? Princess? Duchess? I don't have a clue."

Anna froze, unable to look away from the unexpected argument. How could she when it involved her life so deeply? Queen Ara certainly seemed inclined to give the question a great deal of thought. Anna wanted to scream at her to hurry. Time was so valuable with Maddy held prisoner, but some things couldn't be rushed.

Like royalty, apparently.

After an approximate eternity, Ara glanced from Fen to Anna, then back again. "I will grant each the title of princess, though I worry they lack the knowledge to properly fulfill the role. A lack I will have to correct for all of you."

Anna should have been insulted, but there hadn't been rancor in the queen's tone. Besides, she was right. Anna had gone from a restaurant server on Earth to an

Unseelie princess in a few days, and she wasn't arrogant enough to think she could easily handle the change. That would be as likely as escaping a gun-wielding murderer with a ballet flat.

It *could* happen, but who would believe it?

A tight smile crossed Fen's face. "So it's fair to say the Seelie court has imprisoned an Unseelie princess?"

"It is."

There was nothing about the queen's expression or tone that hinted at amusement, but Anna got the impression it was there, nonetheless. Ara wasn't quite what she'd expected, despite the way the woman had acted in the throne room. Away from court politics and prying eyes, there was an odd longing to the way the queen looked at Fen, and her readiness to accept him despite his resistance was telling.

Ara had loved her son enough to mess up both their lives in an attempt to save him from her father, and she loved him enough now to take his anger without complaint. She had to know Fen might never forgive her. He would be justified if he didn't. But the queen carried on supporting him as best she could.

Maybe as best she knew how.

"You realize I might start a war?" Fen asked. "I'm not exactly great at politics. In fact, I'd say there's a ninety percent chance I'll tell the Seelie queen to fuck off."

"Only ninety?" Anna muttered.

The queen chuckled. "War between our factions is nothing new, and Vek has done that very thing before, though I'll grant he had the weight of experience behind him. Do what you must to retrieve our newest princess."

"But in the throne room…" Fen shook his head. "I thought you disapproved of my mating."

"I was surprised. And I confess I'd had thoughts about the fae houses we might have made marriage alliances with. The Seelie Queen Regent is young and unwed."

Instead of feeling jealous at the suggestion, Anna had to hold back laughter at the aghast expression on Fen's face. If the queen had any idea how shy and awkward Fen could be about relationships, she would have canned that idea even without a mate bond. He never would have survived that many potential courtships.

Fen tried amusingly to find his voice. "Umm."

"I'll retrieve the Heir's Circlet for you before you go," Ara said, kindly ignoring Fen's embarrassment. "Then I'll open the portal to the Seelie palace myself."

By the time the general returned to the room, Maddy's entire body ached from her position—or at least the parts that weren't numb. She could no longer feel her arms, but her shoulders burned relentlessly. If not for her fae blood, she might have had lasting damage to her rotator cuffs.

And that wasn't even counting her thighs and ass. She hadn't considered herself out of shape, but balancing carefully for so long had strained her lower body until her legs trembled. Was there a workout program for being held captive? Because after the last couple of months, it was clear that she needed one.

A new guard who had entered with the general unlatched Maddy and tugged her forward with a grip strong enough to send pain roaring through her numb muscles. Maddy sucked in a breath, but she didn't bother to protest. None of them cared. Her own people, treating her like trash to be hauled out.

This wasn't going to be the presentation to court that her father had hoped for.

Maddy didn't look back to see how Meren fared with the guards. At this point, she almost wished she had let him bleed out, but her conscience never would have allowed it. Were the Seelie so cold about life? They hadn't been willing to train her healing gift, and they hadn't been impressed by her urge to help, though they had made sure Meren hadn't died. A weird choice, really, since they'd probably execute him for treason.

This time, the walk wasn't as long. The guard directed her out of the room and up the nearby flight of stairs until she stood behind the general, who flung open a heavy wooden door and strode through. Maddy was pulled straight into the throne room, and the space was already clear between the side door and the long carpet stretching up toward the throne.

There weren't as many courtiers as she'd expected, but the crowd of regal, richly dressed people reminded her of her grimy state. Why would any of her father's people claim her, whether they'd given a damn about her before seeing her or not? Her jeans were ripped in several places, her shirt had a massive tear across her stomach, and dirt had dried into clumps all along her clothes and in her hair. These glittering, shining Sidhe would see nothing of value in her ragged, half-human self.

Their sneering glances tore through her, but she couldn't do anything besides lift her chin higher and pretend that none of the nobles were there. An attempt unintentionally aided by Meren, who drew every eye as soon as he entered behind her. At least the asshole was good for something.

More warriors in gleaming gold armor lined the carpet leading to the dais, and ten more stood near the throne, five per side. They really weren't playing around. That much protection surely wasn't because of her, but it somehow felt personal. Despite her innocence, Maddy's stomach fluttered and heaved. The two guards nearest the queen held their swords unsheathed—one wrong move, and they would kill Maddy on the spot.

The general stopped in front of the dais and knelt, bowing her head. Maddy's guard jerked her to a halt several paces behind and then shoved down on her shoulder, forcing her to her knees. Like she wouldn't have done that anyway. Her father had trained her in what to expect if she was ever granted an audience. Without prompting, she lowered her head until her chin touched her chest.

Under other circumstances, she would have smiled at the guard's soft, surprised huff.

Behind them, a scuffling sound broke the silence, followed promptly by a man's yelp. Maddy could just see over her shoulder if she tilted her head, so she caught sight of Meren being driven to his knees before she forced her chin closer to her chest and ignored him. If she was lucky, her good behavior alone would mark her as no ally of his.

"I have brought the prisoners as you commanded, Queen Lera."

Maddy frowned at that. The rumors about something being wrong with Queen Tatianella must be true if she wasn't present for something this important. The princess had taken temporary control during the energy poisoning that had afflicted the energy fields for a time, but that poison had been stopped weeks ago. Didn't anyone find the queen's continued absence strange?

"Thank you for your service, General Tobenn."

The queen's voice rolled softly through the room, gentle but unyielding. Fairies and angels and cotton candy danced in that voice, but love and desire and life-dreams lined the edges. Queen Lera could have led humans of yore—and maybe present-day—to their doom in the underhill with a whispered command.

It was far from reassuring.

"Meren I already know," the queen said, as placid and unfeeling as a rock. "But I admit to curiosity concerning our other visitor."

Visitor. Riiiiight.

"Especially one who claims to be of the Clan Cairdai. Look up and state your full name, stranger, and do not bother to lie."

Maddy swallowed against the bile creeping up her throat and raised her eyes. Dammit, Queen Lera was as beautiful as she sounded—and every inch a Seelie Sidhe royal. From the silver crown twined into her golden braids to the elaborate green and gold gown, there was no question of her status.

"I am Maddy a Shayan a Clairen of the Cairdai."

Whispers hissed and swayed around her, but Maddy didn't take her eyes off the queen. Though the general had implied that the court would also judge her, the queen could and would overrule them if she saw fit. Her opinion was everything.

Queen Lera studied her silently for a moment. "That is a heavy claim for one of your stature."

Yeah, she wasn't talking about height. At least she hadn't outright called Maddy a dirty faker. "Please forgive my current state. My mates and I were battling Meren when I was unexpectedly transported away. If my father's petition for a formal introduction is granted, I will ensure my appearance is at an appropriate standard."

The queen's mouth tightened. It might be foolish to throw that implication out there—that the royal court would already know Maddy if they hadn't ignored Shayan's request—but the point had to be made. And it could lessen any doubt that Maddy was who she claimed to be, since a complete outsider wouldn't have thought to mention the petition, if they'd even known.

"You claimed you were fighting Meren, but you were found helping him," the queen said.

Maddy nodded. "Both are true, I guess, depending on what you mean by 'help.' I'm a healer. I can't sit there and watch someone die."

Queen Lera leaned forward slightly. "You stabbed someone and then healed them?"

"I didn't stab him on purpose. We were tossed together in combat, and he landed on the knife I was holding for my own protection." Maddy sighed. She wasn't entirely sure what had happened in the attack, so how could she explain it? "I didn't know where I was when I woke up, but since I'm not a murderer, I decided to try to heal the wound."

A bad life choice, apparently.

"That is a fine story," the queen said. "But one we cannot accept without evidence. This will take investigation. Perhaps if the Cairdai support your claim to a blood connection, your words will hold more merit."

Silence fell, as heavy as the queen's voice was sweet. Maddy glanced surreptitiously around the room, doing her best not to turn her head or appear hopeful. But none of the beautiful nobles in her line of sight stepped forward, and no voice called out support from behind. Oh, her father would be crushed when he learned of his family's final betrayal. They'd never been supportive of his decision to marry a human woman, but they hadn't openly disapproved, either. This, though. This was a final condemnation.

Her heart dropped—and that was before Meren spoke.

"She speaks the truth."

Maddy whipped her head around, unable to stop herself from gaping at him. Did he think he was helping? Why in the hell would the jerk come to her aid? He wasn't even looking at her, but for a brief moment, he met her eyes. No kindness or repentance there, though. Only resolve.

"A life debt repaid," he said before returning his defiant gaze to the queen. "I give my word that she is no ally of mine."

She understood, then. Meren wasn't being nice—he was ensuring she had no hold on his honor. Fulfilling debts, or at least appearing to, was important to the Seelie. But he was a traitor. Why would they believe anything he said?

The queen apparently agreed. "None here trust your sworn word."

"Am I not to be allowed to plead my case?" Meren asked, unflinching.

Maddy turned back to face Queen Lera. Gods, this sucked. Her knees throbbed with pain from the hard stone floor, the only one who would vouch for her was the villain, and there was no sign of her mates. Or her father. Or mercy, for that matter.

"Perhaps we will allow it once we have dispatched your companion to her new home," the queen said. "General Tobenn, you may rebind Maddy a Shayan in the nobles' hold and then escort her to the tower for further consideration."

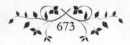

Maddy went cold at that. Like any prison tower, a fair number of the prisoners who went in never came out. Sure, the queen wasn't denying that Maddy might be part of the Cairdai family, but being locked up like a noble wasn't much of a benefit. The only good thing was the shift in her bindings.

The guard jerked her arm until she stumbled to her feet in front of the general, and Maddy barely managed to stay upright as blood prickled its way through her calves all the way to her toes. Then General Tobenn untied one of Maddy's hands so that she could pull her arms in front of her instead of behind, and Maddy couldn't stop her soft cry at the pleasure-pain of that.

Relief and agony flooded her brain as more blood pulsed through her numb, neglected arms. Damn, even her fingertips hurt. If she had access to her magic, Maddy might have been able to ease the ache, but the bindings were re-secured before she could process the switch.

The general gripped her other arm hard enough to leave a bruise, but before the woman could haul her away, Maddy inclined her head toward the queen. "Thank you for the audience, Your Majesty."

She barely had time to catch sight of Queen's Lera's startled expression before General Tobenn jerked Maddy around and started marching her toward the side door where they'd entered. They could deduce what they would of Maddy's manners—she was going to act the way her parents had raised her.

Then the double doors at the end of the room slammed open, and the effect was ruined.

34

When his mother had said she would create a gate to the Seelie palace, Fen had envisioned something a little less…spectacular. A small, hidden alcove or a forgotten place in the basement. Nope. She'd set them down directly in front of the doors to the throne room. Fen had only moments to rush through and disable the two guards standing on each side, swords already clearing sheaths at the burst of magic.

He could have killed them, but he hadn't. Death didn't have to be his purpose. Instead, he'd opened the floor beneath them for a split second and closed the stone around their feet. The huge double doors were so broad that Fen and Anna were able to walk between the floundering warriors without a scratch.

Unfortunately, Fen misjudged the weight of the wood based on its size. It must have been enchanted, for the door flew open beneath his shove and cracked against the wall hard enough to rebound. Nothing like making a fucking entrance.

Well, he might as well use it.

The huge room was only half full, and an alarming number of the people inside were soldiers. But he could barely look at anyone except for Maddy. Fury flared inside him at the bruises on her face and upper arms, especially when Anna whimpered in alarm. Maybe he *could* deal a little death to the warrior hauling Maddy roughly across the room.

"Release her," Fen found himself commanding.

Surprise crossed the guard's face, but although she stopped, she didn't loosen her grip on Maddy. "You dare to issue orders to me?"

Around the room, more swords left sheaths, but Fen didn't draw his own. "You dare to lay a hand on my mate?"

"This incursion will cost you—"

"Silence."

His gaze snapped to the holder of the voice. The queen? There were probably layers of meaning in each whirl of the woman's crown and each stitch of embroidery on her dress, yet none of it had significance to him. But her power was unmistakable.

At a softly spoken command, quiet had fallen, and as she rose with casual ease, the courtiers knelt without question.

"You break our laws by entering uninvited," the lady announced calmly.

"By ancient pacts long-standing, an Unseelie royal may enter to seek redress for a wrongdoing, as you may also enter our court unscathed."

Thank god his mother had made him practice *that* line a few times when she'd explained a few of the terms of the treaty between their peoples. Left to his own devices, he would've said "shit" again. This uppity crew of Seelie—Maddy excluded—didn't seem the type to go for that sort of thing.

"You are an Unseelie royal?" the probably-queen asked, a slight smile making her opinion of him more than clear. "A curious claim. Though I have met most of the royal family, I do not know you."

"I don't know you, either." Fen shrugged, which was only slightly better etiquette than pointing sarcastically at the circlet his mother had placed atop his head. "Queen Ara didn't seem to feel we needed to meet before she named me her heir."

That didn't go over well. The queen's placid expression shifted into anger, and the soldier holding Maddy drew her sword. All around them, courtiers murmured in disgruntled tones, and he thought he caught a few whispers of "the lost prince" before the woman on the dais lifted her hand to silence them.

"I am Queen Regent Lera, ruling with full authority in the name of my mother, Queen Tatianella. Name yourself, and verify this claim."

He almost asked her to verify *her* title, but he stopped himself from that temptation. Barely. "I am Crown Prince Feniarathen an Arafel, granted the Heir's Crown by the Unseelie queen's own hand."

Do not point upward. Do not point upward.

"So the rumors about Ara are true," the queen mused. "By what right do you intrude upon my court when your new ruler has yet to establish formal communication?"

"You're holding an Unseelie princess captive. It seems you've made your own introduction to me and thus my mother."

This time, the murmurs faded to delicious silence without the queen's command. Even Maddy was looking at him like he'd lost his damned mind, and maybe he had. Honestly, he'd expected to feel awkward about confronting the Seelie monarch, but instead of the bravado he usually wore for such encounters, he was nothing more or less than himself.

Without shame or fear—just himself.

"Are you referring to Maddy a Shayan? She has made no claim to being Unseelie royalty."

Fen's smile was purely for Maddy's benefit. "She was unaware that becoming my mate would grant her the title."

Queen Lera studied him, then Anna and Maddy in turn. At this point, he had no clue if Lera was friend or foe, although they could certainly agree about their

hatred for Meren. At least they had that bastard bound and guarded in the center of the room.

"You are the mates she mentioned," Queen Lera concluded after a long, tense moment. "I don't suppose you can supply the reason she ended up in my palace?"

Anna took a step forward. "A strong blast of my magic tossed Rianehd...I mean Meren into her, Your Majesty."

A ghost's whisper could have qualified as a shout in the moment before all hell broke loose. For a solid minute, Fen, Anna, and Maddy were forgotten beneath a wave of raised voices and frightened demands. What was going on? Then some of the conversations around him clarified.

"Rianehd?"

"Not again. Not again."

"My own daughter died defending..."

"She couldn't mean it was Meren?"

A slip of Anna's tongue had revealed the traitor's claim, and the court was far from ready to hear it. The crowd surged forward, trying to get to Meren, and the guards were forced to drive them back while keeping their prisoner contained. Even the warrior holding Maddy released her, apparently deciding she was no longer a threat.

His mate shifted uncertainly on her feet as the angry cries swelled around her. Fen shared a quick glance with Anna, and as one, they hurried toward Maddy before the mood grew even more hostile. But no one was paying attention to her now. Fen untied the knots binding her and dropped the metallic-looking rope to the floor before tugging Maddy gently against him.

She pulled away, an apologetic smile on her lips. "Armor isn't made for cuddling."

Fen released her into Anna's far more comfortable hold, and a moment's peace filled him at the sight of their embrace before the chaos around them trickled back in. Only the queen's authority settled the crowd into some semblance of containment, though even she was visibly shaken. Her voice held no sweetness now.

"Where did you hear that name?"

Anna released Maddy and shifted forward, partially blocking Maddy from the queen's sight. "Meren approached me under the guise of offering training. He introduced himself as Lord Rianehd a Orsed."

Fury shuddered across the queen's frame as she descended from the dais and marched toward Meren. "Sooner or later, you will die for that claim."

For one heart-stopping moment, Fen thought Queen Lera was talking to Anna, but Lera's gaze was locked on Meren. Fen couldn't see the other man's expression, but even on his knees, Meren didn't give the appearance of cowering. *He's been waiting for this.* Meren might not have planned the circumstances, but he'd wanted this confrontation for some time.

A thought that was more than a little worrying.

Something was wrong. Couldn't anyone else feel it?

Anna scanned the crowd, anxious to find the source. Nobles argued amongst themselves or shouted at Meren, who had two of the guards' swords crossed at his neck. Based on the queen's expression, Meren might not have a head much longer. But the conflict unfolding there wasn't the source. Was it?

Then again—

She stretched out her hand to catch at the sudden flow of water magic, but she wasn't quick enough. In a blink, Meren's bonds fell away, and he slipped backward like an errant wave before the swords could dig into his skin. The warriors' blades clanged together, and in that moment of distraction, Meren stood. Mist spiraled around him with an ominous orange glow.

"Water has a way of escaping any barrier," Maddy whispered.

Anna frowned at her. "What?"

"He said that in the holding room, but I didn't know he meant it literally." Maddy rubbed at her wrists, a haunted expression in her eyes. "That rope blocked my powers. I didn't think water could get around that."

Though Anna wasn't close enough to touch Meren's spell, it thrummed against her senses until she wanted to cover her ears. A useless instinct, since there was no actual sound. Could she do anything against this spell? She'd learned how to ground out some of the water magic she gathered, but she had no clue how to deal with something that might be toxic.

"I *am* Rianehd a Orsed," Meren announced. "And I will have this throne."

Queen Lera tipped up her nose. "Insanity. All know you are the eldest son of Nuall."

Fen leaned close, dropping his voice low so that only Maddy and Anna could hear. "Should we slip out of here while everyone's distracted, or nah?"

Maddy lifted her brows, and Anna elbowed him. "Fen!"

"Guess that's a 'nah,'" he said, and drew his sword.

"Oh, fuck," Maddy breathed.

Anna glanced her way. "Why—"

"That's steel, love," her mate whispered near her ear. "Not *peresten*. If anyone else notices…"

Anna shivered. Many of the Sidhe were allergic to iron—and thus steel—so their weapons were made from *peresten*, a metal mined on Moranaia. Yet Fen had come armed with a weapon the Seelie would consider poison. He really hadn't been exaggerating when he told his mother he might get them into a war.

"What are you doing?" Anna sent to Fen.

"At this point, it seems like this is a royal Seelie problem, and I was hoping to get Maddy out of here while the queen and royal guard dealt with Meren." Fen's hand shifted on the hilt of his sword as he eased forward. *"But I get why you both think we should stay, so*

I'm going to end this party early."

"Fen—"

"That's impossible," the queen cried, her fury piercing Anna's thoughts. "Nuall would have noticed that you weren't of his blood."

Meren lifted a hand, and the mist thickened. "Nuall was a fool, easily deceived by my mother. I am Tatianella's older brother. The uncle finally ready to depose you."

"You are a bastard!"

Wind whipped around Lera's body, twisting her skirt around her legs as she cast the air toward Meren. Wind and water—elements that could destroy easily depending on how they were joined. Would the queen defeat her foe, or would they create a hurricane in the middle of the throne room?

Glowing shields snapped around the two guards who had held Meren, and they rushed forward with furious intent. But when the first one swung his sword toward Meren's midriff, the blade slowed as it caught in the mist and began to dissolve. Meren reached through the magical shield and grabbed the guard by the neck as the sword's hilt clattered against the floor.

Anna pressed her hand to her own throat in sympathy when the soldier cried out, but she forced herself not to jump in without considering the problem. There was something familiar about the wretched mist, a hint of some element she'd seen before. But where? What?

No few of the surrounding nobles pulled forth their own magics until the air crackled with it, but when the mist ate through the last of the guard's shields and clung to his flesh, chaos broke out. The crash and hiss of elemental magic connecting with Meren's defenses blended with the screams of the soldier as the putrid mist flowed through his mouth and nose.

It didn't actually eat the man's skin, but when Meren threw the guard's gaunt, lifeless body to the floor moments later, the horror movie vibe was strong. Anna forced her eyes away quickly, but her stomach roiled nonetheless. What that stuff must have done...

The swirl of mist swelled as Meren repelled or absorbed the incoming attacks. He had to have planned for this, and God knew how he'd developed the worst of it. Anna shivered at the thought of how the man might have incorporated Gwragedd Annwn knowledge. At least she'd dodged that trap. But as the mages switched to defensive measures to shield the crowd, she had to wonder if any of them would escape this one.

"I recommend you control your subjects," Meren announced above the noise. "I have no qualms about killing more of them. Oh, yes. You should know that if I die, your mother does, too."

No surprise crossed the queen's expression, only heightened fury. "I will find a way to destroy you."

"Only I can unwind this poison in its many beautiful forms. Isn't that why you've been searching for me? Or did you think I wouldn't hear?" The sickly fog spun faster

around him. "Do you plan to let your guards and courtiers ruin your chance to face me? Though I can't imagine you would dare to kill me with Tatianella's life at risk."

Queen Lera's gaze sliced across the crowd. "None may interfere in this."

To Anna's astonishment, the nobles allowed themselves to be herded closer to the walls by the mages shielding them. Even the soldiers nearest Meren stepped back, although they didn't sheath their blades.

The guard who had been with Maddy caught sight of Fen and froze, her attention falling to the sword he held. Then her expression tightened, and she rushed forward. At least until she heard Maddy's soft call.

"General Tobenn, stop. We are not your enemies."

The warrior proved to be a good leader, for within moments she'd sized the three of them up and given Fen a quick nod.

Anna held her breath as Fen slipped up behind Meren, who was nearly obscured by the mist at this point. It took only seconds, but she might have been waiting an eternity for the steel blade to part through the sickly orange shield. An iron-based metal had to react differently than the guard's *peresten* blade, right? When the sword passed through unhindered, though, she exhaled in a worried hiss.

Wasn't iron supposed to dispel fae magic? It hadn't dissolved on contact, but the metal wasn't making a difference otherwise.

She could just make out the tip of the sword connecting with Meren's back. "Stop this crap," Fen said. "Or I'll stop it for you."

Meren glanced over his shoulder. "Your metal doesn't affect me, boy. Care to see a demonstration of my magic as proof?"

The droplets of mist solidified into something firmer—a globe of water that pitched and waved around Meren. Unlike the blue of a crystalline sea, the liquid was a murky brown-orange-green, a stream polluted with foul magic. The metal blade hissed as the caustic stuff wrapped around it, and as the poison lapped closer to Fen's hand, Anna knew she couldn't wait.

She called upon her magic.

The intensity of Meren's magic almost blinded her inner sight, but Anna let herself flow with it instead of resisting. As soon as she adapted to the strength, the components of the spell began to clarify. The water was bound into a sickly syrup of acid and…disease? Poison?

Large flecks of something like the magic she'd seen in Sparrow's blood danced through the water, but these bits were darker. Harsher and more deadly. No living being could survive this, not in this form.

And it had to be destroyed.

"Not again," Maddy muttered beneath her breath as Anna's eyes glazed over.

The last time she'd seen that expression on her mate, it had been just before Anna sucked in enough power to blast Meren through the air with a ball of water. And while Maddy held no love for any of the Sidhe in this room, she was sure mess-

ing with Meren's spell would be bad for all of them. Water shouldn't pulse with the same ochre-and-moss color scheme of her grandmother's old couch.

Without stopping to think, Maddy grabbed Anna's left hand and reached for the connection between them, one begun even before they'd mated. They'd rarely spoken telepathically before Anna and Fen had contacted Maddy during her imprisonment, but the link waited as though they'd used it a thousand times.

"What are you doing?" Maddy sent.

Anna tightened her grip. *"Look at Fen's sword."*

Squinting against the glow of magic, Maddy gasped. Gods above. The water was corrosive, eating into the metal as it worked its way closer to Fen's hand. Why didn't Fen let go of the damned hilt? Instead, he stared steadily at Meren as though waiting for the perfect moment to do…something. Hell if Maddy could guess what.

"This is related to the poison inside Sparrow," Anna said, her mental voice blank with concentration. *"I'm going to untangle the water. You see if you can do something about the ick."*

Anna's ring warmed against her finger, helping Maddy solidify their connection. She linked her power to Anna's, hoping she could act quickly enough. Maybe it wouldn't work, but she had to try. Her mate was already attempting to suck the water from Meren's spell without waiting for confirmation.

The liquid began to slow its frenetic circles around Meren, and a few water droplets broke away to float toward Anna. Meren spun to face them, fury lighting his face as he caught sight of them. Anna had bested him once, but he had centuries of experience with water. It wouldn't be easy for her to defeat him again.

Queen Lera took a step forward, wind whipping around her with increasing fury as she stared at Anna and then Maddy. Instead of bowing with respect, Maddy met her eyes directly, praying that her resolve would shine through as she tipped her head toward her mates. *Let us*, she thought, but she had no time to consider whether the queen would actually hear her.

Maddy had only that moment before she was forced to focus on containing the poison streaming toward Anna as it broke away from the water. No time for doubts, either. Like it was a true disease, she wrapped her power around each flake, quarantining it with her healing magic.

At least it was easy to focus her magic on one definite goal: purify.

Meren snarled, his hands twisting in unfamiliar patterns as he attempted to reclaim control of his spell. Beside her, Anna stiffened as the water fought against her, and Maddy cursed as her containment began to fail beneath the force of his power.

Suddenly, Fen dropped the remains of his half-eaten sword, and the clatter as it broke on the stone caused more than one shocked cry—and caught Meren's attention. But it couldn't have been intended to distract Meren from Maddy and Anna, because Fen stepped backward, gaze on his adversary, until he could take hold of Anna's other hand.

His thoughts—and magic—merged with theirs in a quick rush. *"There's peresten, copper, and now iron in that maelstrom. Keep grabbing the water, and I'll take care of the earth."*

"What about me?" Maddy asked. *"I don't think I can purify all of this."*

"Continue making sure we don't die."

Maddy almost choked on the laugh bubbling up her throat. *"I'm not the best at healing yet. Lial would have this shit gone already."*

Anna gave her a quick smile. *"Forget being the best. We need you."*

The statement could have been insulting, but instead, it filled Maddy with peace. She didn't have to be perfect. Not at all. As Lial had said, her power was fueled by her will, and there was no way in hell she would let her mates die. Her magic could use what it wanted of her, but she would not yield. If some of the sickness escaped, she would figure it out later.

"Let's do this."

As Anna increased her pull on the water, Maddy closed her eyes and focused on the poison-disease combo. She couldn't manage to nullify the stuff closest to Meren, but the water coalescing in the air between him and Anna was pure. If they could gather it all, maybe...

Then Fen froze the metal particles in the air and forced them toward Meren with a loud crack of energy.

"No!" Queen Lera shouted. "Don't kill him. Capture, but don't—"

Meren's spell cut off, so abruptly the water around Meren dropped to the floor with a splash. She opened her eyes in time to see Fen's bundle of metal condense around nothing. The red-gold-gray lump clanged against the floor before rolling to a stop near the queen's feet.

Meren was gone.

35

Fen stared at the ball of metal in disbelief. He'd been so close to slicing those fragments into Meren's body, but the asshole had disappeared before Fen could spring the trap. The shift had been so abrupt that he hadn't had time to halt the momentum entirely. Instead, he'd pushed the fragments together to make the misshapen lump.

"Hell," Fen grumbled. They had to figure out how he kept doing that.

For a moment, everyone in the room stood so still they might have been shaped into blocks, the disbelief so heavy it defied motion. Only the water Anna still held aloft showed any sign of movement. Then the queen's general advanced on the spot where Meren had stood as she barked out orders to the other guards. A new magic filled the room as several warriors scanned for invisibility spells, but Fen had a feeling it would do no good.

Which Anna confirmed after she dispelled the cleansed water. *"He's gone. I can't sense his water magic now, and he seems to have taken his icky spell with him."*

"Well, let's not volunteer for clean-up duty," Maddy interjected. *"I don't sense any more of the poison, either, but I'd rather not touch anything he left behind. Let their water mages figure it out."*

Fen grinned over Anna's shoulder at Maddy. *"Who's wanting to ditch now?"*

"There's only so much help I'm going to give after they almost locked me in the prison tower," she answered, scowling. *"Which technically isn't off the table."*

His humor dropped like the ball of metal. *"Over their dead bodies."*

"Fen." Anna squeezed his hand until he looked at her. *"Don't kill anyone. I don't want to talk you down from the angst for the next month or two."*

Her words surprised a laugh out of him, which earned an immediate reaction from the queen. Guards on each side, she picked her way around the water puddles until she could deliver her glare up close and personal. He didn't attempt to look repentant. Why bother when he didn't give a fuck?

"You find something amusing about the escape of a deadly traitor?" Queen Lera demanded.

Fen lifted his shoulder. "Not particularly. I was having a private discussion with my mates, one I'd be happy to continue back in the Unseelie court."

Okay, that was a bit of a stretch. Even if the three of them did return to his mother's realm, he had no plans to stand around joking in the middle of a bunch of nobles. But it was the principle of the thing.

Her lips thinned in displeasure. "Maddy has not been given leave to depart. Her claims have yet to be proven, and—"

"Are you fucking kidding—"

"Forgive my mate, Your Majesty," Anna said, her nails pinching the outside of his hand until he shut up. "I imagine his emotions are still high after our enemy escaped, and he is worried for our mate."

That was one way of putting it.

The queen gave him a disdainful glance, but her expression softened as she turned back to Anna. "I should expect no better from the Unseelie, especially one whom rumor has placed in Vek's company. As to Maddy, I'm afraid there are laws I must uphold, whether I wish to or not. She might not have intentionally entered the inner palace, but she did declare herself to be part of the noble house of Cairdai. I must determine if that is false."

Despite another warning squeeze from Anna, Fen couldn't stay silent. "How many centuries of peace with the Unseelie are you willing to risk?"

"You want to begin your time as crown prince with war and death?" Queen Lera asked in turn, her eyebrow lifting.

"It wasn't on my to-do list, but I'll happily wreck your world to save one of my mates." The queen's closest guard lifted his sword, but Fen gave a wide, fang-revealing smile in return. "It's not exactly a threat. Just a fact. Rumor should also tell you I've done worse with less cause."

Queen Lera gestured, and the guard eased back. "An interesting fact to bring up at this delicate time."

Hell, it probably *was* shit timing. Kien's poisoned energy spell hadn't affected the Unseelie alone, and there was no telling how many here had suffered because of it. If the queen realized how involved Fen had been, she would be less inclined to take it easy on Maddy.

Anna tugged her left hand free from Maddy's and held it out toward the queen. Once again, the guards snapped to greater attention, but Queen Lera ignored them. Instead, her gaze fell upon the ring Anna wore—their gift from Shayan. Her eyes widened, and she stepped close enough that she could have held Anna's hand if she reached out. Fen almost felt sorry for the poor, tense bodyguards.

"I see that *you* have been granted the favor of a Cairdai."

Maddy and Fen were quick to extend their own left hands. "My father made these in honor of our mating," Maddy said softly.

A new voice rang out behind them. "Yes, I did."

Fen glanced over his shoulder, and relief filled him at the sight of Shayan stand-

ing beside an imperious, auburn-haired Sidhe man who bore a slight resemblance to Maddy. Both men were dressed in court-style clothing, though Shayan appeared a touch less at ease than his companion. But then, the last time Fen had seen Maddy's father, he'd been dressed in casual Earth clothes.

Just one of many reasons to prefer life on Earth to one in some stuffy court.

"Why has my kin come under suspicion, Your Majesty?" the other man asked.

Curiously, a flush lit across the queen's cheeks as she explained what had happened. All the while, the other Sidhe lord stared impassively at her, only a slight flaring of his nostrils displaying displeasure. Who was he that the queen was almost deferential? Based on appearance, he and Shayan were likely close relations. A brother or uncle, maybe.

"How powerful is your family?" Fen sent to Maddy.

"Distantly noble. I thought." Confusion echoed in her mental voice as she studied the newcomer. *"My father doesn't talk about them much."*

"Maddy a Shayan is a daughter of the Cairdai. I trust my assurances will be sufficient to secure her claim?" the man asked.

Queen Lera smiled. "Of course, Lord Senolai. The royal family holds the greatest respect for you and your clan. Your word is more than sufficient to assure me of Lady Maddy's trustworthiness."

"Good." The Sidhe lord gave Maddy a sharp nod and bowed to the queen. "Then I will return to my forge. My brother will speak for me in this matter."

Before Fen had time to blink, the man had spun away and walked back out the door. Well, then. Either the family had a higher rank than Maddy realized or artisans held more influence here than he was used to. Maybe both? The stranger had mentioned a forge, which could mean he worked with weapons or armor. That sort of thing awarded a power of its own.

Queen Lera faced the rest of the room, and when she spoke, her voice rang through the huge space. "Maddy a Shayan has been claimed by Clan Cairdai and should be no stranger to the inner palace. For their attempts to defeat Meren a Nuall, Maddy and her mates are considered friends of this court. Now. Audience hours are over, and I invite you to depart until tomorrow."

She didn't address Meren's claims except to name him as Nuall's son. Maybe she was hoping that if she didn't make a big deal out of it, her courtiers wouldn't give his claim to the throne credence. Hah. That seemed like a mistake, but what did Fen know about this stuff?

"We will say goodbye, then," Fen offered, as politely as he could when what he wanted to do was haul ass out of there. "Princess Dria told me to assure you that your emissary will be safely returned to you in all haste. Although I guess you'll have to talk it over now that Meren's on the loose again."

But the queen shook her head. "I will speak with all four of you in my private chambers."

He should have known they wouldn't get out so easily.

"Is that an invitation or an order?" Fen asked.

Queen Lera smiled almost sweetly. "Which would be most likely to gain your cooperation? Although I do suppose you could remain out here while Lady Maddy and Lord Shayan comply with my request."

Fen ran his hand through his hair and sighed. After confirming both mates' consent, he nodded. "Let's get this over with."

Her body a weird combination of both aching and numb, Maddy plodded behind the queen and her guards without paying much attention to where they walked. She was too stunned by all that had happened to give the lavish palace much regard. Had her uncle really come to claim her? Why had no one else in the family spoken up when the queen first asked? Shivering, she folded her arms beneath her breasts for warmth. Maybe comfort, too. She'd been so close to being locked up again.

Her father sped up until he walked at her left side. "Maddy?"

"I thought they'd disavowed me entirely," she whispered.

"Sen hadn't made a formal declaration before," Shayan explained gently. "He has been so engrossed in his latest creation that I haven't pushed the matter, especially since I was still waiting for your formal audience. I'm sorry."

She wanted to stop in the middle of the hallway and demand he give her more detailed answers, but she wasn't going to press her luck with the queen. "I guess that's why no one would train me."

Shayan cursed beneath his breath. "We are artisans, not healers. If any close family had the gift—"

"But they don't. And no one else would work with a half-human." Maddy glanced at the ancient tapestries lining the walls. It had made less sense until she'd come here. Until she'd seen how very different their societies were. "It's probably for the best."

He scanned her face, his expression darkening with each bruise he spotted. "Who hurt you? I will demand redress for each mark."

Maddy snorted. "I'm afraid it's mostly on me. They might have put a hood over my head, but I'm the one who tried to explore the room with her face. Anyway, it sucks, but I can't really blame them for the bruises."

She heard a choked sound from Fen, and Anna gave her right wrist a light tug. "You know it wasn't your fault."

"No, it was not," her father affirmed. "I would love to know why General Tobenn is so jumpy. Blindfolding is not standard without good cause, and nothing I've heard would warrant it. Did they do the same to Meren?"

Maddy thought back to when he'd been brought into the holding room and shook her head. "Not as far as I know."

Her father's eyes hardened. "Yes, redress must be demanded."

She couldn't stop glancing over at him, even as they passed through a hallway lined with stained glass windows. But she couldn't have said what the designs looked like since Shayan's face held a story more fascinating than whatever the artist had designed into the glass. On Earth, her father was quiet and steady, but here, he was different. Harder, more unyielding, and a tad bit uncomfortable.

"Are you ever going to tell me why you left?"

He blinked in surprise. "Perhaps, but not today. Probably not tomorrow, either."

"I'll tell you when you're older?"

"Basically." Her father smiled. "But I will say that I don't regret a moment."

At least there was that. "I'm sure Mom will be happy to hear that."

Shayan chuckled. "I'm sure she would."

With each step, the hallways became finer, and the sheer grandness of the place finally captured Maddy's attention enough for closer examination. Like on Moranaia, even the walls were carved with decorations, in this case tiny, exquisite leaves and flowers. Hard floors gave way to thick carpet that softened their steps, and the windows overlooking the city below were interspersed with priceless statues and fine tapestries. She'd assumed the queen had planned to take them to a formal receiving room, not the actual family wing, but now Maddy wasn't so sure.

Before she could ask her father if this was normal, Queen Lera led them into a small sitting room. One guard left, closing the door behind himself, and the other stationed herself against the wooden frame, her hand on her sword hilt. The queen gestured toward the chairs grouped in a loose circle near the fireplace on the far wall.

"Shall we?"

Maddy exchanged *what the hell?* looks with Fen and Anna, but all three of them found seats. This time, Fen placed himself at her right side, and Anna sat on her left. How long would it take them to stop hovering over her after this? Anna shifted her seat slightly closer while Fen stretched his foot out until it almost nudged hers, and she smiled.

Probably a long time.

After Shayan took the chair beside Anna, the queen plopped down in the other seat like a teenager pleading exhaustion, and Maddy couldn't do anything but stare. Especially when Queen Lera tipped her head back against the cushion and shoved her fingers between her tight braids to massage her scalp. Where had the icily formal woman gone?

"Your Majesty?" Shayan asked, shock lifting his tone.

"It's really 'Your Highness,' you know." The queen's fingers rubbed at her scalp so hard it had to hurt instead of help. "Of course, you know that. You're older than I am. Please just call me Lera. For the love of the divine, I miss being called simply Lera."

Not even Fen seemed to have a comeback to that. He, Anna, and Shayan all stared at the queen with the same shock Maddy felt. Something was going on here. Something important.

Finally, Lera sat up, straightening her spine until it looked ready to snap. She lowered her hands to her lap so calmly that the previous moment was almost an

impossible memory. "Forgive my lapse. I am weary beyond words, and now there is Meren's claim on top of it all."

Good grief. Hopefully, there was an explanation forthcoming, because Maddy had no clue what 'it all' might entail. "It's okay."

"No." Lera sighed. "It isn't, but I am beyond my endurance to make it so."

Maddy's father leaned forward. "Is there something I can do to help, Your..."

"I meant what I said about calling me Lera, at least in this room. I can certainly trust Sen's—" A curious blush reddened the queen's cheeks. "Lord Senolai's brother, and by extension, the rest of the family."

Her father didn't question the slip, but Maddy wanted to learn the story behind it almost as much as she wanted to find out about her father's past. She knew better than to question, though. "Trust us with what?" she asked instead.

Lera grimaced. "I need you to examine my mother."

"Queen Tatianella?" Shayan asked. At Lera's wry glance, he snorted. "Of course. Who else?"

Maddy couldn't look away from Lera's exhausted, almost defeated, expression as every rumor she'd ever heard flipped through her head. No one knew why Queen Tatianella had yielded her power to her daughter, and although there had been some grumbling, the Seelie had accepted Princess Lera as regent. Most had assumed that the queen had been afflicted with the energy poisoning, but Arlyn of Moranaia had cleared that months ago.

Right?

This made no sense. "You were about to lock me up in the prison tower, and now you want me to examine the queen?"

"I saw the way you and your mates fought Meren, and the way you purified that poison... I believe you might be able to help, if only to bring clarity to the situation." Lera skimmed her gaze across the three of them, finally settling on Fen. "And you. Whispers tell me the lost prince of the Unseelie worked with Kien during the energy poisoning that affected both realms. Is that correct? If so, you will be able to identify Kien's poison if that is the cause."

Fen's foot twitched against Maddy's. "I owe you nothing, especially after the way you treated my mate."

"Did my general strike you, Maddy?"

"No," she answered honestly. "But the hood didn't exactly help me navigate."

Lera's eyebrows lowered with temper as she inclined her head toward Maddy. "General Tobenn is perhaps overzealous with humans. She will be reprimanded."

"I am as much Sidhe as human," Maddy said softly.

Lera nodded. "So I believe. But the general is...older. My grandfather's ways were different."

Damn. The general hadn't appeared that old.

Then Shayan spoke—and blew Maddy's mind. "Only different among the unpleasant. There's a reason I avoided Tobenn during our schooling."

How…how had she not known her father's age? She'd been aware he'd lived a long time before coming to Earth, but over a thousand years? Maddy struggled to remember what she'd learned about her Seelie history, but after the day she'd had, she couldn't pull up anything resembling an exact date for the old king's death.

"I give my word that she will be dealt with." Lera said, her comment seemingly for Shayan but her focus on Maddy. "So. Will you help me? It is much to ask, but this boon would do a great deal to solidify peace between the Seelie and Unseelie. Similar to your unlikely union."

Maddy closed her eyes as fear and doubt assailed her. She was nowhere near mastery—or even competence—and this was the queen. The most important person in the Seelie realm. Who was she to try to help?

Anna's hand closed around her left and Fen's her right. As their energies mingled, her mind flashed to the moment they had stood against Meren. Maybe if they worked together like that, they could find out what was wrong with the queen. They didn't have to be able to solve it, after all. They could always call in Lial or Vek, who had helped with Sparrow.

Maddy took a deep breath and opened her eyes. "An examination is all I can promise."

36

Anna let Fen and Maddy take the lead as they followed the queen through a door hidden behind a panel and then down a narrow passage. It was only the four of them—Shayan had stayed in the sitting room with the guard. Being shown a secret tunnel was a surprising display of trust. Then again, Lera was counting on them to help with the true queen, so this trust wasn't really bigger than that.

If only Anna had a clue what she was supposed to contribute.

Maddy was a healer. Fen had knowledge of the poisoned energy spell that Kien had imbued in Earth's energy. But what good was water magic? She could purify their drinking water, but that wasn't going to help the queen. She would probably end up observing again as she had when Vek healed Sparrow. If nothing else, she could supply energy to her mates.

The room they entered was huge, and the right side was dominated by a massive bed on a raised platform. It was every medieval-enthusiast's dream. Elaborately carved and painted bedposts held up a gorgeous canopy, and privacy drapes made of the richest fabric Anna had ever seen were tied against the posts with rope that might have been woven from gold.

There was so much going on that it took her a moment to spot the queen's form beneath the piles of blankets. Anna had expected someone older-looking, even knowing about the long lifespans of the fae, but Queen Tatianella could have been Lera's older sister. A very sick and gaunt older sister, anyway.

Lera stopped at the head of the bed and waited for the rest of them to step closer. Maddy and Fen went first since their powers were more relevant to the problem. As they studied the queen, Anna continued to examine their surroundings. She couldn't help herself. Something was…off. It reminded her enough of Meren's icky energy that she shivered.

Then movement from the other side of the bed caught her eye—an attendant of some sort. The lady stood, curtsied to Lera, and hurried from the room without a word, only pausing to grab an ewer on the way out.

The strange energy faded as soon as the door closed. Almost gone, if not quite.

"When Mother first became ill, she tossed and turned a great deal," Lera began. "We struggled to keep her calm and quiet. But the more the energy poisoning dissipated, the more still she became. Now… Well, you can see the now."

Anna didn't know a great deal about analyzing another's health, not the way Maddy did, but even she could see that the queen's condition wasn't right. The blankets barely moved with the woman's breath, and if she was any paler, Anna would have thought she was dead. Why hadn't Lera tried to find help before the queen got this bad?

"You've been giving her water?" Anna asked.

Lera gave her a perplexed frown. "Of course. Although it has been a struggle to get enough water and broth into her of late. It is only a matter of time before the ladies attending her break their oaths of secrecy out of concern."

"And the water was out of that pitcher?" Now even Maddy and Fen were staring at her in confusion, but Anna kept her focus on Lera. "The one her attendant carried out?"

Clarity washed across the princess's face. "Yes. It's something in the water, isn't it? When I learned of Meren's betrayal, I began to suspect he was connected. He had worked his way to a high position in this court, even acting as my emissary at times. He was one of the few I let sit with her, in fact. I wanted him retrieved so I could prove his involvement, especially since it could also be a remnant of the other energy poisoning. I don't know what to think."

Oh, the poor princess. Something about her seemed younger than the other Sidhe, and she hadn't had an easy time of taking over for her mother. If the lady hadn't been a royal from a totally different culture, Anna would have dared a comforting hug.

"I'm not sure, but the water was definitely not normal," Anna said, squelching her overly friendly instincts. "Maybe it's just my inexperience using my magic."

"How about we see what we can find?" Maddy asked, angling herself closer to the bed.

"Wait." Anna grabbed her mate's arm before she could touch the queen. "We're going to join energy, right?"

Maddy nodded. "Right. Of course."

As soon as they gripped hands and joined energy, Maddy's worry hit Anna, along with a nice side of Fen's guilt. *"We can do this,"* Anna sent.

The emotions she received in return weren't exactly confident.

"Fen should connect first," Maddy said. *"And I'll look through his senses the way I did with Meren's polluted water in the throne room. Maybe that will provide some insulation if my power is troublesome."*

Anna expected Fen to argue, but he let out a soft, resigned sigh and shifted closer to the queen. Maybe their combined talents would work or maybe they wouldn't. But in this case, action was better than the alternative.

Fen stretched his hand toward the queen and hoped Lera couldn't see how it shook. They were really going to do this. They were going to use their magic on the queen of the Seelie court, once mortal enemies to his kind and hardly friends now. Not only that, but he might be partially responsible for her current condition. Kien created the poison, but Fen had connected it to the energy field. He'd built part of the web that had put this woman in a coma, and there was every possibility that Meren had manipulated that work.

"Come on, Fen," Maddy muttered into his head, her nerves heightening his anxiety.

Not that he needed a lot of help.

Quickly, he placed his hand on the queen's upper arm and allowed Maddy's power to move through him. A weird sensation like popping champagne bubbles tickled the edge of his awareness, but he didn't mind. Maddy's light could never be a burden.

After a surprisingly short time, she retreated. *"I thought I would find a shard of poison like the one afflicting Sparrow, but I didn't. I checked her body and found no mass of darkness."*

"But?"

"Something isn't right. I just can't tell what."

Fen frowned. *"Let me look."*

He wasn't a healer, but he knew all too well what that poison looked like. He'd channeled it into enough crystals for Kien as the crazy fuck had spread his net of sickness around the world. He'd also been bitten by it when the spell had shattered. Unfortunately, he wasn't adept at scanning people for anything besides the amount of energy he could gather from their blood.

Though Fen did his best, he couldn't find anything conclusive, either. One moment, he thought he detected a hint of dark energy, but it rushed away before he could be sure. What the hell? There had to be *something* wrong with the queen. What else could sicken a powerful Seelie queen?

"You're right," he said. *"But I can't find it either."*

Frustration pooled between them. What if they couldn't figure out the problem? The Seelie queen was in bad shape, and he had to assume the healers here had tried to help. He had no clue if their relations with Moranaia were solid enough that Lial or another healer there would have been called. Was there anyone else who could aid them?

"I'll try again." Maddy's mental voice hardened. *"As often as it takes."*

When his mate channeled through again, Fen stayed in the background, observing her work. Each section she scanned made him uneasy, but the cause slipped away like oil.

Dammit. Why couldn't they figure this out?

Maddy knew she was squeezing Fen's and Anna's hands far too tightly, but she couldn't stop herself. It was that or scream, and that would draw a million of the Royal Guard into the room. But honestly, what else could she do at this point? Darkness freckled the queen's blood like glitter in water, impossible to grasp or contain. What was sustaining it? Where was the origin?

She should have insisted they call for Lial.

After another deep breath, Maddy forced the thought from her mind and prepared to scan again. Maybe if she went really slowly, those trace hints of darkness wouldn't float away. There had to be some solution. If her healing followed her will, then doubt wouldn't help.

Anna's thoughts nudged hers before she could. *"How about we try this together? I found some of what sickened Sparrow."*

Maddy almost rejected the suggestion, but then her earlier comparison flashed through her mind. *Glitter in water.* If there was something in the blood, Anna might have better luck. After all, blood contained a great deal of water. Not to mention that Meren was a possible connecting point, having touched both Sparrow and the queen.

As soon as Maddy gave her assent, they merged more fully, and her ring warmed against her skin as it aided the connection. Together. Somehow, they had to manage.

Rushing through the queen's body on a wave of Maddy's power was…something. Anna gasped as Tatianella's heart filled her awareness. Though she couldn't affect any of the organs the way Maddy could, Anna was able to observe the rush of blood through tissue. The slow, steady beat was hypnotic, so much that she forgot her own task for a moment.

Anna separated her magic from the others' ever so slightly until she could use it to examine the queen's blood. Immediately, she caught sight of the flakes, more numerous than Sparrow's but similar. Would they run from her as they had Fen and Maddy? She opened her power gently until it flowed and lapped with the rhythm of the blood. Only then did she try to draw near to the tiny intruders. She had almost touched one when she realized what it was and retreated.

"It's like the stuff that was swirling around Meren."

Fen's frustration filled her. *"That wasn't Kien's crap. It could be inspired by it, but it's not the same. Guess that confirms that Meren was experimenting."*

Maddy's fingers tightened around hers, and Anna forced her own grip to loosen until her mate did the same. *"We have to get this out of her blood,"* Maddy said. *"Lial might be able to get rid of it, but I don't have a clue. What did you do for Sparrow?"*

"Vek poured in a bunch of life magic," Anna answered. *"Not an option for us."*

"I could try to pull it free while drinking," Fen offered grimly.

"No." An idea clarified in Anna's head. *"That would just transfer the problem to you. What about bloodletting?"*

Fen recoiled. *"That's some medieval shit right there, Anna."*

"It wasn't just done in the Middle Ages, and there are cultures that still do it," Maddy snapped. *"Lial told me about the time he used a similar method to draw iron from Lyr's wound, and that's a lot like what we need to do for the queen."*

"But—"

"I'm not saying we break out the leeches. We just need an exit to pull the toxins through." Anna took a calming breath. *"Stop being a baby. It's not like you're squeamish about blood."*

Once Fen relented, they loosened their connection enough for Maddy to request a bowl and knife from Lera. That was its own fierce argument, but Anna and Maddy finally convinced the princess of the merit of their idea. After that, it was only moments before they had everything they needed to begin the task.

So much fun.

This was going to take hours.

Maddy scowled into the ewer of water as she washed her hands one more time. Fen had used his power to pull the dried dirt away from her body, but she still didn't feel clean. And she was tired. Hadn't she said she was only going to do an examination? But of course, she couldn't leave the queen in a coma any more than she could have let Meren die right in front of her. Sometimes, it sucked being a softy.

With a resigned sigh, Maddy dried her hands on another clean towel and returned to the queen's bedside. This time, her mates would channel through her instead of Fen, and the very idea of being an anchor wore her out. It would work the best, though. They were also going to try to connect without touching so that Fen could keep the queen's wound numb and the blood flowing.

Who would have thought that having a blood elf around during a medical procedure would be so useful? Maybe he should hire himself out to surgeons.

Maddy placed her hand on the queen's upper arm and reached for her link to Anna and Fen. They merged so easily this time that she paused a moment to savor it. Then she and Anna took their metaphorical places at the top of Queen Tatianella's body and waited for Fen to make the cut in her wrist. Only a small one, but hopefully enough.

Anna started first, pushing the flecks of poison through the queen's veins at a slow, methodical pace. Maddy helped direct the actual flow so that the mess wouldn't clump and clog, and once they were a quarter of the way through, she had to use a sedation spell on the queen as she began to stir.

Gather. Push through.

Gather. Push through.

Then purify every bit of tissue she could.

By the time Fen closed the cut, Maddy's entire body was shaking with exhaustion. Even so, she did one last search of the queen's body before removing the sedation spell and pulling her energy free. She opened blurred eyes to search for a chair, and once she spotted one beside the bed, she sank into it without hesitation.

"Maddy," Anna breathed, a strange note to her voice.

Had they failed? Maddy followed the others' shocked gazes to the queen's face, only then noticing that Tatianella's eyes had opened, too. For a moment, no one moved. Then Lera rushed forward with a cry as Fen jerked the bowl of blood away before it was knocked over. A good call. The queen sat up in time for her daughter to envelop her in a hug.

Queen Tatianella blinked, and her blank expression had Maddy worrying that her mind had been damaged by the poison. Had she healed enough tissue after Anna's work was done? Maddy had trusted her magic and will to accomplish the task, but there was every chance she'd messed something up. Wouldn't that just figure?

Then the queen wrapped her arms slowly around Lera. "What happened? Who are these people?"

Lera beamed at Maddy. "You were poisoned, and they saved you."

Maddy's heart thumped hard as a new sensation filled her.

Pride.

"Anna and Fen are equally responsible for healing you, Your Majesty," Maddy finally managed to say.

Tatianella's eyes widened as she studied Anna and then Fen. "A story I must hear. Over a plate of food, I hope. Whatever happened has left me famished."

Maddy could agree with that. But as a bevy of ladies rushed in to help the queen to her changing room and order food, Maddy could only sit there in wonder. She'd done it. She'd used her power, and it had worked.

They were so going to have a celebration when they returned to Earth.

37

When Fen strode into the Unseelie throne room a couple of hours later, he carried a vial of poisoned blood, a letter of commendation from Queen Tatianella, and a metric shitload of worry. There was his fear for Maddy, who drooped with such exhaustion that he'd almost carried her, too. Then there was Queen Tatianella's request for an alliance written beneath the commendation—one she wanted him to facilitate.

Oh, and the matter of Meren out there somewhere. No big deal.

Fen had no clue how long had passed since he'd left, but the throne room was empty of everyone except a handful of guards. No one stopped him as he cut through the door in the back corner and started down the private passageway to his mother's study. He wanted to rush, but he forced himself to slow his pace so Maddy and Anna could walk beside him. If he weren't so tired, he would have run the distance.

Far better to drop this crap on his mother and get the hell out. Unfortunately, he had a feeling he couldn't. Not just because of Ara. It was weird, but something inside him had shifted in the Seelie realm. Maybe it was confronting Lera and then Meren. Or helping to save their queen.

Or that moment after dinner when Queen Tatianella had given him a vial of her tainted blood from the collection bowl and asked him to research what Meren had done—even after Fen had confessed to his work with Kien. But she said he'd earned her trust.

A *Felshreh* prince, heir to the Unseelie throne, granted something as precious as the Seelie queen's blood. It defied all logic.

"I hope this meeting won't take long," Maddy grumbled softly.

Fen lifted her hand and brushed a kiss against her knuckles. "I'll get us out of here as quickly as I can after I leave the letter."

"But what about the—"

"The full story can wait," Fen said, cutting off Anna's words before switching to mental communication with them both. *"I'm not giving her the vial. I don't trust her enough."*

Maddy's hand went limp in his. *"Thank the gods. I know you won't misuse it, but…"*

"My mother is less certain. Believe me, I know."

It was night beyond the window, but Ara sat behind her desk despite the hour. Hell, she looked so tired he had to wonder if she'd been waiting in that spot since he and Anna had left. Quite likely. Ara stood slowly, and her hand drifted to her lower back as though it ached. Her expression, though—that was all relief.

"You've returned," she said, and he could tell from her voice that she'd feared the opposite would happen. "And brought your other mate, I assume?"

It was awkward as fuck introducing them, but Fen made it through with relative politeness. An improvement, he supposed, over the animosity he'd held for his mother for so long. But as Ara smiled at Maddy and welcomed her as an Unseelie princess, the moment was more surreal than anything.

"I'm not sure it's a good idea to give me a title," Maddy said. "Though I have a feeling my father's family is a little more noble than I realized, I don't think I'm suited."

Fen started to reassure her, but Anna beat him to it.

"You're better prepared than I am. You'll do great."

He couldn't resist pulling both women closer until he could slip his arms around their waists. Couldn't they see how worthy they were? Love filled him until he thought he would burst with it, especially when they twined their own arms together behind his back. Fucking perfect.

"At least the word 'shit' isn't likely to feature in your first formal speech," Fen joked.

His mother let out an exasperated sigh. "I am relieved to hear that you've chosen mates with more decorum. However, I would much prefer to learn what happened in the Seelie court."

A reasonable request, but he wished he could avoid it. One more task in a long-assed day.

Well. No time like the present.

Anna trailed her fingers through the water burbling up from the fountain in the corner of the suite's large living room. A shiver whispered across her skin at the contact, but she was too tired to enjoy it. In fact, their exhaustion was the only reason Fen had let his mother show him to his elaborate rooms in the heart of the palace.

"You may make any changes that you like," Ara said to Fen.

Maddy joined Anna beside the fountain, both of them doing their best not to show how closely they were following the argument.

"I'm living on Earth."

"You formally accepted your role as heir. Our people will expect—"

"I'd already been given the title before I returned to Earth with Vek. I don't see any reason for that to change. We have lives there."

"And you are supposed to be facilitating the treaty with the Seelie."

"I never said I wouldn't."

Anna exchanged an amused glance with Maddy, and finally, they both turned. "Couldn't you do what Maddy has arranged for her medical training?" Anna asked.

Ara and Fen gave her such identical confounded expressions that she almost laughed. "But what about you?" Fen asked.

"I can be on my own for a few days, Fen," Anna answered drily. "Besides, I have my own ancestors to hunt down for a little tutoring. We can work it out."

Ara smiled. "An excellent suggestion, although you and Maddy will also need to be here at times. Not only should you be versed in our ways, but it is a good reminder to our people that Fen is mated. He will be a subject of much interest once his negotiations with the Seelie become common knowledge."

That wiped away some of Anna's amusement. She didn't doubt that she could trust Fen, nor did she believe he would be unfaithful. But she remembered the whispered comments he'd received. Other nobles would pester the crap out of him if they thought they could gain any kind of influence through a sexual liaison—or any similar connection.

None of which appeared to worry Fen. "I doubt they'll bother."

"May I assume this solution is satisfactory, then?" Ara asked.

"You just…" Fen rubbed at the back of his neck, his gaze lowering. "You have to know that I have no intentions of forming a close relationship with you."

Ara drew her hands together in front of her waist, the stiffness of the gesture revealing her pain. But the emotion didn't echo in her words. "I understand that you have forgiven Vek."

Fen met his mother's eyes, and Anna's heart squeezed at the hurt and sadness that bounced between them. "He came for me. He tried to talk me out of my bad decisions, and when that didn't work, he ended up saving my ass. My head understands why you handed me off to my father and pretended I didn't exist, but I'm not sure my heart ever will."

Even as she inclined her head in acknowledgement, the queen blinked rapidly as though fighting back tears. "I would do it again to see you safe, and I am happy to bear your anger. You may seek me out or not when you are in residence."

As Ara strode from the room, she wasn't sure who she wanted to hug more—Ara or Fen. Then Fen sank down into an embroidered armchair, lowering his head into his hands, and the queen was forgotten. She nudged her shoulder against Maddy's, and together, they approached their mate.

"Let's go to bed," Anna said.

Maddy ran her hand through Fen's hair. "And that's not a euphemism as far as I'm concerned. I love you guys, but I want sleep."

Fen straightened, a wry smile lightening his expression. "I've gotta agree."

Together, they opened doors until they came across the first bedroom with a decent-sized bed. They undressed quickly—except Fen, who had to find a safe spot for

the vial of blood—and piled together in the center of the bed with Maddy against Fen and Anna at her back.

The best way to fall asleep.

Maddy would have preferred to stay in bed for a solid day, but they rested only long enough to not be walking disasters. Fen had asked Ara to send a message to Vek the night before assuring him of their safety, but Fen was anxious to talk to his uncle. No doubt about the vial of blood.

"Do we even know what time it is there?" Maddy asked.

Fen shrugged. "Don't know, don't care."

"I'm not sure your family will be happy about us popping in if it's the middle of the night."

"Nah, I bet Vek's pacing the outpost like a nervous auntie on childcare duty for the first time." Fen grinned wickedly. "If Dria hasn't put an immobilizing spell on him by now."

Anna moved in front of them and held out her hands. "Let's go see."

They stood together in a circle and linked their energies together as closely as they could. In a quick burst of power, Fen activated his link to the outpost, and Maddy's vision blanked for a moment as the ground disappeared beneath her. She cried out, a bit of an embarrassment since solid ground and her sight returned before the shout had faded from her ears.

The room was small enough that the three of them barely fit around the cluster of blue-green stones in the center. Then Fen slumped against a nearby wall, and Maddy forgot about the pretty gemstones as she hurried to his side. His skin had gone pale, and his breath came fast.

It only took a quick scan, though, to figure out why. "Take some of my energy."

"I don't want to—"

"Be an idiot again?" Anna asked. Again? Maddy's brow furrowed at the odd comment, but Anna explained before she could ask. "He ported us this way when we were trying to save you, and it drained him hard."

"I was only going to say that I don't want to cause Maddy more strain. She went through a lot yesterday."

Maddy wiggled her upper arm beneath his nose. "Then take a tiny bit. I want to go get more sleep sometime today."

She worried that he would refuse, and then they would have to haul him out of here and wander through the caverns until they could find his uncle. Thankfully, Fen sighed and made a tiny slice with his fang so that he could get enough blood to access her energy. Her muscles grew a touch heavier from tiredness, but when he sealed the wound and disconnected, she couldn't tell a great deal of difference.

The informal meeting room was a fair walk from where they'd arrived, but Maddy didn't complain. There was a reassurance to being back in a place she recognized, even if it wasn't hers. She was free of the Seelie court. Truly free. Though Queen

Tatianella had offered her a standing invitation to visit—and a freaking house, for gods' sake—Maddy didn't think she would want to go back any time soon.

Vek and Dria were waiting for them regardless of the hour. As soon as the door closed behind Anna, the couple stood and hurried over. But Fen froze, so abruptly that Maddy almost ran into him. What was his problem?

"Meren escaped."

Frowning, Vek halted. "Did you think I was going to give you a grade on your performance?"

"I know how much you want him dead." Fen sagged, and Maddy didn't think it was from exhaustion. "But even if I'd had a good shot, I'm not sure I could have done it."

It was Dria who stepped forward to settle her hand on Fen's shoulder. "You weren't supposed to. Ralan told us a while back that the task would likely fall to one of Meren's brothers. Or not-brothers, I suppose."

"We did manage to save Queen Tatianella," Maddy offered, hoping to distract Fen. "Oh, and Anna and I are Unseelie princesses now. I think that means Vek can't boss us around."

Fen's uncle laughed. "You wish."

It was going to be okay. As they recounted all that had happened and made plans for testing the Seelie queen's blood, that refrain eased through Maddy until it settled in her soul. Though they had to be on guard against Meren, they could conquer anything as long as they were together. Besides, Meren had bigger things to worry about—like an awakened Queen Tatianella sending every warrior at her disposal after him. He would probably avoid the three of them now that he knew they couldn't be subverted.

And now that he knew that they were capable of defeating him.

Together and apart, Maddy and her mates would train. They would grow and prosper. She wouldn't have it any other way.

One week later

Fen paused at the top of the stairs as a happy shriek rang out. Oh, surely the hell not. His mates, the two best people in the world, wouldn't have started without him. Grumbling to himself, he opened the door at the top of the steps and marched into their living room, only to freeze at the sight of Maddy and Anna doing a victory dance.

While end credits played on the TV behind them.

"Not cool," he said as he approached.

Both women stopped their dance, and Maddy blew a strand of red hair out of her face before grinning. "I beat my save game, not ours. Just in time to keep from giving you spoilers, too."

Suddenly, he wondered if *Death's Curse 3* wasn't a more apt title than he'd given it credit for. He'd certainly been doomed to earn every accomplishment last. Then

Anna danced over to give him a kiss, and he had to rethink the curse part.

"How about we take this upstairs?" Maddy asked, wiggling her brows. "Then we can beat the other save file together."

Well, who was he to argue? If his mates were happy, then so was he.

Character List and Dictionary

Characters

Characters

Alianar (AH-LEE-uh-nahr) – King of Moranaia. Father of Teyark, Kien, Ralan, and Dria

Allafon (AL-uh-fahn) – Lord of Oria, an estate under Lord Lyr's command.

Angela (AN-jehl-uh) – Maddy's human mother.

Anna (ANN-uh) – Maddy's girlfriend and potential mate to Maddy and Fen.

Ara / Arafel (ehr-AH-fehl) – One of the Unseelie king's children and half-sister to Vek. She is also Fen's mother, but she sent him to Earth after he was born.

Aris (EHR-iss) – Husband of Selia and father of Iren. Presumed dead.

Arlyn (AHR-lynn) – Half-blood daughter of Lyr and his potential soulbonded, Aimee, who he met on Earth. Arlyn traveled to Moranaia after her mother's death to confront her elven father and quickly bonded with Kai.

Baza (bah-zah) – A dragon who opposes Kezari.

Caolte (KWIL-chuh) – Brother of Naomh and Meren. Caolte is sworn to protect his brother, Naomh.

Corath (KOR-ath) – Soulbonded of Prince Teyark. A skilled swordsmith and enchanter, Corath's weapons are highly prized.

Delbin (dehl-bin) – A young elf exiled to Earth one hundred years prior in order to escape Allafon's machinations.

Dria (DREE-uh) – Youngest child of King Alianar and Enielle. Dria was sent early to the Citadel, the place where the highest-ranking mages train for battle. At 317, Dria is one of the youngest to complete her training and take her place within a mage troop.

Elerie (uh-LEHR-ee) – Kai's mother.

Enielle (EHN-ee-ehl) – Mother of Teyark, Kien, Ralan, and Dria.

Eri (EHR-ee) – Daughter of Prince Ralan and a human woman. After nearly dying from energy poisoning, her father brought her to Moranaia from Earth to be healed.

Fedah (fay-duh) – Captain of the mage troop sent from the Citadel to help the Moranaian outpost.

Fen (fehn) – Son of Ara and a human man. Fen was abandoned on Earth, where he got involved with Kien's group of outcasts. To atone for working with Kien, Fen helps repair the damage he'd once contributed to creating.

Gessen – One of Dria's few friends at the Citadel. A mage skilled with water and air.

Inona (ih-NO-nuh) – A Moranaian scout assigned to check on exiles banished to Earth.

Iren (EAR-ehn) – The young son of Selia.

Kai –Soulbound to Arlyn. Kai works as Lyr's primary scout.

Kenaren (Keh-NAH-rehn) – Ralan's former lover.

Kethen (KETH-ehn) – Cousin to Vek. Kethen is still in mourning for his son, who died from Kien's energy poisoning.

Kezari (ke-ZAHR-ee) – Dragon companion to Aris.

Kien (KEE-ehn) – Son of King Alianar and Enielle. Power-hungry and determined to someday claim the throne. He finally made his way back to Moranaia and was killed by the king.

Lera (LEHR-uh) – Acting queen of the Seelie court.

Lial (lee-ahl) – The primary healer at Braelyn, Lyr's estate. Lial is renowned for being both highly skilled and easily annoyed.

Lynia (LYNN-ee-uh) – Lyr's mother. A researcher whose magic lies in books and knowledge. She was almost killed during Allafon's attempted coup, but Lial saved her.

Lyr (leer) / Lyrnis (LEER-nis) – Lord of Braelyn. Arlyn's father. After Arlyn's arrival and the subsequent upheaval, Lyr has learned to stop expecting anything—unless it is unusual.

Maddy (maddee) – Anna's girlfriend and potential mate to Fen and Anna. Maddy lives in Chattanooga, Tennessee and is currently buying her friend Cora's shop, The Magic Touch, after Cora moved to Moranaia. Maddy is half Seelie Sidhe and half human.

Meli (MEHL-ee) – Lyr's soulbonded. One of the rare Ljósálfar (Norse elves), Meli guided her king's ambassador to Moranaia to ask for help with the energy poisoning affecting their realm. She ultimately bonds with Lyr and remains on Moranaia.

Meren (MEHR-ehn) – Brother of Naomh and Caolte. Meren is the oldest of the brothers but diverges sharply in ideology. Believing that the Seelie Sidhe should leave their underground realms and reclaim the surface, Meren will do whatever he deems necessary to achieve his goals.

Naomh (NAY-om) – Brother of Meren and Caolte. Works with Kien to keep his people from returning to the surface.

Quaea – Bodyguard to King Torek of the Unseelie. She sometimes acts as his messenger.

Ralan (RAHL-ehn) – Son of King Alianar and Enielle. Eri's father. Ralan is a powerful seer who chose to travel to Earth after his father refused to believe that Kien was plotting murder. Ralan eventually returned to Moranaia to save his daughter from the energy poisoning.

Perim (PEHR-im) – Aris's potential soulbonded.

Retha – Vek's mother. A blood elf like her son, Retha was once sought-after by the king before eventually falling out of favor. She is now happily married to an Unseelie Sidhe.

Rianehd a Orsed (REE-ah-nehd ah OR-sehd) – Mysterious Seelie mage who tries to trap Anna.

Selia (SEHL-ee-uh) – A renowned magic teacher who moved to Braelyn to teach Arlyn how to control her power.

Sen / Senolai (SEHN-oh-lai) – Head of the Cairdai clan and Shayan's brother.

Shayan (SHAY-ehn) Cairdai (KAER-die) – Maddy's father. A lord of a powerful Seelie family who moved lives on Earth with his human wife, Angela.

Tatianella (tah-TEE-ah-NEHL-uh) – True queen of the Seelie court who is mysteriously absent.

Teyark (TAY-ahrk) – Son of King Alianar and Enielle. Soulbonded of Corath.

Torek (TOR-ehk) – King of the Unseelie. Father of Vek and Ara.

Torlahn (TOR-lahn) – A Gwraig Annwn woman who is a relative of Anna's.

Tynan (TIE-nehn) – priest and mind-healer who comes to help Aris.

Vek (vehk) – Prince of the Unseelie. Ara's brother and Fen's uncle.

Common Terms

adai – Seelie word for Dad. From Irish Daid (Dad) and athair (Father)

ahmeeren – Unseelie for my darling or dear

arori – earth-healer

athan ah shols angarn – Unseelie vulgar phrase meaning literally "sun out the ass"

Braelyn (BRAY-lynn) – Lyr's estate

camahr – a cat-like creature on Moranaia

caramuin – Unseelie word for 'beloved'

clechtan (KLEHK-tahn) – a Moranaian curse word similar to 'damn'

daeri – deer

Dökkálfar (DÖCK-owl-vahr) – One of two types of elves in Norse mythology

Dorenal (DOR-ehn-ahl) – Goddess of Portals, the Veil

drec (drehk) – A Moranaian insult. Someone who defiles nature or the natural order.

Ea – Deity of the elements

Eafere – sacred tree of Ea

emeth – Unseelie for "leave"

Eradisel (EHR-uh-DEE-sehl) – one of the nine sacred trees, symbol of Dorenal

fei talef – Ancient Seelie for the otherworld / close other dimension.

Literally meant underground

Felshreh – Unseelie word for blood elf

Feraien – first daughter of the king

graem awn – Unseelie for hold

Gwragedd Annwn (GRA-geth A-noon) – Welsh water fae said to live in lakes.

Gwraig Annwn (grag A-noon) – Singular of Gwragedd Annwn.

isilat (EE-sil-aht) – word meaning roughly "in progress." Used by artisans in shop as a polite way to say that they are in the middle of a delicate process

kehren – a type of fruit native to Moranaia

kinari – Moranaian grain used for bread. Ripens late summer

laial (Lie-AHL) – father

laiala (Lie-AHL-uh) – mother

Ljósálfar (LYOHSS-owl-vahr) – One of two types of elves in Norse mythology

loreln (lor-EHLN) – elite bodyguards of the royal family

Megelien (meh-GEHL-ee-ehn) – Goddess of time and of seers

meregh – Unseelie for kill / destroy

Meyanen (MAY-ah-nehn) – God of love and relationships

mialn (MEE-ahln) – beloved (used for mate or lover)

miaran (MEE-uh-rahn) – iron (literal). Used commonly as an expletive "Miaran dae fe onai" (MEE-uh-rahn DAE fee O-nai) – Iron in the heart. Used as an expletive/curse

"Mor gher Ayanel" (mor gehr AE-ah-nehl) – Blessings of Ayanel. Often used as a greeting

Myern (MY-uhrn) – A title loosely translating to third Duke

nesel – a potato-like plant with a carroty taste

omree – bard, singer

onai (o-NAI) – heart

onaial (o-NAI-AHL) - Dad

onaiala (o-NAI-AHL-uh) - Mom

onraiee – author/writer/creator

peresten (PEHR-uh-stehn) – elvensteel

ruya – Seelie curse word meaning corrupted / to corrupt

skizik – A dragon's partner and helper

slelen – an Unseelie curse similar to "damn"

sonal (so-NAHL) – A specific function in the Moranaian military responsible for scouting the forest and for covert missions. The Taysonal and Tayianeln fall under this branch.

sremed – Unseelie curse meaning a slimy, contemptible person

tarma – Seelie word for a private, safe meeting

Tayianeln (TAY-ee-ahn-ehln) / Tayn – Land Guards

Taysonal (TAY-so-nahl) – A scout who works directly for the head of a branch in some specific capacity. Similar to a Captain but with no one under their command. In Dianore family, this person traditionally acts as a diplomat for the Myern.

Tegreh sil caramuin egem – Unseelie phrase loosely meaning I love you

Tenah – dragonkind / dragon friend

tieln (tee-ehln) – beloved (used with a child, sibling, or parent)

tralt – Seelie for impure

The Sentinels

The Sentinels

Tarah dug the garden keys from the side pocket of her purse and unlocked the private gate. Strangers streamed behind her in hurried clumps, but none of them looked her way as she slipped through and latched the delicately scrolled, wrought iron gate. Or seemingly iron. None of the humans would guess the fence surrounding the garden had been created with *peresten*, a metal unique to the elven world of Moranaia, centuries before. The substitution had been easier to hide in those days, as most things had been.

As soon as the lock clicked into place, peace surrounded her. The ancient trees and carefully tended greenery blocked the interior from view of the outside, but it wasn't just that. Tarah had layered a variety of spells here as the city of London had grown up around her, and one of the newest had been devised to block some of the sounds and smells such a large mass of people inevitably generated. The unmistakable acrid scent of the underground tube system—an iron abomination to an elf, if a necessary and well-run one—was replaced by the tang of old wood and the spicy-sweet smell of the Linden trees.

They shouldn't have been able to bloom in September. While the glamour she'd cast around the outside gave anyone who passed the illusion of autumn flowers and yellowing hedgerows, inside, Tarah's enchanted garden bloomed as she wished. There was enough gloom in the world these days that she hadn't spelled the place to change from early summer in quite some time.

Her tension drained away as she started down the path toward the decorative summer house in the center of the garden. This little side portal to the Veil had been guarded by her family for millennia, long before the city of London had been conceived. Though its strength had waned over the last several centuries due to disuse, Tarah wouldn't neglect her duty to ensure its safety. She'd given up on living primarily in Moranaia for this, but it had been a willing sacrifice. This was no longer a tiny place the humans tended to avoid. Millions surrounded the garden around the portal, increasing the risk of discovery, and Moranaia was too far away for a rapid response to any incursions.

Though it might be amusing to see a gob of Londoners march resolutely through the portal onto Lord Lyr's land. By the time they slowed down enough to notice their surroundings, they'd be fending off arrows. A bit of a culture shock there. They'd be hunting for Way Out signs with a quickness. Well, most of them.

After weaving her way along the trails meandering through the private garden, Tarah made it to the center. The small decorative summer house gleamed white in the thin streams of sunlight shining through the branches. The structure, and another on the other end of the garden, was a lovely bit of vanity she'd had built a couple of centuries back when it had been the fashion to stroll in gardens like this. She'd only known a handful of elves and other fae who had mingled with human nobility back then, but she'd thought it a good idea to build a sanctuary for them here.

Hard to be yourself in a world that didn't believe in you. Literally.

Most of those people had moved on. The ones who hadn't lived in the building she had bought. Flats for fae. It was economical and easy to live close together and share shielding, and having an entire building gave them an excellent excuse to maintain a private garden. Some of her tenants even jogged here.

But not today. Only the swish of leaves and the rare, muffled honk filled the air as she unlocked the summer house and secured the door behind her. Finally free from any prying eyes, Tarah cast a mage globe and set it to hover above her head, illuminating the room. In contrast to the square shape of the outside, a staircase spiraled down from her feet until it reached the center. Mosaics lined the walls, swirls of greenery and flowers she'd paid a great deal to have designed. From here, she couldn't see the end point of the spiral a good floor-and-a-half down, but the swirling blue abstract had been a work of genius—by the artisan, not her. A touch of magic turned it into what it really was.

The portal to the Veil, a magical place that could lead to any fae realm if you knew what you were looking for.

As usual, the room was undisturbed. All protective shielding was intact, and she found no physical sign of disturbance. Brilliant. She might be able to make it through the infernal tube in time to meet Bes at the pub near the other portal on the outskirts of town. That one was stronger than it used to be, thanks to the influx of fae too nervous about coming and going in what was now the heart of a major international city.

Tarah spun to go just as a wave of power hit. But it wasn't from in here, the surge echoing from a greater distance.

It originated from somewhere inextricably connected—and it held the ancient, earthy strength of the dragon.

The first waves had filled him like the rising tide claiming a sea cave—relentless but slow. Enough to stir his senses but not to fully wake. But as he roused, more knowledge of his surroundings seeped through. Countless footsteps, excited voices. So many intruders. He longed to burst from the earth. To spread his wings to the sun and roar his fury through a stream of flame.

He'd been set to guard, and so he had. Until the magic had failed. Until Earth's power had faded to a shadow of what it should have been. Caeregas hadn't had a choice at that point. With the help of the sentinels' priestess, he had put himself into a deep sleep in a form the humans wouldn't bother—his more humanoid fae form. He'd even let them bury him since the ground held no danger for an earth dragon.

After countless millennia, his strength had returned.

And they were defiling his lands.

Still, Caeregas waited until night descended and the people disappeared from his senses. Only then did he part the soil heaped above him and with a burst of air, floated himself out of the hole. For the first time in endless centuries, starlight pierced his eyes, even their dimmer light nearly too much. But he blinked past the pain as he forced his body upright.

The rolling hills glimmered much as they always had, though the trees were somewhat sparser. In the distance, beams of light zoomed by between the hills, and a hint of glow caught against the horizon here and there. But where had all the intruders gone? Was his treasure safe?

Finally, Caeregas called his power forward, letting it surge through him until even his toes trembled. Then he released it. With a moan of ecstasy, he transformed his body until he was his dragon form once more. He stretched his long neck upward, dipping and turning his head to let the breeze caress his scales. His talons dug into the dirt around the hole where he'd risen, now a tiny, insignificant thing.

As a dragon, he barely fit on the mound where his human form had lain, but he would not treat the place with disrespect. Reverently, he closed the dirt over his resting place, rearranging even the grass until no sign of his exit remained. Then he dipped his head low in silent thanks to the ancient humans who had treated him with such care.

They probably hadn't believed he would wake again, but they'd shown him honor anyway. Were their descendants still in this place? Surely not, for they would not have tramped upon the ground with such heavy, irreverent steps. The old ones had known the power pulsing here, and they'd walked these hills with the greatest awe.

His head swiveled unerringly toward the sentinels, though they would be difficult to see even with his keen gaze. It was a short flight from his barrow, barely worth the effort of taking off, but his dragon's body wasn't made for a great deal of walking. He could return to his human form, but the very thought was intolerable after being confined to it for so long.

Caeregas stretched his wings out, letting the wind dance across his scales. He could stay like this forever, had he the time. But it was imperative that he learned the

fate of his hoard and the identity of the intruders who disturbed him each day. There was magic enough now. Somehow, the barrier holding back that magic was gone, and Earth had more than enough energy for even a starved, ancient dragon.

Decided, he took flight, unable to stop himself from spiraling higher until the world stretched beneath him in a darkened blur. Below, objects with lights like eyes sped along the ground in lines, and splotches of stationary lights clumped across the fields in the distance. Houses? Surely not in those quantities, though he supposed it would explain the number of people he'd sensed tramping across the fields so near his head.

Better they than the few who'd dared to dig into his barrow over the centuries. Thankfully, he'd been able to scavenge enough magic to shield himself from discovery, but it had been a near thing. Now that energy was plentiful once more? Maybe he could hunt down those who sought to kill him during his deep rest.

His gaze caught on another stream of lights, these much fainter and slower-moving. Caeregas focused in, much as a raptor would on its prey, and his wing-beats slowed at the sight of the robed humans advancing on the sentinels' location. Were these, then, the descendants of those who had served so long ago? Their numbers were certainly fewer, only nine walking along the path with their candles held high.

This time, he would be there to meet them. And they would have much to answer for.

———————◆—❖—◆———————

"Have any plans for the equinox tomorrow?" Bes asked, his cheerful face highlighted by the soft glow of the pub's antique lamps.

Tarah smiled. Her friend might have come from the elven world, but he'd embraced Earth holidays from the first. Even those most humans no longer observed. He'd pulled her into the local pagan community a few years back, at least the fringes, and she had come to see the appeal. It was the closest they were going to get to openly practicing magic unless humans figured out what to do with the energy that had begun to return a couple of months prior.

She'd even started to think of herself as a witch after attending so many pagan celebrations, although the magic Tarah used was different than what most witches understood. Still, it was as good a descriptor for a modern elf as any other term.

"I'm not going near Stonehenge this year," Tarah answered. "No telling how many people will be there for the equinox. Otherwise, I have no idea. I don't feel like hunting down another high-energy spot, and I'm not in the mood for company for some reason. No offense."

Truth be told, she was tired. It wasn't typical for Moranaian scouts to live on Earth while protecting one of the portals to the Veil, but it was necessary. Instead of making quick trips to Earth from Moranaia, the opposite was the case—Tarah rarely had the chance to step foot on her home world. Lately, she'd felt a deep longing for the ancient, forested mountains where she'd spent her training years.

Maybe if she'd had a companion, things would have been easier. A soulbonded like the myths she'd heard while training on Moranaia. Even her parents, who'd raised her mostly on Earth, had insisted that soulmates were real. Hah. She'd never met any so blessed. But she could see the draw of the tale, a bit of hope to ease the lonely centuries.

Bes seemed to catch her mood, his brows drawing together in worry. "Perhaps you should contact Lord Lyr. Another could guard the portal for a few years if you need a break."

"No," Tarah said at once, even though the idea held appeal. "It's my responsibility. And I do like it here. Truly."

"But?"

Tarah shrugged. "Maybe the increased energy reminds me too much of Moranaia."

It was difficult to believe that only a couple of months before, a barrier holding back Earth's magical energy had shattered. Reports were popping up constantly now of weird happenings, from ghosts walking the streets in daylight to fairies flying through Kensington Gardens. Two of her witch friends had discovered they had fae blood while trying to do private circles, and if the last full moon ceremony Tarah had attended was any indication, humans sensitive to energy were about to join in on the fun. The nightly news was full of stories about brownouts and people protesting the lack of information about said brownouts. Not that the government likely knew that surges of magic were causing them.

She'd almost been trapped in the tube during the last one. Meters underground and surrounded by iron—just the place an elf wanted to be. Fortunately, the power grid hadn't gone down enough to cause more than a stutter in service, but she'd started taking the bus more often than she used to. Better to be safe on that score.

"I'm sure I'll—"

A wave of power washed over her, cutting off her words. The dragon? What... Darkness.

The echoes of chatter and clinking glasses, the scent of cigarette smoke and old wood, the muted light caressing her friend's face—all disappeared from Tarah's awareness, replaced by a red haze of pure rage. For a heartbeat, there was nothing solid in her world. Only feeling. Then she caught flashes of darkness and a hint of ancient stone.

Only a minute must have passed before she was dropped back into reality. Tarah clutched the base of her throat where her pulse pounded. She blinked as the world reordered around her and her senses acclimated to the shift. Her eyes stung from the sudden change in light, though before she'd thought it dim.

What in the worlds had happened?

Bes leaned forward, his fingers curling gently around her wrist. "Tarah?"

"Tell me you felt that," she whispered through lips gone dry.

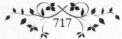

"I detected an energy surge, but it didn't seem that bad." His grip tightened. "You, though. I thought you were going to faint."

Tarah shook her head. "I wasn't. But I wouldn't exactly say I was here, either."

She knew where she'd been transported, at least for a brief moment—Stonehenge. The how and why, on the other hand…Those she couldn't as easily explain. Nor did she have a clue why the dragon she'd sensed earlier would be visiting the ancient stones. They weren't a portal, although the place held its own powerful magic.

"So where were you?" Bes asked.

With a long groan, Tarah pushed back her mug of beer and dropped a ten-pound note on the table. "Let's just say I have to make a trip to a certain monument after all. Mind if I borrow your car?"

Caeregas shifted to human form at the last possible moment, a burst of magic helping him settle his feet soundlessly against the grass. Out of habit, he formed a cloth wrap around his waist in case he encountered any humans. Not that they would concern themselves with modesty if they caught sight of his no-doubt-furious face.

The massive sentinels loomed around him, but they didn't tower as high as his rage. *Gone.* He needed to probe closer, but he was almost positive his hoard was gone.

Had it been stolen by the people who'd toppled so many of the sacred stones? A worthwhile theory since the sentinels' arrangement had been a significant part of the spell guarding his treasure. He'd allowed the humans to worship their gods here, so long as they vowed to protect what was his. After all, the timeless power of the place itself didn't belong to any of them. He was more than willing to share if the oaths were kept.

If.

After a quick scan of the surface, Caeregas ducked low. A pair of humans approached, closer than the group advancing in the distance. He'd seen them as he'd plunged silently toward the center of the scattered stones, but he had no clue what their purpose might be. He had never seen clothing like theirs, though the similarity of design suggested some form of ritual significance or official status. The upper portion in particular had been a shock, the fabric a bright yellow with stripes that gleamed like magic in his sight.

With his keen hearing, the whispered voices reached him well before a human would have heard. "I could've sworn I saw something drop down," a man said.

The other male snorted softly. "Like the hovering lights? Sure."

"I'm not the only one to have seen those," the first man grumbled. "But this was huge. Maybe someone messing around before the equinox? No one is supposed to be here for a few more hours, but…"

"Let's give it a quick look. After dealing with that pair of arseholes trying to run past earlier, I could go for a scuffle."

A click sounded, and a beam of light streamed around the outer ring of sentinels. Caeregas shoved himself low against one of the stones to remain out of view as the men began to patrol the area. Were they warriors or guardians? He'd seen no weapons that he recognized, but that didn't mean anything in this strange time. Centuries—maybe millennia—had passed since he'd been buried. Humans hadn't possessed lights they could activate or extinguish at will then, either. Prudence dictated he study more about this world before acting.

But first, he had to evade this pair.

Caeregas drew in energy from the ancient stone at his back. Ah, what a force! Shivering from the power, he made himself disconnect with the sentinel so he could concentrate. Quickly, he cast a spell of blending around himself, an enchantment designed to bend the eye away from him. It didn't always work well in broad daylight, but even with the humans' portable lantern, the spell would hopefully keep him from sight in the dark.

Before he had the chance to find out, a crackle split the night, and a hollow voice echoed around the space. "David here. Got a group of pagans headed your way."

Frowning, Caeregas sent his senses outward once more, but he didn't detect a third presence nearby. Where had the voice come from? A few of the magic users had devised methods to communicate over distances before Earth's energy had been walled away. Could that ability have returned along with the magic?

Another crackle. Then the first human spoke. "I don't see anything here. We'll catch our early attendees before they get close to the stones."

The humans moved away, their auras receding from Caeregas's mental view in a blessedly short time. But even after he felt comfortable enough to release the blending spell, he remained hidden against the stone. Much of his anger had faded, replaced by confusion. That pair of humans hadn't possessed the same type of energy the ancient protectors had exuded. No hum of magic had surrounded their lantern. No spells of protection or enchanted robes.

How had they come to be in charge of this place?

But despite his questions, Caeregas was no less resolved to discover what had happened to his hoard. Carefully, he crept around a pair of sentinels until he reached a clear spot in the center. Magic pulsed around him from the stones, even with a fair number of them shifted from their original positions. With so much energy now available on Earth, he could reconstruct the entire arrangement until the embedded spells lit up the sky, but that would draw more attention than he wanted. If the humans no longer used this as a worship place, it would be a wasted effort. Especially if his hoard was gone.

Caeregas sucked in a deep breath and placed his palms against the soft grass. Maybe the ground had shifted over time, enough that his quick probe from the air had missed the signs of his hoard. With that thought in mind, he expanded his senses slowly, careful to examine a broader area as he forced his scan downward.

Farther.

His rage built along with his magic as he detected the echoes of the spell he'd left to guard his treasure. Shattered. Gone. A roar of agony tore from his throat. Priceless gems, among the earliest formed on the Earth and excavated by his kind. He'd carved them over centuries. Imbued them with his power. But the worst loss was the precious red beryl, a stone said to attune one mate to another. He'd held onto it well past the time he'd believed he would find a mate.

He pushed his senses deeper with no luck. Someone would pay. If he ever—

Wait. A hint of power caught his attention, so faint he'd almost missed it. Without hesitation, he parted the ground with his magic until he could examine the source. The dark was no obstacle to his sight as the fragment of a bright red scale glimmered up at him, a taunt that brought forth another roar.

Egrenneth.

The wretched wyrm had found a way past his defenses. How had the other dragon survived after the magic faded? Was he still alive? Caeregas hissed out a breath as he sealed the hole without a trace. If Egrenneth lived, he would regret this betrayal.

Caeregas strode from the ring of stones, uncaring who saw him now. The humans had broken their sworn oaths and thus deserved nothing from him. If they interfered, he would kill them. Anything to regain his hoard.

With a thought, he shifted to his dragon form. Perhaps the robed humans advancing on the stone circle would have information. Or the guardians. He heaved himself into the sky, circling high and then gliding low until the group came into view. They would answer his questions if they didn't want to become his dinner.

A snack could only be a good thing before his battle with Egrenneth.

Tarah broke more than one speed limit on her way to Stonehenge. Thankfully, she was able to evade detection with a handy spell she'd learned from Bes on their last road trip. Though she didn't drive often in London, she loved to fly along the roads in a device that required no magic whenever she had the chance. More than once, she'd put extra-strong wards on the portal garden, talked one of her friends into minding the spells, and taken off with Bes to a park or nature preserve for a few days. Each time was a risk, but she deserved the occasional break.

This trip might not be for pleasure, but she'd bloody well get some enjoyment out of it. Her lips curved up as she pressed the accelerator—well, as much as she dared on the A303. She barely slowed as she took the roundabout to the correct road for the Stonehenge car park. Horns followed in her wake, and she extended the two-finger salute out of reflex even though they wouldn't be able to see the rude gesture in the dark.

She had a dragon to deal with.

The thread of power she'd sensed off and on all day flared so brightly to her inner sight now that she had to use a hint of magic to make sure she didn't crash into anything as she pulled off the road beside the locked gate to the car park. Un-

fortunate, though she could understand why they didn't leave it open. There would be people camped out at all hours if they did. A few side roads had been closed to avoid that very thing.

Though the area wasn't particularly busy this late, not even with the equinox so near, Tarah made sure to lock the car after she'd grabbed one of Bes's swords from the boot. Then she jogged toward the second locked gate barring entrance to the visitor center. She'd expected to find a couple of security guards at the least, but the area was eerily empty.

A roar shattered the silence, followed by several faint screams. Well. That explained the lack of security. She didn't bother strapping her sword to her waist, merely unsheathed the blade, dropped the scabbard, and took off running. Not that the sword alone was likely to do much good. Thankfully, she'd started practicing a new spell after hearing rumors of a dragon flying around Scotland a month or so ago. She might not have been part of that search, but she'd thought it prudent to prepare regardless.

As Tarah ran up the road leading from the visitor center to the monument, she formed the spell in the palm of her left hand. She was more scout than mage, but she had made it a point to learn as much immobilization magic as she had the talent for. She had a fairly good catch-and-release success rate in her garden. Of course, memory-altering spells tended to help.

Her lungs burned by the time she made it through the stand of trees surrounding part of the road. She'd grown too soft living in the city, for despite the amount of walking she did each day, she rarely ran like this. But she also wasn't holding back on her speed. She had probably already made it a mile by the time a stream of fire cut through the darkness overhead.

Tarah slowed, stunned by the gleam of orange and gold reflecting against the dragon's white scales. She'd heard the legends, both here and on her home world, but she had never seen a dragon in person. Huge. Majestic.

Not to mention a giant pain in the bum.

Another burst of fire warmed the air overhead. Tarah skidded to a halt near a group of robed humans huddled beside a pair of security guards. One of the humans, probably a pagan or druid out for an early equinox celebration, held a candle aloft with a shaky hand, though whether the light was supposed to ward off or encourage the dragon, Tarah didn't know.

The person had mettle, that was for sure. As the dragon swooped down toward them, even Tarah wanted to run, and she was a trained warrior. But although several of the others scattered toward the stand of trees, the human in the front stood firm. The dragon's wingbeats extinguished the candle's flame when the creature landed in front of them, but none of the people remaining budged.

Tarah kept her spell at the ready, but instinct told her it wasn't time to use it. The dragon hadn't hurt anyone despite the threatening flames, and it could have incinerated the entire group if it had wanted to. So instead, she watched as the dragon mantled its wings and stared down regally from way too far up.

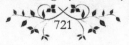

The voice cut through her shields and directly into her mind. *"Who is responsible for the sentinels' care?"*

Several of the humans cried out, and one of them dropped to his knees, palms shoved against his temples. Only the robed person in the front spoke, his voice wavering with fear. "None of us, my lord."

"None?"

Tarah's grip on her sword loosened until it almost slipped from her hand. A male dragon, his voice so resonant and beautiful that she longed to hear him speak again. Her very soul practically vibrated with it, though she didn't believe in such things. Still, she'd never experienced the like. Did dragons have a natural charm? Some kind of glamour? It *had* to be that. She tightened her hold—and not just on her sword. This situation was too dangerous to lose control of herself.

The dragon's head tipped lower, and one eye focused on the human. *"Where is the priestess who tends the stones?"*

"Stonehenge?" the man squeaked, his candle slipping from his hand. "The, ah… The monument doesn't have a priestess. Or priest. Landscapers maybe? I guess you could contact the, um, the English Heritage people? My lord."

Even the dragon seemed to feel sorry for the poor stuttering bloke, because its attention shifted to the only remaining security guard. *"I would know who is responsible for breaking their sacred oath and neglecting their guardianship of this place. I can be merciful to those not involved with the loss of my hoard. Within reason."*

"I knew I saw something," the man whispered before he stumbled forward. "Listen, I don't know what you're talking about with oaths, but I'm sure there hasn't been any kind of hoard here. Just an ancient ring of rocks our ancestors put up thousands of years ago."

The dragon threw his head back and roared until the ground trembled beneath their feet. Two more humans made a run for it, and the guard who'd spoken was so pale that he looked ghostly in the soft gleam of his flashlight. This was not the kind of situation he was prepared for, though she couldn't fault his bravery.

Tarah took a deep breath and then marched around the three remaining humans to stand directly in the dragon's path. He must have awakened recently, and apparently, he'd expected to find his hoard somewhere around Stonehenge being guarded by a priestess. If he'd been around when the monument had originally been used, that meant he was thousands of years old. But where would an ancient dragon have hidden in this area?

His roar faded into silence, and he lowered his head until his eyes pinned hers. *"What have we here?"*

Normally, she wouldn't have revealed much about herself in front of humans, but in a situation like this, why bother hiding? It wasn't as though their night could get any stranger. "I am Tarah Fiele of Moranaia, protector of the London portal. You will cease threatening these humans or answer to me."

722

A puff of smoke shot from his nose. *"One of the Fiele clan. Yes, you do have the look of them. How long has passed since I last saw the surface, elf?"*

The human behind her gasped, but Tarah ignored him. "I can't answer that with any accuracy since I don't know when you disappeared. However, Stonehenge was completed four or five thousand years ago, I believe. If you left something here then, I imagine it is long gone. As are the people who promised to guard it."

She expected the dragon to roar—or maybe blast her with his fire for delivering the news. Instead, he grew so still he could have passed for a massive statue built to celebrate some ancient god. Much like the stones, honestly. So when his claw darted out, the motion was too quick for her to cast her spell before he'd wrapped his talons around her waist and lifted.

Bloody hell.

She definitely hadn't been trained for something like this.

* ⸻ ⊚❧⊚ ⸻ *

Before he had time to consider the ramifications, Caeregas snatched the elf up in his claw, spun away, and dashed across the open space until he found a good spot to take flight. Her shout of surprise rang out, but she was wise enough not to fight as he rose with her into the night. Of all the people he'd encountered since waking, she was the one most likely to help him discover what had happened. Elves lived long, and a close ancestor of hers, relatively speaking, had once visited the sentinels during their construction. This one had to know something.

He flew north, barely taking note of his surroundings. Four or five thousand years. Could that be right? The world had gone on around him for so long, but he'd slept through much of time's passage. Even so, he had stirred periodically, using what energy he had stored to study those around him. Words and thoughts had seeped through even when he wasn't aware, ensuring he would at least be able to communicate when he rose.

But for so long?

The sights streaming by below them suggested that it might have been. Caeregas focused his vision on various scenes as much he could without taking his attention away from his captive, and the objects he identified were far different than anything he'd seen before. Buildings were everywhere, some clumped together in massive villages and others scattered here and there across the countryside. Not small cottages, either—solid habitations with lights glowing from within or from a device on the outside walls. Large paths made of smooth, fine stone crossed the landscape, and close examination of a pair of moving lights revealed some kind of object attached to wheels.

The humans he'd confronted near the sentinels had worn fine garments made of cloth he'd not seen outside of the fae courts and had carried daggers made of steel. When last Caeregas had walked the earth, bronze had only just made its way to the area. Had humans become artisans capable of rivaling the work of fae and dragonkind? Fabric could be explained by wealth, but advanced metalworking could not.

A small, fairly isolated hill came into view. He should be far enough away that the people he'd confronted near the ancient stones would not be able to reach him, and he didn't see any habitations on this particular spot. He could land and interrogate the woman. Though that held its own dangers. She might be able to disable him with magic or maim him with the sword she held.

The easiest solution would be to shift into his human form. Caeregas huffed. He'd barely enjoyed a moment's flight, and now he'd be confined to that small shape once more. Unfortunately, though, the size had advantages he would need. Disarming the elf in his dragon form would risk injuring her. In his fae form, he could rid her of the sword and confine her until she agreed to talk.

As at the sacred stones, Caeregas shifted a moment before his feet touched the ground, but this time, he had an armful of furious woman to deal with. Rightly so, but he couldn't take the time to try gaining her favor. He ripped the sword from her hand before she gained her bearings, tossing it aside as he tumbled her to the ground.

She let out an *oomph* when he landed atop her, and although he'd tried to withhold some of his weight, he obviously knocked the wind out of her. She swung for his head, but not blindly, her palm heading toward his nose with alarming accuracy. Caeregas grabbed her wrists and slammed them to the ground on each side of her head. Only then did he finally meet her gaze.

Every muscle in his body went tense, and deep in his mind, his dragon hissed in pleasure. Her eyes. He'd once had a piece of turquoise like her eyes, and he'd smoothed the stone until the copper striations gleamed in their blue-green setting, much like the hazel lights of this woman's irises. Ah, he had loved that stone. Lost now, like the rest of his hoard.

His hoard.

"How many generations removed are you from the pair who visited the sentinels?"

She glared up at him without a word.

"I do not mean you harm," he said, suddenly aware of how her heart pounded, a thrum he could somehow feel in his own chest. "But I must know what happened. That hoard is all I have in a world I do not understand. More than that, I need a few of those stones now that the barrier is gone. It is bad enough that I didn't prevent the barrier's fall as I should have."

Her eyes narrowed. "Prevent the barrier's fall? What do you know of it?"

"Ah, but I believe I asked a question of you first."

She studied his face for so long that he began to consider other forms of motivation. Perhaps a few threats. Or— "My grandparents guarded the portal to London around the time Stonehenge was completed," she said before he could decide. "They died before I was born, though. If they shared tales of meeting a dragon with my parents, I've never been told."

Caeregas had to force his fingers not to tighten with frustration lest he hurt her. "If your parents live, you could ask them."

"Somehow, I don't think you're going to wait around for me to drive back to London, find my communication mirror, and call Moranaia." A surprisingly wicked smirk crossed her lips. "Although I could treat you to a ride through the tube. I imagine an ancient dragon would adore that experience."

Despite the content of her words, he had an uncomfortable feeling that she was jesting at his expense. "Enough. If you will tell me how to find Egrenneth, I will release you."

She squirmed beneath him, and he froze as heat surged through his body, hardening him against her hip. Her eyebrows rose, and he expected her to chastise him. But she didn't comment on the state of his body.

"Who is Egrenneth?"

That erased his desire at once.

"The vile wyrm who claims the western territory." He couldn't help baring his teeth. "The red dragon. He fought with me for centuries before magic decreased to almost nothing. Somehow, he must have remained active for longer. Long enough to steal my hoard while I lay nearly helpless."

The elf's brow furrowed. "The Welsh have a red dragon as their symbol, but as far as anyone knows, it's a myth. Except..."

Caeregas tipped his face closer, so near their noses almost touched. "Except what?"

"About a month and a half ago, there was a report on the news that a red dragon was seen flying above the Scottish Highlands. The mountains to the north of the island. Then a week after that, a few people claimed to see a red dragon in Wales. To the west."

"The mountains to the north of the island?" He frowned. "You're very familiar with faraway events for an elf who can't fly."

Her sigh brushed his lips. "Trying to explain to you how I know this would take days. Suffice it to say that humans have created far more than you can imagine. News travels much more quickly."

He wanted to ask for more information, but he couldn't let it matter. Right now, he had to investigate whether or not this red dragon was Egrenneth. He should let the elf woman go, shift back to dragon form, and fly to the west as quickly as possible. But instead, he found himself staring into her eyes again. Maybe it was because she reminded him of his precious hoard, but he didn't want to let her go. He longed to bring her with him, though he had no reason or right.

"I will release you as I promised," Caeregas forced himself to say. "But I have a question first."

She held his gaze. "Yes?"

"Come with me." He wanted to brush her hair from her eyes, but he let go of her wrists instead. "If this world is as different as you say, I truly could use aid. Dragons and the elves of Moranaia are not enemies."

She snorted. "About that..."

"Yes, my kind warred with yours after moving to Moranaia, but I was not one of them. I've never left this world, and I have no argument with you. Besides, if you aid me, I will owe you a boon. No small promise from a dragon."

The elf shoved her palms against his chest. "You want to negotiate? You can start by moving off of me."

Though his spirit cried out at the loss of contact, Caeregas stood and helped her to her feet. She could have retrieved her sword and pierced his heart, and he wouldn't have cared. In that moment, staring at the planes and hollows of her beautiful face was enough reward for a lifetime.

And he'd hauled her away like a stray sheep.

Truth be told, the last thing Tarah had wanted was for him to move. His bare chest had been solid and hot beneath her fingers, and the thin bit of cloth he'd formed around his waist had done nothing to hide his interest when she'd squirmed in his hold. Under the right conditions, she could have lain there, her body pressed to his, for a decade or two. Unfortunately, being carried through the sky in his claws wasn't an ideal circumstance, and the threat of a dragon war was too much of a concern to enjoy the moment.

But was interfering in the dragons' argument important enough to travel even farther from the portal she protected? Could she help diffuse the conflict? Tarah studied the somber man standing before her, his gray-gold eyes lined with anger. His long fingers twisted back his fall of pale hair, shimmering like his scales in the moonlight, and worried the strands into a knot before releasing the mass to tumble down his back. Anxiety swirled around him like the soft mist drifting through the air.

She longed to comfort him. Gods, she was going crazy.

Focus.

"What is it about a dragon's hoard, anyway?" Tarah asked, trying to sound flippant. "There's no telling how long it has been gone. Why not get acclimated before you hunt down a bit of treasure? Gold can wait."

"Bit of..." His eyebrows rose. "I do not collect useless baubles for my own amusement. Every stone of my hoard has a purpose, carefully crafted and attuned by my own hand. Each one can be used in its own way to focus my magic. But it is the red beryl I must have. That Egrenneth possesses it is an affront to all I hold dear."

Tarah lifted her hands, palms out. "Sorry. Forget I asked."

"Aid me in this, and I will tell you about the ancient times." He took a step closer. "I volunteered to stay here. A sentinel like the stones. I suspect there is much your people do not know."

In that he was correct. The elves of Moranaia had fled Earth through the Veil between dimensions long before the humans' recorded history. It was after they had left that the Unseelie and dragons had worked together to wall away a large portion of this world's magical energy so that human mages would stop trying to kill each

other—and the fae—with it. But even that was millennia before Stonehenge had been built. Was he really that old?

Only one way to find out.

"I'll need to contact a couple of friends first. I have my own duties that need tending." And Bes would want a chance to retrieve his car before it got towed. "Then I will go with you."

Before he could argue, she spun around and strode a few paces away, tugging her phone from her back pocket as she went. She would call every flat in her building if necessary to find someone to keep extra watch on the portal. Lord Lyr, in charge of any elves stationed on Earth, might not be happy about it, but if she could avoid it, he would never know.

It wasn't every day a girl got a chance to ride a dragon.

And properly this time—not dangling from his claw.

As the beautiful elf stared at him, Caeregas shifted back to his dragon form. It was as natural to him as riding the air currents, yet he felt oddly exposed by her avid gaze. Did she find him unusual? Contrary to what many believed, his kind couldn't shapeshift into just anything. He could change his size as a dragon, and he could shift into a single humanoid form. Some even chose to mate with other fae in their second form, rarely shifting back to a dragon. An unusual choice, though after so many centuries alone, he could finally see the appeal.

Instead of shrinking back with the disgust he'd half-feared, the elf stepped closer and extended her hand. After a brief hesitation, she brushed her fingers along the scales of his foreleg, and he shivered. Tarah Fiele. That was her name. The Moranaian woman appeared young, her brown hair shiny and her skin unlined, but if she had duties here, she was likely much older than she looked. No childish innocent. And suddenly, he wanted her.

Impossible.

He shook aside the foolish longing and connected his mind with hers enough to send his thoughts. *"If you're ready, climb up. It's best to situate yourself at the base of my neck."*

Without comment, she used his foreleg to boost herself. She'd retrieved her sword and fashioned a holder for it out of rope, and the tip rubbed annoyingly against his scales until she got the thing situated. But he no longer feared she would use the weapon against him. After completing her business, she had given her word to help him willingly, and for some reason, he trusted her. He would wager his soul on her honor.

When she spoke into his mind, his claws dug furrows into the hill beneath him, releasing the sharp scent of crushed grass and turned soil. *"What is your name, dragon?"*

"Caeregas," he answered as he heaved himself upward, a hint of magic helping him gain rapid height. *"Once called Caeregas of the Pine, son of the Guardian of the Frozen North."*

Her hands tensed against his neck. *"The frozen north? Do you mean to tell me you were born during the last Ice Age? Scotland's northern mountains were under ice then."*

"I was not." He bared his teeth in a grin when she relaxed against him. Was an elf bothered by such a long life, then? Perhaps she was younger than he'd assumed. *"But my father was. Does my age disturb you? I imagine you've seen your share of centuries. Possibly millennia."*

"I am seven hundred and twenty-three," she replied. *"And I have spent much of that time here, first with my parents and then as guardian of the portal. Old enough, but far from the thousands you have lived. If Stonehenge was begun five or six thousand years ago, what would that make you?"*

Caeregas considered the question and all that it implied. The most glaring was also the most galling—if so much time had passed that even an elf didn't know for sure when the monument had been built, then he had no way of knowing how old he was. Humans hadn't kept records, and few of his kind had remained on Earth after the barrier had been completed. He could be seven or eight thousand years old. Maybe more. Even if he found his calendar stone, he wouldn't know how long had passed since he'd let himself be entombed.

"Lost in time, it seems," he finally answered. *"Tell me what has passed on the surface. I have fragments and hints. Bits of knowledge and pieces of languages, some perhaps long lost. But I need to understand this world, and I didn't comprehend much of the information I gleaned during my rest."*

She patted his neck. *"I'll do my best."*

And as he flew westward, she did.

First, Tarah had him use his camouflaging spell to keep himself out of sight. Then she spoke to him of modern life and the advancements the humans had made since last he had walked the Earth. The most recent were the hardest to believe. Electricity, cars, airplanes. Wireless communication and televisions. Weapons that could be fired through the air, exploding on impact.

He processed it all in numb silence. Below, the things he saw began to make sense. Those were cars driving along roads, and the buildings with lights inside were houses and businesses. Even the seemingly rich cloth worn by the humans was common, available for purchase in some of the structures nestled along the village high streets below. It was akin to magic, the things he learned, and Tarah was the witch who shared their mysteries.

"It is less jarring when you live through the changes," she said softly. *"And some of the old ways do remain. Many will celebrate the equinox tomorrow as their ancestors did in times past. The people you encountered earlier were trying to sneak up to Stonehenge for that very thing, I believe."*

He huffed out a steamy breath. *"The sentinels' spell has been broken, and some of the stones are gone. Why do people return?"*

"Surely you felt the power that lingers? Until recently, those who are sensitive to magic have had to find what remnants they could." She shifted against him, and he almost hummed. *"Now that magic has returned to the world, even the incomplete monument resonates with the power it once held."*

He had noticed that very thing. Perhaps once he had his hoard, he would reconstruct the sentinels. *"The inner portion guarded my hoard, but the outer…that was a powerful shield that protected much of the region from attack. I was supposed to ensure that no one destroyed the structure as the magic weakened, but I could not remain conscious with such little power."*

Her confusion drifted along their communication link. *"Wasn't the barrier created long before that monument?"*

"Yes." A hint of power washed over him—a probe, and one of dragon origin. Egrenneth. But he made no comment, merely changed direction to face the source. *"However, the original barrier didn't drain as much energy. For some reason, more than intended disappeared after several millennia. Slowly at first, but there was enough power for the most skilled human mages to continue their work. There were wooden sentinels then. They were replaced by stone as the energy weakened, since rock is better at channeling and retaining power. Egrenneth offered the bluestone in the center which guarded my hoard. I should have known he had a deeper motive."*

"So you trusted him once."

Caeregas beat his wings harder, ignoring the ache the activity brought to his long-disused muscles. *"Mostly."*

She fell silent, and the night settled around them, a private world that was theirs alone. Then she swayed against him, and peace gave way to alarm. *"Tarah?"*

"Sorry," she answered. *"I'm usually in bed by now, and the rhythm of flight is oddly soothing."*

He examined the area. After skirting a large city glowing with countless lights, he'd had to turn south for a time, and now they flew northwest toward a massive river. He sensed Egrenneth was close, but he was hardly a water dragon. Had he settled somewhere on the other side, waiting for him to cross?

"What is this body of water?" he asked.

"I think it's the Bristol Channel." Tarah wrapped her arms around his neck and leaned over for a closer look. *"Which means we'll be in Wales once you cross. Maybe Cardiff? I've never seen the area from this angle, so it's hard to say."*

The flight—and hearing of the sobering changes in the world—had given his anger time to cool. His first instinct had been to find Egrenneth immediately, but if he had been awake and aware for so much longer, he would have a far better grasp of how to navigate this world. As much as Caeregas hated to delay, a brief rest to regroup would be best, especially with his only guide so exhausted. But he didn't dare stop without finding a fortified location.

He would have to rely on Tarah. Hopefully, she had better knowledge of the area than he did.

As the lights of Cardiff twinkled far below, Tarah tightened her grip on the dragon's neck and fought to keep her eyes open. If she hadn't had to close them to ease the nausea she felt any time Caeregas changed course unexpectedly, staying awake wouldn't have been such a struggle, even with the soothing repetitiveness of

his wingbeats. She wasn't afraid of heights—sitting atop a dragon with no restraints was enough to make anyone ill.

Perhaps it would have been exhilarating with some kind of harness to keep her safe.

At least she and Bes had taken a road trip out here once to celebrate Alban Elfred—the autumn equinox—with a few of their Druid friends. Now that they were close enough to make out familiar details of the landscape, Tarah directed Caeregas to reinforce his shields and fly up the River Taff. They still had two or three hours before dawn, so the old keep at Cardiff Castle was sure to be abandoned. With the roof to the giant round tower gone, it would be an excellent place for a dragon to land.

"I'm not sure if they have security cameras," Tarah said. Then, of course, she had to try to explain what a camera was. The poor dragon had little understanding despite all she'd tried to impart. *"But I have a spell to hide us from those. It's a basic necessity for an elf or fae living in a major city."*

"I will leave that to you, then," he said, his voice gruff with uncertainty.

She didn't blame him for the hint of grumpiness she sometimes caught in his tone. When she had been younger, it had been difficult for her to return from Moranaia during her breaks from training to find the world had changed in her absence. She'd only made it back a handful of times during her last century of training, and even then, she'd often found the city greatly changed each time. Thousands of years? She doubted she would take such a massive shift gracefully.

Tarah cast her invisibility shield around them as he circled Cardiff Castle. Just in time. Without warning, he plunged downward, straight for the mound that held the ruins of the keep. Stifling a shriek, she squeezed her eyelids closed and tightened her arms around his neck as much as she dared. Distracting a dragon mid-descent wouldn't be the best life choice.

Unlike before, Caeregas didn't shift before he landed, so it took her a moment to realize that they'd truly stopped moving. His light, rumbling chuckle vibrated his body beneath her bum, and she sheepishly pried her eyelids open to find herself staring at the dim outline of a stone wall. Even with the castle being in the heart of the city, it was dark in the bowl of the old keep, and Caeregas filled an alarming amount of the space. She glanced up and snorted at the way he'd had to turn his head to avoid smacking it on the wall.

"Dismount so I can shift," he commanded, and Tarah was more than happy to comply.

Her legs ached as she slid down his foreleg, but they held her weight after her feet touched the ground. She eased back toward the wall until her sword clanged against the stone and her shoulder brushed a tuft of grass growing from one of the many cracks. As she jerked away from the itchy blades, her gaze was caught by Caeregas.

In less than two heartbeats, he sank into himself with a snap until his fae form remained. Suddenly, the field in the center of the ruins seemed huge, the walls towering around them so much taller. Tarah could only stare at him, bare save a kilt-like bit of fabric slung around his waist. He stood with shoulders hunched and expression closed—as haunted as this castle had a right to be.

She crossed to him, but she didn't touch him. She didn't dare. Something about him made her want to wrap her arms around him, much as she had as they flew through the sky. But not for her own safety this time. For him. Only for him. If anyone in this world needed comfort at this moment, it was Caeregas.

He leaned close until his whisper brushed against the shell of her ear. "This isn't quite the fortification I pictured when you said castle."

"I imagine only the fae built them when you were last above ground, and then only rarely on Earth," she answered softly. "They were in use. But no one has needed this keep for hundreds of years. Still it stands. There are even a few rooms up that staircase."

Caeregas glanced in the direction she pointed and shuddered. "That is steep for a climb in this form. How could I manage with no talons to grip?"

She peeked down at his bare feet with a grin. "Hiking boots would help."

A light clicked on from the direction of the stairs, blinding in its intensity, and Tarah gave thanks for the spell that would confound any cameras that might be set up. As it was, she thought she caught the echo of voices coming from outside the tower. Bloody hell. They must have been spotted during the descent, the most vulnerable time for this crazy expedition.

"Guess we get to see if there's a spot up there where we can hide." Tarah grabbed his wrist and tugged him toward the base of the stairs. "There's only one entrance to the keep, so if someone's coming up, they'll find us if we try the exit. We can cloak ourselves better in the shadows."

Caeregas scowled, no doubt unhappy with being trapped, but he followed her up the steep and narrow steps to the second stone archway leading to the tower chamber, now empty. Tarah didn't stop there. She started up a narrow spiral staircase tucked in the left wall as quickly as she dared. How had medieval ladies not broken their necks trying to climb these impossible steps while wearing long dresses? She almost slipped a couple of times, and she was wearing trousers.

Finally, she reached an old wooden door with a modern padlock. She could pick it, but there was no way to lock it behind her. If security came up this far, they would see the opened lock for sure. She had to hope the dragon had an idea. With a mental curse, she looked over her shoulder for Caeregas.

But the stairwell was empty.

Caeregas caught her before she passed the doorway to the small empty room and waved for her to cross the rope barring entry. As soon as she did, he tugged her to the side, out of view of the doorway. The windows here were wide but not tall, a problem he could remedy well enough. Tarah watched him with a bemused frown as he placed his hands on the wide stone beneath the glass and used his magic to hollow a spot where they could stand.

A shout sounded from below, and he wrapped his arms around Tarah, holding her close enough for them to sidle into the gap. At first, he was busy weaving a spell of misdirection around them, hopefully strong enough to hide them if the guardians did enter this side room, but as soon as the task was completed, the warmth of her body pressed to his claimed his attention. Her widened eyes met his in the shadowed alcove, the only sound their breaths weaving softly in the narrow space.

Tarah lifted an eyebrow. *"Do you think this will work?"*

"At great cost," he dared to answer. *"I'd thought to find a place for you to rest, but instead, I have brought you into danger."*

Her fingers tapped against his shoulder, and she tipped her head to the side. *"I wouldn't go that far. They'll probably just kick us out if we play it right."*

"I wasn't talking about the guardians of this place." Caeregas slipped his hand beneath the strange, soft tunic she wore and nearly groaned at the feel of his skin against hers, even if it was only her lower back. *"For some years, I lived in my fae form after the lack of energy made it difficult to do as much as a dragon. I laid with human women upon occasion then. It was pleasant enough, but none of those experiences could compare with the fire I experience from a single touch from you. Our proximity tests my control."*

"I…" Her mouth worked, though they weren't speaking aloud. *"I'm not sure if that's a compliment or a threat."*

He trailed his fingers up her spine, only stopping when he reached the hard edge of the sword bound to her back. *"Never a threat, treasure."*

Her body softened against his. Though she had to feel his interest, she didn't shrink from him or try to escape. His past lovers—both human and dragon—had been hesitant of him. The former had feared his power, and the latter had thought he might seek a permanent mating, an impossibility after the few remaining dragons had scattered around the world to protect places important to the barrier. No one wanted to risk being pulled from their assigned location.

But Tarah…something about her felt inexplicably right. Once again, he cursed the loss of his red beryl. The stone would have sung to him immediately if she was meant to be his mate. Suddenly, though, he didn't care what the rock had to say. She was here, warm and perfect. Before he could think better of it, he lowered his lips to hers.

He barely tasted her, so soft was the kiss, but her honeyed flavor would brand him forever. He tightened his grip, and her fingers dug into his shoulders as she lifted up slightly to deepen the contact. He might be misplaced in time, but he was lost in her as their mouths met with greater frenzy.

So lost that the voices made it to the doorway of their room before the sound made it through his dazed head. Struggling for control, Caeregas jerked his lips from Tarah's and tried to steady his breathing. His little elf tucked her face against his neck, her rapid breaths warming his skin.

"I guess we should go all the way to the top," a man said from somewhere beyond the doorway.

"Aye, for certain there's a dragon waiting," another man mocked. "Climbed right up these stairs."

A soft thud followed by an indignant yelp echoed through the door. "Shut it. Weren't people talking about dragons on the news? This was a white one. I swear it."

"And I swear my arse is going to make you pay for making me climb all these stairs for nothing. Come on. If there was a dragon, it flew off while you were finding me."

Caeregas listened avidly to the argument until he could no longer make out their voices. For the first time since he'd awakened, he wanted to laugh. Truly laugh. Once again, some poor lad had accurately spotted him, only to be mocked by his companion. The first, at least, had been redeemed by Caeregas's confrontation with his group. But since Tarah had urged discretion, the latest human would simply have to suffer.

The lights turned off, plunging them into greater darkness, but he didn't let Tarah go. Instead, he widened the stone at his back a bit more, enough to create a seat for himself. It wouldn't be safe for them to stretch out in the open, even in one of the rooms, and he was hardly sleepy after millennia of rest.

"Curl up on me," Caeregas whispered. "Get some sleep. I will keep watch."

"That doesn't seem fair," she replied, though she propped her sword against the wall and settled in his lap.

He smiled against her hair. "Believe me when I say I've had more than enough sleep."

The thin light of dawn trickled through their window when Tarah woke, but she didn't lift her head from Caeregas's shoulder right away. Partially because she was groggy, but mostly because she enjoyed the feel of him, warm and solid beneath her. Who would have thought sleeping on a man's lap in a partially ruined castle could be so comfortable? An underestimated experience for certain, and a wonderful way to start Mabon.

"Happy equinox," she whispered against his neck.

His arms tightened, and he brushed a kiss against her head. "Indeed. All I need now is my hoard to make it complete."

Tarah had to admit that she was eager to see his treasure at this point. It had to be something special to have him so aggravated. "Let's see if we can sneak out of this place, then. Unless you think your hoard is in the castle?"

"No." His chest muscles tensed beneath her cheek. "I sense Egrenneth in the forest beyond the walls. He waits for me deep within."

"I see." Tarah pushed away from him until she could see his face. Some of his tension had eased after their kiss, but now it hardened his expression once more. It seemed their moment was over. "Can you fix the stones you shifted to make our hiding space?"

He frowned. "Of course. Let us stand, and I will show you."

Though she hated to move, she knew she had to. Tarah pushed to her feet, grabbed her sword, and darted out of the way. It turned out to be worthwhile, for watching him use his magic was almost as intriguing as he was himself. She had no idea where the stones had been, but the old wall reformed beneath his hands. Handy, that. And quite likely their best chance of escaping undetected.

They descended the tower built into the side of the round keep, though daylight revealed that it wasn't strictly round. Tarah stared up at the series of walls, so many that the structure appeared circular unless a person looked closely. Moss and grass grew in the cracks, but the building seemed stable. Hopefully, it wouldn't tumble down when her new friend opened a small hole for them.

Caeregas headed for a spot that might have once held a chimney, and she followed close behind. She had no idea where security guards might be this close to opening time—better to be ready to move. So when the dragon created an opening and gestured for her to go first, she darted through without hesitation. Then they crept down the hill and across the space between the keep and the outer wall, where they repeated the process.

The second time took longer since the outer wall was so much thicker, but Caeregas managed to close the gap without causing an alarm. They'd done it. They had made it out of the castle and into the park unnoticed. Well, hopefully. If nothing else, another dragon sighting had no doubt made the news.

Tarah grabbed his arm, halting him in the shadows of the wall. "You fashion your clothes with magic when you shift, right?"

"Yes," he answered with a quick glance at the fabric around his waist.

She was *not* going to focus on the gorgeousness on display. "Can you create something else if I send you a mental image? Your…style…is rather conspicuous."

Caeregas shrugged. "If you insist."

Tarah built the picture in her mind and directed it his way. In moments, he'd refashioned his clothing to a modern kilt worn with a snug, long-sleeved T-shirt and boots. Great gods of Moranaia. He looked delicious enough to almost make her wish she still believed in her people's myths about soulbonding. If that connection she felt to him could be something more…

No. Better not to go there.

"Lead the way," Tarah said, "But don't shift out here. I mean it. A lot of people like to walk through public parks."

"Egrenneth—"

"Is no doubt in some type of human or fae form. Believe me, if there was a dragon in the park, we'd hear the screaming already."

Though he grumbled, Caeregas found them a path around the moat and then marched resolutely in fae form through the park, taking the nearest trail north. Despite her admonition, the only sign of life they encountered was the occasional bird chirp and the distant sound of cars. Perhaps it was too early? Soft light leaked between the sparse, well-maintained trees, gilding the grass with gold. To the left, a

large field opened up before stopping at another line of trees, and buildings peeked through branches on the right.

It should be an everyday sort of place with its paved trails and proximity to the city, and yet there was something magical about the park. Curious, Tarah opened her senses, and surprise had her steps slowing as the unseen became visible to her inner sight. Oh yes, the fae liked to play here. There were more than a few magical beings, from fairies in a tiny grove near the back of the castle to a couple of dryads in quiet spots along the river—and the raging power of dragon a fair walk north.

At least they were going the right way.

"Why do you think Egrenneth would come here?" Tarah asked. "Aside from the lovely energy of this place."

A troubled frown lowered Caeregas's eyebrows. "I am uncertain. A less-populated area would have made more sense."

"My thought as well."

They followed a canal northward, although Caeregas stopped a few times to stare up at some of the buildings on the outer edges of the park. What would these massive structures look like to someone who had lived in the literal stone age? She found herself appreciating the curve of concrete and glass on one long building along their route. Hundreds of years of knowledge had gone into that, skills passed from hand to hand through time.

But sooner than she would have expected, Caeregas ducked into a thick strand of trees nestled near the river. Like the park itself, it shouldn't have been a special place. Then Caeregas stopped beside a wall of energy that shimmered to Tarah's inner sight, much like the shield that surrounded her enchanted garden.

"Going in?" she whispered.

Caeregas surprised her by taking her hand, his warm fingers twining with hers. "In a moment. The equinox approaches. Can you feel the rise in energy?"

"Yes." Tarah smiled. "The midpoint is early this year."

Eyes closed, he lifted his other hand toward the edge of the shield. Minutes passed, and still they waited. New sounds trickled in. She heard the buzz of bicycles on the trail behind them, just out of sight, and the thud of trainers against pavement as joggers took their morning exercise. Somewhere, a child laughed, and a father's voice called out. None of them aware of the magic a few steps away.

Finally, Caeregas nodded and lowered his hand. "There is an opening. Will you enter with me? You have already guided me as promised, so there is no need."

Was he joking? Her curiosity would have been need enough even if she hadn't grown oddly attached to the man. He felt like a part of her in some way she couldn't explain, almost like a kindred spirit. She didn't understand it, and lacking comprehension, she could only go on instinct. Everything within said that she belonged with him, if only for this encounter.

"I'm going," Tarah said, resolved.

She could only hope it wasn't a terrible mistake.

Caeregas hadn't been certain what to expect from the elf by his side, but such adamant enthusiasm was more than he'd considered. It warmed him, even if she had likely agreed for reasons that had nothing to do with him. Entering this place with her felt right. Egrenneth might be irksome, but he wasn't a murderer of innocents. She should be safe.

Together, they stepped through the thin barrier, and the carefully groomed park disappeared, replaced by an older and wilder bit of woodland, so thick that little sunlight made it through. An enchanted forest hidden in a pocket dimension, as he had expected. Clever. But it put Caeregas at a possible disadvantage. Now that they were outside of the humans' realm, Egrenneth might have chosen to shapeshift.

Not good.

As he strolled hand-in-hand with Tarah down a thin dirt path, mage lights hovering overhead like bloated fireflies, Caeregas gathered energy into himself in preparation. He would shift if he had to, even if the other dragon took their conflict back to the human world. He refused to be intimidated.

The lights grew brighter as they walked, more like true mage globes than the flickers along the beginning of the trail. Then the forest thinned, and a clearing opened up before them. Egrenneth stood in the center in his fae form, a shaft of sunlight pouring through a break in the branches to highlight hair the same red and gold shade as his dragon's scales. Caeregas sneered. The wretch's other form should have been a peacock.

Egrenneth smirked, bowing with an obnoxious and unnecessary flourish. "You have finally awakened, brother. Took you long enough after the sentinels' fall."

Tarah's hand jerked in his. "Brother?"

"We share a father," Caeregas admitted reluctantly. "But I have not claimed the useless wyrm for some time. I certainly wouldn't have after he stole my hoard."

"Is that what I did?" A calculating look entered the other man's eyes. "Then perhaps I should suggest a barter. Your hoard for the little elf? Women always did prefer me. In either form."

That. Was. It.

Caeregas sprang forward, his fist connecting with his brother's face before he had time to consider the ramifications. Not that he cared. As Egrenneth's head snapped back, Caeregas shifted his fingers into claws, grabbed his brother by the throat, and lifted Egrenneth until his feet dangled. Caeregas's talons dug into flesh, almost drawing blood, but he didn't release the wretch.

Egrenneth's eyes flashed gold. *"Cer i grafu."*

"Save your insults," Caeregas snarled. "I'll not be going away until you're a pile of useless bones."

He expected his brother to start swinging, for they usually finished their fights in the form in which they began them. But this time, Egrenneth began to shift in Caeregas's hold. Wings snapped wide from his brother's back, and his skin mottled

red with the scales beginning to emerge. Caeregas flung him away, hoping Egrenneth would land against the massive tree behind him. Unfortunately, the rancid wyrm righted himself with a flap of his wings.

Caeregas let his own wings unfurl, his body tingling with the need to shift as his brother leaped over a stone in the middle of the clearing and rushed him. Though he longed to unleash his full form, there wasn't enough space. Fortunately, there was always room for magic.

With a thought, the earth beneath them heaved, reaching upward to wrap around Egrenneth's feet and ankles with a spell only a fully trained earth dragon could break. Caeregas smiled as his brother jerked to a stop, flailing to keep himself from falling forward and breaking his ankle against the unyielding stone gripping him. Too bad he managed to right himself. He would have deserved the pain of a broken bone after stealing Caeregas's hoard.

Egrenneth raised his hand, fire gathering in his palm. "I've had time to play with fire, brother. Care to see how my flame can incinerate a dragon despite our natural resistance?"

He froze. It had to be a trick. Even in fae form, fire barely affected him. Could his brother have done such a thing? "You lie."

"I didn't want it to come to this," Egrenneth said. "But you've given me no choice. Release me, or you'll find out exactly how hot a flame can burn."

Caeregas cursed beneath his breath and extended his magic into the ground, though even he wasn't certain if he would undo his handiwork or cast something else. But Tarah didn't give either one of them a chance to act. As quietly as a breeze, she slipped up beside Egrenneth, the tip of her sword digging into his stomach.

"The softest part of a dragon in any form," she said, a hard edge to her tone.

Egrenneth's eyes widened. "I retract my earlier offer. You can keep her."

"I am not an object to barter," Tarah snapped.

Glacier's wrath, but he should have been the one to point that out. Caeregas winced at the glare she cast him. He'd been distracted by his rage and his desire for revenge, enough that for a moment he'd forgotten the insult his brother had dealt her. "Of course you are not. Human women might have been once, but never our kind. Egrenneth was needling me."

She lifted an eyebrow. "And if he was serious?"

Caeregas started to give a harsh retort, but he hesitated, stealing a glance at his half-brother. The smirk had dropped from the other dragon's face, although the sword tip a heartbeat from puncturing his innards was no doubt responsible for that. Had the man changed so much to suggest trading a person? Truthfully, he had no way of knowing. What would he do if Egrenneth refused to yield Caeregas's hoard unless he handed over Tarah?

An impossibility in any time or place, of course. But would he disavow her? Leave her to fend for herself while he attempted to regain his hoard? He might not hand her over in the truest sense, but not fighting for the woman he'd begun to sus-

pect was his mate was close to the same thing. He simply couldn't do it.

He held her gaze. "Then I would find another time to reclaim my hoard. As much as it would pain me, I could hunt more stones. Even the red beryl, though it might take centuries. I could not, however, find another one of you."

Her eyes softened, but her sword didn't waver. *"I feel the same, though I have no hoard. But it's not necessary. I'm a scout, Caeregas. Some even call me a witch,"* she said into his mind. *"As you can see, I'm not defenseless. I'll help you reclaim your treasure, so long as you aren't planning to sacrifice me for it."*

He couldn't help but grin. *"I've never accepted sacrifices. Virginal or otherwise."*

"Well, that's a relief."

"I don't suppose you could release me and have your lovers' quarrel elsewhere?"

Tarah turned her glare on Egrenneth. "You began all of this with your actions."

"Did I?" The red faded from his brother's skin, and his wings pulled inward until they disappeared. "It was part jest and part test. I'd hoped Caeregas hadn't gone mad during his time underground, especially after I saw the story online about a dragon attacking people at Stonehenge. At a monument, brother? Really?"

Caeregas frowned. "Online?"

"Too bad you didn't find yourself a way to tap into the energy stored behind the barrier as I did," Egrenneth said with a chuckle, though his gaze flicked down at the sword with the action. "Or you would know what I'm talking about. I couldn't pull in enough energy to transform until recently, but I didn't have to go dormant. I've changed with the times."

Caeregas strode closer to his terrible half-brother. "We were supposed to guard the barrier, not steal from it. We are sentinels ourselves, protecting the places of magic and keeping it from the humans. Even Tarah, a Moranaian elf, takes on this mantle, although she shields something different. Taking from beyond the wall—"

"How were we supposed to fulfill our goal with no energy, Caeregas?" Egrenneth snapped, all amusement gone. "I did take my duties seriously. Then the world changed until it seemed a pointless endeavor. I…might have let down my guard. I strayed far from my enclave here and missed the barrier's fracture."

Caeregas studied the beautiful, timeless clearing. "This is your enclave, then?"

The twist of his brother's lips held no humor or mocking now. "No. I am not fool enough to bring you there. I haven't seen you or another of our kind in millennia, but still I would not."

"Then why?" Perhaps Egrenneth was the one who had gone mad, for his actions made no sense. "Why steal my hoard and then let yourself be found here? In the middle of a modern city? Why admit that you failed in your duty to guard the barrier at all?"

Egrenneth's shoulders slumped. "You deserved to know. As far as I can tell, we were abandoned by the dragons who moved to Moranaia after they grew tired of living here. They do not care that we failed or that Earth has magic once more. Do you know how long I have been alone? I am weary of it. And I did not steal your hoard."

His fists clenched at the lie. "Your scale was all that was left behind."

"I didn't say I didn't take it." Egrenneth waved his hand at the large chunk of bluestone he'd leaped over earlier. "I said I didn't *steal* it. The sentinel stones were rearranged after the magic faded to nearly nothing, and over time, the humans became bolder in their explorations. I removed it to this realm until you woke, lest it be discovered."

Caeregas peered at his half-brother, searching for any sign of deception. They had fought several times over the centuries, conflicts over the territories their father had assigned them. Acts of friendship were far rarer. "We were at war not long before my rest."

"Ah, Caer," Egrenneth began, shaking his head. "That fight ended long ago. A useless battle. Even the humans of these lands live largely in peace. In any case, we may argue between ourselves, but I would not let your hoard go astray. Especially not the red beryl."

"What is the significance of that?" Tarah asked suddenly. "That's the second time the red beryl has been mentioned. Is it valuable?"

His skin heated, and he found he couldn't look at her when he spoke. "It is the mating stone. This one is attuned to me and would reveal and bind me to my mate."

Tarah's grip on her sword finally wavered. "A legend, surely, like the bonding necklace I left behind on Moranaia."

For a moment, Caeregas forgot his brother and even his hoard. What did she mean, a legend? "The elves of your land experienced mate bonds when I was last awake. It is difficult to believe that has changed."

"I've never met a bonded pair." This time, it was her turn to flush. "Though I did concentrate on training what little time I was there."

"Then—"

"Figure it out later," his brother interrupted. "If you'll let me go, I'll retrieve your treasure."

Caeregas exchanged a glance with Tarah, and without words, they acted as one. She lowered her blade and stepped back as Caeregas unwound the spell locking the ground into impenetrable stone, an entrapment he'd designed to use against other dragons. All of his kind could shift rock to some extent, an ability that was necessary for shaping the caves they often called home, but working with dirt and stone was an art for an earth dragon. He could do things many other dragons would be unable to replicate.

He half-expected his brother to attack as soon as he was free, but Egrenneth limped straight to the bluestone and knelt beside it. With a quick burst of power, he moved the rock aside and opened a hole. Caeregas caught his breath, too nervous to let himself hope. Could it really be so simple? Had he misjudged his half-brother so thoroughly, or had time truly changed him? A large, ancient stone chest rose from the hole, and the questions no longer mattered. His hoard was safe.

His brother stood and directed the chest through the air with a neat burst of en-

ergy, settling it on the ground in front of Caeregas with a satisfied smirk. "That duty, at least, I was able to complete. Enjoy your treasures and leave me alone. Now that the barrier is gone, I want to explore farther, and it is clear we will never be friends."

Whatever the reasons for Egrenneth's actions, Caeregas couldn't deny that he owed him a debt of gratitude—and an apology. "Forgive me, especially for attacking in such haste. I judged you harshly."

Egrenneth shrugged. "Yes and no."

"I will find a way to repay you."

"As I said, you can repay me by leaving me alone for a while." After closing the hole that had held the chest, Egrenneth walked closer. "But let me teach you a shield I learned first. You can't haul that chest on a train, and it's best no one *else* sees your dragon form. I learned that the hard way."

Could he trust his half-brother? Considering what to do, he stared down at the stone chest he'd wrought with his own magic. Egrenneth could have found a thousand ways to hurt him with some of the gems inside, and he hadn't unleashed his power even under attack. What would be the point of trying something now?

Caeregas met his brother's eyes and nodded. "Very well."

Three months later

As soon as the gate shut behind her, Tarah tore off her coat. Beyond the metal fence guarding her enchanted garden, the London streets were dusted with a touch of snow, but she'd kept the inside of her domain a pleasant early summer temperature. Sometimes, she shifted it to match the vibe of the holidays. Not now. Having a live-in dragon boyfriend had changed a fair number of things.

Her wellies squelched along the wet pavement as she followed the path beside a line of ancient trees and between a tall hedge that bordered Caeregas's place. After the first month, he'd moved into her flat with her, but he still enjoyed retreating to the garden and a decorative guesthouse she'd had furnished. Especially since he could sit in the circle of hedges in his dragon form without anyone on the outside seeing. Not what she'd planned when she designed this section but fortunate all the same.

Today, though, he wasn't sunning his wings in the clearing in front of his house. Tarah loved to stumble upon him like that, although he was oddly embarrassed by it. He'd confessed once that he feared she couldn't accept that side of his nature. She'd gently reminded him that if she could accept his tendency to answer the door wearing a loincloth, she could deal with anything. Honestly, if she hadn't owned the building, they probably would have been kicked out for all the unusual things he did. But he was learning.

Smiling at the thought, Tarah opened the door and walked into the microscopic front room only to freeze at the sight of the stone chest standing open in the center.

Gemstones and jewels of all sizes and colors glistened in the morning light, and despite the shielding on the garden, she slammed the door closed behind her to block them from view.

Caeregas's hoard.

The man in question ducked through the small archway to the bedroom, and his expression lightened at the sight of her. "You're back early."

"I'm sorry," she said instinctively. Despite her curiosity, he hadn't shown her the full extent of his treasure after recovering it, only a few gems here and there. Like the turquoise he'd fashioned into the necklace that dangled on a chain between her breasts. "I didn't mean to intrude."

"You didn't, though I admit I am not done preparing."

Her forehead wrinkled. "For?"

Instead of answering, he began to gather the jewels that were heaped on the floor, settling them all back inside the chest and closing the lid. Then he turned to her, and one corner of his mouth tipped up as he held out his hand.

"Come back with me?"

Baffled, Tarah twined her fingers with his and let him lead her into his bedroom. But she barely noticed the small bed where he'd once slept—instead, she couldn't stop staring at a perfect red gemstone settled on top of a waist-height golden stand. Her heart leapt, pounding its frantic beat in her ears.

It couldn't be the red beryl, could it?

Caeregas halted just out of reach and turned to face her. "I know you are not of my kind, Tarah, but I..."

"Does that bother you?" she asked before he could find the words he sought. This was important. "If that's what I think it is... If the stone works, you'll be mated with me. You'll end up spending most of your time in this form, and our children might not gain the ability to shift at all. Forgive me if I have misread this, but—"

"No." He took both of her hands in his. "You haven't. And I have thought much of what brings me happiness in this new world. My hoard is no longer it. My joy is in you, not a pile of stone. Only you."

"I don't have the necklace my people use for bonding," Tarah blurted. "I don't know if your method will work. I'm not sure my instincts are even correct."

As it always did, his smile lit up her heart. "Shall we find out? You can always find your necklace later. But even if neither work, I'll still love you. I will treasure you regardless."

"I..." The gold in his eyes flared, almost drowning out the gray, as it did when he was trying to hide his worry. And just like that, she knew. "I love you, too."

Caeregas pulled her close, his mouth taking hers. And only later—much later—did they wrap their joined hands around the red beryl, the power within proving what they had both known all along.

They would forever be each other's sentinels.